THROUGH WOLF'S EYES

THROUGH

WOLF'S

EYES

JANE LINDSKOLD

A TOM DOHERTY ASSOCIATES BOOK
NEW YORK

This is a work of fiction. All the characters and events portrayed in this novel are either fictitious or are used fictitiously.

THROUGH WOLF'S EYES
Copyright © 2001 by Jane Lindskold

This book is printed on acid-free paper.

Edited by Teresa Nielsen Hayden

Book design by Songhee Kim

Map by Mark Stein Studios based on original drawing by James Moore

Family tree art by Tim Hall

A Tor Book
Published by Tom Doherty Associates, LLC
175 Fifth Avenue
New York, NY 10010

www.tor.com

Tor® is a registered trademark of Tom Doherty Associates, LLC.

Library of Congress Cataloging-in-Publication Data

Lindskold, Jane M.
    Through wolf's eyes / Jane Lindskold.—1st ed.
        p. cm.
    "A Tom Doherty Associates book."
    ISBN 0-312-87427-8 (alk. paper)
        1. Wild women—Fiction.   2. Human-animal relationships—
Fiction.   3. Inheritance and succession—Fiction.   4. Wolves—
Fiction.   I. Title.

PS3562.I51248 T48 2001
813'.54—dc21
                                                    2001027197

First Edition: August 2001

Printed in the United States of America
0 9 8 7 6 5 4 3 2 1

For Jim,
with Love

A C K N O W L E D G M E N T S

I'd like to thank several people for their help during the development of this book. Christie Golden's eloquent discussion of some aspects of characterization remained with me as I developed certain characters. Phyllis White of Flying Coyote Books supplied numerous valuable references on wolves. Jim Moore was once again my priceless first reader and constant sounding board. Kay McCauley, Jan and Steve Stirling, David Weber and Sharon Rice-Weber never let me give up. Sally Gwylan helped me to conquer time and error. Last, but not at all least, Patrick and Teresa Nielsen Hayden provided thoughtful encouragement and cogent editorial comments.

Special thanks go to Dr. Mark Anthony for fixing my shoulder and to Candy Kitchen Wolf Ranch for giving me a chance to meet several wolves up close and personal.

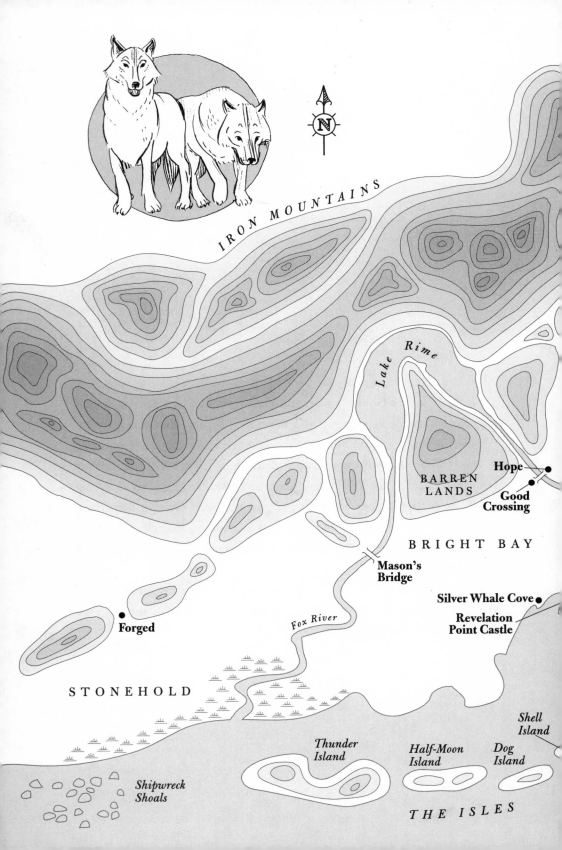

IRON MOUNTAINS

N

Lake Rime

Hope

BARREN
LANDS

Good
Crossing

BRIGHT BAY

Mason's
Bridge

Silver Whale Cove

Revelation
Point Castle

Fox River

Forged

STONEHOLD

Thunder
Island

Shell
Island

Half-Moon
Island

Dog
Island

Shipwreck
Shoals

THE ISLES

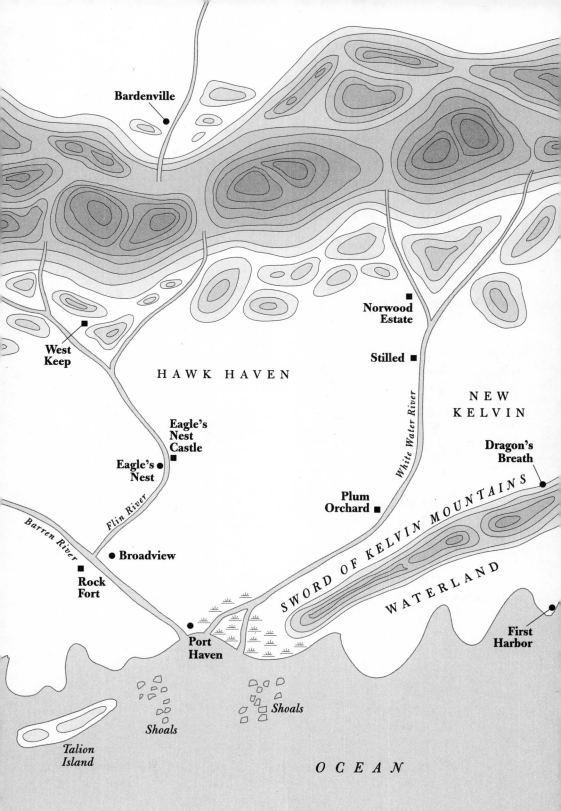

Bardenville

West
Keep

HAWK HAVEN

Eagle's
Nest
Castle

Eagle's
Nest

Flin River

Barren River

Broadview

Rock
Fort

Port
Haven

Shoals

Talion
Island

Shoals

Norwood
Estate

Stilled

White Water River

NEW
KELVIN

Dragon's
Breath

Plum
Orchard

SWORD OF KELVIN MOUNTAINS

WATERLAND

First
Harbor

OCEAN

Map by Mark Stein Studios based on original drawing by James Moore

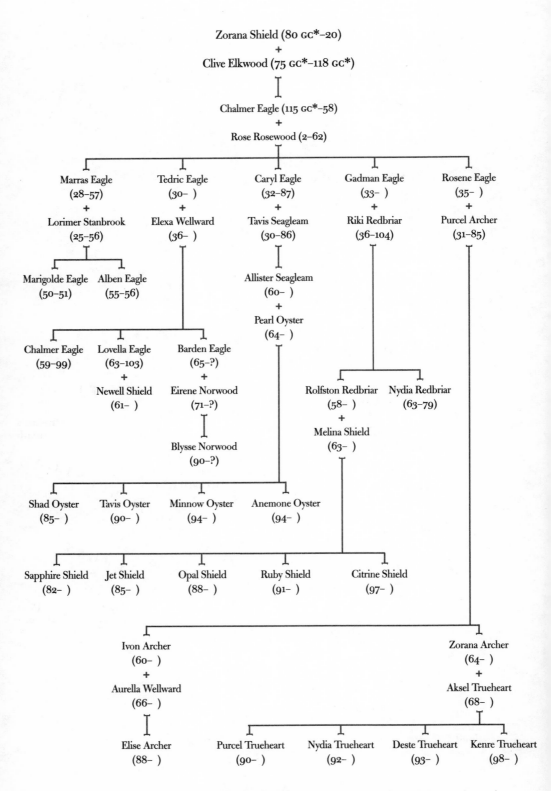

Zorana Shield (80 GC*–20)
+
Clive Elkwood (75 GC*–118 GC*)

Chalmer Eagle (115 GC*–58)
+
Rose Rosewood (2–62)

Marras Eagle
(28–57)
+
Lorimer Stanbrook
(25–56)

Tedric Eagle
(30–)
+
Elexa Wellward
(36–)

Caryl Eagle
(32–87)
+
Tavis Seagleam
(30–86)

Gadman Eagle
(33–)
+
Riki Redbriar
(36–104)

Rosene Eagle
(35–)
+
Purcel Archer
(31–85)

Marigolde Eagle
(50–51)

Alben Eagle
(55–56)

Allister Seagleam
(60–)
+
Pearl Oyster
(64–)

Chalmer Eagle
(59–99)

Lovella Eagle
(63–103)
+
Newell Shield
(61–)

Barden Eagle
(65–?)
+
Eirene Norwood
(71–?)

Rolfston Redbriar
(58–)
+
Melina Shield
(63–)

Nydia Redbriar
(63–79)

Blysse Norwood
(90–?)

Shad Oyster
(85–)

Tavis Oyster
(90–)

Minnow Oyster
(94–)

Anemone Oyster
(94–)

Sapphire Shield
(82–)

Jet Shield
(85–)

Opal Shield
(88–)

Ruby Shield
(91–)

Citrine Shield
(97–)

Ivon Archer
(60–)
+
Aurella Wellward
(66–)

Zorana Archer
(64–)
+
Aksel Trueheart
(68–)

Elise Archer
(88–)

Purcel Trueheart
(90–)

Nydia Trueheart
(92–)

Deste Trueheart
(93–)

Kenre Trueheart
(98–)

* GILDCREST COLONIAL CALENDAR (ALL OTHER DATES HAWK HAVEN CALENDAR)

BOOK
ONE

I

AAA-ROOO! AAA-ROOO!

Distant, yet carrying, the wolf's howl broke the late-afternoon stillness.

In the depths of the forest, a young woman, as strong and supple as the sound, rose noiselessly to her feet. With bloodstained fingers, she pushed her short, dark brown hair away from her ears to better hear the call.

Aaa-rooo! Aaa-rooo!

It was a sentry howl, relayed from a great distance to the east. The young woman understood its message more easily than she would have understood any form of human speech.

"Strangers! Strangers! Strangers! Strange!"

The last lilt of inflection clarified the previous howls. Whatever was coming from the east was not merely a trespasser—perhaps a young wolf dispersing from his birth pack—but an unknown quantity. But from the relay signal that preceded the call, the strangers were far away.

The young woman felt a momentary flicker of curiosity. Hunger, however, was more pressing. The cold times were not long past and her memories of dark, freezing days, when even the stupid fish were unreachable beneath the ice, were sharp.

She squatted again and continued skinning a still warm rabbit, musing, not for the first time, how much more convenient it would be if she could eat it as her kinfolk did: fur, bone, flesh, and guts all in one luxurious mouthful.

AAA-ROOO! AAA-ROOO!

Derian Carter, the youngest member of Earl Kestrel's expedition, felt his shoulder jerked nearly out of its socket when the wolf howl pierced the late-afternoon peace. The haunting sound startled the sensitive chestnut mare he was unbridling nearly out of her highly bred stockings.

"Easy, easy, Roanne," he murmured mechanically, all too aware that his own heart was racing. That wolf sounded *close*!

As Derian eased the mare's headstall over ears that couldn't seem to decide whether to prick in alarm or flatten in annoyance, he said in a voice he was pleased to discover remained calm, almost nonchalant:

"That sounds like a big wolf out there, Race."

Race Forester, the guide for Earl Kestrel's expedition, looked down his long nose at the younger man and chuckled. He was a lean fellow with a strong, steady tread that spoke of long distances traveled afoot and blond hair bleached so white by constant exposure to the sun that he would look much the same at sixty as he did at thirty.

"That it does, Derian." Race stroked his short but full beard as he glanced around their sheltered forest camp, systematically noting the areas that would need to be secured now that big predators were about. "Wolves always sound bigger when you're on their turf, rather than safe behind a city wall."

Derian swallowed a retort. In the weeks since Earl Kestrel's expedition had departed the capital of Hawk Haven, Race had rarely missed an opportunity to remind the members (other than the earl himself) that

Race himself was the woodsman, while they were mere city folk. Only the fact that Race's contempt was so generally administered had kept Derian from calling him out and showing him that a city-bred man could know a thing or two.

Only that, Derian admitted honestly (though only to himself), and the fact that Race would probably turn Derian into a smear on the turf. Though Derian Carter was tall enough to need to duck his head going through low doorways, muscular enough to handle the most spirited horse or work from dawn to dusk loading and unloading wagons at his father's warehouses, there was something about Race Forester's sinewy form, about the way he carried his slighter build, that made Derian doubt who would be the winner in a hand-to-hand fight.

And, with another surge of honesty, Derian admitted that the woodsman had earned the right to express his contempt. Race was good at what he did—many said the best in both Hawk Haven and their rival kingdom of Bright Bay. What was Derian Carter in comparison? Well trained, but untried.

Derian would never have admitted that before they set out—knowing himself good with a horse or an account book or even with his fists— but a few things had been hammered into his red head since they left the capital, things that hadn't been all that much fun to learn, and Derian didn't plan on forgetting them now.

So Derian swallowed his retort and continued removing the tack from the six riding horses. To his right, burly Ox, his road-grown beard incongruously black against pink, round cheeks, was heaving the packs from the four mules. When another long, eerie wolf's howl caused the nearest mule to kick back at the imagined danger, Ox blocked the kick rather than dodging.

That block neatly summed up why Ox was a member of the expedition. Even-tempered, like most big men who have never been forced to fight, Ox had made his recent living in the Hawk Haven military. During the current lull in hostilities, however, he had left the military to serve as Earl Kestrel's bodyguard.

Ox's birth name, Derian had learned to his surprise, was Malvin Hogge.

"But no one's called me that since long before my hair started receding," he'd told Derian, rubbing ruefully where his curly hairline was making an undignified and premature retreat. "But I prefer the name that my buddies in Kestrel Company gave me long ago and, strangely enough, no one ever calls me 'Malvin' twice."

Unlike Derian, Ox felt no inordinate awe toward Race Forester, aware that in his own way he was as valuable as the guide. How many men could shift a battering ram by themselves or do the work of three packers?

"Think that wolf wants us for dinner?" Ox asked Race in his deep-voiced, ponderous way.

"Hardly," the guide retorted scornfully. "We're too big a group and wolves, savage as they are, are not stupid."

"Well," Ox replied, laughing at his own joke, "you'd better tell the mules that. I don't think they understand."

Sir Jared Surcliffe, a lesser member of Earl Kestrel's own family, but prouder of his recently acquired nickname "Doc" than of any trace of noble blood, crossed to claim the general provisions bundle. Like the earl he had black hair and clear, grey eyes, but his height and build lacked the earl's seeming delicacy. There was strength in his long-fingered hands—as Derian had learned when Jared stitched a cut in his forearm a couple of weeks back. Derian recalled that Doc had won honors in battle, so he must have other strengths as well.

"Valet has the fire started," Jared said, an upper-class accent giving his simple statement unwonted authority. "I'll start dinner. Race, shouldn't you see if there might be a fish or two in yonder brook? Earl Kestrel would enjoy fresh trout with his dinner."

Had anyone but Jared or the earl himself even hinted at giving the guide orders, he might have found himself standing a late-night watch on an anthill. Race Forester, though, for all his pride in his skills, knew when he could—and could not—push his social betters.

"Right," he grunted, and departed, whistling for Queenie, his bird dog. The red-spotted hound reluctantly abandoned the station near the fire from which she'd been watching Earl Kestrel's man unpack the delicacies kept for the earl's own consumption.

When the wolf howled again, Derian wondered how much of Queenie's reluctance was due to leaving the food and how much to the proximity of the big predator.

"They say that the wolves in the mountains are bigger than anything found in settled lands," Derian said, talking to distract himself and feeling freer to speculate now that Race was gone.

"They do," Doc agreed, "but I've always wondered, just who has seen these giant wolves? Few people have gone beyond the foothills of the Iron Mountains—those mostly miners and trappers. As far as I know, the only ones to have crossed the range are Prince Barden and those who went with him."

Derian finished currying Roanne and moved to the earl's Coal before answering.

"Maybe in the early days," he hazarded, "when the colonies were new. Maybe people saw the wolves then."

"Possibly," Jared said agreeably, shaping a journey cake on its board. "And possibly it's all grandmother's fire stories. Race *is* right. Wolves and other night creatures do sound bigger when you're camping."

Conversation lagged as the members of the expedition hurried to complete their chores before the last of the late-spring light faded. Part of the reason Earl Kestrel had planned his journey for this time of year was that the days would be growing longer, but after hours spent riding on muddy trails, the evenings seemed brief enough.

Cool, too, Derian thought, blowing on his fingers as he measured grain for the mules and horses. *Winter may be gone, but she's not letting us forget her just yet.*

Ox, who had finished putting up the tents and was now effortlessly chopping wood, paused, his axe in the air.

"If you're cold, Derian, you can help me chop this wood. You know what they say, 'Wood warms you twice: once in the cutting, once in the burning.' "

Derian grinned at him. "No thanks. I've enough else to finish. Do you think we'll get snow tonight? The air almost has the scent of it."

Ox shrugged, measuring his answer out between the blows of his axe. "The mountains do get snow, even this late in the season, but I hope we're not in for any. A blackberry winter's all we need."

Derian frowned thoughtfully. "At home I'd say snow would be a good thing for business. It's easier to move goods by sled and people by sleigh, but out here, on horseback . . . I could do without the snow."

"We won't have snow," announced Race, re-entering the camp from the forest fringe. Three long, shining river trout dangled from one hand. "The smoke's rising straight off the fires. Clear but cold tonight. Derian, you might want to break out your spare blankets."

Derian nodded. He'd slept cold one night out of a stubborn desire to show himself as tough as the woodsman and had been stiff and nearly useless the next morning. Earl Kestrel himself had chided him for foolish pride.

"Our mission is too important to be trifled with," Kestrel had continued in his mincing way. "Mind that you listen to Race Forester's advice from here on."

And Derian had nodded and apologized, but in his heart he wondered. Just how important *was* this mission? King Tedric had seemed content enough these dozen years not knowing his son's fate. And Prince Barden had shown no desire to contact the king.

Earl Kestrel had been the one to decide that knowing what had happened to the disinherited prince was important—Kestrel said for the realm, but Derian suspected that the information was important mostly for how it would affect the earl's private ambitions.

THE YOUNG WOMAN was bathing when a thin, tail-chewed female informed her that the One Male wanted her at the den. The messenger, a yearling who had barely made it through her first winter, cringed and groveled as she delivered her message.

"When shall I say you will come before him, Firekeeper?" the she-wolf concluded, using the name most of the wolves called the woman—a name indicating a measure of respect, for even the Royal Wolves feared fire.

Firekeeper tossed a fat chub to the Whiner. *She* certainly wasn't going to have time to eat it, not if she must run all the way to the den. Ah, well! She could catch more fish later.

"Tell him," she said, considering, "I will be there as fast as two feet can carry me."

"Slow enough," sneered the Whiner, emboldened as she remembered how all but the fattest pups could outrun the two-legged wolf.

Firekeeper snatched a stone from the bank and, swifter than even the Whiner's paranoia, threw it at the wolf's snout.

"Ai-eee!"

"That might have been your skull," the woman reminded her. "Go, bone-chewer. My feet may be slow, but my belly is full with the meat of my own hunting!"

A lip-curling snarl before the Whiner vanished into the brush showed that the insult had gone home. Faintly, Firekeeper could hear the retreat of her running paws.

Her own departure would be less swift. Bending at the waist, she shook the water from her close-cropped hair, then smoothed the locks down, pressing out more water as she did so.

Even before her hair had stopped dripping down her back, Firekeeper had retrieved her most valuable possession from where she had set it on a flat rock near the water. It was a fang made of some hard, bright stone. With it, she could kill almost as neatly as a young wolf, skin her prey, sharpen the ends of sticks, and perform many other useful tasks. The One Male of her youngest memories had given it to her when he knew he was going into his last winter.

"These are used by those such as yourself, Little Two-legs," he had said fondly, "since they lack teeth or claws useful for hunting. I remember how they are used and can tutor you some, but you will need to discover much for yourself."

She had accepted the Fang and the leather Mouth in which it slept. At first she had hung them from a thong about her neck, but later, when she had learned more about their uses, she had contrived a way to hang them from a belt around her waist. Only when she was bathing, for the Fang hated water, did she take it off.

Now she held the tool in her teeth while she reached for the cured hide she had hung in a tree lest those like the Whiner chew it to shreds. Most hides she couldn't care less about but this one, taken from an elk killed for the purpose, was special.

Out of the center she had cut a hole for her head, wide enough not to chafe her neck. The rest of the skin hung front and back, protecting her most vulnerable parts. A belt made from strips of hide kept the garment in place and she had trimmed away the parts that interfered with free movement of her arms.

Some of the young wolves had laughed when she had contrived her first hide, but she had disregarded their taunts. The wolves had fur to protect themselves from brambles and sticks. She must borrow from the more fortunate or be constantly bleeding from some scrape. An extra skin was welcome, too, against the chill.

In the winter, she tied rabbit skins along her legs and arms with the fur next to her flesh. The skins were awkward, often slipping or falling off, but were still far better than frostbite.

Later in the year, when the days grew hotter and the hide stifling, Firekeeper would wear only a shorter bit of leather around her waist, relinquishing some protection for comfort.

Lastly, Firekeeper hung around her neck a small bag containing the special stones with which she could strike fire. She valued these less than the Fang, but without their power she could not have survived this winter or others before it.

Faintly, Firekeeper remembered when she did not live this way, when she wore something softer and more yielding than hides, when winters were warmer. Almost, she thought, those memories were a dream, but it was a dream that seemed strangely close as she ran to where the One Male awaited her.

THE ONE MALE was a big silver-grey wolf with a dark streak running along his spine to the tip of his tail and a broad white ruff. He was the third of that title Firekeeper could remember and had held the post for only two years. His predecessor would have dominated the pack longer except for a chance stumble in front of an elk during a hunt in midwinter along an icy lakeshore.

The current One Male had been accepted by the One Female, who had led the pack alone through the remainder of that winter until the mating season early the following spring. Competition for her had been fierce and one contender had been killed. A second chose exile rather than live beneath his pack mate's rule.

Yet the diminished pack had fared well, perhaps because of, rather than despite, the losses. Fewer wolves meant fewer ways to split the food. New pups had since grown to fill the gaps and the Ones reigned over a fine pack eight adults strong—with a single strange, two-legged, not-quite-wolf to round out the group.

Although she remembered when both had been fat, blue-eyed, round-bellied puppies, Firekeeper thought of both the One Male and the One Female as older than herself. However, though the human had more years than the wolves, the reality was that they *were* adults while she, when judged by her abilities rather than her years, was a pup. Indeed, she might always *be* a pup—a thing she regarded with some dissatisfaction during rare, idle moments.

When she loped into the flat, bone-strewn area outside of the den, the One Male was waiting for her. None of the rest of the pack was visible.

The One Female was within the cave nearby, occupied with her newborn pups. The day for them to be introduced to the rest of their family was close and Firekeeper warmed in pleasant anticipation. Already she knew that there were six pups, all apparently healthy, but everything else about them was kept a guarded secret until the great event of Emergence.

Seeing Firekeeper—though doubtless he had heard her arrive—the One Male rose to his feet. She ran to within a few paces, then dropped onto all fours. When he permitted her to approach, she stroked her fingers along his jaw, mimicking a puppy's begging.

Tail wagging gently, the One Male drew his lips back from his teeth as if regurgitating—though he did not actually do so. All spare food these days went to the One Female and the pups. Firekeeper, who had been made hungry by her swim followed by a swift run, was rather sorry. Many times during the past winter meat had been carried to her from a kill too distant for her to reach before the scavengers would have stripped it.

"You summoned me, Father?" she asked, sitting back on her haunches now that the greeting ritual had been completed.

The One Male wagged his tail, then sat beside her, tacitly inviting her to throw an arm around him and scratch between his ears.

"Yes, Little Two-legs, I did. Did you hear the message howl some while ago?"

"Stranger! Stranger! Stranger! Strange!" she repeated softly by way of answer. "From the east, I thought."

"Yes, all the way from the gap in the mountains, not far from where you came to us."

Firekeeper nodded. She knew the place. There was good hunting in those meadows come late summer when the young deer grew foolish and their mothers careless. There was also a burned place, overgrown now, but hiding black ash and hard-burnt wood beneath the vines and grasses. Every year when the pack hunted in that region the Ones told her how she had come from the burned place and reminded her of her heritage.

"I remember the place," Firekeeper answered, mostly because she knew the One would want to hear confirmation, not because she thought he needed it.

"The Strangers Strange are two-legs, like yourself," the One continued. "A falcon has been following them by day and she relays through our scouts that the two-legs go to the Burnt Place, seeking those who were there before I was born."

"Oh!" Firekeeper gasped softly. Then a question drew a line between her dark, dark eyes. "How does the falcon know where they are going?"

"When this falcon was young she was taken from the air while on migration," the One explained. "I don't know how it was done, but the Mothers of her people say it was so and I believe them."

"Like knows like best," Firekeeper said, repeating a wolf proverb.

"Remember that," the One Male said, then returned to his explanation. "This falcon lived for a time with the two-legs and hunted for them. During that time, she learned something of their speech—far more than the few words they used to address her. From their speech and from the direction they are heading, she believes that these two-legs are not hunters come for a short time to take furs."

"The wrong time for that game, certainly," Firekeeper said. "Your coats are shedding now and make me sneeze."

"That is why those fingers of yours feel so good," the One Male admitted. "Pull out the mats as you find them."

"Only if you remember," she teased with mock hauteur, "not to bite off my hand!"

"I promise," he said with sudden solemnity. "As all of us have promised not to harm our strange little sister."

Made uneasy by this change of mood, Firekeeper occupied herself tugging out a mat, worrying the undercoat loose with dexterous ease.

"Why did you summon me to tell me of the two-legs?" she asked at last. "I know less of them than the falcons do. They are strangers to me. The wolves are my people."

"Always," the One Male promised her, "but since before I was born each One has told those who may follow that there is a trust held by our pack for you. When your people return, we have sworn to bring you back to them. It is an ancient trust, given, so our tales say, to your own mother."

Firekeeper was silenced by astonishment. Then she blurted out indignantly:

"I was never told of this!"

"You," the One Male said gently, "have never been considered old enough to know. Only those who may one day lead the pack are told of this trust, so that they may vow to keep it in their turn."

The human admitted the justice of this, but hot tears of frustration and anticipated grief burned in her eyes.

"What if I want nothing of this trust, given to a mother I cannot remember?"

"You will always be a wolf, Firekeeper," the One Male said. "Meet the two-legs. Learn of them. If you do not care for their ways, come back to the pack. A wise wolf," he continued, quoting another proverb, "scouts the prey, knows when to hunt, when to stay away."

"If I did less," Firekeeper admitted, wiping the tears away with the back of one hand, "I would be less than a wolf. Let me begin by scouting the two-legs. When I have learned who leads, who follows, then I will make myself known to them."

"Wise," the One Male said. "The thoughts of a wolf and the courage as well."

"Tell me where to find them," Firekeeper said, rising. "Call my coming to our kin along the trail that they may guide and protect me."

"I will . . ."

The One Male's words were interrupted by a husky voice from the den's opening. An elegant head, pure silver, unmarred with white or black, showed against the shadows.

"Go after tonight, Little Two-legs," said the One Female. "Tonight I will bring out your new brothers and sisters so that you may know them and they you. Then, fully of the pack, you may be heartened for your task."

Overcome with joy, Firekeeper leapt straight into the air.

"Father, Mother, may I cry the pack together?"

"Do, Little Two-legs," said the One Female. "Loud and long, so that even the scouts come home. Call our family together."

"WE PASS THROUGH the gap tomorrow," announced Race Forester as they gathered round the fire after dinner that night. "Then, we will need to slow our progress. Earl Kestrel . . ." he dipped his head in respectful acknowledgment, "has collected reports from the trappers and peddlers who had contact with Prince Barden. They all agree that he did not intend to go much further than the first good site beyond the mountains. He wanted to be well away from settled lands, but I suspect not so far that trade could not be established later."

Derian, full, warm, and pleasantly weary, asked, "But no one has heard from him since he crossed the Iron Mountains?"

"No one who is admitting it," said Earl Kestrel.

From where Derian sat, the earl was just a solid, hook-nosed shadow. He was not a big man. Indeed, he was quite small, but as with the kestrel of his house name, small did not mean weak or tame. The furious lash of his tongue when he was roused was to be as feared as another man's fist—more so, to Derian's way of thinking. You could outrun a bully, but never escape the wrath of a man of consequence.

He wondered, then, if that had not been precisely what Prince Barden of the House of the Eagle had been trying to do when he left Hawk Haven for the unsettled lands beyond the barrier of the Iron Mountains.

Prince Barden had been a third child and, by all accounts, roundly unhappy about being so. Although King Tedric had his heir and his spare, he resisted having his youngest son attempt any independent ven-

ture. Enough for the king that Barden learn to sit a horse, fight well
enough for his class, and perhaps dabble in some court tasks.

Perhaps when Crown Prince Chalmer had married and fathered a
child or even when Princess Lovella was similarly settled, then Barden
might finally have been superfluous enough to be permitted his freedom.
Or maybe not even then. King Tedric was said to be a very domineering
father.

Ironically, because Prince Barden had been the least noticed and least
dominated by his father, he was the most like the king in temperament.
Prince Barden decided he would not see his life frittered away while
waiting for his siblings to marry (a task, to be fair to them, made more
difficult in that King Tedric wanted a hand in that choosing as well), to
breed heirs, for his father to die. Thus, Prince Barden began quietly
laying plans for a venture of which his father was certain to disapprove.

Sometimes Derian wondered at the younger prince's ambitions. Himself an eldest son, Derian was all too aware of the pressure of his parents'
hopes and expectations. How much easier life would be if they would
just leave him alone! Oh, they were loving and kind—nothing like King
Tedric—but sometimes Derian thought he would rebel if he heard one
more "Derian, have you practiced your . . . handwriting, riding, fenc-
ing . . ." The list was endless.

Even when he wasn't being set to his books, there were quizzes.
"Quick, son, tell me whose crest that is!" Or "Don't hold your knife in
that hand, Derian Carter. A gentleman holds it like so." Lately even his
dancing, which had made him the delight of the womenfolk since he was
old enough to leave the children's circles, had come into question. "Don't
skip so! More stately, more graceful!"

No doubt his parents had dreams of him rising into the lower ranks
of the nobility, perhaps by marriage to some impoverished noble's plain
daughter! Derian groaned inwardly at the thought. *He* fancied the baker's
pretty second daughter, the one with the round cheeks and the saucy
smile.

Maybe, now that he considered it, he was more like Prince Barden than he had thought. Both of them had found their parents' expectations a bit more than they could take, but the difference was that Prince Barden had defied his father. Quietly and carefully he had gathered a cadre of men and women who, like himself, longed for more than what Hawk Haven and her endless sparring with Bright Bay could offer.

Only after the expedition was planned, supplied (largely from King Tedric's own pocket—he didn't believe it good policy to stint too greatly on his children's allowances), and on its way did the king learn that Prince Barden, his wife, and his little daughter had not stayed at their keep in the foothills of the Iron Mountains, but had gone beyond the gap to the other side.

The steward of West Keep delivered the news himself, bringing with him a letter from the prince. Barden's plan had been well laid. Almost every lesser guard, groom, gardener, cook, or maidservant at the keep had been of his party. The steward, left with only his core group, had not dared pursue them and leave his trust untended.

By the time King Tedric learned of Prince Barden's departure, attempting to drag him back would have been futile. Instead, the king disowned his younger son, blotting his name from the books and refusing to let it be spoken by any in court or country. However, Derian knew, as did all the members of Earl Kestrel's expedition, that even in his fury the king had left himself a loophole.

Lady Blysse, Barden's daughter, had not been blotted from the records. She, if the need arose, could be named to the succession. Prince Barden could even be named her regent if her grandfather so wished. In those long-ago days, it had not seemed likely that King Tedric would ever so wish.

But things change, and those changes were why Derian Carter found himself one of six select men seated around a fire, preparing to go through a mountain pass where, to their best knowledge, no human had gone for twelve long years.

He shuddered deliciously at the thought of the adventure before them and turned his attention again to the informal conference around the fire. Earl Kestrel was finishing his diatribe against those who might have defied King Tedric's wrath and made profitable and secret trade with Prince Barden's group.

"It would be to their best interests," he said, "to never speak of their doings. Why risk royal censure?"

"Why," added his cousin Jared, "risk having to share a closed market?"

"Indeed," the earl agreed approvingly. "Forester, as we move deeper into unknown territory, Barden's people may not take such care to hide traces of their comings and goings. Keep a sharp eye out for them."

"Ever, my lord," answered Race promptly and humbly. Then, "My lord, when we find them," (he didn't say what he had said frequently to Derian and Ox, that he thought Barden and his party all dead or fled to some foreign country), "how shall we approach them?"

"We shall scout them," Earl Kestrel said, "from hiding if possible. When we have ascertained their numbers and whether Prince Barden is among them I will choose the manner of my approach. If we find an abandoned settlement, then we shall remain long enough to discover whether Prince Barden and his people are dead or if they have merely moved elsewhere.

"Any information," he continued sanctimoniously, "will be of help and comfort to the king in his bereavement."

And you'll find a way to turn it to your advantage, Derian thought sardonically.

That there was an advantage to be gained Derian did not doubt— neither had his father and mother. This was why they had insisted on Derian's accompanying Earl Kestrel as one of their conditions for setting a good rate for pack mules, a couple of riding horses, and a coach for the early stages of the journey.

As all Hawk Haven knew, King Tedric's paranoia regarding heirs had proven well founded. Crown Prince Chalmer had died as a result of a questionable hunting accident. His sister, Lovella, the new crown princess, had died some years later in a battle against pirates. Neither had left legitimate issue. Prince Chalmer had been unmarried. Princess Lovella had been careful not to make that mistake, but she had delayed bearing a child until she felt she wouldn't be needed as a general.

Now, as King Tedric, still a fierce old eagle of a man, aged, potential heirs buzzed about the throne. The genealogical picture was so complex that Derian was still working out who had the best claim. There was even a member of the royal family of Bright Bay with factions agitating for King Tedric to name him heir.

All Derian was certain of was that Prince Barden, if reinstated to his father's favor, would have the best claim. Lady Blysse, who would be about fifteen now, would have as good a claim as any and better than many.

And certainly lost prince or his lost-er daughter would need a counselor. And who better than the kind and wise Earl Kestrel, who had risked life and limb to bring father and daughter forth from exile?

THAT NIGHT, a few hours before dawn, Firekeeper curled up among the pups so that they would soak in her scent and know her even after an absence. Perhaps it was the hot, round bodies clustered around her own, perhaps the memories awakened by her talk with the One Male, but she dreamed of fire.

Kindled in a shallow pit ringed around with river rock and bordered with cleared dirt. Her fingers ache a little from striking together the special stones from the little bag the Ones have just given her. Deep inside, she feels a shiver of fear as she tentatively nurses the fire to life with gentle breath and offerings of food.

"That's right," says the One Female, her tones level though her neck ruff is stiff with tension at remaining so close to the flames. "Feed it little things first: a dry leaf, a bit of grass, a twig. Only when it is stronger can it eat bigger things."

"Yes, Mother. How do you know so much?"

The One Female smiles, lips pulled back from teeth. "I have watched such small fires being made, Little Two-legs. Only when they are permitted to eat more than their fill do they grow dangerous."

The pale new flames reach out greedily for a twig, lapping her hand. She drops the twig and sucks on an injured finger.

"It bit me, Mother!"

"Tamara! Don't put your hand in the fire, sweetling! You'll get burnt!"

The voice is not the rumble of the wolf, thoughts half-expressed by ears and posture rather than by sounds. These words are all sound, the voice high but strong. The speaker is a two-legs, towering far taller than any wolf.

"I didn't touch it, Mama. I was only looking."

Orange and red, glowing warm and comforting where it is contained within the hearth, the flames taste the bottom of the fat, round-bellied black kettle hung over them. The air smells of burning wood and simmering soup.

"Good girl. We welcome fire into our homes but never forget that it can be a dangerous guest . . ."

Dangerous.

Smoke so thick and choking that her eyes run with water. Coughs rack her ribs. A band wraps around her, squeezing what little air there is out of her. Vaguely she realizes that it is a broad, muscular arm. Her father's arm.

He is crawling along the packed earth floor, keeping his head and hers low. Moving slowly, so slowly, coughing with every breath. The room in the cabin is hot and full of smoke. Something falls behind them with a crash that reverberates even through the dirt floor.

"Donal!" Mama's voice, shrill now with panic. "Donal!"

"Sar . . ." More a gasp than a word. Then stronger, "Sarena!"

A shadow seen through burning eyes, crouching, grabbing her.

"Donal! What . . ."

She is being dragged again, more quickly now.

"My legs, a beam . . . when I went for the child."

"I'll get her out, come back for you!"

"No! Get clear."

"I'll come back."

Outside, clearer air, but still so full of smoke. She is weeping now, tears washing her eyes so that she can see. Mama has brought her outside of the wooden palisade that surrounds Bardenville. Looking back she can see that all the buildings are aflame. Where are the people?

"Wait here, Tamara." Mama coughs. "I'm going to get Papa."

She can't do anything but wait, her legs are so weak. Though the air outside is clearer, she can barely breathe, but she struggles to reassure her mother.

"I'll wait, Mama."

Mama turns. Even smudged with soot, coughing and limping, she is graceful. Tamara watches through bleared eyes as Mama goes into the burning thing that was once a cabin.

Where are the people? Where is Barden? Where is Carpenter who made her a doll? Where is Blysse who plays with her? Where is . . .

Something large comes out of the forest behind her. A wolf. What Mama and Papa call a Royal Wolf, though Tamara doesn't know why. The wolf licks her in greeting, whines.

Tamara points to the burning cabin. "Mama . . ."

The wolf barks sharply. A second wolf, then two more, come out of the forest. Clearly they fear the fire, but they run into the burning settlement. One even runs into the cabin, comes out dragging something that is screaming in raw pain.

Tamara's eyes flood. She hears shriller screaming and realizes it is her own voice out of control, belonging it seems to someone other than herself. She can't stop screaming and all around there are sparks, flames, smoke, and a terrible smell.

She screams and . . .

Firekeeper awoke, the scream still in her throat, the pups stirring nervously around her. Beyond them, a large white shape rose. The One Female nudged Firekeeper fully awake, lapping her face with her tongue.

"Awake, Little Two-legs. The dawn is becoming day. Your journey is before you."

II

GETTING THROUGH THE IRON MOUNTAIN GAP the next day proved only nearly impossible. There was nothing like a traveled path—certainly a blow to Earl Kestrel's conjectures about renegade peddlers—but there was a fairly well used game trail.

"Elk," Race proclaimed. "Moose. Certainly creatures larger than deer. They may summer across the pass and then come east in the winter."

"Delighting our huntsmen to no end," said Sir Jared Surcliffe. "Why do you say they come east in the winter?"

"Just a guess," the guide admitted. "Ocean and mountains both moderate the weather. My thought was that our winters may be milder because we are walled in by mountains on the west."

Derian, recalling some pretty nasty winter storms, bit back a sarcastic comment. He had his hands full with two of the pack mules, stubborn beasts who refused to follow unless dragged. His booted feet ached, and he cursed the boulders and loose rocks that made following the straightest route a fool's dream.

"Must have been tough going for Prince Barden's group," Jared continued. Still mounted, he was leading Derian's Roanne. "They didn't have just a few horses and mules. From what the steward reported to King Tedric, they pretty much stripped the manor of its livestock."

"It *was* the prince's property," Earl Kestrel reminded them with gentle firmness. "West Keep was one of the estates his father had given to him."

Derian grinned despite his weariness. It was to the earl's advantage to make certain that all of them remained sympathetic toward a man who was—realistically seen—at the very least a rebel and perhaps even a traitor.

Not for the first time he wondered just how much King Tedric would welcome back his third child. For some moon-spans now rumors had been flying around the capital that the king was considering putting off Queen Elexa, who was well past childbearing years, and taking a new bride in an attempt to get another heir.

Of course, that would likely anger the queen's Wellward relatives, for she had been, by all accounts, a blameless wife.

They paused an hour or so later so that Race and Ox could clear a path through some growth that moose or elk would likely view as a pleasant snack. Derian trudged down to the nearest brook and hauled water back to the horses and mules.

"A little, not too much," he cautioned Valet, who silently came to help him.

Valet was a small, agile man who, from what Derian had observed, must be made entirely out of iron wire. Equally talented at handling a tea service or a hawk, versed in both etiquette and his temperamental master's moods, he had held up well through the long, muddy springtide journey.

This had come as a surprise to Derian, who had expected, upon first meeting Valet, that the little man would collapse as soon as the going got rough. Who would expect hardiness from a fellow who made his final duty of every evening putting hot coals into a travelling iron and pressing his master's shirts and trousers?

But Valet had proven Derian wrong. When Derian had shared his surprise with Ox, the bodyguard had told him that Valet accompanied

Earl Kestrel everywhere, even into battle. Certainly, Derian would never have learned this from Valet himself. The man rarely spoke three words unless directly addressed.

Even now, though he must have known not to overwater a hot horse, Valet said nothing in reproof (as Derian himself might have), but merely nodded.

As dusk was fading into full dark, the expedition emerged from the pass and onto something like level ground. The light was almost, but not quite, too poor to make camp, a thing for which Derian's aching body was eternally grateful. A cold meal, then sleeping wrapped in a bedroll on lumpy ground, would have been more than he could have borne. Every part of him cried out for hot food, hot water in which to soak his feet, and the relative comfort of a proper tent.

Of course, these things must wait until after the horses and mules were tended, after he had fetched water for all the camp, after he had unpacked the bedrolls, the horse feed, and the party's personal kits.

He couldn't even feel sorry for himself while he worked, for no one else was resting, not even the earl. The nobleman, between mouthfuls of sautéed pigeon with wild mushrooms and lightly braised greens, was estimating how long they could remain away from civilization without replenishing their supplies.

Although Derian had no desire to seem less willing than any of the rest, he was grateful beyond words when, after a meal of journey cake and hard cheese followed by a withered apple for dessert, Jared Surcliffe ordered Derian to remove his boots.

"As you wish, Doc," Derian agreed, "but who will do the cleaning up?"

"Race can handle it," Jared replied bluntly. "I've watched you limping from midday on. He's more accustomed to tromping about over rough ground."

Race, complimented, accepted the menial chore without protest. "I wanted to set some fish traps in any case," he said, gathering up the pots and cups.

The lonely howl of a wolf, answered by a fainter, second cry, silenced for a moment the singing of the night peepers and shriller chirps of the insects. The humans froze in visceral, instinctive fear.

"Take Ox with you," the earl commanded.

Race nodded and the two men departed.

"Think they'll be all right, Doc?" Derian asked nervously as Jared helped him off with his boots.

"I'm more worried about your feet than I am about wolves," the other man replied. "Race and Ox are big men. The wolves should find much easier hunting this time of year."

"The horses don't like all that howling much," Derian said, talking to keep his mind off the sting of hot water on his feet. "But that just makes sense. Wolves probably see the horses as an easy dinner."

"That's something to remember," Doc agreed. "Whoever's on watch should keep a close eye on horses and mules alike."

A few minutes later, he lifted Derian's feet from the water, inspected them, then smeared some ointment on the blisters.

"We'll probably stay in this camp until we locate Prince Barden," Doc said. "I'm going to suggest to Earl Kestrel that you take camp watch so you can wear soft shoes and let these blisters heal."

"Thanks," Derian said, not bothering to mask his relief.

"My pleasure." Doc grinned. "I had the privilege of staying on horseback most of the day rather than picking along the ground dragging a string of mules. You and Ox took most of the punishment there."

"Ox seems fine," Derian commented enviously.

"He's an old campaigner and knows how to pamper his feet," Doc replied. "You should consult him before we continue."

"I will."

They sat in companionable silence for a long moment.

"Doc, do you think we'll find the prince? Honestly?"

Jared shook his head, but his words belied the gesture. "We'll find something—the earl insists."

Later, almost too tired to sleep, dismissed from guard duty for this night, Derian lay in the tent he shared with Ox and listened to the night sounds above the other man's breathing. Deep in his heart, he began to suspect that they would find no one. Nothing in the surrounding wilderness spoke with a human voice.

A howl sounded and was answered by a chorus which continued even as Derian slipped into exhausted rest.

❊

FIREKEEPER SWALLOWED a hurried meal of lightly grilled brook trout while listening to the Ones' parting advice.

"We have sent the pack ahead to hunt for you," the One Female said, her silver fur glinting in the morning light. "This way you will not be delayed along the trail."

"But, Mother," the young woman protested, "you and the pups will go hungry!"

"The One Male will hunt for us," the One Female reassured her, "and we have kept the Whiner near to mind the pups so I can hunt as well. If you are worried about us, remember, the faster you make your trail, the faster the others can return."

Firekeeper nodded.

"Blind Seer waits where the two-legs are," the One Male added. "He learned of their coming from a Cousin wolf who came in panic before them. Blind Seer crossed through the gap to watch the two-legs' coming and send word ahead. He will remain with you. The falcon should be with him, though by now she may have departed to report to the Mothers of her aerie."

"Good."

The young woman dropped to her knees to rub her face in each puppy's fuzzy coat. They looked more like little bears now than wolves: muzzles short, ears small and round. Their blue eyes were still cloudy.

"I'll miss you all," she said, embracing the Ones and punching the Whiner, who had emerged from behind a rock, lightly on one shoulder.

"Sing your news," the One Male reminded her, "and it will reach our ears."

Firekeeper promised to do so. Then, after extinguishing her fire, she departed. As morning passed into bright daylight, daylight into afternoon, noon into evening, she ran east, her gait the steady mile-eating jog of a wolf. When she grew tired, she slowed, walking a hundred paces, jogging a hundred. When even this became onerous, she climbed into the boughs of some spreading forest giant, an oak or maple by choice, and napped.

As promised, her brothers and sisters met her along the way, telling her how winter had reshaped the trails, feeding her if she was hungry, showing her the closest fresh water.

By night, she had met up with Blind Seer. This young, powerful male, some three years old, had been named for his eyes, which never changed from puppy blue to the more usual yellow-brown. For a time, the wolves had thought his vision damaged and had philosophically accepted that he would be among those pups who did not survive their first year.

Blind Seer had surprised them all by demonstrating evidence of sight as sharp as any wolf's. His baby fur had grown out into a classic grey coat shading to ghostly silver at the tips and touched with reddish brown around his face. Content to remain with the pack his first two summers, this spring he was showing restlessness.

Firekeeper knew that the Ones fully expected Blind Seer to disperse this spring, seeking territory and perhaps a mate of his own. The knowledge had saddened her, since Blind Seer had been one of her favorites since he was a pup. Perhaps the fact that he, like her, was marked by a difference had drawn her to him. Perhaps it was that he had never lost a puppyish curiosity about what lay over the next hill.

Now she must face that, different as he seemed, Blind Seer belonged to the way of the wolf in a fashion that she never could. He would follow it and she would go on, as ever, somewhat apart from those she loved best.

The thought sobered her mind even as her long day's journey had made her limbs weary. She was glad that Blind Seer had enough to say for them both.

"The two-legs crossed through the gap today," he reported, leading her to a sheltered place where she might kindle a fire and soften the rabbit he had caught for her over the flames. "What a trial they had of it!"

"Tell," she prompted. "Can we look at them tonight?"

"Better if not," he said. "They have gathered themselves into a circle and they have beasts with them who grow nervous when I close. They have a creature with them, a bitch, but of a breed I've never dreamed existed!"

"Oh?"

"Smaller even than the Cousins," Blind Seer said, chewing on the rabbit fur and viscera she had tossed to him. "Her fur is lighter than even the One Female's: white as a rabbit's winter coat, but spotted fawn-like with fox-red. She is a weird parody of wolf or fox, but there's no doubt that she knows when I prowl about."

"I'd like to see this creature."

"Not tonight. If you wish to study the two-legs, it is best that we do not spook them while they are weary."

"Weary from crossing the gap," Firekeeper asked, "or do they sleep as birds do, simply because the sun has set?"

"Weary from the crossing," Blind Seer replied. "Even before dawn, they started taking down their dens, making their food. They sear their meat as you do, over fire, but take much more time about it."

Firekeeper cut off a haunch of still pink rabbit meat and began eating, leaving the rest over the fire.

"Tell on," she prompted.

"The two-legs have courage, I'll grant them that," Blind Seer said, "and even some wisdom, but no great forest lore. The most skilled of them went ahead and marked a trail. The rest followed, bringing with them the beasts."

"This spotted fox?"

"Not that," Blind Seer replied impatiently. "She went with the scout and shivered when the wind brought her my scent. Other beasts. Large ones built like elk in some ways, but with manes and tails of long, soft hair—rather like yours is when you have not cropped it short."

Firekeeper, who found the constantly changing length of her hair a nuisance, nodded.

"Why do they herd these elk? It seems a great deal of trouble to go to for fresh meat."

"They don't eat them—at least from what I've seen. They sit on them or put their belongings on their backs. These two-legs carry more with them than a raven or jay hides in its nest."

Firekeeper, remembering how she needed the Fang, the stones, the hides, just to stay alive, sighed.

"I will enjoy looking on these things of the two-legs," she said. "Tell more."

"There is not much more to tell. They sleep now, but one of their pack remains awake to guard the rest. If trouble is suspected—as I tested last night—they make a great clamor and all wake."

"Let them sleep," Firekeeper said. "We will look on them come morning."

She finished her meal and waded into a shockingly cold stream to wash clean. Then Blind Seer mouthed her arm affectionately.

"You will need to rest, sweet Firekeeper, but come with me first. Let us sing home the news of your safe arrival. I have found a rise from which the sound carries far."

Firekeeper went with him, refreshed, fed, and excited. They raised their voices in chorus, heard their howls augmented by the Cousins who marked this region for their own, and, after a time, heard a faint reply to the west.

Even when the message had been passed on, they continued singing, enjoying the sound of their voices intertwined in friendship and in love.

❦

UPON WAKING THE NEXT MORNING, Derian was pleased to find that the blisters on his feet had ceased to throb. Still, he was relieved to learn that he had drawn camp duty and so would be able to trade riding boots for soft leather slippers.

"Did you hear those wolves howling last night?" he asked as he stirred the morning porridge, adding bits of dried apple and peach to the glutinous mass.

"Who couldn't? None of us are deaf," replied Race sarcastically. "The monsters must have been readying themselves for a slaughter. I'll bet Prince Barden lost his flocks within the first winter. These woods are full of the thieving brutes."

"My brother was given to the Wolf Society when he was born," commented Ox, "but even he prefers to appreciate wolves from a distance. Such cunning and ferocity is admirable in symbols perhaps, but I don't want to find them on my doorstep."

Over oat porridge and strong mint tea, they traded tales of wolf predation. Race began with the story of the Mad Wolf of Garwood. Doc countered with the story of a wolf pack that wiped out a village one winter when Hawk Haven was but a portion of the larger colony of Gildcrest. Everyone had at least one such story to relate and the telling fired the blood for the day's work.

Eventually, however, Earl Kestrel began briefing them on the activities planned for the day.

"We will search in two teams. I will take Ox. Race, you will take Jared. As we have seen no sign of Prince Barden and his people to the east, I will go further north; you shall go to the west. Based on your report yestere'en, there is a river to the south. Let us wait to ford that until we must."

Race nodded and the earl continued:

"Derian and Valet will mind the camp. This is a good time to attend to the minor repairs we have been postponing. Furthermore, the horses can use a rest."

"How far from this base camp do you want us to go, my lord?" asked Race.

"You must return here by evening. We will each carry hunting horns. Three short blasts will signal a return to camp. Two a request for aid. Remember, if at all possible, save first contact for me. Are there any questions?"

Five heads shook a negative.

"Get ready, then. Valet has made up packets of cold food for the midday meal. If you have anything to be repaired, give it to Derian."

A few moments later, in their shared tent, Derian accepted from Ox some leggings that needed mending.

"Earl Kestrel isn't wasting any time, is he?" he commented. "Yesterday we slogged across a pass still spotted with snow. Today he orders a full day's search, even though a holiday would be a fair reward."

"You forget," Ox replied, checking the edge on the axe he carried with him as both weapon and tool, "that our time here is limited. Even if Race succeeds in augmenting our supplies by hunting and fishing, we need fodder for the horses. It's too early in the year for them to do much grazing."

"I haven't forgotten," Derian protested. "Remember, my folks own stables in three towns!"

"I know," Ox said mildly. "I simply didn't know that you did."

When the others had departed, leaving behind enough chores to occupy Derian and Valet for a week, Derian sighed, regretting now that his blistered feet kept him out of the adventure. Then, sitting cross-legged on the ground, he took a torn shirt into his lap and doggedly began to sew.

⚜

FROM THE CONCEALMENT of thick shrub growth atop a rise overlooking the two-legs' camp, Firekeeper studied the occupants. The animals amazed her, but her response to their keepers mingled astonishment and admiration.

"They are so noisy," she said to Blind Seer, watching one of their number go to a stream for water. "Yet so bold!"

Blind Seer snorted. "What do they know to fear? The red-spotted white animal sees more than any of them, but they ignore her. Did you see their One kick at her when she tried to tell him we were watching?"

"I did," Firekeeper agreed. "I am not certain, though, that he is the One. The other one, smaller, with the hooked nose and silver-shot black hair, they all seem to defer to him."

"True," Blind Seer admitted, "but how could he defeat even the next smallest in a fight? Certainly he couldn't defeat the huge one."

"Maybe they are not a full pack," Firekeeper speculated. "They are all males and how could a pack survive without females?"

"All male?" asked the wolf in astonishment. "How can you tell? They smell of smoke and sweat to me."

"Not by scent," the woman admitted. "I could be wrong, but it seems that I remember ways of telling."

"She is right," came a shrill voice from above them. "Males all."

The speaker was the peregrine falcon, Elation, who had been introduced to Firekeeper soon after sunrise. Elation was a beautiful example of her kind, compact of body, with plumage of a deep blue-grey. Her head was capped with feathers the color of slate and her white throat and underbody were marked with darker bars. Brown eyes ringed with bright yellow missed nothing.

"If you say so," Blind Seer said, immediately deferring to the bird's greater experience, "then it must be so, but I'd prefer to be able to trust my nose."

Ignoring the conversation between falcon and wolf, Firekeeper studied the six gathered below, feeling memories stirring and teasing just beyond what she could grasp.

The men possessed a certain degree of grace, neither toppling over nor lumbering like bears as they made their way about on two legs. Firekeeper knew this was how she herself moved, had even glimpsed her reflection and studied the distorted image of her shadow, but seeing others move this way was a revelation. Before she had always felt vaguely like a freak. Now she felt justified in her choice.

Already Firekeeper had observed many things she planned to adapt to her use. All of the men wore their hair caught behind their heads with a thong—a thing much more convenient than her own short cropping with its heritage of odd-length ends that dangled in her eyes.

The hides they wore were different, too. She didn't think that all their clothing was made from leather, though leather was amply represented. Magpie-like, she wanted to steal some for her own use.

When four of the two-legs left the camp, Blind Seer and Elation followed to learn where they went. Firekeeper remained behind, studying the two remaining.

One was quite tall, the other among the smallest of the group. Neither openly deferred to the other, so she guessed that they were of similar rank within their pack. Wolf-like, she dismissed the smaller one as less important and gave most of her attention to the bigger and stronger.

This one was the second largest of the two-legs, smaller only than the one who towered over the rest as the Royal Wolves did over the Cousins.

A passing thought distracted Firekeeper. Could the two-legs be like the forest-dwellers, each with two kinds? Could the huge man be, in fact, the master of the rest?

After some consideration, she dismissed the idea. The big man had deferred quite openly to several of the others. A Royal Wolf, even a lesser one like herself, would never do so before even the strongest of

Cousins. If the two-legs had a Royal kind, it was not represented among those here.

Or they all could be of the Royal kind . . .

She shook her head as if chasing a fly from her ear. Too much guessing. Too little that was certain. As the Ones taught the pups when hunting, guesses were no replacement for knowledge.

Firekeeper returned her unruly attention to the man below.

He was tall enough to reach effortlessly into the lower limbs of the tree from which the two-legs had hung their food. He was strong enough to control the elk-with-long-hair, even though they outmassed him. After a time, she sorted his attire from himself and could better see what he looked like.

His hair was reddish, the color of a fox's pelt or an oak leaf in autumn. Loosed from its thong, it hung straight, going past his shoulders by perhaps the breadth of two fingers. It was cut so neatly that when it was tied back not a strand strayed from its bonds.

What she could see of Fox Hair's skin seemed lighter than her own, redder as well. His eyes were light, but not blue. At this distance she could not tell precisely what color they were. From the way he moved, the little extra motions he made, the fluidity of his limbs, she guessed that he was young compared with some of the others.

Fox Hair was injured as well, walking as if he had thorns in his feet but not the wit to pull them out.

The smaller man was colored in shades of brown like a rabbit or a deer. Unlike the red-haired man, he had a thin strip of hair growing between his nose and his upper lip. It seemed to bother him, for as he went about the camp doing incomprehensible things with other incomprehensible things, he often pulled at it with his fingers.

So much! And so much unknowable! Firekeeper watched, fascination turning into frustration. In the late afternoon, the other four two-legs returned and more than ever she was certain that the little hawk-nosed man with black and white hair was the One among them.

Blind Seer came and flopped beside her, his flanks heaving with laughter.

"They went hither and yon, over hills and around trees. I'll give it to the tawny-furred one. He knows something of the forest, but he'd know more if he'd heed his red-and-white spotted pack mate. She saw me time and again—when I let her! From her scent, she's of our kind in the same way the foxes are and she had wit enough to stay clear of me!"

Firekeeper listened patiently to her brother's boasting. "Did they find what they seek?"

"No, but Tawny came close. If he goes west again tomorrow, he will find it."

"Hawk Nose is their leader," Firekeeper said. "I am certain of it now. Elation, what did he find?"

"Less than he knew," came the screeched reply. "Time and again, he stopped to study the trunk of a tree or a stump or a pile of rocks. He had the giant collect some things that interested him."

"My two looked at such things as well," Blind Seer admitted. "I think they look for sign of their missing kin. Tell me, falcon, do two-legs do things to trees?"

"Even as your sister does," Elation agreed, "though she is less obvious about her comings and goings. Two-legs cut down trees, pile up stones, make lairs from these things or feed wood to their hungry fires."

"Then these two-legs should be able to find sign of where my ancestors found Firekeeper."

"If the signs are not too old."

Blind Seer turned to Firekeeper. "Will you talk with them tonight?"

"No!" the young woman replied, suddenly panicked. "They are still too strange. Let me follow their movements for a bit longer."

"Well enough," he soothed. "I have not had this much fun since we raced with the young bucks of the Royal Elk for sport."

Firekeeper rose to her feet, aware that she was hungry and very bored from a day spent mostly sitting still.

"Come, dear heart. Hunt with me. Dusk is falling and I have no desire to watch shadows by firelight."

Blind Seer howled in anticipation. "And you, falcon?"

"I have dined on mice and young rabbits, today," Elation said, preening her wing feathers. "I will watch the two-legs until darkness falls. Then I will sleep."

Firekeeper stretched, shaking the numbness from her limbs. Growling low in her throat, she flung herself on Blind Seer. They wrestled for a brief time; then, wild-eyed and excited, they chased each other down the hill.

"Wolves!" said the falcon to herself. "May as well try to understand a storm cloud."

WHEN MORNING CAME, the two-legs began taking down their dens and loading things onto their animals.

"Perhaps Tawny is more clever than I thought," Blind Seer admitted. "Look, he goes ahead with Spots and Mountain to mark a trail."

"He marks it," Firekeeper said when they had followed Tawny for a ways, "as a bear or mountain lion does, by stripping the good bark from a tree."

"Such marks do last," Blind Seer said, "longer than our scent posts, especially when the rain comes. I wonder if he found such marks during yesterday's hunt?"

"He did! Look!" Firekeeper exclaimed, moving to investigate a tree trunk when Tawny and Mountain were safely past. "Here is such a mark, greyed now by weather, but clear."

"Then he reads a trail," Blind Seer said, "and the others will follow his marking. Why doesn't he trust them to see the old trail or the marks of his passage? The last alone would sing to me at least until the next rain."

Firekeeper shrugged. "They are deaf and blind and dead of nose as you have said many times before."

She didn't add that she had long been aware that her senses were less keen than those of the wolves. Her upright manner of travel and a sharper sense for color had provided her with some compensation. Now she was beginning to wonder if her senses were to those of the two-legs as the wolves' were to hers.

Her head hurt a little at the consideration and she distracted herself by concentrating on the problem at hand.

"Do we follow the larger pack," she said, "or these two?"

"Why not both?" Blind Seer laughed. "Elation has stayed with the larger pack, but she can come ahead if we go back. At the pace these move, you and I can dance around them as we dance around a crippled doe."

"True," she admitted. "First then, let us go with these. I wish to see if I can learn more of these signs they are using to find their way."

They did so, learning of piled cairns of rock, appreciating Tawny's skill when he located a pouch of slim sticks with sharp points where it had been cached in a tree.

"He is not such a fool as I thought," Blind Seer said again. "Without scent or sight to guide him, he found that thing."

Firekeeper nodded. "He is searching for things he knows may be," she hazarded, "the way in winter we know that fish sleep beneath the ice or deer hide in their secret yards. He seeks a possibility and sometimes he finds it."

"It excites him," Blind Seer said. "Look how he marks that tree with his scent and cuts the bark away from another."

"At this pace, they will reach the Burnt Place when the sun is at peak or soon after," Firekeeper said. "Let us go back and watch the others."

Blind Seer agreed and they ran swiftly, ignoring the scolding of squirrels and the frightened flight of a doe and fawn. Wolves needed to eat either frequently or heavily, but when something interested them, they could forget hunger. Firekeeper possessed less stamina than her kin, but she had long ago learned to ignore her belly's plaints.

They found the larger, slower-moving group by following the reek of the not-quite-elk. As the wolves slowed, so as not to startle their subjects, the falcon called greeting.

"How goes it with Tawny and Mountain?"

"Well enough," Firekeeper answered. "And these?"

"Slow! So slow!" the great bird shrieked. "These men are like ants though, steady."

"We will watch here if you wish to hunt."

"Good! Then I fly ahead to see what the others do."

Firekeeper was far less bored by the two-legs' slow progress than Elation had been. Other than young possums clinging to their mothers, she had never seen one creature riding another.

"Most other animals," she commented to Blind Seer, "carry their babies in their mouths. Two-legs sit on these elk as if on a rock."

"They go more slowly than they would on their own feet," Blind Seer added. "I wonder why they bother?"

Firekeeper shrugged. "Another mystery."

The sun was slightly past midday when a bleating bellow, rather like that of a moose but not quite so, called out from the west. The sound stirred great excitement among the two-legs, who had persisted in their steady progress, even eating their food while perched upon the backs of the not-elks.

Hawk Nose, the One of the two-legs, took a curving thing the color of antler from where it had hung on his belt and, putting it to his lips, made an answering sound.

"He blows into it!" Firekeeper said, amazed and laughing. "Look how his cheeks round out beneath their hair! He looks like a bullfrog courting in the spring!"

Blind Seer laughed with her, then added, "So these two-legs howl, too, in their fashion. The thing he puts to his mouth makes a fair cry."

"Just as the Fang gives me teeth like a wolf," Firekeeper thought aloud, "this thing gives Hawk Nose the lungs of a moose. Are all their things ways of being more than they could be alone?"

"Two-legs," her brother replied teasingly, "are weak, hairless creatures with flat teeth, no strength, and little wit. This, though, I have known long before seeing these, eh, Firekeeper?"

Accustomed to such jests, Firekeeper sprang on him, forgetting stealth in the joy of the puppy game. Only when they heard the shrill huffs and screams of the not-elk, the shouts of the two-legs, did they think about the consequences of their actions.

"Oh, well," said Blind Seer, mouthing her arm affectionately as they sat up on the leafy ground. "We have frightened them. Let us hunt, then go ahead to where they go. There is no need for this slow progress when we know the trail's end."

"I agree," Firekeeper said. "The not-elk have our scent now and the two-legs will move more slowly if their pack mates are afraid. I want to see what will happen when they find the Burnt Place."

"The beasts are quiet now," Blind Seer observed.

"Then away with us."

They melted silently into the brush and were well away before Jared Surcliffe, coming with great trepidation to investigate the commotion, found their watching place and gathered from a low-slung briar a grey hank of wolf's fur.

✺

DERIAN CARTER WAS IRRATIONALLY RELIEVED when they caught up with Ox and Race. Irrational because this glade was no safer than any other place, but relieved nonetheless because his nerves were still on edge from the ferocious snarling and growling that had broken the woodland peace a few hours before.

Not that he was afraid of the wolves—or whatever the noise had been. In fact, he'd been amusing himself by imagining his return home wearing a wolf-skin cloak. *"This?"* he'd say to Heather, the baker's daughter. *"Oh, I slew it when it attacked the horses. Mad as the Ravening Beast of Garwood, so our guide said. It had been trailing us for days. We'd hear it howling at night, slavering for our flesh . . ."*

He had the story all scripted out, so carefully refined that sometimes he had to remind himself that the encounter hadn't taken place. Still, he'd been glad enough when the earl had decided to increase their pace.

Earl Kestrel's reason for wanting speed hadn't been fear. It had been eagerness. Race's horn blast had signaled that he and Ox had found something. It couldn't be the prince's settlement—in that case, signaling was strictly forbidden lest it ruin the earl's opportunities for an advantageous approach—but it was something.

Now Derian looked around the open meadow wondering just what Race Forester had found and what it would mean to their quest. However, until the horses and mules were untacked and groomed, he wouldn't be free to join the conference.

As a compromise between duty and curiosity, Derian moved to where he could eavesdrop.

"Yes, Race," Earl Kestrel was saying. "Evidently there was a settlement of some size here. Now that you point it out, I see where the palisade must have been. Those mounds of vines and suchlike, those must have been buildings."

"Yes, my lord," Race replied. "Fire did for the place pretty thoroughly, but until we do some digging we can't tell if the fire came before or after the people left."

"How can we tell?" called Ox from where he was helping Valet pitch the earl's tent.

"By what's left behind," Race said. "If we find most of their goods or bones, then we must face that the fire happened when they were here. Graves, too. Survivors would have buried their dead before moving on or left some sort of marker."

"To do less," Jared agreed from where he was tending the cook fire, "would be an insult to the spirits of the departed."

Derian nodded thoughtful agreement. Ancestors were the means by which the living petitioned the natural world. Even if the dead had no blood kin among the living, they still would be the ancestors of the settlement group, meant to be revered even as Hawk Haven still shared with King Tedric and his family reverence for the spirit of Zorana

Shield, who had won the kingdom its freedom following the Years of Abandonment.

Since the discussion had become general, he asked:

"Will we start looking for signs while we still have light?"

"No, Derian," Earl Kestrel replied. "Long enough has passed for vines and young trees to sprout from the houses. Almost certainly, the settlers dug cellars and wells. We do not want to stumble into these in twilight. Tether the horses well away from the ruins of the palisade and check for anything that might harm them."

"Yes, sir. And, my lord?"

"Yes?"

"If we're going to remain here some days, we should make a corral for the horses and mules. Pickets can be ripped up when the ground is soft like this and I dislike the idea of tying them when there are wolves about."

"Good thought. Will hobbles do?"

"For some, perhaps, but not all."

"Very well. Tomorrow, you can begin constructing a corral. I want Ox for the excavation."

"Yes, my lord."

Mentally, Derian kicked himself for making more work; then he kicked himself again for acting like a child. Taking care of the mounts and pack animals was his responsibility and he had done a good job so far, hadn't lost a single beast. Let the earl and the others dig through the ruins and make the great discoveries.

Suddenly he cheered up.

That way they'd be the ones to disturb any angry spirits.

THE MORNING AFTER THEIR ARRIVAL at the Burnt Place, the two-legs began rooting about like young beavers with an undammed stream or bears scenting a honeycomb in a hollow tree.

Firekeeper had admired how quickly they had rebuilt their portable dens and created a little nesting place for themselves at the edge of the meadow. However, when Fox Hair began his day felling small trees and piling them on each other, she was completely puzzled.

Elation clarified his actions for her.

"They plan to stay awhile," she shrieked. Then more calmly, "The fallen trees will cage their riding beasts so they do not stray. Fox Hair is their keeper."

"Oh." Firekeeper was confused; then she thought of an analogy. "Just as a young wolf acts as nursemaid to the pups. I understand. I did think he was junior among them, for all that he is so big."

"And the others," Blind Seer asked with a lazy yawn, "those who root in the heart of the Burnt Place. What are they making?"

"Nothing," Firekeeper replied with certainty. "They are looking for traces of those who once denned there. Didn't Elation tell us that they sought them?"

"True enough." Blind Seer yawned again. "I will sleep while they dig. Wake me if you have need."

"I will," she promised, her gaze drawn irresistibly back to the two-legs.

Today Firekeeper climbed a towering evergreen which oozed strongly scented sap onto her hands and feet. She would have preferred an oak or maple, but their pale green, still growing leaves offered little concealment.

Hidden by the thick, dark green needles, Firekeeper had a clear view of all that went on below. Elation perched nearby.

Sometimes the falcon was able to clarify some incomprehensible behavior; sometimes she admitted herself as confused as the wolf. Sometimes, when the scene below became tedious, she dozed or hunted mice.

Even though the two-legs kept watch around them, they never looked up, never saw the watchers. Firekeeper didn't hold this against them. When she remained still there was nothing to be seen. When she climbed higher or lower, she was careful to wiggle the branches no more than a squirrel might. Moreover, there was a stream between her tree and the Burnt Place. As none of the two-legs or their animals had crossed this natural barrier, none caught her scent on the ground.

That night she climbed down to join Blind Seer, careful this time to keep their greetings relatively quiet. The two-legs had gathered round their fire and she could hear the rise and fall of their voices as they discussed something—quite likely the results of their day's hunting.

She wished she could understand them, but the sounds they made meant less to her than the hoots of the owls awakening for the night or the sleepy chirps of the day birds settling in to sleep.

❦

BY THE TIME DARKNESS FELL that night, all the expedition was subdued and depressed. Race had pulled out his flute, planning to play for them as he had many nights along the trail, but the instrument dangled unused between his fingers. Even one day's excavation had provided evidence that at least some of Prince Barden's expedition, if not all, had died in this place.

"Human bones," Ox said heavily. "No doubt about it. Even if there was doubt, little things confirm that the settlement wasn't systematically evacuated."

"Little things?" Derian asked. He didn't remember ever seeing the big man so depressed.

"Pots scattered where they fell," Ox explained, "a tool kit, a sword with bits of the scabbard burnt hard around it. Things they would have taken with them if they were merely resettling elsewhere."

Race glanced at Earl Kestrel. "We could do some systematic salvage work here."

"Looting, you mean!" the nobleman said sharply. "No! There will be nothing of the kind. Cousin Jared, to what society did your parents give you when you were born?"

"The Eagle," Jared replied uncomfortably.

Derian wondered at Doc's apparent embarrassment, then realized that by giving their son to the society patronized by the royal house, Jared Surcliffe's parents had been openly soliciting royal favor. That would be an embarrassment for a man who took such obvious delight in making his way through his own skills.

"I thought that was what I recalled." Earl Kestrel nodded somberly, apparently immune to his relative's embarrassment. "Eagle joins heaven and earth with his flight; therefore you will take charge of the funeral rites for those who died here. Also, if anyone can be identified, you will keep records of the proof."

Doc lowered his head in acquiescence, but there was a frown visible on his lips.

No wonder, Derian thought. *What the earl means is: "You will do your best to discover if Prince Barden is among the dead." How does he expect Doc to learn that from old charred bones?*

Surcliffe voiced some of the same doubt. "I will try, cousin, but unless the body was miraculously preserved or wears on its bones some bit of jewelry or insignia that has survived the fire, the best I can do is count skulls and pieces of skulls and hope to guess how many died here."

"Very well," Earl Kestrel said heavily. "Men, retrieve not only bones but also anything that might have belonged to the owner."

Race Forester was obviously unhappy about this situation. "I didn't hire on to dig up people's bones," he muttered, almost, but not quite, mutinous.

"I hired you to help me find the missing prince," Kestrel replied sharply, "but if you are afraid of digging, you can do Derian's work with the horses and keeping the camp. Derian, consider yourself reassigned!"

"Yes, my lord!"

"I didn't say . . ." Race Forester began to protest, but a sharp glance from the earl's pale grey eyes silenced him. Disappointment or perhaps sorrow had set the nobleman's usually short temper smoldering. Instead, Race swallowed whatever he had planned to say and occupied himself by taking his flute out and cleaning the stops.

Derian Carter whistled a light air as he fetched the water that night, his previous fear of ancestral spirits quieted by his tacit promotion. Tomorrow Race Forester would haul and carry!

⚜

FIREKEEPER WATCHED THE NEXT DAY as the two-legs turned most of their efforts to excavating the burned-out ruins. Even a steady drizzle that transformed soot and dirt to tacky mud didn't stop them.

"They work like a pregnant mother searching for a perfect den site," commented Blind Seer when he awakened from one of his frequent naps. "Do you think they're whelping?"

"Idiot," she said fondly, tossing a few twigs down at him. "They're carrying out the bones of the ones who died in the fire. Heads interest them especially."

" 'One head, one kill,' " quoted Blind Seer. "How better to tell if they have found all their missing ones? How soon till they find *your* head, sweet Firekeeper?"

"All in my time," she temporized. "Whenever I think I understand them, they do something strange. Today Fox Hair is certainly over Tawny. I heard no sound of fighting. Why then the change?"

"Perhaps they fought while we were out hunting." Blind Seer dismissed the question for something more immediate. "I'm hungry, tired of eating rabbit. The wind is ripe with the scent of some spring-mad buck. Will you hunt with me or must you stay to see each bone taken from the soil?"

Firekeeper considered. "I'll hunt. Elation, will you tell me if they depart from here?"

"One or all?" the bird asked.

"All or mostly all," the young woman replied. "One or two may go hunt for the rest."

When she and Blind Seer returned, full of the flesh of a foolish buck who had cracked his foreleg while fighting his reflection, more skulls and pieces of skulls were laid out in neat ranks. Many were broken, but the two-legs who was their keeper sat fitting broken pieces together into an approximation of a whole.

"Strange," said Firekeeper, "many of the bones must have been burnt entirely. Why do they keep at this crazy hunt?"

"Because," Elation said, swiveling her head so that one golden-ringed eye pinned Firekeeper securely, "from knowing how many are certainly dead they can estimate how many may be dead. It is not unlike judging a wolf pack from two of its members."

"They must know by now," Blind Seer said, licking a trace of deer blood from one paw, "that all or nearly all died here. Firekeeper, you will need to find courage to speak with them before they go back across the mountains."

"I will," she promised, "I will."

But that night, as she and Blind Seer sang home the news of the two-legs and of their own doings, Firekeeper wondered how she could ever dare to approach the strangers.

DERIAN WOKE UP feeling like the aftermath of a New Beer festival. As he struggled awake, he felt vaguely surprised that his mouth was not foul, nor his limbs heavy.

Then he remembered. This hangover was spiritual, not physical, the result of a day spent grubbing in the burned ruins of peoples' homes, bringing out their bones and their belongings, ending any hope that Prince Barden's expedition had survived.

Breakfast that morning was a subdued meal, but at least Earl Kestrel had joined them. The night before he had attended the ceremony for the dead that Jared had improvised, then had retired to his tent. Valet had come over to the main fire a few minutes later and requested silence for his master.

"His youngest sister, you may recall, was Prince Barden's wife," he said before departing.

"I had forgotten," Derian had whispered, appalled that he had thought the earl's mood only disappointed ambition, "if I ever knew."

Ox and Race nodded agreement. Doc sighed.

"Eirene," he had said as if the name itself were a prayer. "Never beautiful, but gentle and sweet. Brave beneath her quiet demeanor. King Tedric didn't care who his youngest son married as long as the bride was from one of the Great Houses."

"So Prince Barden married for love?" Derian had asked softly.

"Yes," Doc had replied, wiping his eyes with the back of his hand. "He did. I'm for bed."

All had nodded. No one felt much like talking in any case. They had performed the evening chores with a minimum of discussion and each had retired to his own tent. Ox had fallen asleep with the ease of an old campaigner, but Derian had heard him muttering in his sleep.

Derian himself had lain awake for some hours watching the shadows against the canvas, trying to imagine what might have happened to all those people. His mind was so populated with horrors that the nightly wolf concert had seemed like a familiar, almost pleasant thing—that is, until he began to imagine wolves dragging roasted corpses from the burned buildings and feasting on the charred flesh.

This morning, however, Earl Kestrel did not mention his sister's death and no one had the courage to offer him sympathy. Instead they listened alertly when, after putting aside his porridge bowl, Earl Kestrel began the morning conference.

"Does anyone have a theory about what happened here? I would like to be able to make a full report to the king."

Poor fellow, Derian thought with surprised sympathy. *Not only does he share our common horror and the loss of his little sister, but also he has to face telling King Tedric his son is surely dead.*

Race Forester offered tentatively, "A fire in the night, I'd say. I'd swear that two of those I uncovered were lying down, peaceful-seeming."

"No one bore weapons," Ox agreed quietly. Soot he hadn't washed away the night before blended in with his scruffy beard, making his face unusually dark. "But how could such a fire start if everyone was asleep?"

"Coals poorly banked, a spark in a chimney, a candle guttering out on a bedside table, a pipe left smoldering," Doc shrugged. "These things and their like have happened before."

"But how did they sleep through it all!" Derian protested, his own voice as shrill as that of the hawk whose cries they had heard periodically over these past days.

"Smoke," said Ox. "Smoke is more dangerous than fire and it rises. Families asleep in the lofts and attics of their cottages might breathe in their deaths without knowing."

"If they trusted themselves to the protection of their palisade," Race said, his voice hoarse, "the fire could have gotten out of control before anyone knew. My lord!" he appealed to the earl, his eyes wide. "Pray tell me that we are not going to spend today as we did yesterday!"

"We are," Earl Kestrel replied, his gaze stern. "I owe the king a full report. You, as yesterday, will tend the camp."

Race sulked, mutiny in his eyes. "It isn't right to so disturb the dead!"

"It is not right," the earl said in measured tones, "to leave them without their rituals."

So passed another day of soot, of painful discovery, of sweaty, back-breaking labor. The only relief was that it was no longer raining.

At the end of the day, Derian was so heartsick he didn't protest when Race shoved a pail at him and demanded that he fetch water from the stream.

Instead he staggered down the newly broken footpath, hardly seeing the ground beneath his feet for the more vivid reality in his memory: a wedding bowl, the names of husband and wife still readable despite the cracking; a tin horse, twisted, but twin to one he had bought his little brother for Summer Festival; buttons lined in a row, though the shirt they closed was ash; a stone inkwell.

And, of course, the bones of the dead.

The stream water was icy cold, fed with runoff from the not too distant mountains. On impulse, Derian thrust his head beneath a little waterfall that interrupted the stream's course. Shedding his clothing as if he could shed the visions with it, he waded into the water, dunking his head again and again, scrubbing the soot from his skin with handfuls of sand.

He could feel his lips turning blue as he pulled himself onto the bank, but his mind was his own again. He could even grin, imagining the expressions on the others' faces when he came into camp stark naked, buckets of water slung from the yoke over his shoulders and his damp clothing in his hands.

Derian was adjusting the yoke on his bare neck when he saw the impossible thing. Across the water, a few yards upstream from the waterfall, was a broad patch of sand, deposited, no doubt, when the waters ran higher.

In the sand, as clear as daylight, was the solid imprint of a small human foot. Next to it, as if the two had walked side by side, were the equally real prints of an improbably large wolf.

III

FIREKEEPER SLIPPED AWAY in the confusion following Fox Hair's discovery of her footprint in the sand. Blind Seer ran with her, but Elation remained faithfully watching the two-legs.

"I have been as stupid as an unweaned pup!" Firekeeper admonished herself aloud. "I knew that they read trails with their eyes, if not with their noses."

"One footprint will not lead them to you," Blind Seer said calmly. "Your trail went from sandbank into the stream, onto a rock, across a pebbled shore, and then up into the tree branches. They may find where the evergreen bled upon you, but its boughs sweep low enough that they may not even look."

Firekeeper scowled, slowed her run to a trot, then stopped completely, leaning her back against a smooth birch trunk.

"As I have planned how I will meet them," she said thoughtfully, "all my dreams have held them ignorant of my existence. This is an adjustment."

" 'When the calf bolts right,' " Blind Seer quoted, " 'it is foolish to run left.' "

"I know," she said, her scowl lightening only some. "Don't you realize that I'm scared?"

"Scared?" The wolf cocked his head to one side, perking his ears inquiringly. "Of the two-legs?"

"Not of them, of what meeting with them will mean." Firekeeper slid down against the tree until she sat on the leaf mold beneath. "All my life, but for shadows I recall only in dreams, I have been a wolf. I knew I was different from my brothers and sisters, but living day-to-day filled my head. I could ignore the differences if I choose."

"And you so chose," Blind Seer said, understanding.

"Yes. Now these," she gestured wildly back to where the two-legs have their camp, "come and my life will never be the same. If I speak with them or if I do not, if I travel with them or if I do not: any choice reshapes the world I have known. Never, never again will I be only a wolf."

Blind Seer scratched vigorously behind one ear. "Then speak with them. What does it matter that they have seen one footprint? I call it a good thing, for your coming when they have believed all their people dead will be a relief."

"I hope so," she breathed softly. "By the blood that runs through my body, I hope so."

❀

INITIALLY, DERIAN'S CLAIM WAS DISMISSED as a prank. Only when he convinced Ox to go look for himself and Ox called Race and the two men confirmed that the footprint was both real and too small to belong to any of their number, only then did the others begin to share his excitement.

"Why would I lie?" Derian said indignantly when they had regathered around the fire.

"No reason." Jared Surcliffe shrugged apologetically. "Our disappointment spoke, not any disbelief in you. After so much pain, so much work for nothing, it was easier to believe you were suddenly given to boyish pranks than to feel hope awaken once more."

Ox grunted agreement. Race nodded. Valet gave a ghost of a smile, and Earl Kestrel, seated on his canvas camp chair, simply brooded over the implications of the discovery. That was all the apology Derian was likely to get, but it warmed him strangely. He'd started out this journey the youngest and most untried. Now they gave him no more consideration than they would to any man.

After a time, the earl cleared his throat and said, "Of course, Derian's discovery changes everything. In the morning, we must begin searching. Race, you are the most skilled in woodcraft. Who would you assign to the search?"

"You, my lord, and Sir Jared know something of tracking, but the one I would choose . . ."

Derian straightened, hoping that Race saw some promise in him.

". . . is your valet. I've watched him. He misses nothing."

Valet blinked, then refilled his master's teacup before reseating himself and continuing to darn a holed sock.

"He does that," Earl Kestrel said with the closest thing to affection Derian had heard in his dry tones. "You may have him if you wish."

"My lord!" Valet said in protest, alarm widening his brown eyes.

"My comfort can wait," the earl insisted. "Come dawn, the four of us will divide the search under Race's direction. Derian and Ox will tend the camp and, if their other duties permit, continue excavating the ruins of the settlement."

Murmured agreement was almost drowned out by the now nightly chorus of wolf howls.

"Poor lost soul," Jared said softly, "out there alone with the wolves on his trail."

"I COULD FAIR HIRE out as a tailor when this journey's done," grumbled Derian, as he took up yet another pair of riding breeches and settled his palm shield into place.

"Derian Tailor doesn't sound bad," Ox replied. He set aside the burned roof beam he'd been shifting and wiped his forehead with his hand, leaving a large black streak on the pink skin. "Though I myself would go for Saddler or Sailmaker. You're working leather now and, by my way of seeing things, those are more interesting jobs than making shirts and breeches."

Derian glanced at Ox and confirmed that the big man was teasing him.

"Well, you would . . ."

His ready retort stuck in his throat for, across the meadow, something—someone—was emerging from the forest.

His first impression was of woodland shadows come to life, for the figure was all browns and blacks. Then it resolved into a person clad in a rough cape of poorly tanned leather; a knife hung from an equally crude belt.

"Ox," Derian hissed softly. "Move slowly. Look to the west."

His caution was merited, for when the big man started to turn, the person moved slightly, poised now to flee.

"Great Boar," Ox whispered. "We've found him!"

"Or he us," Derian replied in equally soft tones. "What do we do?"

"I frighten even those who know me," Ox said, "on account of my size. You handle him and I'll hunker down and keep my movements slow."

Derian nodded, wishing for a moment that Earl Kestrel were there, then with a startling insight glad that he was not. The severe earl with his sharp commands and ordered plans would only frighten this shy creature away.

Carefully, Derian set his sewing aside and rose to greet the newcomer.

"Hello," he said, speaking in the gentle tones he reserved for a frightened horse. "Welcome."

The person showed no sign of understanding, but he didn't bolt. Encouraged, Derian deliberately extended his arms, palms upward, showing that he bore no weapons.

The newcomer mimicked the gesture and for the first time Derian saw that the deeply tanned arms and legs were silvered with countless scars, some just lines, others puckered and seamed. Pity now mingled with his excitement.

"He's been badly used," Derian said softly to Ox.

"He . . ." Ox paused, carefully lowering his voice, though excitement vibrated in every note. "He! I think it's a she, Derian. Look more closely."

Derian did so and for the first time noticed the visitor's nearly hairless arms and legs, the smooth curve of the throat. Either this was a young boy or a woman.

"If you say so," he said uncertainly. "It's hard to tell. That cape is so heavy it hides the body."

The person now took a few hesitant steps closer. Her gait was light and graceful; her bare legs rippled with muscle.

Derian, well aware that the woman could vanish into the forest without warning, matched her approach step by step. Compared with how she moved, his dancer's gait seemed awkward and clumsy.

She stopped at two arm-lengths' distance, studying him with intelligent eyes. Her nostrils widened and fluttered slightly as if she was taking in his scent as well as his appearance.

Derian halted when she did, studying the stranger as she did him. She was of fair height, taller than Earl Kestrel, but then he was short for a man. Her exposed skin was so deeply tanned and weathered that he could not guess what its original color might be, but he guessed from the lack of freckles that she was not as fair as, say, himself or Ox.

He would bet that her dark brown hair had been cut with the knife that hung from her belt. That and a pouch around her neck seemed to be her only belongings—unless one counted the rough hide garment. Wildness emanated from her like a wind from an approaching storm, but her gaze showed rational judgment.

"She's no village idiot," he said to Ox.

"Careful what you say," Ox cautioned. "Who is to say she won't understand?"

Derian was curiously certain that she did not understand, but he nodded.

After more scrutiny, the woman stepped closer. This time Derian held his ground, unwilling to press her. His skin thrilled as she raised a callused hand and touched first his cheek, then his hair, then the fabric of his woolen shirt.

The feel of the last delighted her. Her expression brightened into a wide, unfeigned, childlike smile. For the first time, she seemed human rather than something of the woodlands given form. Derian smiled in return.

This startled her, but only for a moment. She kept her place and continued her tactile investigation. Derian covered his vague embarrassment by saying to Ox:

"She is definitely female. I got a good glimpse of her breasts just now. Small, though. Young, maybe."

Ox grunted agreement. "I'd guess she's been watching us, maybe since we came here. She seems curious but not amazed, like she's confirming things she already knew."

The woman turned her head at the sound of Ox's voice and studied him, but made no effort to go closer. A faint smile shaped her lips as she compared his height with Derian's. Then she touched Derian's clean-shaven cheek and frowned.

With a swift gesture, she mimed the line of Ox's beard, then touched Derian's cheek again.

"She wants to know why you have a beard," Derian interpreted in delighted wonder, "and I do not."

He considered how to answer, then mimed removing his knife from its sheath and putting the edge to his face.

The woman started back, considered, then tilted her head in what was clearly an interrogative gesture. Derian repeated the motions. She smiled and mimed taking out her own knife and chopping at a lock of hair that hung close to her eyes.

"That's it," Derian replied. "You cut your hair and I shave my face."

She was kneeling down, perhaps to examine his slippers, when something made her jump up and back in one fluid motion. Then, silently as she had arrived, she vanished back into the woods.

Only after she was gone did Derian notice that the horses were casually sniffing the air. A few moments later, moving with a woodsman's stealth and grace, Race Forester, followed by the even more cautious Valet, emerged from the forest.

"No luck," he called. "Any word from the others?"

Ox found his voice before Derian did. "No, but she's been here, right here with us. She heard you coming and vanished like a dream."

❦

FIREKEEPER, CROUCHED OVER a kill she was sharing with Blind Seer, spoke for the first time since she had fled the two-legs' camp.

"I couldn't bear it!" she cried. "I was doing well dealing with one, knowing the second was there, but when I heard the others returning, I couldn't bear the thought of being beneath so many eyes. Now I know how a fawn must feel when the full pack cries the hunt."

"The full pack would never hunt a fawn," Blind Seer said practically, "but I understand you. Still, dear heart, I think you have done well."

"I ran," she said bluntly.

"So, go back."

"Not now, not tonight. Tonight I want to sing my story home to the Ones, run for a time in the enfolding arms of the dark, sleep through daylight for a change instead of crouching in a tree like a squirrel."

"Who's stopping you?" Blind Seer asked, chewing on the gristle end of a bone.

She grinned at him, punched him in the shoulder, then grabbed at the bone. He slashed at her, raising a slight blood trail on the skin of her arm, but she had pulled the bone from between his paws. Leaping to her feet, she raised it over her head, wiggling her hips in a puppy frolic.

"Got it! Got it! Slow slug!"

He growled at her, crouched to spring. She kicked him in the nose; he knocked her from her feet. She brought the bone down on his head—hard. He barked in mock anger. She rolled clear. He leapt on her. Together they wrestled, the bone forgotten, the night mad in their veins.

Tension ebbed as Firekeeper played with the blue-eyed wolf. She simply couldn't afford the indulgence and come close to holding her own. Blind Seer's furiously wagging tail proved too much temptation for her. She grabbed it, pulled. He howled in surprise. She rolled back, belly up, throat exposed, laughing, laughing . . .

"I do love you!" she said when she had her breath again. "Why wasn't I born truly a wolf?"

AFTER DERIAN AND OX finished their report, Earl Kestrel half-rose from his seat and bellowed, "You had her and you let her get away!"

"As soon try to grasp water," Ox said bluntly.

"But Derian said that she came close enough to touch him!" The earl's tone was not in the least conciliatory.

"She did at that," the bodyguard agreed, "but still there would have been no holding her, even if we'd had more than a moment's warning of her flight. I've never seen any person move so fast."

The earl was still glowering, but he fell silent long enough for Jared Surcliffe to ask:

"How old would you guess she was?"

Derian spread his hands and shrugged. "Hard to say. Not old. I'd say young."

"Young as in thirty," Doc pressed, "or young as in eighteen?"

"Eighteen," Derian said promptly, "and maybe younger than that. She was female, but didn't have much in the way of breasts."

He'd already explained, glad that the darkness hid his blush, how he'd come to be sure that the visitor was female.

"If my records are correct," Earl Kestrel said ponderously, "there were two young girls with Prince Barden's expedition. One was Lady Blysse. The other was the daughter of two of the prince's associates. I have her name written down somewhere. Of course, there could have been others. Or the young woman you saw could have been a child born after they were settled here."

"My lord," Race offered haughtily, still indignant, for the earl had yelled at him for scaring the visitor away, "from what we've seen of the ruins the fire happened ten or so years ago. There are saplings growing out of the burned houses that are eight years old. The extent of vine coverage speaks for a long passage of time as well."

"Would you say," Earl Kestrel asked Derian, "that young woman you saw was as young as eight?"

"Definitely not, my lord. She had breasts, small as they were. I don't want to be accused of raising hopes, sir, but she could have been right about the age of your niece, the Lady Blysse."

"Dark hair, dark eyes?"

"Yes, sir. That is, her hair was not quite as dark as yours or your cousins'."

Before your hair started turning white that is, Derian added mentally. A small grin at the corner of Ox's mouth told him that his friend was sharing the thought.

"Prince Barden," Jared said with infinite caution, "had dark brown hair. Eirene's hair, however, was pale blond and the child, as I recall her, took after her mother."

"Children often darken with age." Earl Kestrel dismissed the difficulty with a casual wave of his hand. "And this young woman has probably not bathed except by accident."

Derian was offended, as if the visitor were his personal creation rather than his accidental discovery.

"She smelled clean to me, my lord, slightly of sweat and there was definitely the stink of the hide she wore about her, but she looked as if she knew how to wash."

Earl Kestrel shrugged. "Good. It would be a great embarrassment to bring King Tedric his granddaughter and have her ignorant of bathing."

So that's how it's going to be, Derian thought. *We have found Lady Blysse wandering wild in the forest. Now we will restore her to her family. To the king and the Kestrels.*

Thinking of the lively curiosity in the dark eyes, he felt oddly sad and suddenly immeasurably older. For the first time, he understood just how politics used some men and women—and how it consumed still others.

"If she lost her parents when she was young," Doc mused, thinking aloud, "it may explain why she did not speak to Derian and Ox. She may have forgotten how to talk. Such has happened to hermits or ship-wreck survivors who are alone for a long time."

"If so," again the earl dismissed the difficulty as trivial, "she can be taught to speak again when we have her in our keeping."

"And how," Race asked deliberately, "shall we catch this wild child? If she is so wood wise, we could search until winter comes and never find her. I could set snares for her perhaps or dig a pit trap . . ."

Earl Kestrel frowned, considering. A voice so rarely heard as to be almost a stranger's spoke from the shadows at the edge of the fire.

"If my lord would permit," Valet said, lifting his traveling iron from the shirt he had been pressing, "I have a suggestion."

"Speak," the earl commanded, as surprised as the rest of them.

"It would be impolitic to have Lady Blysse tell her grandfather that she had been trapped or snared or handled in any rough fashion. I suggest that we convince her to trust us. Derian Carter said that she admired his shirt, did she not?"

"She did," Derian agreed, leaning forward with eagerness, grateful beyond belief that Valet, at least, seemed to see their quarry as worthy of human consideration.

"We have spare clothing among us," Valet continued, tactfully avoid-ing direct mention that his master possessed three changes of clothing to each one carried by the other members of the expedition. "Make her a gift of a shirt. A man's wool shirt with a long tail would cover as much as the hide Derian described."

"Yes! Let her be clothed from my wardrobe," Earl Kestrel proclaimed, apparently mentally drafting a portion of the speech he would make before the king. "Moreover, since she is timid, let the four of us depart at dawn, even as we did today. Perhaps if Derian and Ox alone are in the camp, she could be lured close once more."

"Depart?" Race asked. "Where to?"

"Perhaps there are other survivors," the earl said. "We can look for sign of them. Certainly we could hunt and so augment our larder. It is early for the fattest meat, but surely a man with your talent can find something worth hunting."

A slightly mocking note in his voice revealed that Earl Kestrel had been well aware of the guide's tendency to flaunt his skills.

Race nodded, reluctant to be away from where the real hunt would be going on, but acknowledging the wisdom of his patron's plan. Besides, he couldn't have won an argument on this point in any case.

Earl Kestrel rubbed his hands together in satisfaction.

"Our plan is ready, then. I suggest that all but the first watch get some rest. Tomorrow will be a long and busy day for us all."

Derian, who had the first watch, began his slow perimeter patrol. When he passed the place where the wild visitor had first emerged from the woods he felt a thrill of anticipation. Would she return tomorrow? Would he be able to convince her to stay?

In the darkness he heard a chorus of wolf howls and knew that somehow they held the answer to his questions in their clear, lonesome cries.

FIREKEEPER'S COURAGE HAD RETURNED to her by the middle of the next morning. A full belly and a warm spring day didn't hurt either. This combination, which tended to make the wolves want to nap, had always stirred her desire to explore.

"Sleep then, Brother," she said, stroking Blind Seer's flank. He looked particularly handsome, for she had pulled out all the clumps of shedding fur. "I will go and visit the two-legs again. Elation said that all but Fox Hair and Mountain have gone hunting."

"Will you come back when they sleep?" the wolf asked without opening his blue eyes.

"I will, but I hope my courage does not fail me and I can remain long enough to look closely at the others when they return from hunting."

"Good. I will sleep then but not so deeply that I will fail to hear your call if they give you any trouble."

Firekeeper ruffled his fur and departed. She made a fast trail going to the two-legs' camp, aware that she felt a strange anticipation.

This is like but not like finding the first strawberries in the spring, she thought. *Like but not like returning to a sheltered place in winter and knowing that I can make a fire and get warm. I don't think I have ever felt like this before. It is interesting and not unpleasant.*

When she reached the trees curtaining the edge of the Burnt Place, Firekeeper exchanged greetings with Elation, then made certain all was safe before going out into the open.

All seemed much as it had the day before. Fox Hair was seated on the ground doing something with one of their soft hides. Mountain was shifting burned wood, bringing out things from time to time and setting them on a cleared space.

There were fewer bones now, she noticed. Most of those that were not burned entirely must have been found by now. She wondered, as she never had wondered before, what those other things might be. She herself had found odd things in the grass when the Ones had brought her here each year, but never before had she wondered about what they were.

Almost as if her impulse guided her feet, she emerged from the forest and trotted over to the heap of rubble. Mountain saw her, swallowed a shout, then held completely still. Fox Hair looked up from what he was doing and, as on the day before, rose very slowly.

He smiled at her. She was fairly certain, at least, that this was a smile, not a baring of fangs. Since she had no idea what her own smile looked like, she couldn't be completely certain, but Fox Hair did nothing aggressive so she decided the expression must be a smile.

Again he held out his arms, twisted them so the palms were upraised and open. She imitated the gesture. They stood like this for the long circuit of a robin's song; then Fox Hair lowered his arms slowly.

He said something to Mountain, who answered him in what Firekeeper was certain was a deliberately hushed voice. Nothing they said made any sense, but there was intelligent purpose behind the sounds.

Now Fox Hair crouched and lifted something from the ground near him. Dangling it between two hands, he held it out to her. The wind caught it, making it flap, but Firekeeper stopped herself in mid-bolt. This flapping thing had offered her no harm!

Seeing that she had been startled, Fox Hair carefully spread the thing flat on the ground between them. He said something, plucking at the soft hide he wore, then pointing to the thing on the grass. Cautiously, Firekeeper extended her hand and touched the thing, feeling the same delightful softness that had met her hand the day before.

Again Fox Hair pointed to his upper body, then, in response to something said by Mountain, he tugged his garment clear from his body.

The skin below, she noted, was lighter than that on his face. It was also rippling with cold, as if the warm spring air were as chill as that of midwinter. But these were things she noted in passing. With deliberate motions, Fox Hair was showing her how his garment dropped over his head, rested on his shoulders, fell down over the torso . . .

She yelped in pleased comprehension. Two quick tugs on her belt freed her from her own cumbersome hide. The Fang's Mouth held between her teeth, she bent and lifted the soft thing from the grass. Finding the opening at the bottom proved a bit difficult, for the soft stuff clung together, but she growled at Fox Hair when he moved as if to take it from her.

Once she found the hole at the bottom, she groped and located the hole at the top. There were holes for the arms as well. After some fumbling and getting tangled and nearly panicking and nearly having to drop the Mouth so her head would go through the head hole, she pushed head and neck and arms all through their appropriate openings.

The garment was light, surprisingly warm, and slightly prickly, like the leaves of a mullein plant in late summer. It felt infinitely better against her skin than the hide had done. Over the animal smell, it was scented with lavender and thyme.

Fox Hair extended an arm toward her and she backed and growled. This was hers now. She was not going to let him take it away. He lowered his arm quickly and she saw that he held a thin strip of hide, much like the one at his own waist. Understanding suddenly that he had been offering her a belt, she snatched it from him.

As she looped it about her waist, threading it first through the Mouth as she had learned to do long ago and finding the task much easier with this even piece of leather, she noticed that Fox Hair was staring first at her, then at his hand as if amazed that she had taken the belt so easily.

She grinned at him. Clearly he had never dined with wolves! Only the fastest and fiercest ate from a kill. Even the meat of her own hunting would be stolen if she wasn't careful. She'd learned that young enough.

Fox Hair answered her smile, but she thought there was something of fear and uneasiness in the tang of his sweat.

WHEN THE REST of the expedition returned later that afternoon, Derian was pleased to see that their wild visitor, although clearly nervous, didn't flee.

Lightly balanced on the balls of her feet, ready to run if anything startled her, she watched the four men file into the camp. Race carried a couple of rabbits, Valet a string of brook trout. When they passed her, Derian noticed again how she sniffed the air, taking in their scents.

Clad in her new shirt and nothing else (he couldn't help but remember his embarrassment when she had stripped right in front of both him and Ox) the young woman looked more like an untidy curly-haired urchin than the wild thing who had first come into their camp. With that strange surge of possessiveness, Derian realized that he was glad that Earl Kestrel's first sight of her would be this way, rather than draped in that awkward hide. He would treat her better, maybe even respect her a little.

"How long has she been here?" the earl asked, studying the woman speculatively.

"Since midmorning, sir."

"And has she spoken?"

"No. We've tried talking to her, but she only makes sounds—whines and growls." That had been both disappointing and a bit frightening. Derian brightened. "She's a wonderful mimic, though. We've been communicating a little by signs."

"Communicating?" The aristocratic brow arched.

"Like about the shirt," Derian replied, "and we offered her something to eat."

"Ah!"

"She eats like a wild animal," Derian admitted. "I've seen neater pigs."

"Mm."

Earl Kestrel's attention was only partially on the conversation. His gaze never left the woman; however, as hers never left him, the clinical investigation seemed less rude. She had taken a position a few steps from the center of the camp, carefully leaving a line of escape open behind her.

Kestrel bowed to her. The woman did not respond in kind. Indeed, Derian fancied she looked vaguely disdainful. Kestrel may have reached something of the same conclusion, for he frowned.

The other three men also had been studying the visitor but more covertly, aware of the penalties for usurping the earl's rights. Derian heard Race comment softly to Ox:

"She doesn't look much like a noblewoman. Acts like one though. There's not a humble bone in that body."

Ox chuckled softly. "I'd noticed that myself."

"She's healthy-looking," Doc said, "despite all the scars. She has a fresh cut on her arm, but it shows no sign of festering. Someone's taught her basic hygiene."

"She is cleaner than I'd expected," Race admitted.

"I'd love a chance to examine her," Jared said, raising his voice slightly to include Derian in the implied question. "We might get a better idea of her age then. From what I can see from here, she's not overfed, not precisely undernourished, but there's little fat on her."

Derian, keeping his own voice soft, said, "She's very cautious about letting anyone close. I don't think it's fear of being touched as much as fear of being trapped."

Ox nodded agreement. "She was interested in touching us: my beard, Derian's hair, the fabrics of our clothing, but she wouldn't accept anything but the lightest pat in return. Even then, you could tell she was letting us out of good manners."

"Interesting," Earl Kestrel said. "Very well, Jared, your examination will need to wait until she trusts us more. She has accepted clothing and food, so we are well on the way. I will not have these advances damaged."

As if, Derian thought indignantly, *you had anything to do with those advances.*

"Secondly," Earl Kestrel continued, "we cannot go about simply referring to this young woman as 'she.' There are very good odds that she is Lady Blysse. Address her accordingly."

" 'Lady Blysse,' " Doc offered, the slightest of grins on his lips, "is a bit of a mouthful for daily use. Given her father's standing with the king and her own probable age at the time of the fire, she was most likely merely called 'Blysse.' I suggest we do the same."

Earl Kestrel, who had been a stickler for protocol even on the trail, glowered at his cousin and Doc hastened to clarify.

"I mean no disrespect, Norvin," he said, emphasizing his own point by using the earl's given name rather than his title, "but if we hope to awaken her memories of herself and of language, we don't want our first lesson to be too complicated."

Norvin Norwood, Earl Kestrel, nodded. "I concede the point, Jared. She will be addressed as Blysse."

The young woman had listened to this byplay with apparent interest, but showed no recognition of the name. Derian sighed. As ever, Earl Kestrel had his own best interests at heart.

"She looks well in that shirt," Jared said. "Is the hide you said she was wearing anywhere about? I would like to examine the tailoring. It might give us a clue as to whether she has a companion or two hidden away."

"I set it over there," Derian said. "I thought she might want it," (he remembered the rapidity with which she had snatched the belt from his hand), "but she lost interest in it as soon as she had figured out how the shirt went on."

Doc crossed to examine the hide. Blysse's jet-black gaze followed his movements, but, though she seemed completely absorbed in watching Doc, when the earl took a step toward her, she sprang back without turning her head, without even apparent volition.

"Like an animal," Race muttered. Then, "My lord, I'll go get these fish ready for the fire."

"Go," Earl Kestrel dismissed him. "The rest of you may go about your tasks as well, but do not come near Blysse. Do not make any loud noises or sudden motions. We wish her to feel safe."

Everyone murmured acknowledgment.

The earl continued, "Derian Carter, come stand next to me. I have noticed that she uses you as a touchstone. If we are together, she may be willing to approach me."

Derian did so, almost hating himself for the subliminal thrill he received from standing shoulder to shoulder with a nobleman. Always before this, in small ways and subtle, the earl had kept his distance from the commoners in his expedition.

Blysse didn't seem to notice, but by now Derian was certain that she missed little.

"What are your conclusions about her attire?" Earl Kestrel asked Doc impatiently, for his cousin was staring at Blysse rather than continuing his examination of the hide.

"She could have done the work herself," Doc said, his deliberately soft tone almost idle but holding beneath it a suppressed excitement. "It is the most simple of constructions, rather like the dresses young girls make for their dolls. The hide—it's elk, by the way, and I wonder how she killed an elk—has been tanned, though badly. It is in one piece; nothing has been stitched on. A hole has been cut in the center rather larger than her head—I expect she didn't like how the rough leather chafed her neck. The rest has been trimmed so that the movement of her arms would be unimpeded.

"This belt," he lifted a twisted piece of leather, "must have closed it somewhat at the sides, if poorly."

"That's right, Doc," Derian confirmed.

"Derian," Jared asked, the quiet excitement now rising into his voice, "did you give Blysse anything other than the shirt and belt?"

"No, Doc."

"Not the knife?"

"No. She had it with her. Never even put it down. Held it in her teeth while she was changing."

Both Doc and the earl glanced at him when he said that, but mercifully, this once Derian didn't blush.

"So you haven't gotten a good look at it," Doc continued. "Then you probably didn't notice that, worn as the sheath is, it is of superlative construction, hardened leather with metal reinforcement. Stamped onto it, I believe, is the crest of the royal house."

"Oh?" Earl Kestrel's grey eyes shone as he understood the drift of his cousin's thoughts. "I cannot see it from here. Is there anything else?"

"Yes," Doc said. "Set into the pommel is what looks like a cabochon gem, a garnet, I'd guess, though it's too filthy for me to be certain. I'm certain I've seen the like before, when hunting with Prince Barden."

Suddenly Derian looked at his discovery with new eyes. Until this moment, he hadn't believed in the earl's dreams, but now it seemed quite possible that this dark-eyed lady of the forest might well be the heir to the throne of Hawk Haven.

IV

FIREKEEPER HAD SLIPPED AWAY to spend the good night with Blind Seer, but before dawn pinked the sky, she crept back again, so silently that even the spotted not-wolf didn't note her return. Lifting the edge of the shelter the two-legs had given her, she crawled back inside and sat on the soft things they had heaped as a sleeping place for her.

She was full from hunting, weary from running, howling, and wrestling with her pack mate. In the dim light that penetrated her lair she saw that her new garment was covered with tiny twigs, bits of leaf, and other forest matter. Fastidious as any wolf, she stripped the shirt off and was pulling the mess from the fabric when sleep took her.

"One character, one sound," a pleasant, melodious female voice says. "Put them together and the words will talk to you."

Tamara looks down at the slate uncertainly. Sweet Eirene has made marks there with a bit of chalk. Tamara recognizes some of the marks, but fitting them together into sounds still bothers her. She feels hot and foolish as she tries, her lips fat and heavy. Her only comfort is that Blysse seems no more enthusiastic than she.

"Mama," Blysse demands, "we want to go outside, Tamara and me."

Outside! Sunlight dappling through the trees. Springtime flowers scenting the air.

"Tamara and I." Sweet Eirene corrects her daughter patiently. She shifts baby Clive to one arm, opens her blouse to nurse him. "After you have sounded out what is written on the slates you may go out."

Tamara looks through the open window with longing, but reluctantly obeys the woman. At least Sweet Eirene keeps her deals, not like some of the other grownups, who seem to believe that the little girls have no more memory than chickens.

Blysse, though as willful as any doted-upon child, seems to know that this is not a time to argue with her mother. Mumbling their attempts to each other, the girls bend their heads, one fair, one dark, over their slates.

"Dog and Hog run with Frog," Blysse announces after a few minutes.

Sweet Eirene smiles at her daughter. "Very good, Blysse. Now, Tamara, what does your slate say?"

"The big pig can dig," Tamara sounds out carefully, wondering why anyone would want to know something so stupid.

"Very good, Tamara." Sweet Eirene offers Clive her other nipple. "Since both of you girls have worked so hard, you may have two strawberries each from the bowl in the pantry."

"Thank you, Mama." Blysse says, hopping down from her chair and running with pattering steps to open the pantry door.

"Thank you, ma'am," Tamara echoes, taking the berries Blysse thrusts at her with pink-stained fingers.

The strawberries are still sweet in her mouth. She sits on the ground outside Blysse's cabin, playing dolls with her friend. Distantly, she hears Barden come inside from the fields.

The prince's boots thump solidly against the new plank floor. A scraping sound is the slate being pushed to one side. A clunk is his heavy pottery tumbler being set on the table.

"It's a beautiful day, Eirene," he says. "Too beautiful to sit indoors and tutor little girls."

"They need to learn how to read, Barden," Sweet Eirene replies. Her voice twangs a little under its gentle melody. They argue about this frequently.

"Let them play," the prince urges. "There's no need to force them along. We have few enough books and they're only four years old."

"Blysse will be five in a few moon-spans. At her age, I could cross-stitch my alphabet. She can barely recite the letters!"

"She can lead a horse, feed a chicken, and tell a weed from a seedling." Barden's tone is affectionate. "Her education must needs be different from that of a lady of Kestrel."

"Maybe." Sweet Eirene's voice is no longer so sweet. She sounds determined. "Barden, I swear that these children will not grow up like wild animals!"

Wild animals, animals, animals . . .

The words echo through Tamara's head and she is kneeling on the ground next to her mother. Mama holds a furry grey ball in her lap. It stares fuzzily at Tamara from cloudy blue eyes.

"Careful, Tamara," Mama says when Tamara reaches to touch the puppy. "This is a wild animal, not one of your toys."

Tamara pats the wolf puppy very, very carefully. "Wild, Mama? It doesn't seem wild. What is wild?"

"Wild is not obeying humans," Mama says after a moment. "Wild is that."

"Wild," Tamara tries the word out. "Wild. Wild wolf. Will the wild wolf bite me?"

"If you poke it or hurt it or tease it," Mama says, "and well it should. But its mother might bite you even faster."

Tamara senses rather than hears the she-wolf emerging from the brush. Her grey head is taller than Tamara's dark one. Her yellow-brown eyes study the girl; then her fanged mouth opens in a panting smile.

"Wild," Tamara says, putting out her hand to pat the wolf. "Wild."

She throws back her head and pipes a thin howl.

Wild.

FIREKEEPER AWAKENED SLOWLY from her dream, feeling it clinging to corners of her mind dense as fog and just as impossible to grasp. The garment Fox Hair had given her was draped across her thighs, puppy-fur soft.

Suddenly she was homesick. Confused and forlorn, she didn't know who she was homesick for. Her pack? Mama? Blysse?

The loud clang of the iron pot being slung over the campfire brought her fully awake. Gratefully Firekeeper pushed homesickness away with anticipation and curiosity.

From outside her shelter, she heard Fox Hair calling in a low voice, "Blysse? Blysse?"

This word was followed by other sounds that almost, coming as they did on the heels of her dream, made sense. So Firekeeper yapped a greeting and pushed her way outside. Fox Hair smiled greeting in return. Then, to her astonishment, his face turned as red as the setting sun.

⚶

DERIAN'S PLEASURE AT LEARNING the wild woman had not fled in the night vanished in a wash of embarrassment when he realized that she had emerged from the tent completely naked. The wool shirt, incomprehensibly covered with bits of bracken, trailed from her left hand. She grasped her sheathed knife in the right.

Moreover, she was staring at him in astonishment, as if he, not she, were displaying himself naked before a company of the opposite sex. Dropping the shirt, she reached out and touched his cheek. Only when he felt the coolness of her fingers did he realize that he must be blushing furiously.

Frozen in shock, he regained control of his limbs only when he heard Doc comment dryly:

"Well, from what I see, I'd concur with the estimate of her age as somewhere between twelve and fifteen. She's thin as a rail, poor child. No wonder she doesn't have much up top."

Derian bent and picked up the discarded shirt, not caring this once if his sudden movement frightened Blysse. His fingers were touching the cloth when he felt it snatched from beneath them.

The woman was glowering at him, holding the shirt close to her. When he straightened, she fixed him with her dark gaze. Then, clearly and distinctly, she growled.

Behind him Derian heard murmurs of astonishment as the other men registered her speed and agility. Then Ox said calmly:

"Well, Derian, she may not want to wear it now, but I'd say that she plans on keeping that shirt."

Coming to himself, Earl Kestrel snapped, "Stop staring at Lady Blysse, all of you! Get on with your chores! Derian Carter, try to convince her to re-don her garb. Then I want to speak with you."

Derian convinced Blysse to dress, helped by the fact that she obviously had intended to do so in any case. With some effort he convinced her to remain with Ox.

Seeing her safe, Derian reluctantly crossed toward the earl's tent. He glanced behind him to check on Blysse and saw her standing behind Ox's bulk, peering out to watch the others as they prepared breakfast and fed the horses.

When Derian reached the area marked out as Earl Kestrel's own, Valet glanced up from the quail eggs he was scrambling for the earl's breakfast to give Derian an encouraging nod. Even so, Derian didn't feel any braver as he announced himself and obeyed the earl's invitation to enter.

Earl Kestrel's tent was larger than the one Derian shared with Ox. It had straight sides and a peaked roof, rather like a small house, whereas the other members of the expedition slept in simple triangular shelters. When Derian entered, he found Earl Kestrel seated on a campstool, making notes in a leather-bound book resting on a collapsible table.

"Be seated while I finish this," Kestrel ordered curtly.

Derian balanced on a second campstool, his hands folded stiffly on his knees. After an eon or so, the earl blotted his ink, sanded the page, and turned to Derian.

"We have a serious problem," he said bluntly, "with the Lady Blysse. We may have located her, but ten years of living like a wild animal have made her unfit for civilized company. At first I intended to head back to Eagle's Nest as soon as we could regroup. Now I see this would be unwise. I want Blysse to be presented to the king as a human being— one who has suffered trials, surely, but as a human being. If we go back now, even with the weeks we must spend on the road, she will still be little more than a freak."

Derian had expected to be reprimanded for staring at the naked woman, for not keeping the woman covered, for something he'd done wrong. These confidences startled him so that all he could do was nod.

"Last night I consulted with both my valet and with my cousin," the earl continued. "They advise that you would be the best choice for the girl's tutor."

"Me?"

"Yes. Thus far, she trusts you more than she does any of us. You are closer to her age. Moreover, you are educated, unlike Race and Ox. Jared and I should return to our homes, at least briefly. Therefore, we cannot teach her."

"Valet?" Derian offered tentatively.

"She does not seem to respect Valet," Earl Kestrel said. "He is very good at what he does, but he himself has noted that he lacks the force of personality to impress her."

"Oh."

"I am offering you an important job, a great opportunity to serve both my house and the throne."

Derian bit his lip, reviewing his options. Could he really civilize this wild woman? What would be the penalty for failure? He was certain that he was still considering when he heard his own voice saying:

"Yes. I would like to try teaching her, sir."

"Good!" The earl briskly rubbed his hands together. "I always knew you had potential as an aide. As you may be aware, after Prince Barden departed, his father sold his property."

"Departed." Was disinherited, you mean, Derian thought, some of his usual sardonic humor returning to him now that the worst shock had passed.

"I purchased West Keep—the place from which Prince Barden departed into the wilds," Earl Kestrel continued. "It should make a fit place for Barden's daughter, my niece, to begin her education. I will speak to Race Forester about his remaining in my employ and staying there to support you. The rest of us will depart, but I will expect regular reports from you."

"How delivered, sir?" Derian asked, his head swimming.

"I will send a courier. He will take your first report and leave a covey of homing pigeons with you. Hopefully, that will suffice."

"Yes, sir."

Earl Kestrel kept talking, but Derian heard little of what he said. He knew he would regret his inattention later, but for now only one refrain kept going through his head.

What have I gotten myself into?

FIREKEEPER SPENT AN EXCITING but nerve-tightening day among the two-legs. Three or four times she ate their food, finding it overcooked and full of the taste of strange plants. It was warming, though, with a warmth that stayed like sunlight in her belly.

When Fox Hair observed her pulling the leaves out of her soft shirt, he brought her another set of garments. This time there were two parts: one to be worn on her lower body and another for the top.

As easily as a mockingbird mimics sounds, Fox Hair communicated with Firekeeper by acting out what he wanted her to know. In this way he showed her that the one part went over the soft shirt, the other over her lower parts.

Thinking the stuff these garments was made from smelled familiar, Firekeeper chewed the material and found that it was indeed leather, but leather that had been made soft and supple, as if the animal were still wearing its hide.

Initially, she wore the clothing in the fashion that Fox Hair had suggested, but she found the combination of two tops along with the bottoms stifling. As much as she liked the soft top, she found the leather one stronger and less likely to accumulate leaf matter. The bottoms protected her legs and rear far better than her hide had ever done, though she missed the feeling of the wind against her skin.

Firekeeper compromised by wearing the leather top and bottoms, setting the soft top aside for another time. When the little brown man made as if to touch the soft top, she growled.

She might not be using it that moment, but she wasn't going to give it up!

During the brightest part of the day, Firekeeper slept for a while, leaving her rested and clearheaded when night fell and the two-legs went into their shelters to sleep. Shedding her new attire, since she was not quite comfortable in it, she slipped out to meet Blind Seer.

They romped for a time, celebrating their reunion with such enthusiasm that she was slightly bruised and soundly scratched. When they had stretched out on some young grass, Firekeeper with her head pillowed on her brother's flank, the wolf sighed.

"What troubles you, Blue Eyes?"

"Elation said that the two-legs plan to depart tomorrow. Tawny has pulled his fish traps from the water and taken down his snares. There are other signs the falcon sees. Although they mean nothing to me, I believe her."

Firekeeper's heart started beating far too fast.

"Tomorrow?"

"Probably as soon as there is light." The wolf thumped his tail on the ground. "Do you go with them?"

It was far to soon to make such a decision, but in her belly Firekeeper knew that the decision was already made.

"I will."

"Across the mountains?"

"Let us see how they treat me in the days it takes to reach the mountains," she temporized.

"But if they treat you well?"

She sighed. "Then I go."

Sitting up, she rubbed the wolf behind his ears.

"I could miss you, Sister," Blind Seer said at last, "but Mother and Father reminded us that all wolves feel the urge to disperse from the pack. Why should our two-legged sister be different?"

"Could miss me?" she said, teasing to lighten this serious moment.

"Could, if I were parting from you," he replied, "but I think I will go with you to see what lies over the mountain. It is long since any but the winged members of the Royal kind went there. Now that the two-legs have come here, why shouldn't I go there?"

Firekeeper howled her delight, thumping Blind Seer so hard that he leapt up and trotted out of range.

"Easy, Sister! Easy!" he protested. "You're not a tiny pup anymore. There's strength in those funny hands of yours."

"Will you come meet the two-legs, then?" she asked eagerly.

"Not yet," he replied cautiously. "Their beasts fear me as we fear fire. Let them grow a bit accustomed to my scent. We should learn, too, if the two-legs also fear wolves. The Cousins who have crossed the mountains don't speak well of them."

"True." She smiled, though, too happy at the knowledge that he would be nearby to worry yet about how the two-legs would take to him. "Have you told the Ones what you will do?"

"How could I?" he replied. "I didn't know until you made your own choice."

"Then let us sing our news to the pack," she said. "The Ones will want to know that we are both departing."

Trotting side by side, they went to a rise from which their voices would carry far. Two voices began a song that became a chorus as it was relayed through trees whose branches reached as if to brush the stars.

❧

"EASY, NOW! Easy, Roanne!" Derian jerked the mare's headstall, but still she danced nervously away from Blysse.

The woman, clad in leather vest and riding breeches, stood barefoot, watching the horse's antics in evident amusement.

"Problem, Derian?" Earl Kestrel asked from where he stood a polite distance away.

"Yes, sir. I'd thought to have Lady Blysse ride my horse while I rode one of the pack animals. We can spare one since we've used so much of the fodder they were carrying. Roanne won't go near Blysse, though."

Exasperated, he punctuated his reply by loosing the mare into the corral, where she promptly trotted to the far side of the enclosure, shuddering her skin as if it were crawling with flies.

"None of the other horses will either," Derian continued. "They're scared stiff of Blysse."

The earl thoughtfully stroked his beard with one forefinger.

"Interesting," he said. "Well, then, until we get a horse accustomed to her, she will have to walk."

He looked as if he was considering declaring that everyone else must walk as well, but self-interest came to the fore.

"Perhaps your horse will grow easier around Blysse if you are in the saddle and she walks alongside."

"Perhaps," Derian agreed doubtfully.

"In any case, how does Blysse seem to take to the idea of riding?"

"Well enough." Derian gestured to where he had flung a saddle across a fallen tree trunk. "I showed her the basics there and she took to them so fast that I think Doc's right. She must have been watching us before she got her courage up to come out and meet us."

"Either that," the earl said thoughtfully, "or she remembers something of her childhood."

A look came into his grey eyes then, a look Derian was beginning to recognize as his facile mind weaving an explanation from the minimal information they had. Earl Kestrel frowned slightly, as if the matter would take more consideration than he could give it now, then addressed Derian.

"Camp is nearly broken. I would take it as a signal courtesy if you would inspect the packing. Ox and Race have done their best, but you are the expert."

Derian hid a grin. Earl Kestrel was taking Derian's promotion quite seriously, a thing that amused Ox and infuriated Race.

"I would be glad to, sir. However, I'm going to ask Blysse to wait here while I do so."

"Wise," Earl Kestrel concurred.

Derian had found it almost too easy to work out some basic hand signals with the young woman. She quickly grasped a nod for "yes" and a shake of the head for "no." A hand held up, palm outward, combined with a head shake meant "stay." A beckoning gesture combined with a nod meant "come." Derian thought that soon the latter two gestures would simplify to a simple hand signal, but for now he wanted to build on what they had.

Now he signaled for her to stay, saying, "I need to go check the horses, Blysse, and you're sure to scare them."

He thought that his pointing toward the horses, rather than his words, transmitted his message, but she grinned agreement. By his way of thinking, there was a touch of wickedness to that grin, as if she understood perfectly well why he wanted her to remain and was amused.

As Derian checked and balanced packs, tightened or loosened girths, he periodically glanced over at his charge. She was sitting on a large rock near the edge of the camp, absorbedly watching the last stages of the breakdown.

When they left, Blysse walked alongside the pack train, staying to one side of Derian, just far enough away that his well-schooled chestnut mare was almost willing to forget her presence.

The young woman's gait was easy and tireless, the sound of her passage inaudible. Race Forester watched her with interest and poorly disguised envy, for she made his claims to woodcraft seem cheap. Knowing how dangerous envy could be, Derian was relieved when Earl Kestrel cleared his throat, and Race shifted his attention to his patron.

"After observing Blysse," Norwood began, "I have come to some conclusions . . ."

Conjectures, Derian corrected silently.

". . . about the manner of her survival following the fire that destroyed the community. I would like to share them with you as you have shared my rediscovery of my lost kinswoman with me."

And so we won't, Derian thought, *mess up your big presentation to King Tedric by offering our own theories.*

After his followers voiced their willingness to listen, Earl Kestrel continued:

"Race Forester's skilled examination of the rings of the trees growing from the ruins places the date of the conflagration at about ten years ago. At that time, Lady Blysse would have been five years old, far too young to have survived without assistance. My theory is that one or more members of the community survived and cared for the child."

His voice deepened and, to Derian's surprise, took on the cadences of a professional storyteller. Like a storyteller, the earl began with the traditional words:

"Envision with me, if you would be so kind, pale light dawning on a morning graced with steady rain. Heaven's water falls on the smoldering wreckage of a community built from youthful dreams. As it extinguishes the fire, it extinguishes the last faint hopes of the builders.

"At the edge of farmed fields stands a small group, perhaps as small as two. One is Prince Barden. His noble face is blackened with soot and ash, his powerful body stooped with exhaustion, his expression ravaged with grief, for those still burning embers hold within their embrace the bodies of his friends and comrades, perhaps the body of his lady wife."

The earl's voice broke there and Derian liked him better for it. Even in the midst of constructing a pedigree for the foundling, a pedigree on which rested Kestrel's own ambitions for advancement, the man couldn't quite subdue his own sorrow at the loss of his sister.

Suspicious then that he was too gullible, that the catch in the earl's voice had just been good theater, Derian glanced at the nobleman, but the tightness around Norvin Norwood's eyes and mouth was genuine. His voice, though, when he spoke again, had returned to his control:

"Prince Barden holds in one of his great hands a small one, that of his small daughter, Blysse. Terrified and confused by the changes the night has wrought, still the little girl tries to be brave for her father's sake. He, in turn, takes courage from the child's need for him.

"After foraging among the ruins for the basic necessities of existence, the prince leads his daughter into the forest. There is no benefit to staying near, yet Barden cannot bear to take himself too far away from this accidental funeral pyre. If he departs, who will make the offerings to the spirits of the dead?

"So he remains and builds a small shelter in which he raises his daughter, letting her help him forage and hunt for what they need to survive in the wilds. Certainly, he made no more permanent provisions for the future. Doubtless, when the traditional two years of sacrifices for the dead were ended, Prince Barden planned to return to his father's kingdom. Once there, if only for his small daughter's sake, he would beg forgiveness for his rashness and ask to be taken back into the fold.

"However, before those two years can pass, something happens to him. Perhaps the heat of the fires that Prince Barden certainly challenged when attempting to save his people seared his lungs. Perhaps he broke a limb or caught an illness while hunting in the freezing cold of winter for food for his daughter. Perhaps it was simply the final stroke of the ill luck that had dogged his young life. For whatever reason, when the two years had passed, the prince was too weak to make the onerous journey across the mountains. Instead, he put his full energies into teaching his daughter what she would need to survive.

"At last, his strength failing him, Prince Barden strapped his own knife about young Blysse's waist, rested her small but strong hand on the polished garnet on the pommel, made her swear to fight to survive even when he had passed on. Taking her to the ruins, he consigned her care to the ancestral spirits to whom he had so devotedly sacrificed. Shortly thereafter, he joined them.

"Perhaps Blysse buried him in the ruins near those he had loved. Perhaps, trembling with grief, she was forced to leave his body to the ministry of the wild creatures. However, like her father, she remained close by the familiar places. There, nearly wild, we found her, and so we return her to the embrace of her grandfather."

Earl Kestrel paused, one hand holding Coal's reins, the other lightly stroking his lip, his gaze keenly observing the reaction of his listeners. Jared Surcliffe was the first to speak. His voice was a bit hoarse, as if he had been holding back tears.

"That's a good explanation, cousin," he said slowly. "It explains much of what has puzzled me: how the girl survived; why she stayed near to this place; why, even if someone had lived to care for her when she was small, didn't that same person take her home to Hawk Haven."

Earl Kestrel bowed his head in gracious acknowledgment of the praise.

"I like the touch about the prince giving his daughter his own knife," Race Forester said, his envy forgotten under the story's spell. "It rings true. A royal prince would have done something just like that."

Derian nodded, but as he glanced at the dark-haired figure trotting alongside his horse, her eyes alive with curiosity, he wondered.

It could have been just like that, but was it?

He wondered if they would ever know and realized with a shiver that discovering the truth was up to him, for if the woman remained a creature of the wilds, the truth would never be known.

◈

THE TWO-LEGS STOPPED traveling toward the mountains long before Firekeeper was at all tired. Still, she was glad for the break, glad for an opportunity to assess what she had learned.

Fox Hair had clearly been made her nursemaid, a role that was apparently a promotion among the two-legs, for it was evident to her that Tawny resented him greatly.

She was rather pleased for Fox Hair, nonetheless. He was amusing and willing to make great efforts in order to befriend her.

After a day of watching the two-legs interact from within their midst, she was certain that they could talk as well as any wolf. Unlike wolves, however, they mostly used their mouths, a thing she found limiting. How could you tell someone to keep away from your food when your own mouth was full?

While the two-legs were lighting their fire and taking all the things off the not-elk that they had put on them with such effort a short time before, Fox Hair motioned Firekeeper to join him by the fire. Although she disliked how the smoke dulled her sense of smell, Firekeeper came over and seated herself on a rock upwind.

While busily washing some vegetables in a container of water, Fox Hair chattered squirrel-like at Mountain, who was setting up one of the shelters. Feeling left out when Fox Hair stopped, Firekeeper attempted to mimic his final string of sounds.

She was a good mimic. So long ago that she did not remember the learning, she had discovered that imitating various bird and animal calls could bring her prey to her, rather than forcing her to seek it over great distances.

Hearing her imitate him now, Fox Hair's eyes widened in an expression she recognized as surprise. In a sharp tone, he said something to her. She did her best to make the same noises back at him.

Hearing her, Mountain laughed and said something to Fox Hair. She mimicked him as well, pitching her voice lower, though she could not reach his great, thunder-deep rumbles.

Fox Hair nodded at this, reached up, and pulled at his mouth in what Firekeeper was certain was a gesture of thought. Two-legs pulled at their mouths a great deal. Those who grew hair there often fingered it or tugged at it.

She wondered if her own inability to grow hair on her face would be a handicap among two-legs, perhaps one as great as not having fangs had proved to be among wolves. If so, she supposed, she could fasten another creature's hair there, just as her Fang had compensated for her other natural shortcomings. However, she hoped that since Fox Hair cut the hair from his face she would be spared this.

Letting his hand drop into his lap, Fox Hair picked up one of the plant roots that he had been washing a moment before.

Slowly and carefully, he said: "Potato."

Firekeeper imitated him perfectly. Fox Hair smiled, picked up another root, this one long and orange.

"Carrot."

She imitated him.

"Onion."

A dozen items later, he began to repeat. Soon she had all the words and could, when Fox Hair pointed to one or another of the items, match word to thing.

Fox Hair grinned his delight. Hawk Nose, who had been watching from a distance, came over and tested her himself.

Firekeeper went through the routine again, aware that impressing this two-legged One was important. Hawk Nose nodded at her when she had finished, then said something rapidly to Fox Hair. Fox Hair replied. His tones, Firekeeper noted, were more measured than when he spoke with Mountain. She wondered if cadence indicated something, perhaps relative standing within the pack.

After they had eaten, Fox Hair drew Firekeeper off to the side and continued teaching her sounds. By full dark, she had learned several dozen more, knew that the not-elk were horses, that the cringing spotted kin-creature was a dog, that the shelters were tents.

She was a little puzzled to find that the same word applied to the small shelters such as the one in which she slept and the larger one in which Hawk Nose slept. They were so different in shape and purpose— Hawk Nose spent much time in his doing more than sleeping—that she thought his should have a different word.

More interesting was learning that the two-legs had names for themselves. Fox Hair was called Derian. Mountain was Ox.

Derian seemed uncertain what to name Hawk Nose. He tried various sounds. Then he shrugged and shook his head, dismissing them all. Firekeeper was fascinated and more than a little confused.

Despite her pleasure in discovering that one could communicate with two-legs, when she heard Blind Seer call, she was eager to leave and join him.

She rose, turning toward the forest. Fox Hair/Derian stood as well, his expression anxious. Blind Seer howled again.

"Come, Firekeeper! I'm lonely!"

Firekeeper smiled and started to walk toward the forest. Derian, to her surprise, for he had never before laid even a finger on her without permission, put his hand on her arm.

She stopped, stared at him, and, seeing concern evident on his features, did not strike him. Perhaps two-legs, like wolves, touched for other reasons than to attack.

Fox Hair gestured in the direction of Blind Seer's cry.

"Wolf," he said.

Blind Seer howled again.

"Wolf," Derian repeated anxiously.

Firekeeper gently pushed his hand from her arm and moved swiftly away. Before she stepped into the darkness of the trees, she turned to Fox Hair and nodded.

"Wolf," she agreed, and slipped into the night.

V

"BUT THIS CAN'T GO ON!" exclaimed Race Forester, eyes ablaze. "Tomorrow we cross the gap; a day or two thereafter we're in populated lands. What happens then when Lady Blysse slips off into the night and runs about in the darkness?"

There was a sneer in his voice when he said "Lady," a sneer just this side of unforgivable cheek, but Earl Kestrel chose to overlook that insolence. No matter how rudely phrased, Race's point was reasonable.

Each night since they had broken camp at the ruins of Bardenville, Blysse had left her tent and vanished into the night. What she did then, no one knew, but she returned each day shortly before dawn.

They had made slower progress on their return east to civilization than they had on the way out. The first day Earl Kestrel had called halt after a half-day's travel, worried that the young woman would not have the stamina to pace the horses any longer. He might also have been prompted by the steady drizzle that had begun with first light and had never ceased—unless turning into intermittent sleet could be considered ceasing.

The second day their start had been late, for the camp had remained on alert for many hours after Blysse had left Derian's side, in answer, it almost seemed, to a howl of a wolf in the darkness beyond. Only on her return had Earl Kestrel fallen into a restful sleep. The third day had been something of a repetition of the second, though Earl Kestrel had permitted Valet to convince him that wakeful watchfulness would do nothing to bring the girl back, that indeed it might do the opposite.

The end of this fourth day of travel found them at the lower reaches of the gap. Tomorrow they would attempt the crossing, a long, hard day's work even for rested men. Although the earl had decreed an extra half-day for rest and preparation, no one was relaxing. Even calm Ox and unflappable Valet kept turning their gazes to the tree line, wondering what strange force might draw Blysse out into the unfriendly darkness night after night.

Derian was the least happy of the lot. Looking at his charge clad in leather vest and rough knee breeches she had made by chopping off a pair of the earl's riding trousers just below her knees, she was a winsome figure, hardly female, impossible to place in any of the categories he had encountered traveling between Hawk Haven and Bright Bay on business with his father.

To some eyes, as she sat busily untangling her brown locks with the comb he had shown her how to use three days before, Blysse could be any girl, albeit a somewhat boyishly dressed one. To Derian, however, she had become more of an enigma for their several days of acquaintance rather than less.

Upon their first meeting she had seemed a wild creature that had taken human shape. By their second, assured of her humanity, Derian had felt proprietary, even protective toward her. By the third meeting, the very one that had ended with Earl Kestrel giving Derian charge of her, Derian had felt certain of Blysse's intelligence and of her peculiar sense of humor.

This day she was a stranger, calm and composed, apparently immune to the human storm that raged around her—as she should be. Although her vocabulary was growing at an amazing rate, what words she had were mostly nouns with a few simple additions such as Yes and No, Come and Go.

"What do you suggest we do?" Earl Kestrel asked Race.

"We should tie her," the scout said firmly. "It's for her own safety, my lord. I don't want her arrow-shot by the first gamekeeper who takes her for a poacher."

"You don't?" the earl's inflection was ironic, but Derian doubted that the scout noticed. Race still believed that his envy of the woman's woodcraft was his own secret.

"No, sir, I don't," Race said earnestly. "Think of the man's shock when he finds a bit of a girl dead with his shaft in her breast and him facing your wrath for doing naught but his duty."

"Indeed," said Earl Kestrel dryly, "not to mention the pitiable situation that Blysse should have survived ten years of privation to die so sordidly."

"That," Race replied, suddenly aware of his tactlessness, "so goes without saying that I didn't bother mentioning it."

"Of course." Earl Kestrel relented. "It has not escaped my notice that you have scouted in the vicinity of the camp following Blysse's return each dawn. Have you found any sign of where she goes or if she is meeting someone?"

"None," Race said, superstitious dread deepening his voice. "She leaves no more track than a spirit would. I've wondered . . ."

Jared Surcliffe broke in, impatient with the earl's game of cat and mouse with the uneducated man.

"If she's a restless spirit? Nonsense! I've examined her more closely now and no spirit would have so many scars—not to mention the cuts and bruises she gains each day. She has clean healing flesh, thank the ancestors of our house, or she would have died from some injury long since."

"If I thought she was a spirit," Race countered defiantly, "would I have suggested putting a rope on her? My lord, it would be no more unkind than the jesses on a hawk or the leash on a dog. It's to keep her from harm in my way of thinking, not to do her some."

"And can you explain that to her?" Earl Kestrel said skeptically. "Derian, could Blysse understand such an idea?"

Derian shrugged. "She's smart, my lord, but we don't have enough words."

"Mime it!" Race insisted.

"When she's never seen—or at least has no memory of—the farmers or gamekeepers you would protect her from?" Derian scoffed. "How?"

In answer, Race lifted a coil of rope and strode over to where Blysse was now interestedly watching.

"I'll show you!" the scout retorted defiantly.

He lifted the rope, uncoiled a section and held it out to the young woman.

"Rope," she said calmly.

Much to Derian's despair, all items for binding, from the thinnest thread to horse hobbles to fish line, had, for the nonce, become rope. Doubtless Blysse thought Race's approach with rope in hand was another attempt to force her to discriminate. Mentally, he kicked himself for not teaching her the word "pavilion" for Earl Kestrel's larger tent that first night. The lack of discrimination seemed to have shaped her attitude toward the refinements of spoken language.

With the ease of long practice, Race made a noose. Then, as Blysse watched in unguarded curiosity, he dropped it over her shoulders and pulled it fast, binding her arms tightly to her sides.

Blysse looked startled, pushing out with her shoulders against the restraint. Her expression when she realized that she could not get free became furious: dark eyes narrowed, lips paling, brows pulled together.

"See, my lord," Race said triumphantly, turning slightly toward Earl Kestrel, leaning back on his heels so that his weight would keep the noose tight. "We can hold her this way and she can walk along or we can set her up on one of the mules. They've grown accustomed to her by now and . . ."

He didn't finish for Blysse screamed, high, shrill, and angry. Her second such cry was echoed by one from the tops of the tallest trees; then a blue-grey streak plummeted toward the gathered men.

Derian didn't think. Balling himself tight, he launched forward, knocking Race to the ground, rolling the other man with the force of his tackle so that the falcon's strike hit the ground inches from where the scout would have been standing.

Race lost his grip on the rope and, as the falcon was taking wing again, Blysse clawed her way out of the loosened noose.

Free, she stood poised lightly on the balls of her feet, Prince Barden's knife in her hand. Her dark gaze darted from Race to Derian to Kestrel then back again to Race.

A low growl rumbling in her throat, she advanced one stiff-legged pace toward the prone man, then another.

Derian rose, imposed himself between her and Race, found that cold, dark gaze now studying him impartially. All their tentative friendship seemed to have vanished like snow beneath the sun.

Blysse's growl deepened, became louder, and she peeled her lips back from teeth. The snarl should have looked funny, for her teeth remained blunt, human teeth, but the menace in her eyes made the expression anything but.

Queenie, Race's bird dog, had been running to assist her master. Now, under Blysse's snarl, she dropped to the dirt, rolled onto her back, and whimpered submission.

Something visceral in Derian understood. He could not demean himself to drop and roll, but he lowered his gaze and stepped slightly to one side.

"Race," he muttered urgently as he did so. "Don't get up! Don't reach for any weapon! If you stay down there, she won't attack you."

"What?" Race continued scrabbling backward in the dirt and leaves of the forest floor, but he didn't get to his feet, nor did Blysse attack. "How can you be so sure?"

"I just am!" Derian replied, resisting an urge to growl himself. "Stay put! Lower your gaze! Don't challenge her or she'll have your head!"

Race obeyed, at least to the extent of not getting to his feet. After Race had clawed his way back a few more paces, Blysse halted. With one last snarl, she kicked dirt at him. Then she shook like a dog after a rainstorm, her anger vanishing as quickly as it had appeared.

She looked at Derian and grinned, then spoke her first sentences.

"Race, dog," she commented conversationally. Then she bent and picked up the rope and shook it. "No rope. No!"

Earl Kestrel spoke for the first time since Race had advanced on Blysse.

"That, I think, quite nicely sums up the matter."

Then he took the coil of rope from her and tossed it onto the fire. Sparks flew as the flames engulfed the damp coils.

FIREKEEPER WAS IN A MERRY mood the next morning. Today they would cross the great mountains. Beneath tonight's stars, she and Blind Seer would hunt where none of the Royal Wolves had hunted in uncounted years. Until then, she had the progress of humans and horses up the steep incline to amuse her.

For once, Derian had abandoned his care of her, his skill with the horses needed to coax them up the slope. She admired his labors with the stupid things, and during a midmorning halt she offered through gestures to assist.

Derian grinned and promptly handed her the rope tied to the head of the smallest but least cooperative of the long-eared horses.

"Mule," he said, pointing toward the creature.

Noting differences in ears, tail, and wickedness of temper, Firekeeper was willing to concede that there might be a need for a different word to separate this creature from a horse, never mind that they smelled so much alike.

"Mule," she repeated, pointing to the animal, then to the others like it. "Mule."

Derian grinned. "Yes. Good."

The last word puzzled her, for it seemed to apply to nothing in particular. She gestured toward the mule's head-rope, wondering if "Good" might be yet another of the useless plethora of words for "rope" that Derian kept thrusting at her.

"Rope," she said, waiting to see if he corrected her.

"Rope," he agreed. Then he made the hand gesture for "wait" and went off to confer with the earl.

While Firekeeper waited, her gaze flickered toward Race, remembering how the man had tried to bind her as the horses were bound. He was keeping a safe distance from her, his spotted dog close about his feet. Their fear pleased her. She liked having some precedence within this human pack, even if over such minor members.

When Hawk Nose shouted the command for them to start, Firekeeper's mule stubbornly refused to move. He stood stiff-legged, lazily chewing a mouthful of leaves, defying her to make him take a single step.

From the corner of her eye, Firekeeper saw Derian approaching, lightly swinging the stick he used to swat the mules across their hindquarters. Determined to move the animal herself, she considered her options.

To this point, she had not tried talking with the animals the twolegs had brought with them. She rarely had bothered speaking with herbivores in any case, finding it uncomfortable to talk with those she might later eat. Now, however, she stood on her toes, rising just high enough that her lips were close to one of the mule's brown-haired, darktipped ears.

"Move!" she snarled. *"Or I'll eat you for supper!"*

Any doubts she had held that the mule would understand her vanished as he threw back his head and brayed in naked terror. It took all her strength, heels dug into the ground, to stop the animal from bolting. With the loose end of the rope, she hit it across the soft part of its nose.

"Walk quietly now!" she ordered. *"Follow!"*

To attempt any command more detailed would be folly, for the stupid animal had suddenly remembered that she was a wolf, not a two-legs. It rolled its near eye at her, uncertain whether to obey or to bolt.

"Follow the others!" she commanded and, after the fashion of its kind it fell into line, comforted in doing what the others were already doing.

Firekeeper whistled comment to Elation, who had been watching the exchange from the trees nearby.

The falcon shrieked laughter. "Mistress of mice and mules! To what lows the proud wolves have come!"

Firekeeper snorted, not deigning to comment further. She was pleased enough to have made the mule obey her. See if the falcon could do as well!

That night and for the nights that followed, she and Blind Seer ranged the far slope of the mountains. This side was not, she discovered with some disappointment, greatly different from the side she had known since her puppyhood.

In one way, however, this region was greatly different. Except for one goshawk, kin to Elation's peregrines, they met none of the Royal kind. The only wolves she and Blind Seer encountered were Cousins. These knew of the Royal Wolves, having ranged west when the hunting was poor in their own territories, and groveled before Blind Seer as a pup before an adult.

Firekeeper found their deference right and natural. What troubled her, having had little contact with Cousins in the past, was how restricted the Cousins' interests were.

They could report in great detail about sources of fresh water, about rival packs, about good hunting, about the danger offered by awakening bears. Beyond that, they seemed to see nothing, to know less. She was shocked to realize that they reminded her more of Queenie, Race's spotted dog, than they did of wolves.

"Are they stupid?" she asked Blind Seer.

"No," he said, lifting his head from the haunch of elk he had been shredding. "They are Cousins. Didn't the Ones teach you about them?"

"Not much," she admitted. "Mostly, they told me to avoid them, that the Cousins would not protect me as did my own pack. I thought nothing of this. Packs often have rivalries."

"That is so," Blind Seer agreed. "However, there is more to our parents' warning than that. Cousins are lesser than Royal-kind in more ways than size. We are wiser, more clever, and possess gifts that the Cousins never have."

He sat up, forgetting his meat in his pride. Firekeeper snatched it from between his paws, winning an appreciative snarl from him.

"Tell me more," she said, tossing him back his food. Her own meal was long finished.

Blind Seer chewed at the knob end for a moment, considering before he continued, "Well, Royal-kind is forbidden to breed with Cousins, even if the urge is great."

"You are?" she asked, surprised. "But they are so like you. They even smell like you."

"Maybe to a human's nose," he replied haughtily. "I tell you, the scent is different, even as the scent of pale roses and dark roses is different."

"If you say so," she said resignedly. "My nose is dead."

"I know," he laughed. "Forget the Cousins, Sister. We can intimidate them if need arises. Moreover, it is spring. Like our own pack, they have pups to hunt for. They will be too busy to bother us."

Firekeeper nodded and for a time all was silent but for the cracking of the elk haunch between Blind Seer's jaws.

"These mules and horses the humans have," she said at last, thinking aloud. "They are certainly Cousin-kind, not Royal-kind."

"I certainly hope so." Blind Seer grinned. "If their Royal-kind are this stupid and docile, there is no hope for the creatures."

"What if the only non-humans the two-legs know," she mused, "are the Cousin-kind? How stupid they would believe all others who walk the earth to be!"

"Does that matter?" the great wolf asked lazily.

"It might," Firekeeper replied thoughtfully. "It might matter very much."

❀

FOGGY AND GHOSTLIKE in the drizzle that fell from the purpling heavens, West Keep loomed before them at twilight, eight days after they had crossed the gap from the west side of the Iron Mountains. Had they been in the lowlands, they would have covered the distance more quickly, but here they were on rough roads, their travel complicated by spring rains.

Derian, who was tired of living in the saddle and sleeping in a tent, welcomed the sight of the keep as if he were already out of the wind, enjoying fresh bread and butter in front of a roaring fire for which someone else had fetched the wood.

Blysse, sitting perched atop a once stubborn mule, gasped aloud when she saw the towering heap of dressed stone. For the first time since Derian had met her she looked completely astonished.

"Hold up for a moment," he called to the others. "Blysse needs a minute to adjust. I think the keep scares her.

"I guess it would be something of a surprise," Derian continued, turning to the young woman. He had learned that she appreciated being talked to, even if she couldn't understand the words. "The bend in the road hid it from view until it was right on top of us."

"Deliberately, I would guess," Earl Kestrel added, twisting slightly in Coal's saddle to face them. "A good strategic move. West Keep has a clear view of the road from its upper towers, but from the road those same towers blend into the surrounding terrain until this last mile."

"Even in daylight?" Ox asked.

"Even in daylight," Earl Kestrel said, as smugly as if he had built the place himself.

Blysse turned to Derian. He hadn't been able to teach her the word "what" and he bet that was exactly the word she wanted now. Instead she raised her hands and gestured wildly.

"Rock?" she asked. Then paused, frowning, "Rock-tent?"

Derian nodded, considering what word to give her. He had tried hard to avoid homonyms, wanting to reserve the confusion of words that sounded alike but meant different things until they shared a larger vocabulary. For that reason, he avoided the word "keep" and chose another.

"Castle," he said, pointing, using the slow, careful cadence he had begun to reserve for new words. "Castle."

Blysse pointed. "Castle. Rock tent. Castle."

She shook her head in amazement. Then, to Derian's surprise, she pursed her lips and gave a low whistle, identical to the one Race used whenever he encountered something he hadn't been ready for: a fallen tree or swollen stream blocking the trail; his fish trap plundered by a raccoon; ants in his boots.

Hearing her, Race laughed, a friendly laugh this time.

"I guess I've taught her something, too," he chuckled.

Derian nodded, an inkling of how he might manage Race brightening the prospect of being left at the keep with Race without the earl's mitigating presence.

Beside him, Blysse was still gaping at the keep. Her brow wrinkled in consideration as she tried to make her limited vocabulary express her awe.

"Castle," she said, gesturing up to indicate its height, then out to sketch the extent of the girdling wall. "Castle ox."

Derian was puzzled for a moment. Then he grinned.

"Castle *big*," he said, stressing the second word. "Ox big."

Blysse nodded vigorously.

"Big," she repeated. Then, after a moment, she added, "Ox big. Valet no big."

Derian's grin broadened as he wondered if it was tact that had led Blysse to pick Valet as her example of small, rather than Earl Kestrel, who was at least an inch shorter and somewhat slighter of build. One thing Blysse seemed to have had no difficulty interpreting were the relative degrees of importance within the little company.

"Ox big," he said, urging Roanne into a walk once more and hearing the rest of the company follow suit, "Valet no big. Valet *small*."

He decided to leave the minor refinement of "not" versus "no" for another time. Abstract concepts were a hurdle he hadn't been certain how to cross. Now that Blysse had provided him with a starting point, he wasn't going to waste it.

They continued their language lesson as the pack train crossed the last mile. At Earl Kestrel's signal, Race rode ahead, blowing his horn to alert the residents of West Keep that their master came unexpected. Derian spared a moment of pity for the garrison if they hadn't kept the place in perfect order. Earl Kestrel was not the most forgiving of masters.

That thought made him redouble his efforts with Blysse, suddenly aware of the earl's grey eyes watching him and the cool, calculating mind assessing his student's progress.

Earl Kestrel had uses for this woman who might or might not be his niece and the best claimant to the throne of Hawk Haven. He would not be forgiving if a mere horse carter impeded his advance. Certainly there would be rewards for success, but Derian was sure that the penalties for failure would be far greater in both degree and kind.

STONE. STONE on the floor. Stone surrounding. Caves made by human hands.

Firekeeper felt some relief when the chamber into which Fox Hair brought her had a ceiling made of wood and two great arched openings in the sides. She rushed to one of these and leaned out, reassuring herself by the sensation of the fresh, wet air on her face that the wide world outside had not vanished.

When her first panic had abated, she noticed that she could see for a great distance from this height. Directly below, several stranger two-legs were leading the horses and mules into a shelter. Beyond the narrow heap-of-stones-piled-on-top-of-stones that Derian had called a wall, there was a cleared area, but then the forest began again.

Even in the gathering darkness she could locate Blind Seer sitting on his haunches in the shadow of a tall tree near the road. The blue-eyed wolf was looking up at the castle, studying its shape. From the tilt of his head, she knew he was quizzical, but not afraid, and his lack of fear for himself or for her gave the young woman courage.

Drawing inside, Firekeeper shook the water droplets from her hair and turned to Derian. He was standing with his back to a fire built in the side of the chamber, watching her with an expression that, had she known it, was twin to Blind Seer's.

"Castle big," she commented with what coolness she could muster.

Derian nodded. A knocking from the side of the chamber where they had entered interrupted whatever he had been about to say. Derian said something Firekeeper didn't understand. Then, apparently in response, a frightening thing happened.

A piece of the wall moved, revealing an opening behind it.

Firekeeper sprang to the opening she had been looking out of a moment before and perched on the broad ledge beside it, ready to dive out and take her chances falling.

Fox Hair seemed amused, not nervous, so she held her pose, watching guardedly. The scent of food drifted in from the opening. That of meat cooked with herbs was immediately familiar. There were other scents that were almost familiar. These teased an awakening part of her, bringing with them a mingled sense of comfort and of longing that made Firekeeper strangely indecisive.

The food was carried by a two-legs nearly as stout as Ox but barely half his height, a person built from rounding shapes that included astonishing, swelling protrusions in the vicinity of her chest. When this person saw Firekeeper she spoke, her voice twittering like birdsong, high but sweet.

Derian made introductions, pointing first to Firekeeper, then to the stranger and back again.

"Blysse, Steward Daisy. Steward Daisy, Blysse."

Obediently, Firekeeper repeated the lesson, wondering why so small a person should have so long a name. Her words released another spate of birdsong from the little person, sounds that held a distinctly cooing note along with the word "Blysse."

Being called Blysse always made Firekeeper feel vaguely uncomfortable, though she had no idea why it should. The words by which the two-legs named themselves meant nothing to her. It was quite reasonable that they employed an equally meaningless sound to name her. But the name Blysse did make Firekeeper uncomfortable, so much so that she longed for the day when she would speak enough human tongue to teach them her wolf-given name.

Steward Daisy departed after making more cooing sounds, and Firekeeper and Derian shared the food on the tray. One of the almost familiar smells proved to belong to something called "bread," a soft, warm substance like nothing else that Firekeeper had ever eaten. She liked it best spread with the salty fat called "butter." Jam, with its taste of overripe berries, was good, but almost too rich.

Satiated, Firekeeper removed a blanket from one of the packs and spread it in front of the fire. A few hours' sleep, and then she would decide how to get out to Blind Seer.

SHE AWAKENED to find the fire burned down to red and white coals and Fox Hair gone, doubtless to his own chamber.

Stretching, she located an oddly shaped container full of water, its neck so tight that she could barely get her hand inside to cup out water with which to appease her thirst.

As soon as Steward Daisy had departed, Derian had shown Firekeeper how the door into the room worked. Now the wolf tested her memory and was pleased to discover that she could open it without help. When she scouted outside, she found a two-legs drowsing on a stool at the end of the hall.

Distrusting this stranger, Firekeeper retreated and considered the window. The drop to the ground below was considerable, but no worse than from some trees she had climbed. Still, the earth below was covered with stone, not soft leaves and forest duff.

Unwilling to risk a broken leg, Firekeeper rooted through the pack Derian had left in her room. Most of the contents were useless, but at the very bottom there was a coil of rope.

Over the past several days, Firekeeper had used rope to guide a mule, to help set up tents, and to tie packs onto their reluctant bearers. Now she anchored the rope to an iron loop on the windowsill and used it to slow her drop to the ground. She ended up with burns on her palms and a long scrape on her calf.

Well pleased, Firekeeper growled the barking dogs into submission and, with a running start and a light foot on the edge of a cart, scrabbled over the wall surrounding the castle.

On the other side, Blind Seer was waiting for her, blue eyes glowing in the darkness.

BOOK
TWO

VI

ELISE ARCHER, DAUGHTER of Baron Ivon Archer and Lady Aurella Wellward, great-niece of King Tedric, was not so much gathering flowers in the royal castle gardens as she was gathering
rumors. However, if her activities were dismissed as such an innocent pursuit, she had no complaints.

Slight, almost fragile of form, peaches and cream of complexion, with
pale golden hair the very shade of early-morning sunlight and sea-green
eyes, seventeen-year-old Elise was just now becoming beautiful.

For the only daughter of King Tedric's nephew Ivon, son himself of
the Grand Duchess Rosene, beauty was hardly the advantage it would
be for a woman of lesser birth. Marriage for Elise was as inevitable as
rain in springtime. Nevertheless, Elise found this new bloom of beauty
a pleasant thing and smiled softly into her bouquet, feeling the admiring
gazes of gardeners and grooms follow her graceful progress.

"Good morning, Lady." "Good morning." "Good morning."

The murmurs followed Elise from damask dark roses to brilliant yellow daisies to honeysuckle vines awash with heavily scented flowers. She
stopped by a bed of gladiolas in a mixture of colors from pure white to
deepest violet with shades of pink and red between.

Shifting her nosegay of roses to her left hand, she fumbled for her gardening clippers and, as suddenly as the High Sorcerer's griffin in the tales of Elrox Beyond the Sea, the head gardener appeared at her side.

"Perhaps I might assist, Lady Elise?"

She smiled, a real smile, though it hid some guile. She had been aware of the spare, sunburned figure of Timin, the master gardener, anxiously tracking her progress for some time now. He had left her alone among the roses, settling for wringing his hands as she clipped a few blossoms, but the gladiolas had drawn him forth.

"Thank you, Master Gardener," Elise replied. "I had intended to add a few pink gladiolas to my bouquet, but these look rather picked over."

There was no reproof in her tone, only mild consternation, but the gardener colored scarlet, then white, as if he had been found guilty of treason.

" 'Twas the arrival of the Duchess and Earl Kestrel that done it, Lady," he managed as explanation.

"You were asked to supply flowers for the banquet tables," Elise helped him along. "I noticed the bouquets. I hadn't realized you'd been forced to raid your flower beds to make the arrangements."

Her sympathetic tone—and the fact that she had admired these gardens since she was a toddler—opened the floodgate.

"I was, Lady," Timin Gardener said. "Never has there been such a springtime and summer for the nobility visiting the king. It seems that as soon as the weather grew pleasant and the roads a bit dry that every niece and nephew of a noble house has seen fit to call. That many receptions taxes those beds I grow just for cutting flowers, it does, pushes me out into the gardens."

Elise nodded sympathetically, but beneath her gentle, compassionate expression she was willing the man to keep talking. Bending to cut her three magnificent pink glads with petals edged in sunny yellow, the gardener continued:

"I exhausted the best of my daffodils and tulips when Grand Duke Gadman brought Lord Rolfston Redbriar and his brood to pay their respects to their uncle early this spring. Boar be praised that Earl Kestrel didn't come calling then. Neither sky-blue nor scarlet are easy to find early in the season."

"There are crocus for the blue," Elise said, considering.

"Too fragile for the banquet hall," the gardener sniffed. "Besides, we had the word that the king wanted Kestrel given highest honors. That takes more than a few crocus wilting among apple blossoms and then me having to answer in the autumn when there's not fruit enough on the trees."

"True," Elise agreed. "House Kestrel calls for stronger colors. It's a good thing Duchess Kestrel waited to ask for audience until the summer."

She stroked the petals of the gladiolas the gardener had handed to her before tucking them in with her roses. The man was mollified, seeing that she was not going to ask for more.

"I don't recall," Elise said cautiously, "such a fuss being made when Earl Kestrel came to court over the winter. He was in and out so much that his sleigh had a permanent berth in the forecourt."

"True enough," Timin Gardener agreed, squatting to tug a weed from among the flowers, then straightening as he suddenly remembered her station.

He spoke more rapidly to make amends. "True enough, Lady, but the word that came down from Steward Silver when she ordered the decorations for the banquet hall was that Earl Kestrel had sent ahead a letter thrice sealed. Once with his personal seal, once with his mother's, and once with the great seal of their house."

Elise nodded, hoping the glow of excitement didn't show in her eyes. Such a sequence of seals indicated a matter of the greatest secrecy.

"I wonder," she said guilelessly, "what business could merit such? Earl Kestrel has been reigning beside his mother at her behest these five years since. His seal is as good as hers in matters of state."

"They say," the head gardener offered, strolling with her down a path bordered in stocks and snapdragons, "that Earl Kestrel journeyed west early this spring, leaving when the roads were still sure to be deep in mud—not the usual time for traveling at all. He only went with a small retinue and none of them are talking about where they went."

"None?"

"None, Lady Elise. To my way of thinking, that's as interesting as if they were talking waterfalls."

"I agree," she said thoughtfully, and carefully turned the conversation to other matters.

LIKE HIS FATHER Purcel, Elise's sire, Ivon Archer, had made his mark by serving in the army of Hawk Haven. That had been a wise move. Although the Grand Duchess Rosene had granted her elder child the title of baron at his father's death twenty years before, Ivon was aware that not everyone in the kingdom appreciated King Chalmer's decision to permit his youngest daughter to marry the dashing war hero who had captured her heart.

Ivon knew that there were many among the six Great Houses for whom his descent from the grand duchess was far outweighed by his common blood—never mind that King Chalmer had made Purcel a baron, head of his own lesser noble house, complete with coat of arms, deed of land, and a name into perpetuity.

It hadn't been so long ago that Queen Zorana had created the Great Houses to reward her staunchest supporters—just over a hundred years. That was long enough for pride to emerge but not long enough for the entitlement to be invulnerable to challenge by upstart houses.

Elise had spent most of her young life in a manor in the capital belonging to House Archer. However, with the first of his war booty the then Lord Ivon had purchased property of his own, for he could not know that his father would die comparatively young, or that he himself would be blessed with only one child. Ivon's own property was held separately from the Archer grant, but, as the years passed and no sibling followed Elise into the world, it was likely that she would inherit both.

Rather than being insulted by Ivon's building his estate, King Tedric seemed to have appreciated his nephew's gesture of independence. Repeatedly, Ivon had earned command of his own company and promotions based solely upon merit. In her turn, Ivon's wife, Lady Aurella Wellward, had made herself indispensable to her aunt, Queen Elexa. Therefore, although just a grandniece and heir to a lesser noble house, Elise had always been given free run of the palace and its grounds.

As a child, this privilege had gained her some mild envy from her cousins. These days, that envy had turned into something sharper.

King Tedric, rumor said, would name an heir to his throne come Lynx Moon this late autumn, for this year the Festival of the Eagle fell then by lot. The king's own children were dead, as was all the line of his older sister, Princess Marras. By the strictest interpretation of the laws of inheritance, the king's heir should be his next sibling or her children, but old King Chalmer had wed Princess Caryl to Prince Tavis Seagleam of Bright Bay in the hope that the marriage alliance would foster peace between the two rival countries.

Neither the marriage nor the alliance had been a success. Princess Caryl had produced one son, Allister Seagleam. Although he was reported to be a man grown with a family of his own, most residents of Hawk Haven felt he was not really a contender for the throne. Who would accept a foreigner when there were native-born possibilities readily available?

In addition to Marras, Tedric, and Caryl, King Chalmer and Queen Rose had produced two other children: Gadman and Rosene. Gadman and Rosene were both still alive, but no one really expected King Tedric to name either as his heir, for both were within a few years of his own advanced age. Hawk Haven deserved more than a temporary monarch after King Tedric's long reign.

Grand Duke Gadman offered in his place a son, Lord Rolfston Redbriar of the House of the Goshawk. Lord Rolfston had five children of his own, so the succession would be secure. Moreover, a Redbriar in his own right, he was married to a member of the influential Shield family.

For her part, Grand Duchess Rosene had two living children: Ivon and Zorana. Both these Archer scions were well married into Great

House families; both had children of their own. Rosene's partisans, of whom the Houses of Wellward and Trueheart were not the least, argued that two possibilities from a line were better than one. However, even these partisans were split as to which provided the best choice: war-hero Ivon, with his staunch popular following, or Zorana, with her brood of four and experience with the domestic politics of the kingdom.

Personally Elise felt that, despite her frequenting the royal palace, she herself had little chance of being named heir, nor had her father and his sister, with their commoner father.

Grand Duke Gadman had married into a Great House, as had his son. Thus, Rolfston Redbriar's claim had the support of both his wife's and his mother's Great Houses, where her own father could only claim the sure support of his wife's.

However, Grand Duke Gadman and his elder brother the king had long quarreled over matters of state. Observers argued that given their past disagreements, King Tedric would pass over his brother's line out of spite. Then?

Then Lady Elise Archer could quite easily find herself heir apparent to the throne of Hawk Haven.

"AND QUICKLY NOW, Blysse, give me your hands." Derian put out his own, grasping those the two-legged wolf awkwardly extended.

She did so, growling quietly to herself, displeased by her lack of grace. In most matters when she compared herself with humankind she was grace itself, but she had yet to learn the trick of this thing called dancing.

Derian pretended not to notice her pique.

"That's right," he praised as she relaxed into his guidance. "Now, three steps to the side. Then when the music gets faster, we spin, so . . ."

One moon's turning and half of another had done great things for

Firekeeper's ability to understand what Derian said to her. Hardly ever now did he use a word she didn't know or for which she could not deduce a meaning. Also now she understood the ways and means of clothing (though not why humans wore so much of it) and how to ride a horse without first threatening it with fear for its life.

Dancing, though, dancing had proven to be a source of constant puzzlement, a puzzlement that ran side by side with delight. In all other things physical Firekeeper felt herself a wind through the treetops when she compared the grace of her movements with those of Race and Derian. When dancing, though . . .

Firekeeper snorted in disgust when—distracted by her thoughts—she trod on Derian's toes. From one corner of the room, Race Forester heard her and chuckled. She forgave him for the sake of the flute he held in one hand.

Music, especially that of the flute, was a pleasure heretofore only suspected in birdsong and burbling brook. Firekeeper had been enchanted the first time she heard Race play, so long ago when they had crossed the mountains with Hawk Nose and his people.

As soon as Race had grown easier around her, Firekeeper had insisted that he show her how to draw the notes from the slender piece of carved wood. It had proven far more difficult than she had imagined. Together, dancing and music raised her opinion of the two-legs until for the first time she was not ashamed to have been born of them, rather than of wolves.

"Turn right, Blysse," Derian called, gently pushing her in that direction. "Then back to me and out again . . ."

Concentrating on where to place her feet, on the timing of the steps, Firekeeper saw Race nod approvingly. They'd made a great deal of progress since the day he tried to loop a rope around her and imprison her in the human world. That progress had all been Derian's doing, for Firekeeper had been content to have Race fear and respect her. Despite her lack of overt cooperation, Derian had coaxed the scout into helping with Firekeeper's education, asking Race to teach her the names for plants and animals, how to shape snares and traps, how to shoot a bow.

Race was pleased when Firekeeper proved to be an apt pupil, was flattered when she showed more interest in his lessons than in Derian's. Eventually, Race realized how little Firekeeper knew of human woodcraft and his envy of her began to fade. When he realized how ungrudgingly she shared her own knowledge, they became friends.

Firekeeper still thought of Race as a lesser pack member, far below Derian and farther below Earl Kestrel. She knew that if need arose she could make him cringe. However, now that Firekeeper had become acquainted with some of the residents of the keep, Race no longer rested quite so low in her estimation.

"Water," she said to Derian when the dance ended. "Thirsty me."

"I am thirsty," he corrected patiently.

"You, too?" she asked, pouring them both full mugs from the pitcher set on the stand at the side of the room. She knew perfectly well what Derian wanted and decided to humor him.

"I know," she said, before he could decide if she had been teasing him. "Say: I am thirsty. Why? Shorter other."

"Shorter," Derian said, "but not correct."

"So?"

"So, would you eat hemlock?"

"No! Hemlock poison."

"That's right. And believe me, Blysse, words used wrong are like poison."

Derian sighed. The little line between his brows deepened as it did more and more frequently since Firekeeper had learned to ask why, instead of simply parroting whatever he said. After several swallows from his mug, Derian tried to explain further.

"Imagine we're hunting," he said. "If you want to make the deer come to you, would you imitate the sound of a frightened deer?"

"No!"

"Would you make the sound of a sick deer?"

"No. But I say 'Thirsty me' not makes fear, not makes sick. Just makes faster."

"Yes, but faster is not always better." Derian waved his hand in dismissal. "Let's leave it for now."

Firekeeper shrugged. "Dance more?"

"Not now. Dinner. Formal attire."

She wrinkled up her nose. "No formal attire. Pinches. Skin no breathe."

"Formal attire," Derian repeated firmly.

Firekeeper knew that he was serious by how he made himself swell up like a bullfrog. When she didn't obey, he simply refused to acknowledge her until she did. She was amazed how something so unlike wolf discipline could hurt as sharply.

"Formal attire," she agreed, consoling herself with the thought that later she could shed almost everything but the leather breeches and vest and run with Blind Seer.

Still, as she permitted Steward Daisy to lace her into a formal gown, this consolation seemed far distant indeed.

EVEN FLIRTING WITH the pretty kitchen maid couldn't keep Derian from reviewing over and over again in his memory the text of Earl Kestrel's latest letter. Despite the grace notes that began a formal missive, the text had been blunt.

> *"Although I concede that six weeks is hardly enough time to break a colt to saddle, much less time to teach the Lady Blysse all she needs to know, the situation here in Eagle's Nest has become critical. Both Grand Duke Gadman and Grand Duchess Rosene are urging King Tedric to name as his heir one of their children or grandchildren. Failing that, they are demanding that he at least indicate which line has precedence over the other.*
>
> *"Furthermore, the faction in favor of Duke Allister Seagleam of Bright Bay is gaining adherents. Among those who have most*

*recently turned to his cause are those who have become weary of the
king's siblings' continued political maneuvering.*

*"If Lady Blysse is to be recognized to her greatest advantage, it
must be before King Tedric names his heir. Afterwards, she could be
accused of inciting civil war. Therefore, I command you to bring
Lady Blysse to me at the Kestrel Manse in Eagle's Nest. In order
that she arrive without notice, you will be met at the Westriver
coach stop by one of your family's vehicles."*

A squeal from the kitchen maid as his fingers involuntarily tightened
around hers brought Derian back to himself. In apology, he kissed her
lightly on the injured members and she giggled and hurried off before
the cook could see her blush.

Still fuming, Derian strode through the halls of West Keep, his boots
ringing against the flagstones.

Damn Norvin Norwood, though! "Inciting civil war"! It would not be
Blysse who would be so accused, but Norvin himself. Unhappily, Blysse
would not be immune to censure. No one who looked into those dark
eyes could believe she was as innocent as she truly was. Derian himself
had his doubts from time to time.

Running up the steps to the highest observation tower wore Derian
out enough that he was glad to pause. Leaning on the stone sill, he
looked out into the gathering darkness. Drizzle was falling, making the
night seem hazy and unreal. In the light from the rising moon—about
half-full tonight—Derian imagined that he saw his charge flitting across
the cleared zone about the keep's walls and darting into the forest.

That was imagination, though. If she was out there, he would never
see her. Time and time again during the first weeks of their stay in the
keep, Race Forester had tried to track Blysse, tried to learn where she
was going. Finally, he had given up, admitting that her skills were nearly
supernatural.

Privately, Derian believed that having learned from Race how he read
tracks, Lady Blysse simply took care to avoid leaving those traces for

which the woodsman would search. Certainly, anyone who could have so much trouble tying a bodice lace or eating with a spoon could not be gifted with supernatural powers.

Remembering the woman's still execrable table manners, her refusal to wear shoes, her tendency to growl at any and all of the keep's dogs, Derian felt a wide, ironic grin light his face.

So Earl Kestrel thought that he could use the woman as a pawn in his political games? He was going to discover that he had a wolf by the tail and daren't let go.

⚜

FAT WARM RAINDROPS greeted Firekeeper when she emerged from her window into the courtyard surrounding West Keep. She cast a glance to right then to left, probing each shadow with her gaze. Race, however, seemed to have permanently given up their game of hide-and-seek.

Slightly disappointed, she climbed the wall and dropped to the damp earth on the other side. No Race here either. Dismissing him from her thoughts, she loped over to the tree line, swung up into the branches of a spreading maple, then crossed from there into another of its kind. The moonlight made the journey easy, so easy that she arrived at the rendezvous before Blind Seer.

The blue-eyed wolf silently glided beside her as she was bending her head to drink from the nearby brook.

"If I were a mountain cat," he said, "I would have broken your back."

"If you were a mountain cat," she replied, punching him on the shoulder, "I would have smelled you a mile off. How is the hunting?"

"Good," he answered. "Even the latest of winter's sleepers are long awake. The deer grow fat on the new grass. I grow fat on the deer. Do they feed you well in your stone lair?"

"Enough," she said, "though much of what they eat tastes odd. Did I tell you that Fox Hair insists I eat as he does now? He's so slow! I could clear the platters while he is spreading butter on his bread."

"Two-legs are not wolves," Blind Seer replied practically. "Their ways are not ours."

"True."

They sat for a while, watching the play of moonlight on the rippling waters of the brook.

"For how long does your trail go with mine?" she asked, suddenly interrupting the silence. "Hawk Nose sent a message this morning and since then Fox Hair has smelled of bitter sweat. I heard him giving orders for supplies to Steward Daisy. When we went out for a riding lesson, he spoke with the groom about the readiness of the horses for the road. I think that soon we three outliers get called to the human pack."

"Do you want my trail to follow yours?" the wolf asked, leaning against her. "You've lived in that great stone lair one moon's death and another's new borning. Surely you've confirmed what the Cousins told me. Two-legs do not like wolves, even little ones like the Cousins. I don't think that they will like me at all."

Firekeeper flung her arm around his great furry neck.

"They will be terrified of you," she said with great confidence. "Never doubt it. Still, I would have you run with me longer. I can dance a few dances and prattle in their tongue, but my blood is a wolf's blood for this veneer of humanity."

"Wolf's blood has always run beneath your naked hide," Blind Seer affirmed. "But I have no wish to see *my* blood spilled by one of those arrows Race shoots so straight."

"No," Firekeeper considered. "This is a problem, but I think, from what Fox Hair has shown me, from the tales he has told me, that where the two-legs den together, there are many such buildings as the keep. There you may not be able to hide from their eyes as easily as you have done here. Best that they know you are my companion. They hold some odd respect for me. It may extend to you, as fear of the adult wolves protects the pups."

"Perhaps," Blind Seer said. "We must think further on this."

"But not for too long," Firekeeper said. "A season is changing, not of the world, but in my life. I cannot turn from the humans until I know more."

"And I," admitted Blind Seer, "cannot turn from you, even if following you should mean my death."

⚜

DERIAN HAD ANTICIPATED having difficulty getting Blysse ready for the journey. What he had not anticipated was having trouble with the horses.

On the morning of their scheduled departure, however, the young woman was calm and collected, but the equines were edgy, requiring the assistance of two grooms to calm them while Derian inspected girths and pack straps.

Chestnut coat burnished and glossy from several weeks of easy living, Roanne snaked back her ears and tried to nip the groom standing nearest to where she was tied.

Race's buckskin and Blysse's grey were hardly any better behaved, though the latter, having been chosen specifically for his placid temper, continued to chew a wisp of hay while rolling a white-rimmed eye at anything that moved.

Lady Blysse, dressed in her favorite battered leather vest and hacked-off trousers, came out of the keep, carrying the saddlebags the kitchen staff had packed for them. Her dark eyes sparkled, dancing with what Derian hoped was anticipation. Seeing the curve of her lips, he feared that it was mischief.

"Give me those packs," he said, surreptitiously eyeing them to see if she might have stolen something.

She did so, and as he was loading the bags onto the pack mule, Blysse cocked her head, catching some sound of which he was unaware. Then, the smile broadening across her face, she loped across the cleared kill zone surrounding West Keep toward the forest.

Race, who had been chatting with Steward Daisy, come forth to see her guests safely on the road, shouted after her:

"Come back here, Blysse!"

The young woman slowed, waving her hand to indicate that she had heard, but kept going.

"Blysse!"

This time she halted right at the edge of the scrub growth bordering the meadow. With her left hand, she made an elaborate beckoning gesture toward something in the woods; with her right she made the sign for Race and Derian to wait where they were.

Derian's heart began to beat faster. He wondered if there might have been more truth to Earl Kestrel's tale of Blysse's survival than even that facile politician had ever dreamed. Could Prince Barden be out there in the forest, ready to emerge only now that he had been assured that his daughter would be treated well?

Derian glanced over at Race and saw that the woodsman had grown pale, his breath coming fast and shallow. Doubtless, being more superstitious than Derian, he feared not a living prince, but a vengeful ancestral spirit. Surreptitiously, Race fingered a talisman hanging from his belt, invoking his own ancestors' protection against this imagined threat.

Oblivious of their reactions, Blysse repeated the beckoning gesture more urgently, drawing forth whatever lurked within the suddenly mysterious trees. Several pounding heartbeats later, without the least whisper of motion, an enormous grey wolf slipped from the cover to stand at the young woman's side, so close that his fur brushed her leg.

A more usual wolf's head might have reached to her waist; this beast's reached nearly to her chest. Moreover, his eyes were not the more usual tawny gold or deep brown of a wolf, but instead a brilliant blue.

Steward Daisy screamed once and would have again, but Race smothered her mouth with his hand. One of the grooms began muttering invocations for ancestral protection. Derian looked at Race and found that, like him, the forester's shock was melting away beneath the glow of comprehension.

"Well," Race said, his taut voice betraying his tension. "Now we know where she's been going every night."

Derian nodded, feeling a grin split the stiff mask of his face. "And is Earl Kestrel ever in for a surprise."

But Norvin Norwood, Earl Kestrel, was not the only one due for further surprises. Even as Lady Blysse took her first step toward them, the great wolf pacing at her heel, a shrill scream pierced the morning air.

A blue-grey blur plummeted out of the sky, resolving into a perfect peregrine falcon the size of an eagle. The bird circled once about woman and wolf, then came to rest atop the baggage packed on the mule. Ruffling its feathers, it shifted from one foot to the other, cocking its head so that it could study each of the humans from brilliant golden-rimmed eyes.

This critical inspection proved too much for Steward Daisy. Sobbing, she fled into the safety of the castle walls. Using her departure as an excuse, the two grooms hurried after; ostensibly to comfort her, in reality to put solid stone between themselves and a woman whose companions were giant beasts out of legend.

Having long since relegated these to a subordinate position in her private hierarchy, Lady Blysse seemed indifferent to their reactions. Her dark gaze was upon Derian and Race. The tightness in her shoulders relaxed only slightly when she saw that neither of them had made any offensive move.

Race's dog Queenie had not been so much the coward as to flee from her master, but as the wolf closed the distance, she cringed and whined. Derian fought back an urge to do something similar by speaking to Race as if this encounter were the most usual thing in the world.

"I'd forgotten until now," he said, "that when I first spotted her footprint, there was a wolf's print beside it."

Race nodded.

"I hadn't wanted to remember," Race admitted, "not once we found her to be but a girl and so ill used."

"Then there were the wolf's howls we heard each night while we were west of the gap."

"Fewer and more distant," Race added, his voice back to normal now, "once we crossed, but still out there, as if they were watching us."

"I guess they were," Derian said, "or at least they were watching her."

"And the falcon," Race continued, "it sure looks like the one that attacked me when I tried to put a rope on Blysse."

"It does," Derian agreed, remembering pushing Race out of the striking range of those talons. "I wondered then, but there's been so much else to wonder about."

"I didn't want to wonder," Race admitted. "I didn't like where that wondering led me."

Listening to their conversation but not commenting, Lady Blysse halted her advance before the horses' panic at the proximity of the wolf reached the point where they might do themselves harm.

Derian wondered that the equines showed even this much control, then realized that they must have been aware of the wolf's presence for a long while, far more aware than the humans had been. What to him was a complete surprise was to them a long-borne menace.

"Well, Blysse," Derian said, "are these your pets?"

"No," she said, shaking her head vigorously and giving Queenie a disdainful look. "Queenie pet. Wolf and falcon are my friends."

Her careful speech showed Derian how important it was to Blysse that he and Race understand her. Even with his constant badgering, she still tended to drop what she viewed as nonessential words. If she was specifying that these animals were friends, rather than pets or property, it was an essential distinction—at least to her.

"Friends," he repeated, taking in a breath so deep that his lungs ached. "Well, I guess you had better introduce us then."

Blysse nodded solemnly, then indicated the wolf. In some distant part of his mind, Derian was amused to see that she used the little court mannerisms he had been careful to teach her.

"This is Not-Seeing Seer," she said carefully.

By this point, Derian wouldn't have been at all surprised if the wolf had spoken with a human voice. It did not. Instead, it took a step forward and stretched out its forelimbs in a credible, non-groveling, bow.

Automatically, Derian bowed in return and Race gave a short jerk in imitation. Smiling now, Blysse gestured to the peregrine falcon.

"This is . . ." she paused, as if having trouble translating the bird's name, "Fierce Joy in Flight."

The falcon didn't bow. Instead it made a soft, mewling cry, quite conversational in tone.

"Pleased to meet you," Derian responded solemnly.

"The same," Race said. To himself he muttered, "I must be dreaming this!"

"No dream," Derian said. "Though it would be easier if it was."

He looked at Blysse. "I suppose that the wolf and the falcon are coming with us."

She looked puzzled, then worked through the essential parts of the question to get at its meaning.

"With us, yes." She put her hand on the wolf's head. "He my kin. Falcon is friend. They go with me."

"The city," Derian said, trying to dissuade her, though he already knew the attempt would be futile, "is not a place for wolves."

"City can be place for wolves," she said stubbornly. "I go to city. Wolf goes with me."

Derian surrendered. Maybe once she saw a town or two she would change her mind. He doubted it, but it was a pleasant fantasy.

"Shall we go, then?" he asked. Then he mused to the air, "The horses aren't going to like this at all."

"I can run with horses," Blysse replied. "Not-Seeing Seer will run near me."

She laughed. "Maybe then, someone think he dog, not wolf."

"There's a chance of that," Race admitted, speaking for the first time since the introductions had been concluded. "At least they'll give a second thought before shooting."

"True."

Derian worried about whether Blysse could keep up with the horses now that the party would be traveling on roads rather than navigating rough woodland trails, but he put the worry by. Either she could or she could not. They'd deal with that problem when it became a problem.

"Well," Derian said, "I'll loosen the girth on your gelding, but he'll be ready if you get tired. Is that all right, Blysse?"

"Yes. No."

She bit her lip, her expression showing the frustration she so often felt when her grasp of the language was insufficient for her needs. Derian waited, knowing he would only add to her frustration if he tried guessing at what she needed to say. After consideration, she began again:

"Yes for horse," she said. "No for Blysse. My name not Blysse. Wolf call me Firekeep. Firekeeper."

Derian had eventually been able to teach her the verb "to keep"—not an easy concept, but one made easier to explain once they were settled where so many things were kept: keys at the Steward's belt, food in the pantry, clothing in a press.

"Firekeeper," he repeated. Then, realizing he sounded much like her, he asked, "Why? Why Firekeeper?"

She touched the bag containing flint and steel hanging around her neck. "King Wolf, Queen Wolf, give me. Teach me."

She scowled, perhaps reading the disbelief in his eyes. Quickly Derian schooled his expression to polite attentiveness and hoped that Race would do the same. He'd gone to great trouble to teach Firekeeper hierarchical titles and had found that she grasped the concept, if not the words, with amazing ease. If she said King Wolf, she meant the wolf with the most authority.

"King Wolf," he prompted, "gave them to you."

"King Wolf, Queen Wolf," she insisted. "No wolf make fire but me. I am Firekeeper."

Derian let this go, his head reeling with the implications of this simple statement. Not only was he to believe that Blysse could understand what wolves said, he was also to believe that they could teach her how to strike fire with flint and steel.

More disturbing still was Blysse's repeated identification of herself with these wolves.

"Blysse . . ." he began, then corrected himself when she growled and the wolf beside her raised his hackles. "Firekeeper, you are not a wolf. You are a human, like me, like Race."

"I am wolf," she said placidly. "Wolf with two legs and no fur, but wolf in blood."

Race put his hand on Derian's arm. "Leave it, Derian. Leave it. We must get on the road and before we do so, you'd better decide whether or not you want to warn Earl Kestrel about this new development with his niece."

"Or if I want to risk Steward Daisy sending word ahead by pigeon." Derian pressed at his eyes, feeling a headache coming on. "How can I tell Earl Kestrel that Blysse . . . I mean Firekeeper . . . thinks she's a wolf?"

"Don't," Race said practically, "but warn him about her unusual companions. We have at least a week on the road to figure out what to do about the rest. More if the weather's bad."

"At least a week," Derian repeated, turning blindly back toward the keep, mentally drafting his message. "This is going to be a very, very interesting ride."

VII

USUALLY, ELISE ENJOYED a chance to meet with her cousins. Being related to the king, even so relatively distant a relation as a grandniece, was a difficult role. There were so few people to whom you were just another person, who could forget that royal shadow looming over you. Being heir to House Archer only complicated the matter.

In all honesty, she admitted, the barony hardly mattered right now. Neither her grandmother Rosene nor her great-uncle Gadman had ever let anyone forget that they and their descendants were royal kin. Theirs had been a harmless enough pretention, one good for the best seats at public games and partners at dances until Crown Princess Lovella had been killed in battle. Then the entire succession affair had opened up, quietly at first, then with greater and greater intensity when King Tedric refused to name a new heir quickly.

Now a gathering of cousins was a little like a gathering of wolves, each knowing that there could be only one head of the pack. Even those like herself who weren't certain they wanted to be that head were even less certain that they wanted anyone else to be so.

"You can almost hear the growling," she murmured to herself, taking a goblet of wine from a tray held by a polite servant and going to sit beside her cousin Purcel.

Named for their mutual grandfather, the war hero Purcel Archer, Purcel Trueheart was a powerfully built youth of fifteen, who had already distinguished himself in several skirmishes, earning himself the rank of lieutenant.

Courage was not Purcel's only asset. His budding tactical sense had also been tested several times. These days, when he was called to his commanders' tents, it was not mere flattery that gave him a place at their councils. Many argued that Purcel was the single best reason for his mother, Lady Zorana, to be named crown princess, for at her death she would be succeeded by a proven battlefield commander.

Watching Purcel slurp down his beer and munch peanuts in ill-concealed boredom, Elise wondered. Warlord, yes, and welcome to it. King? As King Tedric had proven, a good king must be able to reign as well as to command. Both Aunt Zorana and Great-Aunt Rosene argued that Purcel would learn patience and discretion as he matured. Given the familial longevity—the descendants of Zorana the Great seemed to live long lives if they survived their childhoods—Zorana would reign for many years herself before joining the ancestors, and Purcel could learn the skills necessary to be a monarch from her.

Elise wondered, though, if a man who from his youngest years had been praised for quick, decisive action could learn to reflect and consider rather than charge ahead.

Purcel brightened visibly as she seated herself next to him. Two years apart in age, they had become close playmates once she had stopped dismissing him as a baby. Even when he was three and she a mature and thoughtful five, he had loved to trot about on a pony as chubby as he was, playacting the role of a soldier protecting his lady cousin.

"Elise," Purcel said warmly by way of greeting, "want a peanut?"

She took one to please him, though the oily things tended to make her face break out. Purcel seemed immune to this bane of adolescence, though she still nursed hopes.

"Thank you, cousin." She kissed him lightly on the cheek. "How was your ride into the capital?"

"Not bad, the roads were muddy, but we managed . . ."

What followed was a long dissertation on thrown horseshoes, partially washed-out bridges, troops needing to be kept from foraging in newly planted fields, and other minutiae of military life. Elise listened with one ear, nodding when appropriate, her gaze surveying the others gathered in the room.

They were a small enough group given that King Chalmer fathered five children and that each of those children had at least one child. However, Princess Marras's little ones had died as babies. King Tedric's three were gone now, all dying without issue except for Barden, whose name was still a curse to his father.

Princess Caryl, King Chalmer's third child, had been married away into the kingdom of Bright Bay, her father's pledge to a peace that lasted only a few years. Caryl's departure meant that just Grand Duke Gadman and Grand Duchess Rosene remained. Each of these had produced two children, but Grand Duke Gadman's Nydia had died long before Elise herself was born. In memory, Elise's aunt Zorana had named her first daughter Nydia, though the girl was more commonly called Dia.

Just ten of them, unless one counted Allister Seagleam's four children, far away in Bright Bay. Elise found it odd to think that those four—one older than her, the rest all younger—were as close kin to her as were Lord Rolfston's four: grandchildren of her grandmother's brother.

Banishing the faraway Seagleams from consideration, Elise concentrated on the ten gathered here. Any one could become crown prince or princess of the kingdom of Hawk Haven if luck was with them. The chief contenders for that honor were Purcel, as his mother's eldest, Sapphire, as Lord Rolfston's eldest, and herself. However, some courtiers whispered that if King Tedric was going to name an heir why did he need to follow the strict order of precedence? He should choose instead some young grandniece or grandnephew, someone he could shape and teach during whatever years remained to him.

A voice, loud and piercing, cut into Elise's revery.

"Elise! Elise! Darling cousin, you look wonderful!"

Quickly Elise set down her wine goblet, knowing that this gushing greeting would be followed by an equally enthusiastic embrace, and not really wanting to spill wine on her new pale pink, rosebud-embroidered gown.

Sapphire Shield was the eldest of their generation, a buxom young woman of twenty-three with dark, blue-black hair, a pointed chin, and eyes the color of her namesake gem. She had been engaged several times, always into very advantageous matches, but had never taken her vows.

Elise knew perfectly well that politics, not romance, had ruled each of these arrangements, but Sapphire enjoyed mooning about after each broken engagement, acting as if her heart were truly broken. Such behavior might make those who didn't know her dismiss her as flighty and shallow, but Elise was not fooled.

Sapphire Shield was heir to the comfortable holdings accumulated through both her Redbriar and Shield family connections. Riki Redbriar, a scion of House Goshawk, had brought a considerable dowry into her marriage to Grand Duke Gadman, a good thing since members of the House of the Eagle were all essentially landless—merely comfortable life tenants on crown-held lands.

Their son Rolfston Redbriar had made a good marriage to Melina Shield. Melina's dowry had included several nice holdings adjoining lands Riki Redbriar would eventually pass on to her son. Although claiming no title higher than Lady, Melina also brought with her the prestige of the Shield name and membership within the House of the Gyrfalcon for her children.

Queen Zorana the First had been a Shield and the Gyrfalcons were still considered first among the Great Houses. Therefore, as Lady Melina never wearied of telling anyone who would listen, her children were kin to the first queen of Hawk Haven both through their father, who was her great-grandson, and through their mother, who was some sort of cousin.

No, thought Elise, *Sapphire never forgets who she is, no matter how flightily she behaves at functions like this.*

As of this moment, that behavior included a crushing hug, compliments on Elise's dress (including insincere wishes that *she* could wear pink), and other such prattle.

Elise politely prattled back, though she rather wished she could snort, as Purcel did, and stalk off on the thin excuse of needing another tankard of beer.

"So tell me, Castle Flower," Sapphire said, bending her head close to Elise's, "why do you think Uncle Tedric has summoned us all here?"

King Tedric, was, of course, Sapphire's great-uncle, as he was Elise's, but Sapphire often chose to minimize the degree of their relation. Among her peers, she had made no secret that she considered herself practically crown princess already. After all, her father was Grand Duke Gadman's only surviving child and Grand Duke Gadman should have been named King Tedric's heir immediately following Crown Princess Lovella's death two years before.

Elise thought Sapphire overconfident, but there was no gain in telling her so, especially since Sapphire was more likely to become crown princess than Elise herself was, no matter that their relationship to the king was the same. Simply speaking, Sapphire had better connections.

Instead of making excuses to escape after Purcel, Elise considered the best way of answering Sapphire's question. As the nickname "Castle Flower" suggested, Sapphire was among those who assumed that Elise's familiarity with the structure had made her privy to all its occupants' secrets.

"Well," Elise said, looking into her goblet as if the dark red wine held mysteries, "I think it must have something to do with Earl Kestrel, don't you?"

Sapphire, torn between a desire to probe further and a desire to seem to know more than her younger cousin, gave in to the latter impulse.

"I do think so." She leaned so she was nearly whispering into Elise's ear. "The senior porter at the Kestrels' city manse fancies my maid. He told her that a week ago a closed carriage came to the manse. The courtyard was cleared and Earl Kestrel ordered everyone away from the windows. Then someone or something was brought into the manse, cloistered in one ground-floor wing. No one but four servants and Earl Kestrel's cousin, Sir Jared Surcliffe, have been allowed in there since."

Sapphire looked at Elise, but Elise refused to show the least sign that she, too, had heard some version of this tale. Let Sapphire think she knew more than the Castle Flower. She might give away something Elise didn't know.

"They do say," Sapphire continued with relish, "that strange sounds are heard from the closed wing and that Earl Kestrel's bodyguard has been seen in the public markets purchasing great quantities of raw meat."

Elise raised her eyebrows. This last *was* indeed news.

"Truly?" she asked, playing the sycophant gladly.

"Truly," Sapphire confirmed. "My maid's sister is married to the cook for a large tavern in the city and he has seen the bodyguard with his own eyes."

Elise swallowed a flippant impulse to ask with who else's eyes might the cook be expected to see.

"So, what surprise do you think Earl Kestrel has brought?"

But Sapphire had given away as much as she would without getting something in return. She shrugged her pretty white shoulders.

"I have no idea."

Elise was about to suggest something in the line of a bear for the king to hunt when Jet, Sapphire's younger brother, sauntered over to join them.

At twenty, Jet Shield looked five years older, his features rugged under heavy black brows, his hair so thick that it resisted being tied back in a fashionable queue. His eyes were so dark that pupil could hardly be distinguished from iris. When his blood was up, they glittered like the stone for which he was named.

Each of Melina Shield's children was named for a precious gem, an affectation most believed. Some whispered, however, that Melina practiced sorcerous arts thought lost when the Plague caused the Old World nations to abandon their colonies. Certainly the physical appearance of each of Melina's children bore out the latter rumors.

Elise didn't know which tale to believe. Her own mother, Aurella

Wellward, had known Melina Shield since they were both children. Aurella said that she thought that Melina chose names for her children only *after* they were born and some moon-spans grown. Certainly, her confinements at private estates permitted this luxury. However, Lady Melina's old maidservant claimed loudly and frequently that her mistress chose each infant's name as soon as she was certain that she was carrying.

Whatever Rolfston Redbriar thought on the matter, he was not saying. Personally, Elise believed he was too canny to meddle with anything that brought his branch of the family such respect and awe.

"May I join you ladies?" Jet asked, sliding into a seat next to Elise without waiting for an answer. This close she was aware of his scent, something musky and masculine, just touched with a faint hint of pipe smoke.

A year past his majority, Jet had joined his sister in the matrimonial battles. Unlike her, he would doubtless have less time to peruse the selection open to him. Sapphire was a good six years older than Elise, her next equivalent competitor for matches. Although Jet was five years older than Purcel, Zorana was far more aggressive than Elise's father and had already been hinting about making a betrothal for her son. Such hints narrowed the field before the race had really begun.

So Jet turned what was already becoming a practiced smile on his second cousin.

"You look beautiful tonight, Elise," he said. "Your complexion is so well suited to the paler shades. Pinks just make my sister look sallow."

Elise ignored the dig, though she could see Sapphire fuming. It was true, though, that Sapphire was best suited to stronger colors: blues, reds, purples. It was also true that there was no love lost between these siblings.

Long resenting Sapphire's place as heir, Jet now treasured the dream that if his father became King Tedric's successor, he, not Sapphire, would be named crown prince: "Sapphire has trained long and hard," Jet had told Elise, after pledging her to silence, "to manage the estates our family has inherited from both Shields and Redbriars. Why should that training be wasted? Rather, let her continue as heir to our family holdings. I am free to prepare, with no previous bias and no distractions, to follow our father, after his own long reign, onto the throne."

Doubtless Sapphire knew her brother's feelings on the matter. As she glowered at him, too well trained to pull his hair as she would have when they were in the nursery, Elise wished that someone, something, would break this uncomfortable moment.

Her wish was granted. A footman came to the door of the parlor where the grandnieces and grandnephews had been sequestered to await the end of their elders' counsels.

"His Majesty," the man boomed, looking at the carved paneling on the far wall rather than at any one of the ten eager faces now turned toward him, "requests that you attend him in the Eagle's Hall."

Suddenly meek and obedient, the cousins set down goblets and tankards, smoothed hair, surreptitiously checked reflections in mirrors and polished glass. Then, falling into order as they had so many times before, in so many gatherings like, but unlike, this one, the cousins filed from the parlor. Only one voice broke the silence.

Kenre Trueheart, at the age of seven the youngest of the cousins, whispered to his older sister, "Now, Deste, now we'll find out what it's all about."

Smiling softly to herself, Elise could not help but think that little Kenre was uttering the words imprinted on each of their hearts.

SOMETIMES, FIREKEEPER THOUGHT she would go insane. It was the noise. Or perhaps it was the smells. Maybe it was some undefined sense of too many people—just the people, just the humans—forget their dogs and cats, horses and mules, cows, goats, sheep, chickens . . .

She would go mad.

Each day when she bathed in the metal tub that Derian filled for her in the great stone-walled chamber that was her haven in Earl Kestrel's mansion, she checked herself for bite marks. Surely she must have been bitten by some rabid fox or possum. Surely, it was that, something in her blood, running through her mind, setting it afire.

There could not be so many people in all the world.

But the falcon Elation told her with sardonic calm that there were—that this city of Eagle's Nest was large, but not the only such swarming of humans, not the largest even.

But Firekeeper had long been the only human in all the world. She never realized that this was what she had believed. Now she must acknowledge that she had believed herself unique.

Even the evidence of the artifacts—the knife and the tinderbox—these had not convinced her that there were other humans in the world. Now she must face humans in their varied colors, shapes, sizes, and smells.

She would go mad.

Derian entered the room to find her sitting on the floor, her head buried against Blind Seer's flank. She ignored the man. Hoped that he would go away. Knew from the gusting exhalation of the breath beneath her brother's ribs that he would not.

"Firekeeper?"

A finger poked her gently in the side. She growled.

"C'mon, kid."

Hands on her shoulders.

"Today is the day. You don't dare disappoint Earl Kestrel."

Why not? she thought. She had disappointed herself. Why shouldn't she disappoint that small, hawk-nosed male with his arrogant, proprietary attitude?

"Please?"

Derian sounded more unhappy than annoyed. Reluctantly, Firekeeper permitted the smallest tendril of sympathy for him and his predicament to finger through her own misery. Earl Kestrel was always patient with her, even kind in a stiff, wooden fashion that owed more than a little to his fear of Blind Seer. He was not always so with Derian. More than once Firekeeper had heard him yelling at the younger man, berating him for failures incomprehensible to her.

She raised her head from the comforting fur. Derian was kneeling on the floor beside her. To his credit, he was ignoring Blind Seer's baleful blue gaze, having learned that the wolf could be trusted on his terms. As long as Derian did not make what the wolf interpreted as a threatening gesture toward the woman, he was safe.

"Firekeeper," Derian said, catching her gaze and holding it when she would look away, "today you meet the king. Tonight you dine in his halls. It is for this that Earl Kestrel brought you from the wilds. You can't back out now."

"I can," she threatened.

"You can," he agreed, "but I wouldn't like to be you if you do. Earl Kestrel has always had his own uses for you, no matter what pretty speeches he makes for other ears. If you fail him . . ."

She said nothing.

Derian shrugged. "The best you can hope for is being turned out into the streets. You might be fine. So would the falcon, but I wouldn't give Blind Seer a chance, not even at night."

Firekeeper knew too well what he meant. She had seen the city streets, had been taken out into them cloaked and after dark under Derian and Ox's escort. (Fleetingly she wondered why the big man permitted his own to call him after a castrated bull.)

Using curtains of heavy fabric, Derian had made her a concealed place from which she could watch the city traffic without being seen by either the inmates of the manse or the passersby.

So many people!

She felt the mad panic returning and stamped it back. Even so, it filled her voice as she challenged Derian.

"He turn us out," she said sharply. "How he do that? Little man, big voice, no teeth."

"There you are wrong, Lady Blysse." Derian surged to his feet and crossed to where a new gown has been spread on the bed. "Earl Kestrel has many teeth. You just don't know how to see them. Do you think Ox is the only big man he commands or Race the only one who can use a bow?"

She snarled. Derian continued as if she had not.

"You are probably meaner than any one of them—maybe than any two. But in the end, they would win. You would be gone. Blind Seer would be dead."

He shrugged. "Or you can put on this pretty gown, scrub the tears from your cheeks, and let me comb your hair. Then we'll have an audience with the king . . ."

He shook his head in wonder, still struggling with the idea that he was to meet the king. "And then come back here and tell Blind Seer all about it."

She knew he was humoring her in this last. He didn't believe that she could speak with the wolf, understand all that he said to her in return. At Elation's prompting, she had agreed to stop trying to convince him.

"With me?" she asked, rising to her feet in turn. "Blind Seer come with me?"

Derian shook his head. "Not this time. You'll have to settle for me and Ox."

"Blind Seer comes," she insisted stubbornly. "Tell Earl Kestrel, Norvin Norwood, Uncle Norvin—whatever name. Blind Seer comes with me."

Valet spoke from the doorway, his soft-footed arrival having been unnoticed even by the wolves. "Derian, I will advise my master to give Lady Blysse her will in this matter. There are advantages."

Firekeeper spun to stare at the little brown man.

"Do," she said, "and I will make ready."

Valet bowed deeply, an acknowledgment of a deal made and sealed rather than in abasement, and vanished.

"*Well done, Sister,*" Blind Seer said. "*I look forward to meeting this One above Ones. Now, you must make ready. I, of course, am already perfect.*"

"Braggart," she replied in the human language.

The gown she was to wear tonight was made of some soft stuff the color of bone, decorated with thin lines of scarlet and of blue. With it went a wreath of flowers and a string of small round pebbles Derian called pearls.

"A lovely ensemble," Derian commented, lifting the gown by its shoulders so she could inspect it. "I believe that Duchess Kestrel, the earl's mother, selected it at her son's request. It should look good on you—very delicate and virginal."

He chuckled. "Of course the belt knife and the wolf will rather ruin that effect."

Firekeeper cocked a brow at him. They had long settled that whether or not she was wearing formal attire a few accessories were non-negotiable. Her knife and fire-making tools stayed with her and she flatly refused to wear shoes. Even Earl Kestrel had given up in his efforts to convince her otherwise.

She pulled off her leather vest and dropped her breeches, enjoying the small victory of watching Derian's fair skin turn dark red. Then she gestured imperiously toward the fire.

"My bath, Derian," she said. "Then we go see this king."

AS DERIAN HANDED FIREKEEPER into the carriage—an assistance she permitted only because of her difficulties handling long skirts—he imagined many eyes watching them from behind the curtained and shuttered windows of the Kestrel Manse. No matter what the earl had ordered, some would disobey, would peek out. They would tell their fellows of the strange girl but partially glimpsed in the darkness and of the pale grey shadow whose very presence had terrified the horses in the instant before it had leapt into the carriage.

He shrugged. Secrecy wouldn't matter after tonight. After tonight, the entire city would be alive with tales. The only question was what those tales would tell. Would they be about the return of a long-lost grand-daughter to her joyful grandfather, as Earl Kestrel hoped? Or would they be about an impertinent nobleman imprisoned—or perhaps executed—for his presumption in forcing upon the king one he had wished for-gotten?

Derian wished that he had a touch of the gift of foresight. Then, as quickly, he withdrew that wish. Knowing—especially if the news was bad—wouldn't make tonight's ordeal any easier. He would like to know how King Tedric viewed henchmen, though, and devoutly hoped that they were not judged in the light of their master's ambitions.

Tonight, Valet served as footman. Derian would drive the coach, thus eliminating the need to bring anyone else into Earl Kestrel's secret. Ox and Race would provide their only escort.

Turning away as Valet closed the carriage door upon the earl and his niece, Derian spared a prayer to his ancestors that Norvin Norwood would remember to be patient with the young woman. Firekeeper had distinctly disliked the closed coach the times using one had been nec-essary. Then only her strong sense of personal dignity (surprising in one who still could not remember when modesty was appropriate) had kept her from bolting.

Up on the box, Derian shook the reins and felt the elegant team of matched rose-greys step out as smartly as if they were on parade, their momentary fear of wolf scent forgotten. The pre-planned route to the palace carefully avoided the market and the streets where the guild mem-bers kept their shops, so traffic was light. Ox and Race, riding in front, took care of obstacles as they occurred.

At the carriage's approach the palace gates swung open. A rider in the smart uniform of the King's Own Guard trotted his liver chestnut gelding out to intercept them.

"Follow me, please," he said, his tone making the phrase an order.

Derian obeyed, amusing himself by pricing the man's elegant mount and deciding that it must belong to the guard's stables. If it was the man's personal mount, Derian figured he himself should consider going for a soldier. The pay was obviously quite good.

In a private walled courtyard, Derian brought the team to a halt and swung lithely down from the box.

"Take care of these," he said, tossing the reins to a dutifully bored-looking guard standing outside the towering stone archway. "Earl Kestrel will need me."

A wide-eyed look of surprise and sudden anger shattered the man's trained indifference. Clearly, he had not expected to be so spoken to by a coachman.

Earl Kestrel's sharp bark of "Derian!" smothered whatever dressing-down the guard had been planning for the impertinent redhead. Drawing the mantle of the earl's favor around him, Derian crossed to where Valet held open the carriage door. Norvin Norwood stood to one side of the portable steps. Firekeeper crouched in the doorway, her traveling cloak pulled up around her face, her nose wrinkling as she took in all the unfamiliar scents. Blind Seer's head poked around her waist, his own nose busy.

"Derian, if you would explain to my ward," Earl Kestrel said, his tones barely civil with suppressed tension, "that we have an appointment and should not keep the king waiting."

Derian nodded and extended a hand to the young woman.

"Come on, Firekeeper," he coaxed. "There will be time enough for that later. Right now, we need to follow Race and Ox through that doorway."

She looked at him, her dark eyes showing none of the confusion she must feel.

"And see this king?"

"And see *the* king," he agreed with soft emphasis on the article. "Here there is only one."

"Here," she said, gathering up her skirts in massive, unladylike bunches. "I remember. Elsewhere, Blind Seer and I know it is different."

Derian was quietly impressed with how the guards at the door maintained their wooden expressions when confronted with woman and wolf. They passed them through without comment, though the two who led the way down the corridor seemed unnaturally tense. Doubtless they feared being leapt upon from behind.

The castle at Eagle's Nest was an old building as such things were judged in the New World. It had been built some two hundred and twenty-five years before by the family Gildcrest. They had been granted land in this area by a ruler of some faraway nation in the Old World, an old woman who had never and would never see any more of the holdings she divvied up among her followers than their outlines on a map.

However, this Old World ruler firmly believed in rewarding well those who might otherwise become troublesome. If those rewards were located at a great distance and presented in such a fashion that refusing to re-locate to them could be taken as a grievous insult, then all the better.

During the years when the Plague gave lie to all claims of power and dominion, the castle's builders had perished. The castle with its strong walls had been much fought over until Queen Zorana the First had won it and kept it. That possession, almost as much as the loyalty of her people to her, had made her queen then and made her grandson Tedric king today.

And will Blysse be queen thereafter? Derian mused as he escorted his charge down the wide stone corridors. *That, I suppose, is precisely what we're here to learn.*

Then he turned a corner, stepped through a towering door, and royalty was before him. Derian had never seen either King Tedric or Queen Elexa from any closer than a seat in the crowd during some public festival. Up close, he found them both more and less impressive than he had imagined.

Distance had erased lines from both of the monarchs' faces. When Derian raised his head from making his homage on the dense New Kel-vinese carpet at the foot of the steps leading to the thrones, he was shocked to see how ancient they both looked.

Intellectually, he knew that King Tedric was seventy-five years old,

old for even his long-lived family. Queen Elexa was somewhat younger at sixty-nine, but the illness that years before had robbed her of her ability to bear children had given her frailty beyond her age in poor return. Beneath her tissue-paper-fine skin, the blood could be seen running faintly blue. The crocheted lace gloves on her hands could not completely hide the dark splotches of age spots.

Her gaze, though, was kind and compassionate. The gracious dip of her head acknowledged commoners as well as their master.

King Tedric was less kind, more shrewd than his queen. His faded brown eyes flickered over each of them swiftly, leaving Derian with the inescapable impression that the monarch would remember each individual. There was a taut alertness to the agèd ruler that Derian had never noticed when he had gazed upon him from the crowds and something of the eagle in the tight grasp of his bony hands on the arms of his throne.

"So, Norwood," the king snapped, "this girl is the one you claim as Barden's daughter?"

He said the disowned prince's name without any hesitation—a good omen for the earl's cause.

Earl Kestrel nodded. "And these four men can bear witness to her finding, as can my cousin Sir Jared Surcliffe."

"So you said when you came before us with your fanciful tale. Well, I see little of my son in this young woman and less of your sister. Must she bring her dog with her? I am willing to credit your tale of survival in the wilds without such props."

Norwood stiffened slightly. "My ward has her own will, Your Majesty. She did not wish to be parted from the wolf."

King Tedric's lips moved slightly in something not quite a smile.

"Wolf? Never have I seen one so large. Rather, I think, an enormous hybrid."

Derian glanced at Firekeeper, worried that she would react to the insult to her beloved "brother," but the king's diction and use of the unfamiliar term "hybrid" had only confused her. She waited, still patient for now.

Earl Kestrel also chose not to challenge the king and so Tedric continued:

"Now, I have seen the lass. Let me see this other proof you mentioned."

This was the moment that Derian had dreaded over all others. Firekeeper had refused to let the knife—her Fang, she called it—leave her person. Not even when she had slept or bathed had she put it by. No offer of a substitute, longer, sharper, or more ornately made—Earl Kestrel had brought many such, some worth small fortunes in themselves—had moved her.

At the earl's request, Derian had coached Firekeeper long and carefully for this moment. He found he was holding his breath when Earl Kestrel turned to the young woman.

"Lady Blysse," the earl said steadily, "show the king your knife."

The guards to either side of the dais tensed at these ominous-sounding words, but King Tedric, briefed to expect them, only waved his hand imperiously when they would interpose themselves between his royal self and perceived danger.

"Back," he said. "There should be no harm here."

Firekeeper stood where she had risen from her homage to the throne. A slim, even slight figure in her long gown of maiden's white embroidered at throat and hem with ribbons, her cobalt-blue traveling cloak tossed back from her shoulders, the young woman didn't look a threat. Her dark-brown hair was an unruly mass of curls, worn rather shorter than was the fashion. Her only adornments were a simple wreath of flowers and a short necklace of pearls.

Among those gathered in the lofty stone audience hall only Derian and Race suspected that Firekeeper was far more deadly than any of the armed and armored guards, despite their swords and ceremonial halberds. However, Derian and Race could do nothing with their knowledge but wait, tense and ready.

At Earl Kestrel's command, Firekeeper dropped her hand to her waist. There, rather than the more usual girdle of flowers and ribbons, she wore a brown leather belt, much stained from the weather.

"My knife," she said, drawing the weapon and holding it so that Prince Barden's crest and the smooth garnet in the hilt were clearly visible. "Mine!"

The emphasis was clear, even without the growl that trailed the announcement. One of King Tedric's shaggy eyebrows flew upward in astonishment. The queen gasped. Earl Kestrel colored a fiery red.

Embarrassment or anger? Derian wondered.

King Tedric recovered first. "Yours, then. I only wish to see it more closely."

The words barely were past his lips before Firekeeper, despite the encumbering skirts, had flown up the steps to stand at his side. The knife she held inches from his face could have as easily vanished between his ribs, but the king neither started nor paled. Waiting below, Blind Seer thumped his tail briefly in what Derian could swear was muted applause.

The king examined the knife with all due consideration.

"It could be Barden's," he said at last. "It bears his crest and I seem to recall some such blade."

Queen Elexa recovered from her shock and now she, too, examined the knife. "I have seen this before. It was given to Barden by Lovella on his wedding day. She showed it to me beforehand, pleased by its craftsmanship. This one is just its like."

"A knife can be imitated," the king said cautiously.

"Perhaps," Elexa agreed, a faint smile on her lips, "but the knife Lovella showed me possessed a secret. I doubt that any who sought to imitate the weapon merely from its external appearance could have known of it."

"Can you show us what this secret is?" the king asked, interested yet impatient.

"If the girl will let me touch the knife," the queen said, moving a fragile hand slightly.

Firekeeper had been listening, her head cocked to one side, struggling with words and language patterns unfamiliar to her. From the expression on her face, Derian knew that she was growing confused—and when she was confused, her temper grew unpredictable.

"Lady Blysse," he called, without waiting for permission, "the queen doesn't want your knife. She simply wants to touch it. Let her."

"Touch?" Firekeeper said, the hoarseness of an almost growl in her throat.

"Touch," Derian assured her. Shrugging slightly, for he had already committed one social misstep, he addressed the queen directly. "Your Majesty, if you would move slowly, so as not to alarm her."

Accustomed to always being accorded social graces, the queen was less offended by their violation in a good cause than someone of lesser standing might be. Giving Blysse a reassuring smile, she reached out delicately with thumb and forefinger and grasped the garnet set into the pommel.

"Firekeeper," Derian said warningly when his charge stiffened, "hold still."

She did, to his infinite relief. When the queen had difficulty, she even steadied the hilt of the knife so that the queen could twist more strongly.

"There!" the queen said, pleased. Then, directly to the young woman standing before her, "Dear, my hands are not as strong as they once were. If you would grab the stone as I did and twist hard."

Derian doubted that Firekeeper understood all the words, but the queen's gestures were eloquent. Firekeeper obeyed. A firm turn or so and the garnet began to loosen.

Derian had shown the girl how to pull out corks, but a threaded cap was something new and frustrated her momentarily. However, at the queen's urging Firekeeper continued to twist. At last, with a small grating of sand caught in infrequently used grooves, the stone came free, revealing a small compartment in the hilt.

"Not so very large," the queen said complacently, examining the hollow spot, "but large enough to bear a message or some small item. Lovella was quite delighted with it."

"Then without a doubt, this is Barden's knife," King Tedric's gaze was shrewd. "And there is less a doubt that this is Barden's daughter."

Fascinated, Derian watched the king's eyes narrow in an expression far too like Earl Kestrel's for him to doubt the type of thoughts the ruler was entertaining. Norvin Norwood had been right. King Tedric had not at all liked being subject to the manipulations of his siblings and their young kin.

The possible existence of a granddaughter gave the king an upper hand once again. The king smiled, but it was not precisely a kind smile.

"Norvin, bring your ward . . ."

Not "my granddaughter," Derian noted to himself. *He's not ready to grant quite that much, not yet. He wants Earl Kestrel to remember who is in charge.*

"And join my family at table tonight. They have all heard rumors of your travels. It is time that they learn just what you have brought home."

THE BANQUET HALL into which they were escorted some hours later was not the largest room Derian had ever seen. The Guildhall of the Combined Crafts (tanners, leatherworkers, harness and saddlemakers) in the city below was larger. Nor was the banquet hall the grandest room he had seen. The inner chamber where the grandmasters of the smiths held their secret conclaves was grander, its beams gleaming with gilding and sparkling from the tiny silver stars that depended from invisible threads.

This hall, though, surpassed both for mere magnificence. The stone floor was polished to such a shine that the torches in the wall sconces and the candles on the tables seemed to burn twice: once in flame, once in reflection. Referring to the ivory-white marble walls as bare would be an insult, for though they were free from tapestry or curtain, the marble itself was so beautifully carved as to disdain further ornamentation.

In the center of the hall were four long tables set in a modified fan, all of their ends meeting near a head table. The flaring backs of the throne-like chairs set at the center of this head table left no doubt that the king and queen would be seated where they could command the attention of those dispersed along the fan. Derian wondered where Fire-keeper and Earl Kestrel would be placed.

The chief steward was a solid, silvery woman who shared some of Valet's immunity to excitement. As she addressed Earl Kestrel, her voice rang in the nearly empty room like a herald's trumpet.

"The king commands that you and your ward be seated at the head table. The ward is to be at the king's right, you to her right. Your party will be granted a few moments to orient yourselves before the family will join you."

Derian was grateful for those moments. Thus far Firekeeper had been on her best behavior, but there was a trembling tension about her that made him glad that she would have time to scout out the room before it was filled with strangers.

He watched her as she flitted about from point to point, touching the friezes on the wall, fingering the woven linen tablecloths, peeking under the tables as if uncertain what might lurk in their shadow. Blind Seer trotted beside her, more tense, less curious. Derian feared that the wolf might have reached his limit regarding new things and simply strike out at anything that came near.

Clearly the two members of the King's Own who had remained with them shared his concern. Each stood straight with his back against the wall, knuckles white around his halberd shaft. If they found Firekeeper's behavior amusing, no trace of mirth showed on their impassive counte-nances.

Derian ignored them, turning instead to Valet, who, along with Derian, made up the entirety of Earl Kestrel's escort. Ox and Race had been excluded on the grounds that no one else would bring bodyguards. Doubtless they were in some servants' hall even now being plied with ale and rich food by castle staff eager for gossip.

"Valet," Derian said, keeping his voice low, "what am I supposed to do? I'm out of my element here."

"You and I will stand there along the wall," Valet gestured to the stretch behind the head table, "where we can be ready if the earl needs us. Your particular role will be to assist Blysse. If she is about to make any particularly dangerous error, stop her, even at risk of reprimand to yourself."

Derian had no doubt that the errors Valet referred to were not merely social ones, like holding her spoon incorrectly or drinking her soup from her bowl. Firekeeper possessed a quick temper when she perceived offense and he had yet to figure out precisely what *would* give offense.

He was permitted no further time to worry. The towering wooden doors at the far end of the hall were beginning to open and the steward's trumpet voice announced: "Grand Duke Gadman, Lord Rolfston Redbriar and Lady Melina Shield, with Sapphire, Jet, Opal, Ruby, and Citrine Shield."

"Firekeeper," Derian hissed hopelessly, but his charge hurried over to him immediately.

"Stand there," Valet said, his own voice somehow both strong and nearly inaudible. He dared a slight push to center Firekeeper behind the chair where she was to sit. "And wait."

Firekeeper did so and Blind Seer sat beside her, his hackles slightly raised. The woman acknowledged his tension by curling the fingers of one hand in his fur, but her dark gaze was fixed on the eight people entering the room. Derian reflected that the nobles might mistake her unwavering stare for awe, but he knew the young woman well enough to know that to Firekeeper any stranger was an enemy until proven otherwise.

Such care might well be indicated when encountering this particular family. Although the rumors Derian had heard about Grand Duke Gadman and Lord Rolfston credited them with everything from courage to ruthlessness, they were as nothing compared to what was whispered about Lady Melina Shield. In city and countryside alike it was agreed that the noblewoman was a sorceress, one of power the like of which had not been seen since the days when the Old Country still reigned.

Looking at the woman, demurely gowned in mutedly iridescent silk, her fingers resting lightly on her husband's sleeve, Derian was at first inclined to dismiss those rumors as mere superstitious talk. Then he noticed the jeweled necklace encircling the still-firm flesh of Melina Shield's pale throat.

The necklace was short, just a few links too long to be a choker. Polished silver links were hung with five pendants, each holding a single faceted gem. The colors were not harmonious. Indeed a connoisseur might even say that they clashed: brilliant blue; opaque, glittering black; fiery hues like those of a new-lit fire; bloodred, and, lastly, a rich orange-brown, the shade of a fine cognac. Derian did not need to be a gem cutter's nephew to recognize that each of these gems was a pricelessly perfect example of the namestones of each of Lady Melina's children.

Now, seeing the necklace, seeing how each of the scion Shields wore set in a band about their brow a namestone gem to match the one about their mother's throat, Derian believed with a sudden thrill of his terrified soul that Melina Shield was indeed the sorceress gossip had named her. He had little time to grow accustomed to the thought, for the steward was announcing Grand Duchess Rosene and her kin.

Although a widow of seventy, Rosene could still wear soft pinks, for her hair was snow-white and her skin the delicate hues of the inner petals of a newly blossomed wild rose. Her eyes, however, were as shrewd as those of her brother the king and she let her son escort her without hindrance, less from obedience to custom than the better to glance about her and assess the situation.

Baron Ivon Archer, though a mature man, bore himself like the son of a hero, but it was in his sister, Zorana, that Derian saw the true heroic fire. Both of Grand Duchess Rosene's children were accompanied by a spouse and trailed by their get, the youngest of whom might have been excluded from such a gathering just a year or so before. Derian hardly had time to note that Baron Archer's daughter, the Lady Elise, was easily as lovely as any of her more ostentatiously named second cousins when the steward announced:

"Their Royal Majesties, King Tedric and Queen Elexa!"

As no one had taken a seat, no one needed to rise, but when the brass trumpets sounded their fanfare, everyone stood straighter in respect and turned to watch the monarchs enter. Everyone, that is, except Derian's Firekeeper. The loud trumpet call in the contained chamber frightened her, causing her to start back in alarm.

Before she could err further, Derian hurried forward and seized her arm, aware that in doing so he had once again brought himself to the king's attention. He was too busy to worry about this, for Firekeeper's hand had flown to her knife even as she looked about for some sheltered place from which to defend herself.

"Easy," Derian assured her, wishing that his voice didn't sound so loud in the suddenly hushed hall. "Easy."

Firekeeper felt no such need not to be noticed. "What that?"

"Trumpets," he said, letting his own tones match hers. If he could not go unnoticed, then let no one think he had anything to hide. "Like a flute but larger and louder."

"Where?"

"Over there." He indicated with one hand, his other gently guiding her knife back into its sheath.

Firekeeper moved as if she wished to examine one of the instruments. Derian put a restraining hand on her arm, knowing that if she intended to go, no strength of his would hold her.

"Stay," he said, more pleading than ordering. "You can look at them later. Now we owe the king our attention."

"Still?" she asked, blowing out through her nose in what he had learned was exasperation. "We did!"

"And still we must," Derian said patiently.

King Tedric rescued him. "Steward Silver, have one of the heralds' trumpets brought here for my guest's inspection. The rest of you have my leave to be seated."

Even Earl Kestrel obeyed this implicit command and, after examining the trumpet, Firekeeper was willing to do the same.

"Young man," the king said, and Derian realized that he was being addressed. Hurriedly, he bent knee. "Remain at the young woman's shoulder and advise her."

Derian did as ordered, standing at Firekeeper's right, slightly to the left of Earl Kestrel and as far away as was polite from the alarming presence of the king. Still, from where he stood he noticed that the king's white hair was a wig. The realization embarrassed him, as if he had stumbled onto a state secret.

Servants bearing wine and bread emerged from discreet alcoves along the wall. Noticing that none of the nobles seemed to regard them at all, Derian did his best to mimic the servants' impassive expressions, wishing more than anything else to be forgotten. He only moved when one would pour Firekeeper wine.

"Water only," he said softly.

The king, however, cocked an eyebrow. "Do you think my vintage not good enough for her?"

Derian was about to answer when Firekeeper said:

"Wine like sick bird berries. Makes prey."

"She means," Earl Kestrel translated, "that she has observed wild birds eating fermented berries or fruit. They become sick, and sick creatures become easy prey."

King Tedric stroked his angular cheekbone with one finger. "Surely she does not believe that I intend her harm."

Norvin Norwood was too old a campaigner to be discomfited.

"Not at all, Your Majesty, but her prejudices are firm. We have not been able to convince her that wine or beer or any liquor is a fair substitute for water."

The king did not press the point, but directed his attention down the fan of tables where his relatives were watching with as much interest as would be considered polite. Indeed, a few, like Sapphire and Grand Duchess Rosene, were watching with rather more attention than good manners should admit.

"This young woman," said the king with a slight gesture, as if which young woman he meant could be in doubt, "is the ward of Earl Kestrel. At his own initiative and at great personal risk and expense, he mounted an expedition to learn the fate of my son, Prince Barden."

Behind his carefully impassive face, Derian marveled. Those last two words, just a name and a title, but spoken so casually by the king himself, all but rescinded the disinheritance Tedric had passed on his son. From the expressions that flickered across surprised faces at the lower tables not everyone was pleased.

The king paused, perhaps making a similar assessment, perhaps merely to sip his wine.

"Sadly, for myself and for my queen, Norvin has learned that Barden's expedition was a failure. The prince and his followers—all but one—died in the early years of the colonization attempt, apparently in a fire."

At least some of the murmurs of shock and pity seemed to be genuine. Tedric waited for these to subside before continuing:

"The sole survivor was the young woman seated beside me. Believing her to be his sister Eirene's daughter Blysse, Earl Kestrel has made her his ward. His mother, the Duchess Kestrel and head of his household, has confirmed the adoption. Thus, my guest is Blysse Norwood, newest member of House Kestrel."

A hubbub arose at these words. Again Derian was forced to admire the king. He had given a name to the foundling, the same name as was borne by his granddaughter, but he had done so in such a fashion that left open to doubt whether or not he acknowledged the young woman as that granddaughter.

Only Grand Duke Gadman and Grand Duchess Rosene dared to address the king directly, and Gadman's querulous voice was loudest.

"Tedric," he said without formality, "are you saying that this wild-eyed creature is Barden's daughter?"

Grand Duke Gadman was a bent-over, bent-nosed parody of his brother's regal aquilinity. Gossip said, and Derian could well believe it, that the grand duke had been soured by holding no greater honor than that of standby heir for something like seventy years. Unlike Tedric, who had fairly earned his people's respect in battle, Gadman never ventured farther than the fringes of armed conflict, risking his reputation but not his hide.

Yet Derian did not underestimate Grand Duke Gadman as a mere blowhard. By chance, his own brother, Brock, and Grand Duke Gadman were both members of the Bear Society. From the tales that Brock had brought home, Grand Duke Gadman was shrewd, intelligent, and, in a fashion quite different from his brother, charismatic.

"I have said," Tedric replied, a faint smile playing about his lips, "precisely what I have said."

"You say that this girl is Eirene Norwood's daughter," Gadman pressed. "Eirene was wed to Barden. Do you mean to imply that this 'Blysse' is Barden's daughter?"

"Or," Grand Duchess Rosene added stridently, "do you not?"

King Tedric looked at each of his siblings with a weary tolerance that was not without affection.

"I have said what I have said. However, I will now add that because I wish to get to know Lady Blysse better, I am inviting her to dwell in the castle with my family. Earl Kestrel may, of course, take a suite here himself."

Derian's knees weakened. If Kestrel accepted, as he undoubtedly would, then Derian knew perfectly well where he himself was going to be staying. He had thought himself equal to anything, but this was beyond the ambitions of a carter's son. Any thoughts he had of retreating, of making excuses, of risking both parents and patron's ire, vanished as Firekeeper glanced up at him, her dark eyes anxious.

"King say we come here," she said softly. "Blind Seer, too?"

"Blind Seer, too," Derian promised, knowing he would keep his word even if he must smuggle the wolf in some dark night.

The rest of the banquet went much as could be expected. Although Firekeeper's table manners had improved so greatly that Derian had flattered himself that she could pass in polite company—and Earl Kestrel had agreed—the real test cast bright sunlight on their illusions.

The noble company gathered along the tables either turned politely away or openly sniggered. That most of the mockery came from those too young to have polished social skills—young Kenre Trueheart and Citrine Shield, most notably—didn't offer much comfort.

Firekeeper still ate more like a wolf than like a woman and seemed less like a noblewoman than ever.

Of course, Derian thought unhappily as he surveyed this august company from the invisibility of servitude, rumor said that the Princess Lovella had arranged her brother Chalmer's death. Mere acknowledgment would not make Firekeeper safe.

Far from it. If the king acknowledged her, she might be in greater danger than she ever had been in the wilds.

VIII

"THAT BANQUET," announced Grand Duchess Rosene when the family had retired to the suite which had been hers since as a young bride she brought her husband home to her father's castle, "was a nightmare!"

Ostensibly, her audience was restricted to her son and daughter and their spouses. Lady Elise, bearing tea and honeycakes into her grandmother's parlor, retired to a corner after setting down the tray, picked up her embroidery hoop, and was tacitly suffered to remain.

"Whatever does that brother of mine intend!" the old woman huffed, all offended privilege and suspicion. Without a word, Aksel Trueheart leaned forward and began pouring tea, knowing that an in-law's comments would not be appreciated at this moment.

"Precisely what he has achieved, good Mother," replied Ivon Archer, nursing his pipe to life between sheltering hands, "to unsettle us all."

His sister Zorana nodded. "Yes. He has not acknowledged that wild thing as Barden's daughter, but he holds the possibility over us like a whip. Now, we dare not press him to name an heir for fear that he will choose her over one better suited."

Unsaid but trembling in the air was that here, seated opposite each other, brother and sister, were rival claimants.

Grand Duchess Rosene shook her head despairingly.

"Simpletons!" she chided her children scathingly. "Tedric's plan would never be anything so obvious. Already Gadman and I have pressed him as hard as we dare. No, I fear he plays some deeper game."

"What?" Ivon and Zorana spoke as one, their rivalry for the throne temporarily set aside.

"Well," Grand Duchess Rosene said, accepting a cup of tea and stirring honey into it, "some say he intends to put aside Elexa and wed another. Why not this girl? Norvin Norwood may claim her for the Kestrel line, but I see nothing of either Eirene or Barden in this stranger's face. She is too dark for one."

"Certainly he could not wed her!" Lady Aurella, Elise's mother, said shocked. "Queen Elexa is Wellward born, my own mother's sister. The king would not dare put her off in favor of a commoner!"

"Not quite a commoner," Rosene reminded, "for Duchess Kestrel has accepted this 'Blysse' into her household. By adoption, if not by blood, she is Kestrel."

"King Tedric did seem to favor her." Ivon puffed on his pipe, as if reluctant to say more. "I noted how frequently the king's eyes strayed to the stranger. And he did have her seated at his own right hand—far above her station, even if she was a granddaughter."

"Not if that granddaughter is his heir," Rosene said acidly sweet.

Watching her elders, Elise wondered if Grand Duchess Rosene was enjoying stirring up her son and daughter. The old woman's next speech confirmed her suspicions.

"But perhaps you are right, Aurella," Rosene said. "Perhaps it is too much like a storyteller's romance to believe that an old king would shed his barren wife to father a son on a common girl young enough to be his granddaughter. What other use might he have for her?"

"He could," said Aksel Trueheart, "mean to use her to learn our own closest wishes."

Lady Zorana's husband spoke hesitantly, as if uncertain precisely how to phrase his thoughts. Although he was a handsome man and strong, no one held any illusions who was the dominant partner in this marriage.

Some went so far as to jest that Zorana married Aksel simply as a properly pedigreed stud for her brood. Elise, who had often found Uncle Aksel in the castle library poring over old parchments from the days before the Plague, knew him to be more, a self-taught scholar and a bit of a poet.

"Our closest wishes?" Zorana said, her tones no gentler than her mother's. "What do you mean?"

"Forget I said anything," Aksel replied. "A fleeting thought, one I must consider further."

Grand Duchess Rosene, however, would not let the point drop.

"I believe I seized the heel of your thought as it fled, son-in-law," she said. "Think, fools! What better thing to bring us all behind one candidate than to threaten us with a new player whom we desire less? Haven't we all said that we would rather see Rolfston Redbriar crowned king than have Allister Seagleam of Bright Bay elevated above us?"

Murmurs of agreement answered her. The grand duchess continued, setting her cup and saucer down with a rattle as her hands suddenly trembled with excitement.

"Now Tedric has in his own castle one who he can use in much the same fashion without raising the hopes of those who would see a scion of our enemies on the throne!"

"That must be it, Mother!" Ivon agreed. "Blysse Norwood can serve as King Tedric's prod, a reminder of what we get if we do not dance to his tune. My guess is that soon enough we will hear hints of who is her best 'rival' for the throne."

"And if we still resist," Zorana asked, her question less a question than the voicing of a fear, "will he make this newcomer queen simply to spite us?"

"That," Grand Duchess Rosene said, "is completely within the reach of my brother's perversity. I would not tempt him to try it."

"And," added Aksel Trueheart, heartened some by the grand duchess's expansion on his vague idea, "the girl could still be useful to him, even if he does not name her crown princess. He could offer her in marriage to someone—perhaps to his heir, if the heir was unwed, perhaps to the heir's heir, if that one was male and unwed."

"Like our son, Purcel," said Zorana thoughtfully. "Yes. Even if Blysse is never officially named Prince Barden's daughter, some trace of his noble aura will cling to her. There will always be those who will respect her as an unacknowledged daughter of the royal house."

Elise noted with a small smile how Aunt Zorana had shown that her house, rather than her brother's, would be best suited to win the king's favor. She didn't doubt that, beneath his apparent vagueness, Uncle Aksel had entertained similar thoughts.

Certainly, her own father and mother didn't look terribly pleased. Their only child was a daughter, unsuited for a match with the newcomer.

"Would the king," said Ivon, trying to salvage what was beginning to look like a bad situation, "elevate an unknown woman—quite possibly not born from one of the Great Houses—to such heights?"

"Don't be an idiot," Grand Duchess Rosene said impatiently. "If we can seriously consider Tedric capable of making her queen in her own right, certainly we can consider him elevating her to queen by marriage. My dear husband Purcel was common born—though proven hero. My own mother, Queen Rose, was not born of a Great House. My father, King Chalmer, married for love, quite against the wishes of his advisors."

"And that's what worries me the most," Rosene continued after a thoughtful pause. "My brother has ample examples from our own immediate history of kings acting against what their advisors wish."

"Then this time," Zorana put in fiercely, "we must make certain that the king does nothing of the sort."

There was that in her aunt's tone that made Elise shudder and hope that Lady Blysse, now housed somewhere within the castle's walls, locked her doors securely.

❧

EARL KESTREL'S PARTY was given rooms within the section of the castle normally reserved for the king's immediate family. Since the death of Princess Lovella two years before, this wing had been largely vacant and that vacancy was ostensibly the reason for Kestrel's party being housed there. Firekeeper could see that Earl Kestrel was delighted by this mark of favor.

"The tower in which your rooms will be," the silver-haired steward explained to the earl, "is furnished with its own door out into the castle grounds. The king said that all your party is to have freedom of the parks and gardens."

Earl Kestrel nodded. "That is thoughtful of His Majesty. My ward is not accustomed to remaining indoors all the time."

The steward managed a dry smile. "The king expressed confidence that Lady Blysse would be able to control her pet if she took him with her into public areas."

Firekeeper decided that the time had come to speak for herself.

"Blind Seer not a pet."

Derian put a hand on her arm.

"Firekeeper," he warned.

"Well, isn't," she persisted.

Derian shrugged and made some explanation to Steward Silver, using language so complicated that Firekeeper could only catch the gist of his argument. She did learn, however, that the falcon Elation would be welcome at the castle and so went to sleep well content.

THE NEXT MORNING, Derian was nowhere about.

"Earl Kestrel," Ox explained to Firekeeper, "let him go visit his family. His parents."

Ox always spoke carefully, pausing between each word as if she was stupid, not merely ignorant of the language. Firekeeper recognized the essential kindness in the big man, however, and didn't challenge him. When Ox was summoned to wait upon the earl, she sought out Elation. The falcon rested on a perch near a window, watching the little birds outside from sardonic golden-rimmed eyes.

"I wondered how long it would take you to wake up," Elation shrilled.

"Why wake?" Firekeeper replied, scratching behind one of Blind Seer's ears. "There is nothing for me to do. They bring me my food, so I need not hunt. For the first time I can remember, I am warm and fed."

Blind Seer huffed out through his nose. "We fed you!"

"After the strong had eaten," she retorted. "Sometimes there was little enough for me."

"Little enough for any," he replied, "when the strong are finished. That is why only the strong survive."

"I have survived," Firekeeper said, "so I must be strong."

But despite the bravado in those words, there was a singular lack of enthusiasm within her heart. Perhaps Elation heard this dullness, for she shrieked.

"So, eat and grow fat. That is all you wish?"

"Is there else?" Firekeeper challenged without much heat.

"You came away from your pack to learn about the two-legs," Elation replied. "What have you learned?"

"That the world is far bigger than even the Ones imagine," Firekeeper said. "That I can talk human talk after a fashion, but that I fear I shall never be more than a pup among them, even as I have ever been a pup among the wolves."

"And have you acted as other than a pup?" Elation prodded, her beak gaping in mocking laughter. "Have you done other than pad about after your nurse, eating his leavings as if summer will never end? Take care, wolfling, summer may end and leave you within a trap."

"What do you mean?"

"After last night's rumpus, more than Earl Kestrel know that you live.

Remember, I understand human speech better than you do, for those who were my masters one brief season often spoke of weighty matters while they rode with falcons on their gloves. If you are not to be chased hither and yon like a rabbit beneath the falcon's circling flight, then you must make yourself a place within this aerie."

Firekeeper straightened, some vague sense of purpose licking tongues of fire in her soul.

"Do you think I can?" she asked, almost timidly.

" 'Do you think I can?' " the falcon mimicked cruelly. "I think you must and from this very moment forward. Your nurse is away. You can act without risking that Earl Kestrel's wrath will descend on him."

"I have worried about such," Firekeeper admitted. "My missteps seem to bring blows to Derian's head, not mine."

"So I have observed," Elation said smugly. "It is well to protect an ally but not when that protection weakens yourself."

"What," interjected Blind Seer, "would you have Firekeeper do? Somehow I don't think that challenging their One would do her any favors. From what Derian has told us, this is not the way to earn prestige among these two-legged folk."

"It is not," the falcon agreed. "Let me think."

She did so, raising a leg to nibble on the wickedly curving talons of one foot, preening her feathers, chortling and chuckling softly to herself in falcon speech.

"I," Elation announced at last, "shall provide you with the means to meet more equally with those whom you must come to know. Here they consider hunting with raptors—especially the great birds such as myself— a sport reserved for noble folk. We three shall go out into the gardens and I will fly for you as once I flew for my human master."

"What good will that do Firekeeper?" Blind Seer asked dubiously.

"Humans are as curious as raccoons," Elation replied. "Some will come to learn what is happening, younger ones, I suspect, who do not have so much dignity to preserve. Firekeeper can impress them and they in turn will tell their elders that she is not merely a toy."

"Your idea might serve," Firekeeper said thoughtfully, "and certainly sitting in this room does us no good."

"I would," Blind Seer admitted, "like to be outside in the sun again. My patience with cold stone rooms is near ended. Had I loved you less, sweet Firekeeper, I would not have borne them this long."

"Then we are settled," Firekeeper declared.

So it was that when Earl Kestrel came looking for his ward after his breakfast had been eaten and his plans for the day were neatly in place, he found the young woman gone and the door out into the castle grounds standing open before him.

ALTHOUGH A CITY had grown up around it, the castle at Eagle's Nest showed remnants of the days when it had been constructed as a fortification that could, in an emergency, take within its walls all the surrounding population and their flocks and herds as well.

Those days were long past, but not because either the castle or its grounds had grown smaller. Indeed, the descendants of Queen Zorana had jealously guarded their property rights, holding on to not only the gardens, workshops, and stables within the fortified walls but to the surrounding acreage as well. Most of this flowed behind and above the castle, rough land, not well suited for cultivation, but perfect for game parks and meadows.

To one of these lower meadows was where Elation led Firekeeper and Blind Seer, soaring time and again from a padded perch on the young woman's shoulder to check which of the winding paths they should follow. After the coolness within the building, the summer sunshine was welcome indeed. Butterflies congregated around neatly ranked beds of flowers and songbirds nested in trees crowded with ripening fruit. Passage of the three predators caused more than a little consternation, though not one raised hand, paw, or talon to hunt.

"Through that gate," the falcon directed, "beneath the grey stone arch. Step lively, wingless!"

172 / JANE LINDSKOLD

Firekeeper laughed and began to run, forcing the bird to take flight quickly and without great grace. Blind Seer bounded alongside, leaping and almost catching the peregrine by her tail feathers. Once through the gate, they found themselves in a meadow yellow and white with wild flowers, thick with green grass yet unmowed and unbrowned by the greater heat of late summer.

Firekeeper dove into it as she might have into a deep pool, rolling neatly on one shoulder and bounding to her feet without a pause. Around and around her, in spiraling circles, Blind Seer ran, stretching muscles stiff and aching from confinement indoors. He started a rabbit and gave chase, but let it escape since he was not really hungry.

Wolf and woman played in this fashion for some time before a shriek from Elation alerted them to the approach of strangers.

There were two: a male and a female. Neither were adults, of that Firekeeper was certain. She was less certain about their actual ages. Derian had made some effort to educate her on this matter, using as models the few children at the keep and a few others glimpsed along the road or from the windows of the Kestrel manse. After some consideration, Firekeeper decided that the boy was the younger, more from how he deferred to his playmate than from anything else.

That the two had not expected to find anyone else here was obvious from the way they paused beneath the gateway arch. That they were curious was evident from how they stood, hand clasped in hand, staring.

"I wouldn't swear it," Blind Seer said, plopping on his haunches next to Firekeeper, "but they smell familiar. Could they have been among the pack yesterday?"

Firekeeper tilted her head to one side, studying the pair. After a moment, she nodded, a human gesture that was becoming habit with her.

"Yes, I think so," she replied. "They were the two who laughed hardest during the meal. I think they thought my manner of eating amusing."

This last was not something about which she was particularly happy. She had been rather pleased with her progress in human customs. The mockery of these small ones—and the better-concealed reactions of their elders—had proven to her that she still had much to learn.

"Talk with them!" the falcon urged from a perch high in a peach tree. "From what I can see, none of their elders are about. You may learn something here."

Firekeeper nodded, swallowed past a sudden hard spot in her throat, and managed a soft "Hello. Good morning."

Girl and boy exchanged glances. Then the girl stepped a pace forward.

"Good morning. What are you doing in our great-uncle's garden?"

Firekeeper frowned. "Running. The castle is very cold."

The girl took another step forward, her apprehensive gaze on Blind Seer rather than on Firekeeper. She was solidly built, but not heavy, with chubby cheeks and red hair highlighted with gold. In the center of her forehead a dark reddish-orange stone glimmered, set in a band of woven gold. Firekeeper hadn't seen enough of humans to decide if the girl would be judged pretty, but suspected that she was as yet too gawky, too young to be considered so.

Pulling straight the skirt of her mid-calf-length flowered frock, the girl continued her interrogation:

"But do you have permission to be here? These are the king's gardens."

Even Firekeeper could hear the pride in the girl's voice as she said these words, but the wolf thought it a pardonable pride given the importance humans placed on kings.

"I do," she replied. "King Tedric told me last night, when he asked us to stay at the castle."

"Asked you?" began the girl, but the boy interrupted, hurrying forward to tug one of her puffed sleeves.

"Don't you get it, Citrine?" he hissed in what Firekeeper guessed were meant to be hushed tones. "This is Earl Kestrel's ward. This is Blysse!"

"Oh, Kenre!" Citrine protested, looked again, then frowned. "Oh!"

"I am called Blysse," Firekeeper confirmed. "What are you called?"

"I," said the girl, "am Citrine Shield."

"I'm Kenre," the boy said. "Kenre Trueheart. Is that your dog?"

"Wolf," Firekeeper answered. "Blind Seer, because he have blue eyes."

"They are!" the boy said, leaning forward to look, but not closing with the wolf. Firekeeper respected him for his prudence.

Kenre Trueheart was as sturdily built as Citrine, perhaps given slightly to fat where she was not. With his soft light brown hair and big brown eyes, his body all quivering with excitement, he reminded Firekeeper, not unkindly, of a baby rabbit.

"I didn't know wolves ever had blue eyes," Kenre said.

"Most do not," Firekeeper answered, feeling a certain thrill. She was actually talking to humans on her own, without Derian there to intercede or clarify!

The little girl, Citrine, pushed her way through the tall grass. As she came closer, Firekeeper caught her scent, a mingling of soap and flowers, overlaid with the bacon and bread from her breakfast.

"Can I pat him?" she asked, gesturing to Blind Seer.

Firekeeper tilted her head, considering. "He bites."

"Oh! And Earl Kestrel lets you keep him?"

"Blind Seer stay with me," Firekeeper replied, avoiding the awkward issue of permission. "So does falcon."

She raised her forearm, encased from hand to elbow in a heavy fal- coner's glove that Race had bought for her along the road from West Keep to Eagle's Nest. With a showy screech, Elation launched from the peach tree's branches, spiraled upward, then plummeted down to land with deceptive gentleness on Firekeeper's glove. Even so, Firekeeper had to steady herself against the weight of that landing. Elation was to the average peregrine falcon what Blind Seer was to Cousin wolves—bigger, stronger, and far wiser.

Kenre and Citrine both scampered back at the falcon's descent, but curiosity brought them forward almost immediately. Skirting the wolf, they stared up at the falcon, who obliged by intelligently returning their regard.

"It looks like a peregrine," Kenre said hesitantly, "but bigger than any in my father's aeries."

"Kenre's father is a Merlin," Citrine said, confusing Firekeeper to no end. "My father is a Goshawk, though my mother is a Gyrfalcon."

"I not," said Firekeeper, feeling a sinking sensation that this would not be the last time she made this statement, "understand."

Citrine looked delighted rather than exasperated, soothing Firekeeper somewhat, and put on what even the wolf-raised woman had come to recognize as a lecturing tone.

"Each of the six Great Houses has two names," Citrine said. "One is the original family name; the other is the emblem given by King Chalmer the First in the Year Twenty-seven of this Realm."

Seeing that Firekeeper still looked confused, she clarified, "This is the Year One Hundred Five."

"It is?"

"Yes. One hundred and five years ago, Queen Zorana the Great won her last battle with her enemies and founded the Kingdom of Hawk Haven. The losers settled for becoming the Kingdom of Bright Bay."

Firekeeper had understood about a third of this, but the key words, combined with Derian's brief dissertations on the importance of kings and queens, were enough to give her the essential gist.

"So why is Kenre's father a merlin?"

Kenre answered, "My family's name is Trueheart—just like yours is Norwood."

Firekeeper remembered being told something of the kind following a long session with Earl Kestrel and a woman he called Mother and everyone else called Duchess. She nodded encouragement.

"Speak on."

"When King Chalmer—that's King Tedric's father—married Rose Rosewood, he gave titles to the Great Houses as a wedding gift," Kenre said, foundering somewhat.

Citrine came to his aid. "The Great Houses back then weren't happy that the king didn't marry into one of their families."

Firekeeper nodded, though she understood little of this, hoping they would get back to how a two-legs could also be a bird of prey.

"To make them happier," Citrine continued, "King Chalmer gave them a special family name, like nothing anyone else would have. So the Norwoods—that's your family—became the Kestrels."

"Earl Kestrel?" Firekeeper asked. "He is not a bird!"

"A kestrel is a type of falcon, like the peregrine but smaller."

From Firekeeper's fist, Elation shrilled laughter. "*Smaller, stupider, milder.*"

Firekeeper shook the bird slightly.

"So kestrel," she asked carefully, "is name for a bird?"

She remembered now the representations she had seen on the earl's baggage, on his carriage, over the doorways of his manse. Her eyes still had trouble seeing the pictures in human art, a thing that had frustrated some of Derian's attempts to teach her written words.

"That's right," Citrine said encouragingly. "Just like your falcon is a peregrine."

"I know that," Firekeeper answered. "Derian told me. He never told me kestrel was a bird."

"Maybe he didn't want to confuse you with too much too fast," Kenre said with the humble wisdom of someone who often found himself in that very situation.

"Just so," Firekeeper agreed. "He confuses me without trying."

All three of them laughed at this and looked at each other, suddenly relaxed and at ease. Firekeeper remembered something of human manners then.

"We sit," she offered, "over by brook, maybe? You tell me more about fathers who are birds?"

The children readily agreed. Elation soared again to a treetop from which she could keep watch and Blind Seer, quietly amused by all of this, vanished within the tall grass.

"*I will run, scout, maybe hunt,*" he said as he moved away. "*Ox fetches much meat, but it is all dead cold.*"

"Go," Firekeeper replied, "but stay from the town."

"*Gladly,*" the wolf laughed. "*It stinks.*"

When the three humans were seated, bare feet trailing in the water, Citrine resumed her explanation.

"So Kenre's father isn't really a merlin. It's his father's family's symbol."

" 'Symbol,' " Firekeeper repeated carefully. "What is symbol?"

Citrine tapped at her headband, rubbing the stone as if it would help her to construct a definition.

"A symbol is something that stands for something else. My name is Citrine."

"Yes?" Firekeeper said, confused at this sudden switch of subject.

"Citrine is also the name of this stone." The girl indicated the translucent reddish-orange stone in her headband. "The word stands for both me and this stone. Do you understand?"

Firekeeper might have had more trouble if wolf names were not essentially symbolic, though more literally so. She nodded.

"Yes, I think I do. So Kenre's father is not merlin. He is just called Merlin."

"Right!" Citrine beamed. "Kenre's family uses his father's name, rather than his mother's, because the Great Houses outrank those of lesser nobles and Zorana's father was a common archer before King Chalmer made him a noble one."

Firekeeper decided to ignore this for now. It sounded rather too much like some of the lessons that Derian had tried to teach her and she had dismissed as irrelevant to her situation. Uncomfortably, she realized that she might have dismissed the matter of Great Houses and precedence too quickly.

"Easier to know," she said, thinking aloud, "with wolves. Who is first is fastest and strongest."

"Your dog," Kenre said, glancing around nervously, noticing for the first time that Blind Seer was gone, "really *is* a wolf? You're not just saying so?"

"Really wolf," Firekeeper said, having had similar discussions with Derian and Race along the road to Eagle's Nest. "Three years born in my family."

"Your family?" the two children said together.

"Not Earl Kestrel's!" Citrine added.

"No. I am wolf-raised," Firekeeper explained. "Human born. After big fire, my mother gives me to wolves."

"What happened to her?" Kenre asked.

"She died," Firekeeper said, callously blunt toward the memory of this woman she remembered only in dreams. "Wolves say of fire burns."

"Were you very old then?" Citrine asked, pity and horror in her voice.

"Very small," Firekeeper answered. "Smaller than you or Kenre. Little. Young."

Vocabulary exhausted, she shrugged. "So I am wolf."

"And your father?"

"Wolves not say."

"Was he Prince Barden?"

"Earl Kestrel say so." Firekeeper frowned thoughtfully. "I cannot remember."

From the looks the children traded she wondered if she had said too much. Then she shrugged. Let Earl Kestrel deal with it, if the little bird-man could. She didn't want to be queen. At least she didn't think she did.

"Where did you get your knife?"

No one had bothered ask her that before, but Firekeeper knew that the knife was somehow important to the earl and his plans. Since the man had not been precisely unkind to her, she hedged:

"From the One Wolf when I was young, but I do not know where he get. Maybe Prince Barden give to him."

Their elders might have scoffed at such fanciful tales, but Citrine and Kenre were young enough to live on the borders of fantasy. To them, a girl raised by wolves did not seem at all improbable, especially when they had seen for themselves the impossibly huge wolf who shadowed her and the equally large hawk who obeyed her commands though unhooded and unjessed. Moreover, Citrine's mother was reputed to be a sorceress, a thing both of them implicitly believed though the evidence for that belief was shared in whispers.

"That's why you talk funny," Citrine said with the bluntness of the young, "and why you eat . . ."

She stopped herself just in time, but Kenre sniggered and they both fell into uncontrolled giggles before stopping, suddenly aware of the coolness of Firekeeper's dark gaze.

"Like a wolf?" the woman offered dryly.

Citrine nervously tugged a lock of red-gold hair and Kenre paled.

"Well . . ." the girl stammered.

"I do," Firekeeper said, "but I learn human ways. Can you do this?"

In an instant she was on her feet and up into the upper boughs of a gnarled apple tree.

"Or this?"

She hung upside down from bent knees and, in one smooth motion, unsheathed her knife and threw it, burying the blade to the hilt in the soil between the two children.

"Or this?"

She was down again, knife back in her hand, dark eyes wild. In a single bound she was across the brook, crouched on the other bank. Wolves played such bragging games among their kind and she hadn't realized how much she missed showing off.

"I learn human ways," Firekeeper repeated. "Can you learn wolf ways?"

The two children stared in amazement and admiring awe.

"We could try," Kenre offered, eager and intense.

"If our mothers let us," Citrine added, more dubious.

"Those birds of prey symbol humans!" Firekeeper said scornfully. Then she recalled the power they wielded and softened her tone. "Maybe they will let you."

"We didn't realize that you really meant you were a wolf," Citrine said, eager to apologize. "We thought you meant as a symbol. There is a Wolf Society, you know."

"Derian say something of that," Firekeeper admitted. "But I not understand. More symbols?"

"More," Kenre said with another sigh. "My society is the Horse Society."

"Mine is the Elk," Citrine offered.

"But you are not horses or elks," Firekeeper asked, wanting to be certain.

"I wish!" Kenre said wistfully. "When I was really small I thought that was what would happen when I got older, that I'd learn how to become a horse. I went to my first meeting last year and there was nothing like that, just people in fancy costumes."

"Can," Firekeeper asked, her heart pounding very fast at this new and wonderful thought, "can humans become animals for truth, not symbols?"

Her question was awkwardly worded, but neither Kenre nor Citrine had any doubt what she meant.

"Maybe," Kenre said, his voice suddenly soft. "There are stories of sorcerers from the days before the Plague when the Old Country ruled here."

"My nurse," Citrine added, her tones equally hushed, "hints that such magics can be done."

"Oh!" Firekeeper swallowed hard, unable to manage more words around the sudden lump in her throat. To be a wolf, for real and not just in heart!

"It may be," Citrine said quickly, "just a fireside story. That's what my sister Ruby said."

"Ruby," Kenre retorted, speaking what he had heard his older sister Deste say, "is scared of her own shadow. Of course she wouldn't want to believe in magic. It would scare her. Especially with your mother being . . ."

They shuddered together, but didn't offer clarification and Firekeeper asked for none. There were too many new words here, too many new concepts. She held on to just one, one that filled her with delight and made her more determined than ever to learn the ways of humankind.

Somewhere out there might be one who would know how to give her wolf's heart a wolf's body. That was more than enough incentive to make her go on, even if she must win the throne of Hawk Haven to attain her goal!

IX

THE DAY FOLLOWING the grand banquet, Elise Archer sat at home reviewing correspondence and considering how to spend her day. Queen Elexa had requested that Lady Aurella wait upon her and Ivon Archer was once again in conference with his mother and sister, so Elise was alone.

Secretly she was rather glad. Despite her father's ambitions, Elise suspected that either Aunt Zorana or Lord Rolfston Redbriar would be named King Tedric's heir. Further intrigue, on top of last night's session, seemed rather ridiculous.

She was folding a polite refusal of a dinner invitation when her maid came to the door of her solar.

"M'lady, you have a caller."

"Who is it, Ninette?"

The maid, a poor relative several years her senior, meant to serve as her chaperon as much as her maid, frowned slightly before replying.

"A young man. Your cousin, Jet Shield."

"Jet!" Elise considered not whether but where to receive him. "Take him to the summerhouse near the duck pond and have cool drinks and light refreshments brought to him. I will attend him as soon as I have changed into something more fitting."

As soon as enough time had passed that she would seem neither eager nor rude, Elise walked down to the summerhouse. She had combed her hair and donned a pale yellow muslin gown perfect for informal entertaining on a summer morning that already promised to become quite hot. When she was a few steps from the summerhouse, she told her maid:

"Wait for me on that bench, Ninette. I promise not to stray from sight, but Cousin Jet may speak more freely to my ears alone."

Ninette was neither silly nor stupid. She knew as much about the recent political maneuvering as could anyone who was not immediate family and, unlike Elise, still treasured dreams of herself residing within the castle, an intimate of King Ivon's family and, later, confidant to Queen Elise.

"Very good, Lady Elise."

Elise greeted Jet with both hands outstretched, a relaxed informal gesture quite appropriate between cousins. She was slightly taken aback when he instead met her with a deep bow and lightly kissed the air above the hand he gracefully captured in one of his own.

The greeting wasn't precisely incorrect. Indeed, it would be perfectly correct in some settings. However, a summerhouse in the midmorning hours was not one of these.

"Cousin," Elise said, retrieving her fingers. "May I pour you something cool to drink?"

"Thank you, Elise. Whatever you are having," Jet replied. "You look lovely this morning. Cool, peaceful, and tranquil—everything that my father's house is not."

Elise smiled, acknowledging both the compliment and the neat transition into current problems.

"I would be lying," she said, knowing that the same information could be learned from the servants, "if I said that my parents were particularly tranquil this morning."

"Great-Uncle Tedric," Jet said with a small laugh, "pulled a nice one last night. Introducing that girl in such a fashion that we could not question her origin without insulting House Kestrel was brilliant. He is a master of his craft."

184 / JANE LINDSKOLD

"Tedric is," Elise agreed, "a great king."

"Would that I could be as certain," Jet said, his black eyes shining, "that his successor would be as well prepared for the throne. Tedric was King Chalmer's second born, but Crown Princess Marras died a year before her father. King Chalmer had time to prepare his new heir for his role."

"My father said," Elise added, eager to draw Jet out, "that Princess Marras was so distracted from the deaths first of her baby, Alben, then of her husband, Lorimer Stanbrook, that Tedric was his father's right hand for the two years before King Chalmer's death."

"Indeed," Jet said, "just as my sister Sapphire is taken up with the minutiae of learning how to run our family estates. Therefore, I have become my father's confidant in the larger matters of kingdom politics."

That old song again, Elise thought, amused. She murmured understandingly and Jet continued:

"My concern is that whomever King Tedric selects, there will be hurt feelings all around. Rivals passed over may not so quickly forget their own claims and be reluctant to bend knee to one they see as an equal."

The forceful manner in which he tossed a bit of roll to one of the ducks suggested that he might be one of these.

"So you favor Lady Blysse Norwood?" Elise asked, keeping her mien quite serious though she was laughing inside. "If she *is* the king's granddaughter, her claim supersedes all others. No rival would be passed over for one with an equal claim, for no other claim could be equal."

Jet looked shocked for one quick moment before he regained control of his features.

"If Lady Blysse is Prince Barden's daughter," he began, a slight stress on the "if," "then, of course, I favor her. However, there is doubt that she is indeed Barden's daughter."

"Yes?" Elise prompted.

"Certainly! My mother recalls that there were other children included in Barden's expedition. Lady Blysse could be one of these."

Elise nodded. She was certain that some thought other than those raised by Blysse Norwood's addition to the game was burning behind Jet's eyes and she was nearly as eager for him to tell as he was to speak.

"There is a way," Jet said slowly, "to make King Tedric's choice easier for him."

"Oh?" For a fleeting moment, Elise wondered if Jet was hinting that Blysse should be assassinated.

"Yes. Give King Tedric a choice that permits him to unite two of the rival parties for the throne—all three, even, if those involved are properly cultivated."

Elise shook her head. "I don't understand."

"If you and I married, Elise," Jet said, leaning forward and capturing her hand between his own, "then by selecting one of us, King Tedric would really be selecting both of our houses."

Only her mother's careful training kept Elise's mouth from dropping open in shock at this cool proposal. At that moment, a child she hadn't even known still lived within her—a child who had daydreamed of fervent entreaties, of romantic ballads sung outside her window by moonlight, of elegant tokens—died forever.

She gasped something inarticulate which Jet, fortunately, interpreted as encouragement rather than dismay.

"I couldn't believe no one had thought of this solution before," he said, squeezing her fingers tightly. "You are the sole scion of your house. I am the senior male in mine. Surely King Tedric would see the wisdom in selecting us over any of our siblings. He might even forgo the intermediary step of first choosing one of our parents as his heir and name one of us directly."

You, so you believe, Elise thought indignantly, *or you wouldn't be so excited by the prospect.*

"We two are the only ones who could play this game," Jet continued, "and that is to our great advantage. There are no males in your household who could marry one of my sisters. Purcel Trueheart is eight years younger than my sister Sapphire—too great a gap for even Zorana to consider, especially when Purcel is four years shy of his majority."

"But I also am too young to marry!" Elise protested, selecting the first argument that Jet's words suggested. "Marriages are not contracted until the partners are nineteen."

"Consummated," Jet corrected with a unguarded glance that suggested that he had fantasized about the prospect with some of the ardor that had been absent from his proposal. "Some marriages have been contracted long before that date, nor have all the formalities waited until the participants reached their majority. In any case, you're nearly eighteen."

Elise colored. The most usual reason for marriage before the participants were legal adults was an accidental pregnancy. No matter what the obvious political advantages, if she and Jet wed, there would still be whispers, whispers that would not necessarily be stilled when the bride did not deliver a "premature" infant.

"I would not care to make myself the subject of scandal," she said firmly, "no matter how great the prize to be won."

"I understand, lovely cousin," Jet said, pressing her fingers to his lips. "Your scruples do you credit. Still, there is no reason not to arrange a betrothal, is there? King Tedric might even encourage us to marry before your majority. If we wed at the king's command, no one could cast aspersions on your maidenly honor."

Elise frowned. Jet's proposal was enticing. He was handsome, strong, well connected. Though they were cousins, the relationship was not too close. Indeed, just a few years before, she had daydreamed about marriage to him. That had been before she had realized sadly that Lord Rolfston and Lady Melina would not permit their son to remain unmarried until she was eligible.

Certainly, King Tedric could not fail to see the advantages of a match between them. Grand Duke Gadman and Grand Duchess Rosene would both be satisfied, for each would see a descendant ascend to the throne. Only Aunt Zorana would be unhappy, and even she might be consoled at the thought of her niece as queen—especially if Jet was merely consort.

"Would you support me as queen?" Elise asked, pursuing this idea. "King Tedric might not choose to pass over our fathers. Or he might name me his heir. My odds of being named heir—even without any alliance such as you suggest—have usually been considered better than yours. Would you be content if I were queen and you were my consort?"

Jet paused as if to consider, but she was certain he had mulled over his answer in advance.

"Yes," he said at last. "I would support you. Whether you or I were monarch, the other still would be elevated to great honor. Moreover, our child would follow us onto the throne. That is an honor not lightly forgone."

Elise nodded. Until this moment, she had not considered further than her own ascension in the unlikelihood that her father succeeded King Tedric. Now she realized that more was at stake here than the prestige and power of a single lifetime.

As a royal ancestor, great honors would be paid to her even after her death. On the Festival of the Eagle, her image would be paraded with those of Queen Zorana, King Chalmer, and King Tedric. If she was consort, those honors still would be paid to her, just as they were to Clive Elkwood (who had died even before his wife had solidified her kingdom) and to Queen Rose.

Ancestors were always patrons to their descendants, but the people believed that ancestral monarchs were patrons to all their former subjects down through time. As such, they received sacrifices from every family altar, sacrifices that were said to give them considerable power in the afterworld.

Aware that Jet was watching her, the glittering light in his eyes brighter than ever, Elise managed to speak:

"That is an interesting point, Jet. I believe that you *would* support my monarchy if I were named before you."

"And would you support my kingship?" he asked, certain of the reply. "As a scion of House Goshawk, my father outranks yours. My mother is a Shield of House Gyrfalcon, and so outranks your Wellward mother. King Tedric may consider this when naming his heir."

"Those arguments," Elise admitted, "have been raised before—although more usually in your sister's favor. Yes, if we were wed and King Tedric named you his heir, I would support you."

"And if we were merely engaged?" he pushed.

"Engagements," she stated firmly, "have been broken once political goals have been attained—as your sister Sapphire has demonstrated so ably."

Jet scowled. "I am not Sapphire!"

"No," Elise replied easily, "but my parents will not overlook her history, even if I trust you."

As I am not yet certain that I do, she added silently.

"I concede your point," he said gallantly, lightly kissing her hand.

Gently, she drew her hand back, her fingers still tingling from the caress.

"I am a minor yet," she reminded him. "And cannot contract a marriage for myself. If you are serious about this, you must approach my parents."

Jet nodded. "I know. Honestly, Elise, I have not even spoken with my own parents on this matter. I wished first to know *your* heart. When I speak with them, may I say that you would consider my proposal?"

Elise liked Jet better for wanting her consent first, then wondered if he was just being cautious. She phrased her answer carefully.

"Yes, you may tell them that *I* would consider it. I cannot answer for my parents."

Nor, she thought, as they made their farewells and Jet took his leave, *have I said that I would accept—only consider.*

Still, she would be lying to herself if she did not admit that an acute thrill had entered her heart at the prospect of marrying Jet. At this moment, perhaps, his eyes were on the crown, but she liked the thought that in time she could turn them to herself alone.

Being queen would be preferable, but a consort could wield as much influence, especially if she held the heart of the monarch in her hand and bore his heirs within her womb. Humming to herself, Elise left the summerhouse and hurried toward the house, suddenly impatient for her parents' return.

✺

ONCE THE NECESSARY LUGGAGE, including Firekeeper's falcon, was transported to the castle, Derian was given the rest of the day off. He suspected this was so Earl Kestrel could have a chance to work on Firekeeper by himself. Where once that would have troubled Derian, now he accepted it. If Firekeeper could only manage when he was there to defend her, then she was ill equipped to survive in this new world she had entered.

He wondered how much of her own practical view had influenced his thoughts on the matter, and then shrugged. Being free of the castle and of courtly constraints felt good. He had refused the earl's polite offer of a mount—horses were more trouble than they were worth within the city walls—and hurried down the cobbled streets on foot.

His parents' livery stables were conveniently situated outside the city walls, but their home was near Market Square. Today the market was in full swing and he grinned at himself for forgetting that, even as he enjoyed threading through the throng. A few moon-spans before he would have gone out of his way to avoid the crowds, but after his sojourn among the nobility he was glad to be back among the common people.

He immersed himself in the hubbub: the cries of the vendors praising their wares, the scolding of a mother when her child strayed, the pinging of the tinkers' hammers, the heated bartering on all sides. It moved him like music and he danced to it, his steps graceful and his heart light.

At one stall he bought a roll smeared with strawberry jam, at another sweets for his brother and sister, at another a basket of blackberries for his mother. He grinned when a farmer, known to him for years, raised his eyebrows as he noticed the Kestrel crest stamped on the reverse of the token offered in payment.

Derian himself had been fairly awed the first time he'd been given one of those—up until then his pocket money had been the more common guild tokens. Now he took the Kestrel tokens for granted. After all, he was now a retainer of House Kestrel and entitled to use their credit.

Whistling, his basket of berries on his arm, Derian strode down the street toward the large brick house with the cut-slate roof that had been in the Carter family for generations and which, in time, would pass to him. The front door, used only for formal occasions, was closed even on this hot afternoon, but the side door which led into the office was open. He paused in the street, heard his mother's voice rising and falling in the polite but firm tones she used for business, and passed around to the kitchen door.

His eight-year-old brother, Brock, light brown hair bleached from the summer sun, was teasing their sister Damita, who was sitting on the back steps, shelling sweet peas.

"Damita has a sweet-a," the boy sang, dancing from foot to foot, "wants to meet 'im, at the square, but here she sits, shellin' peas. Now do you think that's fair?"

Damita, at thirteen, was as red-haired as Derian, but whereas his own hair was darkening to a subdued auburn, her curls were coppery bright. When Derian had departed with Earl Kestrel, she had been a flat-chested, rambunctious imp, but in these three moon-spans she seemed to have suddenly changed. She looked more a young woman with her hair twisted on top of her head and the definite beginnings of a woman's bosom filling out her summer dress.

Derian paused, his hand on the latch of the white-painted board gate, feeling uncomfortably the stranger. The sensation was not relieved when Damita glanced over and, seeing him, said in polite, bored tones meant to cover her embarrassment at being found barefoot and doing kitchen work:

"May I help you, sir? Business enquiries should be made at the side . . ."

She stopped in midphrase, then erupted to her feet, pea shells flying everywhere. Nearly spilling the stoneware bowl on the step next to her, she darted down the flagstone walk, familiar again.

"Deri! Deri! You're back."

Derian didn't remember opening the gate, but somehow he was inside, hugging her to him. Brock threw one arm around his older brother's waist and hammered on his shoulders, crowing happily.

The initial chaos past, they settled on the steps. Damita automatically began shelling peas again, but her mind wasn't on the job and several times Derian rescued a pod from amid the shucked vegetables.

"I hardly knew you," Damita repeated, "you look so fine."

Of course the leather breaches and heavy woolen shirts he had worn on the journey west wouldn't have done once the expeditionary party was settled at the keep and later at the Kestrel Manse. Earl Kestrel (or Valet, Derian suspected) had sent a new wardrobe along, some of the items not too different from the clothes Derian had worn in his parents' service, some so elegant that they would be out of place anywhere but in court.

For his visit home, conscious that he was representing his new employer, Derian had donned knee-breeches and waistcoat, both of good cotton dyed walnut brown. These were worn over a bleached linen shirt, fine-knit socks, and matching brass-buckled shoes. A striking tricorn hat of dark brown felt topped the assembly.

Damita ran a critical hand over the fabric of his waistcoat and nodded approvingly. "You look like a young gentleman, Deri. That's what I thought you were, standing there at the gate. I thought you'd come about hiring a horse or carriage."

"And you look like a young lady," Derian replied, happy to banish that initial strangeness by voicing it. "You're wearing your hair up now."

"Mother bought me some barrettes for my birthday," Damita answered, ducking her head so that he could admire the carved doe running through her copper locks, "and said that I could wear my hair up for occasions. I thought I was going to the market with Cook . . ."

She paused to glare at Brock, and Derian, remembering the scene he had interrupted, wisely kept silent.

"But Mother said these peas had to be shelled."

Derian, who knew his mother's disciplinary tactics perfectly well, having been on the receiving end of them many times, filled in the picture. Damita had undoubtedly sassed Mother and, as a penalty, had not only been told she could not go to market, but that she must shell the vegetables.

He took a handful of peas from the basket resting between his sister's feet.

"Well, let me give a hand. C'mon, Brock, something wrong with you?"

Brock protested, "It's her job, not mine! I did my jobs: fed the chickens, weeded the kitchen garden, ran messages to the stables . . ."

Derian interrupted. "True enough, but one thing I learned when venturing west with the earl is that when there's a job to be done, everyone pitches in. Many's the night I've sat mending shirts by firelight so that we could hit the trail with the dawn."

Brock, hearing the promise of a story, dropped onto the step on Derian's other side and dipped his hand into the basket of peas.

"Tell us all about it," he commanded.

Vernita Carter found them all there about an hour later.

"Damita," she said, her footsteps light as she crossed the stones of the kitchen floor, "the peas look wonderful and the carrots, too. Since you've finished the potatoes, I suppose you can go to the market for . . ."

She stopped, a sudden smile lighting her face. In her day, Vernita Carter had been regarded a great beauty. Even bearing several children and long days managing the family business had not robbed her of a certain grace and dignity.

"Derian," she said softly, "why didn't you let me know you were home?"

"You had a client, ma'am," he said, rising and giving her his best bow before impulsively hugging her. When had she grown so small? "And I was always told that nothing short of an emergency should interrupt that."

"I think," Vernita replied, drawing back to look him over proudly, "that the return home of my eldest son would qualify. Damita, has Cook come back?"

"No, Mother," Damita said. "If you wish, I could run and find her."

"Do. Tell her we will have an extra mouth for dinner." Vernita gave her son an anxious glance. "You can stay, can't you, Deri?"

"For dinner, Mother, but I must return by bedtime."

Vernita looked temporarily disappointed, but nodded. "Go then, Damita. Take a few spare tokens and buy us all something special for dessert."

"Deri brought blackberries," Brock informed her, bringing the willow basket from the cool room to display the prize, "and candy."

"Then buy something that will go well with them, Dami. I trust your judgment." Vernita turned to her younger son. "Brock, run to the stables and tell your father Derian is here and that he's to come home early for dinner."

"Yes, Mother."

Like a little tawny whirlwind, the boy was gone. Vernita smiled.

"Let me shut the office door and put the sign out referring emergency business to the stables. Then we can have tea and you can tell me everything that has happened since you've been gone."

"Three moon-spans in a few hours," Derian protested with a grin. "Didn't you read my letters?"

"I did," she said, pulling a grubby bundle from a drawer to show him. "We all did. Now you can tell us everything you didn't write."

Derian, thinking how Earl Kestrel had sworn them all to secrecy regarding Firekeeper, nodded.

"There's more there than you might think," he said.

Vernita grinned, a grin to match his own. "Oh, I don't know. We hear things, those of us in trade. And the rumors have been flying thick and fast today."

Derian grinned back and began, "Our expedition did succeed, but only in a way . . ."

Leaving out nothing, for Norvin Norwood's version of the tale must already be leaking from the castle into the city, Derian told of his adventures, repeating a bit when his father and siblings returned, and talking steadily through dinner.

When he ended, there was silence. Then Vernita said softly, so softly that Derian wondered if he was meant to hear:

"Poor child . . ."

At first he thought she meant Firekeeper; then, catching her gaze, he had the uncomfortable feeling that she was thinking of him.

LATER THAT EVENING, Derian walked toward the outer gates of the king's castle with his father. Colby Carter was a thick, broad-shouldered man with a deep inner stillness that came from understanding and working with draft horses and oxen. Brock took after him, while Derian and Damita more resembled their mother.

"I never thought I'd see a son of mine living here," Colby admitted, "except maybe as a groom."

"I'm hardly more, Father," Derian reminded, "but tending to a wolf-woman and her beasts instead of to horses."

"Maybe so," Colby said. He thrust out a muscular, callused hand. "Don't stay away more than you must."

"I won't," Derian promised, wishing suddenly that he could remain longer with his family. "But my duty is yet to Earl Kestrel."

"I know, son." Colby started to turn away, then swung back. "Will your master be expecting you yet?"

"I have some time before I will be quite overdue," Derian replied, puzzled.

"There are matters," Colby continued heavily, "that I had thought to raise with you, but I preferred not to in front of the younger children. Damita is at a flighty age, quick to become moody. Better not give her more to brood upon than the imagined wrongs a girl her age is prone to. Brock is a good boy, but too inclined to chatter."

"And Mother?"

"Knows all that concerns me in this matter," Colby assured his son. "Even that I hoped to speak with you tonight. She won't be worrying if I don't come home at once."

Derian looked down the road back toward the town. "We walked by several alehouses on our way."

"Just what I was thinking," Colby agreed.

A few minutes later found them seated in an out-of-the-way corner in a tavern still busy with the later elements of the market day trade, mostly visitors from out of town who had hawked their wares until dusk and would head for home with dawn. After the potboy had set two mugs of new summer ale in front of them and hurried off, Colby cleared his throat.

"Kings and earls," he said, "are not the only ones interested in this matter of succession. Honest guild members have their concerns as well, as do factions outside our own kingdom."

Derian nodded, having considered some of this himself but, frankly, having been too close to the concerns of his own earl to think much beyond that immediate focus.

"Yes, Father. There's much talk about a candidate for the throne born outside of our kingdom entirely—one Allister Seagleam of Bright Bay. I think, though, you have more than him in mind."

Colby sipped his ale. "True, but let us start with this Allister Seagleam. There are many among the guilds who favor his candidacy above all others."

"Above our native born?" Derian asked, amazed.

"Not so long ago, a bare hundred years," Colby reminded him, "we were one land, the remnants of the colony of Gildcrest. Before the Civil War, we were that colony itself. A hundred years is a long time, true, but not so much that one man cannot easily comprehend it.

"There are those," the older man continued, "who tire of the constant war between Hawk Haven and Bright Bay, those who remember that King Chalmer meant Princess Caryl's marriage to a prince of our rival power to be a pledge for lasting peace among us."

"That peace didn't last much beyond this Allister's birth," Derian reminded his father sourly.

"I'm not denying that," Colby said, "but still, that is the reason for which Allister was born. Many say that since King Tedric's line cannot continue directly, this pledge child should be permitted his destiny. Some go so far as to say that this is why all three of King Tedric's own begetting have died before their father—to clear the way for our great ancestor's vision to come true."

Derian stared at him. "Do you believe this, Father?"

Colby shrugged. "I don't know what to believe. There is sense in that way of seeing things, though, sense that many common folk understand. It doesn't hurt that Duke Allister is the son of the woman who would have been next in line for the throne if she had remained in Hawk Haven. Nor was she ever disinherited, as Prince Barden was. Therefore, her family's claims are strong."

"And if a member of Bright Bay's royal house took the throne of Hawk Haven," Derian said slowly, "there might be an end to war between our lands."

"Should be," Colby agreed, "for there is no indication that Allister Seagleam is unfavored in his own land. They title him duke there and have given him lands like those of a scion of a Great House. Peace would be good for most of the trades. Farmers could live without the fear that their fields may be trampled or plundered by roaming soldiers. The guilds could enforce their standards more effectively. Even such as myself would gain great opportunities from seeing travel open up. Only those few who have made their livings in war would be unhappy, and even if Bright Bay and Hawk Haven were at peace there would not be an end to watchfulness."

Derian frowned. "On other borders, you mean."

"That's right. Up until now, those countries that share borders with ourselves and Bright Bay have been content to let us weaken ourselves by fighting each other. If we were reunited—as one kingdom or as allies through related monarchs—they would be less easy."

"During past conflicts," Derian said, remembering things Ox had told him, "Waterland has sent advisors and marines to supplement our own forces. This is not widely known, but a friend of mine who has served in the military told me about them. The reason given for their presence was training—that Waterland prefers to have some blooded troops among their companies."

"I had heard something of the sort," Colby agreed, "working as I do among traveling folk, tending their animals and gear. Did you know that Stonehold has made a similar agreement with Bright Bay? Ostensibly their reasoning is much the same as that given by Waterland, but I'll tell you, rulers don't worry so much about having blooded troops unless they anticipate a need to use them. Whether Bright Bay and Hawk Haven are reunited by conquest or by peaceful means, our neighbors see us as a possible threat."

"Then is reuniting so wise?" Derian countered.

"The only alternative," Colby replied soberly, "is continuing the cycle of war into uneasy peace and into war again. So it has been all my life and all my father's life. Two of my siblings died from this fighting, both in battles so small that I doubt any but those who won glory in them even remember them, but my brothers died just the same. I begrudge the loss of a son to such circumstances—I even begrudge the death of a horse or ox if there is an alternative."

Mention of the ox made Derian uncomfortably aware of his own Ox, who could have died quite easily despite all his great strength if one of the arrows that had scarred his broad hide had been luckier in finding its target.

"We need a strong monarch," Derian said thoughtfully, "whether this Duke Allister or not. One who can lead us well in war and guide us in peace. Is there anyone among our noble families fit for that task?"

"Not your wolf-girl?" Colby said teasingly. "You've spoken warmly enough of her courage."

"Courage and to spare," Derian agreed, "but not necessarily wisdom, though that could be gained. But can she unite these jealous nobles behind her, even with King Tedric's support?"

"I don't know," Colby said honestly. "All I can do is listen in the market, listen to my clients, listen to the travelers who cross the borders. Now that we are somewhat at peace with Bright Bay—more, I think, because they hope to win our kingdom through inheritance than because hostilities are ended—there are those who travel between the kingdoms once more."

"Merchants, entertainers," Derian said, thinking back to those he had met when working in his father's business, "tinkers, and simply the footloose—and any one of them might be a spy."

"True," Colby said, "but I watch my tongue. I'm but a simple livery stable owner, concerned with my horses and wagons. My wife's the brains of the operation—everyone knows that."

They laughed together at the old joke. Colby was often underestimated, Vernita never. The arrangement suited them both nicely.

"I'll keep your words in mind, Father," Derian said soberly. "And you take care. Some may learn you have a son in Kestrel service and think you more clever than you would wish."

"I will," Colby promised, "and you also take care. There will be those who will resent the kennel keeper of a new-minted noblewoman, especially one who looks suspiciously like she's becoming a princess."

Derian nodded. Without further comment, they finished their ales, settled their score with the tavern keeper, and headed up the hill toward the castle. A few steps away from the gate, Colby gave Derian a bone-crushing hug.

"Come see us again soon, son. Bring your work with you if you'd like. Just don't be a stranger."

"I won't," Derian repeated, his heart lighter than before, though these new twists to the already complex political picture made his head swim.

He turned to watch his father walk down the lamplit streets into the city, then knocked on the iron-bound door. The porter opened it so quickly that Derian knew he'd been watching through his peephole.

"Good visit with the folks at home?"

"Good enough," Derian said. "Wish I could have stayed longer."

"I'm glad to have you back," the porter said with anxious eagerness. "You're Lady Blysse Norwood's man, aren't you?"

"I am," Derian agreed, wondering. He hadn't thought any of the servants knew him as yet.

"Is it true she keeps an enormous wolf as a pet?"

"She has a wolf with her, yes," Derian answered, careful even in Firekeeper's absence not to refer to Blind Seer as a pet.

"And a falcon the size of an eagle, big enough to carry off a small child or a lamb?"

"She has a peregrine falcon of good size," Derian answered, amused.

"Then I'm glad you're back," the porter repeated. "Good to know there's someone managing them all."

Derian hid a grin, pleased enough with this sudden rise in status, but unwilling to let the man think he was mocking him.

"I'll just hurry up then and make certain they're all settled for bed," Derian said politely.

"Good." With a heavy thud of iron-bound oak, the porter swung the door shut after Derian. "First time I ever heard of locking the door to keep the wolf *in*," he muttered.

Running up the wide, smooth stone stairs into the tower, Derian grinned.

X

WHEN ELISE HEARD footsteps coming up the garden path behind her, her heart leapt in her breast. Irrationally, stupidly, with an eagerness she felt was unworthy of the dignity of her seventeen years, she hoped it would be Jet. She hadn't seen him since he made his proposal two days before and the suspense had been unbearable. Although her initial impulse had been to blurt out everything to her mother, the few hours' delay while waiting for Lady Aurella to return from the castle had shown Elise this would be unwise.

Aurella Wellward was a good mother. Since Elise was an only child, Aurella had spent much time with her rather than delegating the more routine matters of her daughter's upbringing to a nursemaid as was more typical in noble houses. Mother and daughter had their disagreements, their times of estrangement, but lately they had been quite close. Still, Aurella was too much a lady of the royal court to not first think of the political maneuvering in Jet's proposal rather than the romantic possibilities.

And Elise so very much wanted to dwell on those romantic possibilities. This was her first marriage proposal (and maybe her only) and Jet was very handsome. She wanted to dream of moonlight rides, of holding hands, of whispered confidences. That was why, even though the sound of two pairs of feet scampering up the graveled path could never be the measured tread of one set of masculine boots firmly striding, her heart leapt and she turned with careful grace to meet . . .

Citrine Shield and Kenre Trueheart ran up, hands clasped, faces flushed. For a moment, Elise preserved the hope that Citrine bore a message from her older brother, but the girl's words dispelled even that fleeting fantasy.

"Cousin Elise!" she said. "Good morning! Your maid Ninette told us you had come to the castle early."

"You're staying here, aren't you?" Elise said, bending to hug each of the children. An only child herself, she had always doted on her younger cousins, viewing them as substitutes for the siblings she herself lacked. The little ones returned her affection openly, so openly that Sapphire had been known to comment cattily that Elise wouldn't like the brats nearly so much if she had to spend more time with them.

"We are," Citrine said, "though Jet's gone riding with Father. Mother and Sapphire are attending upon the queen."

Poor Mother, Elise thought. *Lady Melina would be enough to set me off my breakfast.*

Innocent in her romantic ideals, she didn't reflect that if she married Jet she would see Melina Shield far more often than at the occasional breakfast.

Kenre cut in, "My family's staying here too, but Purcel's out with his troops. I think he's bored."

Elise nodded. "Are you bored too? Is that why you're out and about so early?"

"No," Kenre said, "we're not bored. We've been visiting with the wolf-woman. She likes us."

"Wolf-woman?" Elise asked, but even as the question was shaped she realized who Kenre must mean. Everyone had heard of the great grey wolf who followed Lady Blysse wherever she went—to the discomfort of every resident of the castle other than King Tedric. "That isn't a polite way to refer to Lady Blysse."

"She likes it," Citrine said. "She likes it better than Blysse. The second day we played with her she told us to call her Firekeeper. She said that's her real name, the name the wolves gave her when she was small."

"Want to come meet her?" Kenre asked before Elise could voice any of the dozen questions that Citrine's speech had raised. "We thought you might when we saw Ninette in the corridor. Firekeeper's in the castle meadows."

"How do you know?" Elise asked. "Did you make plans to meet her there?"

"Not really," Citrine said. Grabbing Elise's hand, she pointed up into the sky. "See the bird, way up there? That's Firekeeper's peregrine falcon, Elation. They go out into the meadows in the morning before Earl Kestrel needs Firekeeper so that she can get some air and so Blind Seer can run."

Allowing herself to be towed along—after all, if Jet was out riding with Rolfston Redbriar he wasn't likely to come looking for her loitering among the roses—Elise asked:

"Blind Seer?"

"That's the wolf," Kenre said. "Firekeeper calls him her brother. She gets really mad if you call him her pet. Derian said . . ."

"Derian? Who is that? Her horse?"

Citrine giggled. "Derian is her manservant. He's from the town. He was at the banquet: a tall man with red hair."

Elise remembered this Derian now, a handsome enough commoner standing awkwardly behind Lady Blysse's chair, his face flushing dark red every time his charge made a particularly vigorous social gaffe.

The meadows were outside the castle walls, but Cousin Purcel had explained to Elise at great length how they were far more defensible than they might initially appear. It had something to do with the high cliffs rising behind the fields and the ravines—some natural, some otherwise—that flanked them. In a pinch, Purcel had told her with martial enthusiasm, a few trees could be felled, some pasturage burned to create a kill zone, and the woods and meadows would be almost as secure as the castle itself. This was one of the reasons that the Eagle's Nest was nearly impossible to take by siege. As long as the woods and water were accessible, the besieged could hold out indefinitely.

Every child knew how Queen Zorana had taken the castle by intrigue rather than by force, establishing herself once and forever as the dominant figure in the civil conflict.

A few steps outside of the arched doorway in the stone wall, Elise shook her hands free from the children's grasp. If she was going to meet a rival for the throne, she shouldn't look too undignified. A moment later, she learned that dignity—at least in the way she had been taught to define it—wasn't a concern for Lady Blysse. When the three cousins entered the meadow, this youngest heir to the Great House of Norwood was sitting sprawled in a trampled patch of grass and wild flowers.

She was clad in brown leather breeches cut off just below the knee and a battered leather vest loosely buttoned over small breasts. One tanned arm was flung about the neck of an enormous grey wolf with startling blue eyes. Lady Blysse's face was bright with unguarded curiosity, but she showed no surprise, as if she had been given warning of their coming.

When Citrine and Kenre ran up to her, Blysse jumped to her feet, giving each child a rough but affectionate embrace. Then she looked toward Elise, her expression less open.

"Who that?" she asked.

"This is our best cousin," Citrine said, inadvertently warming Elise's heart, "Lady Elise Archer, heir to the House of Archer. Her father is Kenre's mother's brother."

"Best is good," Blysse replied. Turning to Elise, she offered her an awkward bow after the masculine fashion.

Initially shocked, Elise immediately realized that a curtsy performed in trousers would look quite silly. Indeed, with her dark hair drawn back in a short queue, man-fashion, her bare feet, and her small, neat figure, Blysse looked more like a delicately featured lad than a girl of fifteen.

Elise returned the greeting with a curtsy, only then acknowledging the red-haired man who had scrambled to his feet at her entry. Derian Carter, she thought, had potential to be quite handsome when he grew into perfect comfort with his young man's body. He was attractive even now with his clear hazel-green eyes and fair skin; his hair was auburn rather than carroty.

Derian's bearing was respectful without being groveling, so that Elise found herself returning his bow as she would to an equal rather than to a servant. Somehow, she realized when she turned her attention to Lady Blysse, this had done her no harm in the newcomer's opinion.

"Firekeeper," Citrine was saying happily, "did you catch anything this morning?"

"Rabbits" was the solemn response, "three, but Blind Seer ate them all. He likes his meat blood-warm, but still eats what Ox brings him. I tell him he get too big."

"Fat," Citrine said bossily. Elise caught her breath at this rudeness, but something in Blysse's bearing told her that language lessons must have been a regular part of these meetings.

"Fat," Lady Blysse repeated, then tilted her head to one side. "Why fat? Derian say fat is white part of meat."

Derian spoke for the first time. Elise was delighted to hear that his voice was a pleasant, measured baritone with only a trace of a lower-class accent.

"Fat in meat makes big," he explained, frowning slightly as he tried to keep his words simple. His eyes twinkled as he added, "If we cut Blind Seer open, his meat would have much white."

Lady Blysse laughed at this, punching the wolf hard on one shoulder as if the animal had understood the joke. From a tree branch overhead, the peregrine falcon shrieked.

Feeling a bit left out, Elise essayed, "Does Earl Kestrel know you come out here to hunt?"

"He know," Blysse responded. "Not like when first."

Derian clarified, "Earl Kestrel was not delighted the first time his ward came out here without his express permission. I had been permitted to visit my parents in town, so Firekeeper was on her own. However, he has had to acknowledge that you can't keep a wolf walled up without the furniture taking considerable damage."

"Couldn't the wolf," Elise hazarded what many had stated openly, "be put in the kennels?"

Derian laughed. "The dogs would go mad. Our scout had a bird dog with him on our journey west through the gap. I don't think poor Queenie stopped cringing for a moment—and that was even before Blind Seer started traveling in our company. In any case, I don't think you could get him to leave Firekeeper."

"Or Firekeeper him," Lady Blysse said calmly.

"Oh."

Elise was temporarily at a loss, but fortunately keeping the conversation going was not up to her.

"Firekeeper has an idea," Citrine chattered. "She wants to meet the rest of the family, but she doesn't like banquets."

"Who does?" Elise said with a pose of adult boredom.

Actually, she still found banquets fascinating, especially those attended by embassies from the neighboring kingdoms of New Kelvin and Waterland. The foreigners with their odd mannerisms and turns of phrase— for their initial colonies had not been from the same Old Country as Gildcrest—were infinitely interesting. A career in the diplomatic service was impossible for her, since she was destined to become the Baroness Archer and be responsible for the family estates, but back before she realized no little brother or sister was likely to follow and share the job, this had been her favorite dream.

"Wolves fight each other for their food," Kenre added. "So Firekeeper thinks eating and talking at the same time is silly."

"She has a point," Elise laughed. "What is her idea?"

"Hunting with birds," Lady Blysse said, her tone slightly miffed.

No wonder. Elise thought. *Since we keep talking about her as if she's an idiot. Uncivilized she may be, but she's no idiot.*

"Falconry," Derian said in a tone Elise immediately recognized as that of a teacher reminding a student. Fleetingly she wondered how he came into the job.

"Falconry," Lady Blysse repeated. "Hawking. We go. Me, some of nobles, on horses or walking. Hunt. Talk."

Elise turned to her. "That's a good idea, actually. Most of the nobility of Hawk Haven are fascinated with falconry. I think it comes from the names King Chalmer gave the Great Houses to keep them from fussing when he married a commoner. Anyhow, it is easier to get to know people when you're not sitting around a table or trapped in a parlor."

"Parlor?"

"A room for sitting," Elise laughed.

"So many rooms," Blysse mused. "Wolves have dens for pups. Nothing else. In winter, I use den for fire."

Elise puzzled this out then nodded. "You would need shelter, wouldn't you?"

"No fur." Blysse shrugged. "Cold."

"But you had fire?"

Kenre interrupted. "That's why her name is Firekeeper. She could make fire, but none of the wolves could. They respected that."

Elise glanced at Derian. "Did she really live with wolves?"

The redhead grinned. "She says so. Doc—excuse me—Sir Jared Surcliffe, Earl Kestrel's cousin, said that there's evidence of it. Firekeeper, show Lady Elise your scars."

"All?" Blysse bared her teeth in a brief smile. "If so, then Derian get red."

She thrust out one arm for Elise's inspection. Beneath the fine hairs, her skin was silvered with numerous tiny scars. A few larger ones testified to considerable injuries recovered from in the past.

"Little bites," Blysse dismissed them, dropping her arm. "Also cuts. No fur. Only," she poked at the material of her vest, "bad leather."

"Badly tanned leather," Derian clarified automatically. "Somehow Firekeeper figured out the basics, but while she could keep the leather from going completely stiff, the stuff wasn't good for much."

Citrine and Kenre had dropped to the grass and were sitting in identical attitudes, arms wrapped around knees, their expressions glowing with interest and proprietary pride. Doubtless they saw the newcomer as their special discovery.

Elise shook out her shawl, spread it on the grass to protect her walking dress from stains, and joined them. Only once she was seated did Lady Blysse and Derian resume their seats on the ground.

"Now," Elise said to the general company, "tell me what Lady Blysse has in mind."

"I have falcon," Blysse replied carefully, pointing to the magnificent blue-grey peregrine.

"So I see," Elise agreed. "A peregrine, the emblem of the Wellward house—my mother's house."

"Emblem?"

"Symbol," Citrine said quickly. "It means the same thing, Firekeeper."

Lady Blysse gave a gusty sigh and Elise couldn't blame her. From her own foreign-language lessons, those words that seemed to mean the same thing were the most annoying—especially when you later discovered the subtleties of difference.

"You fly peregrine?" Lady Blysse asked her.

"No," Elise replied ruefully, "though my mother would be pleased if I did. I really don't fly anything these days. Our falconer keeps a little merlin for me. It's more his bird than mine. I don't fool myself."

Derian eased into the flow of her speech so smoothly that he didn't seem to be interrupting.

"Mistress Citrine was telling Firekeeper about how people here fly their hawks. It gave Lady Blysse the idea of having her falcon, Elation, demonstrate her skill."

Elise nodded. "That's a good idea. A few other birds could be flown in their own turn—not too many or they would get upset."

She was out of her depth here and knew it. Falconry—with its bloody successes, the feeding the bird a bit of flesh or warm brains from the kill—had been something she had participated in only reluctantly. To avoid having to reveal her ignorance she turned to her young cousin.

"Citrine, who do you think would choose to go along if Lady Blysse offered to fly her hawk for them?"

"Everyone, I think," Citrine said, momentarily more cynical than an eight-year-old should be. "Even those who don't like blood sport would want to go to get a look at Lady Blysse."

"Good point," Elise said, thinking that if a hawking party was arranged she would definitely see Jet again. She was certain he practiced the art. Perhaps he would fly his own bird, though more likely Sapphire would insist on the honor of representing their family.

"Maybe Opal and Ruby would stay home," Citrine added after reflection. "They don't like getting dirty and even Mother doesn't see us little girls having a chance at the throne. What about your sisters, Kenre?"

"Dia and Deste might want to stay home," Kenre said honestly, "but Mama wouldn't let them. She has no patience with weak stomachs."

He looked a little forlorn as he said this, having recently graduated to an age where his mother no longer accepted weakness even in her baby boy. Lady Blysse nodded agreement with Zorana's policy.

"Weak die," she said. "Strong live."

Looking at Blysse, so confident in her own strength as she sprawled in the grass, an arm flung once more about her wolf, Elise wondered how her relatives would perceive the stranger when they came to know her better. Not all of them, she thought ruefully, would be as fascinated as Citrine and Kenre. Most of them, in fact, would see her as a threat.

THE HAWKING EXPEDITION, when it set out a few days later, was somewhat smaller than Elise and Citrine had dreaded. Of the five children of Lord Rolfston and Lady Melina, the two middle girls, Ruby and Opal, were permitted to remain home. This might have encouraged Zorana to make similar allowances, for neither Deste nor Nydia were forced to attend.

Accompanied by Earl Kestrel, the host of this expedition, King Tedric rode near the front of the party, deep in discussion with his personal falconer about the condition of his magnificent golden eagle, a bird known to be temperamental. Tedric's absorption in this matter—or apparent absorption—effectively prohibited any member of the party from thrusting him or herself into his company.

Derian wondered cynically if this wasn't exactly what the old king had intended. Certainly Sapphire Shield—a stunning young woman who, with her flashing eyes and tendency to flare her nostrils, reminded him uncomfortably of the first horse ever to throw him—would like to remind her great-uncle of her presence. Her brother Jet, however, hardly seemed to notice the king. His attention was wholly on Lady Elise.

Elise looked even prettier than she had at their earlier meetings, Derian thought ruefully, her fair skin flushed pale rose and her golden hair glinting brighter than the light mesh net she had tucked around it. Her laughter reminded him of silver bells or the ringing of crystal goblets. It also reminded him that she didn't even know he existed.

Firekeeper was riding off to one flank on the same patient, if boring, grey gelding who had carried her from West Keep. Much to Derian's surprise, she had agreed to leave Blind Seer in the castle—on the condition that the wolf was not locked in. She hadn't liked leaving him, but she had to admit that the wolf still upset any horse but grey Patience, Roanne, and Race's Dusty. Since the hawking party had been her idea, Firekeeper would compromise to make it work.

That compromise hadn't extended to her agreeing to wear the riding frock Earl Kestrel had suggested, but she wasn't alone in finding skirts awkward for riding. Sapphire and Citrine both wore women-tailored breeches and pretty white blouses, similar to the outfit that Valet had mysteriously managed to procure for Firekeeper. Those worn by the Shield sisters were far more elaborate, embroidered with flowers and birds, perhaps the result of winter labor by the fireside.

Lady Elise had chosen a light gown similar, to Derian's masculine assessment, to the ones she had worn before but somehow subtly more attractive, a thing of pale lavender, laced tightly at the breast. Fleetingly,

Derian wondered how well Elise's legs—long, he imagined—and rounded hips might shape up in riding breeches and decided that she would probably look stunning.

The older women in the party—Aurella Wellward, Zorana Archer, and Melina Shield—also wore gowns and rode sidesaddle. All but Zorana seemed to be treating this as a general outing. Zorana alone followed the preparation of the birds, pausing in her conversation with a weatherbeaten man who—for all his undeniable handsomeness—somehow reminded Derian of a rat.

From one of the grooms, he had learned that this was Prince Newell Shield, the widower of Princess Lovella, just returned from a voyage on *Wings*, the flagship of the Hawk Haven Navy. Although Newell should have reverted to his Shield family title on the death of his wife, King Tedric had deemed it a courtesy to permit his son-in-law to retain the title he had assumed when Lovella had become crown princess.

A tough man, slightly older than his sister Melina, Newell had been an ideal match for the ambitious warrior princess. Although the couple had been childless, rumor said that this had not been for any lack of shared passion, rather because Lovella did not wish to risk the illnesses suffered by her mother during pregnancy until her deeds were as legend.

Although no stories of sorcerous practice were told about Newell as were told about his sister, still, finding the prince gazing at him with curious intensity, Derian felt a cool chill slide down his spine. Newell's pale gaze was fixed yet somehow absent, and Derian found himself booting Roanne in the ribs to remove himself from the direct line of that stare.

Firekeeper rode over to join him, flushed with barely restrained excitement. The falcon Elation sat—unhooded, unjessed, unrestrained in any way—on a perch rigged to the back of the grey's saddle. Only her occasional sardonic squawk as she surveyed her avian competition confirmed that a living bird was perched there, not a product of the taxidermist's art.

"Elation say," Firekeeper commented as soon as they were close, "that men ahead with birds in cages."

"That's for the hunt," Derian said. "Earl Kestrel made the arrangements."

"Hunt? Men?" Firekeeper looked troubled at this, as well she might. Derian had drummed into her that there were numerous ramifications— some vague and terrible, some concrete and demonstrable—for even hurting a human, much less hunting one.

"No, no," Derian laughed. "The birds are to be hunted. This many people on horseback accompanied by attendants and grooms will scare every real piece of game off for miles."

"Yes. Too many," Firekeeper agreed.

"So when we are ready, the gamekeepers will release birds one at a time and the hawks will go after them."

Firekeeper nodded, but he could tell that this was yet another bit of incomprehensible human behavior. Dismissing the mysteries of hunting already caged birds, Firekeeper quickly focused on the real reason for this gathering.

"How, Derian, how I talk with these here like I talk with Citrine and Kenre? How I do?"

He understood her puzzlement, for, unlike the children who had been eager to make her acquaintance, the elders, especially those who saw Lady Blysse as competition for the throne, had been studiously ignoring her. Their excuse, if they were challenged, would certainly be that a young, newly adopted ward of Earl Kestrel was not of their usual circle. They would claim that they were not so much ignoring her as they simply hadn't thought her worth their regard. They'd phrase it more politely, out of deference to Earl Kestrel, but that was what they'd mean.

Derian surveyed the gathering. Elise was too absorbed in the attentions of her handsome cousin to have any thought for Lady Blysse. A formal introduction, such as Earl Kestrel could garner, would be a disaster. Then he noted that one pair of eyes, dark blue but amazingly clear, kept glancing toward Firekeeper. The expression in them was challenging, not kind. Still, Sapphire Shield's interest in Firekeeper was apparent.

Derian saluted Citrine and the little girl rode over gladly, her little, round-bodied chestnut pony jogging over the turf with single-minded enthusiasm. When Citrine had come to greet Firekeeper at the beginning of the ride, Melina Shield had called her daughter away on some pretense and had kept her away since.

"M'lady," Derian said in a respectful tone of voice he didn't bother with out in the meadows, "Lady Blysse would like to make the acquaintance of your elder sister Sapphire. Could you do us the honor of acting as liaison?"

Citrine giggled, then winked conspiratorially, keeping her back carefully turned on the adults. "I think I can get her over here. She's just itching to try Firekeeper—I mean Lady Blysse's—mettle."

Whatever Citrine said to her sister must have been effective, for Sapphire rode over immediately. She made quite a picture in her blue hunting clothes, mounted on a horse whose coat had been dyed a shocking indigo blue—although the mane and tail had been left a silvery white. Sapphire rode well, with natural grace and a certain restlessness. Her every movement was accompanied by the ringing of miniature hawk bells twined into her hair and fastened to her sleeves.

Dangerous, Derian thought, assessing her critically. *Tough and strong beneath all that hair and glitter. She sees something of herself in Firekeeper and that scares her.*

Introductions were made with punctilious correctness. Derian dropped back a few steps, near enough to be at hand if need arose, but effacing himself into servile invisibility. At first he had been bothered that this was so easy to do—especially before some of the more self-important nobles—but now he rather treasured the capacity, for it let him gather knowledge without anyone considering what he might do with it.

Sapphire dismissed formalities with a swiftness that reminded Derian of Elation stooping on unsuspecting prey.

"So, Lady Blysse, my sister told me you think you're a wolf."

Firekeeper shook her head sadly. "Am wolf-raised, not wolf get. Sometimes wish I was wolf."

"Oh?" Sapphire's polished sneer didn't completely hide her curiosity. "Why would you wish that?"

"They what I know best," Firekeeper responded, "and I cannot do what they do."

Sapphire dismissed this revelation as of no importance, her attention shifting to Elation. The peregrine falcon studied her, impudence in her gold-ringed eyes, then made a strange churling sound, almost like a laugh.

"Is that a peregrine?"

"Yes."

"It's rather large for a peregrine." Sapphire sounded miffed. "*I* fly a gyrfalcon—my family's bird. Some are as large as eagles. Are you sure this isn't some deviant cross?"

"Is peregrine," Firekeeper repeated. "Across mountain, animals get larger sometimes."

Derian noticed with some relief that Firekeeper did not attempt to explain to Sapphire her strange theory that there were two types of animals, the royal and the common. Sapphire would not take kindly to the thought that anything she possessed was common.

"I'll buy the peregrine from you," Sapphire said. "It's a magnificent bird."

"No." Firekeeper's response was blunt but her expression was amused, not offended. "Elation is not to sell."

Citrine deflected her sister's pique with a loud squeak of excitement. "We must be coming near the targets. Sapphire, I wonder if your gyrfalcon can outfly Lady Blysse's Elation?"

Derian didn't know whether he wanted to kick or kiss the little girl. He gave a mental shrug. The competition between the young women for a much bigger prize existed. Might as well have this lesser one out in the open as well.

ONCE JET ARRIVED, mounted on a fine black gelding with white stockings and a thin white blaze, Elise hardly noticed falcons, horses, or gathered people. He hovered by her side from the start of the ride, attentive as a declared lover. His first words, spoken almost in a whisper, made her heart beat uncomfortably fast:

"I've finally convinced my mother and father. They will speak with your parents today."

The rest of their conversation was far more routine. Jet was interested in what Elise could tell him of Firekeeper and her wolf. He studied the other woman in a fashion that might have made Elise jealous if he hadn't just declared his intention to have his parents speak with hers about their marriage.

When the time came for the falcons to be loosed, Jet abandoned Elise to claim his own bird. It was a gyrfalcon, as was to be expected, its plumage as black as night. Elise played with the fancy that in the Redbriar-Shield establishment there were servants who had no other job than running about seeking the best mounts, pets, jewels, clothing, and other accoutrements to maintain the theme that Melina Shield had begun with the naming of her brood. In wry afterthought Elise realized that this must indeed be the case and she treasured her own relative freedom of choice and action.

The two gyrfalcons, Blysse's peregrine, and King Tedric's eagle were the only birds being flown today. Initially, Elise had been surprised that Aunt Zorana, normally so competitive, had not insisted on someone from her family taking part. The Trueheart bird, however, was the merlin, a small, comparatively delicate hawk, not known for succeeding with prey the size of the game being taken today. The Archer family, not being one of the Great Houses, did not have a bird of its own so Zorana could not choose that as an alternative.

Purcel and Kenre were both in attendance, the older brother on his big, heavily muscled bay, one of his hands unobtrusively holding the lead rein for Kenre's sorrel pony. Despite the years between them and Purcel's frequent absences, strong affection remained between the two brothers.

Elise brought her own mount alongside her mother's when the first of the pigeons was released.

"Tell me," she said softly, "if the falcon hits or not so I can applaud."

"Squeamish, dear?"

"A little," Elise admitted.

"The other young people are getting on quite well," Aurella said, nothing in her voice giving away her awareness that something like this must have been the entire reason for the outing. "They're over there, arguing about the merits of the different birds. Even King Tedric has joined them. A shame you've chosen to be one of those who stands by and claps for the other's successes."

"I choose," Elise said with a slight mysterious smile, "to fly birds other than falcons."

Aurella's smile was all too knowing. "Earl Kestrel mentioned that his son Edlin is coming up from their lands in ten days or so. Now that he has reached his majority, young Lord Kestrel has more responsibilities on the Norwood estates, especially with his father playing politics in the capital. As I recall, you always did like Edlin Norwood, didn't you?"

Elise had fancied Edlin once, actually, but now she couldn't see last winter's flirtation in her new hopes for Jet. Thankfully, Aurella didn't press, for the heir to a Great House was a far finer catch than a second son of a mere lord. Then the first of the pigeons was freed and no one had attention for anything but the sky.

With a few strokes of her powerful wings, the peregrine Elation mounted into the sky, soared until she was little more than a dot against the blue. The gathered falconers stirred nervously, waiting for Lady Blysse to signal for the pigeon to be released.

"The bird'll flee with the wind," Elise heard someone mutter. "What's that fool girl playing at?"

When the tension was at its highest, Lady Blysse dropped her hand. The pigeon handlers, concealed in a blind some distance from the party as a whole, loosed a panicked bird. It surged toward the sky, wings beating in a desperate race for freedom.

Does it know? Elise wondered wildly.

Then there was a streak from above: the peregrine dropped in a perfect stoop, all the killing force of its descent hitting the pigeon soundly. The explosion of feathers was like a sudden snowfall. As with falling snow, there was no sound.

Then, though Blysse waved no lure, made no call, Elation left her kill, fluttering from the grass to land on Blysse's outstretched glove. Her talons showed a slight line of red, a bit of down. An astonished gamekeeper reported that the falcon had taken not even a morsel from the pigeon.

Watching from just outside the circle, Elise found herself thinking that the rapport between bird and woman was almost supernatural. Apparently she was not the only one to think this. Murmurs of surprise, respect, and apprehension reached her ears. Even the horses seemed edgy.

Elation didn't help matters by turning her head to look at Blysse out of one gold-rimmed eye, her shrill mewling cries sounding too conversational for comfort. When woman nodded as if in reply, the enormous peregrine launched skyward again. Flying beyond where the fowlers crouched with their cages, Elation circled, orienting on some prey invisible to those on the ground, then stooped.

When Elation rose again, her wings were beating heavily, laboring to raise not only herself but a large buck rabbit. With remarkable ease she carried her heavy burden over to Blysse, dropping it on the ground at the young woman's feet before returning to the glove and beginning to ostentatiously preen.

Not to be outdone by the Lady Blysse and Elation, Sapphire and Jet put their heads together, dark curls intertwining like their whispered words. When brother and sister came out of their conference they were both grinning a bit wickedly.

"We'll fly our gyrfalcons together," Sapphire announced to the gathering in general, though her eyes were on Blysse alone.

"Two birds," Lady Blysse nodded understanding. "Two pigeons?"

Sapphire agreed, adding airily, "A shame we don't have anything larger for them to go after—a heron, perhaps. Ah, well. Pigeons will have to do."

Unlike Blysse's unceremonious flying of Elation, there was quite a bit of fuss involved in preparing the gyrfalcons: hoods to be loosened, jesses attended to, the birds themselves to be soothed when they found themselves at the center of a crowd.

Sapphire's female was not blue—gyrfalcons were not feathered in blue and no temperamental raptor would submit to being dyed. Still, the bird was elegant and unusual—pure white with searching yellow eyes. Her eagerness to be away was signaled in how she shifted from foot to foot on her mistress's glove. Jet's black gyrkin was smaller and quieter, but more intense, its gaze already fixed on the sky as if it knew in advance where the prey would appear.

Gyrfalcons differed from peregrines in many significant ways. They were fluffier, seeming bulky, almost fat. Within those thick feathers, their heads seemed too small. The taloned feet they concealed beneath long belly feathers had shorter toes. Yet, though they lacked the peregrine's sleek elegance, they were magnificent birds, huge and haughty. Elise had heard that in some countries gyrfalcons were reserved for kings, a thing she suspected Sapphire also knew, given the pride with which she bore her bird.

Catching sight of Lady Blysse's peregrine, the white gyrfalcon shrieked defiance and rage, echoed a heartbeat behind by the black gyrkin. Sapphire commented with conversational coolness that didn't fool Elise a bit:

"Gyrfalcons have been known to kill other falcons—even eagles."

Lady Blysse replied calmly, "They not kill Elation. Fly your birds."

At the agreed upon signal, Jet and Sapphire released their birds. Black and white, like shadow and reflection, they soared upward, wings beating in fast yet steady strokes until they were above their prey. They soared for a moment, then plunged.

The pigeons didn't have a chance. Hating herself for her squeamishness, Elise turned away at the critical moment, hoping that Jet wouldn't notice.

On the next round, King Tedric's eagle refused to fly at the pigeon, offended perhaps by the indignity of being presented with captive prey, perhaps by the commotion all around. The monarch was not at all dis-comfited. He stroked the eagle's golden brown feathers as he re-hooded it and returned it to the fowler.

"Sometimes," Tedric commented, his gaze almost too nonspecific, "being king means accepting that sometimes things will not go your way."

Elise felt a surge of relief for the soft grey pigeon that had winged its way to the safety of the nearest wooded copse. That relief vanished when she heard Sapphire say in a too sweet tone of voice:

"Lady Blysse, did I hear correctly when you said that you believed that your peregrine could outfly our gyrfalcons?"

Blysse looked momentarily confused, then she said, her voice taut and hard: "Yes."

"Would you be interested in wagering your bird on that belief?"

This time Blysse must turn to Derian for a translation. It took a few moments, during which time Elise noticed Earl Kestrel making his way toward his ward. She was touched by his concern for the girl, but his words when he spoke were ambiguous.

"Dear Blysse, don't do anything foolish."

The look Blysse gave him was far less respectful than those Elise had seen her turn on Derian and she wondered for the first time if Blysse particularly liked her guardian.

Blysse's response was as much to Sapphire as to the earl.

"Is not foolish if is certain."

"Then you accept our wager?" Jet cut in.

The wolf-woman bared her teeth in an expression too vicious to be taken for a smile.

"What is wager if you give me nothing when I win?"

"Win?" Jet barked a hard, harsh laugh. "You tempt the ancestors, Lady Blysse, assuming success."

"What I get?" was the only reply.

"What do you want?"

"Your birds fly after my bird," Blysse said carefully. "Yes?"

"That's the basic idea," Jet sneered.

"If they catch my bird, my bird maybe die, maybe be hurt."

"Yes," Jet's tone had become impatient.

"What if my bird catch your birds?"

"Impossible!"

"What if?"

"There are two of our gyrfalcons to your one peregrine!"

Blysse shrugged as if to say "So?"

"Will you, my Lord Jet," came the calm, neutral voice of Derian Carter, "be willing to accept the loss of your gyrfalcons to the Lady Blysse?"

Blysse nodded, indicating that the translator's words spoke her intention.

Another voice, dry and passionless, yet somehow full of laughter, spoke for the first time:

"It only seems fair."

Heads swiveled to learn who had spoken, but Elise didn't need to look to see that Prince Newell, the widower of the Princess Lovella, was responsible for the comment. When she was very small, she had learned to know that voice and to fear the malice concealed behind its seemingly innocent pronouncements.

Sapphire colored and Jet nodded stiffly. Earl Kestrel interceded then, though the flush on his bearded cheeks made amply clear that he was less than delighted with the situation.

"Then it is decided," Earl Kestrel said. "The gyrfalcons will be released first to give them a moment to gain height. Then Lady Blysse will release her peregrine."

He ended his speech with a quick, angry slash of his hand. Accepting this as the signal, first Jet, then Sapphire released their gyrfalcons. Lady Blysse permitted them enough time to climb to a comfortable rise of air where they soared in easy arrogance. Any bulkiness the gyrfalcons had shown when imprisoned on gloves was gone.

At a word from her mistress, the peregrine Elation mounted the air. Sharp, almost knife-edged wings beat rapidly, alerting the gyrfalcons, which shrieked, infuriated by the intruder's arrogance. They circled for position while Elation was still gaining altitude. Elise felt her heart beating faster, certain that in a moment the sleek blue-grey peregrine would be nothing but a bloody burst of feathers.

It's like us! she thought frantically. *Hunting each other, seeking any advantage!*

Where she had been able to turn away before, she could not now draw her gaze from the sky. The three hawks were well matched in size, but the gyrfalcons had the advantage. Or did they?

Elise watched in astonishment as Elation launched through the gap between the black bird and the white, slipping through an opening so small that the maneuver seemed impossible. Then, wings cutting the air like knives, Elation rose, stooped, and from the power of that stoop came down onto the white gyrfalcon.

Stunned, the white gyrfalcon tumbled in the air, falling, rolling, recovering only inches from the dirt. Even then, all it could manage was to spread its wings, slowing its fall before coming to land with an undignified thud.

Her attention diverted by the falling bird, Elise didn't see how Elation got the better of the black gyrkin, but afterward she would hear that the tactics were similar. The gyrkin came to earth much as its mate had done. It didn't so much strike the ground as land with a sulk, its dignity insulted. Glancing at the two Shield siblings, Elise saw its mood mirrored in their two faces, but where the falcons were merely offended, Sapphire and Jet were shamed.

"Magnificent!" Prince Newell's voice broke the sudden silence. "Lady Blysse, my congratulations!"

Similar compliments followed from the various spectators, but Lady Blysse had eyes only for her two competitors. Waving to them, she invited them to inspect their gyrfalcons. Within a few moments, the verdict was passed that Elation had taken them out with the weight of her body rather than with her talons. Except for a few bruises and offended dignity at finding themselves the prey rather than the predator, both gyrfalcons should be fit for service.

"They're yours now," Sapphire said, anger and embarrassment barely concealed in her polite words. "I hope you enjoy them."

"I enjoy them best," Lady Blysse replied, "if you keep them. They fine falcons. Maybe we hunt with them again sometime."

Jet started to smile, then tensed, fearful that this was some further mockery. Elise felt her heart ache for his injured pride.

"We wagered them," Jet said stiffly. "We can pay our debts."

"What is mine is mine to give," Lady Blysse said reasonably. "Please take."

"As a favor," Sapphire said, "to a scion of House Kestrel, we will do so."

With this, to Elise's relief, the expedition was finally over. The bloody carcasses of the unlucky pigeons were gathered into sacks and Earl Kestrel bowed deeply to the assembled company. In his rich, well-schooled bardic turns of phrase he thanked them all for gracing himself and his ward with their company, praised the falcons that had provided them with such fine sport, and invited them all to attend a banquet that evening. The centerpiece would be the game killed this morning.

The last was a formality, an almost ritual ending to a large hawking party like this, so much so that Elise had already chosen what dress and jewels she would wear this evening. She looked around for Jet, hoping that now that the hunt was ended he would return to her. Her beloved, however, was deep in conference with Lady Blysse and Sapphire, hotly arguing the varying merits of gyrfalcons and peregrines.

Elise's mare was more than willing to trail after the other horses. Although her thoughts were elsewhere, Elise chattered lightly with the other ladies, commenting on the pleasures of the outing. Only after they had returned their horses to the stable attendants and were re-entering the castle did Aurella Wellward say softly into her daughter's ear:

"Lady Melina spoke with me this afternoon about something that may be of interest to you. After you've freshened, would you meet me in my solar here in the castle?"

"Yes, Mother," Elise replied, her heart singing with anticipation and sudden terror. Her feet were so light that she could hardly keep from running up the stairs to her room.

DOUBTS AND FEARS plagued Elise as Ninette laced her into a clean sundress and helped plait her hair into a gleaming coil that would crown her head. When Elise entered her mother's parlor, she hoped that Lady Aurella could not see how nervous she was, but was certain that her rapidly beating heart must give her away.

Aurella was sitting by a round window through which sunlight spilled, transforming the embroidery thread spread across her lap into silken gems. On a frame nearby was the piece she had been working on since the previous spring, a heavy green wool waistcoat embroidered with a hawk perched on a well, a bowman standing to one side. The picture was an allusion to her family joined to Ivon's.

"Come in, Elise," Aurella said, choosing a hank of yellow thread from those arrayed on her lap and returning the rest to her fat, round wicker embroidery basket, "and close the door behind you."

Elise did so, crossing to sit on a chair where she would not block her mother's light. In the winter, the stone flags would be piled deep with rugs, but to counter the summer heat they were left bare and the hard leather soles of her shoes tapped out an almost military tattoo against them.

"Melina tells me," Aurella began without preamble, "that her son Jet desires a betrothal to you. She said that her first instinct was to refuse, but on further consideration she saw that there were advantages. With these in mind, she is willing to permit Jet to become betrothed to you—if your father and I agree, of course."

She paused, snipping off a length of thread before moving to another part of her pattern. Elise held her breath, knowing her mother was not finished.

"I do not know whether or not Melina has consulted yet with her husband. She was careful not to comment on that point as his refusal—real or feigned—would end any decision with no loss of face to anyone involved. My guess, however, is that Jet has spoken only to her. Melina's children must be well aware that without her approval nothing can be done.

"For my own reasons, I have not yet spoken with your father. Before I do so, cruelly raising hopes that have begun to fade, I wanted to know if you had considered the disadvantages of Jet's proposal."

"Disadvantages, Mother?" Elise, her mind alive with images of her handsome suitor and a queen's crown, was shocked.

"Disadvantages, daughter." Though her needle continued stitching elaborate details with the ease of a professional tirewoman, Aurella's mien was as serious as if she were advising Queen Elexa. "For one, you will make an enemy—perhaps lifelong—of Sapphire Shield. She will not easily forgive an attempt to supplant her as the favored candidate for heir. This will cause you trouble even if you succeed in your gambit for the throne, but if, despite your manipulations, she becomes queen, she will be in a position to make you miserable."

"Sapphire will still have her family holdings," Elise said stubbornly. "If I am queen, she will need to placate me—not the other way around."

"Darling daughter, you," Aurella sighed, "are naive. And don't forget, betrothal to Jet will not guarantee that you will become queen. Have you considered your aunt Zorana's potential wrath? Even if you can handle a rival from your own generation, how would you deal with her?"

"Aunt Zorana," Elise said stiffly, her woodenness a cover for the rapid racing of her mind as she considered problems that had never arisen in Jet's rosy depiction of their future, "is the king's niece, true, but once this is settled, surely she will return to ambitions that had been hers before Princess Lovella's death started this play for the Eagle Throne. Aunt Zorana has four children to think of and certainly will court my favor toward their greater benefit. In any case, if I become queen, her son will be the best choice for the next Baron Archer. What advantage would there be to making an enemy of me?"

Aurella shook her head ruefully. "Always, always, your solution is based on the assumption that this gambit guarantees you the throne. I assure you, it may raise your chances, but it provides no guarantee. King Tedric is a strange man, old and fickle, embittered by the loss of the surety that his blood will follow him to the throne. I wouldn't put it past him to pass over all his squabbling nieces and nephews and choose this newcomer Blysse instead. She showed character today and our kingdom is beset by rivals. With Bright Bay at our frontiers, strength and decisiveness may matter more to the king in his heir than possession of the right bloodline. Don't forget, too, that Blysse has House Kestrel to back her. Kestrel may not be as prestigious a house as that of the Peregrine or the Gyrfalcon, but it is as old and very respected."

"And if King Tedric selects Lady Blysse, I," Elise said patiently, determined to demonstrate she had gotten her lesson by heart, "would still have made enemies for myself."

"And for your father and me as well," Aurella reminded her. "Since you are a minor, your betrothal must have our blessing. We will put our heads into the furnace along with you."

"Isn't the possible gain worth the risk?" Elise asked, almost pleading.

"What gain?" Aurella said with deceptive mildness. "The throne of Hawk Haven or handsome Jet Shield for a husband? I think the first is worth the gamble, but I am doubtful about the second."

"Still!" Elise said, leaning forward, her hands clasped so tightly that her knuckles grew white. "Still! Shall we sit back and let ourselves be swept out of the running? Here is a chance to ally our house with another, to make the king's decision easier, for he can please both his brother and his sister by his selection!"

"That is the best point in favor of this match," Aurella agreed. "Then you wish me to speak with your father?"

Elise swallowed, met her mother's gaze, and was overwhelmed by the realization that for the first time she was being spoken to woman to woman, not as a daughter by a mother.

"Yes, ma'am, I do," she said.

Aurella nodded. "Tonight, then, after the banquet."

In a single, swift, graceful movement, Lady Aurella rose, leaving her fancy work behind her on the chair. She was gone before Elise rose from her dutiful curtsy, but not before Elise saw the single tear glittering like dew on her rose-petal cheek.

XI

HANDLESS, FOOTLESS, armless, kneeless, unmoving, unbound. She drifts. Eagle-winged, free to ride air as warm and firm as Blind Seer's fur. Suddenly bound. Unable to move even within human limitations. Time spiralling into memory's clouds.

Smaller, shorter, weaker, afraid, alone, lost. Cold and hungry, the raw meat the wolf has dropped before her as inedible as a rock would have been. The little girl cries and her tears wet against her face are the only thing warm about her. Trembles, coughs, lungs protesting air's intrusion. Wishing she was gone where the others are gone. Shrill whining in her ears, keening of the wolves who have taken her to themselves only to watch her shrivel and fade like autumn leaves under winter's blast.

Dying. That's what she's doing! Dying. The realization comes as a faint surprise, rather like learning that it is her birthday: an abstract thing, anticipated but not understood. *Dying. How very odd.*

Little people die. She'd seen that during the first days when they'd come with Prince Barden into the wild woods. Jeri Punkinhair had died of a cough that wouldn't go away, no matter how warmly his parents wrapped him, no matter how dutifully he'd choked down brews of honey and tree bark, hot broth, stewed herbs. Little people die, twisting and bending like *seedlings that never quite get a start on growing. Now she is dying. She wonders why if this was to come she hadn't been burned in the fire. This new dying seems a dreadful waste of effort.*

Lying on the cold stone floor, coughing from her smoke-seared lungs, weeping until there are no more tears, breathing until there is no more air. Around her, wailing like the mournful moans of the winter wind around the cabin chimney, she hears howling as the wolves voice their despair. Little person, pale flame, soon just so much meat.

She is fading, doesn't even flinch when one arm, then the other is grasped between fanged jaws. Pain can't seem to get through the dying. Astonishment, maybe, just a touch, feeling that the breath of the wolves is warm.

The wolves drag her through the autumn woods, big moon heavy and orange watching from the horizon. Her feet trail behind her, legs as limp as those of the rag doll Blysse carried with her nearly everywhere. She gave it a new name each week, usually the name of some wonderful heroine from the Old Country stories Sweet Eirene told around the fire each night.

Is she become a rag doll? Are the wolves become children? It seems quite possible, there on the twilight fringes of dying. With some faint spark of herself, the little girl holds on to the idea. Even a rag doll has more life than does a dying child.

The moon stops moving in the sky. Then she realizes that the wolves have lowered her to the ground, released her arms. She feels a flicker of regret for the loss of their hot breath. Her own breath is cold and thick, full of slime. The effort to draw in air is not worth the pain. She stops.

Relief is temporary. Something presses against her mouth, forces her to draw in air. She struggles but a heavy and furry weight pins her legs. Eventually, she loses all sensation except for the searing ache of her lungs being forced to draw in breath.

Upon waking she discovers herself bathed in warm mist. Rough hands, coarse but not unkind, rock her gently. Silence wraps her but for a faint hiss of steam and a terrible hacking that she realizes is her own coughing.

Distantly, she feels each curving rib fragile as a twig, bending beneath the racking coughs. The sensation is sufficiently distant that she can dismiss it as unconnected to her relative comfort.

Timelessness passes. Vaguely she knows snowfall and blizzard wind. More immediate is warmth, the caress of those coarse hands. Sometimes voices.

She cannot be permitted to die. We will need her.

Someday someone must speak our talks. Cross between worlds. Separation forever is impossible.

Nearly dead. If she comes back, she will be strong enough to venture into life.

Purpose. And we will teach her, though never will she know our presence. You will be good parents to her, but she is too weak to survive without other aid.

A long journey, this one. Moons will die and be born before it ends.

Awakening into spring. Pale hazes green and yellow on the branches. Scent of blossoms in the warm air. Birdsong and joyful plashing of running water. Running outside on trembling legs, just barely firm enough to bear her weight. Falling. Tumbling against a furry flank that cushions her descent. Strawberries and fish. Warm blood drunk from a rabbit's throat. Crunching stems of watercress. Hot liver.

She has always been a wolf.

THE ANNOUNCEMENT that Lady Elise Archer was to be formally betrothed to Jet Shield was met with excitement and glee by most, a delightful new twist in the engaging entertainment surrounding the selection of an heir by the king. In tavern and shop, market stall and street corner, the townspeople gathered to gossip about this new development. The politically savvy gladly explained to their slower comrades how this gambit would enhance the chances of either Elise or Jet (or one of their fathers) being chosen as King Tedric's heir.

In the manses and suites occupied by the potential heirs of King Tedric, the news was greeted more soberly. Grand Duke Gadman consulted with his son, Lord Rolfston, and daughter-in-law, Lady Melina, about how best to exploit this new twist without completely invalidating Sapphire's claim—should King Tedric not choose to travel down the road that Jet and Elise had made so inviting for him.

GADMAN'S SISTER, Grand Duchess Rosene, sat alone in her private rooms, denying audience to both her son, Ivon, and her daughter, Zorana, steeling herself for the unpleasant but seemingly necessary task of favoring one of her children over the other.

It had not been maternal love but expediency that had kept her from doing so for this long. As long as King Tedric showed no clear favorites, her case was stronger for having two potential candidates in her line. Now Ivon, through Elise, had made a clever play. She hoped that prospect of having Lieutenant Purcel Trueheart succeed in time to the Archer Barony would soothe Zorana.

EARL KESTREL TOOK the news from Valet with the same calm with which Valet presented it. Privately, Norvin Norwood admitted to himself that this plan was a cunning one—one that anticipated a move he had been prepared to make if King Tedric did not acknowledge Blysse his heir. Delay had seemed wise since Tedric had seemed interested in the girl.

Now Norvin Norwood wondered if he had waited too long. In passing, he felt a sudden gladness that his own four children stood between his adopted daughter and the Kestrel duchy. It said something about his own nature that he was unaware of the irony in this thought.

SAPPHIRE SHIELD, SUDDENLY ousted from a position she had viewed as favored, locked herself in her room in the castle. In the hours since her too well informed maid brought her the rumor of Elise's engagement to Jet along with the breakfast tray, Sapphire's mood had shifted from disbelief, to spiteful anger at this betrayal by both parents and brother, to full-blown rage.

Even the trepidation Sapphire had felt when Earl Kestrel had unveiled Prince Barden's presumptive daughter was nothing to this. She dreaded herself discarded, had nearly invaded King Tedric's private rooms to beg him not to forget her claims, put aside that plan as childish, flung herself onto her bed screaming into her pillow and kicking her feet against the feather padding.

Outside the stone walls of the room no one could hear her, but inside the room her maid stood pale and trembling, watching the fit and fearing that her mistress's wrath would be turned against her.

IN YET ANOTHER ROOM there was fury so great as to diminish Sapphire's into nothing by contrast. Lady Zorana Archer tasted the bitterness of certain defeat. There had been times that she had almost felt the crown upon her brow, heard herself proclaimed Queen Zorana the Second. Rolfston's chances had never been as good as he had believed. King Tedric despised him as a crawling worm just like his father, Gadman. Melina Shield ran that family and no one in Hawk Haven would accept a witch as queen.

Ivon was a good enough man, but he had only one heir. Privately, Grand Duchess Rosene had admitted to her daughter that Ivon lacked true regal fire—unlike Zorana, who had been named for Hawk Haven's first and greatest ruler and had modeled herself after her achievements. Since Princess Lovella's death Zorana had even imagined that her ancestress favored her, was guiding her fortunes from the world beyond.

This latest announcement—and her mother's refusal to meet with her—was a betrayal not only of Zorana's hopes but of her private mythology.

Zorana was alone in her chambers when a knock came on her door. Since she had dismissed even her maid, she must answer it herself. Smoothing her hair—though not a bit was out of place, her rages being internal rather than external—Zorana opened it. Prince Newell Shield stood without.

"May I beg admittance, Lady Zorana?"

She opened the door wider in reply. The corridor without was empty. When she sent Aksel away an hour before he must have given orders that she was to be left undisturbed until she herself summoned companionship. Aksel, for all his weakness, had moments of wisdom. He knew that Zorana was not one to lock herself away while secretly craving that others seek her out. Newell, though, Newell she found strangely welcome.

They had been playmates once upon a time, he Lord Newell, son of the duke of House Gyrfalcon, a third son, unlikely to ever be the heir. She had been even lesser ranked, a noblewoman, yes, but not even heiress to her lesser house. When her niece Elise had been born, Zorana became merely Lady Zorana, third in line for the Barony, her title a courtesy she could not pass on to her children. Ambition to be more had germinated then, an ambition unlikely to be achieved through politics but attainable through other avenues.

Some three years or so after Newell Shield had married Princess Lovella there were rumors among the women that there were times the princess, unwilling to trust only in potions and herbals, banned her husband from her bed. At that time, Zorana herself was betrothed to Aksel Trueheart, a marriage arranged for the satisfaction of their houses, not from any affection. Some almost formal pawing in dark corners had awakened in Zorana the terror that she would never feel passion. Then she had seen Newell's gaze upon her, a pale thing that wrapped her like spider's silk: soft and insidiously strong.

They had become lovers during those moon-spans before her wedding, and Zorana had discovered that she was indeed capable of passion.

But Newell had turned from her after her wedding, saying he could not risk fathering another man's heir. Zorana had wondered if the loss of Newell had not been what made her coupling with Aksel so fierce. Certainly Purcel was conceived within a few moon-spans and born slightly before his parents' first anniversary.

Newell had never returned to Zorana's bed, though after a while they had eventually become something like friends. By the time Deste was born, Zorana was feeling some satisfaction from mothering a dynasty that might earn the honors that had been stolen from her.

On this day, though, Zorana forgot what honors young Purcel had already earned, what promise the younger three showed. In the loss of a crown she had dreamed upon her brow, these achievements were ashes. And in this moment of despair, Newell returned to her.

"I thought," he said, crossing to a chair and sitting uninvited, "that you might want some friendly company, company from someone outside of this mess."

He looked older now than when they had been lovers some seventeen years before, his skin showing the lines drawn by long days in sun and weather on land and at sea. Princess Lovella had thought to earn some fame as a naval commander and her husband had voyaged with her. Now the brown hair that had often been bleached tow by the sun was showing grey at the temples. His sideburns and beard were almost completely white. As with some men, this made him more attractive, not less, granting character to his lean features.

Zorana saw the changes and tingled. Here was the face of a stranger, but the eyes that looked out of that face were the same that had once met hers, wild with the passion that sealed their bodies into a single sweaty whole.

"I am grateful for your company," she replied formally, hoping her face did not give away her thoughts. "This engagement is an . . . interesting complication. But you must be delighted, Jet is your nephew."

Newell pursed his lips thoughtfully, as if testing his words before uttering them even in this private place.

"I have never cared for my sister's children as an uncle should," he admitted. "They are too much her creatures, too tightly under her control for me to feel comfortable with them."

His words were so close to Zorana's own thoughts that she did not question them.

"I see," she said softly. "Melina is a strong woman."

"A spoiled youngest," Newell said bluntly. "Always given her way when small and now married to a man who cannot rule her. No wonder the common folk think her a sorceress."

Zorana smiled. "She isn't?"

"No more than I," Newell laughed. "But she has the benefit of the reputation just the same. Or the deficit . . ."

He let the words trail off, but Zorana followed his thought without effort.

"Not all the common folk would be comfortable with a sorceress queen, would they?"

"Nor the noble folk," Newell added honestly. "I have heard words among the rulers of the Great Houses. They think such would be too much like the dark days when the Old World nations ruled their colonies with dark arts as well as honest statecraft."

"Yet Rolfston will not divorce her?"

"For no better cause than ambition?" Newell laughed heartily. "I doubt he could get the king to permit such a divorce. Moreover, I believe he is devoted to Melina in his own way. Their fortunes are hitched together."

"Far easier," Zorana said bitterly, "for them to wed a younger son to a rival and so consolidate two claims."

"To the crown?" Newell asked.

"Of course!"

"More than one family can play at that game," he said, tentatively.

She glared at him. "Impossible!"

"Perhaps I speak too quickly," he said, making as if to rise. "I just thought . . ."

She stopped him. "It is I who speak too hastily. What do you mean?"

"I . . ." Newell paused. She saw him swallow as if the next words were stuck in his throat. "I have always been fond of you, Zorana, in memory of those days we shared so long ago. Childless myself, I find myself looking on others' children as if they are my own."

Zorana felt her face growing hot, thinking how easily—had Newell been less honorable—this might have truly been the case.

"I have just returned from a voyage with our navy. Our kingdom's fleet is small, but we were fortunate and captured a Bright Bay vessel. The captain invited my assistance in questioning our prisoners before they were ransomed. From these I learned how well Allister Seagleam is thought of by his peers. What surprised me more was learning how well he is thought of by our own people. Did you know that he is viewed by some—especially those who have reason to journey between our rival nations—as a pledge child, born to end the wars between us?"

Zorana was cautious. "I have heard some such thing."

"He has children of an age with your own, dear Zorana," Newell said caressingly. "Their grandmother was King Tedric's own sister—they are his grandnieces and grandnephews just as your own children are."

"Just as Elise and Jet are," Zorana said, understanding him and feeling her heart pounding. "And if I betrothed one of my children—Purcel, say—to one of the children of the Pledge Child . . ."

"It might make a claim as persuasive as that offered by the marriage of Lady Elise and young Jet. Moreover," Newell said, rising from his chair and putting his hands on her shoulders, "you would be the best interim ruler in those years following the king's death, before such children could be expected to take on their responsibilities."

"Purcel is but fifteen," Zorana agreed, her voice hushed but the words spilling out faster than she could speak them, "and has a warrior's nature. Even if King Tedric directly named Purcel his heir, it is unlikely our aged monarch could live until Purcel was old enough to take the throne."

"For all Father Tedric's unwillingness to admit it," Newell said sadly, "age has a firm hold on his heart. Allister Seagleam's eldest daughter is four years younger than Purcel. She would be even less ready to take the reins."

Zorana smiled, feeling the crown take shape upon her brow once more. The smile vanished at a sudden thought.

"Doesn't Allister have a son older than my Purcel?"

"Shad," Newell admitted, "is five years older, just shy of his own majority. I understand, however, that he is already betrothed to an heiress of Bright Bay."

"That engagement couldn't be broken without causing much trouble," Zorana said anxiously, "could it?"

"I think not," Newell soothed. "Duke Allister's next son, Tavis, is a few moon-spans younger than Purcel and wholly without Purcel's achievements in battle. I believe he paints pictures or some such."

Relief weakened Zorana so that she sagged to a seat on the edge of her bed. Newell poured her a glass of water from the pitcher on the bedside table and held it to her lips. It seemed the most natural thing in the world that he remained seated beside her when the glass was set by.

"It will not," Zorana said cautiously, "be an easy thing to arrange. I do not believe that I can appeal to my mother, the Grand Duchess Rosene, for assistance."

"That would be unwise," Newell agreed. "If her heart is now set on encouraging young Elise's advancement, she will be hesitant to take this great gamble when she sees a sure thing."

"Yes," Zorana frowned. "Yet I will need a liaison. I cannot ride to Bright Bay myself and make this proposition."

Newell cleared his throat. "If you would permit me . . . I am frequently called into areas where such duties would not be impossible—nor terribly obvious. Your hand need not be shown until all is ready."

"Would you?" Zorana turned and found herself flushing again at his closeness.

"I said before," Newell purred, "that being childless, I must think of others' children as my own."

"There will be details to work out," she said quickly, "letters to draft, conditions to consider, some means of stalling King Tedric's announcement of an heir until we can show him this newest option."

Newell slid his arm about her waist. "That can all be worked out."

"Then we are in this together?"

"Most definitely."

They sealed their agreement with something far more intimate than a handshake.

IN THE TWO weeks following the announcement of her engagement to Jet Shield, Elise tried to believe that she was completely happy. Certainly both in public or in private Jet was as attentive as she could desire. Indeed, in private she became grateful that Ninette was always within call. Otherwise, Jet's ardor might overcome her own good sense. She was startled to discover what fires lurked within her and how easily he could kindle them—sometimes with as little as the brush of his lips across her cheek or a smoldering look that gave a heretofore unsuspected meaning to the most innocent-seeming comment.

Her eighteenth-birthday celebration—a week after their betrothal had been announced—had been a wonderful festivity, marred only by her gathered relatives' sour looks when Elise warmly welcomed Lady Blysse and Derian Carter to the group.

However, ever since the falconry party, Elise had wandered out to the upper castle meadows most mornings, joining in the casual gatherings, teaching the feral woman how to weave daisy crowns and other silly things, and finding herself quite enjoying Lady Blysse's—or rather Fire-keeper's—odd perspective on human culture.

Elise had needed a new friend. Lady Aurella's prediction that Sapphire would be furious with her had come true—a thing Elise had not thought would trouble her so much given how annoying she often found her cousin. Perhaps it was not just that Sapphire had cut out all contact with Elise; maybe it was that she looked so sad, so hurt. Oddly, Aunt Zorana, whose wrath Elise *had* feared, was so contented-seeming that Elise's father was moved to comment (in private) that he wondered if his sister was pregnant again.

As for Ivon Archer, he viewed his daughter with unconcealed pride and joy. Although the necessity of training Elise to manage the Archer estates had forced them frequently into each other's company, they had never been close. Privately, Elise had thought she was a disappointment to her father: too quiet, too scholarly, too uninterested in the martial games he had enjoyed with his own father before the elder Purcel's death in battle a few years before Elise herself was born.

Strangely enough, the fact that Aurella Wellward apparently shared the same weakness that had made her aunt Elexa barren had brought Ivon closer to his wife, but had distanced him from his daughter. Sometimes Elise thought that he privately blamed *her* in some fashion for Aurella's long illness following Elise's birth and her subsequent infertility.

Now, however, that was swept away as if it had never been. Ivon Archer clearly viewed Elise's desire to become betrothed to Jet as a mark of her loyalty to her father and his cause. With that one decision, Elise had removed all the deficits of being an only child, allied her family to their greatest potential rival for the throne, and made her father the most likely choice for King Tedric's heir.

Anticipating with an innocent enthusiasm that reminded Elise not a little of Jet on the day he first proposed, Ivon took his daughter on long rides through the countryside so that they could discuss statecraft. She had learned more about her father in these two weeks than she ever knew before and felt—a little uncomfortably—that he was far more human and vulnerable than she had ever imagined.

But no matter how hugely Baron Archer dreamed, the reality remained that King Tedric had not selected an heir from among his nieces and nephews, nor from among their children. Nor had he sent Lady Blysse away, keeping her thus tacitly beneath the mantle of his favor. Duty to his own estates and family called Earl Kestrel from the castle from time to time, but Blysse remained in residence, a lithe, dark-haired figure, gradually becoming more sophisticated in her manners and seemingly unaware of the shadow she had cast on everyone else's plans.

Fumbling at her throat, Elise fingered the exquisite jet carving of a wolf's head that Jet had given her as a betrothal gift. She had given Jet a token of her own society patron, the Lynx, worked in gold with tiny emerald eyes.

Exchanging society tokens was a long-standing tradition, dating back to when the Old Country still reigned. The exchange of tokens provided a symbolic pledge that one's own society would now be looking out for the soon-to-be wedded partner.

Touching the token, however, did not make Elise decide to seek out Jet. Rather she resolved to go see the real wolf in her life—Firekeeper.

Neither Derian nor Ox answered the door to the suite. Instead, a slightly familiar man with something Kestrel about his dark hair and hawk nose stood in the opening. Slightly disconcerted, for she had been lost in her own reflections, Elise fumbled for words:

"Is Fire . . . I mean Lady Blysse in?"

"Firekeeper's fine with me," the man said, opening the door wider and giving Elise a friendly smile. "Since that's what she insists on being called. However, I'm sorry to disappoint you, but she's not in."

"Oh."

Stepping back, Elise started to make her apologies, but the man continued:

"I think she's in the kitchen gardens. Derian has the day off to visit his parents and so Firekeeper went down to the gardens soon after breakfast."

"The kitchen gardens?" Elise asked, the question coming out despite herself. "Firekeeper?"

"She discovered them sometime after that first hawking expedition," the man replied. "She's completely fascinated by the concept that people can grow their own food. I guess the gardens at West Keep weren't very extensive or maybe she just had too much else to learn then."

He stopped suddenly. "I realize I'm being terribly familiar," he said.

"I, of course, know who you are, but I don't suppose you remember me. Our circles haven't crossed that frequently."

Just as Elise was realizing who this must be, the man made a deep and formal bow:

"Sir Jared Surcliffe, at your service, my lady. I am a somewhat distant younger cousin of the Earl Kestrel."

"Lady Elise Archer," Elise replied with appropriate formality, and curtsies. Then she smiled. "I remembered you just as you introduced yourself. When I was quite small, my parents took me out to the Kestrel estates. You were there, too, and very patiently supervised me and Earl Kestrel's boys while we rode our ponies. Later you took us out fishing by that wonderful stone bridge—the one that looked as if it must have trolls under it. We've shared company since, but I hope you don't mind that that particular occasion is the one I remember best."

"Not at all." Sir Jared grinned, an open expression that made him look much as he had ten years before, not at all like the mature man of twenty-four or twenty-five that he must be. For the first time, Elise realized that there was something vaguely sad about the grown man's expression that had not been present in the boy's. She struggled to remember what she could about him.

"I'm being very rude keeping you standing in the hallway," Sir Jared added. "Would you like to come in and wait, or shall we stroll down to the gardens and make certain that Blind Seer hasn't eaten one of the gardener's sons?"

Elise giggled and was immediately horrified. Jared Surcliffe didn't appear to notice.

"I think," Elise replied, cloaking herself in the shreds of her dignity, "that I would like to go down to the garden. Blind Seer may not be a problem, but the falcon might be."

Jared laughed. "Then if the Lady Archer . . ."

"Elise, please," she hastily interrupted. "No one calls me Lady Archer yet except on terribly formal occasions. I don't need to use the title until I reach my majority."

"And you're not in a great hurry to get there," Surcliffe mused, almost to himself, as he stepped out into the hallway and shut the door behind him. "Now, there is a wisdom one doesn't often see in a young lady."

Elise felt flattered rather than insulted and, as Sir Jared's comment had been spoken quietly, she avoided a direct reply. Instead she walked beside him down the corridors and toward the stairs leading out into the gardens, searching her memory for everything she could remember about her new companion.

Surcliffe, she recalled from her geography lessons, was a minor holding in the Norwood grant. Theoretically, it belonged to the Kestrels, but in practice those small holdings passed from parent to child along similar lines of inheritance followed in other matters. Only if the Surcliffes mismanaged the estate or did something horrible or the line died out completely would the Norwood family dare step in and reassign the land. Thus, for all practical purposes, Jared Surcliffe was a minor noble, never mind that under Queen Zorana's rules restricting titles he did not even merit the title "Lord."

Jared's knighthood was a different matter. He had earned it in the same battle in which Crown Princess Lovella had lost her life. Assigned to the princess's company in a support capacity—as a medic, Elise thought—he had been among the first to see the princess fall. Despite being unarmored and unarmed, Surcliffe had raced out into the field. Using Princess Lovella's own spear, he had held back the attackers until Lovella's troops rallied. Then he had done his best to save Lovella's life through his medical arts.

Lovella's wounds had been too severe to be mended—even by one with the healing talent—but due to Sir Jared's care the crown princess had lived long enough to bid both her husband and her parents farewell. King Tedric—some said at Lovella's express request—had made Jared Surcliffe a knight of the Order of the White Eagle, the highest honor in the land. Elise had been present at his investiture, one figure in the silent and awed crowd. She blushed now to think that she could have failed to recognize him.

She allowed herself some leeway, for the man striding along beside her was very different from the solemn, formally clad figure who had knelt in front of his king and queen to receive their thanks and blessing. He seemed younger, more relaxed, even in some strange way playful. Perhaps, Elise thought, she could almost be forgiven.

Then she realized that Surcliffe was speaking to her and apologized:

"I'm sorry, Sir Jared, I was distracted by my thoughts. May I beg you to repeat yourself?"

"No need to beg, Lady Elise," Surcliffe said. "I was offering you my congratulations on your recent engagement. I've met Jet Shield in passing and he seems like a fine fellow."

Elise nodded. "Thank you. We've known each other since we were children and I've always been fond of him."

Fond, she thought. *Fond! Is that the way to speak of the man who has captured my heart and my hand?*

Yet, somehow, in Jared Surcliffe's company she could not go into the effusions that were so easy when she was among her lady friends. All of them were more than willing to praise every aspect of Jet: his form, his manners, his seat on a horse, even the color of his hair and the line of his eyebrows.

Fleetingly, Elise found herself thinking of her mother and the tear she had glimpsed on her cheek. To distract herself, she asked Surcliffe:

"Are you married, Sir Jared?"

"I am," he replied stiffly, "a widower. My wife died in childbirth three years ago. Our baby died as well. Since then I have occupied myself with other things."

"I'm sorry," Elise murmured, not certain whether she was expressing sympathy for his loss or apologizing for her tactlessness.

Certainly she must have heard about his bereavement! When he had been knighted every aspect of the new hero's character and person would have been discussed both in meetings and in more informal gossip sessions.

"Thank you," Sir Jared said, accepting her sympathy. "My marriage was arranged, but as with you and your Jet, I had known my bride since we were children together. Losing her came as a shock."

They were out of the castle now and crossing the rose gardens, following the path down and around to where the kitchen gardens stood within their stone-walled enclosure. Deftly, Sir Jared turned the conversation to the shade of a particularly lovely yellow and orange rose. Elise replied, telling him how the bush had been brought from New Kelvin when she was but a child, and so they both were saved from further awkward and painful revelations.

❀

"NO, DEARIE," HOLLY Gardener said, coming over to demonstrate. "Don't pull the carrot by the fluffy part at the top. Grasp here at the base, firmly, and give it a tug."

Firekeeper obeyed, eager to do this right. She was becoming desperately fond of this bent old woman with her wispy white hair. Holly was the only person she had met thus far who didn't think of Firekeeper as a potential heir to the throne. To Holly, she was just a girl who wanted to learn about gardens. In her presence, Firekeeper somehow felt younger, but without any of the vulnerability her youth and relative lack of strength had given her among the wolves.

Over the days that Firekeeper had been visiting the gardens and attached orchard, Holly had trusted her with more and more duties. At first Firekeeper had been permitted only to carry baskets and to fetch water from the well, but even these tasks had delighted her, giving exercise to muscles going soft from no greater challenge than occasional horseback rides and her daily romps with Blind Seer.

Lately, Firekeeper had graduated into picking fruit and vegetables. The late-summer harvest was beginning and even with the extra help hired from the town the castle's own staff could barely keep up with their duties. Firekeeper hoped that she could learn to pick the vegetables without harming either them or the marvelous plants that bore them. Then she would free another to do those jobs she had yet to master.

On her second try, the carrot slid freely from the dirt. Firekeeper gazed upon it, fat and orange, lightly dusted with soil, with as much pride as if she had grown it herself.

"Good job, dearie!" Holly said, her praise falling sweetly on Firekeeper's ears, for the gardener could be as quick to criticize as her name plant was to prick unwary fingers. "Now, if you wish, you may harvest the rest of that row. Leave the little carrots to grow into the space left by their fellows."

Firekeeper obeyed. A pack member all her life, it felt good to be contributing to the survival of the whole. Even though most of her days as a wolf had been spent foraging for herself, still the Ones had often trusted her to watch over the pups. Sometimes they even sent her ahead to scout the herds of elk or deer. In the moon cycles that had followed her departure from west of the Iron Mountains, all of Firekeeper's basic needs had been provided for. Moreover, someone else was always more skilled than she in the tasks at hand.

This last had become particularly irksome since they had come to live in the castle. Here, even Derian—who had never been without some task—now found himself idle except for his duties teaching Firekeeper. Firekeeper, however, had a limited attention span for lessons in etiquette and dancing. When she rebelled, Derian had learned to let her be.

For his part, Blind Seer had no difficulty accepting idleness. A wolf proverb stated: "Hunt when hungry, sleep when not, for hunger always returns."

This afternoon, faithful to his creed, the wolf drowsed in the shade of a crab-apple tree whose fruits had already been harvested to make jelly. The garden staff detoured widely to avoid him. Consequently, Firekeeper and the old woman were alone in this particular garden.

Overhead, Elation circled easily above the neat square and rectangular plots, occasionally stooping upon some luckless rodent. The first few times the huge bird had plummeted from the sky, she had scared the wits out of the gardening staff. Now that they had grown accustomed to her, they were rather delighted in having a creature usually reserved for noble sport take part in their routine. They had nicknamed her "Garden Cat"—an indignity the falcon accepted with her usual arrogant grace.

Firekeeper heard a shrill call from above.

"Company coming! Elise and Doc! They'll be upon you in a moment."

Firekeeper sniffed the breeze, but it was blowing from the wrong direction. Even if it had not been, she doubted she would smell anything but the heavy scents of dirt, manure, bruised leaves, fresh vegetables, and hot sunlight.

Carrot in her hand, she rose, turning to face the gate in the stone wall. She greeted her friends as they passed through:

"Elise, Doc," she said with measured solemnity. "What brings you here?"

"Our feet," Jared replied with equal formality. "What else?"

Firekeeper grinned then. "I've been picking . . ."

"Pulling," interrupted Holly, who, like the rest of those Firekeeper named as friends, believed it was her job to correct the wolfling's speech at every turn.

"Pulling," Firekeeper repeated obediently, "carrots. For the root cellar, for the castle, for the winter. Also for the kitchen today and so that the carrots still in the ground can grow wider."

She shook her head, still amazed by the varied wonders of gardening. Elise broke into a broad smile that Firekeeper far preferred to the strained and weary look that had been on Lady Archer's face when she had entered the garden.

"Will you introduce me to your friend?" Elise asked, this both a real request and a subtle prompt for Firekeeper to practice her social graces.

Firekeeper nodded, straightened, and gestured with the carrot. Unconsciously, she adopted the mannerisms of Steward Silver, a woman she quietly admired for her ability to always know the right way through the tangled maze of human social customs.

"Lady Elise . . ." She paused, glanced at Elise. "Or should I say Lady Archer?"

"Lady Archer is best if you want someone to know my social connections," Elise explained. "Lady Elise if you think they already know them, since you know that I prefer to be called simply Elise."

Firekeeper still felt uncertain, a state of mind not helped by Blind Seer's quiet sniggering from under the crab-apple tree. The wolf would not admit that he, too, found human customs fascinating, secure that *he* at least would never be forced to use them. Doc came to her rescue:

"In such circumstances, Firekeeper, I have found that it is always better to err on the side of greater formality."

Elise nodded. "True."

Holly Gardener had been watching this byplay with steady, earth-rooted calm, her hands still busy sorting fresh-picked squash into that which would be sent to the castle kitchens and that which would go to the canning sheds.

Firekeeper began again, "Lady Elise Archer, Sir Jared Surcliffe—may I have the pleasure of presenting my friend Goody Holly Gardener. Holly, these are my friends."

Rising to her feet with the aid of a gnarled piece of thorn wood polished bright with beeswax and long use, Holly curtsied as deeply as her arthritic knees would permit.

"I am honored," she said in her creaky voice, "to have the heir to House Archer and a knight of the White Eagle grace my garden. Will you take a bench in the shade along the wall and allow me to send for something cool to drink?"

Firekeeper shook her head in admiration. She had completely forgotten her duties, but Holly had rescued her with the grace and dignity most of the nobles reserved for their most formal interactions.

It never occurred to her that for Holly Gardener this meeting might be one of those formal occasions. Firekeeper's own awe of the gardener's skill was so great that she placed Holly's worth far above that of the relatively useless members of the court such as Lord Rolfston or his father, Grand Duke Gadman.

Elise answered, "I thank you for your offer of a drink, Grandmother, but I see the well just across the way. Let me get the water and you remain where you are."

Jared grinned. "Not to be outdone, let me lend a hand so that we won't put you too behind in your tasks."

When Holly began to protest, made honestly anxious by the thought of a knight of the realm picking vegetables, he stilled her with a hand on her shoulder.

"Goody, I may have this fancy title, but I am nothing more than a younger son of landholders of a small, rocky estate on Norwood lands. By helping you, I may help myself someday. Please, don't protest further."

Firekeeper held her breath, but there was no need to intervene. Holly settled back onto the low, three-legged stool she used to spare her knees.

"Thank you, son," she said, her smile showing only a few missing teeth. "Tell me about your lands."

"My parents' land as of yet," Jared began, "and then my brother's. I am the third born."

Firekeeper knelt in the dirt and started pulling carrots again, pleased as always to learn something more about how "real" humans—as opposed to those who resided here in the castle—lived. Elise came over with a maple bucket half full of cool well water and silently offered Firekeeper the dipper. She was somewhat clumsy in her task, but Firekeeper recognized that clumsiness as something she saw far too often in herself—unfamiliarity rather than ineptitude.

Jared continued talking while thinning carrots from the row alongside Firekeeper's:

"Let's see, the land was in our family before Queen Zorana established Hawk Haven. Back then it was just a frontier farm—and not one that was doing very well, either. My ancestors had ambition but not much luck in the land they held. At first they eked out their living selling furs and burning charcoal, but that can't go on forever. The animals either die or get smart enough to leave and you run out of hardwood.

"So they had to take to serious farming, a thing that apparently didn't delight my great-great-whatever-grandfather a whole lot. When the fellow who would become the first Duke of Norwood called for volunteers to support Zorana Shield against that skunk, Gustin Sailor, Grandpappy went happily. He did well, too, gaining both booty and honor. When

Queen Zorana created the Norwood grant, my family was given the Sur-cliffe holding in perpetuity."

Firekeeper hadn't followed all of this, but enough so that she had a question: "If they not hunt or grow, how did they eat?"

Doc rose, stretching the kinks out of his calf muscles. "Well, some of them became vassals to the Kestrel family—earning Kestrel credit, some of which was sent home. There's always been at least one member of the family stubborn enough to want to stay and make something of the land. Most recently, my own grandmother decided to set in grapevines. My father has continued their cultivation and we're just getting to the point where we're proud enough of our wine to sell it outside of the Kestrel grant."

Elise, sitting on a bench in the shade, the bucket between her feet, asked, "And you, Sir Jared?"

"Call me Doc, if you don't mind," he said. "The other is so formal."

"Doc, then," she said, "if you don't mind calling me Elise."

"Not at all. I'd be pleased," he replied. "To answer your question, Elise, right now I'm one of those who's earning money to send home. Earl Kestrel has been a good patron. We're nearly twenty years apart in age and not nearly as closely related as he sometimes represents. My parents are both in good health and hopefully will not become ancestors for a long while yet—they're of Norvin's generation. So I've learned medicine and am trying to see something of the country.

"Meanwhile, I send home a portion of my earnings or—even better— hunt out interesting vine cultivars and vintnering techniques and send them along. My brother and sister have stayed closer to home. My sister is an attendant upon Duchess Norwood and my brother apprenticed to a master wine maker for ten years. He's home again now and all afire to put his new knowledge to work."

The talk continued in this vein for a while, Holly Gardener contributing a shrewd thought or two from her vast wealth of garden lore. Firekeeper listened, pulling carrots until they were all thinned, then hauling water to the rows.

After a while, a distant bell announced that the time for the evening meal was drawing near. Elise sighed.

"Duty calls. I have promised my mother that I would go with her and the queen to a banquet at Duke Wellward's city house."

She glanced over at Firekeeper, her blue eyes twinkling, and asked, "Tell me, Lady Blysse, what is Duke Wellward's relation to me?"

Firekeeper growled, very low, very quiet. This new addition to her education, the learning of who were the rulers of the Great Houses and how they related to the players for the throne, made her head ache. Once again, she thought that wolves solved such questions so much more simply. Elise, however, was merciless in her persistence.

"Well, Firekeeper?"

"Duke Wellward is your mother's father," Firekeeper began, "your grandfather. Your other grandfather is Purcel Archer, the hero who died in the Battle of Salt Water in the Year 85. Your grandmother is Grand Duchess Rosene.

"Holly," Firekeeper added inconsequentially, knowing from Elise's approving smile that she had got the complicated scheme of relationships right, "has been telling me stories about Purcel Archer. I think I would have liked him."

Jared Surcliffe grinned. "Given how you have taken to the bow from the first time Race showed you how to use one, I suspect that you would have indeed."

He got to his feet.

"Lady Elise, may I escort you back to the castle?"

She nodded and Firekeeper thought that she saw the faintest hint of a blush touch her cheeks.

"Thank you, Sir Jared."

"Doc," he reminded, and she smiled. Doc glanced over at Firekeeper. "Are you coming back with us?"

"I help Holly Gardener carry the baskets in first," Firekeeper replied. "Then I hurry to the castle in time for dinner. Will Derian be back?"

"Not yet. He has permission to remain out until after dinner."

Bending to pick up one of the baskets of carrots, Firekeeper watched them leave. Behind her, she heard Holly say softly:

"I like that Elise. Maybe she *would* make a good queen after she has some years on her. She's not too proud to carry water to quench a servant's thirst."

"And Doc?"

"I like him, too," Holly assured her. Then she added softly, so softly that Firekeeper didn't think she was meant to hear, "He'd be a far better king than that Jet Shield."

XII

THE HOT SUMMER WEATHER prompted Derian's parents to suggest a picnic along the banks of the Flin River, upstream of the city. The entire family rode there in a wagon Derian remembered as being creaky when he was Brock's age, pulled by an old draft horse to whom Colby and Vernita had given an honorable retirement three years before. Once arrived, they staked out a section for themselves and spent the day following quiet pursuits: tossing horseshoes, rolling hoops, singing rounds and collapsing into uncontrollable laughter when someone became tangled in the words and tune.

Derian drifted into the easy relaxation that came when someone else was in charge and quite capable of doing whatever needed to be done. Quite willingly, he would have stayed along the riverbank into the long twilit evening hours, but Brock rather self-importantly announced that tonight was a meeting of the Bear Society and he must attend. In any case, the gnats were rising, making the grassy verge less appealing.

When they returned to the house, Damita made excuses to go out. She did indeed have a "sweet'a"—or at least imagined that she did, a youth of sixteen who was apprenticed to their jeweler uncle. Next to this beau, the entertainment offered by an older brother—even one who had been living in the king's own castle—had limited appeal. Knowing this,

Colby and Vernita gave in with good humor when Damita asked to go out to the nearby market square, where she would doubtless cluster with a group of girls her own age and giggle at the boys.

Derian's own onetime romance with the baker's daughter had not survived his long absence and his relocation to the castle—especially as he was there in the role of guardian to another girl. His opportunities to cultivate new romances had been limited.

Unlike Ox and Race, who were clearly classed as servants, his role was more that of an attendant, a subtle distinction that ruled out the riotous entertainments the other men could pursue. However, though Derian was slightly more than a servant, he was definitely less than a noble and thus pretty girls like Elise Archer remained out of his reach.

Sometimes this bothered Derian. He found himself brooding that he would become like Valet, a man who apparently had no interests beyond tending his master. But tonight such worries were far away. Derian was content to remain at home and enjoy these last few hours of peace before he must return to his duties.

Once Brock and Damita had departed, the remaining three moved out into the garden. Most of the peaches had been picked and enjoyed, but the narrow leaves of the tree created a pleasant, natural arbor. Derian helped Colby move a few slat-backed chairs and a small, round-topped table into place. Vernita brought drinks from the cool room.

"So, who's the favorite candidate with the guilds these days?" Derian asked with slightly forced jocularity.

The longer he had known Firekeeper, the more he had come to entertain the contradictory feeling that she would be both the best and worst choice for the new monarch. He hadn't been particularly easy with himself when he had learned from his parents a week or so before that the foundling remained high on the list of the people's choices.

"Well," Colby drawled, sipping his chilled tea with an appreciative nod to Vernita, "your wolf-woman is still the romantics' favorite, but those of soberer mind are torn. Some like the idea of Lord Rolfston Redbriar as he is a steady man with a good reputation among his own people. It doesn't hurt that he has a large family, so we won't see a repetition of this uncertainty when he passes on. Others say, and loudly too, that Lord Rolfston is too tightly under the thumb of that sorceress wife of his."

"Derian," Vernita asked, "you've been living in the castle for almost a moon-span now . . ."

"Barely twenty days!" Derian protested.

"Still, long enough to have seen Lady Melina frequently. Do you think she is indeed a sorceress?"

Derian considered this carefully, knowing that his parents were asking his advice and that they would be certain to repeat whatever he said to their friends and trusted associates.

"I have seen no absolute evidence," he said, "but I think that whether or not she is, Lady Melina likes for people to think that she is gifted far beyond those small talents that sometimes crop up here and there. Do you understand?"

"Perfectly," Vernita replied. "She values the awe—even the fear with which she is regarded. I wonder if she realizes that she is hurting her own cause?"

"I doubt it," Derian said. "I don't think she's the kind to ever think even for a minute that she is anything but an asset. Now that her son Jet is engaged to Lady Elise, Lady Melina has not one but two roads to the throne. My feeling is that she's quite smug about it."

"And the young woman Sapphire," Colby asked. "How is she taking having competition within her own family?"

"She isn't thrilled," Derian admitted. "For a day or two she sulked in her room like a child. Then she must have realized—or someone must have told her—that such behavior was not fitting in one who hoped to someday be monarch. She has been much in public since—even invited Firekeeper out for some real hawking and was fairly charming to her, though Firekeeper's Elation did far better than Sapphire's gyrfalcon—but Sapphire's still cool to Elise."

"And Lady Elise," Vernita asked, a slight twinkle lighting her eyes that her own son should be on such familiar terms with the heir to a barony so as to speak of her by her first name, "how does she view the situation?"

"I think she regrets the estrangement from her cousin but is resigned to it. Sapphire Shield is a—to speak mildly—strong personality. I'm certain they've clashed before. But you haven't finished telling me about how the common folk view the field. So far my Firekeeper and Lord Rolfston remain strong contenders . . ."

"And Baron Archer as well," Colby added. "Lady Zorana has fallen behind somewhat, now that there has been an alliance between Lady Elise and Jet Shield."

"What about Allister Seagleam?" Derian asked. "Once you said he was favored by many."

"A few weeks' time hasn't changed that situation much," Colby admitted. "More disturbing are rumors that would seem to indicate that Bright Bay is determined that if Allister wishes to claim his rights he will have support in doing so."

"What do you mean?" Derian asked, sitting up straight in his chair.

"It's the stories coming up the road," Colby said slowly. "You know that we border Bright Bay all along the Barren River."

"Of course."

"Now strategically, the Barren makes a good border. It is rocky most of its length and where it isn't, it's still very wide. There are a few places, however, that are more fordable than others and reports say that a greater concentration of Bright Bay's Stalwarts—or their allies from Stonehold— have been seen in these places."

"I understand," Derian said, watching the map Colby had drawn with his damp fingertip on the tabletop dry into invisibility. "They're watching us, but not yet moving in."

"Right. From my conversations with the army's Master of the Horse— he came by to ask on the quiet if we had any draft animals to sell—the king's officers are aware of the situation but are unwilling to move in lest it prompt the very conflict we would all like to avoid."

"At least," Vernita added, "until King Tedric's heir is selected. It would be a horror if we were to lose the king while engaged in an active war and no one was prepared to take his place. In the infighting for the crown, Hawk Haven could easily be defeated by outside enemies."

"Then," Derian frowned, "the pressure from Bright Bay may force the king to make his decision before the Festival of the Eagle this coming Lynx Moon."

"That," Colby said, "is precisely how I see it. And it may be precisely what Bright Bay wants."

"Or," Vernita countered, "precisely what they don't want. After all an heir chosen may ruin Allister Seagleam's hopes for the throne."

"And we must not forget," Colby added, a wicked twinkle in his eyes, "that Hawk Haven's allies may be putting pressures on King Tedric that we know nothing about. No ruler can be completely indifferent about those countries along the border—even the friendly ones. They can become unfriendly far too easily if offended. It's all rather like running a business."

Derian rubbed his eyes with his hands, thinking of the argumentative and contentious forces gathered at the castle, wondering if any among them could see past the crown's glitter to realize what a tremendous headache wearing it must be.

"I wish we knew," he said, "which way to jump and what the consequences would be!"

"Foresight," Vernita replied calmly, "is the rarest of the gifts and the least understood."

"I wonder," Derian said with an attempt at humor, "if Lady Melina possesses it."

His joke fell flat. Together they sat, sharing in silence the impotence of the common folk when the actions of the great threaten their lives and happiness. Derian wondered what choice he would make if he were King Tedric and was secretly glad that he could leave that choice to the king.

❧

ABOARD A GREAT masted ship anchored off the shore of a small island in the ocean east of the mutual coasts of Hawk Haven and Bright Bay, Prince Newell leaned against the starboard rail. His hair was concealed beneath a seaman's stocking cap; the rest of his person was equally well disguised in a striped jersey and canvas trousers. The disguise worked simply because no one expected a prince to be so clad—especially as the colors he wore were the blue and yellow of a rival navy.

If any were watching him, Newell would seem completely absorbed in studying the eddies created when the water splashed against the hull. Actually, he missed nothing that happened in his vicinity. When a slightly built man crossed the deck with affected casualness and came to stand near him, Newell did not look up to see who it was. Instead he asked rather diffidently:

"Have a good voyage?"

"Yes, thank you," said the man, whose name was Tench. He was a trusted advisor to the throne of Bright Bay. "And yours?"

"Good enough."

Newell's voyage had been, as a matter of fact, less than ideal. He had departed the capital of Hawk Haven two days after convincing Zorana Shield that pursuing her own policy with an enemy power was not traitorous. From the capital he had ridden a series of fast horses to the coast, arriving three days earlier than he had been expected. From there he had helped sail a small, swift cutter to rendezvous with this vessel. At dawn, he would return to that cutter and make the return voyage, all so he could arrive just in time to rendezvous with the Hawk Haven *Wings*, on which he served as Commander of Marines, a task undertaken ostensibly as a means of soothing his broken widower's heart and of giving himself some sense of purpose.

In reality, the game Prince Newell was playing was far more complicated than any of those who associated with him realized, a game that
was meant to make him the next king of Hawk Haven and beyond. The
first step in this process was convincing the government of Bright Bay
that he favored a peaceful resolution of their conflicts. Thus this meeting and the importance of seeming both confident and invulnerable. So
Newell said nothing of his onerous journey, but instead commented languidly:

"And all remains well with Gustin the Fourth?"

All the monarchs of Bright Bay assumed the name Gustin on taking
the crown, men and women alike. It was a curious custom, one that
Prince Newell meant to change when he himself was king of Bright Bay.
That violation of tradition, however, would need to wait until he had
finished with Hawk Haven. One thing at a time.

"All is well with our honored monarch," Tench said. He was a foolish-
looking man who rather resembled a fish, complete with slightly popping
eyes and a perpetually open mouth. "She expresses some concern as to
the situation in Hawk Haven. Although some of her advisors feel otherwise, she is firm in her conviction that her cousin Allister Seagleam is
the only proper heir to that contested throne."

"Glad to know," Newell said languidly, "that she hasn't changed her
mind. Tell your queen that agents interested in her cause have been
working busily. Allister Seagleam should soon receive correspondence
suggesting a way to strengthen his claim to the throne. Her Majesty
should press him to accept the offer."

"Duke Allister," came Tench's stiff reply, "remains difficult. He does
not wish to reign in a land that will not welcome him, no matter how
prepared Her Majesty's military is to support him—no matter how much
the queen presses him."

"Perhaps," Newell said, "we should find a way to make him a hero
in the eyes of both peoples. He would feel himself more welcome then."

What Newell actually planned was for he himself to be that hero. King
Tedric, sadly, would probably not be present to witness those heroics,
but he would hear report of them. The prince was not precisely certain

just what heroic deed he would perform, but he had infinite trust in his ability to manufacture situations to his advantage.

He turned and for the first time looked Tench squarely in the face. "And Stonehold?" he asked, naming Bright Bay's primary ally.

"Remains firm in its support of an independent Bright Bay. However, its ministers are as ever opposed to the uniting of Hawk Haven and Bright Bay. They fear that the larger nation would threaten their own national sovereignty."

"And how shall they prevent this union?" asked Newell scornfully. "Surely sending a few troops to support Bright Bay is a peculiar tactic! What if Bright Bay conquers Hawk Haven?"

"If Bright Bay wins on land," Tench replied, "the victory will be achieved only with Stonehold's support. In that case, Stonehold is confident that it will be able to dictate some of the terms. I believe they favor a partition of the conquered Hawk Haven lands."

Tench added cautiously, "The diplomats from Stonehold have hinted that if Bright Bay permits a marriage alliance with Hawk Haven, Stonehold will be forced to withdraw its military support. Then Bright Bay may be at Hawk Haven's mercy on land."

Fools! Newell thought. *Once Stonehold does that, they lose any chance of subtly pressuring Bright Bay into their way of thinking. All that will remain to them will be force. I must make certain, somehow, that Stonehold does withdraw and then re-enter the field as an opponent. An independent threat would be just the thing to unite both Hawk Haven and Bright Bay behind me.*

Aloud he said, "Stonehold's withdrawal, of course, should be prevented at all cost. This is essential for the delicate balance of power we are relying upon to achieve a peaceful alliance between our nations. If Stonehold withdraws, Bright Bay loses in land power and Hawk Haven may be less willing to treat with it as an equal. Suggest to Queen Gustin the Fourth that even the least rumor of Duke Allister's negotiating with Hawk Haven must be kept the greatest secret."

"I will do what I can," the diplomat said dubiously. "Her Majesty is difficult to guide. She is yet young and impulsive."

"Make her think this secrecy is her own idea," Newell suggested. "Let her think she needs to convince Duke Allister. If she must dominate another's will, she will find she must dominate her own."

"A good thought," Tench replied.

Newell smiled politely. His plans included a future wherein Queen Gustin IV would be his wife. The fact that the headstrong young queen was already married was a difficulty he chose to overlook. Political assassination was not a completely unfamiliar tool to him.

He remembered the days when he and Princess Lovella had squarely faced the terrible consequences that would arise if Crown Prince Chalmer assumed the throne. Despite bearing the name of his illustrious grandfather, Prince Chalmer was an indecisive man. King Tedric had not realized that in the course of educating his son in statecraft he had crushed his spirit as surely as the spirit of a good horse could be ruined by being too severely broken to rein.

Although Chalmer had visited battlefields, he was not a warrior. Lovella was and she feared for her nation if her brother became king. Chalmer's hemming and hawing over the least decision would have meant disaster as his field commanders waited for orders that came too late or were too frequently countermanded.

Since King Tedric refused to acknowledge his son's flaws and promote his daughter over him, then another must do the difficult task for him. Lack of decisiveness was not one of Lovella's flaws. With Newell's assistance, she had engineered her brother's death. Afterward, she had honestly grieved for Chalmer, but, as she told her husband, she had not viewed his slaying as murder, but rather as an execution necessary for the greater good of the state. Simply put, an incompetent commander must be demoted.

Prince Barden had already been disinherited, so only Lovella remained to assist her father. She did her duty well and then, with bitter irony, she died in battle before she could assume the throne, leaving the kingdom in greater peril than it had been in before.

Many a dark night after Lovella's death, Newell had sat alone with only a bottle of strong brandy for company. In his most miserable, most drunken moments he had wondered if Lovella's death had been Chal-mer's revenge reaching out from beyond the grave. When he was sober, those fears dispersed like fog in the heat of the sun. Rapidly, therefore, he learned to stay sober and found himself praised for his strength of character.

Newell was sober when he decided that King Tedric had wronged him by not confirming him as heir to the throne following Lovella's death. Surely he was suited. Certainly he had risked far more to secure the throne than any of those who were now being considered. If Lovella had lived, Newell would have been king. How had her death changed anything?

Newell was sober when he decided that if his rights were not given to him, he would take them. Sober he had remained as he had made his plans, manipulating the policies of Bright Bay with words dropped into eager ears. Sober he had continued as he had watched the political maneuverings of King Tedric's potential heirs with sardonic humor bor-dering on scorn.

Certainly it was symptomatic of the greater chaos that Earl Kestrel thought he could foist off a foundling on the king and convince him to name her his heir. Yet, on meeting Lady Blysse, Newell had rather ad-mired the young woman. For all her lack of manners, there was a buried ferocity to her that reminded him somewhat of Lovella. Never mind. This Blysse Norwood would never see the throne. Indeed, she might well be the very scapegoat he needed. As an outsider, resented by the others, she could easily be blamed for the work of his hands.

Prince Newell chuckled, a dry, humorless sound. His companion checked to see if the sun was vanishing behind a cloud, for surely the day had grown suddenly cooler.

"Now, Lord Tench," Newell said, "I have told you what you want to know. Why don't you tell me . . ."

The next quarter of an hour or so was profitably spent taking notes on the location of certain elements of Bright Bay's fleet, information that Tench gave freely since the two countries were not technically at war.

Wishing to seem the patriot, Newell Shield had given out that his price for supplying gossip about the workings of the Hawk Haven nobility was information that would enable Hawk Haven's navy to avoid accidental clashes with Bright Bay's more powerful fleet. In reality, he hardly cared about such things, except that in some small corner of his mind, that navy already belonged to him.

THE BOWSTRING MADE a sound like a drowsy hornet when Firekeeper released it, but she hardly heard it, hardly felt the slap against her broad, leather wrist guard. Her mind was focused on the target, on the blood-red spot that was its heart. The arrowhead burrowed in three finger widths to the right and she snarled.

"Easy!" Race Forester cautioned her. "It doesn't do to lose your temper. If that had been a deer or a man, you'd have hit soundly."

"Not," Firekeeper replied, "a squirrel or rabbit."

"True," Race agreed, wrenching the arrow from the target. "But at that distance who could know for certain there *was* a rabbit?"

"I," she said with a deliberate calm she did not feel, "would know."

Race nodded. "Yes, I guess you would."

Midmorning had become archery practice time, a thing Earl Kestrel had agreed to willingly since King Tedric might well prefer an heir who would lead in battle to one who must conduct campaigns from the sidelines. For the same reason, Firekeeper was being tutored in elementary swordplay, use of a shield, and some refinements of knife-fighting that her hunting had not revealed to her.

Though she had taken to these elements of martial training with varying degrees of enthusiasm, attempting to teach her lancework had proven useless. As of yet, no horse of sufficient strength and energy had been found that would tolerate her. The patient grey gelding that had carried her from the keep could be coaxed into a walk or even a trot, but certainly not into cantering at a target. Therefore, for now, lancework had been set aside.

A couple of weeks' work had not made Firekeeper an expert in anything. Indeed, other than with a bow or a knife—weapons she had more practice with—she was a greater danger to herself than to any opponent. However, she had learned valuable lessons about how a sword might damage or a shield protect. These lessons could someday be enough to preserve her life.

Blind Seer had taken to practicing with her, though after a few incidents with panicked castle guards they worked together only in the company of Earl Kestrel's retainers.

"I'm not fool enough," the great wolf panted, lunging to get at her beneath the cumbersome shield she carried on her left arm, dexterously avoiding blows from the wooden practice sword, *"to follow where you will lead without learning enough to defend myself. I haven't forgotten, even if you have, how vulnerable my flanks are to arrows."*

Firekeeper tried a shield bash and Blind Seer danced backward, haunches brushing the ground, tail wagging.

"Up close," the wolf continued, *"that's where they'll fear to fire their bows lest they hit their friends, so up close is where I must learn to be."*

He snaked beneath the rim of her shield and clamped his jaws lightly but firmly around her ankle. A single tug and she was flat on her back. Blind Seer leapt upon her and then she pressed the blunt point of her practice dagger into his soft underbelly.

"I cut?" she queried, pushing slightly.

*"You never would have gotten this close if I had **really** crushed your ankle!"* the wolf protested.

"Maybe," Firekeeper replied, *"but Ox has told me of the wonders dying men can perform, even when pain should leave them shivering like a throat-torn doe. You shouldn't allow yourself to forget how vulnerable your belly can be."*

The wolf's blue eyes were hard as ice for a moment; then Blind Seer laughed.

"Call it a draw?" he suggested.

"A draw," Firekeeper agreed.

Derian shook his head in mock dismay at Firekeeper when the woman came in from the practice field covered with dirt and sweat, bleeding from a score of scratches. She knew him well enough by now to know that he really wasn't upset—far from it. He had been more worried when all she had done was eat and grow soft.

"Ox says," he commented, "that you're getting better with a sword."

"Want to practice with me?" she teased. "I show you how good I am getting."

Derian nodded slowly. "Actually, I would. Ox suggested that you'd improve with a different opponent—he said you're learning to fight him specifically, not a general opponent, so I've been brushing up on what I know. For some reason none of the castle retainers will fence with you."

From where he lay on a cool section of flagstone floor, Blind Seer chuckled. *"I wonder why . . ."*

Firekeeper booted the wolf in the ribs.

"You know sword?" she asked Derian, pleased to discover that her fox-haired friend had teeth.

"I'm no great expert," Derian replied, though before he had met real soldiers he had actually fancied himself quite capable. "My parents insisted that I take lessons when I was younger. Sometimes it helps if a pack train owner can help with defense."

"From thieves," she said, remembering various blood-thrilling stories that Holly had been telling her, "and from bandits, highwaymen, and robbers."

Derian laughed. "That's it," he agreed. "What are your plans for the rest of the day, my lady?"

Firekeeper frowned. Derian's latest self-appointed task was making her keep track of her own obligations. She had a sneaking suspicion that this was a lure to make her take her reading and writing lessons more seriously.

"Bath," she said, hedging for time to remember. "Then free until late afternoon. Then dancing lessons with Lady Elise and the other girls.

Then . . ." She shrugged. "Then nothing so important if I can't remember. Right?"

"Then dinner," Derian said seriously, "with Duke Gyrfalcon, his family, and—if rumor is to be believed—emissaries from the court of New Kelvin. This is *very* important. House Gyrfalcon is important in its own right—not just as a source of potential heirs for the throne. Earl Kestrel is working very hard for your cause, trying to show Duke Gyrfalcon that you could be as good a monarch as the duke's own niece or nephew. Furthermore, the New Kelvin emissaries will take report of you back to their rulers, so you must make a good impression."

Firekeeper snorted, more disgusted with herself than for any other reason, but she didn't anticipate another formal banquet with any joy.

"Must I go?" she pleaded.

"Yes," Derian said firmly. "Earl Kestrel is quite delighted with this notice."

"Very well," she said, "to make my guardian happy, I will go."

Derian patted her sympathetically on one shoulder. "I have the tub ready in my room. Hurry and bathe. If you don't take too long, you should be able to spend an hour or so in the garden with Holly. Just don't get filthy all over again."

Firekeeper had a wolf's fastidious nature—a thing that might surprise those who thought of the carnivores as filthy, ravening beasts delighting in blood and gore. In reality, if water was available, wolves bathed after a kill or after eating.

Freshly scrubbed, her hair caught up in a queue behind, dressed in a pair of leather trousers and matching vest, Firekeeper hurried off to the gardens. Holly was resting on one of the benches, enjoying a tumbler of well water seasoned with crushed spearmint.

"I thought you were coming," she said, patting the bench beside her. "Your falcon arrived a moment ago."

"Elation," Firekeeper said seriously, "is not my falcon. She just stay with me."

"It works out to about the same," Holly replied peacefully, "as I see it."

"What are you doing today?" Firekeeper asked, eager to learn more of the mysteries of gardening.

"Mostly resting, child. It's hot this afternoon. I wonder that you don't wear something lighter."

Firekeeper stroked the leather possessively. "It protects. If not wear clothes to protect, why wear at all?"

"I," Holly said with a soft, secret laugh, "would think that you had figured that out by now, but if you haven't . . ."

Firekeeper had heard that type of chuckle before and said scornfully, "I know about mating. This is not the season. I do not need fine plumage."

"For men," Holly replied, a hint of warning in her tone, "it is always the season. Never mind, child . . ."

"What are you doing today?" Firekeeper repeated, feeling that this conversation was taking her out of her depth and, as usual, not liking the feeling at all.

"I was weeding around the acorn squash, but now I'm resting." Holly sipped her drink. "I don't have your energy, child. After all, I'm old enough to be your grandmother."

"Is there still weeding?"

"Always."

"Where?"

Without leaving her bench, Holly gave Firekeeper directions. Once Firekeeper had settled into pulling the runner grass from between the rows of squash vines, she asked, hoping to prompt a story:

"You say you old enough to be my grandmother. Do you have grandchildren?"

"I do," Holly replied. "Do you recall the head gardener?"

Firekeeper had met the intense little man with his fussy manners, had noted his nervous way of eyeing Blind Seer as if he expected the wolf to dig up the rose gardens at the least notice. She was not certain at all that she liked the head gardener but had learned enough castle etiquette not to openly question those in positions of authority.

She grunted a noncommittal "Yes."

"He is my oldest son."

"No!"

"Yes. Once upon a time, I was the head gardener, but when my knees got creaky, King Tedric permitted me to pass the title on to my son, even as my father once passed it to me. It's an inheritance after a fashion, as real as property or money."

"Head Gardener is your son?"

"That's right."

"But he's so . . ." Firekeeper waved her hands, mimicking the head gardener's mincing motions.

Holly laughed, not denying the truth, but not condemning the man either.

"But he is also a very good gardener. I suspect he will learn to relax as he ages. Being around gardens does that to you. In any case, Timin—that's my son's name—has three children of his own. The elder two are already learning the craft. You may have seen them about: Dan and Robyn."

Firekeeper had seen them, hardworking towheads dressed in matching smocks and sandals. Her estimation of Timin Gardener went up a notch. At least he didn't spare his children work to their eventual detriment. The two gardener sprigs took their tasks seriously and if they paused to chase a butterfly or admire a spider's web, they didn't expect others to make excuses for them just because their father was the head gardener.

She'd seen something of what such sloughing off of responsibility could do in Citrine's sisters, Ruby and Opal, and in Kenre's sisters, Nydia and Deste. Those middle girls were becoming spoiled weak things who didn't seem to have any purpose in life but learning how to be noblewomen. They seemed to think a good marriage the best they could do for themselves, unlike Sapphire and Elise, whose training as heirs had made them value themselves for what they could do.

Firekeeper sighed, remembering that the middle girls would be at dancing practice today. She dreaded their sneers and giggles at her missteps, at her inability to hear the guidance the music offered her feet. To distract herself from that dreary prospect, Firekeeper asked:

"Do you have any other children or grandchildren?"

Holly nodded. "I have a daughter who married a fisherman and lives by the seacoast. She has two children and I expect will have more. My younger son hasn't yet married—too restless. He's in the military."

A sad expression flitted across Holly's wrinkled face. "And I had another daughter who is now dead. She was among those who followed Prince Barden across the mountains."

"Oh!" Firekeeper felt strange. "Then I may have known her when I was very small."

"I had thought of that," Holly admitted. "I suppose that's why at first I was so glad to make your acquaintance. In a way, you were a link to my daughter."

"What was her name?" Firekeeper asked, sitting back on her heels, a weed dangling from her hand.

"Sarena, Sarena Gardener. Her husband was Donal Hunter. They had a little girl named Tamara."

She looked so expectant that Firekeeper felt almost ill, for those names meant nothing to her. She hated to disappoint the old woman, but she shook her head slowly.

"I'm sorry. I don't remember. I was very small when the fire came."

Holly wiped away a tear that had somehow appeared on her withered cheek and smiled bravely.

"That's all right, dearie. I didn't expect that you would."

Firekeeper knew that her friend was lying and that truth made her feel all the worse.

XIII

"*AND AS I STAND here on the border between life and death,*" sang
the minstrel, his coat of feathers and twine as marvelous as the
soaring reaches of his voice, "*as here I stand, one hand clutching
the sword blade and the other pressed against the heart of my love,
pushing her back, saving her from death, in the wash of blood across
my face at last I see the truth, dark truth, black as dry blood . . .*"

The minstrel's voice rose, became sweeter still, "*She loves me not at
all!*"

Elise knew by heart the story of which the minstrel sang. It was as
old as the kingdom, the tale of a man whose fingers were sliced off one
by one as he defended his faithless lover.

She hated the first part of the song, always found herself holding her
breath as the man catalogued the cold realities that sliced his soul far
more cruelly than the sword did his hand. Breath trapped aching in her
chest, she waited for the second verse, where the man, accepting truth
in place of the lies that had been so dear to him, watched his fingers
regrow again one by one.

"*Red baptism, dripping from my brow, through the rose of new vision, I
see her laughing at my pale offering—bent fingers on our cottage floor . . .*"

Seeking to distract herself until the hopeful verses began, Elise glanced at Jet, wondering how he was responding to this classic story of love and betrayal. In the several days that had passed since she had visited with Firekeeper and Sir Jared in the castle gardens, she had found herself giving Jet many such glances: wondering what he thought and dreamed, dreading that he was hollow but for ambition.

Elise had always imagined herself in the place of the man in the song, the faithful one, believing in love despite all obstacles. Now she dreaded that she might be more like the faithless lover than she had ever dreamed. She shoved these thoughts away in real terror, discovering that she had become a stranger even to herself.

Now as she looked upon her betrothed's black-browed face, she thought he looked bored. Then she realized that Jet was not watching the minstrel at all, that what she had taken for boredom was carefully guarded neutrality. Following the direction of Jet's gaze, she saw that a soldier had mounted the king's dais and was handing Tedric a letter many times folded and secured with bright seals. The woman's uniform was dusty and her face expressionless—or was there a touch of pity on those dirty features?

Gamely, the minstrel continued his verses, but no one heard him and only Kenre Trueheart, too young to have wondered what messenger would dare interrupt the king at his meat, patted his hands together in applause when the entertainer made his awkward bow and gratefully ducked behind a curtain concealing a door out of the banquet hall.

Afterward, Elise remembered this unfinished ballad as a bad omen.

❧

KING TEDRIC AND QUEEN ELEXA departed the hall almost as soon as the packet was placed in the king's hand and a few words were exchanged with the weary messenger. The gathered nobility was courte-

268 / JANE LINDSKOLD

ously invited to remain and continue enjoying the entertainment, but no one had ears for the music. Hands reached for goblets of wine by reflex rather than to savor the fine vintages.

Steward Silver escorted the messenger from the hall with a swiftness that made any cross-examination impossible, but this did not keep conjecture at bay. If anything, it added to it. Fragments of information were welded into improbable theories.

Elise listened to the scattered scraps that drifted up and down the long tables:

"The stablemaster said that she came in without escort and her horse was blown. It may be ruined."

"They have the messenger sequestered in a private room. Steward Silver herself is waiting on her. No one else is being permitted close. I wonder what they fear the messenger will say?"

"My maid just happened to be passing down the hallway when a servant came by carrying the messenger's soiled uniform. She said that she's certain that it bore signs of a battle. One sleeve hung as if nearly sliced off."

"Did you see the king's expression when he spoke with the messenger? There must have been some terrible tragedy!"

Initially, Elise was as eager as any of the others to gather scraps and piece them into a crazy quilt of possible event. Then a sudden weariness and unnamed sorrow seized her. Making her excuses, she left the hall. She was heading for her rooms when she remembered that Ninette would be waiting there, eager to continue the cycle of gossip and conjecture.

Although the evening was dark, Elise slipped out a side door into the garden. The moon was half-full and bright enough to navigate by, though the garden seemed robbed of color. By moonlight, Elise found refuge among the roses, their scent heavy in the hot, damp summer air. She bent her head to breathe deeply of their perfume. When she raised her head, she discovered that she was not alone.

A slim figure leaned against an arched trellis overgrown with pale roses. Even in the dim light, Elise could tell the figure was another woman, dressed in a long, formal gown. When the woman moved, Elise knew her.

"Firekeeper," she said softly.

"Yes," came the equally soft reply. "I saw you come out. What is happening?"

"News from the army, I think," Elise said. "I don't know any more than that. I don't think anyone knows any more."

"Oh." A long silence, then Firekeeper asked, "I don't understand."

"Neither," Elise admitted, "do I. How can they build such elaborate pictures out of guesses?"

She glanced around. "Where is Derian?"

"Inside, making guesses." Firekeeper's laugh was throaty. "He doesn't worry about me in the darkness, especially since Blind Seer is always near. He said he worries about those in the darkness who might meet me!"

Elise laughed in turn. "Shall we walk then? My head is muzzy with wine and too much talk."

She saw the pale oval of Firekeeper's face nod agreement. Side by side, they strolled down the curving paths. More than once, Elise felt Firekeeper's hand on her arm, steering her away from a collision with a bush or other obstacle.

"Can you see in the dark?" she asked.

"See, like in daylight?"

"Yes."

"Not really." Firekeeper shook her head.

Elise heard rather than saw the motion, felt the breath of air against her bare shoulders.

"I cannot see in the darkness," the other continued. "More I know how to see the dark, to know what is there. Wolves hunt much at night, so I must learn darkness or I must starve."

Elise heard Firekeeper stumble, heard a soft curse, smiled, wondering if Derian had taught it to his charge intentionally.

"Why," Firekeeper asked plaintively, "do women wear these dresses?"

Elise might have laughed, but she could hear the frustration in the other woman's voice.

"Because," she offered slowly, "dresses make a woman look attractive and graceful."

Firekeeper snorted. "I am not graceful in a dress."

Having seen Firekeeper treading on her hem on the dance floor, Elise could not deny the truth of this statement. Moreover, Elise had learned that the other didn't understand polite social lies.

"No, you are not," she admitted, "but that's because you have never learned to walk in a skirt. You must shorten your stride just a little, not step out like a soldier on parade."

"I am not so noisy as a soldier," Firekeeper protested.

"No, you are not. You're even graceful in your own way—like a panther or a wolf—but not like a woman."

"But I *am* a woman," Firekeeper responded in the tones of one to whom this was still a matter for debate. "How can what I do be not like a woman?"

Unlike her cousin Sapphire, who rode well and enjoyed hunting, Elise had always preferred quieter pursuits. Still, she recalled some of Sapphire's loudly voiced frustrations when Melina had moderated her daughter's wilder behavior. Although she disliked Melina, Elise found the very arguments Melina had presented to Sapphire rising to her lips.

"You cannot escape that you are a woman," she began.

"I wish I could," Firekeeper muttered, but Elise continued as if she hadn't heard.

"Since you cannot, you cannot escape the expectations that our society and our class places upon women."

"Why?" Firekeeper said querulously.

"Just listen to me for a moment," Elise insisted. "Since people will expect a young woman of a noble house—and you are of one ever since Duchess Kestrel permitted her son to adopt you—to know certain manners of behavior, you must know them."

"Circles," Firekeeper complained, "like a pup biting its tail. I am this so I must be that. I am that so I must be this. Tell me, how will this little foot walking keep me alive?"

Elise resisted the urge to reply, "By keeping you from falling on your face." She already knew that the literal-minded Firekeeper would respond that this problem could be avoided by letting her wear what she wanted.

"Consider," she offered, "what you told me about learning to see at night so that you could hunt with the wolves. Learning to wear a gown, to walk gracefully, to eat politely . . ."

"I do that!"

"You're learning," Elise admitted, "but don't change the subject. All of these are ways of learning to see in the dark."

"Maybe," Firekeeper said, her tone unconvinced.

"Can you climb a tree?"

"Yes."

"Swim?"

"Yes!" This second affirmative was almost indignant.

"And these skills let you go places that you could not go without them."

Stubborn silence. Elise pressed her point.

"Why do you like knowing how to shoot a bow?"

"It lets me kill farther," came the answer, almost in a growl.

"And using a sword does the same?"

"Yes."

"Let me tell you, Firekeeper, knowing a woman's arts can keep you alive, let you invade private sanctums, even help you to subdue your enemies. If you don't know those arts, others who do will always have an advantage over you."

"All this from wearing a gown that tangles your feet?"

"If you know how to wear it," Elise leapt onto a stone bench, her long skirts swirling around her like bird's wings, "you can seem to fly."

THE NEXT DAY, King Tedric summoned into private conference those heads of the Great Houses who were in the capital or their representatives. He also included his brother and sister, Grand Duke Gadman and Grand Duchess Rosene. Anyone else was denied entrance, a thing that forced several of the competitors for the throne to swallow their rage when Earl Kestrel was admitted as representative for his absent mother, the duchess.

Some hours later, the conferees emerged, uniformly somber. Yet, despite the solemnity, the same inner glow lit the eyes of Earl Kestrel, the grand duke, and the grand duchess, leaving observers to comment that the king must have said something decisive regarding the appointment of his heir.

As soon as the conference had ended, Earl Kestrel summoned Firekeeper and Derian to him. At his orders, Ox mounted guard at the door and Race was sent to linger near the entry from the gardens, just in case someone tried to slip in from that direction. With his usual tact, Jared Surcliffe had made himself politely absent.

"The king has sworn us to silence about what occurred at the meeting," Kestrel said, "but Lady Blysse, you must be prepared."

Firekeeper cocked an eyebrow at him, "For silence?"

"No, to act!" Earl Kestrel calmed himself with visible effort. "Bright Bay has sent an emissary escorted by a considerable armed force to our southern border, into the contested area near the twin towns of Hope and Good Crossing. King Tedric is resolved to meet with this emissary himself. Since this action will put him in great danger, the king has submitted to the request of the Great Houses that he settle the matter of his heir before he departs. From the way he kept glancing at me as he spoke, Blysse, I believe he means to choose you!"

Firekeeper flushed, her heart suddenly pounding. She thought of all she had learned to do, how much more she had learned that she could not do. And over it all, seductive as the scent of a hot game trail, was the realization that the power of a queen was all she needed to make what she could and could not do moot.

"But I cannot . . ." she began.

Earl Kestrel cut her off. "Of course you can. You must! If the king wishes you to be his heir, you have no choice in the matter. I shall continue to advise you, as I have ever since I rescued you from the wilderness. You will not be alone in your great responsibilities. Indeed, since you are but fifteen you must have a regent until you are nineteen. I am likely to be that person, since I am your guardian . . ."

He was rattling on in this fashion, Firekeeper ignoring most of his words, when Ox thumped on the door. Valet glided over and opened it.

"Someone is here with a message," Ox announced loudly. "Says it's not written."

"Let the messenger enter," Earl Kestrel said grandly.

A man in castle livery came through the door, bowed deeply, and announced: "King Tedric and Queen Elexa request that Lady Blysse Norwood come to their chambers one hour from now. She may be escorted as far as the door, but they wish to meet with her in private."

Earl Kestrel was so keyed up that a fascinating mixture of emotions—delight, annoyance, fear, and finally smug satisfaction—glided unguarded across his hawk-nosed face. Firekeeper took advantage of his distraction to reply:

"Tell the king and queen that I will be there."

Any momentary annoyance Earl Kestrel might have felt about his privilege being usurped vanished in his greater elation.

"Wonderful!" he crowed as soon as the messenger had departed and the door was secured.

He was about to say more, but Firekeeper held up a hand.

"I must get cleaned and dressed," she said, her tones haughty. "This is most certainly a formal occasion."

"Yes!" Earl Kestrel slapped his palms together smartly. "Absolutely. Valet! Ring for hot water. Prepare my best jacket and trousers. Ox! Find Cousin Jared. Tell him I wish him to be part of Lady Blysse's escort. He should put on his uniform and order of knighthood . . ."

Firekeeper escaped while Earl Kestrel was still shouting orders.

"He do," she said to Derian, "everything but sing and spread his tail feathers."

"This," Derian replied, clearly a bit stunned, "is the culmination of all his plans."

"I wonder," Firekeeper said softly, "if it is the coming together of all of mine as well?"

❧

GRAND DUCHESS ROSENE summoned her son and daughter to her, along with their spouses. As a matter of course, Ivon brought Elise and Zorana brought Purcel. The younger children were kept away lest they inadvertently carry gossip.

When Jet Shield arrived at the door of Rosene's suite, his demeanor that of one who expects to take part in a family conference, even the acid-tongued grand duchess could not turn him away, no matter that her expression showed that she thought he was there more likely as a spy for his grandfather than out of a desire to be near Elise at this crucial time.

Elise was glad to have Jet there, no matter how of late she had doubted the sincerity of his affection. The glitter in her grandmother's washed-out old eyes frightened her a bit. She imagined that Grand Duke Gadman wore the same expression and wondered how King Tedric had survived to such a ripe age while the focus of so much malicious ambition.

"Tedric refused," Rosene began snappishly, "to read us the full text of the letters borne to him by the army messenger. He said they were too long and too filled with repetition."

Her dry sniff was commentary enough on how much she believed *that*! She continued:

"In essence, Bright Bay wishes to meet with someone in authority to discuss a matter that will be to the benefit of the mutual peace of our nations."

"I thought," commented scholarly Aksel Trueheart, "that we *were* at peace."

"Only technically," Rosene replied with a glance at her daughter as if to say, "How do you stand him!"

Aunt Zorana, however, seemed very calm, almost unnaturally so. From a woman who had been infuriated by the reduction of her hopes for the throne, she had become so self-contained that some had wondered aloud if she was indulging heavily in drink or one of the exotic drugs the New Kelvinese cultivated beneath green glass within steam-heated greenhouses hidden in the valleys of their mountainous realm.

"Although we do not have a declared state of war," Grand Duchess Rosene continued when Zorana remained silent, "our interests continue to clash. There have been numerous skirmishes over contested territories, robberies by bandits who may well be Bright Bay raiders, and blockades of our sea-lanes by their fleet. Now, suddenly, though war is undeclared, we are being offered a means to peace. What might that be?"

Elise heard her voice speaking as if it were separate from herself. "A marriage alliance—like Jet and mine."

"That is correct," Rosene agreed with an approving nod. "That is also the only thing that I can see drawing Tedric out of the security of his castle. Allister Seagleam is wed and has children of his own. Doubtless, the alliance would be between one of his children and one of Tedric's grandnieces or nephews."

Elise wondered if she was imagining the calculating look in Jet's eyes, as if he was recalling how easily Sapphire's engagements to various scions of Great Houses were broken when some more promising liaison became available.

His next words, the first he had spoken since making his greetings to his prospective in-laws, did nothing to reassure her.

"How old are Allister Seagleam's children?"

Aunt Zorana answered, her tone oddly caressing, "His eldest two are sons—one just your age, dear Jet, the other the same age as my Purcel. His twin daughters are quite young, younger even than my Deste."

Elise was quite certain she didn't imagine the malicious glance Aunt Zorana shot at her brother as if to say: "See, if you hadn't been so eager to use Elise within our own kingdom, you would have had the perfect offering for King Tedric."

If Jet felt any disappointment at this news, he didn't show it. Instead he commented blandly, "My sister Opal would be just the age for either of these sons. She's three years my junior."

To Elise's surprise—for she hadn't needed a dance card to see that Aunt Zorana's own children, if a bit young for betrothal under usual circumstances, meshed quite well with those of Allister Seagleam—Aunt Zorana only smiled blandly.

"I'm certain that Uncle Tedric will not overlook that point."

At that moment, a sharp rap sounded on the door. Before any could rise to answer it, the heavy door flew open and Grand Duke Gadman, followed closely by Lord Redbriar, burst into the room, shoving his way past protesting guards.

"I don't suppose you've heard," Gadman almost shouted at his sister, "closeted in here with your minions, plotting . . ."

"Heard what?" Rosene replied, her tones more moderated but no less forceful.

"While you have been plotting, Tedric has stolen a march. He summoned that girl Blysse Norwood to his chambers. They are to meet in less than an hour!"

Feeling curiously outside all of this, as if her own prospects and those of her father were unconcerned, Elise noted that the rivals had been united for this brief moment by an even greater threat. Only one person's expression was less than shocked—Aunt Zorana's. She actually looked pleased, though that pleasure was mingled with a trace of apprehension.

"He can't name that foundling his heir!" Grand Duchess Rosene proclaimed. "We must protest!"

"I've already demanded to see him," Gadman said bitterly. "He refused me."

"Perhaps if both of us . . ." Rosene suggested.

"I can't see how it will hurt to try," Gadman agreed.

The two bent figures stalked forth, their heirs trailing them like an agitated flock of ducklings. Elise moved more slowly, unable to remove Aunt Zorana's strange expression from her mind.

⚭

AN HOUR WAS BARELY ENOUGH time for Firekeeper to bathe—a thing made necessary by her usual morning romp with Blind Seer—and don a gown hastily pressed by Valet.

Escorted by Elation, who soared overhead screeching loud commentary, Derian dashed out to find Holly Gardener. The old woman asked no questions as she provided flowers for Firekeeper's hair and girdle, but something in her ancient eyes told Derian that rumors had already reached the gardens.

"Wish her luck," Holly said as she pressed the cut flowers into his hand.

"I will," he promised. "Whatever luck is."

There was a brief argument when Earl Kestrel, resplendently garbed in frock coat, waistcoat, and knee-breeches of the Kestrel red and blue, learned that Firekeeper planned to bring Blind Seer with her.

"He comes," she insisted. "The king know of him and give him freedom of the castle."

Earl Kestrel relented, muttering, "If the king wishes the wolf kept without the door, doubtless he will have left orders to that effect. Ancestors preserve me, but by now everyone in the castle must know that she won't leave the beast behind!"

Derian resisted adding, *Just as everyone knows that the real issue here is whether or not you can dominate Firekeeper!*

When they set off for the king's private chambers, the party encountered an unexpected obstacle. A milling throng of the king's relatives blocked the corridor—less intentionally than by their mere presence. Their mood was ugly. Clearly, the king had refused to meet with them.

Upon seeing Earl Kestrel, Grand Duke Gadman snarled, "There is no way we will allow this foundling to be named heir! No matter what you say, there is no proof that you didn't just pick this girl up in some gutter, stuff her in a gown, and teach her the basic rudiments of table manners!"

Firekeeper said nothing in response, studying the grand duke as if he were merely some curious species of beetle who had crossed her path. Not all of her companions were so silent.

"Our word is not proof enough?" Sir Jared asked with dangerous dryness; his Order of the White Eagle gleamed on the breast of his Army dress uniform.

Even in his self-righteous fury, Grand Duke Gadman was reminded that Jared Surcliffe's honesty was not open to question.

"I suppose . . ." he hedged, fumbling for an apology that would not admit that he was ever really in the wrong. "You must agree that the girl, the circumstances . . . most unusual . . ."

"I do agree to that." Sir Jared filled the gap followed by this weak attempt. "Certainly we can open this matter of Lady Blysse's finding to question when you find another gutter brat who lists among her peculiar assets being attended by a wolf. Now, will you let us through?"

This reminder of Blind Seer's presence parted the crowd. They filtered past in a thin stream as the Kestrel party moved forward.

Derian reflected that it was a measure of the gathered nobles' anxiety that they had overlooked the wolf at all, for Blind Seer had grown no smaller, nor had the fangs he showed in a deliberately sarcastic yawn grown any less sharp.

Only Lady Elise walked by the Kestrel contingent with something like a friendliness in her bearing. She even reached out a hand to pat Blind Seer's grey fur.

"You look very elegant and graceful," she said to Firekeeper as they passed. "Quite the lady."

Derian wondered why Firekeeper seemed so very pleased.

FIREKEEPER HAD FEARED that Earl Kestrel would try to inveigle himself into her meeting with King Tedric. Frequently the earl reminded her of a lesser wolf in a large pack, always trying to cut into the head wolf's share of the kill, always testing to see if this was the moment to challenge for primacy.

She was pleasantly surprised when he motioned her entourage to a halt in the hall and did not even try to press into the waiting room.

"Lady Blysse Norwood," he announced to the officer of the King's Own standing to one side of the door, "to see His Majesty."

"She is expected," the officer said. "Pass through, Lady Blysse."

No mention was made of Blind Seer and Firekeeper did not bother to ask permission. She nodded to her escort, adding a reassuring smile for Derian, who looked quite worried.

"Thank you for bringing me."

Earl Kestrel replied, "We will wait here to escort you back when His Majesty has concluded his business."

For all the calm formality of his words, the earl's eyes shone with anticipated glory.

Let through without question or search into a luxuriously furnished waiting area, Firekeeper went into the king's parlor.

Unlike the waiting room, it was simply furnished. A cluster of fine chairs upholstered for comfort, not for ostentation, rested on a thick rug.

In the center of this loose circle was a low table set with light refreshments. Light shone in from open windows curtained with gauze against glare and insects.

From outside of one of these windows came a brief squawk that told Firekeeper that Elation was watching.

Three people awaited her: King Tedric, Queen Elexa, and a man Firekeeper recognized as someone important in the King's Own Guard. All three rose to greet her, a courtesy Firekeeper appreciated since she knew that it was not her due—would not even be her due if she were the king's heir. She accepted the gesture as it was meant, a welcome meant to put her at her ease. When bows and curtsies had been exchanged, King Tedric motioned her to a chair.

"Be comfortable, Lady Blysse, or would you prefer that I call you Firekeeper?"

"Firekeeper is what wolf call me," she replied with singular tact—for her. "Blysse what Earl Kestrel call me. Please take your comfort."

Queen Elexa smiled. "Then we shall call you Firekeeper here in private, but in public, so as not to hurt Earl Kestrel's feelings, we shall refer to you as Blysse."

In this, Firekeeper recognized the elaborate etiquette that established rank, so like and yet so unlike the groveling and playful biting used for the same purpose by a wolf pack.

"Let me present to you," King Tedric continued, "one of my most trusted advisors, Sir Dirkin Eastbranch. By rights, Sir Dirkin should be commander of the King's Own, but his own choice has been to accept lower rank so that he will be free to follow my most frivolous command."

"Rarely," Sir Dirkin said in a voice that came from deep in his chest, "have Your Majesty's orders been frivolous."

King Tedric laughed and Firekeeper sensed a long-standing joke. Dirkin Eastbranch was a tall man with chiseled features that included the squarest chin Firekeeper had ever seen. Something about his upright posture reminded Firekeeper of a tree, a resemblance enhanced by the weathered texture of his skin. Like many soldiers, he was clean-shaven, but his brown hair was long and thick. She still had difficulty guessing human ages, but she suspected that Dirkin was older than Doc, maybe even as old as the earl.

"By now," King Tedric said as Queen Elexa leaned forward to pour early-pressed cider into elegant glass goblets, "you will have heard that I plan to travel south to the border of our kingdom and Bright Bay."

King Tedric paused to let his guest reply. Firekeeper didn't say anything, but sat looking alert and interested. She knew that Earl Kestrel was to have said nothing of the king's plans to anyone and refused, for all her occasional annoyance with her guardian, to betray his indiscretion.

After a moment, King Tedric continued, a slight smile that she might have imagined just touching his lips.

"To tell you something that I did not mention during this morning's conference—and that I would prefer did not leave this room—Allister Seagleam, my sister Caryl's only child, has requested a meeting with me."

By now Firekeeper had memorized the complete list of competitors for the throne and heard their various merits argued so many times that she had no trouble placing this one.

"The Pledge Child," she said, remembering what Derian had told her, "some say the favorite of the common folk."

This time she was certain that the king was pleased. Queen Elexa also nodded approval, saying:

"Not all our nieces and nephews would speak so openly of Duke Allister. Most seem to feel that we should deny him. What do you think?"

Firekeeper shrugged, remembered this was not an elegant reply, then shrugged again. "How can I say until I have met him?"

This won a small, quickly swallowed, chuckle from Sir Dirkin.

"That is precisely what we think," King Tedric said. "I have prayed long and hard at the shrine to my ancestors and I have come to the conclusion that I would be betraying my father's dream if I did not at least meet with the man whose very birth is the result of my father's hopes for peace.

"However, in order to assuage my Great Houses, I have had to prom-

ise that I will not leave for such dangerous territories without first assuring that the succession is safe. They believe that in this way they will
make it impossible for me to name Allister Seagleam my heir, for how
can I name one heir and then denounce him or her without reason in
favor of another?"

Firekeeper nodded to show that she had understood.

"So, Lady Blysse," the king continued, "would you like to be queen?"

XIV

PRINCE NEWELL MIGHT HAVE KNOWN even before King Tedric did what news was contained in the letter sent by Queen Gustin. Whether or not this was the case, it was certainly true that he was determined to be on the spot when the representatives of the two monarchies met. This was quite critical to the fruition of his plans.

Therefore, the prince made mysterious and cryptic comments to the captain of *Wings*. These comments made that faithful if unimaginative man quite certain that once again the prince was placing his life at risk for the good of the Crown. Since *Wings*'s captain had repeatedly benefitted from the information that Prince Newell had brought to him, news that had made *Wings* the most successful ship in Hawk Haven's small navy, he was willing to do without his Commander of Marines for a time.

If it also crossed the captain's mind that the reserve commander was a less willful man with far fewer highly placed and important connections and thus far easier to overrule in matters of tactics and suchlike, the captain was not likely to say this to Prince Newell.

Instead, he assigned a couple of sailors to lower the small cutter that was the prince's own property (although Newell was generous to a fault in sharing it with other officers for their need and entertainment), told the quartermaster to grant the prince anything he needed within reason from ship's stores, and bid Newell fair winds and fast sailing.

Racing before the wind toward his destination, Newell was assisted in his tasks with sail and line only by Rook, his personal manservant. Rook was a sandy-haired, quiet, forgettable fellow, as efficient as Earl Kestrel's Valet, although somewhat quicker with a knife in the back in a dark alley. Newell had caught him robbing the bedchamber of Duchess Merlin during a house party at the Norwood country manse. In return for not being turned over to Duchess Kestrel's executioners, Rook had sworn Prince Newell his abiding loyalty.

Skin stinging with salt, eyes red with concentration, Newell Shield distracted himself from discomfort by meditating on those things that set him apart from his competitors for the throne. As these were also the qualities he felt would make him a superior king, it was a pleasant self-indulgence.

For one, he thought, tightening a line around a brace and tacking slightly, they were sheep whereas he was a wolf. All one had to do to be sure of this was observe the lot of them flocking around King Tedric, baaing compliments and waiting for the monarch to grace one of them— or one of their lambs—with title and kingdom. They thought that blood was merit enough.

He admitted that a few of them, Ivon Archer, in particular, had distinguished themselves for their own achievements. Rolfston Redbriar, though, he was a real bleater—had been since they were all children gathering with the rest of the extended nobility for the Festival of the Eagle.

Little sister Melina had Rolfston neatly in line. Sometimes Newell was almost certain Melina *was* a sorceress—not that a woman would need to be one to direct Rolfston. No matter the truth, the reputation had garnered her a certain measure of respect. It was to Newell's own advantage that Melina had never realized that respect based on fear can only go so far, especially for a younger daughter of a Great House with no prospects for inheritance.

And then there was sweet Zorana. She was a lusty lady. It had been delightful to renew their intimacy. Yet in the final assessment, she had done nothing more to advance her position than bleat and baa—and breed. Four living children! He wondered at Zorana's lack of wisdom. It was not as if she had a great deal to offer her brood in the way of prospects. Purcel would make a good career in the military even before he inherited, but what did she plan to do with the rest?

Newell laughed and salt spray splashed into his mouth—make them little ladies and lords with a queen for a mama! Doubtless when he was king Zorana would be making sheep's eyes at him and hinting that she'd be quite happy to poison Aksel Trueheart and become his queen—and provide him with a tidy little line of ready-made heirs in the process. The idea would have its merits, but he was going beyond Hawk Haven for his queen.

The thought of Gustin IV with her long sunset-gold hair, laughing eyes, and breasts like a ship's figurehead stirred him, soaked with cold seawater as he was. She would be somewhere in her late twenties now, ripe but far from withering. There was no way a woman with a body like that could be barren, no matter what rumors said. Her lack of children had to be the rooted in that effete husband of hers.

Newell had heard that a woman became lustier in her middle years, especially if she hadn't borne a child, as if her body was telling her to hurry up and be about it. He looked forward to finding out if that tale was true.

If everything went according to plan he'd be bedding Gustin by this next summer—those Bright Bay folks would just need to be reasonable regarding mourning periods for her late husband. After all, a king shouldn't need to wait about getting an heir.

Prince Newell smiled into the sun, high and gold like the one on the coat of arms of Bright Bay's royal house. He'd already designed the arms for his new kingdom—a fresh design that eschewed both eagles and suns. He'd already planned so much. Now, at last, he was going to have a chance to make those plans reality.

❦

"QUEEN?" FIREKEEPER REPLIED, thinking more rapidly than she could ever remember doing before. Unknown to her, for the first time since soon after the fire that destroyed her parents, her thoughts took shape in human words and symbols. A bridge was built.

"Queen," King Tedric repeated steadily. "The one who will rule here after I join the ancestors."

And Firekeeper thought of power with a greater reach than her single Fang. Of humans groveling before her as a wolf did before the Ones, of the power to command, of that power turned to find the answer to the question that had nipped the edges of her mind as the pack nipped at the heels of an elk, and from that last image came her answer.

"No," she said. "A queen should be to her people as the Ones are to the pack: the greatest strength to guide and preserve through winter. I could not be a queen. I do not yet have the wisdom."

She looked squarely at the king, awaiting his anger, for she knew that he had offered her a great honor and she had cast it away like a too small fish into the stream. Tedric, however, was nodding agreement. Queen Elexa looked hesitant, but Firekeeper thought she was pleased. Only Sir Dirkin maintained a face of wooden impassivity.

Feeling as if she was stalking some elusive prey, Firekeeper curled her fingers in Blind Seer's ruff, awaiting developments.

King Tedric asked, "Are you certain about this, Firekeeper? Your young wisdom could be guided by advisors until it grew. I would appoint such and many others would offer their wisdom unasked."

This was Earl Kestrel's vision voiced. Still Firekeeper must shake her head.

"I am a wolf. Perhaps two-legged kind take leadership before they can lead, but for a wolf that is folly and such folly is death—not just for the wolf but often for all the pack."

Now King Tedric smiled a sour smile. "Would that all my nieces and nephews were raised wolves, Firekeeper. All they think of is the honor and the power, not the responsibility. That is why I must meet this Allister Seagleam. My father laid the foundation for his birth. I must see the structure that has risen on that foundation before I reject it entirely."

As Firekeeper struggled to follow the king's imagery, she realized that her afternoons in the gardens with Holly had taught her a great deal. Through them, she had come to understand the hidden preparation that rested beneath so many human endeavors. It was a different way of living from the season-structured roaming of the pack, yet a valid one for frail humankind.

King Tedric continued, "Yet even as I follow this course, I must be faithful to my own responsibilities. Queen Elexa can reign in my absence, but even with her firmly in charge I cannot leave the relative safety of this castle without naming my heir."

"Who?" Firekeeper asked, wondering which of the many will finally become the One.

The old man bared yellow teeth in an expression that reminded her very much of a wolf and answered with a question:

"Can you read, Firekeeper?"

"No." She shrugged. "Derian tries, but the black marks on the page won't talk to me."

"Or," laughed Queen Elexa, her thin elderly voice heard for the first time in a great while, "you will not speak with them. That is closer to the truth as I have heard it from Aurella Wellward."

Firekeeper stared at the queen, her eyes round with indignant astonishment. "How she speak of me? I have not spoken three words with her!"

"But her daughter is your friend," the queen replied. "Every scrap of information about you, my dear, has been gathered and traded, shared and twisted every which way. You do not think we have left you to go your way unnoticed, do you?"

Actually, this was what Firekeeper *had* believed, for ever since the king had granted her freedom of the castle she had felt herself unimpeded but for the ever-watchful presence of Derian. If anything, outside of the small circle of friends she had been able to cultivate, she had felt herself slighted. Queen Elexa's words revealed a spiderweb of human chatter as complex and useful as birdsong in a spring woodland.

Before she had time to contemplate this further, King Tedric was speaking:

"Although you do not read, you seem to understand the idea of reading—that the black marks on the page talk with the voice of the writer."

"I do."

"Then this is my intention. Before I leave, I will write the name of my heir on a special document called a will. Two copies shall be made. One will travel with me. The other will be sealed and locked away, to be opened only if I die. If I do not, then I am free to change what is written. If not, I have fulfilled my responsibility."

"How," Firekeeper asked, tentative before these mysteries, "will they know one piece of paper from another?"

"The marks of writing are distinct from person to person," Tedric said.

Like scents on a trail, Firekeeper thought. *All deer smell like deer, but one deer smells more like itself than it does like all others.*

"Furthermore, both copies of my will and the boxes into which they shall be locked will be impressed with my personal seal. No other will be able to forge those marks."

"I understand," Firekeeper said, having seen similar arrangements on the documents that Duchess Kestrel sent to her son. "Why not just tell before you go?"

"For two reasons," the king replied. "One is that I may decide that Allister Seagleam is the best person to be king after me. If I publicly designate one person as my heir, then renounce him or her for no reason other than I have found another I think would be better, I may create a feud between factions."

"But better is better!"

"Not all see this as simply as you do," the king said sadly. "And they are more correct than you are. Rulership of humans takes more than strength and wisdom. Sometimes it takes more uncertain qualities like charisma or political allies."

"If you say," she agreed.

"I do."

Momentarily, the king looked so stern that Firekeeper had to resist the impulse to lick the underside of his jaw and beg forgiveness. Then he continued:

"The other reason for not naming my heir openly is that I will create a danger for myself."

"Why?"

"Once I name my heir, I become a danger to that heir because I could change my mind and name another. The heir personally might not fear my changing my mind, but there would be others who would think it wisest to end my life before I could select a rival. Needless to say, I hope that whoever I choose would not countenance such behavior, but the heir might not even know what was done for his or her benefit."

Firekeeper shook her head, feeling it buzz with undesired complexities. She could not believe Elise—for example—would wish her greatuncle dead, but eager, watchful Ivon Archer was another matter and he was nothing beside sour, spiteful Zorana.

Sir Dirkin broke his own silence to add, "There are too many plausible ways that an elderly monarch could die while traveling or in an unexpected spate of battle. I have vowed to protect King Tedric from these, but that restricts my own freedom greatly."

"Therefore," King Tedric said, "I have a request to ask of you."

Firekeeper was surprised. She had thought that once she refused the king's offer to make her queen he would be finished with her. She had not realized that all the talk that had followed was anything more than the tongue wagging of the type Earl Kestrel was so fond of.

"Ask," she said, remembering the courtesies offered from Royal Wolf to Royal Wolf. "You have fed me and I have grown fat in your keeping. If I can feed you in turn, I will."

A small smile flitted across King Tedric's face, but instantly vanished and he replied with equal formality:

"Come with me to Hope. Be ears and eyes for Dirkin and myself. Those skills your upbringing granted you have not escaped my notice. One of the difficulties I suspect will result from my naming my heir only in my will is that many of those who believe themselves potential heirs will choose to join my train. Those who believe themselves the chosen one will wish to stay close so as not to lose in comparison to Allister Seagleam. Those who are less certain will still wish to be nearby in case some valorous deed or great service to me might bring them into my favor.

"I cannot refuse any of them without causing more speculation. Those who were refused would plot behind me—wondering if they were left behind to preserve them from danger or merely because they were no longer of use to me. They would envy those who went in my train. I wish I could refuse them all, but to do the latter would rob my forces of three able commanders—Norvin Norwood, Ivon Archer, and Purcel Trueheart—and in my heart I dread that these negotiations cannot end without bloodshed."

Firekeeper nodded solemnly. "I will go with you."

Sir Dirkin reminded her, "You will be placing yourself in danger. There are those who will hate you for this meeting, believing that the king has selected you his heir. Those who would resort to assassinating a king would think still less of assassinating a rival."

"Let them try!" Firekeeper said, hand falling to the knife at her waist.

Blind Seer—who had learned enough of human speech to follow this talk, though the shape of his mouth would not let him speak it as well— growled fierce agreement. If the falcon in the tree outside flapped her wings in agreement, only Dirkin, silent and watchful, noticed.

"I will watch my Firekeeper!" Blind Seer said in wolf-speech and it almost seemed that the king and his advisors agreed.

"I know you will take care," Tedric said, "and that your companions, human and otherwise, will guard you. Still, the danger is real and must be accepted."

"I accept it then," Firekeeper said with a shrug, "but I will still come with you and help Sir Dirkin watch."

"And I would have you watch my kinfolk as well," King Tedric said, "for the death of even one under suspicious circumstances could create the very feuding I am hoping to avoid."

Firekeeper nodded agreement, but she could not resist saying:

"Wolves solve these matters more simply."

"But wolves are not humans," King Tedric replied, "and I am hoping that my humans are not wolves."

EARLY ON THE MORNING following Firekeeper's meeting with King Tedric, Derian Carter was sent into the city by Earl Kestrel. Although he had a list of errands to run, he was also at leave to visit his family.

"The earl is a fair master," he explained to his mother around a mouthful of freshly baked oatmeal cookies, the fat, round cookies lavishly supplied with raisin. "As he plans for us all to depart along with the king's train, he has given those of us who will attend him leave."

"Does Earl Kestrel simply continue trailing in the king's wake, hoping for him to select your Firekeeper as his heir?"

Derian shook his head. "Some perhaps, but he has also volunteered his services as a commander of cavalry and the king has accepted them."

"And you?" Vernita asked eagerly. "You ride as lightly as foam on the crest of a wave—are you going as a member of Earl Kestrel's unit?"

"No," Derian replied. "I continue as attendant upon the Lady Blysse."

A mixture of disappointment and relief flitted across Vernita's pretty face. She asked carefully:

"And are you content with this?"

"Perfectly, Mother," Derian assured her, although at first he had been hurt and angry, knowing from his moon-span of residence in the castle that he rode as well or better than most of the King's Horse. He could even shoot a bow from the saddle, though his skill with a lance was less expert.

Patting his mother's hand, he repeated to her what Earl Kestrel himself had said when Derian dared protest:

"Earl Kestrel says that I am the only person Firekeeper truly trusts. The earl hates admitting this, but it's true. She has made a few friends, but I am the one she returns to again and again for explanations."

"Is it not perhaps time for her to learn to trust others?" Vernita hazarded.

Derian shook his head ruefully. "Mother, three and a half moon-spans ago she was a wild animal, eating raw meat, sleeping in the open, drinking blood as readily as water. We have succeeded in putting a veneer of civilization over that animal, but the animal is there, ready to burst free."

"I have seen her," Vernita said doubtfully, "just once and that from a distance as she rode in an open carriage with the Lady Archer. One seemed as much the lady as the other."

A full-throated laugh burst from Derian at the comparison between delicate Elise and Firekeeper.

"Oh, Mother, appearances are deceptive. I remember that day. Firekeeper had been invited to dine with Duke Peregrine and his family at their city manse. A house guard, improperly prepared for her or perhaps merely determined to show how he would dare what the King's Own Guard would not, tried to take her knife. Quick as breath Firekeeper punched him squarely in the nose, then followed through with a kick that nearly shattered one of the man's knees. Then, pretty as could be, she curtsied to the shocked duke, apologizing for spilling blood on his carpet."

Vernita's green eyes widened in shock. "As well she should!"

"No, Mother." Derian could hardly keep from laughing further at the memory. "You don't understand. Firekeeper then went on to explain that she would have punched the man in the gut but she didn't want to hurt her hand on his dress corselet and she had to take him out quickly because Blind Seer was heading for his throat."

"She brought that wolf to a duke's manse?"

"Blind Seer goes everywhere with her: bodyguard and companion both. I spoke out of line when I said that I was the one person she trusted. She trusts me to guide her actions, but Blind Seer she trusts with both body and heart."

"You speak as if the wolf is a person," Vernita said. "You've spent your entire life around animals. I don't think you would do this lightly."

"Never, Mother." Derian shrugged and bit into another cookie. "Blind Seer is as much a person as I am—and not just in Firekeeper's opinion. I've watched him since Bear Moon when Firekeeper first introduced him to me and Race. Blind Seer is as clever as any human—and more so than many I've known."

"Oh."

The monosyllable was noncommittal, but Derian grew defensive.

"Mother, she talks to him and he to her—I am certain of it! Queen Zorana's edicts encouraged us to forget everything that came before the Civil War. Mostly I agree with her wisdom. Our nation started fresh, without all the deadwood of Old Country traditions that would have weighed us down. I doubt her wisdom where it applies to the history of our own lands since the earliest days of colonization.

"Lord Aksel Trueheart gives regular lectures to those who wish to listen—much to Lady Zorana's embarrassment. Perhaps Firekeeper's arrival spurred Lord Aksel in that direction, but of late the topic has been what the New World was like when the earliest settlers arrived. Their records to a one agree that in those days there were animals far larger and far wiser than any we know today. Then, some fifty years after colonization began, almost to a one they vanished. Where did they go?"

Vernita humored him. "Across the Iron Mountains?"

"That's what I think," Derian replied, flushing slightly as he realized he'd been ranting. "That's exactly what I think. I think they figured out that they couldn't compete with our bows and arrows, our swords and armor, with the magics of the Old World wizards. Those who admitted it left. The rest were slain."

Footsteps on the wooden floor announced Colby's arrival.

294 / JANE LINDSKOLD

"I heard similar stories when I was a boy," he said, joining them at the table and pouring himself a mug of beer, "from an old, old woman who belonged to my society. She claimed to have them from her own mother, who had lived in the foothills of the Iron Mountains and seen some of the wise beasts herself. Human life is short and memory a chancy thing, but I believed her. She had a relic, a bear claw long as a scythe blade. It was an impressive thing."

Vernita grinned at husband and son. "I consider myself cautioned to keep an open mind. Colby, you're home early."

"Brock came and told me Derian was here. We've heard enough at the stables of the king's planned departure for me to guess that this might be Derian's last visit for a while, so I turned the day's work over to the journeymen with promises that you would review their books yourself."

"Thanks," Vernita said dryly.

"In any case, I want to go hear King Tedric's farewell speech."

"Is that today?" Derian asked, surprised. "The word I had is that he doesn't depart for another few days yet."

"He doesn't," Colby replied, "but apparently he has decided to scotch rumors by speaking with the people himself now, rather than later."

"Wise," Derian said. "Just this morning in the market I heard some remarkable tales, including one that he was dead and this journey was simply an attempt to conceal the fact until the nobility could fight out who would be his heir."

"That one will be easily ended," Colby agreed, "but I wonder what new ones this will begin?"

"I can't say," Derian grinned, remembering. "Actually, I'm curious about what the king will say myself. Firekeeper met with him yesterday, but she refused to say anything of what passed between them. The earl was nearly mad with rage and frustration."

Both Vernita and Colby looked as if they wished to ask more, but they respected Derian's professed ignorance. After all, hadn't he just finished boasting that he was the only person Firekeeper trusted?

Derian sighed inwardly. Let them keep their illusions. On this matter, Firekeeper had been as persistently mute as a stone.

"Let me close the office," Vernita said, "and call Damita and Brock in. We may as well go as a family. The younger ones don't seem at all aware that they're living in important times for the history of Hawk Haven."

THE PAVED ASSEMBLY AREA outside the speaker's tower of Eagle's Nest Castle was normally more than large enough to hold those who came to hear news from the royal court. Here, once early in the morning and again at sunset, a herald stood on a platform within the tower and made announcements. Most of the time these were routine, hardly more important than the crying of the hours. Other times they included some interesting tidbit: the resolution of a crucial court case, the passage of a law, the birth of a child into the nobility. Each week a post-rider carried the same news to every surrounding township.

The assembly area was usually strained to capacity when at midday on each full moon, King Tedric himself came to the speaker's tower. From this lofty perch, but full in view of his subjects, he reassured his people that all was well and gave the blessings of the royal ancestors.

Today, the usual idlers and newsmongers could hardly find a place to stand. It seemed as if most of the town and a fair portion of the surrounding countryside had come to hear the king's speech. Pressed into the throng, craning his neck to get a good look, Derian was once again made aware of how much more—well—noble the nobility looked from a distance.

At this distance, most of the lines on King Tedric's face vanished. Those that remained gave his features a look of regal dignity. No one could tell that the snow white hair was a wig or that his eyes were yellowed with age. Crowned in gold and diamonds, Tedric looked the storybook picture of a king, and Derian was aware of the covert glances of respect directed at he himself from neighbors and friends who knew of his employment in the castle.

It's as if, he thought wryly, *I'm somehow improved by having been close to that old man once or twice. I doubt their opinion would change if they knew the king doesn't even know me from the other servants.*

Standing a few steps back from the king were several members of the court. Derian recognized Queen Elexa, attended by Lady Aurella, Steward Silver, and Sir Dirkin Eastbranch. He knew that the rest of the court would be standing in the interior courtyard, unable to stay away from this important speech, although doubtless court gossip and rumor had revealed everything that would be said.

Indeed, initially there were no surprises for Derian. As he had in private conference the day before, the king informed his people of his proposed journey to Hope in order to confer with diplomats from Bright Bay.

A soft murmur swept the crowd at this news. Not everyone was, like Derian's family, in a position to hear the earliest hints of travel. Except for occasional journeys to family estates or to the seats of his Great Houses, the elderly monarch had not left Eagle's Nest for years.

The king continued, informing his people that Queen Elexa would administer daily business in his absence, but that he would be in regular contact with her through carrier pigeons.

"My heir," he said, his still powerful voice carrying easily over hushed throng, hardly needing the amplified repetition from the heralds to be heard at the farthest reaches, "has been named in my will, a copy of which remains here in Eagle's Nest, a copy of which goes with me. I shall not reveal who I have selected in any other fashion at this time."

From this astonishing announcement, he moved onto the formal blessing from the ancestors, but Derian hardly listened. Although most around him stood with their faces upraised to accept the power of the blessing, a few could not resist whispering.

He goes to meet with the Pledge Child!

Allister Seagleam will be our next king! Why else wouldn't the king name his heir publicly?

There'll be unhappiness in the court tonight!

Pledge Child . . .

Over and over those two words were repeated, rustling like dry leaves in the hush, practically taking on the force of an incantation from an Old Country tale.

Moving through the crowd after the king had retired, Derian listened to the gossip and conjecture, wondering at the fidelity of an image. Allister Seagleam was hardly a child any longer. Indeed he was a man grown with grown sons, but the image of a child born to fulfill a promise of peace persisted. Even if King Tedric named Allister Seagleam heir, could any man live up to such a legend?

AS KING TEDRIC HAD PREDICTED, immediately after the announcement that his choice of an heir was to be known only upon the reading of his will, rapid arrangements were made so that many of the candidates could join the royal train.

Grand Duchess Rosene's fury when she learned how her brother had resolved the matter was magnificent to behold. When she finished raging, she began issuing orders.

"Although I wish to go, it would be an undue risk at my age. Tedric should have more respect for his own aging bones. If Bright Bay wishes to negotiate, he should insist that their emissaries come here."

Rosene had made the same argument to her brother to no effect. Tedric had refused to even admit that there was sense to her position, thus increasing her pique. Now, Rosene shored up her diminished sense of self-importance by assigning positions to her family members as a general might order troops.

"Aurella, of course, must remain here with Queen Elexa. To have her do otherwise would be to our own detriment."

Elise thought that it was a good thing that her grandmother could not read minds, for Elise knew that there was no way, commanded or not, that Aurella Wellward would leave the queen at such a time. Aurella's loyalty to her Wellward aunt might even exceed that to her husband's family—Ivon and Elise herself excepted.

"Ivon, of course," the elderly matriarch continued, "must be with his troops. If Ivon's name is the one on that sealed document Tedric was waving about so arrogantly, he was most certainly chosen at least in part for his martial prowess. No need to undermine that reputation at this critical moment."

"Thank you, Mother," Ivon said dryly. To his credit, much of his attention had been given to reviewing the roster that had been delivered to him soon after the king's announcement.

"Purcel will also be with his company," the matriarch continued. "Therefore, upon Zorana and Elise falls the responsibility of keeping an eye on my brother. You must make certain that Tedric makes no unwise decisions, that he does not overlook the value of his own kinfolk in favor of a glamorous newcomer."

"Your wish is as my own, Mother," said this newly mild Zorana. "Aksel can remain here to guard our interests and watch the smaller children."

"Fine. He is useless on a campaign—nothing like the Truehearts who bore him. Your son's talents clearly come from the Archer side of the family."

Zorana nodded, not even bristling at this dismissal of the father of her children.

"I don't think any of your other children need to be taken along," Grand Duchess Rosene continued to her daughter. "They are young and almost certainly out of the running."

"I am bringing," said Zorana with a flash of her old fire, "my daughter Nydia. If I am King Tedric's heir—as is still possible despite your recent dismissal of my chances—Purcel as my heir will need to shift his focus to national matters. Nydia will then become heir to our family properties. It is time her education is expanded."

"Nydia is," protested the Grand Duchess, "but thirteen. Until this point you have not cared overmuch about her education, even though she would follow if Purcel was killed on one of his military ventures."

"I care now," Zorana said firmly.

The tension in the air between mother and daughter was a palpable thing. Elise imagined that she could pull it, tug it, twist it like taffy until it grew white, hard, and immobile.

Grand Duchess Rosene was the one to relent. "If you wish to expose your thirteen-year-old daughter to the risks of a traveling military encampment, so be it. Perhaps," she added sourly, "we should also include Deste and little Kenre. Are you certain that you are not ignoring their education?"

"As to them," Zorana said, her mildness now a mockery, "I shall be ruled by you, but I thank you for your concern. Perhaps you may devote some of your time here in the capital to their lessons. You shall have little else to do."

Offended, Rosene swept out, unwilling to discipline her daughter in these sensitive times. Zorana took her leave a few moments after. She spared a completely false smile for Elise.

"We shall be much in company, Niece. Certainly, your cousin Sapphire will not welcome you into her pavilion and I wonder if Jet will be so much about. He has himself to prove, you understand."

"Certainly, we follow the example of our elders," Elise answered with a flicker of her own malice. "I wonder sometimes if Purcel does take after his mother's side of the family. He is such a *noble* warrior."

This curiously mild Zorana did not deliver a scathing reply, as the one of a few weeks ago might have, but the glower she directed at Elise still shot a shiver of fear into the young woman's soul, one that lasted even after her aunt had departed.

"Was that wise?" Ivon asked, distracted from his papers. "Your aunt Zorana has been much disappointed of late. It is the hungry wolf that bites."

"True," Elise admitted, thinking of Firekeeper and knowing that this was true.

"And speaking of wolves," Ivon continued, his thoughts following the same course, "you have a great advantage on this campaign. You alone have a foothold in the Kestrel camp. Do not forgo that contact now that

King Tedric has made his decision. Personally, I cannot believe that he has chosen Lady Blysse, but if he has, we must cultivate her. Make yourself her familiar; learn what you can."

Aurella added. "Do not forget that you are growing into a pretty enough young woman. Earl Kestrel has surrounded his ward with men. One of them may talk freely to you even if Lady Blysse will not."

Elise nodded, but she doubted that Derian could be moved in his loyalty to Firekeeper and the wolf-woman would confide in no other. Sir Jared, perhaps . . . A tingle of anticipation melted the ice in her soul at this excuse to speak further with the knight.

"Yes, Mother. I will remember what you have said." She paused, uncertain if she was really asking for advice or merely being clever. "But should I risk this? What if Jet is offended?"

"Jet Shield plays his own games," Aurella said dryly. "As he always has. He will only treasure you the more if he thinks others value you. Still, keep Ninette nearby. Give Jet no reason to question your honor."

Ivon Archer stood and began gathering his papers. Then he turned to his daughter, a wry expression, not completely without sorrow, on his face.

"Welcome to the adult world, my daughter. Whether or not we win the crown, you will always need to know how to use people against each other. Such is our duty to our barony. My father won lands and titles for us with his keen arrows in battle. To preserve those honors, our weapons must be more subtle."

Elise dropped him a deep curtsy. "Then we will go together into this new battle, Father. Let us not flinch from whatever we must do to honor our noble ancestor."

Ivon clapped her on the shoulder and was gone. When Elise glanced at Aurella she saw no sorrow, no unexplained tears upon her mother's cheek, only a stern countenance lit brightly from within by pride.

BOOK
THREE

XV

SEVERAL DAYS ON THE ROAD put Firekeeper into the best shape
she had been in since she left the wilderness to reside in West
Keep. Indeed, she realized that she might be in far better condition
than she had ever been, since her body at last had ample food with
which to build its strength.

In the wilds, she had hardly ever had enough to eat. Summer's glut
quickly vanished as soon as the first frost killed the plants with which
she supplemented her diet and forced the little animals into hiding and
hibernation. Stealing the occasional squirrel hoard (and eating the squirrel when possible) did not make up for the loss of sweet fruits and slow,
fat rodents. Without the generosity of the wolves, she would have shriv-
eled into nothing, her body consuming itself in a desperate effort to keep
lit the spirit's fire.

Three moon-spans of steady eating had changed Firekeeper from a
slat-sided, feral waif into something recognizable as a young woman. A
thin coating of fat now padded her muscles and buttocks. To her slight
consternation, she was even developing small, round breasts. Despite
devouring more than many grown men at any given meal, regular exercise
had kept her from becoming soft. She could still climb like a squirrel,

swim like a fish, and outrun a trotting horse—and she did so on a regular basis.

Each day, the king's train started moving as soon as dawn crossed into pale daylight. It was mighty thing, ostensibly meant to provide for the elderly monarch's comfort and security, in reality meant to impress the Bright Bay diplomats with a reminder of what Hawk Haven could bring to bear if treachery was intended.

Scouts preceded the entire body, fanning out to the sides. Race Forester was often among them and he was the only one who was ever aware of Firekeeper's presence in the surrounding woods.

Following the scouts were wings of light cavalry, the riders armored in leather, armed with bows as well as swords. The heavier cavalry rode closer to the king's carriage, the dust they stirred considered a fair trade for the safety their presence offered.

Here, too, rode the members of King Tedric's court, some in carriages, some on horseback. Elise traded back and forth between the two conveyances, but her cousin Sapphire remained on horseback. Sapphire wore armor after the fashion of the light cavalry, the leather portions dyed deep blue, the metal protecting the joints polished to bright silver. A long sword was sheathed across her back, its pommel set with a bright stone that some said was a sapphire and others insisted was merely glass. Over one arm or slung from her saddle she carried a shield with her personal device: a silver field emblazoned with an octagonal sapphire.

Her brother Jet was similarly accoutred, though his chosen colors were black and gold. Firekeeper was amused to discover that while most of the soldiers were half in love with Sapphire, they thought her brother a fop and pretender.

Groups of foot soldiers were interspersed about the column, some guarding the creaking baggage wagons, some trudging in the rear. Progress was so slow that these men and women had time to argue, sing, gamble, and pursue rivalries between units.

This provided Firekeeper's first exposure to a mass of the common folk and she found them fascinating. Despite her usual dislike of crowds, she frequently went among the soldiers. Some resented her for behaving neither as a noble or a commoner, or from fear of Blind Seer, but Purcel Trueheart welcomed her—perhaps at his mother Zorana's request—and so the soldiers tolerated her at first. Later, she made friends among them and these welcomed her for herself.

At Derian's insistence, each day Firekeeper rode some hours on Patience, the grey gelding, amusing herself by practicing archery from the saddle. Her greatest delight, however, was when riding lessons were finished and she could dismount. Pacing the caravan on foot, she was free to investigate interesting parcels of woodland, spear fish from brooks, and in general to behave in a fashion that would drive insane any caretaker less accustomed to her ways than Derian.

At first Earl Kestrel had tried to restrict Firekeeper's movements, but he was too busy with his own responsibilities to enforce his commands. Later, King Tedric privately informed his vassal that Lady Blysse had his express permission to go where she wished. The earl, believing this yet another indication that his ward was the chosen heir, happily acceded.

Blind Seer caused numerous problems simply because all the horses and dogs were uniformly terrified of him. The dogs simply rolled over and groveled, rarely essaying an attack even when they outnumbered and outmassed the wolf. The horses, however, refused to compromise with their terror unless Firekeeper wasted a considerable amount of time talking to them—a task she found boring and repetitious since the stupider horses needed to be frequently reminded that the wolf wouldn't eat them. Even Patience, Roanne, and Race's Dusty were skittish at first, reacting to their fellows' fear.

Firekeeper resolved this frustrating situation by remaining away from both the cavalry and king's mounted companions as much as possible. If she wished human companionship, there was plenty among the soldiers. The placid oxen who drew the supply wagons were less imaginative than the horses, more ready to accept the wolf as an exceptionally large—and rather less annoying than most—dog.

Firekeeper's daily attire was a modified version of the knee-length leather breeches and vest that she had favored since her introduction to human-style clothing. She still ran barefoot, never having lost the leather toughness of her foot soles. Nor did she need gloves, for her long-fingered hands were as callused as any farmer's. To Firekeeper's delight, her dark brown hair finally had grown long enough to be tied back in a respectable queue. A few clips, gifts from Elise, kept the straggle ends from her eyes.

Since armed conflict was possible, Earl Kestrel insisted that his ward be outfitted with some sort of armor. Firekeeper had rebelled against the jangling weight of mail. However, after a vivid demonstration by Ox of how armor could prevent a sword from penetrating into the vitals, she had agreed—when necessary—to wear leather armor similar to that worn by Sapphire Shield, though less gaudily colored.

Except for riding lessons and weapons practice, during these days of travel Firekeeper was free to run wild, bare of foot and head, silent as the wind. Yet, despite her enthusiasm at being released once again into the woodlands, Firekeeper did not forget the task the king had enjoined her to perform. In daylight there was little she could do, but at night she left her bedroll and glided among the pitched tents, growling the curs to silence and taking shameless delight in eavesdropping on her fellows.

In this fashion the wolf-woman learned many strange things. Sapphire Shield, who by day rode straight and tall on the blue-dyed horse with its silver-white mane and tail, regularly cried herself to sleep each night. Lady Melina Shield frequently stole away into the woods where, believing herself unwatched, she danced in the moonlight and dipped glittering gemstones into pools of strongly scented liquor.

Jet Shield, in the guise of courtship, frequently pressed himself on Elise. When Elise refused him more than hot kisses and pawing at her breasts, Jet found relief among the women who trailed the caravan.

When night brought privacy, Lady Zorana vigorously tutored her daughter Nydia in deportment, schooling the thirteen-year-old so fiercely that Nydia, to this point ignored in favor of her older brother, was driven into sullenness one step shy of rebellion. At these moments, Zorana whispered to her, promising the little girl great things until she sweetened and was willing to memorize signals and responses that would puzzle Firekeeper more but that most human rituals still puzzled her.

Elsewhere, Firekeeper learned that King Tedric's old bones did not permit him to sleep easily unless he was dosed by his personal physician. Then nothing would wake him for some hours. In contrast, Dirkin East-branch never slept—at least not that Firekeeper had seen. He was also the only one among the king's retainers who seemed to notice her comings and goings, greeting her with a silent smile and a slight raise of one eyebrow.

Nighttime was not Firekeeper's only time for discovery. She developed greater respect for Earl Kestrel when she realized that the soldiers he commanded honored him for his courage and wisdom, not merely for his title. From Doc she learned something of the arts of treating cuts and bruises, of wrapping sprains, of salves and ointments. From Race and Ox she continued to learn human arts of survival and war. From Derian she learned humor and to play at dice.

In all her memory, these days of travel became some of Firekeeper's happiest, filled with new things and with fitting of them into a larger pattern of human society. No longer did she think dance and music were the only things worthwhile about the human way. Yet deep-rooted in her heart was the desire to be other, to run on four fast feet, to raise night-seeing eyes to the moon, and sing her praises from a wolf's heart.

ARRIVING IN HOPE, Prince Newell Shield was delighted to learn that King Tedric's party was not expected for some days yet. Advance riders were contracting with the locals for facilities and supplies. Some were specially delegated to treat with the town leaders.

Although technically part of Hawk Haven, Hope had changed hands so frequently—even since the Civil War ended some hundred and five years before—that its residents viewed the entire issue of citizenship with a cynical eye. If they felt a strong kinship with any group they felt it for the citizens of Good Crossing, Hope's sister city across the Barren River. There had been times when Good Crossing, too, had been part of Hawk Haven, times when Hope had been part of Bright Bay.

An even greyer area of loyalty was Bridgeton, a massive stone bridge on which shops and even houses had been built. Before the end of the Civil War, there had been a bridge here—the "good crossing" for which the original town had been named. In the century since the end of the war, the original bridge had been widened repeatedly until the small midriver islands on which the pilings were set had all but vanished.

Bridgeton was dominated by the Toll House in the center. Although no attempt was made to stop river traffic, enough commerce passed over Bridgeton's mighty span to keep it mended strong and its coffers full. Neither monarchy had attempted to restrict Bridgeton's business, for the bridge was ideal neutral ground for negotiations. At less peaceful times, the army that commanded the span also commanded the perfect place from which to police the river.

Prince Newell rather liked the locals' cynicism. Hope and Good Crossing both were home to dubious segments of the population, men and women who found a close, easily crossed border extremely convenient. It was home to deserters, thieves, smugglers, practitioners of doubtful customs, and just plain free spirits. The more law-abiding citizenry—which were the majority—put up with the scoundrels because of the money they brought in, and because people who had nowhere else to go would accept taxation (a rarity elsewhere in Hawk Haven) and poor treatment.

The law-abiding elements also delighted in the economic benefits derived from the permanent army garrison on the eastern fringes of the town. The army officers, aware that alienation of the townspeople was a good way to find themselves fighting alone if an invasion attempt was made, turned a blind eye to anything that did not clearly threaten Hawk Haven's border. In return, the underworld regularly supplied information about troop movements in Good Crossing and elsewhere in Bright Bay. It was an arrangement that worked for all.

Not wishing his presence to be known quite yet, Prince Newell had Rook arrange for rooms in the Silent Wench, a tavern with many doors and a reputation for discretion. Although this reputation was well earned, Newell took no risks. Both Rook and Keen, his assistant, were ordered to disguise themselves and give false names. Newell went the further step of never venturing out of the tavern before sunset.

In many towns in both Hawk Haven and Bright Bay such behavior would be either foolhardy or a guarantor of boredom. Hope was not a typical town and with diplomatic contingents from the rival nations converging upon it, even those rules it usually upheld were broken.

Following a long day's sleep, sorely needed after journeys on water and land, Newell Shield sauntered down to the conveniently dim-lit tavern. He doubted that his own mother could recognize him in this light, but nonetheless he kept a greasy leather hat securely on his head, the wide brim shadowing his eyes. Slouching in a corner booth, calling for food and drink in harsh accents, he trusted that no one but Rook and Keen would know him for the widower prince of Hawk Haven.

While he ate, he listened to the gossip, but the Silent Wench was renowned for her discretion and those who stayed there were not the type to give much away. Paying in guild tokens which Rook had acquired back in the port and at Eagle's Nest, Prince Newell ventured into the night. A soft cough from the shadows told him that Keen trailed him, but Newell looked neither right nor left.

Keen was a round-faced, slightly soft-looking man in his late twenties. By preference, he wore his straight brown hair loose to his shoulders and cut blunt across his brow rather than pulled back in a fashionable queue. Keen's close-cut beard had the same glossy sheen as an animal's coat and his large, brown eyes seemed guileless and gentle. That was all deception. Violence brewed beneath that innocent gaze, as more than one woman lured into Keen's bed had discovered. Newell found him very useful.

Those who walked alone through the streets of Hope at night were either drunks or fools or very confident of their own strength. Newell clearly did not belong to either of the first two categories and so no one bothered him.

He strolled along, noting that the Night Roost Inn displayed the scarlet eagle of the Hawk Haven royal family. Here, then, stayed the advance guard for the king. The laughter he heard through the taproom's open window was doubtless that of their guests, locals wined and dined to make them glad to grant favors on their monarch's behalf.

It took Newell longer to find Stonehold's presence, for although Stonehold was no more at war with Hawk Haven than was Bright Bay, when there had been war, Stonehold had regularly supported Hawk Haven's rival. Discretion regarding their representative's presence in Hope was wise, for only the most open-minded could believe that it would be to Hawk Haven's benefit. But Newell found the Stoneholders by snooping among stables and kitchen yards, swapping tall tales with burly men with soldiers' bearing yet conspicuously out of uniform. Many were deserters or mercenaries, but at last he found those whose telltale accents gave their origin away.

Having found Stonehold, it didn't take more than another hour to find those who were spying for Bright Bay. These hid their accents, refrained from the nautical jargon with which even the most inland-dwelling salted their language, and dressed as neutrally as he did himself. They were ready with their money, buying drinks and food, encouraging conjecture and speculation in the hope of learning something to their advantage.

Though Newell drank wine and ale as offered, tonight he said nothing beyond commenting on the weather or the quality of the local vintages. Tonight he was taking the pulse of the situation and finding it racing. Humming to himself, just slightly drunk, he ambled back to his room at the Silent Wench.

❀

THE FIRST NEWS that King Tedric's party received when they arrived outside Hope before noon on the fifth day of travel was that Bright Bay's contingent was not expected in Good Crossing until late the next evening. This advantage of a day and a half did not mean that there wasn't plenty to do.

King Tedric, along with his closest advisors and personal staff, would stay within the permanent fort to the east of Hope: the Fortress of the Watchful Eye. Although the great stone-walled structure could contain more, the king told his commanders to set up in the surrounding open zone surrounding the fortress. No one complained, for the late-summer weather, though sometimes muggy for marching, had been so clement that camping was a pleasure.

Earl Kestrel ordered that his personal encampment be set up at the fringes of the field, on the side nearest the cultivated areas. Part of his reason was a desire to keep Blind Seer away from the bulk of the army, part because the cavalry companies were stationed on the other fringe, near to the river where the horses could be watered with ease. The earl's light mount, Coal, had joined Roanne, Patience, and Dusty in grudgingly accepting the wolf and thus Norvin could skirt the larger army encampment and ride between his areas of responsibility with relative ease.

Derian was assisting Valet and Ox with setting up tents when Race Forester arrived. More than willing to show off his skills to those who could appreciate them, Race had accepted a temporary scout's commission, reporting directly to Earl Kestrel. He looked good in the brown trousers and green shirt of the scouts, the Kestrel arms—a shield divided top to bottom into narrow blue and red bands, blazoned with a gold hunting horn—over his heart.

Race's ego had not been hurt at all during his association with the scouts and he was swaggering a bit when he joined the others, evidently bristling with gossip.

"Lend a hand," Ox said with the good humor that rarely left him, "and tell us what you've learned."

Race grinned and grabbed a tent pole. "Half of Hope's folk already believe they know why we're here. The other half claims not to care. My gossips say differently, that Hope is glad to have us here. Whatever happens with the negotiations, they expect to come out the victors. The wine and ale merchants have been importing from anywhere they can get it, anticipating that once the troops are in place commerce will be slowed."

"As it will be," Ox said. His back muscles bulged as he hauled the earl's pavilion onto its frame. "Before Earl Kestrel dismissed me this afternoon—saying with his usual kindness that he'd be in meetings until sunset and there was no need for me to just stand about—I heard enough about security precautions to know that no one is getting near any place King Tedric will be without careful searching."

"Well," Race commented, "tonight will be the last night without rules. The army commanders have permission to release up to two-thirds of their troops for a night on the town. Those who volunteer to stay back will get bonus pay."

"We're not eligible for that," Ox said, pointing at Valet and Derian with his bearded chin, his hands being full, "as we're personal retainers. Are you for a night out or bonus pay?"

Race shrugged. "I haven't decided. I thought I'd learn if Earl Kestrel has any preferences."

Pausing in his own work, Derian glanced skyward, located Elation soaring on the warm winds, and knew that Firekeeper was safe. He'd gradually come to rely on the peregrine for such signals and suspected that they were offered deliberately, that the bird knew how difficult it was for him to track the wolf-woman and was assisting him.

Despite how he had defended Blind Seer's intelligence to his mother, the thought made him uneasy, as if he were standing outside of a door into a new world. If he accepted that a falcon was voluntarily helping him do his job, he must accept that many things he had thought simply old tales just might be true. If you accepted beasts that were as intelligent as humans, then were the horrors and wonders told of in some of the other stories far away?

Idly, Derian waved one hand in greeting and was certain he saw Elation dip wing in acknowledgment. To distract himself he said:

"I suppose the negotiations themselves will be held on Bridgeton?"

Race nodded. "That's right. Advance parties agreed to that easily enough. They'll be using the Toll House and traffic under Bridgeton itself is being halted entirely during the meetings."

"I bet the guilds love that!" Derian whistled. "And what is being done about the shops and residences on Bridgeton itself?"

"On our side," Race said, raising his eyebrows eloquently on the word "our," "advance negotiations have succeeded in renting space on rooftops and in front of shops. I understand they tried to get everyone to agree to shut down, but the guilds were having none of it. I expect that Bright Bay did no better."

Ox grumbled, "Two towns—three if you count Bridgeton—united in nothing but their desire to oppose the forces that surround them."

Valet said softly from where he was stirring the fire, looking for embers to heat his iron:

"And I, for one, don't believe for a moment that they're not interested in these negotiations. If ever Bright Bay and Hawk Haven make peace, the first casualty will be this arrogant trio. We must not forget that."

Race stared at him in amazement, then said, "Valet, you don't say much, but when you do, you sure say a mouthful."

LATE THAT AFTERNOON, when Derian was grooming Roanne and coaching Firekeeper as she sparred with Ox, Doc came into their camp.

Like Race, Sir Jared had taken a temporary commission, but his was with the medical corps. His uniform was the brilliant scarlet that served both to mark him out as a medic and to hide the gorier side effects of his calling.

Unlike Race, Doc didn't wear the Kestrel badge, but the one granted to him when he received his knighthood: a hand palm upraised and impaled with several arrows. Beneath that was pinned a brooch in the shape of an eagle outlined in scarlet enamel, the wing feathers worked in silver, the beak and talons in gold, and the eyes perfectly faceted diamonds.

Doc slipped Roanne a piece of carrot, then said to Derian in a hushed voice, "I'd like to speak with you privately when you're done."

"I'll meet you there," Derian tossed his head to indicate a hillock about equidistant between their camp and a copse of trees that skirted the field, "as soon as I have this done."

Curiosity made Derian finish more quickly than he should and by way of an apology he gave the chestnut mare another chunk of carrot. Seizing a water bottle, he ambled to where Doc leaned against a slender tree trunk.

"What's up?" he asked, sitting beside the other man. "You look grim."

"Do you know Hope well?" was Doc's answer. "I haven't been here for some years."

"Pretty well," Derian replied. "I haven't been here for about a year, but I've come the last several with my father. You can get some good deals on stock this time of year from folk who don't want to feed them over the winter."

"Legally owned?" Doc asked, curious despite his evident preoccupation.

"Not all," Derian admitted, "but quite a few are. There are wild horses in the plains to the southwest. Some cross into Hawk Haven, but the best herds are found in Bright Bay. Import is legal, but elsewhere you pay a fee at the border. Here . . ."

Doc nodded. "I see. Well, I need your help. The Surgeon General and the king's personal physician have asked me to purchase something for them."

He hesitated and Derian said quickly, "I won't say a word to anyone, not even Firekeeper if you don't want me to."

"I'll take your word on that," the knight said, and Derian felt his heart swell with pride.

"Go on," he said, a bit more gruffly than he had intended.

"The king," Doc said, still hesitant, "is not a young man and this journey has not been easy for him."

Derian decided to help him along. "Lady Elise told Firekeeper and me—she didn't want to talk about it with her aunts, they having their own agendas—that she was worried. She said King Tedric looked grey and tired."

"Lady Elise," Doc said, a glow banishing his worried expression for a moment, "has good eyes for this. She has studied some of what I've been teaching Firekeeper, saying that if there *is* trouble, ancestors forfend, she wants to be able to do more than hide in the fortress."

The glow vanished as Doc went back to his immediate concern.

"King Tedric's heart is not strong," he said, as if admitting to treason, "not diseased, simply tired. As long as he took limited, healthful exercise and rested well it did not trouble him. However, both have been denied to him.

"There is a tonic that has been helping him. Unhappily, the king's physician did not anticipate so great a need and he has nearly exhausted his supply. Some of the ingredients are rare and not of the type the Surgeon General would stock in quantity for the field hospital."

"So they want you to buy some," Derian prompted.

"Yes." Jared smiled. "In short, I need to find an apothecary who will not gossip, preferably one who is loyal to Hawk Haven. Can you help me?"

Derian considered. "What are the ingredients you need?"

After Jared had told him, Derian smiled encouragingly. "Some of those are used for horses as well as people. We can buy those from a farrier

I know and none the wiser. The last few . . . Yes, I think I know the person to deal with. My father buys fragrances from her for my mother."

"Fragrances?" Doc said dubiously.

"Don't worry," Derian assured him. "Hazel's a healer as well. Perfumes are her hobby. My father swears her attar of roses is superior to anything you can get in Eagle's Nest."

Doc nodded. "Very good. Now, remember, not a word of this to anyone."

"I promise." Derian's eyes sparkled. "If any of the others ask me what we were talking about, I'll say you wanted my advice on the best way to court a girl."

To his great amusement, Sir Jared Surcliffe colored nearly as deep a red as his uniform.

They left camp that evening as dusk was falling. Derian had made a quick trip into the town and assured himself that both farrier and apothecary were going to be open that evening.

"Extended hours," he told Doc as they walked into town that evening, both of them dressed casually as if joining the men on leave. "Who would miss a chance to do business tonight with all these soldiers with money to spend and only one night to spend it?"

"I'd forgotten that not all of them would go to taverns and brothels," Doc confessed.

"Nope," Derian said cheerfully, caught up in the general air of festivity despite his awareness of the importance of their mission. "Many will end up there, but some simply want a decent meal or to augment their kits. Others will be shopping for gifts to send to the family back home. Smuggling being what it is here, this is the perfect place to find something exotic and wonderful."

When the two men reached the town proper, they had to thread their way through streets crowded with exultant soldiers. It was too early for many to be very drunk, but they passed at least one brawl: two men, slugging at each other with such narrow focused concentration that they hadn't noticed that the whore who was the reason for their dispute had left with another man.

"I'm glad," Doc said, "that Firekeeper agreed to remain behind."

Derian laughed. "I think I solved that one rather neatly. I took her with me this afternoon. She was horrified by the crowding and stench. When I told her it would be worse tonight, she was happy to stay away."

As they moved along, several times they encountered former patients who offered to buy Sir Jared and his friend a drink. Other soldiers, often those with whom Derian had raced horses or thrown dice of an evening, called out to the pair to join them.

"We'd better accept some of their invitations," Derian advised, "unless you want to look like you're on duty."

Doc agreed somewhat reluctantly, but Derian kept an eye on the flow of traffic and made their excuses.

"I've got to stop by a farrier and pass on some information for my family business," he said. "Coming, Doc? This fellow has some fine horses, better than the one you're riding."

Doc shrugged. "I guess so. Just remember, my commission doesn't cover a private mount."

They made their exit neatly and Doc gave Derian an admiring punch on the shoulder.

"Nicely done, young man. Cover story as well as an excuse to leave."

"At your service, Sir Jared," Derian laughed.

"What excuse do you have in mind for our trip to the apothecary?" Jared asked with a grin.

"Perfume, of course," Derian replied lightly, "for that girl you were asking me about."

This time he decided not to ignore Jared's blush.

"Dare I guess who is on your mind?" he asked. "It won't go any further."

"Please don't let it," Jared begged. "I've tried hard to hide my feelings, but she is betrothed."

Elise's name hardly needed to be spoken.

"A political arrangement," Derian said firmly.

"One she asked for," Jared countered, "if rumor is correct."

"One she may regret, if I read her right. Jet is not all Elise imagined him to be. I think she has learned more about him over the past moon-span, especially since she has been traveling in this company."

Derian hesitated, wondering how much he should say. Ninette, Elise's maid, was one of the few women in this entourage who was not in uniform, above his station, or a prostitute. Although Ninette was not really his type, Derian enjoyed female company and had found himself drifting into visiting with her. Teasing and flirtation had progressed into something like confidences, offered since Ninette shrewdly recognized Derian's sincere liking for her mistress.

Jared remained somberly unconvinced and so Derian went on, "Jet frequently seeks Elise's company when the day's travel is over. Lately, I've noticed that she finds reasons for them to visit in public."

"She is a lady," Jared protested indignantly, "not some tart!"

"She is a young woman," Derian persisted steadily, "and a woman's blood can run as hot as a man's with no fault to her but that she risks a child and a man does not. Ninette tells me that Elise was not always so chary of time alone with Jet."

Jared colored, clearly torn between indignation at the thought that his ideal could be vulnerable to passion, and hope that she indeed did not favor her betrothed.

"She . . ." He stopped, unable to go on.

"You told me once you were married," Derian said. "An arranged marriage to a girl you had known from childhood."

"Yes." Doc's monosyllable was guarded.

"And are you telling me that you and your betrothed never touched before the wedding? No kissing games? No little trial runs, a blouse opened maybe, a hand guided to touch?"

The light was too dim for Derian to be certain, but he felt sure Doc was blushing again. Shining Horse Hooves! He himself had played the same games and more, and he could feel his own color rising. It must be that talking about a thing was more embarrassing than actually do-ing it.

"Don't fault Elise for having the same impulses," Derian continued, despite his embarrassment, "especially with a man she has been smitten with since she was a girl. Take hope instead that she no longer welcomes such games."

Doc said nothing, but in the flickering light from a freshly lit street-lamp, Derian caught the hint of a smile.

"Here's the farrier," Derian said, glad to have an excuse to change the subject. "Come along and look at the horses."

Their stay lasted well over an hour, extended because the farrier was busy with a group of cavalry women, each of whom was replacing items from her kit, several of whom wanted to try the paces of a horse or two. Knowing that Doc didn't want to draw attention to himself, Derian chatted up one of the stablehands, tried out a horse or two himself, and even convinced Doc to relax enough to examine a colt with great potential.

Derian did indeed have business messages from his father to the farrier and would have delivered them that afternoon but for the opportunity this gave him to draw the farrier aside. Then he asked to see the man's stock of horse medicines. Taking covert signals from Doc, he investigated the wares and made his purchases.

Once they were out in the street with their packages, Derian said, "You'll need to speak with the apothecary yourself. I know something about these ointments, but nothing about the rest of the stuff you mentioned."

"That won't be a problem," Doc replied. "With what we've already purchased, she'll have a harder time guessing just why I need what I do. Especially," he grinned at Derian, "when I add a small order for attar of roses."

The apothecary's shop was set back from the street behind a small herb garden that provided advertisement for her wares. Climbing roses in red, white, and pale yellow covered the front of the shop, still heavily in bloom despite the lateness of the season.

"Some say," Derian commented, as they passed through the gate, "that the apothecary's a sorceress."

Doc looked quite serious. "I wouldn't be at all surprised if she is talented. It is late for roses to be so heavily in bloom."

Despite Derian's own turns tending the family kitchen garden, Derian had never considered the significance of late-blooming roses. Without further words, he opened the shop door.

As elsewhere in the town, business was brisk, but Hazel Healer herself recognized Derian as a regular customer and left her assistants to handle the walk-in trade. A woman in her mid-fifties with strong features that would never be called pretty, nonetheless, her confidence and friendly smile made her handsome.

"Here's an old customer," she said. "Is Colby with you?"

"Not this time," Derian replied. "He's waiting to make his trip until the upcoming negotiations are through. I'm here with my new master, Earl Kestrel."

"As the wolf-girl's keeper." Hazel smiled. "Yes. I'd heard something of that. Come into my workroom and tell me more."

Derian could not have wished for better and he motioned for Jared to follow him. Once they were in the workroom, Derian made introductions.

"Mistress Hazel Healer," he said, "I would like to present my friend, Jared."

Doc had asked not to be introduced with his full name and titles, but here again gossip had gone before them.

"Sir Jared Surcliffe," Hazel replied, making a deep curtsy. "I am honored."

With a slight shrug for Derian, Doc returned her greeting with a bow. "And I am to meet you. Derian has spoken well of you and of your shop."

"Thank you, and don't look so surprised that I know who you are. I'm from Eagle's Nest myself originally. Many members of my family live and work at the castle. I have seen you there myself, years ago."

"Would I know any of your family?" Jared asked politely.

"Unless you frequent the grounds, Sir Jared," she said, "I doubt it. My cousin is Head Gardener now and, if the Green Thumb passes on, one of his children will follow in turn."

Derian grinned. "I know your aunt, then," he said. "Goody Holly Gardener. She has befriended my wolf-girl, as you called her."

"Firekeeper," Hazel said, twinkling at his surprise, for Lady Blysse's wolf-name was not commonly known. "Aunt Holly wrote me when she heard you were coming here with the army, asking that I help as I might. She never realized that you and I have been friends since you were but freckles and red hair."

She poured them tiny crystal glasses of her own cherry cordial and they settled down to visit. Despite the relaxed atmosphere, Derian was surprised when Doc himself opened the question of the necessary herbs.

"Mistress Hazel," Doc said, "I am in great need of several rare—and expensive—items for my medical use. I would like to purchase them from you or, if that is not possible, have you act as my agent in their purchase. I am willing to pay more for your complete silence in that matter—and will do so, although I do not think such is necessary."

Hazel, who a moment before had been laughing so hard at one of Derian's stories that he had worried she had imbibed too much of her own distilling, grew immediately serious.

"Tell me what you need," she said, "and unless it violates my guild's code, you will have it."

Their conversation became technical then. The one thing Derian was certain of was that although Hazel did not say so, she had both a good idea what Doc was preparing to concoct and for whom. Nor did she ask questions when Jared bought a small jar of her famous rose attar.

When they departed the shop, Doc's purse was much lighter, for he had insisted on paying market rates and a bonus besides, and the two men had several more bundles to stuff into their jacket pockets.

"Come and see me again," Hazel said at the door. "Bring Firekeeper. I'd like to meet her."

"If I can, I will," Derian promised.

"And I with him," Jared added. "I think you have much you could teach me."

"Gladly," she said with a contented smile. "Gladly."

The streets were emptier now, but the noise from the taverns louder. The two men walked briskly along, aware that human predators seeking human prey would be prowling. Sober and in company, they were not precisely worried—there was easier prey about—but they saw no reason to invite trouble. None sought them out, but others were not so lucky.

Past the market area, where residences mingled with businesses and warehouses, they were drawn up short in their steps by a shrill scream of pure terror.

Derian whirled, orienting on the sound. Doc pointed down a narrow alley at whose far end was just visible a flicker of light.

"There!" he said, starting to dash that way.

"No, you fool!" Derian said, grabbing his arm. "It could be a trap—a bait and hit!"

Doc shook him loose. "Then I'll fall for it!"

Cursing himself for behaving as no city-bred man should, Derian ran after him. Their boots splashed in noxious puddles of unseen mess. Doc bumped a pile of trash that squeaked and spewed forth rats. Then they were in the open again.

They found themselves in a narrow street on which just about every streetlamp had been blown out. In this scattered light, a young woman, her black hair a cloud about her shoulders, was holding off three men. Only the fact that she bore a sword and shield while they were armed with knives had made this possible.

Even as Derian and Jared realized what was going on, the boldest of the attackers darted forward. Raising his knife he made a murderous slash. The woman blocked with her shield, but as she did so the second darted forward and tangled her sword with his cloak. The third was about to disarm her when Doc, unarmed except for his courage, went charging forth.

His bellow halted the attackers in midmotion. The woman took advantage of the momentary confusion to solidly bash the first man with her shield. As he crumpled unconscious, she spun, perhaps more from exhaustion than from skill, and Derian got a good look at the device: a octagonal blue sapphire on a silver field.

"Hold on!" he yelled. "Rescue's here!"

Jared's momentum carried him into the second man, who dropped his cloak and reached for his knife. Derian would have liked to keep an eye on him, but found himself confronting the third man, the one who had been about to take Sapphire's sword. The long knife in the bandit's right hand glittered wickedly, but Derian didn't feel fear, only a dreadful clarity of focus on that shining silver edge.

"Haallooo!" he hollered, drawing his own knife, a more utilitarian item meant for cutting rope or minor trimming of hooves. Fortunately, what it lacked in length and grandeur it made up in sharpness. His first blow sliced his opponent along the left upper arm—a miss since he'd meant to stab him in the chest, but effective enough.

His opponent hit as well, a long slash down Derian's right side that ruined his waistcoat and spilled packets of the farrier's medicines onto the cobbles but otherwise did no damage. They sparred for several moments longer, during which time Derian became aware that Sapphire had joined Doc and the two were dealing effectively with the remaining bandit.

Still, Derian wondered if they could reach him before his luck ran out. Practice with sword and shield he had; he'd even been in the occasional tavern brawl, but never before had he been in a close-up fight with death or maiming as the goal. The thought was fleeting, passing through his brain as he and his nameless opponent traded blow and counter, dodged and struck as if they were partners in some weird, unchoreographed dance.

Sometimes Derian felt his blade hit something solid. Sometimes he was the solid thing hit—and hurt. More often there was the empty swish of air against his knife.

The dreadful clarity of the first few seconds was fading now, replaced by vagueness. Blood was sticky on Derian's left arm. His own or his opponent's? The face before him kept fading in and out.

Faintly, Derian heard a low howl, saw his opponent's expression of focused cruelty transform into one of pure terror, and then a dark and terrible shadow leapt onto his opponent.

When Derian looked again, there was a raw, red hole where the man's throat had been and his body was limp, tumbling onto the street, blood gushing once from that terrible hole, then ebbing to a dribble.

A slim arm grasped Derian firmly around his waist. He struggled, and a familiar voice said:

"It's me, Derian!"

"Firekeeper?"

"It's me," she said, her voice fierce and choked. "The fight is over."

To his eternal relief and eternal embarrassment, Derian Carter took one look at Firekeeper, saw the splash of red blood across her face, and collapsed into a dead faint.

XVI

FIREKEEPER VANISHED BEFORE THE NIGHT watch arrived so resolving matters with the Hope town guard took less time than Derian had dreaded. Sapphire's three attackers were known criminals, unwanted elements even within Hope's comparatively easygoing structure. Moreover, two of those who had been attacked were members of the Hawk Haven noble class and the third was a personal servant of Earl Kestrel.

After asking very few questions, the night watch took the thugs away—one dead, two living, though one of these was badly concussed—to the jail.

At Sapphire's request, the men did not take her to her own tent, but to the Kestrel camp at the fringes of the larger Hawk Haven encampment.

"I need," Sapphire explained, "a chance to clear my head. Mother will have questions. I need to know the answers."

Derian thought it odd that a woman of twenty-three should be so worried about what her mother would think—especially when the woman considered herself a fitting candidate for the throne—but he was too aware of his place as Sapphire's social inferior to ask any questions.

Instead, ignoring his own wounds, he concentrated on his duties as host. Guiding Sapphire toward that same hillock on which he had conferred with Doc just that afternoon, Derian explained:

"We won't wake anyone out here. Doc, go get your gear so you can look at her wounds."

Jared Surcliffe took Derian's order as a matter of course, and if Sapphire looked offended at the young redhead's presumption, Derian pretended not to notice.

"Earl Kestrel," Derian said, seating Sapphire where she could lean against a rock and trying hard not to notice a spreading stain of blood along her side, "is standing watch tonight with his cavalry force so that one more could go on leave into town."

"I heard him being toasted in the tavern," Sapphire commented, keeping her voice steady. "His men do love him. Strange, for he's such a dour sort." She paused, "And, by the way, thank you for coming to my aid."

"I was just following Doc's lead," Derian admitted, though her smile made him feel awfully good about himself.

" 'Doc' being Sir Jared?" Sapphire asked.

"That's right, Mistress. That's what we called him on our trip west and it just stuck."

"West . . ." Sapphire looked at him, perhaps saw him as a person for the first time. "You are?"

"Derian Carter, Mistress," he said, wishing he didn't feel so tongue-tied. Sapphire was as different from Elise as night from day, but no less captivating. "I work for Earl Kestrel."

"That's right," she said. "I remember you now, the red-haired youth who tends Lady Blysse."

Derian privately approved of her presence of mind. He'd heard her call Firekeeper a few more uncomplimentary things when she thought no one was listening. A crunching of boots on grass and a detached star of lantern light announced Jared Surcliffe's return.

"Valet was awake," he said, "and had hot water on to make some tea to bring the earl. I borrowed some. Now, Mistress Sapphire, if I could attend to your wounds."

Inventory and treatment of their various cuts and bruises took some time. Sapphire, thanks to sword and shield, had escaped with mostly minor injuries, but a knife slash that had gotten through her guard and sliced the fabric of her shirt on her right side looked nasty. She also had countless bruises and nicks on her hands caused by wielding her sword and shield without gloves.

Derian had several small nicks of his own, none impressive, but all painful. His head ached abominably. Doc had escaped virtually unscathed.

"Mistress Shield," Doc explained unashamed, "came to my rescue."

"After you came to mine," she reminded him. "Again, thank you both."

Jared produced a flask of good brandy from one of his pockets.

"The lady can use the cap for a cup," he explained, pouring. "I also suspect that Valet will be here with the tea tray momentarily. Don't worry, Mistress Sapphire. He'll never say a word to anyone—not even Earl Kestrel—the soul of discretion, our Valet."

Sapphire accepted the cup gratefully and passed the flask to Derian.

"It doesn't matter overmuch," she said. "My mother will know and that's enough."

Derian swigged directly from the flask before passing it back to Jared. The strong liquor cleared his head and made him instantly bolder.

"If you don't mind my asking, Mistress Sapphire, but how did you come to be out there alone? You've never struck me as one to take foolish risks."

"I appreciate that," she said. "I . . . I went out with my brother, Jet. I wanted to see something of the town and everyone else was going somewhere interesting. Jet didn't want me to go with him, but I convinced him that I had as much right as he did to enjoy myself.

"He let me come with him—I guess since he couldn't stop me—but I soon understood why Jet didn't want me around. His plan was to get drunk and then . . ."

It was dark, but in the lantern light they could see her glance down in embarrassment.

Doc cut in, "We understand, Mistress."

Derian thought he sounded offended. Doubtless Sapphire would believe he was offended for her, which couldn't hurt, but Derian suspected Doc's indignation was for Jet's insult to Elise.

"As soon," Sapphire continued, "as Jet got drunk enough, he ditched me. I wandered around a bit and found myself in that poky little street. Those men jumped me."

"A good thing you had your sword and shield," Derian said, allowing a slight questioning note to enter his voice.

"Luck," came the blunt reply. "I had scarred the paint on my shield during our journey here. The armorer had white paint with him, but not silver. I decided to see what someone in the town could do . . ."

Ruefully, she looked at the newly battle-scarred shield. The delicate silver work was scored in multiple places and there was a large dent the size of a man's head.

"I understand better now," she said, false cheer in her voice, "why white is a preferable substitute for silver, at least for in the field. I shall make the change tomorrow and keep the silver field for show."

They toasted her choice and as they did so Valet shimmered up rather like magic with tea, cookies, and fruit neatly arranged on a tray. He set this on the rock behind Derian and vanished again.

"A remarkable man," Sapphire said. "May I pour?"

"Please do," Doc replied.

"What I would like to know," Derian asked the listening night, "is how Firekeeper happened to be there when we needed her."

Firekeeper stepped from the darkness. Blind Seer, his fur slightly damp, was with her.

"Tea?" Sapphire asked the newcomer, unable to keep a slightly frosty note out of her voice. "I see that the remarkable Valet has supplied a fourth cup."

"Thank you," Firekeeper said, accepting the proffered cup and hunkering down on her haunches.

"How *did* you happen to be there, Firekeeper?" Jared prompted.

"I follow," the wolf-woman said, "practicing cities. It isn't too hard at night once the people go inside, but in the crowds . . ."

She ended with an eloquent shudder.

"And Blind Seer?"

"He stay in the narrow places between buildings mostly," she said. "Is there a word, Derian?"

"Alley," he supplied automatically. "Why didn't you join us sooner?"

"You were doing so well," she said with a fey grin. "I not want to hurt your fun. Then the man you fight hit you in the head . . ."

"Is *that* what happened!" he muttered, remembering how everything had gotten dreamy.

"And Mistress Sapphire was giving a good fight to her man, so we came to help."

"We?" Derian asked carefully, remembering the nightmare vision of the bandit with his throat torn out, of Firekeeper's face smeared with blood.

"Blind Seer kill the man," Firekeeper said with indignant self-righteousness. "You tell me this not a thing to do!"

Sapphire had softened at Firekeeper's compliment to her skill. "Were you hurt?" she asked, refreshing Firekeeper's tea.

"No." Firekeeper looked almost disappointed. "I not get to fight."

Sapphire looked at her own dented shield, at the bandages on her side and hands. "It isn't nearly as much fun as it looks."

Jared and Derian nodded agreement. The wolf-woman did not seem at all convinced and the great shaggy beast at her side opened his fanged jaws in what Derian could swear was laughter.

BARON IVON ARCHER HAD TAKEN FULL ADVANTAGE of his rank to insist upon a good position for the Archer pavilion, although he himself would be splitting his time between his command and numerous conferences, returning there only to sleep. Given her strained relations with both Sapphire and Jet Shield, Elise had ample reason to be grateful for this.

Along the road, she and Ninette had shared a fairly small tent pitched between her father's tent and Aunt Zorana's. It was a very proper arrangement, one that offered some protection from Jet's increasingly impatient advances, but one that also guaranteed that she would hear every noise in the surrounding tents.

Her father, she discovered, snored—as did his manservant. Aunt Zorana insisted on being sung to sleep by her maid. Ninette rose repeatedly during the night to answer nature's call. After these intrusions, Elise felt a certain guilty pleasure that the heir to a barony could command not only room for a large pavilion, but a certain degree of space surrounding it. Ninette still chaperoned her—and Elise was glad for her company—but at least with her on the other side of a curtain Elise was not so aware of the other woman's nocturnal micturitions.

On the first morning following their arrival, Elise woke after the sun had risen. She was trying to guess the hour by the position of the sun shining through the pavilion's canvas when Ninette lifted the dividing curtain and peeped around it. The other woman's eyes were shining with excitement and Elise was certain she had some interesting gossip.

"Good morning, Ninette."

"Good morning, Elise. I have water on for tea. Would you like some?"

"I'd be grateful," Elise said, swinging her feet to the carpet at the side of her cot.

The camp bed had been an improvement over sleeping on pads on the floor of a tent barely large enough to stand in, but still some of her muscles protested. Stretching and enjoying the luxury of being able to spread her arms over her head, Elise slipped into her morning robe and went to join Ninette in the pavilion's common area. The curtain in front of Baron Archer's sleeping niche was lifted, revealing the section to be empty.

"My father?" she asked Ninette, crossing to where tea is brewing in a cozy pot.

"Rose before dawn," Ninette replied, "and has gone to inspect his men. He said to remind you that the contingent from Bright Bay is expected this evening. You are to stay within the bounds of our encampment unless expressly summoned into the city."

"As if," Elise said, sipping the raspberry leaf tea, "I would want to go there. Doubtless it's full of rascals looking to take advantage of this situation."

"Your cousin Sapphire," Ninette said, lowering her voice and glancing at the canvas walls for shadows that might indicate listeners without, "went to town last night. She had quite an adventure."

With Elise's encouragement, Ninette told the full story of Sapphire's encounter with the bandits. She'd already been over to Earl Kestrel's encampment and coaxed a few details from Derian—prompting him to tell her the truth by offering him some of the rumors that were already circulating within the small servants' community among the nobles' pavilions.

"Lady Melina," Elise said thoughtfully, "must be furious. I wonder whether she's more angry at Sapphire for getting attacked or at Jet for leaving his sister?"

"I couldn't say, Elise," Ninette admitted. "I have gone out of my way to avoid her. Lady Melina's lady's maid had a red mark on her cheek the shape of a hand and little Opal had clearly been crying."

"Wise," Elise said. "What time is it?"

"An hour past full sunrise, my lady."

"And we are not expected anywhere?"

"Sir Jared Surcliffe indicated that he would be at the hospital center until midday. After that, he would be happy to continue your and Lady Blysse's tutorial in the treatment of wounds."

"Send him a message saying you and I would be glad to take him up on his kind offer. Say that unless we hear otherwise we will meet him at the Kestrel encampment."

"Very good."

"Then why don't we have breakfast here in the pavilion? Afterwards, perhaps, we can use the luxury of being stopped in one place for longer than a night to bathe and wash our hair."

Having finished these pleasant domestic tasks, the two women, their hair still wet and scented with the marigold petals and rosemary leaves with which they had rinsed it, stole away to a natural solar created by a grouping of boulders near one edge of the camp. By climbing over the outer rocks, they found a little hollow, perfect for two, open to sun and sky though invisible from without. The walls of the Watchful Eye loomed to their south, between them and the river. Wise tactics dictated that a clear zone be kept around the fort, so no troops were stationed anywhere near their refuge.

"Doubtless," Elise explained to Ninette, spreading her hair on a flat rock to speed its drying and pillowing her head on one of the cushions they had brought with them, "the army would have removed these rocks but for their great size and their distance from the walls. Even a good archer would be pressed to make an accurate shot from here."

"I hadn't thought of that, Elise," Ninette said, spreading out her own hair to dry. "I simply noticed these yesterday when we were pitching camp and decided to investigate, thinking they offered possibilities for discreet privacy within limits."

Elise, knowing her ever-romantic cousin had been thinking of rendez-vous with Jet, colored slightly. She hadn't quite been able to explain her changing feelings toward him, even to Ninette—perhaps especially to Ninette, knowing how the other woman dreamed of Elise as queen.

She settled for murmuring something grateful but noncommittal and gazing into the sky. There was much to consider, both regarding her own personal predicament and the impending conference. Elise was weighing the advantages and disadvantages of being invited to the initial conferences when voices interrupted her meditations.

Ninette started to her feet, but Elise cautioned her to silence with a finger raised to her lips. There had been something in those voices, something familiar, something angry, that made her wish their presence to remain unknown. Rolling over, her drying hair chill against her neck, Elise crept to one of the gaps between the towering rocks and peered out. Sight confirmed what her ears had told her. Lady Melina Shield stood without preparing to pass judgment on her son and daughters.

Already it was too late to make a graceful exit, for the words streamed from Lady Melina, pungent and furious. In any case, Elise was not certain she wanted to depart. Jet had taken advantage of his position as her betrothed to listen at Archer family conferences. Certainly she had as much right as he did!

Ignoring Ninette's trembling gestures that they could get away by climbing over some other rocks, Elise instead motioned for her to begin braiding her wet hair.

"We will not skulk away," she said softly into Ninette's ear. "That would be a confession that they have greater rights than I do—and no matter how well Lady Melina thinks of herself, they do not!"

Ninette subsided and began plaiting Elise's long hair into a pair of thick braids. Elise ignored the tugging at her scalp, all her attention on the drama unfolding without.

"I wonder," Lady Melina was saying, evidently not for the first time judging from the sulky expressions on her three children's faces, "that a woman as closely descended from the family that produced Queen Zorana the Great could bear such foolish children. It must be your Redbriar father's contribution."

"Our father's great-grandmother was Queen Zorana herself," Jet growled. His dark eyes beneath his handsome brow were bloodshot. Elise might have felt more pity for him if she hadn't suspected he was nursing a hangover. "She is our great-great-grandmother. Can you claim closer kinship?"

"Impudence," Melina sighed. "A shame you have so little cause for it, my stupid son. Doubtless when Queen Zorana married Clive Elkwood, the strength of the Shields was diluted and diluted again when King Chalmer insisted on marrying a commoner. Pity that King Tedric's lot all died. My brother Newell might have returned Shield strength to the royal line."

Elise could tell that Melina was toying with her brood, taunting them, insulting them. She wondered that the elder two took it so calmly, for neither was known for patience. With a slight shiver, she realized that they feared the little woman who stood there, her gaudy gemstone jewelry glittering in the midmorning sunlight.

"But Tedric's children are dead and Newell never got a legitimate heir." Lady Melina drawled the word "legitimate" with a special glower for her son. "Doubtless like some he has spilled enough seed into anonymous loins."

Elise felt her face grow hot. Though Jet had never gotten that close to her, she felt herself shamed by implication.

"Sowing wild oats," Melina continued in her silky, furious voice, "is well enough for common soldiers but for a boy whose only hope for the crown is his betrothal alliance with another family it is not only irresponsible, it is near treason!"

She grasped the jet pendant depending from the multi-stone necklace around her throat and closed her fingers around it as if those slender fingers could crush it. Jet's eyes widened in unfeigned terror and Elise imagined that she felt heat from where her betrothal gem rested against her skin.

"Treason against the crown you could wear and treason to the father and mother who would wear it before you!"

In a single easy, graceful movement Lady Melina removed a fine chain silver bracelet. Then she took the jet pendant from its place on her necklace and attached it to the chain. Swinging it pendulum-like, she crooned in a voice that transfixed her listeners.

"From this moment forth, Jet, my son, your loins are bound. Your staff shall not rise. Your blood shall not heat. Until you prove yourself worthy of power, know yourself impotent! This is my curse!"

Elise bit her lip to hold back an involuntary cry of fear. She should be grateful, but this ritual gelding spoke of black sorcery she had thought vanished from the land.

A small whimper of what might have been laughter, but could equally be a strangled scream, slipped from Sapphire Shield's lips. Melina turned her gaze upon her eldest daughter, pitiless despite the bandages visible beneath the bodice of the young woman's gown and the gloves that offered mute testimony to the cuts and bruises on her hands.

"And you," Melina sneered with even more contempt, "you pitifully ambitious chit! I've watched you riding your great blue stallion, armed and armored like some warrior maiden from a nursery tale. How did you like your first taste of battle?"

"I won," Sapphire retorted, clearly speaking with effort. "Two of the three men fell to my blows."

"Yet you screamed for help like an infant," came the cold reply, "screamed and brought to your aid our greatest rival for the throne: Lady Blysse herself, that flea-bitten waif who has insinuated herself into King Tedric's favor. You brought Lady Blysse and her lackeys."

Sapphire tried to protest, but Melina surged on, her hand coming to rest on the blue stone in her necklace.

"Do you think I enjoyed thanking a common carter for assisting in my daughter's rescue? Do you think I enjoyed being reminded that a lesser scion of House Kestrel has been awarded a knighthood that none of my children will ever have the courage to win? Sir Jared rushed to your aid though unarmored and not even bearing a knife! You brag that you defeated two common thugs, yet were it not for the three who raced to your aid, I doubt that you would have taken out even one!"

Between clenched teeth Sapphire said defiantly, "When have you even stood before even one opponent?"

Melina remained pitiless. "I am wise enough to know that a woman can have other strengths—that wisdom and knowledge grant their own powers. You, however, you care for nothing but posing. You resent Jet's competition instead of seeing that it matters not which of you wears the crown. Whoever wears it, my will shall rule!

"Better," Melina continued after pause pregnant with menace, "that you limit your ambitions to the inheritance you will take from your father and me. When you inherit your lands and country manses, then you may prance around in arms and armor to your full delight. For now, remember your place and do not put yourself at risk. I might decide that you are not worth preserving after all."

She twisted the blue stone at her throat and to Elise's horror the blood drained from Sapphire's face. This was not faintness on her cousin's part; it was as if for a moment Sapphire's body was robbed of blood and breath. Melina changed the sapphire for the jet stone on her chain. After a horrid moment while the sapphire swung back and forth, glittering like a fragment of the ocean deeps, Melina said in almost conversational tones:

"I curse you, my daughter, Sapphire, with pain. Though the wound in your side has been treated, though it is clean and good ointments soothe the flesh, though Sir Jared has the talent of healing, still you shall feel pain there, dull and throbbing as it is even now. If you should defy me further, then the pain shall become sharp and keen, as hot as when the knife first sliced your flesh. Thus pain shall tutor you in prudence until I judge you have learned your lesson."

Sapphire's hand flew to her bandaged side and she gasped as if for a stark moment a knife had freshly reopened the wound. Melina bared her white teeth at her daughter, grimly satisfied.

As Melina reattached the pendants of jet and sapphire onto their places on her necklace, her gaze fell upon Opal, and the girl, to this point silent and stolidly calm, paled and trembled.

"And you, Opal," Melina said. "Take these punishments as a warning unto you. Obey me and perhaps someday I will favor you with lessons in my craft. Disobey and know my wrath."

"Yes, Mother," the little girl whispered. "I understand."

Melina pressed her hand once again to the gems on her necklace. "I conjure and bind you all to silence on these matters. The day has not yet come for my art to be revealed to the masses. Speak of these doings and it shall be as if red ants bite your tongue. Even as you suffer, the truth you sought to reveal shall be refashioned into clever falsehood that shall honor me and defame you."

"Yes, Mother," came three subdued responses.

"Follow me. We have work to do before the diplomats from Bright Bay arrive."

Only as Elise watched the four Shields turn back toward the encampment did she realize that she had her fingers pressed to her mouth as if to keep even the faintest sound from coming forth. Even as she struggled with her fear, Elise could feel a terrible resolve forming within her, a resolve she dreaded almost as much as she dreaded Melina's dark arts.

Oh, Mother! she thought frantically. *You never knew how wrong you were about Lady Melina. She is a sorceress, her powers as wicked as sin!*

A terrible thought came to Elise then. What if Aurella Wellward did know? What if her tongue had been conjured into silence by Melina, even as Melina had bound her own children? Who could be trusted to be free of the sorceress's power? How many others might have been so silenced?

At last, Melina and her children were safely gone. Pulling herself with effort from her thoughts, Elise became aware that for some time now Ninette had been murmuring to herself, only now daring to permit her frantic whispers to become audible.

"Oh, ancestors, protect us from evil magic! Wolf, Elk, Raven, Bull, Horse, Puma, Bear, Dog, Hummingbird, Deer, Lynx, and Boar: Gracious Ones, shelter us from harm. Estrella and Rozen, Jinette and Tunwe . . ." Ninette continued reciting her personal ancestors back to the days of Queen Zorana and then began on those of the House of the Eagle, for they were believed to protect all their subjects from harm.

Patting Ninette on the shoulder, Elise joined her in her prayers. Even as she recited the familiar litany, Elise suspected that the answer to those prayers might come in a form as mysterious and terrible as the powers themselves.

AFTER A NIGHT OF ROAMING the richly stinking streets of Hope, after bloodshed and battle, sleep could not enchant Firekeeper. Blind Seer at her side, she darted through the fringes of farmer's fields, haunted the forests, and swarmed up the spreading branches of a thick-leafed oak to howl defiance at the moon. Only when dawn drifted into full daylight—a late-summer day promising muggy heat rising from the river before mid-day—was Firekeeper willing to sleep.

She preferred the forests, cool even in the hottest parts of the day, especially when compared with the interior of a canvas tent. Derian had protested, more because Earl Kestrel had punished him for permitting such wildness than because he saw any harm in her choice.

Yet, despite her affection for Derian, Firekeeper had persisted. Stone walls when there had been little other choice had been tolerable; a canvas box when the trees beckoned a few yards away was not.

Elation had provided compromise, alerting Derian to Firekeeper's location and keeping a golden eye bright for the earl. Should Earl Kestrel begin to harangue Derian, Firekeeper could reappear before he was fully warmed into his subject.

The earl's need for Firekeeper outweighed his desire to assert his power, so she could protect Derian. Now that she had known Earl Kestrel longer, she realized that there was a certain fairness to him. He assumed that Firekeeper obeyed Derian and thus Derian was doing his job if Firekeeper did as the earl commanded. If she did not obey, Derian would be punished.

Firekeeper obeyed nothing but her own impulses, but it didn't bother her if Earl Kestrel believed her controlled.

So as she had since the march from Eagle's Nest to Hope began, the wolf-woman slipped into the forest. In a tangled copse of young maple saplings, not far from a narrow thread of a stream, she pillowed her head on Blind Seer's flank and fell instantly asleep.

The past night's events would not leave her mind to rest. Looping like embroidery thread through a needle's eye, they stitched out a pattern that gradually mutated into something approaching nightmare.

Shadows and rocks underfoot, round rocks, smooth like those in a streambed but these are wet by other than good, clean water. The stream that runs over these rocks is horse piss and dog piss, man piss and cat piss, vomit and sweat, manure and spilled beer, the rotted sap of dead vegetation and the salt of ancient tears. Even when the rain falls it cannot remove the stench entirely. It settles into the crevices between the rocks and waits for heat to bring it forth.

Barefoot, Firekeeper runs from cobble to cobble, feet light and silent. There are no twigs to snap here, no leaves to crumble and crunch. She feels like a shadow given life and Blind Seer padding beside her is heralded only by the panicked barking of dogs in their pathetic yards. Their appeals to their masters bring them no help, no praise, only angry threats and the occasional thrown shoe.

Partly from pity, partly because their barking annoys the night, Blind Seer silences the curs with a growled command. In their secret hearts the dogs are grateful. They retire to doormat or kennel, wrap their tails about their noses, and try to believe they are as ignorant as their masters as to what friend of the darkness walks the streets.

Each place where Derian and Doc halt is a delight of newness to nose and eye. The tavern at twilight invites care; it is a busy place. Wolf and woman sniff about the stableyard, steal scraps from the trash heap, and marvel at the variety of people coming in and out the doors. Leaving Blind Seer below, Firekeeper swings onto the roof to peer into windows on the upper story. Nothing she sees through the bared windows is precisely new, but much is educational.

So it is with the livery stable and the heavily scented gardens of the herbalist, Hazel. Then comes the return through the night, the scream, Sapphire Shield fighting in fierce earnest, the scent of her sweat cutting sharp and acrid even through the pong of the streets.

Indecisive, Firekeeper lurks in the shadows, uncertain whether this is a fight in which another might be welcome. Only when Derian is endangered does she throw etiquette to the winds and bound forth. As she catches him in her arms, the blood streaming from his wounds alternately red and black in the lamplight, Blind Seer leaps upon the attacker.

A man is not a wolf. There is no thick ruff to protect his throat. He is not even a deer with great cabled muscles beneath a thick hide. He is not even a rabbit who can sometimes shake loose leaving a mouthful of fur. A man is a pitiful naked beast. One snap and the red blood is running onto the cobbles, overlaying their stench with a rich new scent.

Blind Seer vanishes. Firekeeper remains. When Derian comes to himself, she sees horror and fear in his eyes. Deep within her, despite the exultation of victory, she is troubled.

Horror and fear in his eyes. A body: the throat a raw red hole through which life gushes and is gone. Fear and horror in her heart. A raw red wound gushing life. Hot and blurring in her eyes, tears salt on her tongue. Hot and terrible in her belly, hunger refusing the question of right and wrong, living and dying.

Where is the sweet sticky beverage? Day after day, it had been forced between her lips. Slowly life had returned with it. Breath had no longer tormented her lungs. Then there had been milk, sucked from the teat of a she-wolf, girl-child nursing side by side with blind balls of fur that grew far faster than she.

Blood flowing life-hot from a gaping neck wound, steaming in the cold of an autumn day. Around her she hears the Ones growling at the pack to keep their distance. Despite hunger, the girl cannot drink blood, not with the memory of the doe's soft brown gaze upon her, with the sharp stink of her panic as the wolves closed upon her still fresh, not with her last terrified leap for freedom, doomed before it began, imprinted on her mind.

The girl's stomach roils. The doe's eyes had reminded her of her own, of those of a sweet-voiced, soft-bodied woman even now becoming a dream. If she drinks, she kills that woman again.

"So, is the life to be wasted then?"

The girl has no idea who is speaking to her. The voice is familiar, but her memory slides around it, as unable to grasp its source as her hands are to pick the sunlight from a stream.

"I can't," she sobs. "I'll be sick!"

"Sick? You are sick now. Sick unto dying. How much longer do you insist that others do your living for you?"

"Why live when so many others die?" the little girl retorts, remembering the cooked-flesh smell of that almost forgotten woman. "Why me?"

"Fire spared you for a reason. Why can you not accept this?"

Though calm and measured, yet there is a note of impatience in the voice.

"How can I live on others' deaths?" And the death of which she thinks is not just the death of the doe, but the death of those others in the fire.

"We all live upon death, even the deer. There is no escaping that part of the cycle. Your dying will not save the deer. Your dying will not reverse the fire. Your dying will only slay others someday."

"What!"

"Nothing more can be said on that matter. Trust me."

"Why?

"I have need of you. Enlightened self-interest is the best reason I can give you."

"I don't understand."

"Nor should you. All you should know is that your dying will serve no one. Your living may serve many, not the least of which are those who have labored for your life. Now, drink!"

"I can't!"

"The doe dies for nothing?"

"Let the wolves eat her!"

"Why them and not you? Why are you less worthy of life?"

"I . . ."

"Drink! The heat and liquid will do you well. You are nearly starved from your stubbornness."

"Let the wolves have her!"

"Foolish human! Very well! If the wolves are to have her, if the wolves are to live, then I name you a wolf. Be a wolf. Forget that ever you were human. Your heart is a wolf's, your appetite a wolf's, your memory a wolf's. Strange wolf you may be, but if only a wolf may live, then you must be one!"

Hot blood, slowing to a trickle. The wolf dips her human head, laps at the stuff, sucks deeply, finds an appetite for life in the blood. Chews hun-

grily at the still-warm flesh, finds strength for living. Only when she is sated does she stop growling the others back from her right. Only then do her parents call the rest of the pack to share the bounty.

When they are finished, there is doe no longer, not even bones, for these have been cracked for their marrow and the splintered segments chewed into dust. A single doe isn't much to the hunger of a wolf pack. Before the night is over, they will hunt again, a two-legged wolf running beside them, eager now to be in on the kill.

XVII

AFTER THREE DAYS' RESIDENCE IN HOPE, Prince Newell Shield
flattered himself that he understood the budding political situation
better than any of the central players. Although a century of sporadic warfare following hard upon the chaos of civil war had brewed
hatreds between Bright Bay and Hawk Haven, largely these were
personal—hatreds for the ugly deeds done in battle or of one person for
another—not the terrible abstract fear and horror with which both night
fears and some enemies were regarded.

Perhaps this was because legends of the Old Country monarchs who
wore crowns carved from skulls and wielded scepters worked from human thighbones remained fresh—real enough to raise thrills of terror
when some old grand could say, "It was in my own grandmother's day
that this was so," and be right.

Perhaps this lack of hatred was because the goal of these battles,
skirmishes, and frays had always been reunification, not conquest. When
monarchs strove to bring the errant sheep back into the fold, they could
not resort to the rhetoric of hatred and alienation lest this raise doubts
in their people's minds as to the wisdom of reunification. With eager
predators prowling on the fringes, neither Bright Bay nor Hawk Haven
could risk razed countryside and slaughter of local inhabitants. Too easily

then would the conqueror find itself in danger of conquest as it sought to solidify its expanded holdings.

Did anyone but himself realize that those who feared and hated were the very allies who supported one side or the other while really supporting none but themselves?

Prince Newell sniggered into his pewter tankard of ale. Blind! Blind! That was what both Tedric and Gustin IV were. As their predecessors had done, they accepted aid from nations who in their most secret hearts desired not their allies' success but their failure.

Still laughing quietly to himself, Newell rubbed his fingers along his temples, delighting in the clarity of his vision. He, he alone had wisdom! The rest were as blinkered horses dragging their burdens through crowded city streets, as sheep who blindly followed the slaughterhouse goat to their own deaths!

Should such willfully ignorant creatures have the rulership over thousands of souls? Ancestors, refuse! He knew his duty and had already taken steps to achieve a position from which to carry it out.

First there must be newly awakened doubt between the various factions for Hawk Haven's crown. He had hoped that Sapphire Shield's death would do the trick. The men Keen had hired to follow her and Jet had been told to make it appear that an animal had savaged her. Ostensibly this had been to draw suspicion away from human hands— Keen had been posing as a love-maddened, rejected suitor when he contracted the thugs' services.

Needless to say, there had been a better reason for such theatrics. Newell himself had intended—if no one else arrived at the conclusion—to hesitantly suggest that young Lady Blysse had murdered the one regarded by many as her greatest rival for the throne. Blysse's habit of slipping off into the night was well known by now. Not even her faithful lackey Derian Carter would be believed if he swore that he knew where she was every hour. His laxness regarding her had been commented on, even by those who knew that Blysse had the king's favor.

Sapphire's death should have weakened Blysse's support as well as eliminating one of Newell's own rivals. He was still disappointed that the thugs had bungled. Keen, however, had made certain that they would not live to tell tales.

After going bail for the two survivors—not a difficult a thing to do in Hope, where the local authorities did not wish to seem to care more about assault on a noblewoman than on a commoner—Keen had murdered the men and tossed their bodies into the Barren River. If any wondered about the deaths, they should end up thinking that one of Sapphire's legion of admirers had done the deed. Newell would make certain they thought so even if they didn't on their own.

Although he had been less than successful in the first part of his plan, Prince Newell was progressing with the second part. This was to make at least one of the allies betray that its deepest loyalties were to none but itself. After consideration, he had elected Stonehold for this role for the logical reason that it was Bright Bay's ally, not Hawk Haven's. For now Hawk Haven provided the foundation for Newell's own prestige and influence. He did not care to weaken that, though neither Waterland nor New Kelvin were any more honest in their motives for alliance.

For the third part of his plan to work there must be conflict that would bring the prince shining to the fore. Newell fancied a battle would do the trick, one wherein Stonehold would show its true colors. Perhaps weakened by loss of their ally, Bright Bay would join forces with Hawk Haven. Alternatively, the battle could take place between three armies. In either case, Hawk Haven's army should come forth victorious—they must, for they alone would be unweakened by the defection of a traitorous ally.

And in that battle Prince Newell planned to lead. His would be the great deeds. Based upon them, he would be hailed the new king of Hawk Haven by popular acclaim. Rook and Keen were already sounding out the gathered armies for those soldiers who could be easily bribed or influenced to shout Newell's praises loudly—and at the proper moment.

Among the many deserters who resided in Hope and Good Crossing there were those who could be bought and instructed to insert themselves among the troops when added numbers would be welcomed, not questioned. Their voices would shout loudly for Prince Newell, for he would promise them pardon and honor. With the army firmly behind him and the added weight of his own noble title, none would dare resist him.

Then graciously would Prince Newell offer the conquered (or newly weakened) Bright Bay a chance to come under his sweeping wing. He smiled, imagining the meeting with lovely Gustin IV, perhaps grief-stricken from her husband's sudden death. Surely he could arrange that little detail if it seemed meet. If Queen Gustin suspected assassination, so much the better, for then she would fear him and the power he wielded off the battlefield.

There was, of course, the small problem that King Tedric still lived and must continue to live until the very day of the battle in question. The mad old man had secured his succession while leaving his prospective heirs spatting. All to the good for Prince Newell, for united in their distrust of each other they would not look to him as a rival. Once Newell was the hero of war and peace a mere name scribbled by a quivering hand on a piece of parchment would not bear the weight of his deeds.

But King Tedric must not die too soon.

The sound of a cautiously cleared throat brought Newell from his revery.

"Master," murmured Rook, "all is prepared for your departure. Keen is sweating the horses even now. Rumor has confirmed that the two diplomatic parties will meet at a reception in Bridgeton this very evening—a reception hosted by the citizens of Hope and Good Crossing."

Newell's lips curved in a cruel smile at this news, for he was the one who had inserted such an idea into the minds of the Guild Heads and other influential residents of the twin towns. It had been easy enough to join the fringes of their meetings, for they usually met in public houses. It had been easy enough to make a suggestion from some shadowed corner of a crowded room, even easier to play upon the emotions of the ambitious or fearful.

The prince doubted that even now any of those who were busy supervising the decoration of the Toll House's central courtyard—watching as trays of sweets and meat pasties or kegs of wine and ale were set into place—were in the least aware that the idea to so subtly emphasize Good Crossing and Hope's own power was not solely their own.

"Very well." Prince Newell rose, drawing up his hood to hide his features. It would not do to become careless when the game was nearly won. "Let us go. I believe I shall call upon my father-in-law before the festivities begin. I am certain that he will want me at the reception to support him in this time of trial."

"Who else can he trust?" Rook answered seriously, but a wicked gleam in his bright eyes belied that sincerity. "Who else among our noble king's contentious court has only the best interests of the nation at heart?"

Laughing then, arm in arm like two roisterers who had supped too deeply of an afternoon, they stumbled from the tavern. None noted their going but the barmaid who gathered up the coins left in payment for their drinks; none even thought of them thereafter. Certainly none equated the one who laughed hardest with the salt-stained and road-dust-coated prince who rode into the Hawk Haven encampment late that afternoon on a tired horse, his entourage only a single servant, so great had been his eagerness to reach his father-in-law's side at this time of crisis.

FIREKEEPER WAS DRAWN FROM happy dreams of her childhood by Derian's voice saying things she had long dreaded to hear:

"Rise and shine, Firekeeper. Formal attire for the reception tonight. Earl Kestrel expressly told me to make certain to scrub your feet."

Dragging herself from joyful participation in a full pack hunt, Firekeeper reluctantly rolled over. Late-afternoon sunlight was spilling down through the oak leaves. Absently, she noticed that the edges of some of the leaves were turning orange and yellow. Despite the present heat, the trees knew that autumn was coming.

Feeling a bit like one of those trees herself, Firekeeper pulled herself to her feet.

"I have never slept so before," she commented to Blind Seer. *"I didn't even hear old heavy-foot Fox Hair coming."*

"I heard him," the wolf reassured her, *"and knew his step. Otherwise, I would have awakened you."*

Elation whistled in shrill laughter and launched into the sky. Waving to the bird in thanks, Derian looked at Firekeeper with what the wolf-woman now recognized as an affectionate grin on his face.

"Stop growling and groaning," he said. "You've bathed daily, I know, but a good scrub won't do you any harm. Valet has a kettle on over the fire and we've permission to use Earl Kestrel's pavilion for your ablutions. I've even bought you some lavender scent."

Firekeeper bristled. Among the human customs she couldn't understand was that of covering one's own perfectly good scent with something derived from some tree or shrub.

Derian laughed. "You don't have to use it if you don't want to. I'm certain Ninette or Lady Elise would be happy to have it."

"You think I should?" she asked, brushing leaves from her hair. "Wear scent? Will Earl Kestrel be happier?"

"He might be," Derian allowed.

"Then I wear," she said, adding hastily, "a little only."

Derian clapped her on the shoulder. "You're becoming a real lady, Firekeeper."

Remembering Elise's lecture on social graces, Firekeeper was quite pleased. She was sitting on one of the campstools in Earl Kestrel's tent, scrubbing the black from her bare feet with a boar-bristle brush, when Elation's shrill cry announced that Lady Elise was coming, accompanied by Ninette. A few moments later, Elise herself was raising the tent flap and requesting entry.

"Come to chaperon us, Elise?" Derian asked, rising politely to his feet in greeting. He'd been sitting to one side mending a small tear in the hem of the gown Firekeeper was to wear tonight.

"Everyone in camp has heard of your valor last night, Derian," she said lightly. "I doubt that such a hero would molest a young girl."

Firekeeper snorted through her nose, but Derian, more skilled than she in hearing the nuances of human intonation, frowned.

"Is something wrong, my lady?"

"Yes. No. I . . ."

Firekeeper dropped the brush and crossed to Elise. The other woman was clearly in pain, her expressive blue eyes widening in surprise as her hand rose to touch her lips.

Elise began again. "I came to thank you both for saving my cousin. Sapphire can be both ambitious and obnoxious, but she is brave and honest as well."

"That," Firekeeper said with certainty, "is not just what you want to say."

"No," Elise agreed, licking her lips nervously. "But I don't think I should try to say anything more now. Tell me, are you going to the reception tonight?"

"Am," Firekeeper agreed, not satisfied with this evasion, but willing to accept it for now. "Earl Kestrel requests I do the honor of accompanying him to reception for the diplomatic parties. I am not certain I understand what this is but he asks and it is a small enough thing."

Derian brought forward a campstool and offered it to Elise. Firekeeper could see that he, too, was unhappy with Elise's sudden change of the subject. Unlike Firekeeper, however, he was too aware of his social position to press a noble lady into confidences.

"Sit for a bit, Lady," Derian said, his use of her title twice in such a short time underscoring his unease. "Even better, ask Ninette to join us and you both can advise me in how to dress Firekeeper's hair. It's getting long enough now that it escapes my skill."

Firekeeper expected Elise to refuse, but Elise suddenly smiled.

"Would it be too much trouble for Earl Kestrel if I brought all my dressing here? My father is away with his troops and my tent seems so lonely."

"She is afraid," Blind Seer growled from where he had been napping outside the tent. *"Her scent is sour with fear."*

Before Derian could vacillate, Firekeeper leapt in.

"Yes. Tell Ninette to bring. Valet can help if she needs."

Now it was Elise's turn to look uncertain, as if she suddenly dreaded her own request, but Firekeeper left her no room to change her mind.

Hurrying outside, she found Ninette huddled by the cook fire as if the day were quite chill. Valet was filling her teacup. Firekeeper caught the scent of skullcap, wood betony, lavender and lemon balm. She cocked an eyebrow, knowing this concoction was used to soothe a troubled mind. Whatever had happened to Elise had affected her maid as well.

"Valet," Firekeeper said, "please if you have time, go to Lady Elise's big tent—pavilion—and bring her gown and other things for tonight's reception. She and Ninette are to dine with us this evening so they can tell Derian what to do with my hair. They will go straight from here to meet Baron Archer for the reception."

Imperturbable, Valet nodded. "Very good, Lady Firekeeper. I am certain that Earl Kestrel would approve."

"I wonder," Blind Seer commented, *"what nose he uses to smell fear, for he smells it as surely as do I."*

"And I," Firekeeper agreed.

She returned to the pavilion and her interrupted foot scrubbing, but no matter how subtly she and Derian phrased their questions, Elise would say nothing more about what was evidently troubling her. Ninette's only reply was to tremble so violently that she could hardly handle her combs and cosmetics.

"I am learning to lie," Firekeeper said to Blind Seer, *"for otherwise how could I refuse to say what I think when I see these two so bravely afraid?"*

"You are," the wolf said, *"becoming human. Tonight while you are at*

this reception—where I think I would be less than welcome—I shall cast about. Perhaps I can learn where she went, who she saw."

"So many people here, so many to blur the scent," Firekeeper said doubtfully.

"I can but try."

IF EARL KESTREL WAS RELIEVED when Firekeeper informed him that Blind Seer would not be attending the reception, he was too well-mannered to say so. Firekeeper didn't think she needed to tell him that Elation would be on guard, tracking them from the air and then watching from some perch high above the crowd.

All three of the wild creatures had their wind up, Elise's fear touching nerves honed to hear warning in crow call or squirrel scolding. Never mind that most of the time the warnings were against *them*—still, they had learned to heed and to take care. What frightened one so deeply might mean danger to all.

Baron Archer came to meet his daughter at the Kestrel camp, adding his considerable social weight to an escort already heavy with earl and knight, for Jared Surcliffe was also of their company. Tonight bodyguards and caretakers were left behind, an agreement that pleased the rival powers only slightly less than the alternative. Knowing that Derian was deeply concerned, Firekeeper found a moment to comfort him.

"Don't worry, Fox Hair," she said. "I am to be the perfect lady, just like Elise. Look, I have even put my Fang here—"

She hiked up her skirt to show the sheath strapped to her right thigh.

"—not around my waist so the guard will not be frightened."

Derian laughed and almost managed not to blush. "You are a little savage," he said affectionately. "Behave. Remember, your manners reflect on me."

"Haven't I promised?" she replied, evading actually promising. "Elation will watch from without. If I am in greater trouble than I can handle, she will rescue me."

Derian groaned, "Great! Now I'm really relaxed."

The Toll House on Bridgeton, where the reception was being held, was a huge building. It straddled the entirety of a bridge so wide that its span was lined with houses and shops on either edge. Room remained between the buildings for carts and foot traffic to pass in two directions.

In its time, the Toll House had been fortress, shop, and administration building. Tonight it was an unofficial palace, flaunting the peculiar semi-independence of Hope and Good Crossing to those who would claim the towns as their own, while forcing acknowledgment of those qualities in the very use of the twinned cities for this meeting.

Walls of polished river rock were adorned with pitch torches, their yellow-orange light sputtering slightly in the gusts of river wind. The paired arches at the base of the structure, each wide enough to admit a heavily laden cart, glowed like the mouths of some sea demon from Old World legend. The flags and pennants flying from the poles on the roof high above were invisible except as snapping black forms that blocked the wheeling constellations.

The Toll House was actually two buildings standing back to back, a wide neutral zone between them. This courtyard was where the reception was being held tonight. For light, chandeliers the size of wagon wheels had been slung from great cables strung between the two buildings and more torches were set on the walls. In this light, the guests could admire paving stones scrubbed as clean as the deck of a ship and adorned with thick carpets.

Long tables bent slightly beneath the weight of the food and drink spread upon them. Light music performed by scattered musicians filtered its way between conversations, creating an illusion of privacy.

Here, tense beneath her superficial composure, Firekeeper witnessed the first meeting of King Tedric of Hawk Haven with his nephew, Duke Allister Seagleam of Bright Bay. She had been long enough among humans by now to see them with something closer to their own eyes.

From that newly expanded perspective, crowned in silver set with rubies and gowned in regal scarlet trimmed in white, the elderly monarch looked quite august—no longer merely an old man as Firekeeper had first seen him. Yet even in the torchlight her wolf's eyes could see that the king's lips were faintly blue and his fingers, when he had extended them earlier for her to kiss, had been cold as ice.

Beside his uncle, Allister Seagleam cut something less of a impressive figure. His greying blond hair, though neatly tied back, showed a tendency to escape its bounds, framing his features with wisps of straw. Nor did the sea green and gold he wore suit him, making him rather sallow. In the artificial light, Allister squinted, reminding Firekeeper a bit of bookish Lord Aksel Trueheart. Yet there was confidence in his bearing and nothing either servile or groveling in his bow.

"Uncle Tedric," he said, and his voice carried in the sudden hush spreading through the courtyard. "I am honored to have the privilege of finally meeting you."

King Tedric did not bow in return, but opened his arms. "You have the look of my sister about you, Allister. Something in the shape of your mouth, I think. Her hair, too, was light."

Accepting the kinsman's embrace with dignified grace that did not overstep the bounds of familiarity, Allister replied:

"No one has told me of that resemblance before and I am pleased to learn of it. May I present my wife, Pearl Oyster, and our children?"

While Allister was introducing a lady as plump and pale as the full moon and several children who resembled both of their parents to varying degrees, Firekeeper's attention wandered. Everyone else was watching the proceedings with great interest. Firekeeper noted that a fierce look, almost a hunger, crossed Lady Zorana's face as Allister presented his sons.

Zorana looks as if she will eat one of them, bones and all! Firekeeper mused silently. *Yet from what I have been told, she will be lucky to get near the plate.*

With skill that did not quite reject the rest of the company, King Tedric drew Allister and his family aside. From what Firekeeper could overhear, all they were discussing were family matters, including the daily life of Princess Caryl in Bright Bay. As the wolf-woman drifted restlessly about the courtyard, accepting food—but never drink—from the footmen who circulated with trays, she was amused to learn that almost everyone else thought that high matters of state were being settled in that private gathering.

As she walked around the courtyard, Firekeeper was astonished to discover that humans come in different colors. Until this point, she had thought they were all basically like herself: light skin shading into reddish brown with exposure to the sun, hair mostly in brownish hues though occasionally lighter or redder. Here in the courtyard, apparently as representatives of some of the interested countries she had only known by name, were people with skin the yellowed shade of grass in the winter and hair as fine as silk and black as a raven's wing. Their eyes were shaped differently, too, slanting somehow.

There were also people so fair that they made her look dark, their skin a rosy pink flushing red from sun or wind. These people had hair so light that it almost glowed. Their eyes were very round, so that Firekeeper felt her own must seem heavy-lidded. These round eyes shouted with blue or green beneath brows so pale that they seemed a dream of a shape. These people were large, though trim about the waist and hip, where the Winter Grass people were small and delicate.

Finally, just three or five among the many, there were people who in coloring were quite like those of Hawk Haven or Bright Bay, but their attire was so strange that they seemed the most alien of all. Men and women alike shaved the front of their heads and grew the hair long behind. The exposed skin was colored in elaborate patterns that extended over their faces. They wore long, straight robes embroidered with complicated patterns in many colors and their shoes curled at the toes.

Viewing the contrasting humanity pleased Firekeeper. She had thought that humans might be like deer or rabbits, limited in their coats and forms. Learning that they were more like wolves—who could be any color from snow white to mingled shades of grey or brown to night black, who could have eyes the color of pine tree tears or maple leaves in autumn or a piece of the summer sky—was quite a relief. Deep inside, Firekeeper felt that homogeneity was for prey animals, not predators.

When viewing the passing scene palled, Firekeeper sought her companions. Earl Kestrel was deep in conversation with some military counterpart from Allister Seagleam's escort: one of the Winter Grass men, someone he had apparently met before on the field of battle. Their verbal sparring, which barely kept the blade in the sheath, amused Firekeeper for a time, but eventually became filled with references to events far beyond her ken.

Doc was part of a group that included Lady Elise, Jet Shield, and several representatives from the guilds in Hope and Good Crossing. Their discussion bored Firekeeper almost immediately, largely surpassing her command of the language. When everyone burst into laughter for the third time at some witty comment that had not seemed at all funny to her, Firekeeper gave up in disgust.

Her vague hope that there might be dancing to liven the evening gradually dying, Firekeeper moved to one side of the span to where she could watch the water flowing beneath the bridge. The torches reflected in the black water made it seem as if the stars themselves had descended to eavesdrop on these monumental human affairs.

Seeing her alone, the falcon Elation flew down from one of the Toll House towers to perch on a jutting abutment below the line of sight of the party.

"*Having fun?*" she whistled.

"*Not much,*" Firekeeper admitted. "*I wish that humans solved their problems as wolves do. A quick fight must be better than all this blather.*"

"*Human fights,*" Elation said seriously, "*are not always quick. They do not always know when to surrender or how to accept surrender when it is offered. Believe me, once you have seen humans at war, you will understand why this blathering—as you name it—has its place.*"

"*Hush!*"

Even through the mingled drone of music and conversation, Firekeeper had heard someone approaching from behind. The step was not one she knew, and the wind was from the wrong direction to carry scent, so she wheeled to confront Prince Newell Shield while he was still a good number of paces away.

"You're like a cat, Lady Blysse," he said with a friendly smile. "Or should I say like a wolf?"

"Wolf," she replied stubbornly, though she knew no answer was expected.

"Mind if I join you?"

She started to shrug, remembered her promise to Derian that she would do her best to be a lady, and said instead:

"That would be kind of you."

Prince Newell leaned his elbows against the stone rampart and stared down at the water. After a cautious moment, Firekeeper returned to her previous attitude. Below, hidden in the darkness, Elation kept her silence.

"Where is your wolf? I thought you went nowhere without her."

"Him. He is outside. This place is close and crowded. He would not like it." She left out mentioning that many of the people would also not like him. Prince Newell didn't need to know that she would moderate her actions for anyone's comfort.

"I believe I sympathize with your wolf," the prince said after a moment. "For a sailor like me, parties like this are very trying."

Firekeeper remembered not to ask why and instead smiled politely. Prince Newell continued, offering the answer she hadn't asked for:

"I suppose it's the chatter, but that can't be it. On an oceangoing vessel we're packed more closely. Sometimes dinner at the captain's table—especially when the wine has gone around a few times—gets quite noisy. No, I expect that it's the tension. Everyone here wants something and dreads that someone else will get it. That's why I was so surprised to see you over here. I thought you'd be checking out the young men from Bright Bay."

The word escaped her lips before she could school her puzzlement. "Why?"

Prince Newell chuckled heartily, his manner the same, she realized, as she had seen him use with little Citrine during the falconry party.

"Why because young men are interesting to young ladies—and these two more than most—they could be a secure way to the throne."

"Oh," she replied, understanding, "like Elise and Jet."

"That's right. I'm certain that Baron Archer is wishing he could sever that engagement ever more the longer the king spends talking to Allister

Seagleam's family. Doubtless my sister, Melina, feels the same way. But they've made their beds and their children must lie in them."

His laughter this time was somewhat coarse. Firekeeper wondered how many times the bottle had gone 'round the table for him this evening. From her point of view, the betrothal between Elise and Jet was a problem—largely because Elise did not seem happy. It had not escaped Firekeeper how often Doc found excuses to talk with Elise. Nor had she overlooked that Elise seemed much more cheerful when Doc was about.

Turning from the rampart, she glanced over the gathering until she located Elise. Yes. There she was, Jet close at her elbow, talking in quite a lively fashion to several important guild representatives. They looked delighted, but Jet seemed bored, his gaze frequently wandering to where the Oyster twins were now venturing into tentative conversation with his sister Opal and his cousin Nydia Trueheart.

Prince Newell followed the direction of her gaze without difficulty.

"Yes, there is our young Jet, rearing against the lead rope—despite the fact that little Minnow and Anemone are something like eleven years old. Lady Archer has her betrothed firmly in hand though. He cannot leave her side without giving grave insult to her family—an insult which King Tedric cannot fail to perceive. Tell me, Lady Blysse, who are you sweet on?"

His tone was playful, but she had learned when someone was fishing for information. She had been asked this question or some variation on it by everyone from the queen to Sapphire's maid. Only the queen seemed genuinely interested.

"No one," she said. But her thoughts, as they often did, flitted to Blind Seer. "There is no man I think sweet."

"Yet you are a young lady, surrounded by men. Surely it is time Earl Kestrel got you a maid. That strapping redhead might have done when you were just a . . . at first, that is, but now it must raise questions of propriety."

What she wanted to ask the prince was why should he care what people thought of her, but Firekeeper had learned something of manners. She replied courteously:

"True. Today Lady Elise was kind and came to help me gown and do my hair. Ninette, too. I shall need a maid soon."

"Perhaps," he said in avuncular tones, "I can help. I still know many reliable servants from the days when my late wife and I maintained an estate. These days, alas, I am much the wandering bachelor."

Firekeeper knew that this was a cue to flirt with him. It was as obvious as the song of a cock robin in the early spring or the sparring of two young bucks with the velvet barely off their antlers. Yet she could not bring herself to play this game. Wolves mate for life, usually only after blood has been spilled and great battles fought. Courtship was too serious a matter to play at with a man she was quite certain she didn't even like.

Therefore, she was greatly relieved when she noticed Doc casting about, having noticed at last that she was missing. She lightly waved her hand to show where she was and made a quick curtsy to the prince.

"Forgive me. Sir Jared is seeking me, perhaps for Earl Kestrel."

She used titles and honors as protection against her flight being halted. The prince did not stay her retreat but only looked after her, the look of quizzical amusement on his face changing to one of calculation as he returned to staring into the river. He might have thought no one could see him, but the falcon Elation watched from the darkness below and whistled softly as she beat her wings in retreat.

The reception did not extend past Firekeeper's level of endurance. The guilds of Hope and Good Crossing had made their point. No one would forget to calculate their wealth into the coming negotiations. Representatives of the various contending forces had met and now knew each other as more than tantalizing names. Old rivals had re-met, new rivalries perhaps had begun. All in all, it had been an interesting, if not precisely enjoyable, evening.

Only Doc seemed pleased with the outcome of the night's entertainment. As they walked back to their camp, Firekeeper noticed with some amusement that he was humming.

⚜

EXHAUSTED AFTER THE EVENTS of the previous day—discovering the truth of Melina's sorcery would have been enough without the strain of visiting with her at the reception the night before—Elise had trouble sleeping. At last she gave into Ninette's pleading and joined her in a cup of tea doctored with an infusion of herbs which dragged her restless mind below the threshold of nightmare.

Consequently, Elise slept into late morning and woke with a muzzy head. Ninette was still asleep and Elise decided to wait upon her for once. The other woman had been as shocked as she had been and was far more terrified. Unlike Elise, Ninette was not a baronial heir and clearly felt that while Melina might withhold her hand from Elise, she might well make an example of her servant.

Both Ivon Archer and Aurella Wellward held that any noble who could not perform at least the basic tasks of cooking, sewing, and the like was dependent on her servants and so would become a slave to them. Therefore, Elise, had no difficulty tending to her own needs.

Her father's valet had left a kettle to one side of the cook fire so there was warm water for washing. Elise set another above the coals to heat water for tea, then stoked the fire until a cheerful blaze crackled beneath. Once again, the late-summer day promised to become quite hot. The air here near the river was already thick and humid. It didn't promise well for tempers when the conferences began.

Gowning herself in a light muslin dress with long sleeves of the same material that should help protect her skin from insect bites, Elise wished that there were a way for her to attend those conferences. Rumor and report were no substitutes for actually seeing the expressions on people's faces or hearing their intonations as they spoke.

Doubtless she was not the only one who felt that way and doubtless

King Tedric would refuse anyone he could in order to be able to refuse those he genuinely did not wish to attend. She supposed this must be an advantage of monarchy over the odd, oligarchical system used in Stonehold or the plutocracy of Waterland. Right now, however, she would give much for something like New Kelvin's parliamentary monarchy, where the reigning monarch—always a king, an odd concept—must answer to someone other than himself.

When Ninette awakened, Elise had porridge and tea ready. Over the other woman's protests, she insisted on waiting on her. By the time Ninette had finished eating and dressing, there was color in her cheeks and the tendency to blanch whenever she heard one of the Shields' voices, carrying over from their not too distant pitch, had vanished.

"Last night," Ninette admitted, sweetening her tea with pale gold clover honey, "I couldn't stay here alone. The baron's man had gone to play at dice with some other retainers, you see. Usually, I'd find some of the other lady's maids, but I couldn't bear the company of that creaky-voiced old crone who attends on Lady Melina. She's always hinting about her mistress's powers, especially to us younger ones when she thinks we're getting above ourselves."

Elise, who had been terrorized by the same old woman when she was a child, nodded sympathetically. She knew that it would make no difference to that one that Ninette was well-born, her only fault that she was the daughter of a younger son with a tendency to gamble.

Encouraged by Elise's sympathetic murmurs, Ninette continued, "I went over to Earl Kestrel's camp. I hope you don't think it improper of me, given that they are all men, but the earl's valet is very polite—even courtly—and Derian Carter may be brash, but he never oversteps himself."

"Were they the only ones there?" Elise asked.

"Yes. Ox had gone with Earl Kestrel, as you recall. He couldn't attend the reception, of course, but he waited with the horses. The other man, the scout . . ."

"Race."

"That's right—Race Forester—wasn't there. I think he spends much of his time with his fellow scouts. He may even have been on duty."

"Doesn't Sir Jared have a manservant?"

"Not that I have seen, my lady. I don't think that, for all his honors, he is very wealthy."

"No," Elise agreed. "That is probably true. He mentioned that his family grew grapes somewhere in Kestrel lands. That's hardly the basis of a fortune."

"Then you don't mind that I went out?"

"I think it was the smartest thing you could have done," Elise assured her. "The question is, what should we do next?"

"Next?"

"Yes." Elise thought for a time, sipping her tea.

She had decided not to tell Ninette about the curious pain she had felt when she had impulsively tried to tell Firekeeper and Derian about what she had witnessed. The woman was terrified enough without wondering if she herself was cursed.

Touching the carved piece of jet that hung around her neck, Elise wondered if she might have been particularly susceptible because of her link—however slight—to Jet. What if they *had* become lovers as he had pressed? Would taking his body into hers have increased the power his mother might hold over her?

She shuddered, feeling again that curious mixture of guilt and relief when she realized that Melina's curse served, evil as it was, to protect her from Jet's advances. Last night had been the first he had not tried to convince her to go for a walk in the woods or to duck into his tent. Either the curse had dulled his desires as well as his ability to act on them or he had feared that she would notice the difference in how his body expressed its ardor.

She felt a stranger to herself as she realized again how much had changed in her feelings toward Jet. At first she had only kept him at a distance out of a sense of propriety and—she honestly admitted to herself—a desire to test his devotion before surrendering. Never had she

362 / JANE LINDSKOLD

dreamed that Jet would fail that test. In her fantasies, he had become more and more ardent until, showered in gifts, poetry, and song, she had given herself to him gladly.

Instead, Jet had become impatient, even sniping, hinting that she was a tease or even unable to respond to his attentions. This had been rather insulting. She might be unpracticed, but her mother had told her about the mechanics and she was certain there was nothing wrong with *her*!

As their courtship had extended, Elise had tried to overlook the occasional innuendos that hinted her betrothed visited the camp followers, but learning that he had been in a brothel when his sister had been assaulted—and apparently not for the first time in his life—had been a real blow. Jet was nothing like she imagined and she was bound to him by her own wish.

Elise was too honest with herself to accept the tempting notion that Jet's behavior was a result of his mother's machinations. The idea was tantalizing, inviting her dream to take on new life. In that new fantasy, she would rescue him from the sorceress's control, grinding the jet emblem on his forehead into dust beneath her heel. Then he would fall to his knees before her, swearing his undying love, and become the man of her dreams.

No. As much as she wished that were the truth, Elise must honestly admit that the truth of Jet's character—no better, but no worse than many a young man of his age—had been there all along. Hadn't there been the rumors about why Duke Redbriar's granddaughter vanished from the social scene? Hadn't Trissa Wellward hinted at things when she and Jet were keeping company some years ago? Hadn't Trissa been devastated beyond proportion when Melina Shield put an end to the relationship?

Hadn't there been the time, back when Elise herself was fourteen and playing hide-and-seek with Jet and his siblings, that he had found her hiding place and used that privacy to steal a kiss and fumble at her breast? At the time she had been flattered and curiously thrilled that the handsome older boy had seen her as a woman. Now she realized that his behavior was all of a type.

No. Jet had only been a hero from a romantic ballad in Elise's own imagination. She forgave him and herself, but that didn't change that if they married he would likely be unfaithful and difficult. If Melina Shield ever raised the curse, that is. . . .

"We must stop Lady Melina," Elise said softly. "Otherwise what she said is perfectly true. Whoever is on the throne, she will find a way to rule. Even now, the most likely contenders include her husband and two of her children. Hawk Haven must be ruled honestly, not through sorcery."

Ninette blanched, but to her credit did not try to dissuade Elise. Perhaps in the privacy of her own thoughts she had been reaching the same decision. Setting her teacup on the tray, Ninette asked simply:

"How?"

"First, someone else must know what we do," Elise said. "Otherwise we may join those who are bound to silence."

"Who?"

Elise had been about to suggest her father, but the sudden shrill cry of a falcon, heard as if it called greeting while passing over their pavilion, was inspiration.

"My father might or might not believe us, but I'm certain that Derian and Firekeeper would. Let's start there."

"How about Sir Jared? He has the king's ear."

"Then him as well, if he is present." Elise snatched up a straw bonnet. "Let's go. If I wait too long, I'm going to lose my nerve."

And I hope, she thought as they left the pavilion, *that in telling this I don't lose my tongue.*

XVIII

WITHOUT, THE SUMMER MORNING had become quite hot and thick, but within the thick cobblestone walls of the Toll House, the temperature was comfortable. The windows at either end of the room in which King Tedric and Allister Seagleam were meeting were open, curtained in fine woven fabric to keep out both insects and the river miasma. Bowls of rose incense burned in front of each window as a further precaution against river ills, giving the room the scent of a well-born lady's private chamber.

It is, thought Allister Seagleam, *a strange ambience for a meeting between two men.*

King Tedric had suggested—and Allister readily agreed—that their first conference be kept as small as possible. They had settled on themselves, two assistants to take notes, and two guards to watch the doors and handle the inevitable interruptions. These were effacing themselves as much as possible, so Allister had the curious feeling that he was alone with his uncle.

Today's meeting was being held on the Good Crossing side of the Toll House, technically within territory owned by Bright Bay; thus Hawk Haven had already made the first concession. Looking at the steady old man seated across from him, Allister felt that King Tedric had lost nothing. Last night he had only noticed the king's courtesy and majesty. Today he saw more.

King Tedric was evidently ill. Perhaps the malady was nothing more than advancing age, but, like many of Bright Bay's nobility, Allister had studied some medicine. Those lessons were meant to enable him to act as a medic if caught far from shore on one of the sea commands that any able-bodied member of the nobility took as a matter of course. Today they showed Allister the paleness of the king's face, the slight blueness around his lips, and told him: "A weak heart. Uncle Tedric must resolve this contention on the matter of his heir or leave his kingdom in chaos when his heart fails him."

Resembling more than a little the eagle woven into the brocade fabric of his waistcoat, King Tedric leaned forward and said with a curious bluntness that was not impolite:

"So. I have named my heir. Why are you here, Nephew?"

"Because, when we asked for this meeting," Allister answered steadily, "you had not named your heir. I was born to be your heir—or at any rate the heir to Hawk Haven. I thought you should have a look at me before you made up your mind."

King Tedric nodded. "I see you. Why should you be chosen over someone I have known all his or her life?"

"Your father, my grandfather, King Chalmer, arranged for my mother to marry my father so that a prince and princess of both kingdoms might reunite the realms."

"That's true. Do you think it would work?"

Allister saw the faintest twinkle in the old man's pale eyes and answered honestly:

"I don't really know. I have been told that many of your people believe that I am heir to Bright Bay. You know and I know that I am not. I do not think that Gustin the Fourth will step down in favor of me, even if you granted me your throne. However, there is hope that perhaps one of my children might wed one of Gustin's children—and as of yet she has none—and so in time resolve the separation."

"Trusting to an unborn child and the actions of not just your generation but your grandchild's generation to bring the solution." Tedric sighed. "That is a slim hope. The best thing would have been to wed you when you were of age to one of your cousins, my daughter Lovella, perhaps, or Rosene's Zorana. Marras's daughter would have been ideal as she was already in line for our throne, but poor Marigolde didn't live beyond her first year."

"That might have been ideal," Allister agreed, "but by the time I was a young man, it was already evident that the experiment was a mistake—that suited as they were by birth and age, my parents were not suited by temperament. They lived apart from shortly after my birth, but Princess Caryl was forced by politics to remain in Bright Bay, an alien princess in a hostile country. She might have been accepted eventually, but Mother was not a tactful woman . . ."

"None of King Chalmer's other children were," Tedric said grumpily. "Why should Caryl be different?"

Allister hid a smile. "And she made many people hate her. These would have refused to follow me as king even if the union of which King Chalmer and Queen Gustin the Second had briefly dreamed had come to pass. My father was among those who hated Princess Caryl—as well as the ambivalence of his own position. Another powerful group who opposed Mother was the family of Crown Prince Basil's wife, who saw Mother's marriage to Father as an attempt to unseat their daughter as queen-to-be. Indeed, Crown Prince Basil wasn't delighted by the thought that his younger brother might be set above him at the whim of his mother—a resentment that grew stronger after I was born and Uncle Basil and his wife remained childless."

"They were quite right to resent you," King Tedric grunted. "I have often thought that if my father and your grandmother wished to make this great plan work they should have wed their heirs, but that would have been a greater gamble. This one left them the elegant pretense that the marriage was merely of noble to noble, not of heir to heir."

"True," Duke Allister said, "but because they did not take that gamble, Gustin the Fourth is ruler after her grandmother and father rather than I."

"Do you resent that?" King Tedric asked.

"Not really," Allister answered honestly. "I grew to manhood knowing that I was issue of a failed venture. Neither of my parents were unkind to me. My father assured that I was granted name and title. My mother schooled me in the traditions of both my countries."

"Both?"

"She did not wish me at disadvantage in anything."

"That's Caryl."

"It's strange," Allister mused aloud. "My parents died within a year of each other—both in their mid-fifties. Neither could remarry, of course, but as far as I know neither ever became seriously involved with another person. Mother pined for Father, I think. I don't know whether she had focused so much of her energy on hating him that when he was gone she lost all reason for living or whether she secretly loved him."

"Your father died at sea?"

"That's right. It's a very usual death for a member of the Bright Bay nobility. Most of our wealth comes from the sea and we join our people in harvesting it."

Allister was acutely aware of King Tedric studying him. His first impulse was to look away. Then he squared his shoulders and met the old man's gaze.

"Tell me, Allister," the old king said, "do you want to be my heir?"

"Not," Allister replied with an answering bluntness of which he was certain Queen Gustin would not approve, "without the approval of your people. Otherwise, I am inviting worse, not better, for your people and for those of Bright Bay."

"I notice you do not say for your people and for mine."

"I told you, my mother reared me to think of both countries as my own. Although I have lived all my life in Bright Bay, it is difficult to escape such early indoctrination."

Allister wondered if he had said too much. He had selected the clerk who sat scribbling notes a few places down the table, but the man was duty bound to report to Queen Gustin. She might well consider his making his own terms—when her orders had been to do his best to win the Hawk Haven throne—an act of treason. King Tedric hadn't seemed to mind, but Allister's home and lands were not within King Tedric's kingdom.

"For you to be accepted within Hawk Haven at all," Tedric said after a long pause, "you would need to be allied with one of our Great Houses. I would offer you one of my own children or grandchildren, but I have none. If I had any, I would not be sitting here with you."

"I suppose not," Allister agreed. He wondered about the wolf girl of whom he had heard. Some said that she was Tedric's granddaughter, others simply a contrivance of Earl Kestrel's. He decided to wait to ask about her until he could introduce the subject gracefully.

"I have," Tedric sighed, "nieces and nephews of your age, but they are married and you are married. Beginning this proposition with several divorces would undo any good we could do."

"True."

"Thus we move to the next generation, playing games with young lives as my father played with the lives of Caryl and Tavis. Do we want to risk that?"

"I don't know."

Allister thought of the letter from Zorana Archer folded within his breast pocket. The longer he spoke with the king, the more he was certain that she had acted of her own accord, not with the king's knowledge. Should he tell the king? What might Tedric's reaction be? Would the king thank Allister for his honesty or would he condemn him for treating with—or perhaps for misrepresenting—one of his nieces?

Allister waited, knowing that he could not wait too long or the moment would pass. King Tedric accepted a glass of sweet pear cider from his clerk and continued thoughtfully:

"Are any of your children married?"

"No."

"Betrothed?"

"My eldest, Shad, is betrothed to a girl of good family in Bright Bay. It is a political arrangement."

"Aren't they all," the king said breezily.

"I understand that your father married for love."

"And was forced to distribute titles to appease his angry Great Houses. These days most marriages among our Great Houses are alliances. Sometimes they work out quite well. Elexa has become my right hand, though initially we did not care for each other. Other times these marriages do not work at all and create trouble for the families."

"Ah."

"Are you indicating that Shad's political betrothal could be broken if necessary?"

"Queen Gustin would probably insist."

"I see."

A knock sounded on the door without. King Tedric's guard—Sir Dirkin Eastbranch, Allister recalled—went to answer it.

"Yes?"

A note was passed in. Sir Dirkin carried it to the king, who broke the seal and read it. Smiling wearily, he passed it to Allister.

"As you can see, my physician is reminding me that my heart is not strong and that I should rest. As much as I am enjoying this conversation, I believe I should obey."

"As you wish, sir."

"We will both be hounded by questions. I, for one, shall tell my people we are still feeling out what the other wants and needs. You may tell yours whatever you wish."

"I believe you have spoken the simple truth, Uncle."

"One last thing."

"Yes?"

The king studied his gnarled fingers. "I am unwilling to contract too freely with young lives as was done in my father's day. Within my kingdom, perhaps, but across the borders is a different matter. I suggest we hold another gathering—a dance perhaps—so I can see how everyone behaves."

Allister could hardly believe what he was hearing. A dance? At such a critical time? King Tedric read something of his expression.

"You forget, good Nephew. I have named my heir. My meeting with you is simply to see if I will change my mind. If we are to make monumental decisions, let us not make them in haste."

Allister bowed. "I agree."

On that accord they departed. Messages would be sent back and forth arranging the next meeting and the ball to be held some days hence, as soon as arrangements could be made. Followed closely by his men, Allister descended the Toll House stairs and departed.

He was so busy composing how he would reply to various questions from the Bright Bay contingent that he did not notice the anxious concern with which the generals of Stonehold watched him pass.

PRINCE NEWELL SHIELD INITIALLY had been more than a little put out at being kept from the king's conference with Allister Seagleam. Surely he hadn't come all this way to be balked at the door! Somewhat mollified when he learned that everyone was being refused, he decided to put his morning to good use.

The two generals from Stonehold had come to last night's reception already edgy and Newell had taken it upon himself to make them more so. That there had been two of them had caused him some difficulty at first, but there had been no avoiding that situation.

Stonehold assigned all posts in pairs, a parallel to their governmental system. One of the pair was drawn from stock originally from the Old Country of Alkyab. The other was a scion of the Old Country of Tavetch. When the Plague Years had begun, Alkyab and Tavetch had been among the first countries to abandon their colonies. Faced with powerful neighbors, all still receiving support from their founding countries, their colonists had banded together.

Perhaps if physically they hadn't looked so different, the two cultures

would have merged, but the people *were* different. The people of Tavetch were tall, heavily built, massive people with a tendency toward blue
or green eyes and fair hair. The people of Alkyab were small, even petite.
Their skin was the yellow-tan of old ivory, their eyes dark and slanting,
their hair jetty dark.

Their religious customs differed as well. The fair-haired Tavetch wor-
shipped a sun deity possessed of three aspects who, according to their
legends, was wed to a lunar goddess whose face changed each day as
the face of the moon changed. The stars were the children of these deities
and danced messages regarding their parents' wishes for humanity in
elaborate patterns on the night sky.

The Alkyab were, as the descendants of Gildcrest saw things, far less
superstitious. They, too, understood that one's ancestors were one's li-
aisons with the complicated and incomprehensible forces that ruled destiny and fortune. True, the Alkyab built temples to their ancestors (rather
than the descendants of Gildcrest's less ostentatious family shrines) and
governed marriages by a complex system having to do with figuring
degrees of relationships. These differences were an acceptable eccentric-
ity given that the Alkyab's ancestors had come from lands unknown and
so the Alkyab were the ones with whom Newell Shield felt more comfortable.

Therefore, at the reception Prince Newell had made his first overtures
to little General Yuci, a skilled horseman and commander of cavalry.
Yuci had been arguing with Earl Kestrel about the merits of various
methods of training horses to withstand the noise and chaos of battle
when Newell came up. Yuci was several strong glasses of wine past what
his slim frame could bear and Earl Kestrel had seemed sincerely grateful
at being rescued.

Under the guise of finding the general somewhere in which to sober
up a bit, Newell had steered Yuci to a quiet corner and proceeded to
alter his perception of events.

"Of course," Newell had begun blithely, "King Tedric is delighted to
meet Allister Seagleam. He despises all his other nieces and nephews,
never could get on with his brother and sister, you know."

Later, seeing Elise Archer laughing at a joke made by one of the guild representatives, Newell commented: "She seems terribly innocent, doesn't she? She grew up around the royal castle and there isn't a secret she doesn't know or an intrigue to which she isn't privy."

When Lady Blysse drifted from the party to watch the river, Newell represented the young woman's adolescent boredom as the sullen silence of a cruel and calculating mind. He dropped rumors about her upbringing among wolves, hinted that the creature who usually trailed her with such fidelity was an evil familiar spirit.

So he went, telling a tale on this one, sharing a confidence about that one. He spared his sister Melina's family a little, wanting to seem a loyal soul, but still managed to dredge up the rumors about Melina's use of magic.

By the end of his chat with Yuci, Newell was well pleased. Nothing he had said about anyone had been precisely untrue—or had at least been within the realm of common gossip. He knew, however, that hearing it from his lips—from the lips of a prince of Hawk Haven—would give even the most outrageous tales credence. Eventually General Grimsel had joined them and Newell had experienced the pleasure of hearing his slander repeated and amplified.

Yes, last night's game had been a good one, a delightful way to pass a portion of the reception. Today, however, refused a place at his monarch's side, Newell had something more serious in mind. If last night he had set the logs on the fire, today he planned to add the kindling.

At Newell's request, the Stonehold generals agreed to meet the prince at a nice little tavern on the Bright Bay side of the river, near where one of the regular ferries docked. They arranged for a private dining room and refreshments. Newell—as he saw it—took responsibility for the entertainment.

He doubted that Grimsel and Yuci saw their meeting in exactly that light. Doubtless they were nervous at meeting with a prince of a nation that was not on the best of terms—if not openly at war—with their own.

Had he not found their presence so useful, Newell might have even felt sorry for them. The generals' simple tour abroad to train Bright Bay's army and to command the mercenaries that augmented that same army had mutated into a political crisis.

Newell imagined how they must have felt when Queen Gustin IV commanded her army to accompany Duke Allister to Good Crossing. Even if they had wanted to demur—and they would have found that difficult—there would have been pressure from Stonehold that they be on the spot to learn everything as it unfolded.

After greeting his hosts and inquiring after their welfare, Newell jumped right to the reason he had called this meeting, judging that he could hardly string their nerves any tighter without fueling an explosion of some sort.

"Thank you both, Generals, for making the time to see me."

General Grimsel, a tall woman, built in every way on the heroic scale, with eyes of transparent blue, returned his greeting with some terseness. Her own infantry idolized her for her past deeds. The Bright Bay troops she had trained were less happy with her, seeing through her surface heartiness to her basic dislike of them, realizing that she saw them as aliens, rather than allies.

Cavalry commander Yuci, neat and trim despite the previous night's binge, was more polite.

"We always have time to learn things that may be of interest to Stonehold. That is what you said in your note this early morning, isn't it? You said you had something to tell us that would be of interest to Stonehold."

Newell nodded. "I did and I do."

"Pray," Grimsel said, pouring herself a mug of summer ale from the pitcher set in the center of the table, "tell us."

Newell bobbed his head again. Then in the slightly breathless tones of a storyteller who wasn't certain of his audience he began:

"Well, you know the true reason for the split between Bright Bay and Hawk Haven, don't you? I mean, it wasn't just a natural outgrowth of the years of unrest following the Plague."

"No?" Grimsel said, her tones bored.

"No," Newell replied, still eager. "There had been any number of factional squabbles from the time the last Old Country nobles left— people fighting to establish holds or to keep what had been given them or just for the right to loot what had been left behind.

"Out of these, three figures—Zorana Shield, Clive Elkwood, and Gustin Sailor—had risen to the fore. While they were working together it seemed pretty certain that all of Gildcrest's colonial lands would be reunited under a single government. Then things split down the middle and we ended up with two kingdoms."

General Grimsel frowned a sturdy frown, no longer precisely bored but clearly puzzled as to what bearing this discourse on factionalism over a hundred years past could have on current events.

"I had heard," Grimsel said, "that is, we were told—that there was a differences of opinion in how the campaigns should be conducted. In the end, some chose to follow Gustin Sailor, some to follow Zorana Shield. So two kingdoms were born rather than one."

"That," Newell gave an approving smile, "is the story in all our history books. It is completely true but omits a rather interesting point."

"I had also heard," General Yuci added with a slightly embarrassed cough, "that Queen Zorana—Zorana Shield then—had excited the love of both Gustin Sailor and Clive Elkwood. She favored Elkwood and in a fit of pique, Gustin Sailor went his own way and took his followers with him."

"That," Newell said, trying to sound as if he were amused but politely concealing that amusement, "is the story told in all our romantic ballads. The truth is darker, more dangerous, and more believable."

"Oh?" asked General Grimsel, refilling her mug from the pitcher in what she clearly thought was a casual gesture.

"I learned the true story only because I was wed to a member of the royal family," Newell said, playing the generals before setting the hook. "No one but members of the royal family are ever told the story by order of Zorana herself. My late wife, the Princess Lovella, knowing that I would rule alongside her one day, confided the tale to me. She was very concerned about how I would take it, for she believed that hearing this tale was what had unmanned her brother, Crown Prince Chalmer, leading to his untimely death."

"What was this secret?" General Grimsel pressed, anxious now lest Newell say nothing more.

Prince Newell dropped his voice and looked uneasy. "I'm not certain I should tell you this, but I'm hoping that if you know the truth, perhaps you will recognize how important it is that Bright Bay and Hawk Haven not be rejoined."

General Yuci's dark eyes glittered with what might have been intensity but what Newell feared was laughter.

"Perhaps you have your own advancement in mind, Prince Newell? Very well, I can understand such motives. Tell on."

"And quickly," Grimsel added.

Newell feigned a mixture of anger and embarrassment—a man caught intriguing but unwilling to back out.

"The real reason that Gustin Sailor split from his associates," he said, "was that Zorana Shield and Clive Elkwood believed firmly that everything that stank of Old World sorcery should be destroyed. We all know how the rulers kept knowledge of the higher orders of magic from the colonists."

The two generals nodded, willing to let him digress now that he was on the point. Such restrictive policies had been fairly universal, for the power of high magic was what had permitted the Old Countries to dominate the residents of their colonies.

Newell continued, "And we all know that most of them took their magical materials home when they left."

Again nods.

"That didn't always happen." Newell saw the generals exchange surprised glances. "According to the tale King Tedric told Princess Lovella, one day some years after the departure of the Old Country rulers of Gildcrest, Zorana Shield chanced upon an isolated vacation retreat in the

376 / JANE LINDSKOLD

foothills of the Iron Mountains where the residents had succumbed to the Plague. Danger of contagion was long past, but the illness must have come upon the residents suddenly for none of their magical trinkets had been destroyed or sent away."

Newell glanced at his audience. Neither looked either bored or inclined to laugh. He continued, satisfied:

"Zorana burned the books and scrolls, but there were a few items, a ring, I think, and maybe some sort of wand—Lovella was vague. There may have been more. Before Zorana Shield could destroy these items, her allies joined her. They quarreled, Clive Elkwood supporting her, Gustin Sailor furious at the waste. When it became clear that there was no resolution possible, Gustin acted.

"In the dark of night, he stole the items and fled to the southeast, near the bay where his strongest base of power lay. Later, those who thought he had done right rallied to him. Zorana Shield already had a solid following in the lands north of the Barren River, lands still held today by her Shield kindred. To the delight of the balladeers she married Clive Elkwood.

"Thus the break between our countries—for though they weren't really countries yet the Barren River gradually became a boundary between factions. It would take several more years before Zorana Shield and Clive Elkwood solidified their hold on the lands north of the Barren River. After they had, they went after Gustin Sailor. He now held most of the lands south of the Barren—though his interest lay especially along the coast and in the Isles.

"When Zorana and Clive went after Gustin, that's the period we usually call the Civil War, though ideologically the split had happened several years earlier. The Civil War was fought for something like four years. Clive Elkwood died in one of those battles, but Zorana was firmly at the head of their faction so the fighting went on. Finally, peace seemed easier than continuing to fight—you must remember that some of these people had been fighting for fifteen years or more.

"With peace, the Barren was confirmed as the border between Hawk Haven and Bright Bay. Zorana's followers had been calling themselves the Hawks, because they were resolved to fly free without magic's bondage, so their new kingdom was called Hawk Haven."

Newell fell silent and General Yuci prompted, "And Gustin Sailor, of course, he became King Gustin I of Bright Bay, but what happened to the magical relics?"

Newell looked tense and grim. He milked the silence for a few moments more then said:

"Despite trying repeatedly, Zorana never managed to retrieve them from Gustin. The good thing is that—according to what Princess Lovella told me—no one in Bright Bay has ever possessed the talent to employ the relics. To this day they remain curiosities in the Bright Bay treasury, protected by the Seal of the Sun and brought forth only upon the coronation of a ruler. Even then, they are only seen by a select few. I've asked around and what I've heard from those few makes me believe the story. Bright Bay has Old World magic."

General Grimsel swore a thunderous oath. "Old World magic! If someone learns how to use it, they could destroy us all!"

"And," whispered General Yuci, "in Hawk Haven there are those who are sorc . . ."

Yuci stopped then, remembering that Newell's own sister was a reputed sorceress. Newell politely pretended not to have heard. He'd done what was necessary.

Stonehold now had an excuse to be at odds with Bright Bay. Whether they would use that excuse to declare war on Bright Bay, to withdraw their mercenaries, or merely to attempt to dictate domestic policy he didn't know. What he was certain of was that Stonehold's rulers would not let the opportunity pass them by. Soon enough, Bright Bay would be seeing her ally's true colors.

"It is an outrageous tale!" protested General Grimsel loudly, perhaps to cover for her own too thoughtful silence.

Newell rose to take his leave. "I thought you needed to know the truth—to know why it is so dangerous to let these nations be reunited."

"You are a true friend to all humanity," General Grimsel said. "Stonehold will not forget this noble act."

"Thank you, General."

General Yuci favored him with a deep bow but said nothing. Newell wondered if he was still shocked by his recollection of Newell's own familial reputation for sorcery or whether he was simply keeping his counsel.

Prince Newell straightened his hat, bowed, and departed, not wishing to dilute the impression he had made. He had no doubts that Stonehold would do its best to confirm what he had said, but about that he felt no qualms.

*It **is** an outrageous story,* Newell thought as he left the two generals to their certain consternation. *The funny thing is, it is also completely true.*

DESPITE ELISE'S RESOLVE to act immediately, circumstances conspired against her. First, she encountered her cousin Sapphire. Since witnessing the events of the afternoon before, Elise's feelings toward Sapphire had undergone a revolution. No longer did Sapphire seem a pushy older cousin but something of a valiant heroine, striving to maintain her identity despite crippling pressure from without.

The trouble was that Sapphire's feelings about Elise hadn't changed at all. To Sapphire, Elise was still the upstart who conspired with her own brother to steal a march on her. Elise drew in a deep breath:

"Good morning, cousin."

"Good morning—though from my reading of the sun," Sapphire commented unkindly, "it is nearly noon."

"True," Elise replied mildly. "It is. I suppose I do not have your constitution. Last night's party was too much for me. I am not accustomed to such hours or such strong wine."

Sapphire paused as if examining this comment for some subtle insult. Failing to find one, she smiled.

"I am about to go riding," she said reluctantly, certainly remembering Melina Shield's recent reminder that Sapphire had a duty to her family, not merely to herself. "Would you like to join me? It would sweat the wine out of you properly."

Riding was the last thing Elise wanted to do, but she would be an utter fool to reject such an offer, especially since she had resolved to rescue Sapphire from her mother.

"Let me change," she said. "Ninette, ask one of the grooms to bring around my palfrey."

"I'll take care of that," Sapphire offered. "I was going to saddle up the Blue."

Elise thanked her. As she changed into riding breeches—the pretty frock she had worn to go on Firekeeper's hawking party so long ago was back in Eagle's Nest—Elise cautioned Ninette to say nothing to anyone.

"I won't, Elise," the woman said earnestly. "I think I'll take my sewing and go join the lady's circle. I won't be so scared in daylight and maybe I'll learn something."

"You are brave," Elise said, kissing Ninette on one cheek. "Do that, but keep your own mouth tightly sealed. I wouldn't have harm come to you for all the world."

Riding with Sapphire was surprisingly enjoyable, though, of course, Sapphire must show off her superior skill. Elise found it easy to give her cousin the praise she clearly craved, for when Sapphire thought herself unwatched her hand often fell to her side as if to quiet the pain of her wound.

They visited Ivon Archer and Purcel Trueheart among their troops. Here, Elise learned, Sapphire had developed quite a following. They found the same when Elise suggested that they visit Earl Kestrel's cavalry unit. Despite a large proportion of the riders being female, here too Sapphire was a favorite.

Perhaps she is not all bluster and pose, Elise thought. *Perhaps beneath that showy armor and boastful talk does beat a warrior heart. The question is, is that also the heart of a queen?*

When they returned to the encampment, the nobles' enclave was buzzing with news. Nydia and Opal ran out to meet them.

"The king met with Allister Seagleam this morning," Dia announced.

"And," Opal cut in, "they have arranged that there will be a great ball in a few days. All our noble folk and officers will be invited."

"And all of theirs," added Dia. "They're also inviting important people from the towns."

"And Mother thinks," said Opal with a guarded glance at her older sister, "that the purpose is to see who might make a marriage with one of Allister's children."

"Our mother thinks so too," Dia added, and her expression was strange, a mixture of anticipation and what Elise was certain was fear.

"Since none of us brought appropriate clothing," Opal said, a real thrill of delight in her voice this time, "we are all to go to town this afternoon and visit the shops. Messages have been sent ahead and it is rumored that a great bazaar will be prepared for our pleasure."

"And Lady Blysse," Elise said when the three excited girls paused for breath, "has anyone told her of this grand event?"

Glances between the two made clear that not only had Blysse not been told, the tacit decision had been made *not* to tell her. Elise was slightly surprised when Sapphire said:

"She has not been, I see. Very well. Elise and I will ride to the Kestrel camp and tell her."

Before there could be any protest, Sapphire reined the Blue around and Elise's palfrey was quick to follow.

"Blysse," Sapphire said, "saved my life—she and her men. I will not have her slighted in such a petty way."

Elise glowed with delight. Perhaps her cousin did have the heart of a queen as well as that of a warrior.

"May I offer you a hint?" she said.

"What?"

"Lady Blysse likes her friends to call her Firekeeper."

Sapphire looked offended for a moment. Then a slow smile spread across her face.

"Her friends, you say. Very well. I will remember that."

SHOPPING TOOK THE REST of the daylight hours. It was not merely a female expedition. Most of the noblemen and officers had come no better equipped. The informal bazaar was filled with men and women examining bolts of fabric, conferring with seamstresses and tailors, and shooting each other shy glances as if wondering what the other sex would think of their finery. Festivities extended into twilight with impromptu dinner parties in most of the finer inns.

Hope was up to the challenge. The resident clothiers recruited nearly everyone who could use a needle to work in their shops. They were forced to compete for labor with the jewelers and cobblers, as well as the purveyors of food and drink. Despite all this ingenuity, many of those invited found themselves forced to mend and polish their own attire and many of the locals had to make do with last season's gown or waistcoat rather than the new one they craved.

Yet minor disappointments could not quell the festive spirit. The merchants of Hope (and her sister city Good Crossing) saw half a year's earnings or more flow into their coffers. This in turn made them able to be more generous with those they hired. Even the hard feelings raised when merchants lured away workers in their neighbors' employ were dismissed as points scored in a rather rough and tumble game.

Normally, Elise would have delighted in such a shopping expedition, especially when she discovered that due to extensive smuggling through the area fine goods imported by the sailors of Bright Bay were far less expensive here than they were in Eagle's Nest. The excellent wools of Stonehold were also well represented and, although the weather was too warm for wool, Elise and her father purchased several bolts of fabric to ship home.

Yet, despite such distractions, the thought of the conference she must arrange for later that night was rarely far from Elise's thoughts. During a visit to an herbalist who also distilled the most wonderful floral scents, Elise managed to slip Derian a note. His quick nod and a light of interest in his greenish-brown eyes acknowledged her message and agreed to the suggested arrangements. Then he switched back into servile invisibility with such skill that she could hardly believe he was the same man.

Later than evening, when the parties had broken up, Elise pleaded exhaustion and went to her pavilion. Fortunately, Baron Archer was one of the night officers, so no one would miss her. Even if they did, Ninette would cover for her.

Elise skirted the fringes of the camp until she came to the edge where the Kestrel tents were pitched. She avoided these, going out into the fields to a cluster of rocks that had been appointed as their meeting place. Derian, Firekeeper, and Sir Jared were already there with a shielded lantern and a pot of tea.

"Valet," Elise said to Derian, "is making his mark on you."

Derian grinned. "To think that when I first met him I judged him a useless mouse of a man. I know better now."

Firekeeper, from at the fringe of the circle of light where she sat with her arm thrown around Blind Seer, had no patience with such niceties.

"All day, Elise, you have smelled of fear. Last day, too. Tell us why."

Elise laughed nervously. "I hope that everyone does not have your nose, Firekeeper."

"Not just my nose. Blind Seer, too. If someone has frightened you, we will frighten them back."

"Thank you," Elise said, genuinely grateful. "But it's not as simple as that. Might I have a cup of tea?"

Part of her reason was to win a moment's more respite. Part was remembering what had happened when she had tried to tell before. While Derian poured, she began, telling them of how she and Ninette had gone out to the cluster of rocks near the Fortress of the Watchful Eye.

"We hid ourselves because we did not want to invite the attention of the soldiers. However, we were not the only ones to have marked out those rocks as a good place for privacy. Melina Shield came there with Sapphire, Jet, and Opal."

Without wasting words, Elise told how Melina had scolded her children. She was grateful for the darkness when she must relate how bluntly Melina had berated Jet for his sexual exploits, but she must be honest or risk leaving out something that might assist them.

Thus far, any pain she had felt could have been imagined or dismissed as the slight burning of the tea, but when she began to tell how Melina had cursed Jet, a sharp hot sensation, precisely as if her tongue had been bitten, caused her to cry out.

"Lady!" Jared Surcliffe jumped to his feet. "What is wrong?"

She waved him back. "Part of this tale, I fear."

Digging the nails of her right hand into her palm, Elise continued. She tasted blood by the time she had finished telling of Jet's cursing, but memory of Sapphire's courage shamed her into going on. She, too, had thought herself worthy to be queen. She might not be a warrior, but surely she was not without courage.

Firekeeper's soft voice from the shadows broke through her pretense.

"I smell blood on your breath," she said. "What causes this?"

Elise felt tears begin to slide down her cheeks unbidden, as if Firekeeper's detection of her pain had freed them.

"A third curse," she said, each word a throbbing stab. "To guard against . . . any telling what . . . Melina has done. Jet and I . . . she didn't know . . . but still."

The pain was horrid. Perhaps because this curse was the one that had affected her personally, the sensation of biting ants was so acute that she could even feel their little feet tromping on the swollen flesh of her injured tongue.

"Quiet," Derian urged Elise, pouring her more tea and holding the cup to her lips. "Rinse your mouth and spit. Don't be proper."

Sir Jared had vanished, returning a moment later with his medical bag in his hand.

"Chamomile and sage," he said, drawing out two packets. "Both good for the mouth and throat. Chamomile has soothing properties as well. Do we have more hot water, Derian?"

"In the kettle by the fire."

"I get," Firekeeper said and was gone and back before anyone could answer her.

Sir Jared's potion did seem to help. At his urging, Elise first rinsed her mouth with a tincture of sage, then drank more in a tea blended with the chamomile and some honey.

"Don't talk yet," Sir Jared said when she started to thank him. "Let us see if the pain is as intense if you respond to our questions. We have enough information to begin."

Elise nodded. "Good idea."

"Melina Shield cursed her son Jet with impotence. Lovely." Jared paused. "Did she know that you were there when she cursed him?"

"No."

"Any pain?"

"No."

Actually, there might have been a twinge, but Elise wasn't going to tell him. He might refuse to go on and she needed to tell this.

"Good. Now, based on what you said before, you think that because you and Jet are betrothed, her magic was able to touch you."

"Yes."

"Have you asked Ninette if she feels similar pain?"

"No. She is so very frightened."

"We'll still need to test this." In the lantern light she saw him frown, then look embarrassed. "Lady Elise, are you and Jet . . . lovers?"

"No." Did she imagine it or was Sir Jared's expression a bit too pleased to be merely relief?

Derian cut in. "Elise wears a betrothal pendant. It's made of the same jet that he is named for, the same stone that the sorceress used when she cursed him. Could there be a connection?"

"There might be," Sir Jared said. "Lady Elise, take the pendant off."

Elise had not removed the carved wolf's head pendant since the betrothal ceremony. Even when she had bathed or slept, it had remained in place. She felt curiously reluctant to take it off now, an almost physical nausea that roiled the tea in her stomach.

To combat the nausea, Elise summoned an image of Jet bedding some light woman, her own lynx pendant swinging from his neck or tossed casually on a bedside table. Deliberately, she built the details, fueling what she didn't know from her imagination until she roused an answering anger.

Quickly, before she could lose the will, Elise lifted the chain from about her neck and set the pendant on the rock beside her.

"That was difficult, wasn't it?" Jared asked. "Interesting. When I was betrothed and later married I had no such difficulty removing the associated jewelry."

"My father takes his off all the time," Derian added. "Especially when he's working with the horses, yet he adores Mother."

Sir Jared nodded. "I think you have guessed right, Derian, that pendant, as much as anything, may be what Lady Melina used to channel her spell. Tell me, Elise, did she do anything in particular during the ceremony or soon thereafter?"

Elise tried to remember. She had attended numerous betrothals in her capacity as heir to the Archer estates. In recent years, her father had been tutoring her in how to perform the ritual since, as head of the family, it would someday be her duty.

"Not during the ceremony," she said, "but afterwards she drew me aside and made quite a fuss about the pendant. She asked to see it."

"Did you take it off?" Derian asked.

"Yes. I had no problem with that—except for a girl's romantic heart flutters, that is." The only pain Elise felt as she spoke was disdain for herself. "Melina held it up to admire the carving. She told me that I should be proud to wear it always since it marked me as a member of her family. Now that I think about it, she swung it back and forth, much as she did when she . . ."

Elise hid a wince as a faint but certain bite pierced her tongue near the tip.

"Cursed her children," she finished steadily.

"Her children, you say," Sir Jared nodded. "Time for question and answer again. Did she curse Sapphire as well?"

"Yes."

"Not with impotence. That would hardly be appropriate. What with?"

"Pain from her wounds." Elise was certain that the ant bites were less sharp now. "Pain and inability to heal until Lady Melina releases her curse."

Jared swore, invoking his society patron—the Eagle, Elise noted in passing—and a long line of Surcliffe ancestors. Firekeeper spoke for the first time since volunteering to bring water.

"What happens if Melina Shield dies?"

Firekeeper's intention was obvious. Though she was but a shadow in the darkness, they could see her hand resting upon her knife. Blind Seer's hackles were up and his fangs gleamed white as he snarled.

"No one knows," Sir Jared answered. "The curse may last forever without her to lift it. It may die with her. Great magics were never taught in the New World. Most of what our people had were inborn talents, like my gift for healing or Holly Gardener's green thumb. Some were trained in sorcery but those with the most promise were taken back to the Old World for their final training. Legend said that they were bound not to reveal their arts to anyone."

Derian whistled softly. "Bound. That's just what *she* did to her children. I doubt they could get around that."

"We need to know more," Elise said, feeling panicked, "but how will we learn! If we were at home, I might consult the library. There are musty tomes there, dating back to before Queen Zorana captured the Castle. Aksel Trueheart often roots around in them gathering information for his history."

"I wonder if that library or someplace similar is where Melina got her knowledge," Jared mused. "You're right, Elise. We can't go ahead in ignorance. We may do more harm than help."

"We have time," Derian said. "Not a lot, but some. King Tedric won't leave or make any great changes until after this ball, so we have time. I think I know where to start. Hazel Healer strikes me as a wise woman. I saw lots of books in her workshop and not all were about herbs."

"Good," Sir Jared said. "Happily, with the ball to prepare for, no one will think it at all odd if we call on her. They'll just think the ladies are shopping for scent. I have the excuse of searching for odd medicinal herbs. Indeed, since Sapphire was assaulted, everyone is traveling in larger groups."

Firekeeper had risen to her feet. "Tomorrow then. Early. Derian may think we have time, but wolves hunt when they are hungry and I am very hungry."

She turned then and in a few steps was gone.

Elise sighed. "I wish I could be as sure as she is."

"She's less certain than she seems," Derian said. "I think."

Aware of her trembling hand, Elise lifted the betrothal pendant from the rock and put it back on.

"I can't be seen without it," she said. "Good night, gentlemen."

"Good night, Elise," Derian said.

"Let me walk you back to your tent," Sir Jared suggested.

"No. Better no one sees us together. There is enough uncertainty tonight. I'll be fine."

She smiled at him. "Have Firekeeper call for me in the morning. My aunts dislike that Sapphire and I insisted on bringing her shopping today. No one will press to accompany us."

"What about Sapphire?" Derian asked.

"I think she has a dress fitting early. Don't worry. Now, good night."

As she hurried back to her pavilion, Elise thought about the look in Sir Jared's eyes as she had turned away. Concern had been there, and admiration, and something more. A sudden warmth touched her cheeks as she realized that he might be the admirer who had anonymously left her a small pot of very expensive rose attar scent.

XIX

WHEN ALLISTER SEAGLEAM AWAKENED, he realized with something like astonishment that he was actually looking forward to his meeting with King Tedric. He listened with half an ear as Sir Tench briefed him on various things he should and should not do, kissed Pearl and assured her that the sketches for her new gown and those for the twins looked wonderful, tossed said twins in the air while they shrieked at this assault on their eleven-year-old dignity, and then drew Shad and Tavis aside for a private word.

"You'll be escorting your mother into the town today, I expect."

Shad, a serious-looking young man of twenty who had his mother's rounded lines and fair coloring—but no longer any of her plumpness— nodded.

"That's right, Father. She is insisting on having us all fitted for new clothes. I think my dress uniform should do quite well, but Mother is acting as if this ball is Queen Gustin the Fourth's coronation all over again."

"It is, Shad, especially for our family," Allister replied. "However, if you wish to wear your dress uniform, tell Pearl that this is my wish as well. If you do choose to wear it, make certain that every button and line of braid is as perfect as if you were expecting an inspection by the Lord High Admiral."

"I will, Father," Shad said earnestly. His recent promotion from ensign to lieutenant was the most important event in his young life. Allister understood. He had also struggled to prove himself though hampered by high birth and outlander blood.

Tavis, at fifteen, had yet to enter the Navy formally, though like any youth raised in Bright Bay he swam like a fish and sailed as if the masts and lines were extensions of his own body. He scuffed his shoe along the ground and looked sidelong up at his father. Beneath his thick golden lashes, his eyes were the exact shade of a the sea before a thunderstorm.

"I suppose," Tavis said gloomily, "that I have no choice but to let my mother doll me up in lace and brocade."

"None at all," his father said sternly. "It is time you realized that you have a responsibility to this family. Think about this little fact while I am away. If a marriage alliance is made between our family and one of the royal scions of Hawk Haven, you are as good a candidate as your elder brother—better in many ways for he is already betrothed."

Tavis looked at his father wide-eyed. Although a second child in Bright Bay prepared for the possibility of becoming heir far more stringently than his counterpart in Hawk Haven might, Tavis had passed from boyhood onto the threshold of young manhood secure in the knowledge that he was protected by the double bulwark of father and elder brother.

"But I . . . but the girls . . . but Mother said," he stammered.

"But nothing. I say all four of you must conduct yourselves as if the entire fate of our family rests upon you alone. You boys have been taking this upcoming ball less than seriously. I hereby order you to start doing so."

"Yes, sir!" snapped Shad.

"Yes, Father," Tavis said slowly, but his expression assured Allister that he would obey.

Allister could pity the boy. Born into another family, Tavis would probably have become a musician or poet, a burden to be cherished lest he starve but cherished nonetheless for the evidence that he had been blessed by the ancestors with a special gift. Tavis, named for a grandfather he had never met, now must take his own part in the political games to which his namesake had been sacrificed.

"I must go now," Allister said. "Make me proud of you and know that I will not treat with your lives lightly, but remember also—there is a part of our lives that does not belong to us. It belongs to our country and to our families. That is the price we pay for titles and honors common folk do not have."

He turned then, resisting the impulse to tousle their heads. For a moment, twenty and fifteen though they might be, his sons had looked very much like little boys.

TODAY ALLISTER MUST CROSS the courtyard between the sides of the Toll House to mount the stairs on the Hawk Haven side of the building. A woman he recognized as Lady Melina Shield was busy discussing potential decorations for the ball with one of Lord Tench's assistants. The matter under discussion seemed to be whether or not the emblem of the royal family of Bright Bay should be displayed given that the queen herself was not in attendance.

More of this eternal political maneuvering for position, Allister thought. *And I am beginning to think that it matters as little to Uncle Tedric as it does to me.*

At that very moment, he made up his mind to tell King Tedric about Zorana Archer's letter. After greetings were exchanged, he began on this immediately.

"Yesterday, Uncle Tedric, when the physician reminded you of your health, I was about to tell you something rather interesting. Lest we get distracted today, I would like to begin with that piece of business."

"I am quite curious," the old monarch said equably. "Speak on."

"Some twenty or so days ago, I received a letter from a member of your court. It was carried by private courier and delivered in great secrecy. The letter suggested that it would be to the mutual advantage of the writer and myself to arrange a marriage alliance between our families. She . . ."

"Ah, she," King Tedric murmured. "Do go on."

"She stated that she herself was already married," Allister continued, somewhat nervously, for the old eagle's face was completely unreadable, "but that she had several children of marriageable or near marriageable age. She then went on to name these children and note something about each."

King Tedric coughed dryly. "It must have been a veritable tome."

"The missive did run to several close-written pages, Your Majesty," Allister admitted. "Next she expressed considerable knowledge about my own family, including the knowledge that my son Shad was already betrothed—a thing that astonished me a little, as the betrothal is fairly recent and I had not thought the news would have reached your court.

"Then she suggested the combination of her children and mine would be—in her opinion—to our mutual advantage. She signed the letter and impressed it with her personal seal so that there would be no doubt of her identity."

"Do you have this letter still?"

"Yes, Your Majesty. Queen Gustin, to whom I confided this information . . ."

"You did. I see."

"Queen Gustin ordered me to give her the letter for her state archives. I refused on the grounds that it was a personal communication to me in my capacity as the head of my family, not in any of the positions that I hold for the Crown."

"Very correctly, I'm certain." King Tedric smiled slightly. "And I'm certain also that as a monarch Queen Gustin was rather piqued."

"I'm afraid she was, Your Majesty."

"I much preferred when you referred to me as Uncle Tedric or, failing that, King Tedric. Don't worry, Nephew. I'm not going to bite heads off just because you brought this to me. Not your head at least . . ."

For a moment his smile faded and Allister was reminded again that the eagle was a bird of prey. Then King Tedric was sternly affable again.

"Do you plan to show me this remarkable document?"

"If you will agree to leave it in my custody."

"I will. I can hardly respect your rights less than did your own monarch. I would come out rather badly in the comparison."

Allister reached into his inside jacket pocket and removed the several sheets of vellum.

"Thick enough to stop an arrow," King Tedric mused. "If you would bide a moment, have a cup of something to drink, I will just quickly review this."

He pulled a pair of reading spectacles from his own breast pocket and did so. Allister sipped water flavored with mint and rose hips, hoping by the Bull's Wide Forehead that he had done the right thing.

At last, King Tedric set the letter aside and sighed. Removing his spectacles, he methodically put them away, saying:

"Zorana. I thought it might be her when you began. She's ambitious and her ambitions were sadly stifled when Baron Archer and Lord Rolfston agreed to betroth two of their children. They knew I could hardly overlook the opportunity to flatter three of my Great Houses. Lord Rolfston's wife is a Shield, you see, while Baron Archer's wife is a Wellward. Lord Rolfston himself is a Redbriar on his mother's side."

"Oh." Allister felt a bit out of his depth here. In Bright Bay the noble houses all had one name, the same as their house emblem. His case was rather an exception. Normally, he would have taken his mother's family name since Seagleam was reserved for members of the royal family—all but for the monarch, who became a Gustin. However, he couldn't well be an Eagle in Bright Bay, so he had been granted a dispensation to bear his father's name. His children, however, were Oysters.

"Zorana," King Tedric repeated the name, a little sadly it seemed to Allister. "I will need to speak with her. In the meantime, what do you think of her proposal: her Purcel and one of your little girls?"

Allister spoke carefully. "Remembering that we are not talking a romantic alliance here, but a political one, I suppose the first and most important question is what do *you* think of her proposal?"

King Tedric looked at him blankly, then roared with laughter, an amazingly deep and rich sound coming from such an apparently frail body. Worried that Tedric would do himself harm, Allister glanced around, but even Sir Dirkin, normally as expressionless as a piece of wood, seemed to have a small smile on his face.

"Nephew! Nephew!" the king gasped when the worst of the laughter had passed. "Where did you learn to speak so bluntly?"

"From my mother, your sister," Allister replied honestly. "I told you that she did not make herself popular among the nobility and she did not do that by remaining meek, quiet, and demure."

A few more snorts of laughter and then the king said, "And so this is how you honor Caryl's memory. Very good. What do I think about this proposal? I think that it has potential."

"I would only agree to it myself," Allister said seriously, "if I had your word, both verbal and written, that the boy Purcel would be named your heir and that my daughter would have settled on her land and money. There would remain the question of a regent. Purcel will not reach his majority for another four years. If the ancestors call you to join them before that time, someone must be designated in advance. Would your people accept me? Would his mother accept a third party?"

Tedric waved his hand to slow Allister down. "I can see that you have given this matter a great deal of thought, as well you should since you have had twenty-some days to think about it. Let me reply to your comments one at a time."

"Very well, Uncle. Forgive my impetuosity. I have had few people with whom to discuss this matter. Queen Gustin requested that I keep it a state secret. Only myself, my wife, and the queen's advisor Tench are privy to the letter."

"Zorana has also kept her peace," Tedric said, "although not without a certain gloating calm. Now, your first demand before you would agree to this alliance is that I name Purcel Archer my heir. I can see that. It would protect your daughter to a certain extent, especially from her mother-in-law's vagaries of mood. If Zorana was to be queen with Purcel to follow her, she could always pass him by in favor of another. Very good. I could agree to naming Purcel my heir directly.

"I could also agree to settling some property and goods specifically on your daughter. Purcel is a warrior. Although we can hope that this alliance would make peace between our nations, warriors do die in battle. Your daughter should have some security of her own.

"Regent would be a more difficult matter. I am not certain my people would accept you as sole regent nor do I like the idea of two regents. We have enough divisiveness without encouraging more. Zorana has proven herself able, but too willing to act outside of channels. I believe I would need to select from outside of all of those currently concerned in this matter. There would be too many hurt feelings otherwise."

Allister nodded. "I see—as well as someone who has only observed matters from outside can see, that is."

"I might have suggested Earl Kestrel," the king said, "but that he involved himself by hunting out Lady Blysse and so involving himself."

"About her, Uncle . . ."

"Yes?"

"There are so many stories. What is the truth?"

"The truth, as much as I am willing to admit," the king said, a twinkle in his eye, "is that Lady Blysse—Firekeeper as she prefers to be called—is the genuine sole survivor of an expedition into the lands west of the Iron Mountains. She claims to have been raised by wolves. If you had seen her table manners when she first arrived you would have no doubt of the veracity of that statement."

Clearing his throat, Allister pressed, "I heard that she is followed everywhere by an evil familiar spirit in the shape of a giant wolf."

"That is partly true," the king conceded. "She is followed almost everywhere by an enormous grey wolf with blue eyes. If it is not a familiar spirit—as I believe it is not—then we must reconsider those old tales from the early days of colonization which claimed that the animals in those days were larger than any seen today."

Allister knew he was skating on thin ice, but he must ask. "Her name is 'Blysse.' That was the name of Prince Barden's daughter. Is she . . ."

"Blysse," the king interrupted, "is what Earl Kestrel named his feral foundling—one might say with the memory of my granddaughter in mind. Duchess Kestrel agreed to adopt the girl into the Kestrel House, therefore, Blysse can claim the title 'Lady.' As to whether or not she is my granddaughter . . . that remains to be seen."

"I see," Allister grinned. "You are less blunt than my dear mother, Uncle."

"I have learned to be. I am a king."

"True. Rumor said that the name on that piece of paper—the one on which you named your heir—is that of Lady Blysse. They say that you summoned her to you soon before your departure and met with her in private."

King Tedric bared his teeth in something too fierce to be a smile. "The latter part of that is true. As to the former, I shall say to you what I have said to everyone else: nothing."

Allister leaned back in his chair, knowing that he had pushed as far as even his uncle's curious good humor would permit.

"Shall we then turn to other matters, Uncle Tedric? Sir Tench hinted to me that Queen Gustin would very much like you to know that the smugglers operating through these paired cities of Hope and Good Crossing are not operating with her sanction. She wondered if some sort of agreement might be reached to limit their activities to the mutual benefit of our treasuries . . ."

King Tedric nodded and motioned for the clerk to start taking notes. The rest of the morning passed in politely formal discussion of matters of state. Only as Allister was rising to leave did King Tedric push Zorana's letter over to him.

"Don't forget this, Nephew. And give my best wishes to your family."

Allister smiled. "And give mine to yours, Uncle, to all of yours."

Even those, he thought as he trooped down the stairs and across the courtyard, *who run about like wild things and howl at the moon.*

❀

DESPITE THE URGENCY OF THEIR BUSINESS, Firekeeper didn't awaken Elise at dawn, having learned from Derian that Hazel Healer was not likely to be able to meet with them until the morning was quite old. Moreover, it would look as strange as a wolf in the treetops if they were all to troop off to a perfume shop at that early hour with the ball still some days off.

Knowing both more and less about magic than her companions assumed, Firekeeper needed no warning to be cautious about arousing Melina Shield's suspicions. So she and Blind Seer hunted, though the hunting was poor here on the edges of the town, and swam in a millpond some miles from the camp. Then they trotted back at a leisurely pace, arriving just in time for breakfast.

Such rituals completed, they gathered Elise and Ninette and walked the track to town. The beaten dirt road was busy enough, but most of the traffic was related to the routine of the military. Exchanging greetings with those they knew, they made no secret of their destination, hiding their purpose in plain sight, as Derian had suggested.

Hazel was waiting for them and ushered them into her private workroom. When they took seats beneath the hanging bunches of dried herbs, Firekeeper must fight a powerful urge to sneeze and, from his place beneath her chair, Blind Seer grumbled protest at this olfactory assault.

As soon as they were settled, Hazel began, her expression somewhat severe. "I understand from Derian's note that you wish to consult me about a matter of great delicacy and great secrecy. Let me save you some trouble. I do not dispense abortifacients except in extreme cases when the life of mother and child both are at risk."

Firekeeper was completely puzzled, but evidently what Hazel had said meant something more to the others. Derian turned vivid scarlet. Elise and Ninette both blushed and looked away. Only Doc remained composed. He replied:

"Your assumption is quite reasonable, Mistress Healer, given what you know, but let me assure you that we have come to consult you about something quite different—although no less grave."

Hazel's severe expression vanished. Now she looked both worried and relieved.

"Very well. You have my promise of silence. Start telling me what your problem is while I set a pot of tea brewing."

In deference to the pain Elise would experience telling her own story, Sir Jared began. Ninette volunteered specific details and Firekeeper noticed with interest that she seemed to feel no pain whatsoever. Hazel noticed this as well and, as soon as the narrative was ended, she asked the maid:

"You don't feel any pain, Ninette, even when you talk about specific aspects of the curse?"

"No, Mistress Healer. My heart beats terribly fast and sometimes I feel so afraid that I think I will fall down in a dead faint, but I don't feel any pain."

"Then I must be right!" Derian said excitedly. "The betrothal stone—that's the means by which the sorceress is affecting Elise!"

Ninette said, coloring slightly, "I guess I should also admit that as soon as the Lady Melina started droning her curse, I looked away—buried my face in my hands. I don't know if that might have helped."

In response to the unasked question Elise volunteered, "I never looked away. I was curious and angry—I wanted to know what was going on. Another thing you should know, all through the ritual Ninette never stopped muttering prayers to her Society patron and to her ancestors. I was only aware of it afterwards, but when I think back on the situation, I remember the low drone of her voice behind me."

Ninette nodded in confirmation. "That's right, I did pray. Mother always taught me to do that when I had night fears. I guess I felt like a little girl again, faced with real sorcery."

Pouring tea, Hazel considered. Then she rose and, reaching up onto a very high shelf, took down a book.

"Magical powers," she said without preamble, "did not vanish from the world simply because Queen Zorana ruled that higher sorcery would not be practiced in Hawk Haven. They still manifest today, mostly within families and then we only recognize magical power when it takes the shape of what we call talents.

"My family has a strong talent for working with plants—the Green Thumb, as it is usually called. There are other talents: a touch of precognition or clairvoyance, perfect sense of direction, healing, a strong empathy for animals . . ."

Firekeeper was surprised when Hazel paused and looked at her.

"I wouldn't be at all surprised if Firekeeper has that last gift and maybe others. It would explain her survival and her ability to communicate with animals."

Derian, Elise, and Ninette looked as surprised as Firekeeper felt but Doc only nodded.

"I'd thought that might be the case, maybe because I have the healing talent myself. It would be impossible to test, of course. Firekeeper's own story of her upbringing provides an alternate explanation."

From his place on the floor Blind Seer commented to Firekeeper, *"He speaks as if these talents are restricted to humankind, but the Royal Beasts may have them as well. Ah, well. Doc is not a bad man, only filled with human arrogance toward other bloods."*

Hazel, of course unaware of this comment, continued, "The House of the Eagle has never—to my knowledge—shown evidence of being talented. Neither have the Shields. However, Melina Shield's other parent . . ."

"Her father is Stanbrook born," Elise said.

"I don't know much about what talents the various Great Houses might have," Hazel said apologetically. "After Queen Zorana decreed a reign based on rejection of such Old World things as elaborate titles and magical power, even those families that had talents went out of their way to play them down."

Firekeeper thought this was the time to ask something that had been troubling her.

"Everyone say that Queen Zorana want no titles, but still there are king, queen, duke, duchess, all and more. These seem like titles to me."

"Good point," Doc answered, "but you should study how it was before Queen Zorana's reform. She eliminated some titles and the custom of one person bearing more than one title. Before that, a single person might have five or six titles: King of this, Prince of that, Duke of this, that, and the other thing, Baron of this . . ."

"All one person?" Firekeeper asked, not at all certain she wasn't being teased.

"All one person," Doc assured her. "It's sort of a variation of the way you call me Doc, while my associates call me Sir Jared, and those who knew me when I was a boy and some of my friends call me Jared. Different names for different situations."

"It is easier for wolves," Firekeeper snorted. "One name, one person."

"Unless you are the One," Blind Seer reminded her. *"Then you are the One Male or the One Female, but you still have a personal name. Our Pack's One Female was Shining Coat. I have this on the best authority."*

Firekeeper kicked him.

"We're getting off the subject," Elise said somewhat anxiously. "Mistress Hazel, you were saying that it is possible that Melina Shield might have inherited a talent for sorcery from House Kite."

"Yes, but there are other options as well." Hazel opened the book in her lap and ran a finger down a closely written page. For once, Firekeeper regretted not being able to read, for the others clearly had some idea what Hazel was doing. At last she halted.

"Here it is: trance induction." Hazel looked up and continued, "The good news and the bad news is that from what you describe, Lady Melina may also be performing something that, while rather like magic, is not magic at all. It is an art that enables one person to control another person's mind through suggestion. As with many other practices, trance induction fell out of favor after the retreat of the Old Countries, but some healers advocate it to help with the control of pain or certain detrimental impulses. That's why it's mentioned in this book."

"What does trance induction do?" Elise pressed. "Why is this good news and bad news? It sounds all good to me. If Lady Melina isn't a sorceress, we may be able to defeat her."

"The reason it isn't all good news," Hazel replied levelly, "is that if legend is correct, all magic that isn't locked into a specific physical item ceases to function after the caster is dead. You remember what happened in the comic song about Timin and the Flying Goat, don't you?"

Everyone but Firekeeper nodded and she decided this wasn't the time to ask for details.

"Trance induction is used to create a suggestible state in the mind of the subjects," Hazel continued. "When the subjects have been made suggestible, then they can be convinced to do almost anything—especially if deep inside they wish to do this thing anyhow. Since the person's own mind is really in charge—just under someone else's direction—breaking the power of the person who induced the trance doesn't remove the suggestion any more than a newly built table reverts to raw lumber after the carpenter hangs up his tools."

"Oh." Elise's small moan of dismay was echoed around the room.

Hazel frowned. "That's why it isn't necessarily a good thing if Lady Melina *is* using trance induction. If she is, she has been working on the minds of her primary subjects—her children and, I would guess, her husband and close servants—for years. That hold will not be instantly broken. The only way to break that hold would be to convince her subjects that she has somehow lost her power over them."

Derian drummed his fingers against his teacup, making a little ringing sound. "I suppose we could tell them," he said dubiously. "Tell them about this trance induction, I mean."

"Lady Elise," Hazel ordered suddenly, "you've heard my explanation. Now, talk about how Lady Melina laid the curses."

Obediently, Elise began to speak, but the sudden twist of pain that contorted her mouth was an eloquent answer to Hazel's test.

"But it *must* be sorcery," she protested. "Lady Melina only spoke with me briefly. How could she have induced a trance in such a short time?"

Hazel looked at Elise with a trace of pity. "Because, Lady Elise, you were quite willing to believe that Lady Melina had power to command you and because she was telling you to do something you already were inclined to do. What newly engaged young woman doesn't feel pride in her betrothal token and want to wear it always? Lady Melina simply reinforced the impulse you already held in your heart."

Elise looked sad. "I wonder if she knew about Jet's unreliability and decided she'd better assure my loyalty herself? If I'd been a stranger who knew nothing of her reputation as a sorceress, then Lady Melina's task would have been more difficult."

"I think so," Hazel agreed. "Of course, it might have been sorcery and the jet pendant the focus for her charm."

"Take off the necklace," Firekeeper urged. "Talking was easier then yesterday, I think."

Elise lifted off the necklace with its jet wolf's head and set it on the table next to her empty teacup. Firekeeper wondered if anyone else saw the trembling of Elise's hands.

"Lady Melina said . . ." Elise began tentatively, "that if anyone spoke of what she had done . . ."

She stopped and frowned. "The pain is less but still there."

"So we don't have a definite answer," Derian sighed. "It could be that a spell has been laid on Lady Elise or it could be that she has been made to believe that a spell has been laid on her. What do we do?"

Silence followed through which Firekeeper could hear the shoptalk without, the comings and goings of people buying medicines, perfumes, and spices. Seeing that no one else was going to offer a suggestion, she said:

"Why not do something for both? Melina use the pendants on her necklace to cast spell or to make believe she cast spell. If we get necklace and destroy with great fuss," she looked doubtful, uncertain that she was expressing herself well, "then the way of the control would be broken, too."

Doc's dour expression lightened. "You have a point there, Firekeeper. That necklace is the key—at least to Lady Melina's control of her son and daughters."

"But what Firekeeper suggests is very dangerous," Ninette piped up, trembling at the very thought. "Lady Melina never lets that necklace out of her sight. Her maid said once she wears it even in the bath and to bed."

Firekeeper sprang to her feet. "So we take it!"

"That may be what we have to do," Derian agreed. He didn't look happy. "I wish we could test the effectiveness beforehand."

"Could we," Elise said, "have my necklace duplicated? A substitute she has never touched wouldn't have the same power, would it?"

Firekeeper decided not to mention things she had heard about the sympathetic resonances between types of stone. Maybe that was just a wolf legend and didn't apply to human magic. In any case, she thought that Melina was more likely to be a trickster than a sorceress. She hoped so—her own knowledge of human sorcery was a bit shaky.

Hazel extended her hand. "Let me see the carving. If it isn't too complicated, I know someone who might be able to do the work. Jet isn't a terribly hard substance, thank the Dog."

That same almost invisible quiver in her hand, Elise picked up the pendant and handed it to the healer.

"It's intricate, yes," Hazel murmured after a few moments' inspection by the sunlit window. "But my friend may be able to do the job. He's a local, but I've known him for a long time and I think he's trustworthy."

"Think?" Derian asked.

"Yes. He dabbled in some shady dealing, usually with smugglers and thieves, but in his own business he has a very good reputation."

Elise decided. "I'll do it. Thank the Lynx for this ball! It makes all sorts of strange shopping trips possible."

"Derian," Hazel said, "you know your way around Hope. I'll write you a note saying you represent someone who needs private work done. You can run over there, get my friends's answer directly, and then retrieve Elise. In the meantime, ladies," she smiled, "can I interest you in any of my wares?"

APPARENTLY THE JEWELER —one Wain Cutter—was quite accustomed to confidential commissions. He expressed only slight surprise when Elise explained what she wanted done.

"Usually, I get asked to do something like this," he said, peering narrowly at the wolf's-head carving, "after the lady or gentleman has lost the piece. Then all I have to go on is a description. This is much easier."

Taking out a thin piece of charcoal, he started making a sketch on a piece of smooth white board. Firekeeper moved behind him so she could watch, fascinated as he drew the piece first in a front view then in both right and left profiles.

"It's a nice bit of carving," Wain said as he worked. "Very nice, but after seeing this young lady's companion I can think of a half-dozen things I'd do differently."

"Don't," Elise pleaded. "It must be as much like the original as you can make it."

"I understand," Wain said peaceably. "Good luck for you that I already have some nice jet in stock. Got it from a trader who came down from the Iron Mountains. Prime stuff and I can offer you a good price."

Derian stepped up then and Firekeeper let her attention drift as the intricacies of haggling began. She knew she should make an effort to learn this skill, even realized that the thrill of getting a good price for something must be similar to that of a successful hunt, but she couldn't escape the feeling that the strong should take, not ask. Even her own acceptance that she was not one of the strong hadn't undermined her faith in this division of property.

Blind Seer, apparently asleep out in a patch of sunlight in the gem carver's yard, sensed her restlessness.

"What are we going to do about this Melina Shield?"

Firekeeper moved to sit next to him. *"I wish I knew. Things were simpler in the wolflands."*

404 / JANE LINDSKOLD

"*Only because you were a pup and others made your decisions for you.*"

"*Hmm.*" She considered and accepted the veracity of this. "*Still, I favor the simple solution. We should attack this Melina, you and I, some dark night and take her necklace. Or, even better, I could slip into her tent and take it while she sleeps.*"

"*You could,*" the wolf agreed. "*Then what?*"

"*Then we destroy it and the spell is broken.*"

"*And if it is not a spell, if it is this trance induction?*"

"*Still, Melina will no longer have the necklace. Her frightened pups will see she no longer has power over them.*"

Blind Seer snorted. "*They think the power is in her, not in the necklace. That will do nothing and she will have another necklace done. No, Little Two-legs, the answer is not so simple.*"

"*Maybe not,*" Firekeeper agreed with a sigh. "*I haven't forgotten the promise I made to King Tedric. Each night I prowl, but no one seems to hunt him. The attack on Sapphire was the only attack we have seen and I know too little of cities. Everyone seems to think that such human predators thrive therein like beetles beneath a rotting carcass.*"

"*True. But we will not cease in our vigilance.*"

"*Of course not. Besides, I like roaming about at night.*"

She rested her head on the wolf's flank and lay there with her eyes closed, trying to come up with solutions. From inside the shop she heard Elise say to Derian, her tone distinctly wistful:

"I wish I was Firekeeper. Look at her there, not a worry in the world."

Firekeeper didn't disabuse her. Let Elise take comfort in such fancies if she could. Soon, she suspected, they all would have very little time for any consideration of such niceties.

ON SOME LEVELS, Prince Newell Shield was a very happy man. Through discreet questioning, he had received the impression that his pet Stonehold generals were leaping through their hoops of fear and superstition just as he had planned. At least one courier had been dispatched to their central command and carrier pigeons had been sent in advance of the courier.

Without telling him anything of this, General Yuci had pleaded with Newell to delay any permanent alliance between Bright Bay and Hawk Haven. When, later, Yuci expressed his delight that the ball had been scheduled for several days after King Tedric and Duke Allister's initial meeting and thanked Newell for using his influence to assist their cause, Newell accepted his thanks, not wanting to embarrass the good man, even though logistical concerns—rather than any machinations on *his* part—had been the reason for the delay.

He was less happy about events within King Tedric's own court. On the afternoon following his second meeting with Allister Seagleam, King Tedric had summoned Zorana Archer to wait upon him in his chambers within the Fortress of the Watchful Eye. The noblewoman had gone to the meeting with a triumphant glow in her eye and a proud arch to her neck—reminding her sometime lover rather of a warhorse. She had returned with the air of a beaten cur.

Rumor had quickly spread—for King Tedric had not kept their conference any great secret—that she had been severely berated for usurping his prerogatives. The king had not specifically said that Zorana had ruined the chances of one of her sons and daughters being privileged with a marriage alliance, but bets around camp were firmly against her.

In her disgrace, Zorana had focused her attention on grooming her son and daughter for the ball. She was also avoiding Newell, though whether out of anger or embarrassment, the prince wasn't certain. He figured he would smooth things out during the ball, when his attentions would be interpreted by observers as mere courtesy.

Newell was unwilling to trust to Stonehold alone for his success. There was still too much harmony in the Hawk Haven encampment for his taste. Lady Elise was treating Lady Blysse more like a sister than a rival for the crown. Sapphire Shield was speaking to her cousin again. Elise remained rather cool to Jet, but that was understandable given that the young idiot had been foolish enough to shame her by going to a public brothel.

The two other girls—Nydia and Opal—seemed to be treating the unfolding events as if they were a drama which they were observing rather than living. Maybe he could do something with that. The men—other than Jet—were pretty much out of his reach. Earl Kestrel, Baron Archer, and Purcel Trueheart all had been dutifully attending to their commands within the army—eager, no doubt, to show the king what responsible and mature kings or regents they would make.

As if they were all carved pieces on a game board, Newell moved this one here, considered pressing that one there. . . . Over and over, he arrived at a plan only to reject it. Finally, only two pieces remained: Jet and Lady Blysse.

Could he contrive to make it appear that Jet and Blysse were romantically entangled? He rejected that almost immediately. Blysse barely spoke to Jet and Jet seemed to have lost his balls since the night his sister was assaulted.

Maybe Newell should entice Jet out. Late . . .

The pieces of the puzzle began to lock into place. Out late . . . Behaving shamefully . . . What would little Blysse—that dangerous Firekeeper—do if she saw Jet with his arms around a couple of light ladies? Wouldn't it be reasonable for her to fly into a fury at this added insult to her beloved friend? Consider what her wolf had done to one of Sapphire's assailants. And, of course, there would be a witness, unimpeachable as daylight: Prince Newell Shield himself.

The prince laughed, heartened once more. Now he simply needed to find a way to put his plan into action. It would take honing, especially developing a way to confirm that Lady Blysse would not have a convenient alibi for her whereabouts at the time of the attack. Still, the rewards were too great for him not to attempt to carry this out.

Surely if Lady Blysse killed Jet that would end her friendship with

Elise. Sapphire, no matter how grateful for Blysse's role in saving her own life, would certainly be infuriated. She might even challenge Blysse to a duel. That would be just lovely. They might both end up dead or maimed. And as an added bonus, everyone would be distracted from whatever Stonehold might be stirring up.

Newell smiled and resisted the impulse to rub his hands together like a craftsman anticipating a day in his workshop. Step One: Talk to Jet. Step Two: Find a way to get Lady Blysse out of the way. Step Three: Sit back and enjoy the bloodshed.

Glancing across the encampment, he saw the king's carriage moving across the grounds, doubtless taking the king to another secret or semi-secret conference. Newell shook his head sadly.

The king really should have kept him closer at hand. It was really Tedric's own fault that the prince was left with so much time to pursue his own plans. He considered telling Tedric this at an appropriate moment and smiled. That news might even trigger the necessary fatal heart attack. Wouldn't that be perfect!

XX

DESPITE COMPLAINTS FROM BOTH staff and participants that they had not been given enough time to prepare, the ball was held on the third day following King Tedric's first meeting with Duke Allister Seagleam of Bright Bay. Obviously, Derian mused as he rubbed polish into dress shoes bought especially for the occasion, there were advantages to being a king.

Such thoughts distracted him from the fact that he was distinctly nervous about his role in this evening's planned entertainment. He would have been content to attend as he had now attended so many grand functions—as Firekeeper's nearly invisible servant.

At first that invisibility had bothered him, but now he admitted there were times that he revelled in it. Unnoticed, he heard and saw things that no one bothered to hide from a servant.

He knew, for example, though he had spoken of it to no one, that Lady Zorana was carrying on a flirtation, if not more, with Prince Newell. He knew that Lady Sapphire's maid took snuff—a thing that would horrify her mistress. He knew that Baron Ivon Archer had a fondness for strong brandy in his evening cup of tea—and that sometimes he skipped the tea completely.

Derian was honest enough with himself to admit that he might not be so happy with his state if there were not plenty of people above the level of servant who treated him as an equal. His early hopeless crush on Elise had faded and now he felt about her as he might a sister. Doc had not put on airs with his return to society and remained the same forthright and direct man he had been on the road west. And Firekeeper remained impossibly herself.

Tonight, however, Derian must leave off his servant's anonymity and step onto the floor as a member of the party. Someone—he suspected Firekeeper—had told Earl Kestrel that Derian was an excellent dancer. Knowing that many of the officers invited to attend would not wish to dance with any but those whose political loyalties they were certain of, the earl had commanded Derian to join the party, to fill in where needed so that no lady need stand out more than one dance.

"Lucky me," Derian muttered; then he felt instantly ashamed.

Earl Kestrel had been generous, standing the bill for an entire costume beginning with a new tricorn hat and including a white ruffled shirt, a tailored waistcoat cut from brown and green brocade, dark green knee-breeches, raw silk stockings, and the very same wide-buckled shoes that Derian had just finished rubbing to the satin polish that his father had insisted on for the best of their horse leather.

Once dressed, Derian joined Earl Kestrel. Out of his cavalry commander's uniform for the first time since they had left Eagle's Nest, the earl was dressed in court attire. His dark blue knee-breeches might have been bought in town, but the waistcoat striped in Kestrel blue and red with a hovering hawk embroidered on the right breast must be from his own wardrobe. Derian did not put it past Valet to have found room to pack the waistcoat away among more practical attire—just in case.

When Derian arrived, Valet was setting Earl Kestrel's tricorn on his head, just as carefully as if he were finishing a work of art.

"You will do, my lord," Valet said, surveying the final effect with muted satisfaction. "I suppose one cannot expect too much when forced to attire in a tent."

Earl Kestrel gave one of his rare smiles. "I am certain I look fine." Seeing Derian he added, "Run your eye over that tall redhead, though to my way of seeing, he looks quite a bit finer than the sunburned young man who has been with me these past weeks."

"Good evening, Earl Kestrel," Derian said, flabbergasted at this unaccustomed praise. Valet winked at him and adjusted the line of Derian's waistcoat.

"You'll do, Derian Carter."

Earl Kestrel nodded. "Thank you, Valet. Derian, shall we go? Lady Blysse is with Lady Archer. I told the carriage to meet us at her pavilion."

As they strolled to where the rest of the nobility was encamped, the soldiers stopped cooking their dinners or playing at dice to comment on their attire. Taking his lead from the earl, Derian did his best to respond appropriately or not at all. Still, he was certain that by the time they reached Elise's pavilion his ears must have been as red as his hair.

Baron Archer was waiting outside the tent for them, smoking his pipe. "Good evening, Earl Kestrel. Good evening, Mister Carter."

They answered and then the earl added, "Blasted hot, isn't it? I could have danced for joy when I heard that jackets were unnecessary for this event. I don't think my valet was pleased, but then he's a stickler for form. Still, I held my ground."

Baron Archer chuckled and tamped out his pipe. "The carriage is ready and the young women should be with us momentarily. Ah! Here they are even now."

Derian managed to keep his mouth from gaping open by sheer force of will, having been alerted by faint giggles from within that something must be up.

First to emerge was Elise, resplendent in a gown of silvery satin with side panels of glowing green. Her golden hair was piled high on her head and adorned with a few tasteful white rosebuds. The jet wolf's head was nestled in the hollow of her throat, the only spot of darkness in a confection of light. Although he looked carefully, Derian could not tell if the jewel was the original or the promised replacement.

The woman who followed her must be Firekeeper, but she was like no Firekeeper that Derian had ever seen. The gown in which she was attired was pale blue with rose piping about the throat. To conceal the scars that marked her every limb, the gown's sleeves were long, but constructed of a loose diaphanous gauze that revealed the grace of Firekeeper's arms while hiding their flaws. Above the modest neckline of her gown she wore a strand of polished lapis beads—an early gift from Earl Kestrel. Her dark brown hair was now long enough to be worn upswept but a few tendrils had been left to curl about her temples.

Derian was not the only one stunned to silence. Earl Kestrel stood gaping for a moment before offering his arm.

"Lady Blysse, you look lovely," he said.

Firekeeper smiled and Derian could almost swear that she blushed. Baron Archer gave an approving nod, knocked the last ash from his pipe, and offered his arm to his daughter.

"Earl Kestrel and I," he said, "are fortunate to have two such lovely ladies to escort. Come along. We don't want to be late."

Trailing the others, Derian glanced back over his shoulder. Standing in the door of the pavilion, Ninette waved cheerfully, mouthing:

"Have fun!"

Standing beside her, his tail just a little low and his ears cocked at a forlorn angle, Blind Seer watched them leave. Seeing Derian's gaze on him, he managed a quick wag before his brush drooped again.

Poor guy, Derian thought. *More and more Firekeeper's going places where he can't follow. I don't blame him for not liking that at all.*

Above him he heard a shrill whistle and could swear that Elation, soaring in the darkening sky above, was agreeing with him.

THEY WERE NOT LATE, but neither were they the first to arrive. In order to round out the festivities and keep the ball from being too obviously what it was—a chance for King Tedric to review his great nieces and nephews in company with each other—a number of military officers and important citizens from the two towns had been invited as well.

Especially for the townsfolk, this was the event of a lifetime, something they would be telling their children and grandchildren about two generations hence. *The night I was invited to King Tedric's ball I saw . . .* No wonder they didn't want to miss a single moment.

Derian rather wished that he could miss a moment or two. Whispered comments, half-heard, made him acutely aware that he was masquerading as a nobleman. What was he but a carter's son?

Background music was playing softly as their party moved through the reception line, greeting King Tedric and Duke Allister as representatives of their respective monarchies, and Mayors Terulle and Shoppe of Hope and Good Crossing as heads of the twinned towns. When the orchestra struck up the overture to a line dance popular since before the days of Queen Zorana, Derian began to fade back, alert for a woman in need of a partner.

A hand lightly plucked his sleeve. He turned and saw Lady Elise, a bright flush lighting her cheeks.

"Will you dance this one with me?" she asked. "Jet is doing everything he can to pretend he hasn't located me just yet in the crowd and I don't want to end up slighted."

Derian swept a deep bow. "I would be honored, my lady. Forgive me for bluntness, but your betrothed is an ass."

"I should call you out on that," she said with a light laugh that didn't fool him at all, "but my father cautioned me that this could be an opportunity to make a good impression."

"Indeed," he replied in what he hoped were courtly accents.

As they took a place at the bottom of a set, Derian noticed that Jet had nearly pounced on one of Allister Seagleam's young daughters: Anemone, he thought, but it might well be Minnow.

Derian quickly made a joke, hoping that Elise wouldn't notice Jet's tactlessness. The fellow to his right, a nervous townsman, picked up on the quip and soon they were all laughing. When counting off of sets of four began from the top of the line, they were cheered to find themselves in the same set.

The dance began rather roughly, for although the Star Waltz had been around for a long time, it had clearly evolved differently in the two monarchies. The variety that the lead was familiar with was the Bright Bay version. Fortunately, the residents of Hope and Good Crossing seemed to know both forms and helped Derian and Elise along.

Derian found himself easily swept into the next dance by the simple expedient of trading partners with his new townsman friend. That lucky man nearly stepped on his own feet when he learned that he was dancing with the future Baroness Archer. Derian's partner was slightly disappointed when she learned Derian was no one so famous, but he tried to make up for this by being a sprightly and talented dancer.

By the third dance, Derian had forgotten that he ever felt nervous or out of place. From long habit, he kept an eye on Firekeeper. Not surprisingly, given her presumed favor with the king, she was not short of partners. Elise was also doing well. Jet came through for the third dance and the rules of etiquette that dictated that even an engaged couple shouldn't dance more than two dances together gave them an excuse to stay apart without seeming to slight each other.

Relaxed now, Derian was more than happy to fulfill Earl Kestrel's commission that no woman be left without a partner. When the music began again after an intermission, he noticed a stately though somewhat older woman standing alone. He strode over and had already begun to ask her to dance before he realized that his prospective partner was Lady Melina Shield, the reputed sorceress.

With her silver-streaked, blond hair swept up in an intricate knot interlaced with a strand of multicolored polished gemstone beads, and the glittering diamond-cut gems of her omnipresent necklace displayed upon the white skin of her throat, Melina Shield looked quite well—past her first prime, certainly, but possessed of a calm and control that made the prettier younger women look somehow gauche and coltish.

Having begun, Derian could not back away. He continued after a pause he hoped was interpretable as awe at realizing who he had chanced upon:

". . . and so I was hoping that your ladyship would deign dance this piece with me."

Melina smiled and he felt the full force of her considerable personality.

"I would be happy to so honor you, young man. Let us hurry. The dance is about to begin."

When Derian would have politely joined at the bottom of the set, Melina led the way toward the nearest set of four.

"Excuse me," she said, breaking in so that they became the second couple and everyone below must fumble to reorient themselves with new partners. Derian didn't doubt that a few couples who had positioned themselves advantageously so that they might flirt during the interweaving of the figures were rather put out. If Melina Shield cared, she did not say.

Fortunately for Derian's piece of mind, this dance was one of those where the couples ended up dancing with their opposite number in a set as often as with their own partner. Even so, as progress through the intricate steps brought him once again back into contact with Lady Melina, it was all he could do to not stare at her necklace. Could one of those stones really be capable of inflicting impotence on a man? Could another inflict agony on a brave young woman?

He kept the thoughts as far from his mind as possible, terrified that Lady Melina might be able to read them. Glancing down the long line he caught a glimpse of Sapphire Shield—dressed in a sweeping gown of brilliant blue overlaid with a light gauze in the golden-yellow of House Gyrfalcon. Without knowing everything Elise had confided, he might think it merely his imagination that Sapphire favored her wounded side as her partner wound her under his arm or walked her through a stately march.

Lady Melina apparently thought Derian's silence respect for her and concentration on the particularly intricate forms demanded for this piece. Derian was relieved and rather glad that his sister, Damita, wasn't there to brag how he had mastered this one several years before and won the Hummingbird Society–sponsored contest as a result.

When he escorted Lady Melina off the floor, Derian discovered he was soaked with sweat. After fetching Lady Melina a cup of punch, he was glad that her bearing made quite clear that he need not remain. He chatted with Doc for a few minutes, then with his acquaintances from the first

set. The orchestra warming up reminded him that the dancing was to begin again. He was dropping back to see who might be left out when he
noticed King Tedric beckoning to him.

At first Derian was certain that the king was summoning someone
beyond him, then that the king—recognizing him as essentially servant—
needed an errand run. Hurrying toward the low dais from which King
Tedric was watching the dancing, Derian bent knee almost before he
was there.

"Rise, Derian Carter," came the king's somewhat high old voice, giving Derian his first shock. Despite having lived among the court for a
moon-span and more now, he had never thought that King Tedric
recalled his name.

"Come and sit beside me and talk for a while. It is difficult being old
and able to dance only a few sets. I had quite as fine a leg as you when
I was your age."

Caught in this second shock, Derian recovered himself before he could
bolt in panic. *Him* sit with the king and speak with him? Only the
recognition that he would be guilty of a great insult to the monarch kept
him in place.

On legs that suddenly felt as if they had been carved from wood,
Derian mounted the few steps and sat on the chair toward which the
king gestured. He felt as if every eye in the room must be on him, but
when he stole a surreptitious glance toward the floor he saw that nearly
everyone was caught up in the unfolding dance.

Nearly everyone. Lady Melina cast a speculative glance his way and
from the slight grin on Earl Kestrel's face his patron hadn't missed the
situation either.

"So, young Carter, are you enjoying yourself?"

"Yes, sir . . . I mean, Your Majesty."

"Sir is just fine. I was knighted once, long ago, for deeds I performed.
I was terribly thrilled. That was long before I knew I'd be king one day.
Long before poor Marras lost her will to live."

"I know the story of how you won your knighthood," Derian said,
momentarily less afraid. "It was in battle."

416 / JANE LINDSKOLD

"Yes, in battle, against these very people with whom we are now dancing. Tell me, Derian Carter. Should I put one of our enemies—or former enemies—in the position to rule our people?"

This time all Derian could do was gape. King Tedric waited a moment, then continued:

"You see, I was sitting here, watching the dancing and thinking on that question. I was wondering what my people would want me to do. Then I saw you down there, dancing away, and I thought to myself: 'Young Derian has been living in the castle for a good time now. He has made friends with some of my potential heirs and has met others. Most importantly, he is one of my people, scion and heir of a hardworking trade family. I shall ask his opinion.' So here you are. Answer me truthfully. I won't harm you."

With effort, Derian made his lips obey his racing brain. He remembered his conversations with his parents, the gossip he had heard in the markets and in the square when King Tedric announced his intention of making this journey. Carefully, he framed his reply:

"Well, sir, they do—I mean lots of the people back in Eagle's Nest—they think making Duke Allister your heir is just the thing for you to do. They call him the Pledge Child and have great hopes for his ascension to the throne bringing peace and goodwill between our lands."

King Tedric nodded, coughed slightly, accepted the cup of wine handed to him by his omnipresent guard, and said, "Yes, Pledge Child, I heard that term back when Allister was first born. I took reports that it was still in common use with a grain of salt. So my people dream yet of my father's great vision coming true. I would hate to disappoint them."

Accepting a goblet for himself without even realizing he was doing so, Derian asked:

"Can you avoid disappointing everyone, sir? There are so many conflicting claims."

"Claims? I wouldn't call them claims. I would call them ambitions—for themselves or for their children. You still haven't answered my question, Derian Carter. Should I make Allister Seagleam my heir?"

"I don't know, sir." Derian met those shrewd old eyes for the first time. "I don't know him."

"Yes. That is the trouble. None of us really know him. He seems an affable enough fellow here and now. Is it an act?"

"They say," Derian offered, "you can judge a man by his children or his dog."

"True. Pity his dog isn't here. His children are old enough to have learned to act as they think they should rather than how they are. Let's talk for a moment about those you *do* know. How about your charge? How about Firekeeper? Should I make her my heir?"

Derian swallowed hard. He knew what Earl Kestrel would want him to say. Knew, too, what he was going to say.

"I don't think so, sir. Not unless you can be sure you'll be around to educate her. She's as honest as the day is long and brave as a wolf, loyal, too, but those things aren't necessarily the qualities a monarch needs."

King Tedric chuckled dryly. "Interesting. She didn't think she was ready to be monarch either. I'm certain that Earl Kestrel would think differently."

"He has hopes for her, sir. You can't blame him for that."

"I don't. I respect him for his ambition while condemning him for it at the same time. I'm certain that he honestly hoped to find Barden alive when he went out into the western lands. Barden would have been able to make a case for himself or for Blysse. Firekeeper with her odd habits and weird upbringing is a much less easy piece to situate advantageously on the board."

The king's use of Firekeeper and Blysse as separate names for seemingly separate individuals had not escaped Derian. Knowing that he was out of line, but unable to resist, Derian asked:

"Sir, do you think that Firekeeper is your granddaughter?"

A smile that might be called mischievous curved the old man's lips.

"If I told you what I think would you swear to say nothing of this matter—not even to Firekeeper herself? I have my reasons at this time for withholding public admission one way or another."

Derian's heart, which had slowed its panicked thumping, now felt as if it was going to burst out of his chest with excitement and fear.

"You have my word of honor, sir, sworn on my society patron, the Horse."

"Very good, then. I accept your word." The king bent his head so that his lips nearly touched Derian's ear. "Firekeeper is not my granddaughter, Blysse, but I know who she is."

Disappointment, relief, and curiosity warred for a moment, then Derian asked:

"Who?"

The king leaned back slightly. "Firekeeper is the daughter of two members of my son's expedition. Her mother was the daughter of a lady you have befriended: Holly Gardener. She was named Serena, after a maternal aunt who died young. Firekeeper's father was Donal Hunter, a steady man with a gift for the bow and a love of the wilds. They said of him that he understood animals so well it was as if he could speak to them. Firekeeper's birth name was Tamara, after her deceased paternal grandmother."

Hearing this, the world spun behind Derian's eyes then righted itself. Once he had heard this, the truth seemed obvious. It would explain so much about Firekeeper—he couldn't think of her as Tamara. Another question burst forth before he could school his tongue.

"Sir, how did you know?"

"When I was a boy," King Tedric replied, unfazed by Derian's effrontery, "Holly Gardener was one of my playmates. I knew her and her sisters well. Firekeeper has the look of Holly's youngest sister Pansy at that same age, though she takes after her father's mother as well. I saw the resemblance nearly at once and confirmed that Serena had been among Barden's recruits. Tamara—like Blysse—is listed among the records."

Catching Derian's surprised stare the old king chuckled. "We were not so grand then. The Great Houses were still learning to feel their importance. My own mother, Rose, was not from a Great House. Holly's family was related to my mother's—cousins, I think—and came into castle service because they possessed the Green Thumb quite reliably. Their relation to Queen Rose is one reason why they hold their place in perpetuity, for as long as the Thumb continues to manifest in their line. Thus far it has not failed them. Nor would I banish them if it did. Their knowledge and wisdom means far more than a chance talent."

"I wonder," Derian said, thinking aloud, "if Holly knows . . . knows, I mean, who Firekeeper is?"

King Tedric nodded. "I am certain that she suspects, but, like me, she knows that Firekeeper is best preserved by doubt about her origins. The Gardeners have little they could give Firekeeper even if they did claim her. Best then that Firekeeper keep to her recent alliances. Earl Kestrel is ambitious, but he would never deny basic support to one he has taken as his ward."

Thinking of a father who disowned his youngest son for disobedience, Derian's expression grew unhappily thoughtful.

"What are you thinking about, Derian Carter," the king asked sharply. "Have I misjudged Norvin Norwood?"

"No, Your Majesty," Derian fumbled, then forged ahead. "I was wondering how you could . . . I mean why you . . . why you disowned Prince Barden."

The king looked angry for a moment, then sad. "I was hasty, infuriated that he would act so without my express permission, angry, too, that he did not trust that I had a place planned for him in the governing of Hawk Haven. I was younger then and maybe I believed myself immortal. It has been so long—ten years or more are still ten years, even to a man of my age—that I am a stranger to that sour, proud man. I have lost both son and daughter. That changed me. Now, I would give anything to not have driven Barden away, but it is too late and my heir must come from among those."

He made a sweeping gesture at the dancers twisting through the latest intricate form.

"What do you think of Lady Elise? Would she make a good queen?"

"Please, Sire," Derian begged. "I'm just a carter's son. I'm not fit to advise kings."

"That you would say that at all makes you fit. And you are not just a carter's son. Earl Kestrel does not hire dead weight. If he has kept you on it is because he sees good in you—good beyond your ability to coach Firekeeper. Now, will you disobey me? I want your opinion!"

Derian chewed his lower lip before speaking. Despite the wine, he felt dreadfully sober, so sober that he knew he was out of his depth.

"I know Elise mostly as a friend . . ." he began.

"Good. Friends see sides of each other that elderly and terrifying great-uncles do not. Speak up, Derian! Or are you in love with her and afraid to admit it?"

"No." Derian straightened. "I'm not. I was taken with her at first— she's kind and sweet when you get to know her and she was the first noble lady I was close to, but now that I know her better I realize we're not suited. She's much better for me as a friend."

"So, you didn't cease to love her because you found fault in her?"

"No, sir, not at all! What I loved was the idea of a titled lady with golden hair. When I got to know Elise I found she was much more than that—just a person."

King Tedric nodded. "And young men don't fall in love with people. I believe I understand. Tell me what you think of her as a potential queen."

It hadn't escaped Derian that the king was skipping his nieces and nephews and moving directly to their offspring. Was this because he had rejected the others or because he was asking Derian about those Derian was most likely to know well?

"Elise," Derian began slowly, "is a good person. She knows her way around the castle and its people already."

"Castle Flower," the king murmured.

Rightly guessing that this cryptic comment didn't need a reply, Derian continued:

"That's already an advantage over Firekeeper. A few days ago, I'd have said that Elise's greatest weakness was a lack of courage, but now . . ."

He trailed off, realizing he shouldn't say exactly how he had learned of Elise's deeper reserves.

"Now I know differently. She may be a bit squeamish, but she's not lacking courage."

King Tedric didn't press Derian to clarify, but after a thoughtful pause during which he studied the young woman below as she whirled through the steps of a particularly fast dance, her face alight with laughter, he said:

"So, you think Elise should be queen."

Derian blurted, "I don't think she *wants* to be queen, Sire. I think she might have once, but now I'm not so certain."

"And you don't think that someone who doesn't want to be monarch should be forced to do so."

Derian fumbled to explain, "Princess Caryl didn't want to go to Bright Bay and marry Prince Tavis and so that didn't work out too well. I was just thinking that this might be a bit the same."

"Hmm. And how about Jet Shield? Do you think he should be king?"

"Him?" Derian couldn't keep the disgust out of his voice, no matter how he tried to school it. "He's too ambitious. He wants it *too* much."

"So I should neither choose someone who doesn't want the task nor someone who does. That is quite a conundrum, Mister Carter. How shall I resolve it?"

Derian could feel himself turning bright red, but he pressed on, determined that if he was going to have to go through this peculiar interrogation he wouldn't flub it completely.

"Your Majesty, what I'm trying to say is that the best candidate would be someone who wants to rule but for the good of Hawk Haven, not solely for his or her own good. Someone, like Elise, who doesn't want to rule is going to do a bad job because either she isn't going to pay attention to the small details or she's going to resent them."

King Tedric snorted. "Even I—and I wanted to be king—even I grow tired of those small details."

Derian persisted. "Someone who wants to rule because he'll have titles and honors . . ."

"And power, don't forget power."

"And power. That type of person is equally a bad choice because he's going to make decisions based on how they'll affect his own importance. He's not going to care about how they affect the people who live under his rule. Eventually, they'll realize this. Common folk aren't as innocent as some of your noble folk believe."

"Yes. I know. My mother never let me forget that. I wish I had thought to drill that into my nieces and nephews, but then I never thought that I would be forced to pick one of them or their offspring to follow me. So, is Jet's only flaw his ambition?"

Shrugging, feeling himself already in so far that he could not get in much farther, Derian said:

"I think if he were made king no matter whose head wore the crown his mother would wield too great an influence."

"I saw you dancing with Melina earlier. So you don't like her?"

Derian shook his head. "I don't know her well enough to say that, sir. I do know that her children respect her with a respect that is akin to fear."

"So you're offering me a criticism that would apply to any of Lord Rolfston's children—and perhaps to Rolfston himself. You narrow my choices dramatically with that small statement."

Stubbornly Derian said, "One of the first to befriend Firekeeper was little Citrine. She made no secret that her mother commands more than a mother's respect. I don't know the others well, but I think the same must apply."

"Interesting thought, young Carter, and one not altogether alien to my observations."

King Tedric added nothing more and Derian waited quietly. The orchestra and dancers were taking another intermission. As they milled about sipping their chilled wine or punch, their gazes—surreptitious or not—often rested on the king's dais.

All at once, Derian's self-consciousness came back to him. When he glanced at the king, however, Tedric seemed unaware of the scrutiny

from below. Perhaps a king must learn to live with such continual observation. If so, Derian was suddenly glad that he had betrayed Firekeeper's
weakness to the monarch. His wild wolf-woman could never live so.

"Well, Derian Carter," King Tedric said at last. "I had a mind to
question you further. It is refreshing to be counseled by one who speaks
only of individual merits and never of who is related to whom except as
that is related to those merits."

Derian colored. "Thank you, Sire."

"Don't think for a moment that those relationships don't matter. They
do. However, it is easy to forget that this one's daughter or that one's
son is also a person possessed of personal weaknesses and strengths.
Don't you forget that when you are older."

"No, Sire, I won't."

King Tedric stretched slightly and smiled benignly at the young man.
"Now, you have given me good counsel. What do you wish for your
reward? I offer you anything within reason."

"Nothing, Sire. I am honored, really."

"Tosh, of course you are, but still I wish to give you a gift."

An idea slipped into Derian's mind, as wild and insane as any he had
ever had. Even as he tried to dismiss it, he knew he would ask and
accept the consequences.

"Then, sir, I ask for the necklace that Lady Melina Shield is wearing
this very moment, the one she always wears."

The expression in King Tedric's pale eyes was shrewd, not startled,
and Derian wondered how much the old man knew, how much he
merely suspected. All the king said, however, was:

"I fear I cannot give you something that does not belong to me. If
you so covet the necklace, why not have one made? Despite the pride
with which Lady Melina wears it, it is not so impossibly unique."

Derian drew in a deep breath. It had been too much to hope that he
and his friends' problem would be so easily solved, but even as he
nodded his acceptance of what the king had said Derian wondered if
Tedric had just shown him a way out of at least part of their problem.

Tedric continued, "Since you cannot think of something yourself, let me choose. Dirkin, come here."

Sir Dirkin Eastbranch, who had been standing such silent witness to all their conversation that Derian had never noticed his presence, stepped forth.

"Your Majesty?"

"Give me one of the counselor rings. The men's ones."

Sir Dirkin reached into a leather pouch at his belt and drew forth a gold ring. The band bore the royal eagle cast directly into the metal. Set in the center was a cabochon-cut ruby. King Tedric's personal emblem, an eight-pointed star, was incised into the stone and inlaid with a thin bead of gold.

"Here you are, Derian Carter," said King Tedric, fitting the ring onto Derian's right index finger. "You are now among those who may request my ear at any hour of day or night. I know that you will not abuse the privilege. Understand that this is a personal privilege. When I pass on to my ancestors, you may keep the ring, but the privilege will vanish unless the new monarch chooses to renew it. In return for this honor, I inflict on you the added burden of making yourself available to me when I feel desire of your counsel."

For the second time in a very short while, Derian discovered that he could not speak. King Tedric chuckled.

"A poor gift, you may think, giving you added duties under the guise of a reward."

Derian found his tongue. "No, Sire. Really. I am so honored. I don't . . ."

"Don't worry too much," King Tedric said and placed a wrinkled hand on his shoulder. "Have the ring sized as soon as possible. You wouldn't want it to slip off."

"Yes, Your Majesty."

"And say nothing of our conference to anyone—even to Earl Kestrel or Firekeeper. If asked, simply say that I was bored and wanted a bit of common conversation."

"Yes, Your Majesty."

"Now, Derian Carter, give me your arm and help me to the dance floor. The orchestra is warming up. I believe I will claim Lady Blysse for this dance. It will keep my contentious nieces and nephews guessing. Unfortunately, it will also raise poor Norvin's hopes unduly, but he is strong enough to survive the eventual disappointment."

As Derian helped King Tedric down the few steps and signaled for Firekeeper to join them, he couldn't help thinking that the old man was rather calculating, even a bit wicked. It was an unsettling thought that maybe even a good king—or perhaps *especially* a good king—might need to be so.

XXI

ELISE AWAKENED THE MORNING after the ball aware that something momentous had occurred, but a moment passed before she remembered what had happened. Then she remembered: Derian and the counselor ring, King Tedric dancing the last dance of the evening with Firekeeper. The terrible fury in her father's eyes. How he'd refused to ride back to the encampment in the same carriage as Earl Kestrel and "those upstarts" even though it meant crushing into a carriage with Aunt Zorana, Nydia, and Purcel.

Purcel had finally gotten out, saying he would walk back. He never showed up back at the nobles' enclave. Later they learned he had walked all the way back to his unit in his dress clothes rather than deal with his mother and uncle's fury.

Elise thought that Purcel had been wise. The angry counsel, practically of war, between her father and Aunt Zorana had lasted long into the night. They'd even invited Lady Melina and Lord Rolfston to join them. When Elise had dared speak up for Firekeeper, saying they couldn't very well blame *her* for accepting the king's invitation to dance, her father had sworn at her and sent her to her tent.

Given how reserved Baron Archer usually was and how affable he'd been toward her since her engagement to Jet, Elise was truly hurt. Still, she'd kept her tears to herself until she had reached the safety of her curtained-off bedchamber. Then she had let them flow. Her father's man might report her collapse to Baron Archer, but at least no one could accuse her of acting like a child in public.

Secretly, Elise had been rather glad to be sent away. She didn't want to hear the familiar bickering again. Moreover, knowing what she now did about Lady Melina, she had no desire to spend time in her company. Elise's only fear—a fear that returned to her with full wakefulness—was that her father would forbid her to see Firekeeper and Derian.

With her morning pot of tea, Ninette brought Elise word that Baron Archer had requested her company as soon as she was dressed.

"Did he say 'request'?" Elise asked. "Or are you being polite?"

"He said 'request,' " Ninette assured her. "And he seems milder this morning. Perhaps he's sorry for shouting at you that way."

"Perhaps," Elise replied, but she didn't feel very hopeful. Baron Archer had always been vaguely disappointed that his heir was female— and a softhearted female as well. When Aurella contracted an illness similar to that which had rendered Queen Elexa sterile, he had resigned himself to not having sons, acting instead as a second father to Purcel, who was as similar to his bookish father as Elise was like Ivon.

Ivon Archer was waiting stern and formal in his military uniform when Elise stepped out of the pavilion.

"Good morning, Elise."

She dropped a curtsy. "Good morning, Father."

He frowned at her excessive formality, but he couldn't precisely chide her for being too polite. Instead he grunted:

"Come, walk with me. I wish to speak with you about last night."

Elise obeyed with deceptive tameness. Still, her heart skipped a beat when she realized that her father was walking toward that same cluster of stones where she had witnessed Melina Shield ensorcelling Sapphire and Jet. What would she do if Melina was there? Then she calmed herself. With almost all the resident nobles living in canvas tents, those rocks were the obvious place for a private conference.

Indeed, when they reached the rocks, the area appeared to be empty.

Elise, however, spared a moment to peek into the hidden space from which she had unintentionally spied on Lady Melina, garnering a strange look from her father in the process. The space appeared to be empty and Baron Archer did not comment on her actions. His mind was busy with other matters.

"Elise," he said, "you disappointed me last night when you spoke up for that foundling of Norvin Norwood's. I know you have befriended her—though I am at a loss to understand why—but that is no reason to side with her against your own kin."

With effort, Elise kept her silence. Silence, her mother had once told her, was the best weapon when your opponent had all the strength. She wondered now if Lady Aurella had meant specifically her husband.

Baron Archer continued, "Yet, you will have an opportunity to redeem yourself."

Here it comes, Elise thought. *Stop seeing that girl and her low-bred companions and . . .*

She was so busy with her own thoughts that she almost missed what her father was saying.

"Since Earl Kestrel's party trusts you, you will have the opportunity to continue to call on them. I fear that my evident anger last night makes such casual social contact on my part suspect."

He frowned, but that was as far as he was going to come to admitting that his behavior had been rude and ungentlemanly toward either daughter or peer.

"Therefore, I order you to continue your visits. Attempt to learn everything you can about their plans. Find out if the king has made any promises. Whether King Tedric intends to make Lady Blysse his bride, the bride of one of Seagleam's brats, or ruler in her own right will affect my own actions."

Momentarily his expression turned pleading. "Remember, Elise. I am worried about this not only for myself, but for you as well. I would like to see you made queen with Jet as your consort. No foundling should be able to take what is ours by blood right."

Elise, however, refused to be mollified. Ironically, though her father's

THROUGH WOLF'S EYES / 429

commands were the opposite of what she had dreaded moments before, she was coolly enraged.

"So, a few hours ago I was a traitor to you," she said, her tones as measured as the steps of last night's waltzes. "Today you wish me to spy on my friends. I see you still see me as a traitor, but betrayal is fine as long as it is to your advantage."

Baron Archer gaped at her. "Elise, you misunderstand . . . I spoke in anger last night."

Elise ducked within a bubble of almost preternatural calm, speaking with her gaze fastened on the towering stone walls of the distant fortress.

"You did," she agreed, "but your very words to me a few moments ago show how poorly you regard me. Very well. If you feel that way, you have your choice. Permit me to redeem myself in my own fashion or disown me as your heir."

Baron Archer began to speak, but she breezed on as if she hadn't heard him.

"Just remember before you lose your temper and make such a drastic move that I am your sole child. Without me, that crown you crave so deeply is lost to you. Remember, too, that King Tedric came to regret similar rashness."

Despite the cruel thrust of her words, Elise delivered them in a tone so detached that it was almost clinical. She might be Hazel Healer diagnosing what herb poultice would best treat a rash.

"Well, Father," she said when Ivon Archer did not reply, "what is your wish?"

When she turned her gaze to him at last, she found that he was studying her, neither angry nor pleased, but with a care that she never recalled seeing directed to her.

"I think," Ivon Archer said, "that disowning you would be foolish. Remember before you grow too triumphant, that it remains an option."

"I won't forget," Elise said, her inner calm wavering slightly. "But I also cannot forget the tone in which you called me a traitor and then dismissed me like a small child. I am your heir, just a year short of my majority. I think I am owed more consideration."

"Perhaps," her father said grudgingly. "For now, I lay no task on you. You retain your freedom and your title."

"I won't thank you," she said, "because both are mine, not to be taken from me by anyone—not even you. As for Earl Kestrel's entourage, I will continue to visit with them. If I learn anything that I am not expressly requested to keep in confidence, I will be happy to share it with you."

"Thank you," Ivon said, a spark of last night's anger lighting his eyes, "for your gracious condescension."

She thought she heard him mutter, "You little bitch," but his voice was low enough that she could pretend to have heard nothing.

"Well," Baron Archer said, brushing imaginary dirt from his trouser leg, "I have duties to perform. May I escort you back to camp on my way?"

"I would be honored," she said, offering him a neutral smile and resting her hand on his arm. Nothing further was said during the interminable length of that walk.

LATER THAT MORNING WHEN ELISE met Firekeeper and Derian she gave an abbreviated account of the events both following the ball and this morning. When she finished, Derian commented:

"And the odd thing is, the king made no such promises as everyone seems to imagine. He only wanted to hear my opinion—as a commoner—on various issues."

"Including the succession," Elise said teasingly.

Derian looked with unwonted seriousness at the ruby ring on his finger. "I was asked not to say."

Elise nodded and changed the subject. "I'm amazed that you had the courage to demand Lady Melina's necklace as your reward. That was clever."

"It didn't work, though," Derian replied. "Still, I've been thinking about what the king *did* say. I don't know if he meant it as a hint, but his idea of our having an identical necklace made was brilliant. It solves the problem of Lady Melina missing her own."

"I suppose Wain Cutter could do the work," Elise agreed. "This should actually be easier. Still, even if we got it, how would we work the trade?"

Firekeeper offered, "I could do it. Every night I go among those tents. Blind Seer terrifies the dogs. None even bark any longer. Get the necklace. I will trade it."

"You've been skulking among the tents?" Elise asked, amused yet vaguely embarrassed. What might Firekeeper have seen or heard—especially before Jet lost interest in her?

"I have," the wolf-woman said. "All through the camp I go. Sometimes I learn things. Mostly, I just walk and put into my memory scents and sounds."

Derian added, "I believe she can do it, Elise, but to pull this off we need as exact a description of the necklace as we can get. Wain Cutter said that he can work from a verbal description, thank the Horse, but a sketch would be better. Did your young lady's training include such skills?"

"It did," Elise said, "though my teacher never praised me highly. Still, I can manage something. Also, Melina likes to go into town and she's never without that necklace. Wain Cutter could easily get a good look at her then."

"That's going to mean trusting him," Derian cautioned.

"He's not stupid," Elise retorted. "That necklace is famous. He may well guess without our admitting precisely which necklace we want copied."

Derian nodded. "Very well. You get the description. I'll sound out Wain when I go into town today to have my new ring sized."

He touched it almost reverently. Elise hid a grin.

"You're a bit overwhelmed, aren't you?" she asked.

"More than a bit." Derian looked at her squarely. "I realize I'm not the first to be given one of these, not even the first common born. King

Tedric has always had counselors from among his subjects. But you're born to such honors. You can't imagine what this will mean to my family. My mother is likely to insist on my keeping the ring in the family's ancestral shrine when I'm not wearing it. The king's trust is a great honor."

Elise suddenly realized that she had been being a bit of a snob, a trait she has come to despise in others.

"It *is* a great honor," she said firmly, "and your parents will be justified in their pride. King Tedric chooses widely but never foolishly."

Firekeeper shook her head, as if wondering that this much attention was being paid to a shiny thing with no virtue as a tool.

"Talk does not get us any further with necklaces," she reminded them. "Elise must learn the look of the necklace in perfect. Derian and I will talk to Wain Cutter. Then I will talk to Doc."

"Why talk with Doc?" Derian asked.

"He has powders to bring sleep. Lady Melina not sleep alone. Sometime her maid sleep in her tent, sometime her husband, too. On the night of the change, Elise must give all some powder to sleep."

"I thought," Derian teased, "that no one ever hears you when you go among the tents."

Firekeeper stared at him as if he was an idiot.

"This is important, Fox Hair, like the first hunt in spring after winter starving. We take no risks just as the One does not hunt alone when there is a pack."

Elise nodded, suddenly somber, quietly afraid of the role she must play but agreeing with Firekeeper's wisdom.

"She's right. We don't dare take any risk. My relatives may think the matter of the succession is settled, but we know how tenuous it is. King Tedric doesn't know what we know. It is our duty to make certain that a sorceress cannot rule from behind the throne."

Derian curled his fist tightly as if daring the ring to slip free. Elise thought she knew what he was thinking. So much rested on their shoulders. Were they really up to the challenge?

❀

ALTHOUGH NOT EXPRESSLY PRIVY to the counsels of his fellow nobles, Prince Newell shared their indignation and frustrated anger. He'd
actually been enjoying that thrice-cursed ball. The food and drink had
been excellent, and many of the women fair. Since his ambitions reached
far higher than marriage into the family of Allister Seagleam, he hadn't
wasted his time dancing with eleven-year-old girls.

Just for the fun of renewing his acquaintance with Lady Blysse he had
asked her for a dance. She had accepted, but he could feel her dislike
of him in the lightness of her fingers on his whenever the ritualized
motions demanded that they touch. By the end he was rather sorry he
hadn't asked her for a waltz.

Other women, even Lady Zorana after he whispered a few sympathetic
words in her ear, were far less reluctant to dance with a prince. Unable
to continue the flirtation with Zorana in such a public place, Newell had
been in the process of cultivating the acquaintance of the pretty daughter
of a local silversmith. She was intimating that she was willing to do more
than dance when the ripple of gossip through the room alerted Newell
to a new element in the game. He had turned in time to see Derian
Carter, dressed like a gentleman in an outfit that must have set his patron
back a good bit, mounting the steps of the dais from which King Tedric
watched the festivities.

Mindful of his health, the king had taken part only in the Star Waltz
which had opened the entertainment. Appropriately, his partner had
been Pearl Oyster, the plump but still winsome wife of Allister Seagleam.
Inviting everyone to continue on, King Tedric then had made his way
up to the makeshift throne that had been prepared for him and indul-
gently surveyed the others at their pleasure. Needless to say, just about

everyone who was anyone made an excuse to mount the few steps and speak with him, but only young Carter had been invited.

That invitation ended the evening's pleasure for Newell. The lovely young thing he had been flirting with previously now held as much interest for him as might a painted doll. When King Tedric chose to close the evening by dancing with Lady Blysse, any joy Newell might have salvaged from seeing his Hawk Haven competitors equally crushed vanished.

Only Allister Seagleam seemed untroubled by this turn of events and that was quite understandable. The king favoring Lady Blysse did not mean an end of his hopes. At fifteen or so, she was a good age to be wed to either of his sons. Newell had noted that both Shad and Tavis had taken their turns partnering the foundling. Of course, they had each danced with all of the other eligible contenders for a polite political marriage and a few tentative friendships seemed to have begun.

During one of the intermissions, Purcel Archer, Sapphire Shield, and Shad Oyster got into a heated discussion about the various merits of combat on land and on sea. Jet flirted shamelessly with Minnow and Anemone, not precisely forsaking Elise, for the manners of a grand ball insisted that an engaged couple mingle with everyone and not remain selfishly absorbed in each other. Tavis Oyster apparently found an unexpected friend in Nydia Trueheart. When Newell had drifted near—ostensibly to get a new glass of wine—they had been discussing the merits of various New Kelvinese poets.

But any hopes the parents of these sprigs might have entertained had been dashed when King Tedric chose Lady Blysse for his dance partner.

Newell's fury that next morning was not mediated when he considered how hopeless his attempts to discover a way to distract or disable Lady Blysse had been. Her unwarranted dislike of him had made it impossible for him to chat her up and thereby drop a hint that she go hither or yon so as to be neatly away while Newell's lackeys pulverized Jet. Her illiteracy had robbed him of that favorite tool of conspirators, the anonymous note. That damned wolf which shadowed her whenever she was not in company—and often when she was—made it unlikely that he could simply have her hit over the head and put out of the way.

As a last resort, Newell had taken advantage of the crowded ball to slip a tincture of valerian (a preparation known to encourage drowsiness) into Lady Blysse's fruit juice. Raising the cup to her lips, she had suddenly wrinkled her nose and dropped the entire thing—cup and all—into the nearest waste bin.

So the morning following the ball, foiled and frustrated, Newell sent a note to Lady Zorana asking if he might pay a call in private. Before going to meet her he summoned Keen and Rook to him.

Without preamble, Newell growled, "I've been going about this all wrong. Why should I try to frame Lady Blysse and rely on others to condemn her? She needs to die."

Keen cocked an eyebrow.

Rook simply said: "Indeed, sir."

"Yes. This afternoon, I'm going to take Lady Zorana for a ride."

Keen, always one for a double entendre, grinned slightly.

Ignoring the other man's smirk, Newell continued, "Once I have Zorana deep in the woods, one of you—Keen, I think, since no one knows he works for me—is going to kidnap her.

"Keen, when you attack, I will appear to defend Zorana. I'm afraid I'll have to take a split lip or black eye or my defense won't look convincing. Just don't hurt me so much that I can't join in the battle if the Stoneholders come through. That's more important than any little mischief we may do here."

Keen nodded.

"After a bit, I'll feign to be knocked out," Newell went on. "You take the lady. I'll go for her help."

His henchmen knew better than to interrupt, so Newell surged on.

"I'll go directly to King Tedric, suggest that we keep the incident quiet. If he doesn't suggest that we enlist Lady Blysse, I will. She is certain to go tearing off without any more backup than her damned wolf. When they reach wherever you're holding Zorana, shoot Blysse with an arrow or two. Don't let her or that beast get close. Then flee in apparent panic, leaving your prisoner behind. I'll come later with a rescue party. Questions?"

"Where should I take Lady Zorana?" Keen asked.

"There must be a woodsman's hut or something. If there isn't, tie her to a tree. Knock her out if you want. At least gag her to keep her from screaming. Just give her to understand that you have someone delivering a ransom note and she'll be freed when you get your money."

Keen nodded again, his eyes shining.

"Wouldn't it be better," Rook asked, more willing to question, secure in his position as senior aide, "to kidnap someone like Lady Elise? Lady Blysse likes her. I don't think Lady Blysse cares for Lady Zorana one way or another."

"Who she cares for hardly matters," Newell snapped. "She'll do the king's bidding. Besides, I don't know if I could get Elise to go with me. She's been a stuck-up little bitch since she was just a snip, never could take even a tease. Even if Elise would go with me, it would look suspicious. Zorana, however . . . We go a long way back."

Keen chuckled. "It'll even give you a good excuse for losing the fight. Right, boss? I mean, caught with your pants down and all."

Newell glowered at this joke at his expense, but he had to admit that Keen had a point.

"Good thought," he agreed reluctantly. "I had wondered how to justify my being defeated by one man."

Keen laughed. "Don't worry, boss. I'll be implying that there are two or three more around."

"Disguise yourself," Newell ordered. "I don't want Zorana killed, only roughed up a little so this threat will seem convincing. Rook, you stay completely out of sight. Both of you bring bows, swords, and knives. When Lady Blysse comes to the rescue, I want her very dead."

Rook nodded. "I had appropriate tools laid by against our proposed assault on Jet Shield. Since you have yet to invite Lady Zorana, we have some time to prepare. I'll go ahead secretly and find a defensible place to hide the lady. I don't think we'll need to tell you where in advance."

"No. I'm trusting that Lady Blysse's nose—or at least her wolf's nose—will lead her there."

"Then, unless you have further orders, I am gone."

"Go. I will send Keen after you if for some reason Lady Zorana is unable to join me."

That lady, however, proved more than amendable to a ride in the countryside and dismissed her personal attendant to mind young Nydia. Zorana fussed a bit, making up a basket with light refreshments, and Newell was content to wait, knowing that this would give his men the time they needed to prepare.

"I had thought," Zorana said when they were safely away from listening ears, "that the day Elise became engaged to Jet was the worst in my life."

"Last night must have been terrible," Newell said, soothing his own anger by pouring salt on Zorana's wounds, "seeing the king so publicly favoring someone other than one of your own."

"You don't know a mother's grief and frustration!" Zorana replied dramatically. "I do everything I can for them. I even nursed hopes that tonight would be the realization of my dreams. Purcel was visiting quite nicely with one of Duke Allister's sons. I thought such decorous behavior far better than the opportunistic flirtation in which Jet Shield was indulging. Certainly, Duke Allister would be more interested in a proven warrior who can maturely discuss men's business than in a young rogue."

"Certainly," Newell murmured, allowing his spirited red roan to match the brisk pace of Lady Zorana's dapple grey. The dapple grey seemed to have caught some of her rider's feisty mood and had to be discouraged from breaking into a trot.

"And then just as I was allowing myself to feel hopeful—and encouraging Nydia in her friendship with young Tavis—then that Derian Carter was summoned to the dais."

Newell listened with half an ear as Zorana recounted the events of the night before, noticing her difference in emphasis. Again he was struck by how her ambition overwhelmed her good sense. How deeply had she embraced his little fantasy that the mere age of her children made them the most suitable matches for those of Allister Seagleam! How eager had she been to ignore how many political matches these days were being made without due consideration for the relative ages of bride and groom.

King Tedric had indicated his disapproval of such matches but not expressly forbidden them, so dukes and duchesses paired up their available children like toy soldiers ranked on the nursery hearth rug.

Thinking of deep embraces and matches stirred brutal excitement both in Newell's groin and within the darkest reaches of his mind. They were well away from both camp and town now. Even while gabbling away, Zorana accepted his lead toward the forests maintained as a game preserve on the fringes of Hope. Once they were deep within its shelter, privacy was virtually guaranteed.

Virtually. Zorana had been too interested both in her woes and in her desire for privacy to notice the figure that had been shadowing them all along. A man on foot could easily pace a walking horse, especially if he didn't wish to get too close. As requested by his master before they departed, Keen had remained near.

Seeing a sheltered glen near an attractively babbling brook, Newell suggested to Zorana that they "let the horses have a drink and a rest." Their easy pace hadn't even sweated the animals, but Zorana agreed with a coy smile.

Tying their mounts to a tree, Newell loosened their girths and removed their bridles, pleased with the glade. There could hardly be a more ideal place for a tryst—or an assault. Trees and shrubs provided both shade and a screen from observation, but warm, green sunlight filtered through. The ground underfoot was thick with springy moss. When Zorana took a rolled blanket from behind her saddle, Newell smiled. It was rather pleasant to be the seduced instead of the seducer from time to time.

Excusing himself for a call of nature, he walked into the woods. As he expected, Keen met him almost at once.

"Is all ready?" Newell murmured.

"It is. We've got a place and Rook even had the sense to rub our boots and clothes with lavender oil so later the wolf-chit won't be able to identify us."

Newell made a mental note to reward Rook for his initiative. Despite his own depending on Blysse's tracking abilities and his suspicion that the rumors that she could speak with her wolf were true, he had overlooked this weak point in his plan.

"Good. Bide until you can convincingly take us both," Newell reminded Keen.

Keen nodded, his brown eyes glittering almost feverishly.

"Keep your pecker up, boss."

Newell had never considered himself an exhibitionist, but the thought of Keen and possibly Rook out there in the shadows watching his lovemaking stirred him strangely. When he returned to her, Zorana had spread a thick blanket on the moss and poured two glasses of white wine. The remainder of the bottle was chilling in the brook.

Taking his goblet, Newell brushed his fingers against hers. As he sipped, he locked her eyes with his own, holding her gaze until a blush began to creep up her throat.

"What are you looking at?" she asked, and her voice was husky.

"You, lovely lady. Just you."

"Want a better look?" she invited and untied the ribbon lacing her bodice. Newell set down his glass and freed her breasts from their prison.

The next few moments were a welter of sensual impressions: his hand on her naked breast, her mouth on his tasting of wine and salt, her arms pulling him closer. She was as eager as he was, so it wasn't long before he was bare-assed: naked but for his shirt which she had slid her hands playfully beneath.

Women's garments were more complicated, but Zorana had made things easier by removing several of the more involved undergarments in preparation. Newell had a moment to wonder if she did this in advance or while he was in the woods; then he was topping her and even the watchers were forgotten in a more immediate obsession.

He was thrusting his way to completion, Zorana alternately moaning and whimpering her own response, when a hard hand fell on his shoulder and a rough voice said:

"Enough of that. I've a use of my own for the lady."

Newell *couldn't* stop and despite Zorana's sudden shriek of alarm, he continued where his body led. Hands grabbed him and pulled him forcibly off Zorana. Newell surged to his feet, truly insane in that moment of frustrated need. He swung wildly and missed. Keen's first blow caught him solidly on the side of his face. Newell stumbled backward a few steps, then charged forward again. Keen punched him in the gut and the prince fell to his knees retching.

Zorana was busy shoving down her skirts, shrieking hysterically. There was a wild look on Keen's face that cooled Newell's lust and made him suddenly afraid that this neat little plan was going awry. Keen looked as if he could kill him. Newell's next punch was driven with the force of fear and Keen lurched.

"Damn you," Newell hissed in the other man's ear. "Get control of yourself!"

And Keen did. Clubbing his hands together, he effectively battered Newell to the ground. However, Newell could feel that he was pulling the force of his blows somewhat and though there would be bruises, nothing should be broken.

Keen leered down at Newell as the prince fell and dropped a piece of paper onto his chest. "Take this to the king. It gives our terms. Got it?"

Newell groaned. Keen kicked him. Though he didn't put much force behind the kick, coming on top of Newell's other injuries it still hurt.

"Passed out," Keen sneered, according to script. "Lily-livered as well as a wimp."

Lying on the ground, hurting so much that real unconsciousness would be welcome, Newell heard Keen continue in silky tones:

"Stop screaming, Lady Zorana, and come with me. I'll take you to a nice place and we'll wait there for the mail to be delivered."

Zorana said shrilly, "You're kidnapping me?"

"Detaining you, rather." Newell heard Zorana jerked to her feet. "Now come along quietly. If you're a good girl, I may even reward you by finishing the job your inconsiderate friend there didn't."

Keeping his eyes shut and his breathing shallow, Newell considered the very real probability that Keen would rape Zorana. It wouldn't be Keen's first rape and he did have provocation.

Ah, well. As long as Keen wasn't about his fun when Lady Blysse came along. Newell had learned long ago, if you wanted to dance, you must expect to pay the piper.

Later, when the sounds of their footsteps and Zorana's whimpering had diminished, Newell hauled himself to his feet. He staggered to the brook, where he splashed cold water on his face. There was wine left in the bottle and he felt a bit better once he'd drained that to the lees. He hoped that Keen hurt at least a little. Surely at least one of his own blows had gone solidly home.

Re-bridling and tightening the girth on the red roan took considerable effort. Then Prince Newell pulled himself into the saddle. He'd be to the Watchful Eye by dusk. By using the most convenient gate, he'd also avoid the bulk of the Hawk Haven encampment. He ran his tongue around his teeth, reassuring himself that they were all in place. Then he smiled and urged the roan into a fast walk. Everything was going according to plan.

XXII

IN RESPONSE TO KING TEDRIC'S summons, Firekeeper came running to the Watchful Eye. It was some measure of the urgency of the king's summons that the gates swung open upon her approach and that none of the armed and armored guards who stood their posts attempted to slow her or question the rightness of the great, grey wolf bounding at her side.

Overhead, the falcon Elation soared in defiance of the rules normally governing diurnal and nocturnal creatures. Glimpsing her broad wings silhouetted against the orange face of the rising harvest moon, more than one soldier touched an amulet pouch or totem necklace and muttered that the days of black sorcery had returned.

But Firekeeper had no time for these. King Tedric's message had said for her to come as rapidly as two feet could run and for Derian to follow at his own pace. They were to speak to no one—not even Earl Kestrel—about the reason for their going.

So Firekeeper ran through the gate into the stone-flagged courtyard, through the arched doorway into the fortress building itself, then padded quick-foot up the broad stone steps. Silent guards directed her with gestures, and even those with whom she had laughed and thrown dice during the slow journey to Hope said not a word. Grateful she was for their guidance, but Firekeeper could have found her way without it for the scent of the king and the medicaments of his sickroom heralded his presence to her more brightly than trumpet calls.

For all the speed with which she had run, Firekeeper arrived in the king's presence barely winded, only the rising and falling of her nascent breasts beneath her leather vest giving testimony to the speed at which she had flown over the ground.

Gracefully, she bowed to King Tedric, for she had come to respect him far more than ever she would have dreamed possible at their first meeting. Beside her, Blind Seer stretched out his forelimbs in a deep wolf-bow, but his blue eyes remained alert so Firekeeper would be protected even while she abased herself.

And when she raised her head, shaking back the wild tangle of dark-brown curls, she saw what her nose had already told her.

King Tedric had a visitor before her and that visitor was wounded. Yet, though Firekeeper knew that according to the laws of etiquette Prince Newell was due a bow in turn she refused him the homage. There was that about Newell that she did not trust and she would not lower her guard before him, even with Sir Dirkin and his ready sword present.

Instead Firekeeper said to the king:

"I am here as you wished, King Tedric."

"Do you remember of what we spoke before we left the castle, Firekeeper?" the king asked with the directness she admired in him.

"Every word, every breath."

"One of those things I feared has occurred," he said, and she noticed how tired and ill the old man looked. "My niece, Lady Zorana Archer, has been kidnapped—stolen—by men who would exchange her safety for money. She was taken while in the forests to the northeast of this fortress. The message the men sent said that they will hold her in a safe place until we send money."

Firekeeper listened but her gaze rested for a moment on Prince Newell. He had clearly been in a fight. One eye was blackening; his upper lip was swollen fat. Rather than lolling in his chair with the indolent ease she knew was customary for him, he sat stiffly straight as if his body hurt him.

Beneath the scents of blood and sweat, Prince Newell smelled of wine and of something else that it took her a moment to place. However, she had not slipped her way between the tents of the camp followers without learning the scent of mating humans.

Blind Seer had reached the same conclusion as she. *"This prince is the one who lost Lady Zorana. My nose says they were interrupted at their dalliance."*

Thus Firekeeper did not ask how Lady Zorana came to be taken but asked instead:

"Do you wish me to find her, One, or do you wish me to bring money to her takers?"

"Find her, bring her back if you can. I would prefer not to pay to redeem her." Tedric added hastily, "This not because I do not value her, but because then others would think to do the same."

Firekeeper shrugged, only partly understanding this but trusting the king's wisdom in how to deal with his own kind. What she did not trust was the small smile that had touched Prince Newell's mouth when the king asked her to find Zorana.

From what Firekeeper knew of human pride, especially male pride, Newell should be demanding that the rescue was his right. Perhaps he was more wounded than he smelled. Perhaps he had the wisdom to know that a wolf was wiser in the woods than any human.

"I go," she said.

King Tedric nodded. "I will send Derian Carter after you with reinforcements. My counselors and I agree that it is best that as few as possible know that Zorana has been taken. Not even her children have been told. I have sent word that she is visiting with me so they will not worry."

"Derian is good," Firekeeper said, "but Race Forester has eyes to see even in the woods at night. He will know how to find the signs I will leave him for they will be signs he taught. I will send Elation to him if you will write a message for her to carry."

King Tedric reached for quill and paper. "The peregrine will fly at night?"

In reply Elation glided through the open window and squawked complacently, holding out one foot as if to grasp the message once it was ready. Firekeeper grinned.

"Elation is like Blind Seer, among the greatest of her kind. She will find Race Forester. If you tell him to meet Derian near the wood they will save time."

King Tedric continued scratching quill across paper. "I have already done so, Madame General. Sir Dirkin, reach me the sand so I can blot this, then a tube so that this falcon does not crush the paper in her talons."

Prince Newell spoke, his speech sounding odd as he forced the words through his swollen lip.

"Again, I beg Your Majesty, let me go with the rescue party. I realize I would only slow Lady Blysse, but surely I can sit a horse and ride with the others."

"You have already done enough this afternoon," King Tedric replied with an ambiguity that Firekeeper quite admired. "I refuse your request. You will remain here and a healer will be sent for to tend your wounds."

Turning away, eager to be on the trail before it lost its freshness, Firekeeper said:

"Get Doc—Sir Jared—he knows how to keep silence."

King Tedric's agreement in her ears, she fled down the steps and into the gathering night.

The brilliance of the harvest moon, even though its face lacked fullness, still gave her ample light to run full out until they reached the forest. Blind Seer ranged ahead until he found the signs they sought.

"This trail bears the recent scent of horses. Two went in, only one of those two came out. Prince Newell's scent is here as well. His blood was spilled on the ground."

The wolf sniffed more deeply and added, *"There is another scent here, too, the scent of lavender masking a faint scent of humans—males. At least one smokes a pipe."*

"Cry that trail," Firekeeper said as she plunged into the forest, all senses alert, *"even as we run. Your nose is keener than mine. I will follow this horse trail and leave marks for Race to find."*

Breaking slightly from the path, Blind Seer padded silently through the bracken at the trail's edge.

"Lavender Scent's path followed the others, but he took care to stay from sight. Here I find where he waited behind a tree. Here he paused. Ah! I see why. The ground is open beneath this Grandmother Oak. He waited until the horses were farther ahead before showing himself. In the ways of hiding, this one is a master. Remember that as you run, sweet Firekeeper."

"I will," she promised, *"but even my dead nose can smell the reek of lavender and the wind kindly blows toward us. We should have warning before he can leap upon us. I wonder why he took such great care to hide his shape but left his scent so blatant?"*

Blind Seer coughed derisive laughter. *"He hid himself from human prey. They use their eyes and ears, but their noses smell nothing. Doubtless this scent he wears is such as those blended by Hazel Healer, meant to adorn the wearer."*

"Perhaps," Firekeeper replied, but the worry stayed with her and made her slow her gait slightly and watch with even greater care. She wished for Elation, but the falcon could not see anything through the spreading canopy of tree branches. If those who had taken Zorana remained beneath their shelter, the falcon would not be able to find them any more quickly than those on the ground.

At length wolf and woman came to a small clearing tucked off to one side of the trail. The dapple-grey palfrey tethered to a tree to one side jerked against her rope when she smelled Blind Seer, but her relief at human company—even that of so dubious a human as Firekeeper—outweighed her fear.

Giving the mare a brisk pat on one shoulder, Firekeeper told Blind

Seer—for the wolf would never lightly speak to a horse—*"This frightened one says that there are no humans here. She is alone and afraid but we must leave her behind. She would only slow us. The others can gather her up."*

Blind Seer was busy snuffling the glade. *"Prince Newell came here with Zorana. They rutted upon the blanket and were interrupted by Lavender Scent. They fought. Here is Newell's blood on the moss and here again. I do not smell that of Lavender Scent."*

"Here is something else," Firekeeper added, pointing.

Pinned to a tree trunk was a piece of white bark on which black marks had been made.

"This was done with a burned stick," she said, sniffing. *"Alas, it cannot speak to me. We will leave it for the others. Perhaps it will hasten their trail. Come. We have learned all we can here. Can you catch their trail when they left?"*

"As easily as you breathe," the wolf boasted, leading the way. *"There are two trails now—Zorana's is added. No, there are three! Here a second human/lavender scent joins the first. This one was waiting in the tree."*

Firekeeper padded after Blind Seer and noted the marks left on the ground. She made a broad arrow sign in the dirt that Race would be certain to see, and followed.

"They hunt in a little pack, then. This second one was not needed for the rutting Newell was easy prey." Firekeeper snorted in derision. *"I hope I am never so human as to be ruled out of season by my loins!"*

Blind Seer laughed. *"You are human, Little Two-legs, but even humans can moderate themselves. Most simply do not care to do so."*

They ran in silence then, Blind Seer easily guiding them and Firekeeper leaving sign for those who would follow. At times this was hardly necessary for Lady Zorana had left pieces of her clothing behind her. The first time Firekeeper spotted a scrap, she thought the bit of fabric had snagged accidentally on a jutting twig. By the third bit, she knew that Lady Zorana was deliberately marking her trail. The tiny shreds of lace could be torn from her riding habit fairly soundlessly and yet their whiteness shouted the way.

"*Good for her,*" Blind Seer said when Firekeeper told him. "*She always struck me as having some heart to her.*"

Sometime later Firekeeper said, "*I smell smoke.*"

"*Burning pine,*" Blind Seer added, "*such as two-legs use for torches. Walk slowly now, with care. The lavender scent is heavy here. They may have dug traps or set snares.*"

They found nothing so subtle. Soon flickering lights, like grounded stars, could be glimpsed through the trees.

"*What madness is this?*" Blind Seer said as soon as they were a bit closer. "*Do they shine their denning to all and sundry?*"

Once Firekeeper would have agreed that this was madness. There in the center of a well-cleared glade was a gamekeeper's cabin, the cages in which the pheasants and grouse were kept lighter forms surrounding the solidness of the central building. Lashed to every sizable tree were makeshift sconces holding brightly burning pine torches. But Firekeeper had come to understand humans far better than once she did.

"*No, there is wisdom here. Humans see little in the darkness. Any who could track them this far at night would follow that trail to its end. Thus Lavender Scent and his pack mate have lit the grounds all about the den wherein they keep Zorana. Their eyes will be accustomed to the fire brightness, but those like us who come through the darkness may be blinded.*"

"*And even,*" Blind Seer agreed, "*if both see the same, those within are at advantage, for all who cross into the lit space will be seen before they can reach the cabin. This is a good game, sweet Firekeeper!*"

She agreed. Her heart was pounding within her breast and every nerve was as alive as ever it had been. She could hear muffled voices from within the cabin: deep male and the sobbing of a female.

"*How do we take Zorana away?*" Blind Seer asked. "*Shall we wait for Derian and the others to join us?*"

"No," Firekeeper said decisively. "*I do not like the sound of Zorana's cries. There is terror in them and despair. The others may be long coming yet.*"

"*Then how do we take her away?*" Blind Seer repeated. "*I will not* cross that bright circle. Too easy for an arrow to find my heart and you did not wear your armor."

"Neither did I bring a bow," she brooded, "but I hunted much game before I knew how to use one. What do you think of this? I will climb out along the branches of the tree that stretches farthest over the clearing. From there I will throw rocks at the cabin. Perhaps they will come out."

"Stupid," the wolf replied. "Why announce ourselves only to have you shot like a squirrel? Think better."

She scowled at him. "This fire is our enemy. In darkness we are any two-legs' better."

"Then the fire must die first," Blind Seer said sensibly. "You are Firekeeper. How do we kill it without killing ourselves or burning down the forest?"

Firekeeper considered and rejected numerous plans based on the unavailability of buckets, bags, and bowls. Then she grinned:

"Fox Hair will love me for this. I will take these leather breeches and cut them into two bags. My vest is of soft leather. I can fashion another small bag quickly enough. Strips of leather will close them and I will hang them over three torches. Then I shall slash them open: one-two-three. Three torches will gutter and fail—that should be enough to create a wedge of darkness to hide us. In that moment, we strike."

"You take a great risk," Blind Seer said dubiously.

Firekeeper was already stepping out of her breeches and making the legs into bags. She cocked her head toward the cabin.

"Listen to her weep. That is not just fear—someone treats her badly. Zorana has been no friend to me, but Kenre Trueheart is our friend and he loves his mother. Go with care, dear one. See where the cabin looks out into the night? We will put out the torches where those within the cabin will have the least chance of shooting arrows at us without coming out themselves."

"You are too kind," the wolf grumbled, but he went and by the time she had her three bags filled with water he was ready.

"The cabin sits four-square in the glade, flanked with bird cages to rear and out behind. The door faces north. There are windows on all sides. Though they are shuttered, a watcher could have them open quickly I think."

"Or they may have made arrow slits," Firekeeper added, remembering such security arrangements in West Keep and in Eagle's Nest Castle.

"If you put out the torches to the west," the wolf continued, "the approach is slightly shorter. After you cover the ground, the cabin itself would be your shelter."

Firekeeper nodded and hefted the bags. "They leak some," she said critically, "but they will do. Keep to the shadows, my dear."

"I will make the pheasants and grouse our allies," Blind Seer said with a trace of laughter beneath his growl. "Be careful yourself. Your naked hide near glows in the moonlight."

Firekeeper snorted as she scrabbled up and anchored the bags above the torches. When she had fetched water, she had removed her underclothing lest its pale color make her visible and then rubbed herself carefully with wet dirt from near the brook and knew she was nearly as mottled in color as the wolf himself.

"Go then" was all she said. Raising her Fang, she slashed the first bag open. The other two were ripped open in quick succession, nor did she pause to see how well her plan had worked. The light had dimmed, the hunt begun.

Dropping nearly to all fours, Firekeeper raced across the ground, eschewing some stealth for speed. An arrow passed over her head, confirming her guess that the kidnappers had constructed arrow slits.

To her right she heard avian squawks of terror and knew that Blind Seer had released the caged birds. Their terrified fluttering filled the grove with shadows and her mouth with down. Nonetheless she howled with glee.

"Well done!" she cried, then she was upon the cabin.

At that moment she was all wolf and the human clamor from within mattered no more to her than did the plaints of the game birds. Pressing her back against the rough wood of the cabin, Firekeeper studied the shutter to her left. Something darker was pressed against it, peering out.

Dropping below the level of the sill, she crept into position, then bounded up, thrusting the Fang's blade through the shutter slats. A shrill scream of pain rewarded her, but she was already gone.

Darting around to the back she thudded her body's weight against the shutter there. It didn't break open, but a shout of alarm rose. She did not wait to see how those within would deal with that supposed intrusion, but dropped back to the west side. Picking up a chunk of firewood, she threw it with all her might against the shutter. A few slats broke and there was another shout.

She was about to continue this game when a call rang out through the night.

"Stop what you are doing at once or we will kill the Lady Zorana!"

Firekeeper had expected something like this. Her goal had been to keep those within guessing, nothing more. She trusted that they would be reluctant to kill their prisoner—after all, what would protect them thereafter? However, in a panic many a mother animal had smothered her own young. Therefore, Firekeeper proceeded with caution.

The cabin had a stone chimney on the east side. Firekeeper swarmed up this, finding toe- and handholds with ease. Once on the roof, she moved with great care, keeping her weight on the center beam. Using the Fang, she pried away several of the shingles until she found a crack between the roof boards through which she could peer. Within, the cabin was lit by several lanterns so she had no trouble seeing what was going on.

Two men prowled restlessly within, glancing out through the shutters, hands dropping to their swords at every sound. Each also had a bow. Arrows were set ready beside every window.

The men's faces had been blackened, but one had a broad slash on the cheekbone below one eye. Blood still leaked from the wound and from time to time he dabbed at it with a folded piece of cloth. Firekeeper spared a moment's regret that her blade had not gone in a bit higher.

Lady Zorana lay tied to a narrow bed set in the center of the room. The bodice of her dress was open and her skirts were hiked up over her naked lower body. She had stopped weeping now and watched her captors with single-minded hatred.

452 / JANE LINDSKOLD

A fourth person—an older man Firekeeper recalled as one she had encountered in the forest from time to time, usually messing about with birds or setting snares—was tied to a straight-backed chair. His eyes above his gagged mouth look frightened and a spreading bruise along one cheekbone gave ample reason for that fear.

Watching the two men prowl, Firekeeper considered what to do next. She had hoped to find Lady Zorana near one window or another, but the kidnappers had anticipated that. Still, the cabin was not so large that Zorana could not be reached easily enough from either window. The old man should not be left to die either.

Firekeeper knew that she must find a way to distract the men without giving them time to kill their prisoners and she must do so quickly. Derian and the others could arrive any moment and their presence could drive the kidnappers to foolishness.

Deciding, she dropped to the ground once more. Blind Seer met her instantly.

"Blind Seer, I want you to go find Derian and stop him from coming further. Those kidnappers are afraid, but not yet panicked. They may act rashly if further pressed."

The wolf growled agreement, but he wasn't pleased. "And what will you do alone, Firekeeper?"

"I will set a fire," she said. "The cabin is wooden but for the chimney. I will kindle a fire here where they will not see. Then I will drop smoking damp stuff down the chimney to force them out. I can carry straw in the ruins of my breeches. To make their choice easier, I will set fire to this western shutter before I go to the roof. Then they will have trouble east and west and me above."

"Will you then leave the others to burn alive?"

"No. I will break in the southern shutter and cut them free. I don't like breathing smoke, but I can hold my breath long enough."

"Dangerous," Blind Seer replied, but she had already begun to gather her kindling and straw. "I will go find Derian, then. Someday you must learn to write. Then I could carry a message telling them to be silent."

Firekeeper nodded acceptance of his criticism, blowing on the spark she had struck. By the time she had a flame licking the tinder, the wolf had vanished. As she fed her flame, Firekeeper wished she could just steal one of the torches, but knew that the burning brand would make her too fine a target as she carried it across the clearing.

When the flame was stronger, she kindled a bit of the western shutter, kneeling below the lowest edge until it caught. Then, taking her smoldering straw onto the roof, she stuffed it down the chimney. The effect was immediate and satisfactory.

Coughing. Then a male voice choked out:

"Coming down the chimney! Stomp it!"

Firekeeper stuffed down more straw to make this last more difficult. Darting to her peephole, she saw the man with the cut face tromping on the straw. Then the other man noticed the smoke eddying in at the window.

"The cabin's on fire!" he shouted, racing to see if he could put it out. "Grab the woman and get out of here!"

This last suited Firekeeper fine. She waited until she saw Zorana's bonds had been cut, then went to the edge of the roof on the south side. The eaves were lower here. Grabbing the roof edge she swung down, her feet toward the shutter, forcing the full weight of her descent into the wood. It splintered and she was through, keeping her balance with the ease of one who had spent her life climbing trees.

The wounded man stood by the bed. Despite the smoke and the fire now reddening the west shutter, he reacted to Firekeeper's arrival by turning his knife in his hand and throwing it at her. She dodged, but she had not even her hide for protection and the blade sliced a furrow across her rib cage.

Before she could feel the pain, Firekeeper charged forward, her Fang in one hand. The momentum of her charge knocked the now unarmed man off his feet. She stomped on his hand, wishing this once for boots, and pushed Zorana back toward the south window.

Zorana stumbled that direction, hampered by her skirts. Then, seeing the other prisoner, she stopped and began fumbling with his bonds.

"Out!" Firekeeper howled at her.

Then she howled again, returning to battle. Kneeing the wounded man in the face as he struggled to rise, she flung herself at the second man as he surged toward her, a sword held high in both his hands, the blade arcing down toward her.

Firekeeper had nothing with which to parry. The first man was clawing at her legs, making dodging nearly impossible. In desperation, the wolf-woman did the only thing possible and darted under the arch of descending blade.

This move kept her away from the sharp edge, but the hilt struck her soundly between the shoulder blades, knocking the breath from her lungs. Firekeeper fell into the swordman's arms in a parody of an embrace. She could feel him turning the sword in his hands, knew he meant to stab her in the back.

Going limp was almost too easy. Before the man could arrange the clumsy blade in order to stab, Firekeeper had dropped to her knees on the floor, landing almost on top of the wounded man. He grasped at her, trying to reestablish his hold.

Firekeeper kicked herself clear but the exertion caused her to choke on the now smoky air. The air within the cabin was thick with smoke. The sound of crackling wood as the fire claimed the west side of the cabin and moved toward the roof loudly snapped in her ears.

The man with the sword seemed to realize his own danger for the first time.

"Get out!" he yelled to his comrade and turned to run. The wounded man struggled to his feet, eager to follow. Firekeeper made no move to stop him. In all honesty, she was not certain that she could.

Dragging herself to her feet and turning weakly, she saw that Zorana must have disobeyed her, for the tied man was no longer in his chair. Through the smoke, Firekeeper glimpsed him clambering over the windowsill. She followed, wondering why this seemed so weirdly familiar, wondering if she would ever catch her breath, thinking vaguely that fire was a very chancy ally indeed.

Then she felt packed earth cool beneath her feet. After a few staggered steps forward, the air, too, cooled. She breathed it in gratefully, though every gasp caused the place where the sword hilt had struck her to throb. Her head cleared with each breath, then Blind Seer was beside her.

"Little idiot," he said fondly. *"Come away. Zorana and the gamekeeper are safe but the kidnappers have escaped and the cabin is lost to the flames. Derian and the rest fetch water now so that the fire will not spread to the forest. The falcon Elation has carried a note back to King Tedric, telling him all is well."*

Staggering slightly, glad for the wolf's strength beneath her hand, Firekeeper followed.

FAR LATER, RESTING ON A CUSHION on the floor of King Tedric's room in the Watchful Eye, Firekeeper learned the rest of the tale as told by Lady Zorana. As had Firekeeper herself, Lady Zorana had been bathed and given a loose linen shift to wear.

While the wolf-woman lay still, Doc's hands traveled over her various scrapes, cuts, and bruises, applying ointment and bandages as was appropriate. From his touch emanated a strange coolness that seemed to go to the heart of the pain and ease it at once.

"And so after the brute had beaten poor Prince Newell until he crumpled unconscious on the moss," Lady Zorana said, "he and his fellow dragged me through the forest and imprisoned me in the cabin. They treated me badly . . ."

She paused and colored. King Tedric asked in level tones that somehow conspired to make the brutal words gentle:

"Did they rape you?"

Zorana shook her head. "No, Uncle, but they handled me most familiarly, making free with my person. I think if rescue had not come they might have steeled themselves to the deed, but they rightly feared pursuit."

King Tedric frowned. "I wonder that they feared pursuit before morning. Had I not summoned Lady Blysse, none could have found them so swiftly. Pray, continue, Niece."

"When Lady Blysse arrived," Zorana said, glancing at the young woman, a curious mixture of gratitude and resentment on her face, "the men were ready to slay me rather than risk themselves. They swore they would kill me and one stood over me with a knife at my throat until the noises without died away. Lady Blysse was clever, though. Smoking them out was a good idea."

Firekeeper nodded in acknowledgment of the praise. Zorana continued:

"They cut me loose and prepared to escape. When Lady Blysse came in through the window shutter—and such a figure you've never seen, naked as the day she was born but for a knife belt, mud smeared on every inch of her skin—I hastened to escape through the broken window. First I paused to cut loose the gamekeeper. That poor man had done no wrong beyond living where those ruffians wanted to be yet they had beaten him and tied him to a chair, making him unwilling witness to their depravities. How is he, Uncle?"

King Tedric turned to Doc. "Sir Jared?"

"The gamekeeper is resting," Doc replied. "His bones couldn't take the battering. His jaw is broken and several ribs are cracked. Saddest perhaps is that his mind has been swallowed by fear of any man. The townsfolk tell me that he was always simple. That's why he was given that job. Weeks at a time he would never see a human being. Then two strangers come and steal his house to molest a lady. I had to call in a female healer from one of the cavalry units to treat him. He just started screaming whenever he laid eyes on me."

Zorana said firmly, "I will arrange for the gamekeeper's care, for he took those injuries because of me. My husband and I have lands he can care for if he wishes to leave here. If he doesn't wish to leave, I will pay for his home to be rebuilt and for help recovering his birds."

King Tedric nodded. "So be it. Is that the end of your story, Zorana?"

"Almost. When the gamekeeper and I escaped from the cabin, we found that other rescuers had come. One man took us in charge. The rest went to put out the fire."

Derian Carter cleared his throat and the king acknowledged him.

"Firekeeper left a trail clear enough for Race to follow even by torchlight," Derian said. "We found the grove from which Lady Zorana had been kidnapped and stopped to read a copy of the ransom note that had been left there. When we drew near the cabin and heard the noise from within we would have gone charging in, making things worse from how Lady Zorana tells it, but then Blind Seer appeared. By scaring our horses so he could drive them like cattle, he made it known to us that we should approach the back of the cabin. That's how we were there when Lady Zorana needed succor."

"Thank you," the king said. "I had wondered why you were so conveniently placed. Lady Zorana, Lady Blysse, Prince Newell, can any of you identify these ruffians? Though they were stopped short of their intention, still I would have them hanged."

Firekeeper shook her head regretfully. "Not even by scent, King Tedric. All they smelled of was lavender and the oiled ash they had smeared on their faces."

"They were disguised," Lady Zorana agreed, "and took care never to call each other by name. I would say that each had borne arms in his time and that they were of Hawk Haven not Bright Bay. They had not even the accent you hear in this border region."

"That is useful," King Tedric acknowledged, "as is the knife slash that Firekeeper left on one of their faces. Prince Newell, have you anything to add?"

The prince shook his head sadly. He reeked of anger and remorse, but Firekeeper couldn't escape the feeling that he was not being wholly truthful.

"I was attacked when my back was turned," he said.

"I guess you could call it that." Blind Seer commented dryly. Firekeeper smothered a giggle in her hand.

"And never saw my attacker clearly. I agree with Lady Zorana that he knew something of combat. The way he went for me was not the random flailing of a barroom brawler."

Sir Dirkin frowned. "Unhappily, unless we find the man with the fresh knife cut, we are at a complete loss. Too many residents of these twinned towns are deserters or fled criminals. The towns' policy is to protect them. My guess is that they are already away across the river into Good Crossing. We shall not see them again."

"You think them opportunists then?" King Tedric asked.

"I don't know what I think them," Sir Dirkin replied, "but I expect that they will not take similar risks again."

"I see," the king said, and once again Firekeeper had the feeling that he was not saying all he thought.

Doc rose and bowed. "Your Majesty should rest, as should my patients. For all her courage in reporting so clearly, Lady Zorana has been sorely abused. I would like to dose her with an herbal mixture to help her sleep without dreams. I also suggest that she stay here within the fortress so that she will feel secure."

Lady Zorana looked as if she wished to reject such coddling but was only too well aware that she needed it. King Tedric saved her dignity by saying:

"I command that Zorana take your recommendation, Sir Jared. Place yourself on call in the anteroom to my chamber, where you may be available if anyone has need of your services. The rest of you are dismissed. Remember, speak nothing of tonight's events except to keep rumor from exaggerating them beyond measure. Now, good night and thank you."

He gestured for Firekeeper to close with him and whispered in her ear, "And be careful, little wolfling. There is wickedness abroad."

She bowed to him and with a thoughtful hand twined in Blind Seer's ruff followed Derian and Race back to the Kestrel encampment.

PERHAPS LADY ZORANA'S KIDNAPPING and the daring rescue would have been ferreted out by the nosy despite the best attempts of those involved to keep the secret, but something happened to eclipse her adventure. The next morning shortly before noon, news came across the river that Stonehold was withdrawing its troops from where they were bivouacked with those of Bright Bay.

Lady Zorana, returning from the Watchful Eye, brought additional news to her brother. Despite the fact that others must be spreading the same information, Zorana acted as if what she was reporting were privileged information.

"Word has come to the Watchful Eye," Zorana said, her voice low and breathy with excitement, "that Generals Yuci and Grimsel have sent a letter to Queen Gustin—with copies to her representatives here—having to do with their discovery of something about Bright Bay of which the Stonehold government seems to strongly disapprove. They have demanded that Queen Gustin the Fourth come meet with them immediately. They say that if she does not the alliance between Stonehold and Bright Bay otherwise will be forever broken and war declared between their nations."

Baron Archer cocked an eyebrow, but for all the steadiness with which he stuffed his pipe neither Elise nor Zorana was fooled. He was as surprised as anyone by the recent change in events. Silence merely provided him with the opportunity to calculate what these changes would mean to Hawk Haven.

Seeing that her father wasn't going to give his sister the satisfaction of a reply, Elise asked her aunt:

"How can they make such demands, Aunt Zorana? Certainly foreign generals aren't in a position to order a queen about—especially in her own land!"

Zorana looked quite serious. "Foreign generals can try, Elise, if their army provides much of the strength of that queen's army. Never forget, Bright Bay is powerful on the sea—a rival for Waterland most say—but for a long time now her army has depended on Stonehold for both troops and officers. The withdrawal of their troops from among hers is a reminder to them of that dependence."

"An unwise dependence, I've always thought," commented Ivon Archer, "but it was an arrangement that enabled Bright Bay to fully exploit her own rich naval resources. Stonehold has seafront, but no ports deep enough for large ships, so her people benefitted, too. Still, I've often wondered how much time would pass before Bright Bay became a vassal state of Stonehold in fact if not in name."

"Then," Elise pressed, "can Stonehold dictate to Queen Gustin?"

"The question," her father replied, "is not *can* they—that's just what they have done. The question is whether or not Queen Gustin will permit herself to be given orders by them and what her decision will mean for the rest of us."

Later, arriving at the Kestrel encampment, Elise wasn't surprised to learn that news of this new development had reached the earl's retainers before her. After exhausting speculation on how this new event might affect the negotiations between Hawk Haven and Bright Bay, Derian, Firekeeper, and Elise shifted to their more immediate problem, planning the next step in their private campaign against Lady Melina's sorcery.

Elise was showing them the sketches she had made of the necklace when Valet came out toward their makeshift conference center.

"Derian," he called from a polite distance, "a messenger has just arrived from King Tedric. You are requested to meet with His Majesty and other of his counselors at the Watchful Eye at your soonest convenience."

"Ladies," Derian said, looking both proud and nervous, "will you excuse me?"

"Of course," Elise replied, as Firekeeper nodded. "Enjoy yourself. We'll take these sketches into Hope. If there is to be trouble, then all the more reason for having Sapphire freed of her mother's control."

And you, as well, Derian thought, but he said nothing.

AFTER HURRIEDLY CHANGING INTO CLEAN SHIRT and breeches, Derian strode toward the Watchful Eye. He noticed the occasional puzzled glance flicked his way and heard one man say to another:

"I know he's the newest counselor, but where's the heir?"

Derian smiled quietly to himself. Let them stay a bit confused. He was beginning to understand that governing was not unlike horse trading—you held the advantage best when even your friends were a bit off balance.

Earl Kestrel, already present at the fort, greeted Derian with the courtesy, but not the condescension, of patron to dependent. He gestured to a seat beside him.

"Is all well in our camp?"

"Yes, sir."

At that moment, the king's secretary rapped for silence and they all stood as King Tedric entered the room.

He can't have had much sleep since last night, Derian thought. *Doc and the other medicos must be furious.*

King Tedric, however, didn't look as if he needed anyone's coddling. Standing before his chair, leaning slightly against the table in an attitude that seemed belligerent rather than weak, he began the meeting.

"You are all," he said without formality, "aware of the changed situation between Stonehold and Bright Bay. In the interests of forestalling rumors, I have summoned you here. My secretary is going to read you several documents, the contents of which I expressly wish to be shared with the men and women in your various households and commands. At a time such as this, rumor and misinformation are our greatest enemies. Farand, please begin."

He sank into his chair and Lady Farand Briarcott, a pinch-nosed woman with snowy hair piled high on her head and a voice that could command troops—and had indeed done so—rose, paper in hand:

"This first missive," Lady Farand announced, "comes from the First Equal of Stonehold. It is also signed by the Second Equal and the members of the advisory cabinet.

" 'To King Tedric I, Monarch of Hawk Haven, Knight of the Eight-Rayed Star . . .' "

"Skip that unzoranic nonsense and read the text," the king snapped.

Lady Farand gave a curt nod, ran her finger down the outer margin, and recommenced:

"Through our loyal generals, Yuci and Grimsel, information has come to our ears that gives us to realize that the support we have

granted to the nation of Bright Bay was done while that nation deliberately maintained a foul and most unreasonable deception.

"We have written to Queen Gustin the Fourth requesting a meeting with herself. Until she grants this meeting and the results of said meeting are satisfactory to our needs, we will withdraw the military support which to this time we have granted Bright Bay.

"If subsequent to our meeting with Queen Gustin the Fourth, Bright Bay persists in her foolish and dangerous practices, we will have no choice but to declare war upon her. Moreover, in light of these discoveries, we hereby warn you as ruler of Hawk Haven that any efforts to support, succor, or in anyway ally with Bright Bay will cause us to view you in an unfriendly light.

"We have confided some measure of our concern on these matters to the countries of New Kelvin and Waterland, noting that we believe that the government of Hawk Haven is well aware of the deception practiced by Bright Bay and that its refusal to share that information constitutes an unfriendly act uncomely between allies.

"Note that if you remain neutral toward Bright Bay so we will remain toward you and your people."

Derian hardly heard as the secretary read off a long list of the titles and names belonging to the distinguished signatories. As soon as Lady Farand finished, voices were raised, some nearly shouting frantic questions. King Tedric banged for silence.

"Listen to the rest of the correspondence," he demanded. "You may find some of your questions answered therein."

Lady Farand unfolded a shorter missive stating, "This one is from the Plutarchs of Waterland:

"To King Tedric . . .

"Recent discoveries of foul secrets held by the Crown of Bright Bay lead us to encourage you to stay away from entanglements, whether civil or military, with that nation:

"Waterland has always found it profitable to support your

*kingdom's continued freedom from Bright Bay's encroachment,
especially upon the seas where our vessels could offer our aid and
protection. However, if you continue to treat with Bright Bay
without insisting on the destruction of their foul hoard, we shall
view you as one with them, no matter how separate your boundaries.
Your ships shall be to us as their ships: our rightful prey.*

"We trust that a man of your great years and well-respected
wisdom thinks as we do in this matter. Signed . . ."

The missive from New Kelvin, Hawk Haven's other ally, was much
the same, though in this case the threat was to withdraw the economic
support and favored nation trading status which Hawk Haven had hereto
enjoyed.

Derian was already quite confused and anxious when Farand Briarcott
unrolled the final missive, a personal letter to King Tedric from Allister
Seagleam.

"Uncle Tedric,

"By now you must have heard the accusations of deception and
foul play being heaped upon Bright Bay by Stonehold. I hardly
know what to say. If there is any deep secret, I know nothing of it. I
came here as I told you, in sincere hopes of building a bridge
between our nations—in hopes of fulfilling the charge laid upon me
at my birth.

"Now I must wait until Queen Gustin the Fourth decides how to
answer these demands. In the meantime, my family is held not quite
prisoner in our residence by guards supplied by our own people and
supported by those members of Queen Gustin's court who do not wish
to risk that any small action of mine might be interpreted by
Stonehold's spies as an excuse for war. As we are no longer free to
come and go, I fear I can no longer attend our planned conferences.
I deeply regret this.

"In hopes of resolution of this strange situation, I am, your
nephew, Allister Seagleam."

Lady Farand's reseating herself seemed a signal for the hubbub to erupt once again. King Tedric let the confused babble go on for a few moments, then recognized a senior army commander:

"Your Majesty," the man said, "what is this? Do you know of any dark secret?"

"In answer to your first question," King Tedric said, " 'this' is a warning to us from our three neighboring countries that if we meddle in any way, peaceful or not, in the affairs of Bright Bay, we will find ourselves viewed as enemies as well.

"As to your second question: How could I know what dark secrets Bright Bay conceals? I have never been there."

While Derian was admiring the fashion in which the king had avoided a direct answer to the latter question, Ivon Archer was recognized:

"Your Majesty, I recommend that we prepare to attack Bright Bay as soon as Queen Gustin arrives to negotiate with Stonehold. If we take her, we have her kingdom. War between our peoples would be ended. If there is something in Bright Bay's treasury—this 'foul secret' alluded to—we will then be in a position to turn it over to Stonehold. All wars will be ended."

"I agree with that," said Rolfston Redbriar, not to be outdone. "Everyone knows that Bright Bay's power is on the seas, not on the land. Since Stonehold has withdrawn her troops, we could defeat Bright Bay's remaining force handily. We already have a base of operations set up here at the Watchful Eye. Stonehold does not. Moreover, we have the Barren River between ourselves and Bright Bay. Stonehold, even if it brings in reinforcements, will share ground with those it seeks to conquer. The very countryside will rise against them. We are secure in our own lands. Our supply lines need cross no enemy territory."

There was more clamor along similar lines. Derian could practically feel the blood-lust rising and wondered if Stonehold had anticipated this reaction on the part of Hawk Haven. Gripping the edge of the table hard, he listened and said nothing, feeling more than ever a mere carter's son. At last King Tedric banged his gavel on the table and said, his tones dry and ironic:

"So I am to understand that most of you are in favor of taking advantage of this situation to invade Bright Bay, never mind that our own navy would be forfeit to Waterland, never mind that New Kelvin has promised economic repercussions and could quite possibly offer more than that if it felt threatened."

No one moved for a moment; then Prince Newell asked to be recognized.

"As one who has recently served with our navy," said the prince, "I would like to offer my opinion on Waterland's threat."

"Speak," King Tedric said.

"Our navy," the prince said, a feverish light in his eyes, "could be warned of what we intend to do. Our ships could temporarily withdraw into secure waters, leaving Waterland's fleet to futilely sweep a vacant sea. When the reunification of Bright Bay with Hawk Haven is completed, our newly augmented navy will be large enough to deal fairly with Waterland's."

Derian saw many of the soldiers nod and smile in approval of Prince Newell's vision. Hawk Haven's weakness upon the seas had long been a sore point among the military, but a nation with only one major harbor and no offshore holdings could not expect to compete with nations like Bright Bay and Waterland, overblessed as they were with ports.

"Thank you, Prince Newell," King Tedric said. "If we do move against Bright Bay, certainly we will take your advice and warn the navy in advance."

Derian thought that the prince looked a bit deflated, even a bit miffed, to hear his dream of naval domination reduced to such a simple point. King Tedric didn't allow the prince time to retort. Instead he asked his assembled counselors:

"You all seem to believe that we could easily conquer Bright Bay. Tell me, though, is creating three enemies where before we had none— for we are at peace with Bright Bay never you forget—is that a fair trade?"

"Peace," spat an old soldier, his exposed skin fairly seamed with scars, "peace that erupts in border raids and banditry, not to mention privateering upon the seas! Call that peace if you wish. I call it war."

"Peace," said young Purcel Archer, his voice light in contrast. "I wish I thought we were at peace. However, if we truly believed what we had with Bright Bay was peace why did Your Majesty need such a large and heavily armed escort just to meet with your foreign-born nephew? Doesn't that speak of a tension greater than that of peace?"

"What both of you say," King Tedric sighed, "holds an element of truth, but peace—even peace with border raids and armed tension—kills far fewer men and women than even one pitched battle. Think carefully before you advise this course."

A slim woman not much older than Derian himself but wearing a uniform decorated with honors up and down the sleeves, said into the silence following the king's statement:

"Your Majesty is correct. My fellows should remember that Waterland and New Kelvin have long supported us—as Stonehold has Bright Bay— not from love of us or of our way of life but from fear of what we might become if we were one nation with Bright Bay. Think you. You see a touch of that fear now directed toward Bright Bay. Do you think it would fade to nothing if we conquered our old rival and so became the great country that they have long feared? Neutrality is the answer to this difficulty. Let Bright Bay pay for her sins—whatever they are—herself. Perhaps then she will have the humility to leave us to our lives and the border raids will cease."

There were a good number of muttered agreements at this, mostly from the very grizzled veterans—those who knew what a pitched battle could be—or the very young officers who were beginning to dread the learning.

"Yet that neutrality means," said Prince Newell, his voice as clear as a bell, "that we will resign ourselves to forever being at war. We can do this—we have for over a hundred years since the end of the Civil War. Yet I find myself thinking of my aunt's son, this Allister Seagleam who came to us with such touching hopes for peace. Are we to leave him and his children—two of them just small girls—to the mercies of Stonehold's army because we fear the future? I say then that we are not worthy of that future! I say war now for those little girls. War now for a future of peace! What good are allies who support us merely to keep us weak? I say defy them and show our strength!"

An unguarded cheer greeted the conclusion of this stirring speech. King Tedric, however, only smiled dryly:

"So, Prince Newell, you believe we should conquer Bright Bay in order to preserve her against an army that has not yet declared war. That is an interesting policy. However, it is good to see how many of you would go to war to protect my nephew's little girls."

After this evaluation, King Tedric fell silent and all the room fell silent with him in respect of the burden that was his alone to bear. They might counsel, but the king alone must decide.

When Tedric raised his head from his hands, decision was written in the aged lines on his face.

"War it shall be." He raised his hand to still the cheering that arose at these words. "Not a war of conquest, a different war than any you have suggested. We shall start our way to peace with Bright Bay by offering our support to her in this time of trouble, by giving our support to those who came here to treat for peace.

"When or if Queen Gustin the Fourth comes, she shall encounter us not as enemies, but as those who are willing to maintain her rights against those who would take them. If false allies are to be unmasked and flouted, then we must be well on the way to making true ones. Are you with me?"

The cheer that greeted the conclusion of this speech was pure acclaim, so loud and ready that it made that which had answered Prince Newell sound like the thready wail of a newborn kitten. Even as his own voice joined the cry, Derian wondered to find tears on his face, streaming from eyes he had been certain must be bright with joy.

XXIII

MY NATION IS ON THE BRINK OF WAR, Elise thought. *Some of our troops have crossed the Barren River and stand between our former enemy and their former friend. Others make a tight cordon along the banks of the Barren and scouts patrol the farther reaches lest we miss some hint of invasion while our attention is centered here. My nation is on the brink of war and what do I do? I go shopping for jewelry.*

She smiled ruefully, knowing how unjust she was being to herself. Still, there had never been a time in her life that she so regretted being unskilled with a bow or sword and being rather squeamish at the thought of killing another living thing.

Five days had passed since King Tedric made his decision to support Bright Bay if Stonehold enforced its threat to answer Queen Gustin's refusal to speak with their representatives with arms. The necessity had become rapidly apparent, for Queen Gustin's refusal to meet with Stonehold had come a mere two days after Stonehold's initial demand had been made.

Gustin's letter (a copy of which had been sent to King Tedric) simply refused to permit an outside power—no matter how friendly—to give her orders. Her response had been blunt, leaving no room for misinterpretation. Forced to either declare war or have their threats called as a bluff, Stonehold had attacked.

They had been rebuffed for two reasons. One, Good Crossing's walls had held—though they would not hold against another such press. Two, King Tedric had his troops ready to march. As the first volley of arrows had been fired, Bridgeton had opened her broad span to permit Hawk Haven to come to aid Bright Bay.

Stonehold's relatively small army—for Yuci and Grimsel only had those troops which had been withdrawn from Bright Bay's own army—had been unable to take a walled city while being attacked on their flank by a second, stronger force. Still, they had done considerable damage. Good Crossing's walls were no longer unbreached, forcing Duke Allister to bring his troops out into the fields surrounding the city.

A large, relatively open area to the south and west of Good Crossing had become the acknowledged battleground. Stonehold had pulled back to the southern edge while the combined forces of Hawk Haven and Bright Bay held the area outside of Good Crossing and along the Barren River.

Elise's own role in all of this martial activity had been comparatively insignificant. While others dashed hither and yon—important in armor, freshened blazons on their shields—she wound bandages or blended ointments and tinctures for the infirmary with inexpert hands.

Baron Archer had hinted that Elise might do well to return to Eagle's Nest, where she would be safe if Stonehold managed to cross the Barren. Elise had pretended not to understand those hints and her father had let the matter drop. Doubtless he had come to realize how unjust he had been in hotheadedly branding his daughter a traitor, but he could not press her to leave this sensitive area without risking that she raise the matter once more.

At least the commanders of Bright Bay's troops had been wise enough to accept the help offered by Hawk Haven. Allister Seagleam had taken advantage of his place as senior noble present to become effectively commander in chief of the Bright Bay forces. His first command had been that his officers work with those of Hawk Haven. Yet, despite Duke

470 / JANE LINDSKOLD

Allister's efforts to smooth things over, tempers were short and trust shorter still.

Duke Allister's task might have been easier if Lord Tench, the queen's advisor, had remained, but he had departed on a fast horse to advise Queen Gustin as to the situation. It was still uncertain whether Gustin IV would come to Good Crossing at all. On that matter, the rumor mill was most vocal and most contradictory.

Some said the queen was on her way from Silver Whale Cove, armed and armored and leading a host of noble knights, fronting a band of blooded marines. This was a favorite among Bright Bay's troops—never mind that Bright Bay's nobility was more comfortable on the command deck of a ship than on horseback and that those marines would be scattered among dozens of ships.

Or the queen was waiting in her castle in the capital, afraid for her life. She would deal with the situation once others had risked life and limb. This was the favorite of the more cynical elements of Hawk Haven's forces.

Or yet, the queen was coming in disguise and on a fast horse, ready to negotiate terms that would keep her nation independent now that Stonehold had actually used its teeth. This was the favorite of those on both sides who had actually thought about the text of Stonehold's demands.

Or the queen had fled to safety in the Isles. The queen was already present but keeping her exact whereabouts secret. The queen was dead or ill or pregnant. The queen didn't matter—what mattered was force of arms upon this one field.

That last was what Elise herself dreaded would prove true. The situation seemed to have progressed beyond what rational words and negotiation could achieve. Armor had been polished, swords sharpened, arrows newly fletched. The only seemingly impossible thing in all this chaotic and unpredictable situation was that these would be returned to armory, sheath, and quiver unblooded and unstained.

Her thoughts running thus, Elise needed Ninette's tap on her sleeve to alert her when they had reached Wain Cutter's shop. Over the past several days, Elise had grown quite comfortable with Wain. Whereas on their first visit she had hardly noticed him as a person, now she found the thoughtful calmness of his hound-dog features comfortable in the midst of confusion and the way he rubbed his bald pate when working his way through a problem rather endearing.

Wain had set to work on their second commission as soon as they had given it to him. His first step had been locating gems of a size and color to match those in Zorana's necklace. He had been lucky with the sapphire and the ruby, but a citrine of the deep cognac shade favored by Lady Melina had been difficult to find, and he had been forced to cut the gem himself. The opal had been gained after negotiations with a rival across the river and then cut down to match the others. The jet he had also cut himself—though from a different piece than that which had supplied Elise's new betrothal pendant.

Although Derian had accompanied Elise that first morning to explain the new commission to Wain Cutter, the developing military situation had given him no time to join her since. If he was not in some meeting, he was making Firekeeper buckle on her armor or acting as reserve farrier for Earl Kestrel's command.

Firekeeper was busy as well. Elise rather suspected the king had given the wolf-woman some task or other, for she often vanished for entire half-days. One of the tasks Firekeeper was almost certainly performing was scouting, and Elise doubted that Firekeeper remained on Hawk Haven's side of the river or that all the reports she delivered were restricted to the ostensible enemy's readiness.

Yet it was Firekeeper who made certain to check with Elise several times a day and Firekeeper who had not forgotten in the new turmoil that within their own camp, a few long paces away from the pavilion in which Elise herself slept, was one who might be more dangerous than any army.

Now Elise bent her head over the finished necklace that Wain Cutter proudly spread out upon a piece of white velvet for her inspection.

"I finished it early this morning," he said, "rose before the dawn. Couldn't get it off my mind, dreamed of it even. I got the feeling that it wanted to be made and that I shouldn't be holding it up."

Elise nodded comprehension, though she didn't really understand such obsession.

"It's lovely," she said honestly, admiring the gentle curve of silver with the five diamond-shaped pendants hanging down, "but the silver looks just the slightest bit scratched."

"Patina," Wain explained hastily, rubbing his pate in quick circles as if polishing the baldness. "That's what that's called. It makes a piece of jewelry look not so new. Soft metals like silver and gold often acquire a patina after they've been worn for a time."

He colored and Elise knew why. If you were asked to duplicate a famous—even notorious—piece of jewelry by people who swore you into secrecy, it wasn't a great jump for even a slow mind to guess that maybe a substitution was planned. And Wain Cutter was not a slow man at all. He hurried on, talking fast as if to cover an awkward pause in the conversation that hadn't yet occurred.

"Of course, if you're wanting it looking bright and new, I can shine it up and buff out the patina."

Elise smiled at him. "No, the patina is perfect. You're right. It gives the piece the look of an old family heirloom rather than something commissioned by that market woman who discovered she was the only heir to a duke."

There was a popular comic song about that very situation. For generations tavern drunks and small children alike had enjoyed reeling off the long list of the things the market woman had ordered when she had discovered that she was to be a "duchess fine."

The words of one verse rose unbidden from Elise's memory and she had to resist the urge to hum along with the jaunty tune:

> *A sweeping gown of fine brocade,*
> *A long-maned, elegant pacing jade,*
> *An ivory board on which games were played,*

> *For these all in future coin she paid,*
> *That soon to be duchess fine!*

But resist Elise did, for Wain was unhooking the sapphire pendant and showing her its catch.

"Getting these right was the biggest trick," he was saying, "for you told me that each pendant needed to be removable with some ease, yet remain firm set the rest of the time. I appreciated those sketches you made for me."

Elise nodded acknowledgment. It hadn't been at all easy to see how the pendants were held in place and had meant spending far more time in Lady Melina's company than she had desired. Fortunately, Lady Melina, like everyone else, was eager to demonstrate her support of King Tedric's war and had spent many hours in the infirmary.

There Elise's persistence had been rewarded. She had contrived to tangle into Lady Melina's necklace a stray end of linen thread from the bandage strips she was cutting, snagging both the opal and ruby pendants. Greatly annoyed, Lady Melina had rebuked her sharply, then permitted her to untangle the mess to make amends.

Afterward, Elise had nearly fled the infirmary to sketch the details before she forgot them. She didn't doubt that Lady Melina believed she scurried off to sob at the harshness of Her Ladyship's words, but in the interest of the greater good, Elise could live with a little loss of dignity.

"Very fine work, absolutely marvelous," she said, meaning every word of her praise. "I am amazed you could do such complex work from an amateur's sketch."

"There's a logic in it, my lady," Wain said complacently, "that guides a crafter through the job. Your sketch was a map, but my skill taught me to make sense of it."

"Then the necklace is ready for me to take?" Elise asked.

"It is." With a final proud and affectionate glance at his creation, Wain tucked it into a little bag of dark red velvet.

Elise paid him in a mixture of credit tokens, some bearing the Archer mark, others that of the Eagle, still others the local guild mark. Before he had been called to other duties, Derian had changed the Kestrel tokens he and Firekeeper possessed into local marks, thereby muddying the trail should any wonder why Lady Elise had spent such a great sum. Some Archer marks were necessary, however, for Elise had excused her frequent visits on the grounds that Wain was making her a bracelet to bring back to Lady Aurella.

Wain gave her the bracelet as well, a pretty thing of cut gemstones set upon a heavy silver band. He had adapted it from a design he had been working on before their new commissions had distracted him. It was complex enough to excuse Elise's visits and yet not too expensive for her already strained purse.

Thanking the jeweler, Elise forced herself to visit several more shops before returning to camp. There she settled herself to rolling bandages and listening to the anxious gossip of the noncombatants while waiting for Firekeeper to make an appearance.

The wolf-woman glided into Elise's pavilion late that night, long after Elise had snuffed out her candle.

"You have it," she whispered after she had woken Elise.

"I do."

"And you will put sleeping herbs into Lady Melina's food and that of Opal and the nurse?"

"I'll try." Even though she was whispering, Elise could hear the note of doubt in her own voice.

"You must," Firekeeper urged. "When you do this leave this stone . . ."

Elise felt something flat and vaguely oval-shaped set next to her on the cot.

". . . on the ground outside of your pavilion just the other side of your sleeping. I will find it there and know that we may hope that they are sleeping deep."

"I will," Elise whispered. "It may take a few days to find an opportunity."

"I know. That's why I bring the stone. Good luck. I know you will be brave."

There was a faint stirring of air and Elise knew she was alone again. For a long time she lay awake, staring into the darkness, and wondering if she was indeed the least bit brave.

ALLISTER SEAGLEAM KNEW SOMETHING that no one else knew. He knew which of the rumors about Queen Gustin IV was true. He knew, but the knowing brought him little comfort. Tench had returned the evening before—cautious, worried, little Lord Tench who was Lord Tench rather than Tench Clark because of his service to Her Majesty, first as her secretary when she was Crown Princess Valora, later as a trusted member of her diplomatic corps.

And with him Lord Tench had carried letters: letters commanding generals to hold fast and obey Allister Seagleam as they would her royal self; letters to other nobles in the entourage who might not think this a good idea; letters to Allister's children telling them to obey their father and be the firm deck under his feet in this tossing storm. Lastly there was a letter to Allister himself telling him much the same and assuring him of the queen's support.

This was the letter for public eyes, for possible spies. Allister Seagleam doubted that even Lord Tench had read it—though he was certainly privy to the contents of the others. Gustin IV had left nothing to chance, however. This letter was triply sealed and encoded. The key to this code had been given to Allister by Gustin herself when he had departed Silver Whale Cove to meet with King Tedric. She swore that no one else knew it and Allister believed her. From a small girl, Gustin had been good with numbers and puzzles. She was quite capable of constructing and employing a code without any assistance.

Once he had decoded the letter, it read:

"Dear Cousin,

"I wish I could come to your side—and indeed to the forefront of this battle that has been thrust upon our people. Sadly, I cannot. What Stonehold accuses us of may indeed be true as they see things. There are secrets known only to the monarchs of Bright Bay. To share them even with you, cousin, would be treason. If in some mysterious fashion Stonehold has learned one of these secrets, I certainly cannot confirm the rightness or wrongness of their knowledge by rushing to Good Crossing at their command as might a kitchen maid called to task by cook for breaking a platter.

"So here I remain. Soon you will hear tales that pirate activity on the coast forces me to remain in the capital. Part at least will be true. Here I must remain until either you come home victorious or Stonehold's generals batter down my door.

"Tench tells me that King Tedric has offered his alliance for the nonce and that you in my name have accepted it. I shall support you in this, even before those who whine about your foreign blood. They are asses. You did the only thing you could—accept a new ally when an old turned against you.

"Standing fast is only part of your duty. You must drive Stonehold out. I realize that military command was never your ambition, but I know you well. You have a fair mind and will weigh the advice given to you by those who do know that art before deciding a course of action.

"As soon as this war is resolved, I will reward you as you deserve. For now, I fear you will need to settle for my thanks."

The formalities which ended the letter were fluff and vanity. Allister stared at the missive for quite a long while before folding it into thirds, smoothing it flat, and tucking it into the interior pocket of his waistcoat. Then he headed outside to attend to the duties assigned to him, not altogether certain that Queen Gustin IV, guardian of dark secrets, was as worthy of his loyalty as she clearly believed she was.

◈

IN THE MIDST OF THIS MARTIAL PREPARATION, Lady Elise Archer, heiress to a barony earned by her grandfather in battle, went into the fray herself, but her battleground was a dinner party and her weapon a flask of fine-ground powder.

It had been easy enough to arrange the party. Ever since the entry of Duke Allister Seagleam and his brood into the competition for the throne of Hawk Haven, the alliance between the family of Rolfston Redbriar with that of Baron Archer had been strained. Nor had Jet Shield's failure to behave as a properly betrothed young man should helped the situation.

So when Lady Elise had chosen not to spend overmuch time with her betrothed, she had been well within her rights. Equally so, when she invited her betrothed and his family, including sisters and father, to dine with her in the sumptuous Archer pavilion, they were not likely to refuse.

Baron Archer dined with them, but before the sweets and cheese he returned to his command. Lord Rolfston, never wishing to seem less the warrior than his rival, excused himself soon thereafter. Soon Jet and Sapphire also departed, each having accepted temporary military posts. Sapphire now rode with the cavalry under the command of Earl Kestrel. Jet was learning to hate drilling with the foot soldiers and to hate even more their sly smiles as they invited him night after night to join them on visits to the camp followers' tents.

Elise was glad to see them go. Sapphire's pain was obvious to her though her cousin hid it bravely. Elise feared that her own sympathy would seem too knowing and so guarded her own words and then worried that she seemed cold. Every word Jet spoke, every courtly gesture he made infuriated Elise, but this fury was directed not at him, but at herself for allowing romanticism and ambition to overwhelm her native good sense.

Their departure left Elise with Melina and Opal just as she had planned. She brought out a cunningly crafted miniature game board. For a while they played hopping pegs and gossiped just as if they were at home. When Ninette brought out elegant goblets of strongly flavored mint cordial, Elise dissolved the sleeping powder into two of them. Lady Melina and Opal, absorbed in counting the score and arguing over the values of various strategies, never saw her.

When Melina drank her goblet to the last honey-green drop, Elise felt like dancing. Opal, ever her mother's shadow, did the same. Glancing at Ninette, Elise hid a smile at the sign the other woman made her. As planned, Ninette had shared her mistress's hospitality with the sour crone who waited on Lady Melina. The signal meant that Nanny too had drunk the sleeping draught. Elise's part in the exchange of the necklace was completed.

And indeed after another round of their game, Lady Melina yawned, delicately patting her lips with a beringed hand.

"I apologize, dear Elise. It must be all your good food on top of rising with the sun. I am so tired I can hardly keep my eyes open."

Opal blinked owlishly. "Me, too. May I beg to be excused?"

Elise feigned drowsiness herself. "Of course. Let me walk you back to your pavilions. Ninette will dash ahead and tell Nanny to expect you."

She escorted her guests back and returned to her own tent, brimming with triumph. Then she set in place the river cobble Firekeeper had brought her the night before. It was a pretty thing when seen in daylight, greyish white, veined with black, smooth-polished by the rapidly flowing waters of the Barren.

Elise settled in to wait for Firekeeper to arrive and claim the substitute necklace. Surfeited with success, she worked a piece of embroidery near a lamp to pass the time.

Time passed. Ninette finished cleaning up from the dinner party and came in to help Elise braid her hair for bed. More time passed. Ninette went into her own curtained alcove and blew out her candle. Still more time passed. Elise finished one rose and began on another. She heard the guards change shifts and fought sleep.

After the second guard shift, Elise was no longer tired. She realized that something had happened to delay Firekeeper, perhaps for the entire night. It need not be that the wolf-woman was in any difficulty. Undoubtedly she had been sent scouting. She might not return before dawn. Elise pricked the canvas and drew some pink thread through, her mind racing.

She could not hope to give Lady Melina the sleeping drug twice and go undetected. Perhaps it was her own nervousness, but the more she remembered the sorceress's gaze the more it seemed to her that beneath the drowsiness there had been a hint of suspicion. The embroidery canvas dropped unheeded into Elise's lap. She knew what the only course of action left to her was, but she took another several minutes to work herself up to it.

Then, moving like one in a dream, Elise rose from her cot. Among her clothing were some riding breeches dyed dark forest green and a matching long-sleeved blouse. Donning these, Elise then stepped into the soft leather house slippers she wore around the tent, for she was no Firekeeper to go barefoot. Lastly, she tucked the substitute necklace into the band of her breeches.

Walking softly on the carpeted floors of the pavilion was easy. She left her lit candle on the table, protected by a tin shield, and stepped into the night.

Outside, the stars and moon were dimmed by light high clouds that raced along, pushed by a wind unfelt by those on the ground. Elise waited until her eyes adjusted to the dimmer light, then moved purposefully toward the Shield encampment.

There were many more tents here than in her own doss: a smallish one for Jet, one large enough to stand in for Sapphire and Opal, a square-bodied one for Lord Rolfston, and a fine pavilion for Lady Melina. Sometimes Opal slept with her mother. Other times Nanny did so. Only Lord Rolfston must negotiate to share his wife's sleeping space. Lady Melina claimed he snored.

When she passed his tent Elise had to agree. The deep, steady vibrations shook the air even through the muffling of thick canvas. Within, the noise must be terrible. Elise fought down a nervous desire to giggle. Then the realization of what she was about to do hit her and she sobered instantly.

Reaching Lady Melina's pavilion, Elise ducked inside before she could lose her nerve. The air was thick and muggy with trapped breath. The interior of the pavilion seemed so dark and close that she nearly panicked and ran outside again, never mind her mission. Then she stilled herself.

Over the last several days she had been in here many times, usually fetching something Lady Melina had forgotten. Opal hated running errands for her mother and such a menial task was beneath Nanny's dignity. Both had been happy that the newly dutiful daughter-in-law was willing to do it.

Now Elise called the floor plan into her mind's eye, counted the steps as she had done earlier when she had intended to pass the information on to Firekeeper, never dreaming she would need it for herself. At six steps, just as she had estimated, her hand touched the curtain. Another three steps and she could hear Lady Melina's breathing. There was no mistaking the characteristic scent of lilacs that permeated her bed linens.

Firekeeper claimed to know how to see in the dark, but Elise had no such skill. Instead, she moved her hand to where the top of Melina's head should be. Slowly, carefully, she brought it down until she touched ever so lightly the top of the older woman's head. Tracing her fingertips along the sleeping woman's hair, Elise estimated where her throat must be.

The next step was something she never would have dared if she hadn't known Melina was drugged. She touched her again, hoping to feel the body-warmed silver of the necklace. Instead she felt skin. Again. Again skin. A desperate terror rose within her. What if Lady Melina took the necklace off after all and stowed it away? What if this was all a terrible mistake?

Resisting the impulse to flee, Elise tried again. On her fourth try, she touched metal. A sob of relief rose unbidden in her throat. She swallowed it before she made any but the faintest sound, then stood like a stone, listening. All she heard was the steady, distant roar of Lord Rolfston's snoring.

Reaching with both hands now, Elise slid her fingers along the necklace until she felt the clasp. Undoing this without being able to see it proved nearly impossible. Her hands fumbled until she pretended that she was reaching up behind her own neck, undoing a similar clasp as she had hundreds, even thousands of times before. The clasp opened and she slipped the necklace off.

Grasping the necklace in her teeth, Elise quickly took the counterfeit from her waistband. Thankfully, it was warm from contact with her body. She placed it against the sleeping woman's throat. Melina stirred restlessly, muttered something.

Hurriedly, Elise fastened the clasp. The original necklace still held between her teeth because she did not trust herself not to drop it, Elise turned slowly, walked three steps, and found the curtain.

The doorway out of the pavilion was comparatively easy to find, the variance between dark and darker easy for her adjusted eye to see. Six steps and she was to the pavilion door and outside. Not wanting to cross the Shield compound again, she slipped behind Lady Melina's tent. Now she dropped the necklace into her hand, holding it so tightly the metal dented the skin. Elise was nearly back to her own tent when she realized someone had followed her.

Sapphire Shield, clad in a long sleeping gown that looked black in the faint starlight but was almost certainly dark blue, stood in the open ground in front of the Archer tent watching her. She motioned Elise into Elise's own pavilion. Elise obeyed, not because Sapphire held her bare sword in her hands but because she wanted the relative privacy. Her father and his man were with Baron Archer's command. Only Ninette was within and she knew everything of importance.

When they were inside, Sapphire said in low tones:

"I saw you coming out of my mother's tent."

"Yes," Elise said calmly, revealing what she held in her hand. "I've stolen your mother's necklace."

482 / JANE LINDSKOLD

Sapphire's eyes narrowed in suspicion. Even in light from the single candle on the table, Elise could see her hand move restlessly along the hilt of her sword. A pang of pure terror soured Elise's stomach. What other controls might Melina Shield have put on her children? But Sapphire said only a single word.

"Why?"

The truth rose unbidden to Elise's lips. "I want to set you free."

Sapphire's eyes widened. "How much do you know?"

"Enough. Enough to know about pain that never fades from wounds that seem to be healing and about the biting of ants."

"We must do it tonight," Sapphire said. "Before my mother learns anything is different."

"I left a substitute," Elise said with pardonable pride.

"I'm certain it is beautifully crafted," Sapphire said, "but can we be certain it is enough?"

Elise shook her head. "No, we can't, but I know nothing about how to perform a disenchantment."

A husky voice spoke from the doorway. "Hazel Healer may know. We must ask her."

Firekeeper stood in the doorway, the oval river rock in her hand.

"I only just come," she explained, "from across the river. I see this, then I hear. You not need me after all, Elise."

Elise nearly crumpled, her knees suddenly weak as she realized that all her risk had been for nothing. Then she straightened.

"I handled it," she said simply. "And my cousin is right. We need to do something with this as soon as possible."

Firekeeper turned. "Then I am away to Hazel. Can you two come to her house or do I bring her here?"

Elise glanced at Sapphire. Sapphire frowned thoughtfully.

"The road to town is going to be watched and we'll be obvious. There's no rule against our going to town, but I'd prefer not to raise comment. These tents with their canvas walls are as public as a street."

A wicked grin lit the wolf-woman's face. "Why not the forest? I think every sort of thing goes on in that forest. I meet you there with Hazel."

"Do you think she'll come?" Elise asked.

"Oh, yes," Firekeeper grinned again, and Elise found herself thinking what a predatory thing a smile could be. "I will ask her very nicely."

ELISE TOOK ADVANTAGE OF THE WALK to the edge of the forest to tell Sapphire everything she knew, including what they had learned from Hazel about both trance induction and enchantment. In return, Sapphire told her a little about what it was like being a daughter of Melina Shield.

"I'm not certain I have ever had a choice of my own in my entire life," Sapphire said. Her tone was blunt, without a trace of whining. "And much of the time I'm not certain I even minded. While others worried about what color to wear, I always knew. My jewels, my horses, my pets, even my playmates were all neatly chosen within two parameters: whether they were blue and whether they fit the traditions and mystique of my noble ancestors."

"And you never minded?" Elise asked hesitantly.

Sapphire shrugged. "It didn't seem much different from how everyone else I knew lived. My parents didn't encourage us to cultivate friends outside of the Great Houses. There was even some debate about your suitability, you know."

"Oh?"

"Yes. Archer *is* a lesser house, but in the end Mother decided that the close relationship to the Crown could not be ignored. Moreover, your mother is a Wellward and intimate with the queen."

"I see."

Sapphire's tone was so matter-of-fact that Elise found it easy not to take offense. Her cousin was reporting history—past history—not getting in a subtle dig.

"When did you start," Elise asked, changing the subject, "resenting your mother's control?"

"Not until recently," Sapphire admitted, "not until you and Jet pushed me down in the running for the Crown and diminished me in her eyes. Then I got angry at her as well as at you."

"Not at your father?"

"Father," Sapphire said in those same level tones, "doesn't matter. He has never mattered. He may be the king's nephew, the only son of Grand Duke Gadman, but he doesn't matter—except that he has good connections and came with generous holdings."

They had reached the forest trail by then. Casting about with the narrow beam from their lantern, they found a fallen tree trunk set alongside the path several paces within the fringe of trees. The lack of bark and low polish along its upper surface testified that they were not the first to employ it as a bench.

Once they were seated, they turned the lantern low so as not to waste oil. A chance play of light touched the faceted sapphire set in the band on Sapphire's forehead.

"I never asked," Elise said, "but I've always wondered, doesn't that headband get uncomfortable?"

Sapphire laughed softly. "You know, I don't even notice it, no more than you notice your shoes if they fit well. I've been wearing it—or one like it—since I was a year old. I'd feel strange without it—naked."

"You wear it even to sleep or bathe?"

"Always," Sapphire assured her. "The only time I haven't worn a headpiece like this is when I removed one to replace it with another."

"Does your mother make any sort of fuss then?"

"You're thinking of sorcery, aren't you?"

"Well, yes."

"She does, actually," Sapphire admitted. "The stone from one headband has to be set into the new one—even *our* family can't afford to replace precious stones of the first water as fast as children grow."

Snob! Elise thought defensively. Then she felt rather bad. Sapphire was taking a stand against her mother, the person who had defined every waking moment of her life. Certainly, she had the right to hold on to some scrap of pride. Then an uncomfortable thought slipped its way in beneath Elise's sympathy.

What if she isn't taking a stand? What if she's just trying to learn what we know and then plans to turn us over to Lady Melina?

Unbidden, Elise's hand touched her lips as if already the fiery bites of red ants were lacerating the tender flesh. And Sapphire continued, her voice soft but steady in the darkness:

"Mother had studied how to set the stones herself and while she did so I had to sit by and wait. She always gave me something to drink, something rather sweet, that made me feel dreamy. After a while, I'd stop feeling anxious about the funny feeling along my brow where the sapphire should rest."

Sapphire paused for a moment, then whispered, her words barely audible, "When I was very small, I thought I stopped existing when the stone wasn't there. I was Sapphire—somehow that stone was me—when it wasn't touching me, I was no longer myself. I wasn't anyone."

"It hasn't always been the same stone," Elise said, "has it?"

"No." Elise felt her cousin shudder so violently that the log vibrated beneath them. "Until I was about Citrine's age it was a different stone, a smaller one. Then Mother decided that the smaller one didn't make the same impression. I still remember when she took the band off and, instead of removing the stone to set in the new band, put it to one side.

"I screamed when she started setting the new stone. What I felt was raw panic. I shook. I was nauseated. Tears nearly choked me.

"Only when Mother let me hold the little stone did I calm down. For a while, she let me carry it in an amulet bag like the common folk use. Then she took it away. By then I was comfortable with the new stone, even liked it better. The color was more vibrant and the cut better. People admired it. I didn't miss the old stone anymore."

"And the new stone," Elise asked, "that's the one you're wearing now."

"That's right."

"I hope you can give it up," said Hazel Healer, stepping out from the shadows, Firekeeper a pace behind her, "because that is going to be the first step, whatever we do."

The cousins jumped and Sapphire asked, "How long have you been there?"

"Longer than you have," Hazel answered easily. "Firekeeper was probably to my house before you changed out of your nightdress and found a lantern. She is very direct, she is. My mare is used to night calls, and I keep my bag packed and beside her in the stables. Even with taking the road around the camp, we made good time. No one stops a healer, you see, not even army pickets."

Elise felt Sapphire relax slightly and smiled. Her own heart was thudding in her chest but she was obscurely relieved now that someone else was there to share the responsibility.

"You were doing so well," Hazel continued, "telling Elise about your mother that I didn't want to interrupt, but time is running short. The sleeping draught Elise gave your mother should last all night, but varying metabolisms react differently to drugs. Therefore, I interrupted as soon as our course of action became clear."

"Clear?" Elise asked.

"That's right." Hazel didn't elucidate further. "Firekeeper said there is a glade a bit deeper in where a light wouldn't be seen so we can turn up the lanterns. She's gone ahead to kindle a fire."

Elise looked around and, indeed, the wolf-woman had disappeared.

"Still with us?" she asked Sapphire.

When Sapphire bent to pick up their lantern, Elise saw that her cousin was dreadfully pale beneath her tan, but when she replied her voice was steady. "I'm with you. I'll walk first with the lantern. Let Mistress Healer come last leading the horse."

In the glen where—as Elise would later learn—Prince Newell and Lady Zorana lingered for dalliance and met with disaster, Firekeeper had a steady fire burning within a ring of river rocks. A small copper pot—hardly larger than an apple and polished so bright as to look almost pink—was slung over the flames.

"From my emergency kit," Hazel explained, tying her mare, a brown horse unremarkable for anything but its calm, to a bush. "You won't believe how often you need hot water fast and the best thing available is a kettle large enough to make stew for an entire harvest crew and cast of thick iron besides. Now, let's get comfortable."

Under her calm authority, Elise positioned her lamp and two more from Hazel's gear so that, without shedding undue light outside of the glen, they had enough that they could read each other's expressions. Firekeeper brought over a couple of logs to act as benches and when the water boiled Elise brewed rosehip tea. Sapphire set more water to heat and then Hazel indicated that she was ready to continue.

"From what you told Lady Elise," she said to Sapphire, "the sapphire—indeed the entire headpiece—is symbolic to you of the identity which your mother has crafted for you. Is that right?"

Sapphire nodded. "Of who I am."

"And who you are is someone under Lady Melina's control," Hazel stated unapologetically. "And don't try to deny it. I saw how you favored your side while you were helping set up our little parlor here. I've spoken at length with Sir Jared about his talent. Your injury should be mending now without pain. The wounds were superficial, though ugly, and were treated almost immediately."

Sapphire bit her lip, then nodded stiffly. "It has been fourteen days. Very well. I accept that my mother has the ability to inflict pain on me, pain I shouldn't feel. I'll even admit that she's done it other times, though I never remember feeling this angry about it before. What I want to know is do you think this is sorcery or that trance induction that Elise told me about?"

Hazel sighed. "I wish Elise hadn't told you quite so much. It will make our task more difficult. To be blunt, I don't know. However, I don't think it matters . . ."

"Doesn't matter!" Sapphire said with a fury that Elise realized was mostly fear. "It doesn't matter whether my mother is a sorceress or merely skilled in some form of controlling the mind? How couldn't it matter?"

Hazel ignored the anger and answered the question. "Because the tool which she used to effect her control is the same in either case. It doesn't matter because if we can—if you can—destroy that means, then the hold should be broken."

I wonder, Elise thought uneasily, *just how much Hazel is bluffing. She didn't seem to know this much when we consulted her ten days ago.*

"I've been reading about related matters ever since Elise brought her own problem to me," Hazel said as if in answer, "and have consulted most privately with various colleagues. Lady Melina's fondness for the showy gesture—for using her power over you to enhance her own reputation rather than keeping it quiet—may be her undoing. However, I can only show you the way. I cannot do any more."

"What," Sapphire said, "as if I can't already guess, do I need to do?"

Hazel ignored her for a moment. Removing the boiling water from over the fire, she poured some into a round pottery cup, then shook in powder from a folded paper packet. This done, she covered the cup and asked:

"Elise, how much trouble did you have telling Sapphire about your discovery of Lady Melina's powers?"

"Not much," Elise replied, slightly puzzled at this change of subject. "I felt shy, of course. It's hard to admit you've been spying on people, even by accident."

"But you didn't feel any pain? No ants biting your tongue?"

"No!" Elise was surprised. "But why should I? Sapphire already knew the truth."

Hazel turned to look at Sapphire. "Tell me, is that the usual way with your mother's curses? Do they work only when you try to talk to the uninformed?"

Sapphire shook her head. "I haven't really tried, not for years, but we never could talk about what she had forbidden, not even to each other, not without bringing down the curse."

"So, you see, Elise," Hazel said, "what you did is remarkable."

"Do you think it's because we replaced my jet piece?" Elise asked eagerly.

"Yes, I do. When you removed the means by which Lady Melina had laid her hold on you, that hold was broken."

"Then all I need to do," Sapphire said, her disbelief evident, "is take off my coronet?"

"I fear not," Hazel said sadly. "Lady Melina's control over you is of much greater duration and her curse laid upon you directly. For you to break her hold, not only must you remove the sapphire from your brow, you must destroy it."

There was a long silence. When Sapphire spoke her voice was no longer that of the confident, even arrogant, warrior and noblewoman but of a very young girl.

"I can't!" she wailed.

"Then you are doomed to remain bound."

"Wait!" Elise said. "Sapphire was talking to me before with no trouble. Maybe the hold is already broken."

"No," Hazel said sadly. "Think back. She told you about very general things. The closest she came to anything sensitive was when she mentioned her panic whenever the sapphire was removed—she said nothing that couldn't be dismissed as superstition. I'd guess Sapphire knows her own limits very well."

"I do," the other admitted dully. "Perfectly."

Firekeeper, who had hovered at the edge of the firelight, her back to them so as not to diminish her night vision, spoke for the first time.

"So we are ended before we begin?"

"No," Sapphire replied with sudden stubborn decisiveness, "I won't let myself be."

Her hands rose to the elegant band about her brow, rose, fell, and rose again. Elise could see them shaking as Sapphire fumbled for a catch.

"It's beneath the stone setting," Sapphire said, her voice a weak semblance of normalcy. "Nice bit of design, really."

Hazel strained the mixture in the pottery cup and offered it to Sapphire. "It will calm you. I suspect it's similar to what your mother gave you."

"Then I don't want it!" Sapphire snarled.

With a violent tug she snapped the strap. Elise heard a slight metallic ping as the silver wire parted.

The torn strip dangling from her hand, Sapphire asked, "And now?"

"And now," Hazel replied, "I'm afraid you're going to need to crush or break the stone. That won't be easy. Sapphires are quite hard, not as hard as diamonds, but almost."

"Gem cutters manage," Sapphire said, the words sounding torn from her. Unable to speak further, she put out her free hand in a mute request for tools.

Hazel said apologetically, "I couldn't get a gem cutter's wheel in the middle of the night, but I do have a hammer with a steel head. We can use a large river cobble for an anvil."

Firekeeper brought the latter, pausing to put her hand on Sapphire's shoulder. Even this slight delay had started Sapphire trembling again, but she stiffened at Firekeeper's touch.

Elise wondered if Sapphire could not bear pity—or what she perceived as pity—from a potential rival. For whatever reason, Sapphire steadied enough to kneel and place the damaged headpiece flat across the cobble, the blue gem in its center glittering like a single eye in the lantern light.

Raising the hammer, Sapphire swung with all the power of muscles trained to use of sword and shield. A thin cry slipped out between teeth locked in a death's-head grimace. The bright steel arced down, a blur rather than a solid thing. There was the sound of metal hitting rock, a sharp stink as of sulphur, a crack . . .

Elise stared in disbelief. Sapphire's blow had struck the cobble, not the sapphire, splitting the rounded stone in two. Bending forward, her long black hair masking her face, the hammer clutched in both hands, Sapphire was whimpering hysterically:

"I can't, I can't, I can't . . . It will kill me if I do. My soul . . . I can't." The repetitious rhythm of her chant was more terrifying than any scream could be.

"You must!" Elise pleaded, hearing her own voice shrill despite her efforts to keep it level. "You must!"

"I can't!" Sapphire snapped, sitting straight in a sudden motion like an arrow shot from a bow. "I can't . . ."

And her voice sank again.

In the shocked silence, Firekeeper's return with a new cobble seemed as prosaic as a shopkeeper polishing counters on a slow day. She crouched beside Sapphire, removed the split cobble, and placed the headpiece in the new cobble's center.

"I think," the wolf-woman commented sardonically, "that you are like the Whiner in my pack. She is great hunter except when anyone bigger face her. She even afraid of me!"

Firekeeper's laughter made plain how ridiculous she found the thought of any wolf fearing a naked, clawless, fangless creature like herself.

"I'm not afraid of you!" Sapphire gasped, her gaze still downcast, safe within the sheltering tent of her hair.

"I not say you are, but your mother, she the great One of your pack and never will her pups rise to challenge her. Never even will they disperse to found their own packs. You are poor, sad creatures: can't piss, can't eat, can't breed without mama's word."

That "mama" was said with a rich sneer to Firekeeper's voice, a sneer that Elise noted did not reach her face. Sapphire only heard the mockery and some faint shred of pride in her responded.

Raising her head, she glared at Firekeeper. "You dare! I am a Shield and grandniece to a king."

"You are a weak-spined, mewling pup," Firekeeper said savagely. "You dine only on the regurgitated pap from your mother's gut. You crouch so in her shade that you fear a blue rock! A rock!"

She laughed, a cruel sound from deep in her belly, and from the shadows Blind Seer sniggered agreement.

"I'll break your head!" Sapphire shouted, leaping to her feet and swinging the hammer at Firekeeper.

Firekeeper blocked her, hand grasping the descending forearm and squeezing, forcing the infuriated woman to face the glimmering blue eye of the sapphire on the rock.

"A pup," Firekeeper said steadily, "attacks a butterfly to show how big he is. So you attack me naked and unarmed as I am—you with steel death in your hands—because you are a pup. If you are so terrible, smash that blue stone."

"I thought you said," Sapphire retorted, twisting but unable to get free, "that it was just a stone."

"Then why," came the reasonable voice, just showing the edge of the effort Firekeeper was exerting to hold the larger woman in place, "don't you break it?"

She let go then and Sapphire's own twisting spun her to the ground in front of the makeshift altar with its mute sacrificial victim across it. With one hand Sapphire caressed the faceted surface as if it were the face of a lover, perhaps recalling the years during which it had adorned her brow, the fairest gem of its type in all the land.

Then Sapphire grasped the hammer with two hands, raised it above her head, and brought the steel head down with the force not only of her arms, but of the entire weight of her body behind it.

Elise surged to her feet, unable to look away, unable to remain still, knowing in her heart that if Sapphire missed this time, if the gem refused to break, if she lost courage at the last moment, that there would never be another attempt, that this was the last chance and if it failed everything—even the stealing of Lady Melina's necklace—would have been for nothing.

When the hammer rose, a fine blue dust littered with tiny fragments of gemstone sparkled on the river rock, brighter even than the tears that glittered in Sapphire Shield's eyes. But Sapphire did not weep, only said:

"I guess I'd better have the matching stone from Mother's necklace. We'd better do a thorough job of this."

Elise wrenched the pendant holding the sapphire from the band. Not bothering to remove the gemstone from the silver that framed it, Sapphire smashed it, her first blow breaking the diamond-shaped stone, her second thoroughly flattening the silver and breaking the gem to pieces.

Rising to her feet a bit unsteadily, Sapphire looked at Firekeeper. "Still think me a pup?"

"I think you a great woman," came the reply, and Firekeeper bowed low. Beside her the enormous grey wolf bowed as well.

Hazel said then, "Do we destroy the rest of the necklace here and now, or should we preserve it for the others?"

"I think," Sapphire said, "that it must be preserved as proof that this can be done. It's going to be hard enough to convince my brother and sisters as it is."

"And you," Hazel asked, "how do you feel?"

"Like I've jumped off a cliff only to be caught by water at the bottom and nearly drowned. My knees are shaking, my head is throbbing, and," Sapphire grinned, "my side has stopped hurting. I don't think I've felt better in a long, long time."

"How do you plan to hide from Lady Melina what you've done?" Elise hardly recognized her own voice when she spoke.

"I don't. It's time Mother realized that her control of me is over and here in this camp with King Tedric near at hand she should moderate her response to what she will see as my rebellion."

"Do you plan to tell her what . . . what we . . . what you . . . suspect?"

Sapphire shook her head. "Not at all. There's no need. I think I'll just tell Mother that I got tired of her taste in jewelry."

The laughter that followed this announcement was too loud, too ragged to be cheerful, but it held a bravado more warming than the bright yellow-orange flames of the campfire.

XXIV

PRINCE NEWELL SHIELD NOTED his sister Melina's outrage when Sapphire stopped wearing the gem-studded headpiece that had been hers since she was small, and thought Melina's reaction disproportionate.

Certainly a young woman of twenty-three—one who had been her mother's cat's-paw for her entire life—should be expected to rebel at some point. Melina should be grateful that Sapphire had chosen to discard a piece of jewelry rather than, say, one of the numerous titled young men Melina had betrothed to her, only to break the engagement when one more advantageous seemed possible.

He told Melina as much and her rage was so great that he deemed a retreat advisable. Calling for Rook to saddle the red roan, Newell went out to look for signs of war.

Things seemed promising. From Keen, who was recovering from his cut face hidden in a tavern in Good Crossing, Newell had learned that Bright Bay's troops were nervous and demoralized, trusting no one, not even—as the five days following the first battle with Stonehold produced no sign of Queen Gustin or her young husband, King Harwill—their own monarchs.

Allister Seagleam's role as commander in chief provided the troops no particular comfort. The duke had no great reputation as a warrior on land or at sea—although he had done nothing of which to be ashamed, either. Moreover, they resented him somewhat. The Stalwarts had marched out on a mission that should have been mostly play, to escort the Pledge Child to his uncle. Never had they dreamed that they might need to fight and, though Duke Allister was not responsible for the current situation, they blamed him nonetheless.

Additionally, knowing too much about a strong opponent was never a good thing for any army—and Bright Bay's Stalwarts of the Golden Sunburst knew far too much about Stonehold's Rocky Band. After all, until a slight eight days before, Stonehold's troops had been not only comrades under the same banner, but also the source of most of Bright Bay's noncommissioned officers: the sergeants and corporals who made things work when idealistic officers gave impossible commands.

The Stalwarts must feel, Newell thought, cupping his hand around his pipe and striving to light it despite a freshening wind from the north, rather like children who suddenly found themselves challenging their teachers. He liked the image and played with it as he gave up on the pipe and cantered Serenity along a road running west then turning south along the edge of the rough foothills west of Good Crossing.

If Stonehold was bringing in reinforcements, they might be visible from this general direction. Stonehold's border with Bright Bay was the Fox River, a river as broad and difficult to span as the Barren itself. Indeed both the Fox and the Barren had their source in Rimed Lake, high in the mountains to the west. The same volcano whose eruption long ago had split Rimed Lake into two fat lobes had spilled molten rock down its eastern side, creating the Barren Lands, a place where nothing grew but those determined plants that could subsist on dirt caught within crevices in the basalt.

Even at the foot of the flow, where Newell now slowed Serenity to a more cautious pace as the road roughened, the volcano's influence could be seen, but here trees had managed a roothold and a struggling forest had grown up. He felt secure continuing south under the cover of the trees, knowing that Hawk Haven had posted scouts throughout this area.

Moreover, the day was pleasant. Here, away from the river's immediate influence, Newell noted a kiss of autumn in the air. Good campaigning weather, but the harvest would be ripening, making foraging easier for both sides.

He was thinking about how he would handle an extended campaign through this area when a flicker of motion caught his eye. Drawing Serenity up, Newell was poised either for flight or to take cover when a rather grubby woman stepped from cover. She wore the green uniform of the scouts, her arm banded in Kite blue with a chestnut stallion embroidered upon it.

Newell didn't recognize her, but she clearly knew him.

"Prince Newell," she said, her voice was rusty, as if she hadn't spoken for hours. "I am Joy Spinner, scout under the command of Earle Kite, posted to this point. May I ask your business here?"

"I came to check the situation," Newell said honestly. "I grew restless in camp. There were no signs that Stonehold would make a major push today so I decided to see if there were any signs of why they were waiting."

Finishing his speech, Prince Newell unscrewed the top of his wine flask and offered Joy Spinner a pull of the dry white wine within. The scout accepted, then looked at him squarely with eyes the color of violets.

"Your timing is fine, sir," she said. "My ancestors must have put you on the road. You see, not long ago I spotted something interesting to the south. I don't dare leave my post to report it—we've had trouble with Stoneholders trying to slip through here—but I think King Tedric and Duke Allister should know."

"And your relief?"

"Not due for hours. Even the officer who's checking the posts isn't due for a while."

"What have you seen?" Prince Newell asked, a tingling in his breast making him certain that this very moment was the beginning of his time to be a hero, even as he had dreamed.

"Let me show you," Joy said. "Your horse will be safe here."

They crept through the brush to the basalt outcropping from which

Joy had been keeping watch. It was a good lookout, set higher than much of the surrounding area but offering perfect concealment. Joy checked something with her long glass, then handed the glass to Newell.

"Look there, just where I was. Site along the road as it leaves the field along which Stonehold is encamped. The road itself vanishes when the land dips, but it heads roughly south, bending a bit east. I won't say more—I want to know if you see what I do."

Prince Newell did as Joy had requested, finding the road easily enough. Over the past five days he had pored over the superior interior maps of Bright Bay supplied by Duke Allister over the grumbling protests of some of his advisors. These maps, added to the information Newell had already memorized from Hawk Haven's own maps, came to him as he obeyed Joy Spinner's instructions.

One of the reasons that the Fox River made such an effective barrier between Bright Bay and Stonehold was that it flared out into a broad marshy delta many miles before it met the ocean. In the summer these marshes bred disease. Even in the winter one had to be an expert to navigate them without grief. No large force, especially one with horses and armored troops, could cross through them.

The middle stretches of the Fox were too broad and deep to be forded, even in the autumn when there was no snowmelt to augment the flow and when irrigation of fields had lowered the river further. The Fox was bridged in several places, the nearest of which was due south and east of Good Crossing.

Mason's Bridge was hardly close—indeed, miles of Bright Bay–held lands lay between their current battlefield and the bridge. Reports from the south, however, informed them that Stonehold had secured Mason's Bridge before the local Bright Bay pickets—hardly more than toll collectors—even knew there was trouble between the countries.

Since then, the other bridges across the Fox—or at least their northern ends—had been secured or destroyed by troops sent out from Silver Whale Cove. These now patrolled the Bright Bay side of the Fox, reducing the chances that Stonehold would abandon their attack on Good Crossing and strike for the capital. This necessary expenditure of troops had further reduced those reinforcements which Bright Bay could bring to the immediate battle and had increased the low morale of the Stalwarts, who once again found themselves the lesser part of an army defending their own country.

Now Newell traced the road more by memory than by sight, quickly spotting what Joy Spinner had seen. The Stoneholders weren't foolhardy; they knew that the less their opponents could see the better. The troops marching along that road showed no metal that might flash in the sun; their wagons were tarped over to conceal what they carried. The road they traveled was packed, but even so many feet raised a thin column of dust.

Prince Newell drew in his breath with a sharp hiss. "So Stonehold sends reinforcements to augment those who currently hold the ground south of Good Crossing! Surely Bright Bay's people will rise against them!"

Joy Spinner spat eloquently. "The folk of Bright Bay look to the ocean, not the land. Too long have they relied on Stonehold mercenaries to keep Hawk Haven from claiming their lands for our own. All those poor farmers and herders will look to defend will be their harvest and flocks. If Stonehold's Rocky Band will cross and leave their livelihood unmolested, then they will let them pass."

"And judging from the supply wagons," mused Prince Newell, "the commanders are wise enough to not give the common folk of Bright Bay reason to turn soldier. Stonehold's Rocky Band is well disciplined. They won't loot the lands through which they pass—especially if they know that supplies await them at the end."

"And with the supplies being protected by columns of troops," Joy added, "no farmer will be tempted to turn bandit. They've thought it through all right. Some of their reinforcements may travel more slowly, but everything will get here intact."

Prince Newell handed Joy the long glass and turned back toward where Serenity waited.

"I wonder," he said thoughtfully, "just when those wagons started their trip?" He shook himself. Now was a time for action, not speculation. "Scout Spinner, trust my horse and myself to carry the message as swiftly as we can. I think the time for stealth has ended."

Joy nodded. "Good. I will keep my post. Ride safely, Prince Newell. Doubtless someone else has seen the signs, but we may be first."

Newell smiled. "First or last, the news is still important."

As Newell swung into the saddle, Serenity pawed the ground, catching his rider's excitement and eager to be away.

"I will see you in Hope!" Newell cried. Touching his heels to the red roan's flanks, he was away.

He did not look back, nor did he doubt in the least that he cut a perfectly dashing figure.

SERENITY WAS NEARLY FRESH, for the morning's ride had been easy and the gelding was in good fettle. Newell pressed his mount to speed wherever the road permitted. No matter what he had said to Joy Spinner, he wanted to be the first with the news. Even if he was not, eagerness would count for something.

Both Newell and Serenity were nicely sweated and covered with road dust when they arrived outside of the commanders' pavilions in the encampment outside of Good Crossing's walls. Stumbling from the saddle on legs tired and sore, Newell tossed Serenity's reins to the first guard he saw. Then he gasped:

"The king, where is he?"

"Within," the guard replied, "in consultation. What . . ."

Newell looked sternly at him. "Tend my mount, good man. My news is urgent and for King Tedric's ears alone."

Such vagueness was certain to start rumors. Prince Newell trusted that his dutiful discretion would have the troops swearing to each other that Stonehold was arriving within the hour, armed with war machines meant to batter the walls of Good Crossing until one stone did not stand on another. Why else would a prince ride so hard and look so grim?

Sir Dirkin Eastbranch paused in his steady pacing about the perimeter of the king's pavilion to nod to his subordinate.

"Let the prince pass," he said.

Pleased, Newell pushed back the curtain door, knowing that in a few minutes he would be able to collapse into a comfortable chair while servants pulled his boots off his aching feet and put a glass of wine into his hand. Such pleasures were good indeed, especially upon what might well be the eve of war.

TWO MEN LISTENED WHILE Prince Newell gave his report. It was a small enough audience, but as one of these men was King Tedric and the other was Duke Allister, the prince felt sufficiently rewarded for his hard ride. He even forgot that his aching feet had not been tended. King Tedric had apparently dispensed with servants for the moment.

When Newell finished his report, King Tedric frowned:

"Estimated numbers?"

"I'm not precisely certain, Your Majesty," Newell replied. "I was catching glimpses through the trees. Several companies, well armed, I believe. I'd guess that when they're added to those Stonehold has pulled from their recent service throughout Bright Bay they'll be a match for what we have gathered here."

"Your report," the king said, "confirms speculations that we have had from our spies—reports that to this point have been but rumors. You have done well, Newell."

The prince bowed and tried to look humble rather than gloating.

Duke Allister managed a wry grin. "Evidently Generals Yuci and Grimsel doubted that Stonehold could defeat us with those forces they already had in place so they risked our own reinforcements arriving while they brought in their troops."

King Tedric nodded wearily. "A reasonable risk for them to take. The distance from Hope to Eagle's Nest is easily as far as that to Mason's Bridge. Troops from my more northern lands have even farther to travel. True we can and have drawn troops from the more southern parts of the kingdom, but we cannot strip our border with Bright Bay any more than you can strip yours with Stonehold."

Duke Allister nodded, accepting that despite Hawk Haven coming to his country's aid perfect trust would not occur instantly. Leaving this issue unspoken, he added thoughtfully:

"And what use would a victory be to Stonehold if she lacked the forces to occupy Good Crossing after her troops had taken it? Now they have their greater force and supplies to sustain them. Doubtless their commanders have left troops back along the road south so that further reinforcements can be brought through as needed."

"I wonder," Prince Newell said, attentive despite his honest weariness, "how those wagons managed to come so far so fast?"

Duke Allister sighed. "I suspect that many crossed Mason's Bridge and began the trip north days before the troops, maybe even as early as the very day that Queen Gustin was sent Stonehold's ultimatum. We have active trade with Stonehold—indeed, much of our steel and iron comes from there, for the Barren Lands are metal poor and block our access to the Iron Mountains your own nation mines."

"So," Newell frowned, "not even a heavily laden wagon would seem curious—not even if it clanked with quantities of finished metal."

"The only people who would look at those wagons would be the toll collectors, whose interest would be in judging how much each wagon should pay for crossing into Bright Bay," Duke Allister said. "We can send a pigeon to our garrison near Mason's Bridge for confirmation, but I think we have enough of a working theory to plan upon."

King Tedric unrolled the best of the maps of Bright Bay.

"Even if," he said, tracing his finger along the road south, "Stonehold has brought in fresh troops and more supplies, the length of their supply line home remains their greatest weakness."

"Yet we can't get our army around the mass of their army to get to those supplies or that road," Newell put in practically, rather enjoying pointing out the worst aspects of the situation. "Our troops would be spotted too easily as they crossed the open zone around Good Crossing. Generals Yuci and Grimsel did not strike me as tactically dull. They, too, must realize that their supply line is their vulnerable point and will be alert to efforts to harm it."

"They must," Allister agreed, "and yet they will wait to lessen their dependence on supplies from home until they have no choice. Looting and pillaging would awaken a new enemy all around them. Farmers armed with pitchforks or old spears scavenged from the family's ancestral shrine may not be much of a threat to a prepared army, but they could become a dangerous nuisance."

"And with the harvest ready to come in," Tedric added, "those farmers will be more easily enraged. No one, not even the most peaceful grower of wheat, likes to see an entire year's work vanish into someone else's mouth."

Prince Newell cleared his throat and asked anxiously, "How long do you think the Stoneholders will give us before they attack?"

"Until tomorrow," Tedric replied bluntly. "Perhaps they will wait until the next day, but from what you reported their troops were marching steadily, though not at a forced pace. Most should be ready for action after a night's rest."

"Might they attack tonight?" Allister asked.

"I think not," Tedric said after a moment's thoughtful pause, "but if they do, we will have ample warning—warning beyond the usual sounds or lights of their approach."

The king's thin smile held a hint of the indulgent grin he reserved for one favored person.

With a surge of envy, Prince Newell realized that Tedric meant that he expected Lady Blysse to bring Hawk Haven warning. Newell's envy turned into a peculiarly uncomfortable form of fear as he realized that the wolf-woman must have been scouting for the king ever since this war had been declared—and perhaps even before. What might she have seen?

He endeavored to look bluff and hearty.

"It's good to know we'll have warning, Sire. Our men will sleep better for the news."

"Whatever news you are envisioning spreading, Newell," the king ordered sternly, "keep it to yourself. One reason that Allister and I have kept our conferences as small as possible is that we cannot be certain who—especially among Bright Bay's forces—may still feel allied to Stone-hold."

"You must remember," Allister said a touch sadly, "that until a mere handful of days ago most of my nation's troops viewed Stonehold as a friend and her army as teachers. Although most are angry and offended by the recent betrayals, still, there must be some—maybe even some officers—who retain loyalty to those who taught them."

"And," Newell added bluntly, "who still hate us."

"Well," Allister said, "you *were* the enemy."

King Tedric sighed. "Newell, go gather the officers. It's time we gave a briefing."

"Yes, Your Majesty!" Newell replied, saluting smartly.

As he was leaving he heard the king say to Allister:

"I have a thought how we might deal with that supply line. Tell me what you think of this . . ."

RACE FORESTER CAME TO DERIAN Carter late that afternoon while Derian was checking the shoes and feet of the horses who—if all pro-gressed as anticipated—would carry their riders into battle tomorrow.

At Earl Kestrel's express command, Derian himself wasn't going to fight. He didn't know whether he felt relieved or angry. For the first time since Firekeeper had been given into his charge Derian felt as if he'd been demoted from a man's place to that of a boy.

Because of this, the sight of Race, clean-lined and military in his scout's uniform, made Derian scowl and dig at the stone lodged in Ox's bald-faced chestnut's shoe with rather more intensity than he should. The normally placid horse shuddered his skin and muttered equine warning. Queenie, who had been sniffing around the horse's heels, flinched away.

"Good afternoon to you, too, Derian Carter," Race said, leaning against one of the hitching posts and scratching Queenie behind the ears.

"Oh, Race," Derian said, flinging the stone away and pretending to notice the scout for the first time. "I didn't see you coming."

"And no wonder with that mountain of horseflesh hanging over you," Race said easily.

Derian, knowing he had been being rude, felt rather embarrassed. He pulled out a curry comb and began grooming the chestnut's coat.

"Ready for tomorrow, Race?"

"I suppose so," Race said. "For a bit there I thought I might be drafted into the archers at the last moment—someone had been bragging about how good I am with a bow—but the commander of scouts insisted he couldn't spare me."

"Great."

"Yes, it is rather nice having people argue over who will get your services." Race paused. "Isn't it?"

"I wouldn't know," Derian said stiffly.

"Oh?" Race drew closer and lowered his voice. "Then I must be the first to get to you. Derian, how do you feel about going into battle tomorrow?"

Derian kept his voice equally soft, though he felt like shouting in surprise and indignation.

"Me? I can't. Earl Kestrel has demanded that I stay with the horses. He says that both his and Duchess Merlin's units are short of farriers and my skill with horses far outweighs my skill with a sword."

Despite himself, Derian heard the bitterness in his voice.

"As if," he added, "Earl Kestrel has even noticed how I've kept in practice all these moon-spans."

"He's noticed more than you might imagine," Race said, "and he's said no more than the truth. There are few men—especially of your years—who are as good with a horse."

Derian grunted, accepting the compliment but not being particularly graceful about it. Race punched him in the shoulder with affectionate bluster.

"Young idiot," Race said. "Did you ever think that Earl Kestrel might want to keep you alive? King Tedric has made you one of his counselors. That's important not only to the king, but to the earl. Norwood's been preening ever since you were named—pointing out to his peers whenever he can that he knows how to pick a good man. But whether or not he wants to keep you alive, that's all out with the wash. There's been a change of plans."

"Change?" Derian suddenly felt frightened. It was one thing to scowl and brood about being overlooked when you were safely out of danger; it was quite another when that danger was immediate again.

Race nodded. "I was to tell you quietly if my commander hadn't gotten to you. I guess he hasn't. Are you about done with those nags?"

"About."

"Meet me at our camp," by this Race meant the new Kestrel camp on the southern bank of the Barren, "when you're done. Make sure you finish up properly because you might not make it back here tonight."

Derian did as Race had suggested, going over each horse carefully and consulting with the farrier from Hope—the same from whom he and Doc had bought medicine just days before—as to the strengths and weaknesses of the war mounts. These were huge, fierce horses, often intolerant of any but their handler, and working with them took special consideration.

Only when he was certain that he had discharged his duty to Earl Kestrel did Derian head for the camp, but he did so at a quick trot that was nearly a run. Overhead he heard Elation shrill something like laughter. The great peregrine had taken to following Derian about more often now that Firekeeper was scouting for the army and a beacon overhead would not be either welcome nor wise.

Arriving at the Kestrel camp, Derian found Race and Valet waiting for him. As before, their camp's location had been selected to permit Firekeeper to come and go without Blind Seer panicking the rest of the army. Backed against the Barren River, downstream from Good Crossing, they were the farthest group east but for the pickets who patrolled the camp's border.

506 / JANE LINDSKOLD

Across the river, Derian could see lights glowing in the Watchful Eye and along the northern side of the river. For the first time he realized that evening was gathering. Tomorrow if all rumors were correct, there would be battle, a massive thing that would make the battle a few days before—now called the Battle on the Banks—look like a minor skirmish.

And he might be in it. Not wanting to introduce the matter, Derian commented:

"I always meant to ask why we built the Watchful Eye on our side of the river but Bright Bay never built any similar fort on their side."

Valet poured him a cup of mulled cider and commented, "When the Civil War ended, Bright Bay received Good Crossing. Hope didn't exist then—just a few houses and farms as I understand it. The Watchful Eye was built to house the garrison that would protect this newly vulnerable point."

He fell silent, having been far more talkative than was his wont. Race added:

"Good Crossing had a watchtower—it's part of the walls now—and was a whole lot bigger. Hope grew up pretty fast, though, what with smuggling and tolls and soldiers to supply. I've heard that when it got to be a town rather than a cluster of houses they called it Hope because folks there hoped they wouldn't get attacked."

"My father," Derian said, "told me it was named for a hope for peace and reunification."

"Maybe," Race shrugged. "I'm no historian. Anyhow, thanks for getting here so quickly, Derian. I've got your marching orders, if you'll take them."

Derian nodded, swallowing cider despite the lump that suddenly appeared in his throat.

"Go on," he said.

"I was told to tell you that this was a request, not an order," Race began. He stopped, scratched his beard and started again. "Sorry, I'm not much good at speeches."

Derian wanted to strangle him, but waited with what patience he could muster.

"It's been decided," Race began again, "that Stonehold's biggest weak spot is that they've got a long way to go to get in their supplies. The king and the duke, though, they don't want to send the army after those supplies. They figure it would be too easy for Stonehold to defend them."

"Would it?" Derian asked.

"Well, I haven't been over there myself," Race said, "but from reports we've got they've got their wagons drawn up alongside the road that leads back to Mason's Bridge. They're keeping the road mostly open, but their camp is all along there as well as along the southern end of the field outside of Good Crossing.

"Now," Race continued, "if our army does succeed in breaking Stonehold's lines and going through we'll get those supplies, no question. The thing is, we may not break those lines, at least not right away. It might take days of fighting."

Derian refilled his mug, mostly to hide a shiver.

"And during those days," Race said, "they'll be bringing in more supplies and maybe even build good defenses for what they have. So, what King Tedric and Duke Allister have decided is that at the same time the main armies are hitting each other out on the field, a small group—one that could circle wide around the eastern fringes of the Stonehold camp and come in where they'll only have guards, not a whole army—that small group could come in and destroy as many of the supplies as possible."

Derian nodded. "That makes sense. If the group could get through, they could do real damage."

"Right." Race nodded. "Now, the problem is that the king and the duke figure that there are spies in the main army."

"Our army?" Derian asked, a little shocked, even though his common sense told him that this must be so. After all, didn't Hawk Haven have spies around Stonehold's army?

"If the spies got wind of this flank maneuver," Race said, "they would certainly tell their chiefs and perimeter patrols would be beefed up. So the raiders are being drawn from people who have the skills but aren't part of any regular units. Take me, for instance. I'm with the scouts, but I haven't given up my primary allegiance to Earl Kestrel. There's another scout—one who came with Earle Kite's group—who's also semi-independent."

Derian could see where Race was heading. He decided to anticipate it.

"And me? I'm one of Earl Kestrel's people, too."

"Right." Race puffed his chest a bit. "I told my commander that you'd learned a lot from me on the trip west—and more from taking care of Firekeeper."

"Is Firekeeper part of this, too?" Derian asked, momentarily dismayed that his true worth was actually as a watch on the wolf-woman.

"Actually," Race seemed embarrassed, "she's not. They discussed it and decided that Blind Seer would spook the Stonehold animals. It's happened a time or two already, when Firekeeper's been scouting for the king, but it hasn't mattered then because the two of them just took off before the guards could be sure of anything."

"Whereas we need to stay," Derian said.

"Another reason is that Firekeeper," Race shrugged, "just doesn't know how to pick a target. She wouldn't know how to figure out what's valuable and what's not. She's also fairly reluctant to kill people."

"A good thing," Derian said dryly, "given how good she is at killing game."

"True," Race agreed hastily, "but we can't have someone distracted by needing to give her orders or clarify a target. All the raiders need to be capable of initiative. King Tedric has spoken with Firekeeper already and she's agreed to stay out."

"I hope she listens to him better than she does to me," Derian said, recalling how Firekeeper had followed him and Doc into town.

"I think she will," Race said. "I think this entire concept of war has her rather confused."

Valet added quietly, "I agree. She is most distressed."

"I hadn't noticed," Derian admitted, "mostly because she's been away so much and I've been with the cavalry mounts where she doesn't dare come—not with Blind Seer."

"Talk with her," Valet urged. "You will have time before our departure."

"Our?" Derian looked at him. "Are you going along on this raid, too?"

"Earl Kestrel," Valet said with a faint sigh, "has requested I join, recalling how Race praised my woodcraft when we were seeking Prince Barden."

Derian grinned, assured despite himself. It seemed impossible that anything could go wrong if Valet was taking part.

"Who else?" he asked. "Us three, the scout Race mentioned, and . . . ?"

"About a dozen other people chosen for both their skills and their certain loyalty," Race said. "It's not been easy to find what we need, especially on short notice and with most of those assigned to the army ruled out lest they be missed. Still, scouts are harder to pin down and my commander has found clever ways to cover for those we're taking. The other members are personal attendants on various of the nobles who have arrived with their troops. You'll see them all at a meeting tonight."

"Meeting?" Derian asked. "Won't that be risky?"

"We've a safe place," Race assured him. "Anyhow, it would be more risky to go in without a chance to plan, practice, and meet each other."

Derian thought fleetingly of Prince Newell's man Rook and hoped he wasn't being included. The times their paths had crossed—which hadn't been often—he had not liked the man any better than he had liked his master. Derian decided not to ask. If Rook had been ruled trustworthy, then it was not Derian's place to question.

Instead he looked out across the camp, watching the glow of the campfires, listening to the rise and fall of voices, the sound of weapons being sharpened, of meals being prepared. In the middle distance, a clear baritone voice began a mournful song.

It's for real, Derian thought. *I'm going to war.*

He rose then and went to check his own armor and weapons. There wasn't any time to waste.

XXV

GOOD CROSSING WAS THE WESTERNMOST town in Bright Bay. The reason for this was that no one could live in the Barren Lands. Out of the Barren Lands flowed the Barren River, widening as soon as the waters reached less rocky land, like a broad-shouldered man stretching after a day in a cramped coach.

Long ago, those rapid-flowing waters had carried enormous boulders downstream. These, over even more time, had collected other rocks, dirt, and detritus, becoming small islands that would one day entice colonists to rest the supports for a bridge upon them. Around the bridge a town would grow up and someday the bridge itself would be a town.

Firekeeper found the ways and reasons for human settlement astonishing. It was so unlike the roving ways of the wolves, like but unlike the nesting of certain birds who would return to the same tree or cliff edge year after year.

She thought about this as she stood with Derian on the hills to the west of Good Crossing, hills that were themselves the last remnants of the Barren Lands. Because the soil here was rocky, these hills had never been cultivated. Because the trees that grew on them were stunted and twisted, they had never been cut for lumber and only rarely thinned for firewood. Since the soil east of the Barren Lands had been enriched by the ash from the long-ago volcanic eruptions, it produced not only good timber but good farming. So this poor excuse for a forest had been left alone.

Surrounding Good Crossing there was a large, cleared area. In happier days, this had provided public grazing for the town, the place where market wagons clustered before the opening of the city gates, and the home of the horse fair held once in the spring and once in a autumn.

Until a few days ago, Firekeeper had crossed those fields almost every night while gathering information for King Tedric. Now she was amazed at how different the place seemed—transformed since the almost impulsive Battle of the Banks into an acknowledged battleground.

After that battle, Stonehold's forces had retreated as far as the southern edge of the field, arraying themselves along the field and spreading to either side of the broad north-south road that would ultimately arrive at Mason's Bridge. The road had a grassy margin along it, bordered here and there with saplings or by hedges protecting farmers' fields or by orchards.

Firekeeper looked back and forth between the two camps. In the camp outside of Good Crossing, the scarlet and white shields borne by Hawk Haven's rank and file blended with the sea green and yellow of Bright Bay. On the other side of that cleared area, which to Firekeeper's eyes looked no different from any other patch of cleared ground, neither scarlet and white nor green and yellow could be seen, but only the triple chevronels of Stonehold—red, purple, and blue on a field of white.

Even through the long glass that Derian had borrowed from Race, the array of flags and pennons was confusing. Ever since King Tedric had departed from Eagle's Nest to meet with Duke Allister, Firekeeper had been studying various insignia, trying to learn how to tell person from person by their signs, and occasionally regretting her refusal to learn to read and write.

Her memory was good, far better than that of most humans she had met, but it was schooled to recall scents and sounds more than visual images. Notes would help her to remember, or at least provide a better sense of how human symbols worked.

"I don't understand, still," the wolf-woman admitted to Derian. "The simplest, yes. Hawk Haven's soldiers bear the shield split side to side on the slant: red and white. King Tedric's colors."

"Scarlet and silver are the preferred heraldic terms for those colors," Derian said teasingly, "but red and white will do."

"And those of Bright Bay carry shields of green and yellow, split on a similar slant, but opposite," Firekeeper gestured, miming a line that started high on the left and dropped to the right.

"Very good. Sea green and gold—yellow in this case—are the colors of the royal house of Bright Bay," Derian said.

"And Stonehold soldiers," Firekeeper continued, "have on their shields what looks like three skinny mountains against a snowy sky, colored one each red and purple and blue."

"Yes."

"But some shields—no matter the color of the background—have something drawn on the middle of the shield. A star—or what *you* call a star—or a flower—though I have never seen such flowers—or animals."

Firekeeper's snort showed what she thought of these last as representations of the true beasts and beside her Blind Seer laughed.

"The basic shields," Derian explained with the enthusiasm of a youth raised in the capital city for whom heraldry meant not just symbols but real people—some of them heroes, "are carried by the rank and file. The shields with a simple blazon—the star or flower or animal—are carried by the officers."

Firekeeper nodded. "This so those they command may know them when helmets are pulled low, but Earl Kestrel is an officer and yet his shield is different yet more so. It bears the same blue and red bands set side by side with the golden hunting horn that he shows on his flag and even on his clothing."

"That's because he's heir to a Great House and entitled to bear his own house's colors instead of those of the king," Derian said. "If you look to where Elise's father stands with his archers you will see that his shield is different again: white with an archer upon it shooting a scarlet arrow from his bow."

Derian pointed. "If you look you'll see that there are others carrying Earl Kestrel's red and blue stripes. These are troops raised from his lands, his local militia. There aren't many of these because Norwood lands are all the way cross Hawk Haven—in the area bordering New Kelvin. Most of his troops have stayed home to patrol banks of the White Water River, just in case the New Kelvinese get to wondering if we're watching our flanks. Still, there were some based at the Kestrel Manse in Eagle's Nest and they've come along so that Kestrel can demonstrate its support of the king."

Firekeeper nodded, noting that what Derian said of the Kestrel colors was true of the other Great Houses as well. She resigned herself to confusion, wondering how anyone could keep all of this straight. In addition to those devices she had come to know there were so many new ones: mostly devices designating military companies or personal devices such as Sapphire's gem-blazoned shield.

"I have a new respect for heralds," she said to Blind Seer. *"When we were in at the castle they seemed stuffy, self-important sorts. Now I see how useful their knowledge is."*

Blind Seer grunted agreement. *"I wonder what keeps one soldier from carrying another's shield or stealing a great noble's banner?"*

"A good question." She repeated it to Derian, who replied:

"In the heat of battle one soldier will often seize another's shield, especially to replace one lost or damaged. However, the imposture couldn't continue after helmets were removed."

"But deliberately change," Firekeeper pressed, "to make oneself more important."

Derian laughed. "That would be its own penalty, for those with reputation enough to merit a personal coat of arms are usually the target of many soldiers. Killing a common soldier is useful, but killing an officer or a noble may strike fear in those who depend on his or her commands."

"I see," Firekeeper frowned. "You speak lightly of killing and even laugh. Have you ever killed anyone?"

Derian sobered. "I have not. Honestly, I'm wondering if I'm a great coward for being so glad that my place will be off the main field."

"I don't think you're a coward," Firekeeper said, looking out over that strip of empty land and thinking of the coming battle as Derian had described it to her. "I think you show great good sense. What will they fight for? How will they know who has won?"

"Our troops fight to defend their position and to drive the others away," Derian explained. "Their troops fight to take ground and make our soldiers lose heart."

"Then we will win," Firekeeper said confidently. "We are here already and have nowhere to go. It is easier, too, for more of King Tedric's troops to join this army here."

"True," Derian said, "as far as that goes. But the damage done to land and property is all ours to take. If this war stretches on, we are hurt by those damages."

"Long? I thought this war was to be this afternoon!"

"This battle," Derian said heavily. "Wars are made of many battles or sometimes of only one."

"Which is this to be?"

"I wish I knew," he said. "I bet King Tedric wishes that he knew, too."

"Is there any way to make the war end without many battles?"

"Never start," Derian said, then regretted the flippancy in his tone. "I take that back. If that quick wisdom was true our country and Bright Bay would not have been spatting these hundred years and more. Sometimes a war is needed to clear the enmity as a thunderstorm clears a late-summer sky—or so they say."

Firekeeper grunted, politely noncommittal about what she thought about this bit of human wisdom.

"The other way wars are won," Derian continued, "is if one side captures a place or person so important that the other side will surrender rather than risk their destruction: a king or queen or perhaps someone like Duke Allister Seagleam, who has taken his queen's place here. I have heard that in New Kelvin there are buildings so revered that the New Kelvinese honor them more highly than any living thing."

"Buildings?"

"So they say," Derian shrugged, "but then New Kelvinese are mad for old things and older customs."

Firekeeper caught her breath in excitement. "Do the Stoneholders have a king here? Where is his sign?"

Derian shook his head. "It's not so easy, Firekeeper. Stoneholders are ruled by two people, not one, and by a council in addition. Moreover, none of those august personages are here as far as I know. They've left Generals Yuci and Grimsel and their troops to fight the battles for them."

"I don't," Firekeeper admitted, "understand."

"I'm beginning to think," Derian replied, reaching over and squeezing her shoulder, "that neither do I."

WITHIN A FEW HOURS, a field battle was no longer a thing to be imagined. High in the concealing branches of a twisted oak on the hilly ground west of Good Crossing, Firekeeper watched.

She was alone now but for Blind Seer. The wolf was prowling at the base of the tree trunk, too nervous to sleep, though the early afternoon was filled with lazy sunlight. Like her, he had come to care for many of their human friends—to love them as an ersatz pack—and to see these friends risk their lives so lightly for so little was maddening.

Derian had gone to his post—to join the raiding party from which Firekeeper herself had been asked to keep clear. She had agreed, reluctantly acknowledging the wisdom of King Tedric's arguments, but at Firekeeper's request, Elation was with Derian, providing both guard and messenger should their friend come to harm.

Both Elise and Doc were serving in the hospital tents erected to the rear of the Hawk Haven–Bright Bay lines. Ox was at Earl Kestrel's side; Race and Valet were with Derian. Sapphire and Jet were both bearing arms on the field. Even Lady Zorana was pulling a bow under her brother's command. Various spare nobles had been delegated to run the king's messages to the commanders on the field.

Alone of all those she had befriended, Firekeeper had no place in this war. Her skills with sword and shield, while admirable for the scant training she had been given, were not good enough for her to serve in the ranks without being more of a liability to her allies than to the enemy. Although she was more skilled with a bow, she could not bring herself to do as Baron Ivon's archers would do—stand in a line and loose arrows on command, hoping to hit some anonymous figure on the other side. Slaughter so impersonal made the wolf-woman shiver and feel sick.

Through the long glass, Firekeeper saw Duke Allister near the center of Bright Bay and Hawk Haven's allied armies—riding out among them as chief commander of all those assembled. She wondered how Duke Allister felt about his tasks and the deaths that would occur upon his word. She wondered if King Tedric regretted not being out there himself—he had seemed so very angry when the physicians had adamantly refused to risk him any nearer to the battlefield than a tent at the rear of the lines. She wondered if she was even human to so little understand war.

And troubled by such thoughts, she watched from the limbs of her towering oak. A thin shrill blast as from a hunting horn pierced the air. This was followed by a flight of arrows, one coming so rapidly after the others that the horn call seemed the source of that black-shafted hail.

Though slim and light in the air, the arrows landed to deadly effect. Firekeeper cringed as on both sides soldiers crumpled and screamed. After a few more volleys, archers slung their bows across their shoulders and lifted their fallen fellows, carrying dead and wounded alike toward the rear lines. Then she heard the trumpet call signaling the next movement in the battle.

From the flanks rode out the cavalry. Mounted on a dark sorrel far heavier than familiar Coal, Earl Kestrel led the right wing onto the field. Riding slightly behind him on a bald-faced chestnut selected more for strength than for beauty or grace was Ox. The big man bore the Kestrel banner in one hand and a sword in the other.

Ox has no shield, Firekeeper thought anxiously. *No shield but the speed and skill with which he wields his sword. Yet I could swear that he is laughing and urging the others on.*

Her gaze turned then to the other flank, where a woman she had met only in passing led the left flank of the cavalry charge. This was the Duchess Merlin, a woman young for her position—barely twenty-four. Her grandfather and father had both died in their forties.

There had been those who had argued that House Trueheart would do better with an older, steadier person at its head to help young Grace learn her way about her responsibilities—among those had been Zorana Archer, who had nominated her husband, Aksel Trueheart, the duchess's uncle. Grace, however, had been twenty-two when her father died and so was legally eligible to take her place among the heads of the Great Houses.

Many had expressed surprise when Duchess Merlin had arrived personally leading the reinforcements raised from those who usually patrolled her lands. Derian had reported that the king had said that the young duchess needed to prove herself and that she fully understood the risk she was taking. On her arrival Duchess Merlin had presented the king with a document not unlike the king's own will, naming a regent for her year-old son should she die on the field.

And how many others, Firekeeper mused, watching the slender duchess on her sturdy dapple grey charge into the opposing line of mounted soldiers, *are out there fighting not because they believe in preserving Bright Bay's territory from Stonehold, but because they have something to prove? Surely Sapphire Shield fights to earn glory rather than for Bright Bay. And perhaps Jet hopes that valor in battle may remove the ignominy of his behavior on the night of the brothels.*

When Sapphire Shield had requested to join Earl Kestrel's company, the earl had welcomed her, not so much, Firekeeper knew, for her skill—though Sapphire rode as well as many of the cavalry troops—but because the soldiers loved her for appearing like a figure out of legend: for the blue steed she rode, for her dyed and enameled armor.

Sapphire's renunciation of the stone that had glowed so long on her brow had done nothing to lessen the tales growing up around her. Though two days had passed, the skin where the headband had rested for so long remained as white as new-fallen snow. Already some whispered that Sapphire had battled evil sorcery and won.

And yet, even those who shiver deliciously at the tales don't believe them, not deep inside. How strange.

The infantry waded into the gaps left by the clash of cavalry. Here was where Rolfston Redbriar fought and here was where he died, slain by a practiced sword slash from a grim-faced woman with a dogwood blossom painted above the triple chevronels on her shield. Neither Sapphire nor Jet, each elsewhere on the field, knew that they were now fatherless.

Melina was right when she told Rolfston Redbriar not to be a fool and join the battle, but he would have nothing of her wisdom—not when Ivon Archer fights both as an archer and then on foot. I wonder if somehow Lady Melina will turn even this tragedy to enhance her reputation.

In the infantry was where many other people Firekeeper had met were fighting: men and women with whom she had tossed dice or who had proven their courage by stroking Blind Seer's head. It bothered her that she could not tell one from another even with the long glass. Helmets and armor, combined with shields held to protect vital spots, turned each figure into a blood- and dirt-smeared variation on the rest.

Firekeeper found herself watching the cavalry instead, for horses were distinct where humans were not.

She watched, fingernails digging trenches in her palms, as Earl Kestrel's sorrel was belly-wounded and tumbled screaming to the ground. Had Ox not been near to lift the body from his earl, Norvin Norwood, too, would have died there. As it was, Earl Kestrel struggled to his feet and eschewed his own safety to cut his horse's throat before turning to face those who saw an unseated cavalry officer as fair game.

Prince Newell, mounted on a rust-colored steed splashed with white on legs and face, rescued Earl Kestrel by dashing close enough to shield-bash the soldier who was raising his sword to strike, though this left Newell himself vulnerable.

Ox tended to the soldier who would have stabbed Newell, receiving in return an ugly slash that laid open one side of his jaw. Ignoring the red rain that came forth, he beat his way back to the little earl's side, finally shoving him into the saddle of his own sturdy chestnut. Then, scooping up the banner pole, Ox raised the Kestrel crest so that the earl's troop would take heart from the knowledge that their commander was safe.

Once unremarkable, now the little scrap of land was watered with blood, mostly in trickles and dribbles but sometimes in terrible gouts where soldiers or steeds had been mortally wounded. The hot, coppery stink came even to where Firekeeper sat and soon she thought she could bear no more. Yet she remained anchored to her perch, held by a fierce desire not to cheapen the sacrifice of those who were fighting by hiding like a rabbit.

So she was there to see when Duke Allister's aide, a man she vaguely recalled as Lord Tench, was slain by an arrow meant for the duke.

Duke Allister's group was mostly afoot now—perhaps to make the duke less visible. Had Allister Seagleam not turned to answer some request from a bloodied retainer, had Tench not moved to listen to what was being said, the arrow might have landed unnoticed in dirt already churned by many feet, already littered with countless arrows from earlier attacks. But the arrow hit Tench squarely in the back, a mortal wound that left the others in his vicinity scattering for cover. And Firekeeper was down from her sheltering oak before Tench hit the ground.

"That arrow could only have come from near here," she cried to Blind Seer. *"That was no chance shot! Let us find the archer. I have no love for those who kill brave soldiers from a distance and from cover."*

Blind Seer gaped his fanged jaws in a vicious smile. *"I am with you, Little Two-legs, but the smells of blood and sweat and fear thicken the air. I cannot find this archer by scent alone. Use your knowledge of the archer's craft and find him for us."*

And Firekeeper nodded, calling to mind every trace and trick for use of the bow that Race Forester had taught her. Her teacher's skill had been honed by the need to live by his hunting and her enthusiasm for his lessons had been avid; otherwise she might not have found the place from which the assassin's arrow had been shot. But having all her life—at least her life as she remembered it—needed to survive by dint of quickness and cleverness, Firekeeper remembered precisely the path of that arrow as it had streaked through the fair sky.

"It is not so unlike finding the lark's nest by recalling how she darts into the sky from cover," she said to Blind Seer, mentally tracing the arrow's path. *"We will find the archer there in that clump of maples— ahead a bit, closer to the battlefield. Doubtless he has hidden in the tree boughs as I did here."*

"The ground between is opener than I like," the wolf replied, already lowering himself to slink close to the earth as the pack would when stalking a herd of elk. *"I mislike how your tall two-legged shape will stand out."*

The feral woman stroked his thick ruff. *"There is no avoiding that risk. We can only hope this archer's thoughts are for his prey alone. Keep to what cover you can, dearest one. Remember his skill with the bow!"*

Together they left their shelter. Blind Seer, belly so close to the earth that the stubble groomed his fur, took the most direct line, but Firekeeper dropped back to approach the clump of maples from behind. Once in the open, she ran like a deer or a wolf—for one was much the same in short bursts; it must be for the one to live by hunting the other. And it was doubtful that even if the archer in his lofty blind had seen her he would have been able to fit arrow to string in time to take aim.

Despite having more ground to cover, Firekeeper arrived slightly before the wolf. No scent betrayed the archer, but the scuffed bark of the largest tree in the clump testified to his presence. Blind Seer crouched below as she leapt onto the tree trunk, scrabbling upward like a squirrel, her bare feet finding purchase where most climbers would have found none.

"If he jumps down," Firekeeper called to her companion, *"catch him, but leave the killing to me. I liked not how the humans looked at you in fear when you killed the one who would have slain Sapphire in the town that night."*

Blind Seer howled softly in agreement and this gave the archer warning of Firekeeper's coming. He was well placed on a platform jury-rigged across two thick boughs and traded bow for knife as Firekeeper's hand emerged from the leaves, casting as if searching for a firm hold to continue the ascent.

A human would have died without seeing the hidden archer's face, but Firekeeper was not a human in such things. Though the archer had moved with stealth, she had heard the soft tap as the bow was set down, the slight scrape as knife left sheath. The questing hand had been a feint to draw his attack.

Her Fang was ready in her free hand, her feet securely braced on a lower limb. When the archer's knife flashed to where her arm should be, her Fang met his own arm right at the shoulder joint.

Though the archer wore armor, it did him no good. The Fang pierced the light leather in the interstices between the heavier sections, drawing both blood and a cry of pain. Yet the archer kept both his balance and his blade. Stumbling back onto the platform, he seized his quiver. When Firekeeper leapt onto the branch, he hurled it at her. She parried with one hand, keeping the Fang ready to bite again in the other.

They faced each other then and Firekeeper knew the man. This man had taken care to be unobtrusive in his comings and goings about the Hawk Haven camp, but she had taken equal care to know something about the entourage of each noble.

"Rook!" she exclaimed, startled, for what was Prince Newell's manservant doing here, attacking his master's commander?

Rook's reply was to lunge forward, perhaps hoping to take advantage of her momentary surprise. Firekeeper's defenses, though, were as automatic as breathing—they needed to be, for in the wilds she would not have breathed long if she needed to think about defense. She dodged the blow and counterstruck. Already she knew that she did not want to kill Rook—alive he could talk—but he had no such consideration for her.

Rook was larger and had better footing. He might be stronger, though Firekeeper was discovering that she was stronger than most humans she encountered. However, stronger or not, Rook outmassed her, not a trivial consideration in a duel where one could win merely by making the other fall. But Firekeeper was at home in the trees, almost as much at ease as she would be on the ground, especially in a spreading, broad-branched old tree like this maple. Reluctant to leave the sure footing of his platform, Rook was greatly handicapped.

Below, Blind Seer leapt into the air, snapping his jaws loudly. He could not reach the upper branches where the two humans tussled, but Firekeeper saw how his growls and snarls unnerved her opponent.

"Surrender," she suggested, nicking Rook's forearm on the underside so that the blood ran from between the lacings. "You cannot run. Blind Seer will wait for you, even if you defeat me. Surrender and I swear you will live to speak with the king."

Rook considered and even glanced out at the battlefield as if expecting to see King Tedric there. Unwilling to risk killing him, Firekeeper did not press beyond nicking Rook again, this time along the back of his neck where his helmet and collar did not quite meet.

Perhaps it was this, perhaps it was a foreboding that surrender or not he would eventually become her prisoner, but Rook snarled:

"I surrender! Do you promise you or that beast will not kill me until I have seen the king?"

"Seen and spoken with," Firekeeper agreed, "if King Tedric wishes to speak with you. And if you surrender faithfully."

"I will," Rook said, laying down his long knife.

Not trusting him overmuch, Firekeeper bound Rook with his own bowstring there in the treetops.

"This can be your prison," she said, "until the battle is done."

"Seal his mouth!" Blind Seer called, leaping and snapping still for the pleasure of it. *"He may call for help otherwise."*

Firekeeper agreed. As she bound Rook's mouth with cloth torn from his shirt, she thought she saw dismay as well as anger in the man's eyes.

"A good reminder," she said to the wolf as she dropped down beside him and rubbed his head. *"I wonder if his master knows of his treachery?"*

She looked out over the still raging battlefield, hunting for Prince Newell and his rust-red steed. Duke Allister, she noted in passing, was back in command, framed by four soldiers who must be very brave because they intended to intercept any arrow meant for their commander—with their own bodies more likely than not. Sir Dirkin Eastbranch was one of these four, doubtless participating in today's battle at his king's express command.

Lord Tench's corpse lay on the ground to one side, still facedown, though the arrow had been broken off, probably in a desperate attempt to stanch the blood and save his life.

"I don't see Prince Newell," Firekeeper said, puzzled. *"Nor is his war mount among the dumb brutes lying dead on the field. Where could he have gone?"*

"Perhaps he has retreated wounded to the hospital," Blind Seer suggested.

Firekeeper turned the long-glass in that direction, but saw no sign of the rust-red horse or its rider. Troubled now, she cast wider and finally, at the very rear of the line, she located the horse. Prince Newell's shield hung from the saddle harness, confirming that she had not been mistaken.

"Newell is with King Tedric," she said. *"Perhaps he reports on the progress of the fighting."*

But something troubled her even as she offered this explanation. She remembered how Rook had scanned the battlefield before surrendering. Recalled how he had insisted on speaking with "the king," not with "King Tedric."

Little things, she thought, *but a strong bird's nest can be built with nothing but slim twigs and rabbit fluff.*

Beginning to run, she called to Blind Seer, *"Come away with me, sweet hunter. Suddenly, I am very afraid."*

No one but a few frightened horses seemed to notice when woman and wolf came running down the hillside and went darting through the rear lines toward the scarlet pavilion pitched as a command center for the aged king.

As Firekeeper closed with that pavilion, however, she noticed a strange thing. The guards who should stand flanking the door to the pavilion or pace a patrol outside of it were standing a good number of feet from the structure. Standing there as well were some of those who had been acting as messengers for King Tedric: nobles and castle staff alike.

Lady Zorana raised her bow when Firekeeper would cross the perimeter around the pavilion, her expression grim.

"No one may interrupt the king, not even you, Lady Blysse. He is in deep and confidential conference."

"No!" Firekeeper swallowed a snarl of frustration. "Not with Prince Newell?"

"That's right." Lady Zorana looked slightly puzzled, but her bow and that deadly arrow remained steady.

Other of the guards were drawing weapons as well. Realizing that even she and Blind Seer could not take out so many—especially when she wished these people no harm—Firekeeper decided to risk the arrow. Feinting left, then ducking in the other direction, she dashed for the pavilion. She hadn't reckoned on the skill of the daughter of Purcel Archer.

Lady Zorana corrected her aim while Firekeeper was still pounding across the open ground. The wolf-woman heard the bowstring sing out and leapt up, but Zorana's aim was true. Only the fact that Zorana had not wished—despite, or perhaps because of, her political rivalry with the king's presumed heir—to kill Firekeeper preserved the young woman's life. The arrow plowed across the flesh on the outside of Firekeeper's left thigh, cutting a deep furrow through skin and muscle.

Ox's courage when she had seen him wounded sprang to mind, balancing but not diminishing the searing pain. Firekeeper had been hurt many times before, but most of those injuries had been of the pummeling variety. When she had been cut, it had rarely been deep. Nothing in her experience had prepared her for the sensation of muscle being neatly sliced and of control vanishing.

Yet she leapt forward on her strong leg, relying on her arms as she had when a pup. Carried by momentum, she pitched through the pavilion's door. Blind Seer bounded beside her, alert, though whimpering his concern.

Firekeeper nearly surrendered to the pain when she saw what awaited her within. Prince Newell bent over the high-backed chair from which King Tedric had commanded his forces. The king's form was still upright; his hands still grasped the carved arms of the chair, but his eyes were shut. There was a pallor to the king's face that Firekeeper did not like at all and he did not seem to be breathing.

Prince Newell straightened when he saw her.

"Lady Blysse," he said, his tone for a moment as casual as it had been when they met at the ball. Then it altered, filling with concern and shock. "You've been wounded!"

"The king," she said. "What have you done to the king!"

"Nothing," he responded. "I was telling him about the attempt to assassinate Duke Allister when His Majesty collapsed. I fear the news was more than his heart could take. I was attempting to revive him."

Firekeeper knew nothing of medicine's deeper mysteries, but it did not seem to her that Newell had been reviving the king. Why then was the king's wig knocked to one side? Why was there none of the sharp stink of stimulants that she recalled from her visits to the king's chambers? Why were the king's pale lips slowly shaping one word?

"Help . . ." Tedric hissed.

"He lives!" she said to Blind Seer. *"Quickly! Get Doc!"*

"But Prince Newell!" the wolf growled in protest. *"He reeks of treachery!"*

"Go!" Firekeeper repeated. *"You must not be here when I deal with him."*

And the great grey wolf slipped beneath the edge of the pavilion's scarlet fabric and was gone. From without Firekeeper heard cries of alarm, but she could not attend to them. Her argument with Blind Seer had taken half the time it would have in human words but still she had wasted too much time.

"I think," Newell was saying, already drawing his sword and lunging at her, "the shock of your death, little Blysse, will finish my job for me."

Firekeeper leapt back, knowing that she could hope for no assistance, even if those outside overcame their reluctance to disobey the prince's orders. They would see her as the attacker and Newell as the bold defender. Yet she could not abandon the king, unarmed and lightly armored though she was, not after the proud old Eagle had asked her for help.

She leapt back, stumbling on her wounded leg. Normally she could have gotten clean away, but slowed as she was the sword's sharp point deeply scored the leather armor across her belly. Silently Firekeeper thanked Derian, who had insisted that she wear the stifling stuff, even if she was not to be in combat.

Drawing her Fang from its Mouth, Firekeeper dropped low, coming within the compass of Prince Newell's arm, too close for him to bring the sword to bear. He was more heavily armored than she was, but she jabbed the blade between two metal plates and through the leather. It grated against a rib, then slid in.

Her reward was a grunt from Prince Newell and a kiss of warm blood on her fingers. The prince jerked back before she could pull the blade free, leaving her unarmed, her only weapon damming the wound in his side.

Not only weapon, she reminded herself. *Have I not called myself a wolf?*

More cautious now, Prince Newell held his sword as much to guard as to attack. He must indeed regret the shield he had left hanging from the rust-red charger's harness.

Blood loss was making Firekeeper light-headed, but she remained enough herself to know that she could not charge again. Instead she lifted a small table. The papers that had covered it fluttered to the ground and began sopping up her blood from where it puddled on the rugs.

Throwing the table, then a footstool, Firekeeper took advantage of Prince Newell's dodging to close a few more steps. Her leg didn't even hurt now; the pain was as much a constant as her unwavering desire to protect the old man in his high-backed chair.

In the background she heard the sound of someone entering the tent. From the corner of her eye, she glimpsed one of the King's Own Guard. Knowing that in any moment she might have another enemy, Firekeeper grabbed a medicine bottle, a carafe half-filled with red wine, a tray, and hurled them one by one with the pinpoint accuracy of one who had lived by that skill.

Prince Newell was wholly on the defensive now, unable—or perhaps merely unwilling—to close as long as she had ammunition. An angry red mark spread on one cheek where a heavy pottery goblet had broken against the bone. His lower lip was bleeding.

There was the sound of more people entering the pavilion, but thus far no one interfered. Firekeeper's vision was beginning to blur now: fading in and out so that she had moments of great clarity and others where she could hardly see the man whom she no longer recalled by name, recalling only that he was her prey and that this was the most important hunt of her life.

On the periphery of her attention, Firekeeper heard shouts and screams. Considered that they might be important, dismissed the thought as a distraction from her task.

Relentlessly, she dragged herself after her prey, throwing whatever came to hand: scraps of pottery, bits of blood-soaked paper, a solid metal box. Then, suddenly, the tips of her fingers scrabbled vainly in the plush of the rugs. For the first time, she realized that she was on the floor, her weight resting on the knee of her sound right leg and on her right arm. Her left hand quested blindly after something to throw.

A shadow fell over her. In one of those moments of perfect clarity of thought and vision, Firekeeper recognized Prince Newell, battered and bloodied but still alive. Grasping the hilt in both hands, he was raising his sword to pin her to the ground, thus to end her crawling forever.

A dark red eye, bright and wet in his side, looked down at Firekeeper—the garnet set into the hilt of her Fang. With her last strength, the wolf-woman surged just high enough to grasp the knife handle. Shoving the blade in with desperate power, she twisted. The force of Prince Newell's own descending thrust ripped the Fang free.

Then hot, terrible pain forced her face into the bloodied rugs. She knew nothing except that faintly, at the very edge of her hearing, a wolf was howling as if his heart must break.

XXVI

EVEN BEFORE THE THIN WAIL of the trumpet signaled the first exchange of arrows, Derian and the other raiders had been long gone. They had left via Good Crossing's river gate huddled beneath a tarp on the deck of a cargo boat. To an observer, theirs would appear to be just one of many small boats filled to capacity with those who had decided that it was safer to be away from the city, just in case the defenders did not hold.

However, unlike most of these boats, which went downriver to land at the usually placid hamlet of Butterfield, their boatman carried them only as far as a small cove hidden from the city—and, they hoped, from any observers—by a thick tangle of willows.

Derian felt dreadfully exposed as he climbed from the boat onto the shore, uncomforted by the fact that not even most of the river traffic seemed to notice their detour. Rationally, he knew they were invisible, but he fully expected a roving band of Stoneholders to leap out upon them.

His back tensed against this imagined threat, he steadied the boat as the others climbed ashore. Each raider carried a bow and arrows, a knife, and a hand weapon of choice. Each was lightly armored, any metal dulled, any light tanned leather rubbed dark with soot. None carried a shield, for these would slow them and the raiders had to move quickly and use what cover they could.

Traffic on the road east from Good Crossing, a road that roughly paralleled the Barren River, was nonexistent. In an effort to keep Stonehold from pressing east should they break the army at Good Crossing, the road had been barricaded with fallen trees where it left the open grounds around the city. In any case, no coward or refugee was going to chance a land journey when the river was so near.

Race Forester led them away from the riverbank and across the road, then through a gap in a hedgerow bordering a farmer's fields. The grain was high and—Derian thought—close to being ripe. It made an admirable shield from anything.

He glanced up, catching a glimpse of what he thought was Elation lazily riding the air currents far above. Firekeeper had told Derian that the falcon would be there keeping an eye on him and that she would bring Firekeeper if needed. Otherwise, the bird was to stay high enough that she would not draw attention to herself or to the raiders.

Derian thought it was nice that his death would be avenged, but other than that he didn't think the great peregrine would be much help. Realizing that he was woolgathering, Derian forced himself to pay attention as Race reviewed their plans.

"We're going to make our way back," Race said, "just about all the way that boat carried us, but this time we'll angle inland south and west. Jem"—the scout nodded toward a burly, bent man who looked as if his nose had been hit with a potato masher—"has done a good deal of scouting over on this side of the Barren and is going to take us through orchards and fields."

"And folks' barns," Jem grunted. "We won't touch a road and the Stoneholders"—he spat—"won't see us until we choose."

Between practice sessions last night, Derian had talked for a while with Jem, the only Bright Bay scout in their strike force. Jem passionately hated Stonehold because of how a Stonehold sergeant had violently beat him some years before. His smashed nose was only the most visible of his injuries.

When he had recovered enough to walk, Jem had defected to Hawk Haven and by now was well known and well trusted by the garrison at the Watchful Eye, who knew him for a smuggler who would smuggle information as well as goods.

"I know not all 'holders are like that sergeant," Jem had told Derian. "I know it in my head, but in my heart I hate 'em."

Derian dragged his attention to the present.

"Stay out of sight," Race reminded them. "The army's providing a distraction for us, but that won't mean everyone's staring toward the front lines like kids watching a puppet show. Some will remember their duty to guard, some won't want to watch, others will have jobs that will take them through the camp. Still, they won't be watching every wagon and supply dump. Those are our targets."

Derian nodded, his mouth dry. Then he fell into place. In front of him was Joy Spinner—the scout from House Kite—and behind him was another scout, a man called Thyme. Valet was toward the back and Jem out front. Race, nominally in command though this raid demanded initiative as well as obedience, moved alongside Jem, ready for trouble.

Jem's chosen route, however, was clear. Those who owned the farms they crossed were either absent or reluctant to notice an armed group that was so evidently just passing through. The barns they cut through were empty of any livestock other than the occasional chicken or cat. In a surprisingly short period of time the raiders were behind the Stonehold lines and drawing up on their encampment.

In the near distance, shouts and commands, the clash of metal, and the screams of the wounded confirmed that battle had been joined. They came sharply to Derian as he closed on his own battlefield, a reminder of the penalty for failure.

Jem led them through an orchard, the upper boughs of the trees heavy with unpicked fruit, the air smelling of cider. It came up right to the edge of the Stonehold camp. Doubtless even the strict rules against pillaging hadn't kept the soldiers from stealing the more easily picked fruit.

Derian didn't need Race's hand signal to remind him to keep to cover. As on the banks of the Barren, he felt dreadfully exposed, even though he knew that as long as he kept his movements slow and steady only the most alert guard would be likely to spot him through the intervening apple trees.

He knelt behind one of the trees, studying the camp through the veil of low-hanging branches.

The Stoneholders had not unloaded most of the recently arrived wagons. That made sense. If the Rocky Band won today's battle, they would be moving forward to take new ground. If they failed, they needed to be ready to retreat. Many of the tarps covering the wagons had been thrown back, probably to inventory the contents and to haul out what was immediately needed. Those wagons that remained covered clearly contained fodder, for hay poked out at either end.

There's my target, Derian thought. *I'm sure I can hit a haystack and even slightly green hay will burn nicely.*

He gestured his choice to Race and the scout nodded. A few moments later, he signaled for them to string their bows. Each raider carried several arrows specially prepared for fire. Five of their number—Valet was one—carried clay pots containing coals. As they had rehearsed the night before, they broke into clumps of three and set their arrows tip-down into the coals.

First, Derian reminded himself, *light the arrow. The smell of burning shouldn't alert the guards, because they'll have campfires of their own. Wait for Race's signal to shoot. Shoot all your prepared arrows. Then decide whether you can constructively do more or whether the best thing you can do is clear out.*

Neat orders. Tidy. Simple when they were just diagrams drawn in the dirt rather than directed toward a living camp that looked far too much like the one you had left behind.

The Stoneholders didn't look like monsters, just like soldiers. The guards were alert, scanning the orchards though more than one spared a glance toward the battlefield where their comrades were fighting. Some of these guards were clearly walking wounded, reassigned after the Battle of the Banks.

A few had dogs with them, heavy, thick-bodied brutes meant for guarding not hunting. Derian was glad that Race had left Queenie behind. The bird dog wouldn't have a chance against these animals. They might even give Blind Seer a good fight. The dogs had a better chance than the guards of spotting the group creeping through the orchard, but the light wind blew from the north and Stonehold's camp was rich with odors so the dogs hadn't scented the raiders.

In addition to the guards, there were other Stoneholders in the camp, men and women who hurried about purposefully fetching stuff from the wagons, darting in and out of tents, hurrying along with serious expressions on their faces. There was even a fat woman washing socks in a cauldron slung from a tripod over a fire.

I've been around Firekeeper too long, Derian thought. *People just look like people.*

The arrows in the pot had just caught when Race's signal to shoot came. Derian fired, fumbling a bit because—despite practice the night before—he'd never fired a burning arrow with any speed. To his right, Valet shot off two shafts with neat precision before Derian had readied his own second arrow. When Derian tried to hurry, Valet said softly:

"Make it count."

Derian slowed. His first arrow had landed in his chosen haystack and fire began to catch the hay. He sent another arrow at the same stack— after all, you didn't use just one piece of kindling to start a cook fire.

As he reached for a third arrow, Derian realized that Valet—having finished with his own prepared arrows—had been poaching Derian's. Momentarily angry, Derian would have laughed at himself if he hadn't been so nervous. What did it matter who fired the arrows as long as they were shot?

Only as he was lowering his own bow did he realize that one of the dogs from the Stonehold camp was charging toward him. Its long-muzzled face was set in an ugly, fang-barring snarl that reminded Derian of Blind Seer.

If this had been a ballad, Derian would have reached for an arrow from his quiver and smoothly fired, dropping the vicious canine in its tracks. Instead, Derian yelled and swung his bow. The string popped, stinging as it slapped against his face, but the solid shaft hit the dog soundly along head and neck. The dog reared back on its haunches, yelping in surprise and pain. By the time it attacked again, Derian had dropped the bow and drawn his sword.

Here the practicing he had done with Firekeeper and Blind Seer came to his aid. He *knew* how the dog would attack; indeed, he nearly misjudged because he expected one of Blind Seer's more subtle feints. This animal didn't feint or dodge. It came straight in, trusting its speed and ferocity.

Derian's sword laid it open along one flank. His second stroke took off its head.

"Very good, sir," Valet said from beside him. "And thanks."

Derian grinned, feeling wetness on his face where dog blood had spattered. Excitement made his own blood race and his head feel light. He might have dashed foolishly to where the Stoneholders were turning to face the dozens of fires blazing throughout their camp if Valet hadn't held him. Suddenly, he realized that the attack had come to them.

Stonehold guards were surging into the orchard, determined to find the source of the fire arrows. A short distance away from where Derian and Valet were half-hidden by the same tree, the scout Thyme, who had shared their pot of coals, was trading sword blows with a Stoneholder. Race was entangled with another, disadvantaged by his lack of a shield. Joy Spinner lay curiously still on the ground, an arrow in her back and one of the dogs sniffing at her pooling blood.

The excitement left Derian as quickly as it had come. He glanced at Valet.

He wanted to yell, "Let's get out of here!"

Instead he managed, "What next?"

Valet pointed. Fire was spreading through the Stoneholder's supplies. In some places it had been beaten out or drenched with water from one of the butts distributed with military order among the tents. In other places it had spread to the saplings and shrubs that bordered the road. Hot leaves and twigs dropped down, rekindling the blaze.

Derian looked where Valet had pointed. At the west edge of the Stoneholders' camp was a makeshift corral holding, at rough estimate, at least two dozen draft horses. The fire was spreading near them, feeding on the fodder in the wagons parked conveniently close and on the wagons themselves. The huge, normally placid animals were panicked, rolling their eyes, wheeling and plunging, screaming like frightened women or small children.

Kicks from powerful hind legs had broken out sections of the corral, but mostly the horses had simply crowded as far as possible from the flames. They were strong, but not brilliant, bred to trust people to do their thinking for them.

"Loss of those horses," Valet said, "would hurt Stonehold badly."

Without a second thought, Derian headed for the horses. Never mind that the Stoneholders' cause would be hurt! Those horses had done nothing but haul wagons. He couldn't let them burn to death—especially not in fires he had set.

Even in his sudden fury, Derian didn't forget he had to cross most of the Stonehold camp to reach the imperiled horses. Joy Spinner with the arrow in her back was reminder enough of the risk he was taking.

But in this case, fire and the chaos it had engendered actually helped Derian. Once he slunk past the closest guards and entered the Stonehold camp, most people didn't look twice at him. His light armor wasn't banded with any crest. Rubbed with soot as it was, Derian looked as if he'd been fighting the fire.

That's just what he did as he darted through the camp, Valet a few steps behind. He stomped out a grass fire where a hot twig fell, tipped the kettle of socks—somehow forgotten until now—onto a heap of burning laundry. He was just a red-haired youth with a scared look on his face, running toward the fire. The enemy was outside.

Am I the enemy? Derian thought. *Not to those horses.*

Others had noticed the horses by now, but they were more interested in combating the fire rather than dealing with the massed equine terror. One grizzled sergeant actually gave Derian a quick grin of praise when he saw him heading into the corral.

"Take care, son," he shouted, never turning from where he was throwing water onto some hay. "They're fair panicked and won't know friend from foe."

I certainly hope they don't, Derian thought.

Glancing around with a practiced eye, he quickly spotted a horse that seemed marginally calmer than the rest—a big, black gelding with white stockings and a broad white blaze. Derian could feel the horse's strength when he grabbed his halter and tugged. The horse balked and Derian, remembering what he'd been taught, grabbed a rag—doubtlessly used to rub down the horses—and blindfolded the animal.

The horse didn't magically become unafraid, but now it was at least willing to be led. Even better, several of the other horses, seeing that there was a human in charge, seemed inclined to follow.

Derian grabbed Valet by the arm and shoved him at the black gelding.

"Take this one out!" he ordered, shouting over the crackling of the fire and screams of the horses. "I'll see what I can do to urge the others on."

Ever efficient, Valet produced a bit of rope from about his waist and slipped it through the horse's halter as a makeshift lead line. Feeling the tug at his head and Derian's hand slap his haunch, the black permitted himself to be led by the small man.

Derian's self-appointed task was nearly impossible, but Derian had been around horses since before he could walk. His mother had carried him slung from a saddle when he was an infant—him on one side, a saddlebag on the other. His first job had been in the stables, the first present he could remember had been a pony. There were times Derian believed he could think like a horse—and he tried to think like one now.

Horses feared and hated fire like any intelligent creature should. Derian offered them a way out. He pulled at their halters, turning their heads away from the nearby flames, urging them away. They might not understand his words, but they understood that a human was taking charge. And being herd animals, once the first few were heading somewhere, the rest wanted to follow.

Ancestors! Derian thought. *We're actually getting away with this!*

"What do we do with them?" Derian asked Valet when the little man returned to help. "Won't the Stoneholders just recapture them when the fire's out?"

"I suspect," Valet said, slipping his lead rope through another halter, "that the local farmers will be happy to give the horses new homes."

Derian nodded. Although his eyes streamed from the smoke, he could see that the newly released horses were heading into the stubble of a harvested oat field on the west side of the road, equal parts eager to escape the fire and to settle down to some interesting foraging. Stonehold might reclaim a few of their horses, but not many—not if the farmers who owned that field and others like it had any say.

As he eased the last horse out of the corral, Derian glanced back over his shoulder. The Stoneholders were getting the fire under control. The fodder for their horses was gone, though, along with bedding, many tents, and a good bit of food. There were dead guards on the ground, too. Not all of the raiders had contented themselves with stealing horses.

Not all of the raiders had gotten away, either, Derian learned when he and Valet rejoined the others at the barn that had been designated as their meeting place. Joy Spinner was dead; so were three other scouts whose names Derian hadn't even learned. Jem was missing; so was another of the scouts.

Race was there, his arm in a rough sling. Thyme lay on a stretcher made from a horse blanket and the shafts from two spears. He was unconscious and there was blood on his lips. Most of the other raiders bore wounds, though none so grave.

Derian was surprised to find that his broken bowstring had raised a huge welt across his face and that he had burns on his hands. He hadn't felt any of it during the action. Still, he was better off than many of the others.

Taking one end of the stretcher holding Thyme, Derian tried to keep his tired feet steady as Race led them back toward the river road. Several of the scouts had their bows out, ready for ambush. None came.

The battle still raged and the fires still burned.

❧

IN THE INFIRMARY TENT, Elise wrapped a bandage around a newly stitched wound in the forearm of a cavalry officer from Duchess Merlin's company. The face she saw in front of her was not that of the wounded woman, but of her cousin Purcel as she had seen him only a few minutes before: still, white, and dead.

He had been brought in by bearers from the battlefield. A glance at the blood soaking the stretcher's taut canvas and running from the young man's slightly parted lips had told the story, but the bearer, perhaps knowing her Purcel's cousin, perhaps merely to assuage his own grief and shock, had blurted out:

"He was alive when we picked him up, Lady Elise. Laughing a little even, trying to buck up our spirits. We moved him careful-like, very careful. Then he gave a soft cry and coughed. Just like that, he was gone."

Elise had started to cry, had wanted nothing more than to sit there beside the still, cooling body. Who would tell Kenre? What would Aunt Zorana do? A firm hand had touched her arm. She had looked up to see one of the field medics, a man she didn't even know by name though today they had worked as closely as brother and sister.

"I'm sorry," he had said, "but you could best honor this man by saving some of those who served with him. We are so very short of trained hands that we can't spare even a pair."

And Elise had staggered to her feet, knowing that Purcel would understand. By the time she reached the infirmary, she had blinked the tears from her eyes, but their stiff, dry tracks remained. Remained as she picked up bandages and began wrapping fresh wounds, remained as she murmured calming words she didn't even hear, remained as if they had been seared onto her face.

Suddenly, Elise's patient drew her breath in sharply.

"Did I hurt you?" Elise apologized, fearing that in her preoccupation she had been clumsy.

"No!" the woman gasped. "Behind you. A wolf!"

Similar murmurs, whispers, and even a few screams sounded beneath the hospital canopy. Elise turned and saw Blind Seer standing at the edge of the canopy, his head up and his tail wagging.

Everything about the beast shouted: "I am not here to hurt," but Elise saw hands searching for weapons and several of the wounded trying to get out of their beds.

"Stay still," she called, remembering her own first reaction to the enormous blue-eyed wolf. "That wolf is a friend."

Leaving her patient, she crossed to Blind Seer. Behind her she heard the regulars, those who had been with King Tedric since he left the capital, explaining to the new arrivals: "That's Lady Blysse's wolf. He's safe. Well, not safe, but he won't hurt *us*. See how he wags his tail at Lady Archer?"

Elise ignored them and spoke directly to the wolf. "What do you want? Where's Firekeeper?"

Blind Seer whined, groveled, then tugged delicately at the edge of her skirt.

"I'll come with you," Elise assured him. Immediately, Blind Seer dropped the fabric and began to trot toward one of the surgeries.

These were partially enclosed tents meant to keep out dust and distraction, not like the convalescent shelters, which were left open to light and air. Not until they ducked through the door of one did Elise realize who Blind Seer wanted. Sir Jared was busy with a critically wounded man. His face was strained, as he pressed his hands to a savaged abdomen and visibly willed the sutured flesh to heal.

Healing talent can help, but not when the person is already dead, Elise thought. *Oh, Purcel!*

Sir Jared turned just as Blind Seer nudged her and whined.

Elise called to him, "Sir Jared?"

Hearing her voice, to her amazement, Jared Surcliffe actually smiled.

"Yes, Lady Elise?"

"Blind Seer wants you rather urgently. Please come or I'm afraid he'll drag you with him."

Sir Jared did not ask questions, but obeyed. A few of the other physicians looked as if they might protest, but the combined prestige of baronial heir and knight silenced them.

Outside the tent, Blind Seer barked once and trotted in the direction of the king's tent, Sir Jared at his heels. Elise was about to follow when a familiar voice—almost shrill with strain—shouted:

"Elise! Sir Jared! Medic!"

Sir Jared hesitated, causing Blind Seer to growl, his hackles rising. Elise pushed the knight between the shoulder blades.

"Go!" she urged. "I'll handle this."

Grabbing one of the emergency kits from a long line stacked on a bench, Elise hurried toward the voice. Wounded were being carried off the battlefield on every side, but one pair crystallized her attention. Sapphire Shield was helping a young man off the field. It took Elise a moment to realize that her cousin's companion was Shad Oyster.

Sapphire's showy armor was streaked with blood—at least some of which seemed to be her own—caking field dust into clumps. Shad was nearly unconscious. Still, his limbs were all intact and he was not gushing blood, making him, no matter his social standing, a lesser priority than many others.

Elise guided them to a prep area explaining, "Unless he is in danger of death or of losing a limb, he must wait."

"Right," Sapphire said, and assisted Shad to something resembling comfort on the dirt. Folding her cloak under his head, she patted his hand reassuringly.

"The Blue and I were on the south flank," she said, turning some of her attention to Elise. Words spilled from her lips, though her gaze remained distracted.

"We fought for I don't know how long. Then there was one of those gaps that happen. I heard someone saying that Lord Tench had been shot. I looked in the direction of Duke Allister's command center. Everyone there was taking cover, but I didn't like the look of a group of Stonehold cavalry that was pushing that way. Earl Kestrel didn't either and shouted for us to get between them.

"We did. Somewhere in that, I was unhorsed. The Blue panicked— I hope he got away. I kept my sword and shield, though and kept backing toward the command center. That's when I met Shad doing pretty much the same thing."

She started helping Elise undo Shad's armor. When they lifted the breastplate off, Elise was relieved to see no evidence of an abdominal wound. She'd already learned how ugly those were—and how hard to treat.

Purcel!

Sapphire continued talking as she worked. Elise wondered if the flow of words was meant to stem similarly horrific thoughts. Did Sapphire know yet that her father was dead? Did she know about Purcel? For the first time, Elise remembered that Jet, too, was out there on the battlefield. Love must be dead—if ever it had lived—for her to have forgotten him so entirely.

With an effort, she focused on Sapphire's words:

"Earl Kestrel and his group stalled the cavalry charge or I wouldn't be here, but some Stonehold infantry took advantage of the horses kicking and milling to slip around the edges. They were heading for the commander again and no wonder. Duke Allister may have taken his training at sea, but he has tactical sense. Our side might have cut and run if they learned he was down—nearly did when the rumor came that he had been shot. Shad, though, he bellowed just like he was on deck in a storm, telling everyone that Duke Allister was alive."

Mopping blood from the young man's pale face, Elise found it difficult to believe that Shad could summon that much force. He looked exquisitely fragile now. Still, there was no blood on his lips and his gut was sound.

"How can I help?" Sapphire said, interrupting her own account.

"Try to get a little water into him," Elise said, "but slowly. There may be injuries I can't see."

Sapphire took the proffered water bottle, reminding Elise in her gentleness of the days they had both nursed dolls. Then the regular bustle of hospital and distant battle was pierced by a deep, mournful howl.

"Blind Seer!" Elise gasped, keeping herself to her duty with effort. "Something has happened to Firekeeper."

"I hope not," Sapphire said, but she too remained where she was needed.

Perhaps to distract herself from how the water dribbled down Shad's face or from the implications of that mournful howl, Sapphire continued:

"I'm not bragging, but it got down to few enough of us. Then a lucky blow slipped through and caught Duke Allister in the head. Shad went crazy, slashing at the man who'd done it. The commander was only stunned though. Someone got a bandage around his head and tried to get him to command from the rear but he insisted on staying. That's the kind of courage Duke Allister has. He knew what would happen if he left.

"I was crossing blades with some Stoneholder when Shad went down so I don't know exactly how it happened. Afterwards, someone told me that he took the flat of a sword squarely on the side of his head. I guess it's lucky that it wasn't the edge, but whatever did it, he went down like a bull under the hammer.

"Duke Allister ordered me to get his son off the field and I did. The duke wasn't playing favorites—not a bit—but I knew he couldn't very well fight a war with his son dead or dying at his feet. How is he?"

For a confused moment, Elise thought her cousin meant the duke, but then she recovered:

"He's breathing. His brain has obviously been shaken. Still, I see no deep wounds. I'm no doctor, but I think there's hope."

Sapphire smiled and got wearily to her feet. "Then I must report back. The commander will need to know. And . . ."

Her voice trailed off. "What is that?"

Elise looked where Sapphire was pointing, seeing a thick cloud of dark smoke rising in the west.

"Fire?" she said. "What does that mean?"

"It means," Sapphire said, straightening her helmet and arraying her much dented shield, "that if we press now the battle may be over."

Elise looked after her cousin as she ran toward the battlefield, understanding.

"The battle," she whispered, hardly daring hope, "and maybe even the war."

Then she remembered Blind Seer's howl and, calling for an aide to tend to Shad Oyster, she ran in the direction of the king's pavilion.

A splatter of blood on the ground outside the pavilion heralded the scene she found inside. Elise's overshift of bloodstained raw cotton (no medical uniform could be found for her when she volunteered) was her passport past the guards, for it marked her as someone from the hospital. Only after she was heading through the door did she hear one comment to the other:

"Was that Lady Archer?"

Within, the pavilion was crowded with those who had been delegated to stay near the king. Elise saw Aunt Zorana, Opal Shield, and Nydia Trueheart among the faces, but despite this usually talkative company, the pavilion was curiously silent, all attention fixed on the middle of the room. There Sir Jared knelt over a patient lying on one of the several carpets that had been spread for the king's comfort.

King Tedric himself held the lamp that lit the medic's work and Elise did not need to see Blind Seer pressed flat on the ground near the patient's head, whimpering with rather more pathos than one would expect from such an enormous beast, to know that the woman facedown on the floor was Firekeeper.

The crowd parted to let Elise through. She moved immediately to Sir Jared's side and asked:

"What can I do?"

"Hold this open," he said, not even glancing at her. "I need to make certain it's clean before I stitch it up."

Elise grasped the separators as she had been taught earlier that day, holding open a deep and ugly slice in Firekeeper's left thigh. While Jared sloshed something pungent into the raw opening Elise glanced at Firekeeper, but though the wound must have burned horribly, the younger woman did not stir.

Firekeeper's eyes were not so much closed as not open. A faint white line could be seen beneath the shuttered lid. An ugly wound in her back near her left side testified that a mere leg wound alone hadn't felled the wolf-woman so profoundly. Her armor and clothing had been partially removed, the sword cut cleaned, but little else had been done.

"Firekeeper saved my life," King Tedric explained, his voice quavering. "Prince Newell came. I believe he hoped to shock my heart into bursting, but failing that I think he would have taken more direct means. I don't know how Firekeeper knew, but she came charging in here— Newell had sent everyone away, saying he had something for my ears only and who was I to doubt him? There are state secrets he knew because of his marriage to Lovella."

"Knew?" Elise asked, letting the wound close when Jared signaled and then holding the edges in position so he could stitch.

"He's dead," the king said. "Firekeeper killed him even as he stabbed her in the back."

"Didn't anyone try to help her?" Elise asked indignantly.

"I was unable to do so." The king sounded as if he was apologizing. "Newell came closer to bringing on a heart attack than he will ever know. When the guards came in, I could not get the breath to speak. All I could do was keep them from interfering. Sir Jared, how does your patient?"

"There's not much I can do about the back wound," Jared said, his hands busy. "I think the sword blade missed most of the vitals, but I don't like the blood on her lips. A lung may have been nicked. Still, my talent may help keep internal damage from worsening."

Blind Seer moaned and sniffed Firekeeper's hair.

Elise asked, "But this on her leg doesn't look like a sword cut."

"Arrow," Jared said briefly.

"I did it," Lady Zorana said, coming forth and taking the lantern from King Tedric's hand. "Sit, Uncle. Do you want Lady Blysse's valor to end for nothing?"

The king reluctantly obeyed, leaning forward to keep watch over the proceedings. Zorana went on to Elise:

"Lady Blysse came charging up and without any explanation insisted on going into the tent. We told her the king was in conference, but she wasn't having anything of it."

"So you shot her?" Elise heard the incredulity in her voice.

"You may be comfortable with feral women and wolves," Zorana said in angry defense, "but some of us are not."

"She's also Lady Blysse and has lived with us for moon-spans now!" Elise protested.

Sir Jared glanced up. "Elise, please fight with your aunt later. I need you now."

Elise complied, but her anger didn't diminish. Only later would she calm enough to wonder if Purcel's death might have so shaken his mother that sane judgment had failed her.

At last, Sir Jared lifted his red-stained hands. Unasked, Elise poured water for him from a carafe, noticing for the first time how everything portable seemed to have been thrown about. Her gaze fell on Prince Newell's corpse, on the ugly red mark on the side of his face, and she thought she knew how the mess had been made.

Sir Jared said, "Your Majesty, I don't think Firekeeper should be moved except perhaps from the floor onto a cot. I'll need to commandeer your pavilion."

"It is hers," the king said. "I would remain here to guard her, but I fear I have a war to fight."

Elise realized that King Tedric knew nothing of the fire to the west. "Sire, if you're strong enough, you should go out and see what messages may be waiting. Just before I came here it seemed as if the enemy camp might be on fire."

"Lend me an arm, Opal," the king said immediately, turning to his grandniece. Elise noted absently that he didn't seem surprised by her news. "I'm strong enough if I have someone to lean on."

"The rest of you," Jared snapped, clearly expecting to be obeyed, "get out. Two of you take the corpse with you. Get me a cot, clean bandages, and more water."

The gathered nobles, even Lady Zorana, obeyed. Zorana, however, paused long enough to hang the lantern from one of the pavilion beams.

"Whatever you think," she said to Elise. "I do regret my part in this. I thought I was right—that's all I want you to realize—but I was wrong."

Elise nodded. When Zorana turned to go, Elise said to Sir Jared, "I'm not leaving."

"I didn't mean you," he said. "You're medical staff."

Warmed by his confident assumption that she had a right to be there, Elise confided, "I would have never thought I could do this work. I hate hawking or hunting, get all squeamish. My father is quite fed up with me."

"Squeamish?" Sir Jared shrugged. "Not when it counts. I've found you a steady assistant. It's a pity you're to be a baroness. I'd like to see what would happen if you had further training."

Elise raised an eyebrow. "There is no law against a baroness learning medicine. It could be quite useful."

He coughed. "I apologize."

Two guards came in then with the requested cot and gear. As they were setting it up, there was a shrill, avian cry from above.

"Elation," Elise said. "Then Derian . . ."

The tent flap all but flew open and the redhead dashed in. He was sweaty, reeking of smoke and horses. Blind Seer greeted him with another whine.

"Is she going to be all right?" Derian asked, flinging himself on the rug next to Firekeeper.

Jared said, "I hope so, but it's too early to tell. She's taken several bad wounds and lost a lot of blood."

Derian groaned. "I tried to get here faster. We heard Blind Seer howl, but we were still quite a ways off. Then we had trouble getting through the camp. Everyone was running here and there—a new push was on— fresh soldiers were needed. I nearly got hauled out there myself, but Elation kept diving at everyone who came close. What happened?"

They told him as, with his help, they moved Firekeeper onto the cot. Blind Seer promptly positioned himself directly under his pack mate and no one dared try to move him. The fierce desperation in the wolf's blue eyes was more eloquent than words.

"Poor guy," Derian said, doing what no one else had dared and actually patting the wolf on the head. "She's going to make it, fellow. After everything Firekeeper has survived she isn't going to let a couple of pompous noble-born asses kill her."

He glanced at Elise. "I'm not going to apologize for calling your aunt pompous."

"Just as long as you don't include me in that assessment of the nobility." Elise forced a laugh.

"Not you," Derian promised. "I don't even think it."

"Now that we've got her on the cot," Sir Jared said, "we should get the rest of Firekeeper's clothes off of her. Lady Elise can . . ."

Derian interrupted. "I've seen Firekeeper naked plenty of times. I think the minx used to do it on purpose to make me blush. Elise can chaperon if you want, but I'm here and I'm not leaving."

Jared patted the younger man. "Why do you all think I'm trying to get rid of you? I'm grateful for your help. Do you think you could tell Blind Seer not to bite us? Firekeeper may cry out as we move her."

"I think he understands," Derian said, taking out his knife and carefully beginning to cut away leather and fabric. "I just wish we could understand him better. He could tell us how Firekeeper knew the king was in trouble."

To his complete surprise, Blind Seer crept out from under the cot and, going to the door of the pavilion, barked once sharply. They heard Elation cry response; then the wolf returned. To everyone's astonishment, the peregrine falcon was walking with deliberate care after him.

She shrilled softly, almost cooing as she inspected Firekeeper. The wolf, busy fitting himself back under the cot, gave a low bark. Elation came to Derian and tugged at the cuff of his riding breeches with her beak.

"No," the young man replied. "I will not follow you. I'm staying with Firekeeper. Do you want someone to go somewhere with you?"

The peregrine drew her entire body up, then down, bobbing her torso in a fair facsimile of a nod.

Derian stepped to the door of the pavilion.

"Guard, get me Valet, Earl Kestrel's manservant. If you can't get him, I'll settle for Ox or Race Forester."

When it seemed that the guard might protest, Sir Jared snapped, "Do it!"

Derian returned to his task, saying to the falcon in passing, "Just a couple minutes. I'd have sent you after them, but I think you need someone to explain."

Grinning rather weakly, he looked at his friends. "You try tending to Firekeeper for nearly five moon-spans and see if you're not talking to animals at the end."

Elise saw the tears that filled Derian's hazel eyes as he looked at the unconscious woman, and politely pretended not to notice.

Valet arrived almost immediately. Elise noted that the usually immaculate manservant was nearly as grubby as Derian.

"That guard said you desired my presence," Valet said politely.

Derian nodded. "Follow Elation. I think she knows where something important is. I don't know more. Can you go in safety?"

Valet nodded. "The battle is over. The fire demoralized Stonehold's troops. To their credit, they didn't like fighting soldiers who were in many cases their friends. General Grimsel—the big blond woman—had been killed, earlier. Not much was needed to break their morale. General Yuci surrendered to Duke Allister a few moments ago."

The rush of relief that filled Elise was so powerful that her hands started shaking. Biting down on her lip, she steadied herself and continued with the delicate task of removing Firekeeper's undergarments without leaving fibers in the wounds that might later encourage infection and scarring.

"So it's over," Derian said for all of them.

"Not yet," Sir Jared replied with the sad wisdom of one who had been through fighting before. "That battle is ended. Now we need to know if the war is over as well."

XXVII

ALLISTER SEAGLEAM BRUSHED PEARL'S HANDS away from straightening the bandage that still wrapped his head.

"Enough, dear," he said firmly. "I realize it is hardly approved head gear for an audience with the queen, but the doctors say I must keep the wound lightly covered. There is too much risk of infection, especially here where the horses attract so many flies."

Pearl folded her arms over her chest, just slightly pouting. "I only wanted you to look your best for your meeting with Queen Gustin, Allister. This is the first time in the two days since her arrival that she has granted you a private audience. Given all you have done for her, that is hardly just!"

Allister patted his wife's hand, thinking that for an arranged marriage really this one had worked out remarkably well.

Pearl was actually concerned about the slight to him, not because it was a slight to herself or to her family, but because of her fondness for him. How many couples could claim that after twenty-two years of marriage and four children?

"My dear," he said, bending to kiss her round cheek, "Queen Gustin *wants* to play down her debt to me. You cannot have forgotten her reception when she arrived at the head of her marines, can you?"

"And I hope I never will!" Pearl laughed, her good humor restored. Then she frowned. "Though perhaps the townsfolk throwing rubbish at her from the walls was a bit much."

Allister nodded. "It was, but who could blame them? They are simple folk who place their trust in the Crown. This was not the first battle fought in the shadows of those walls—only the biggest."

"And the only one where Hawk Haven fought beside us rather than against us," Pearl mused. "Yes, when an enemy turns out to be a friend, is it any surprise that late-coming friends suddenly seem like enemies?"

"No, it is not." Allister paused thoughtfully. "My dear, what I want to say to the queen today may put me on the list of those she sees as enemies. One word from you and I will hold my tongue."

Pearl raised an eyebrow. "That bad?"

"That bad."

"Have you spoken to the children about it? Shad, at least, is old enough that you should consider his opinion before doing something that will affect his future."

"I have. He encourages me."

As he should, Allister thought, *for if I pull this off it will make his fortune.*

"And have you spoken with Tavis?"

"A little. Right now he is still adjusting to the realities of war. He did not fight, but in acting as runner he saw plenty of bloodshed. The concept that true heroism and true horror can and do exist together is a large one for a romantic fifteen-year-old to grasp."

Pearl nodded. "It is. I had wondered at him spending so much time with the soldiers all of a sudden. At the ball he avoided them; now he sits by their firesides for hours, listening to stories and asking questions."

A discreet knock at the door reminded Allister that the time had come for him to depart for his appointment.

"Do you really want me to do this?" he asked, putting on his tricorn at a rather rakish angle over his bandage.

"Perhaps you should tell me just what it is you plan to do," Pearl sighed, but something in her shrewd gaze made him think she had guessed.

Allister turned back from the door he had been about to open and said softly, "I plan to tell Queen Gustin that she must make me her heir and, if I predecease her, that my surviving eldest must take over as crown prince."

Pearl stood on tiptoe to kiss him, her eyes very bright. "You saved her kingdom. What else would be reward enough?"

But as Allister went out the door he could not fail to see that Pearl was trembling and knew that she feared she would never see him again. Queen Gustin was not always a just monarch—only a successful one.

After the second battle of what people were calling Allister's War, the grateful town of Good Crossing had made much of her defenders. Needing a secure command center, Allister had accepted the loan of a mansion from a real-estate speculator who had imagined all his investments torched and battered by Stonehold's invading army.

Flanked by his bodyguards, Duke Allister trotted briskly down the mansion's broad, stone front steps. Cheering greeted him the moment he passed into the sight of the people gathered outside his temporary headquarters.

Day and night, idlers waited outside the place, hoping for a glimpse of the Pledge Child, the valiant commander in chief. Winning the battle had made Allister a hero—nor had it hurt the duke's prestige that both himself and his eldest son had been injured fighting in defense of Bright Bay.

However, what had helped Allister Seagleam's reputation the most was that Queen Gustin IV had not been present for either battle. When rumors had spread that she had not been fighting pirates but had been within a day's ride of Good Crossing for several days before the fighting began, escorted by a host of blooded marines drawn from her best ships, Allister's reputation had soared even as hers had plummeted.

Waving to his admirers, Allister accepted a hand up into the carriage that would rattle him through the cobble streets to where Queen Gustin resided in sumptuous quarters in the Toll House. In the carriage, he made casual comments that he could not remember a moment later, his thoughts focused on the meeting to come.

It was not as if he hadn't seen the queen in the days since her arrival. There had been countless meetings: with King Tedric and his officers, with General Yuci of Stonehold, with members of the local guildhalls. During all of them Queen Gustin had been faultlessly courteous, deferring to her cousin's greater knowledge of the situation while making clear that she was his ruler and that she believed that his triumph was best seen within the context of her reign.

Allister supposed it had been that attitude—that combined with the current situation regarding King Tedric's own heir—which had made him consider what he would demand as reward for his services. He knew that he was being foolhardy, but he also knew that he could not go back to his former situation. It had taken him over forty years to be something more than a failed pledge. The need to continue building the bridge between Hawk Haven and Bright Bay was a desperate fire within him, hot in breast and mind.

Cheering admirers ran alongside his carriage and greeted him as he dismounted from it at the Toll House. Even while acknowledging their good wishes, Allister knew that those noisy praises were doing him no good with the queen.

Arriving at the tower room where Queen Gustin IV was holding audience, he was admitted at once. Queen Gustin rose from her paper-strewn desk, holding out her hands to greet him in a familiar embrace.

"Welcome, cousin," she said. "I am so glad that matters of state at last relent enough to permit us a private talk."

Queen Gustin IV was regarded by many as a lovely woman. Certainly her eyes were the blue of oceans and her hair the red-gold of honey just as the ballads said, but a calculating expression rarely left those blue eyes. At twenty-eight her figure was still firm and buxom and her smile merry, but that smile came infrequently these days and to him, who had known her since she was a child, it possessed a studied cast.

"I am glad to see you, too," he replied.

"And Shad, is he recovering?"

"Nicely. He took a solid blow to the head, but several of the medics possessed the healing talent. Give him a couple days bed rest and he will be up and about—though the doctors suggest he do nothing too strenuous for a moon-span or so if at all possible."

"I am glad to hear he is doing so well. Sit down, Cousin Allister. We have much to discuss."

Allister did so. An unobtrusive servant took his hat and set out a tray with peach cider and cups.

"Leave us now," Queen Gustin ordered.

The man—a marine, Allister thought—bowed and departed.

"I don't know how to thank you for the work you have done for me these past days," she began.

Here is where you could make your demands, Allister, he thought, but all he said was:

"Thank you. Bright Bay is my country, too."

"There are those back at court who are remembering that Hawk Haven is your country, as well," Gustin said, just a bit slyly.

"My mother's," he replied. "I have never crossed its borders, not even as far as over this bridge."

"Yet report is that King Tedric embraced you like a long-lost son."

"King Tedric was kind to me for his sister's sake and for the sake of peace between our nations," Allister replied.

"And has he made you any offers?"

"We had not reached that point before Stonehold grew nervous and our negotiations were suspended."

" 'Grew nervous'—that's an odd way to say 'Declared war.' "

"They did not declare war," Allister said, "until it was evident that Your Majesty was not going to treat with them."

"They had no right to meddle with a completely internal issue!"

"I agree, Your Majesty. I was merely responding to your statement."

Queen Gustin IV glowered at Allister, reminding him irresistibly of the autocratic little girl with whom he once had played at make-believe. She hadn't liked being criticized then either—not even by implication.

That very well might be the problem of raising someone to know that she can expect to rule someday, Allister thought. *Of course, the opposite problem is what King Tedric faces—choosing a successor from those unprepared for the responsibility.*

"Negotiations with Stonehold are progressing," Queen Gustin said, "slowly, but progressing. A pair of ministers empowered to sign a treaty should arrive tomorrow. They are bringing with them a fine sum to compensate us for our losses in soldiers and goods. If all goes well, Stonehold will begin withdrawing the following day."

"Very good."

"Although we have promised her a share of the compensation, Hawk Haven is being a bit more difficult about stating exactly when her troops will withdraw," the queen continued thoughtfully, "and I am not in an advantageous position to set dates and times. Even with the reinforcements I brought with me, the Stalwarts of the Golden Sunburst are less impressive without Hawk Haven's army intermingled with them. Without Hawk Haven's support, Stonehold might decide not to depart after all."

Allister forbore from commenting.

"Indeed, I would have Hawk Haven's troops remain until Stonehold's are gone and Mason's Bridge secured, but I can extract no promise that they will withdraw at all." Queen Gustin frowned. "Have you any suggestions as to how we might resolve this problem?"

This is it! Allister thought, taking a deep breath.

"Yes, I do," he said, and was amazed that his voice did not shake. "Hawk Haven has proven a true friend to us. They need equal proof that we will be a true friend to them."

"And," Gustin said, her tone just a touch sardonic, "do you have any idea what we might do to give them this assurance?"

"Make me your heir," Allister said coolly, "for I have shown myself their friend. In the event I predecease you—as is likely—my heir must take my place as your heir.

"In return, I will convince King Tedric to wed to his own heir one of my children—who I will immediately designate my own heir. Thus, upon Tedric's death—which sadly cannot be too far away—a child Bright

Bay born will sit upon the throne of Hawk Haven. When I become an ancestor, the reverse will be true. By then our nations will have grown accustomed to—perhaps even come to anticipate—the idea of a union between our peoples and all should progress smoothly."

Allister managed to complete this long speech mostly because Queen Gustin was far too astonished to interrupt. When he stopped, she exclaimed:

"I should make you my heir? Why should I care for a union?"

"Promise of a union will permit us to forge an alliance with Hawk Haven, an alliance that will give King Tedric's people the incentive to provide Bright Bay with military support without taking the further step of becoming conquerors—a thing that is otherwise far too tempting.

"If my plan is followed, you will reign as long as you live. Then I— or more probably my heir—will assume the throne. Since that same heir will quite likely already be king or queen of Hawk Haven, our kingdoms will be reunited under one ruler and my royal grandparents' dreams will at last come true."

Queen Gustin was too self-disciplined to start out of her chair, but she did slam her cup of peachy down with such force that the tray rattled. "This plan is insane! I forbid you to mention it to anyone."

"I'm sorry, Your Majesty," Allister replied levelly. "I have already discussed something like this with King Tedric in the context of my permitting one of my children to marry his unnamed heir."

That's stretching the point a bit, he thought, *but the clerk who attended the meeting will not be able to say for certain that something of the sort was not discussed in private. There is no need for her to know that I've written Uncle Tedric telling him my plans and nearly begging for his support—and for sanctuary for me and my family if I fail.*

"Oh, you have . . ." She fell into thought. "And has this tasty bit of treason been mentioned to anyone else?"

Allister answered calmly. "Not in so many words, but several of my callers these past days have expressed hope that some such plan may be in the making. I have only been able to say that I believed Your Majesty a good and wise ruler with the best interests of her nation at heart."

"Oh, you have . . ."

"I could hardly say more when Your Majesty and I had not yet spoken in private."

So there! he thought with what he knew was childish vindictiveness. *Ah, well. Her neglecting to give me a private meeting was equally childish.*

Still, he was privately embarrassed. He was a grown man of forty-four, not a child.

Queen Gustin had not seemed to hear the reproof in his retort. "We had not, had we? And if I do not agree to make you my heir? What will Hawk Haven do then?"

"I couldn't say."

"But that doesn't mean you don't know . . . and their troops already on our soil and the local people lauding them as saviors."

Allister replied sternly, "Hawk Haven deserves such praise. Their army fought and many died in defense of Good Crossing. We could not have held the city without them. The Battle of the Banks would have been our disgrace, not the first action in a victorious war."

"Perhaps," Gustin said hotly, "they merely fought to keep Stonehold from crossing at Bridgeton and threatening their own lands."

"Don't be an idiot," Allister retorted sharply. "Stonehold was already stretched to the limits of their supply line. If anything Hawk Haven stood to benefit economically by Stonehold's conquest of Good Crossing."

Queen Gustin's cheeks had flared hot and red at the sharpness of Duke Allister's words, but his fame as the hero of the recent war protected him. She could have him neither executed nor arrested without bringing the rage of the local populace down upon her.

Allister, who had regretted his lack of tact as soon as the words slipped out, saw the red fade from the queen's cheeks to be replaced by an ivory white pallor that was no less furious.

"Economically?" she replied, the word coming out as a cough. "I suppose you mean by supplying Stonehold's army."

"I do," Allister said, watching her guardedly. Queen Gustin seemed to be under control now, so he went on pedantically, giving her more time to cool. "The raiders who burned Stonehold's supplies performed an act that was as decisive an element in General Yuci's decision to surrender as anything done on the battlefield. All of them, by the way, were residents of Hawk Haven."

"Including among their numbers," Queen Gustin said, cooler now, but needing to vent her fury, "a carter, a manservant, and a criminal, if I read the report correctly."

"Yes, I suppose you could say that," Allister replied, deciding not to protest too strongly. "Earl Kestrel permitted several members of his personal entourage to take part in the battle."

"Kestrel . . ." Gustin murmured as if trying to place the name, though Allister did not doubt she knew precisely of whom they spoke.

"Kestrel," Allister repeated dryly. "The man who led the left wing of the cavalry charge and fought bravely despite ribs broken when a horse fell on him."

"I remember him now," Queen Gustin said. "Norvin Norwood. He's also the man who brought back some foundling and tried to claim she was King Tedric's granddaughter, right?"

"Yes. There is some evidence in favor of his claim. I've met the young woman. She's quite remarkable."

"Rumor said she's nearly dead from injuries taken when she assaulted Prince Newell Shield."

"At last report," Allister replied, a trifle more sharply than he had intended, "Lady Blysse is expected to live, though she will be convalescing for some time. Prince Newell, as you may have heard, was attempting to assassinate King Tedric. From what one of the late prince's servants confessed, Newell had planned to have himself declared king."

And I don't suppose we'll ever know just how much you knew of his plans or whether you would have supported them. Oh, Valora, I wish I could trust you!

"We can't treat with Stonehold from a position of strength," the queen mused aloud, "without the support of Hawk Haven. Now you tell me—or at least imply—that Hawk Haven's continued support is contingent upon my naming you my heir. Tell me, why shouldn't I make my treaty with Stonehold, get them gone, and then dismiss Hawk Haven?"

"Well, Your Majesty, they might be difficult to dismiss."

"True. And they might even ally themselves with Stonehold and complete the conquest. Our army could not withstand them both."

Allister nodded. "I do not like to dwell on the idea, but the possibility has occurred to me. Still, I believe that King Tedric would prefer to ally himself with us with eventual reunification in mind. We share a common heritage—common ancestors—so to speak."

"Yet he could be a conqueror with half our lands as his booty," Queen Gustin said, "far more quickly than if we travel the route you suggest."

Allister Seagleam shrugged. "True. However, conquered lands might be hard to hold. Once secure with part of Bright Bay, Stonehold might decide she wants the whole. We have the ocean ports their own land lacks."

Queen Gustin laughed bitterly. "Stonehold might want the whole, just as Hawk Haven has decided she wants the whole. Yes, I can see how King Tedric might take warning from his own example. Tell me, Allister, why shouldn't I just prolong negotiations until King Tedric dies? His new heir might prove more tractable."

"Or he or she might not," Allister countered, fascinated despite himself with this weird byplay. He could feel Gustin hating him for the position in which he had put her, yet she persisted in asking for his advice. "And King Tedric, while possessed of a weak heart, is not in any immediate danger. Some have suggested that the stimulation of this journey has actually strengthened him."

"Delightful . . ." Gustin IV sank her polished white teeth into her little finger, as if pain was the only distraction that would keep her from screaming. "So my only choice is to make you my heir."

"I never said that, Your Majesty," Allister replied firmly, "only that I thought that solution provided the best way to secure an alliance with Hawk Haven that will prove for our mutual benefit."

Queen Gustin fell silent for a moment, then looked across at him, her face eerily expressionless, a portrait cast in clean, white porcelain.

"You may leave, Duke Allister," she said with cool formality. "Thank you for your services. Send my commander of marines up to me as you are leaving."

Allister did as ordered, wondering what thoughts had lain behind that lovely mask and dreading that he must soon learn.

❦

DERIAN SAT AT FIREKEEPER'S BEDSIDE occupying the restless patient by drilling her in the alphabet—alternating these lessons with basic heraldry when she grew frustrated.

Annoying as the wolf-woman's impatience could be, Derian took it as a good sign that she had energy enough to get angry. For two days following her struggle with Prince Newell, Firekeeper had lain still and silent, hardly responding to any stimulus, no matter who her caller or what news she was told.

A few things had sparked her interest: praise from Earl Kestrel, who had knelt by her bedside holding her hand, tears actually running down his cheeks into his neat black and white beard; learning that Rook had been taken and had confessed—in return for a promise of imprisonment rather than execution—the extent of Prince Newell's plotting; the story of Derian's own adventures, told with great enthusiasm by Race Forester.

But for most of those two long days she had simply lain still, neither restfully sleeping nor truly awake, suffering with every breath. Derian or Elise or Doc had kept vigil by her cot, wiping the bloody spume off her lips, moistening her throat with dribble of water, and talking to her when it seemed she might actually hear.

On the third day, Firekeeper had begun to recover, reacting with small signs of pleasure when Doc had ordered her cot moved out into the warm autumn sunshine. Today—the fourth day since the end of the decisive battle of Allister's War—she was sitting propped against carefully positioned pillows and fretting because Doc would not let her get up— and because Blind Seer and Elation had nominated themselves enforcers of the physician's orders.

Doubtless Doc's healing talent had been instrumental in assisting Firekeeper's recovery, but he had refused to take full credit. Indeed, he had confided to Derian that without her own indomitable desire to live, Firekeeper—like so many of those wounded on the battlefield—would have died.

Derian had taken his turn digging graves for the dead of both sides. The continuing warmth of early autumn would not permit the bodies to be carried home to their families, but still the dead's spirits must be properly honored. Sitting by Firekeeper as she had slept, Derian had lettered temporary gravestones—wooden plaques that would be set in place until the stonecutters could finish the permanent headstones.

As he worked, Derian was inexorably reminded of those anonymous graves west of the gap. Now he knew two more of the names that should be there: Sarena Gardener and Donal Hunter. Silently, he vowed that he'd learn the other names and return someday to set a permanent gravestone in that burned glade.

"Scarlet beside forest green blazed with . . ." Derian was prompting Firekeeper when footsteps crunching up the path announced callers.

Elation squawked and Firekeeper said:

"Sapphire Shield and Shad Oyster." A wicked twinkle lit her dark eyes. "Elation say they were holding hands when they were farther, but have let go now."

Derian wagged a finger at the peregrine falcon. "You're a worse gossip than any market-wife."

The falcon, who continued to follow Derian about his errands until Derian couldn't decide whether he felt honored or pestered, screeched at him and Firekeeper chuckled, stopping abruptly as if the intake of air still hurt her damaged lung.

"We can't precisely knock," Sapphire called, halting a short distance away, "but Elise said that Firekeeper was entertaining callers."

"As long as she stays in bed," Derian said, rising and bowing. "Would you like me to withdraw?"

"Not for my sake," said Shad in a pleasant light baritone. "I've wanted to meet you. That was a brave deed you did, Derian Carter."

He offered his hand as if he were not a duke's son, but just another man. Derian accepted the handclasp.

"The real credit should go to the scouts," Derian said firmly. "They fought the enemy. I shot a few arrows and freed a few horses."

"Not having killed doesn't alter the courage you showed in going behind the lines," Shad insisted, and Sapphire nodded agreement. "And given that the diversion caused by the fire probably saved my father's life I am particularly grateful."

"Thank you," Derian replied, dismissing the topic of his own heroism by turning to Firekeeper. "Have you met Lady Blysse?"

"At the ball," Shad said, "I believe I had the pleasure of a dance."

"No dancing now," Firekeeper commented sadly, "not yet. Your father is well?"

"If having Queen Gustin the Fourth furious with you can be taken as well," Shad said proudly, "yes, he is."

"And you," Firekeeper said to Sapphire, "I was told your father died. I am sorry."

"Me, too," Sapphire admitted. "I miss him more than I had thought possible. Mother has already departed for home with Opal. The dual blows of losing her husband and having her brother proven traitor were too much for her. She said she will retreat to our country estate for a time."

"Good!" Firekeeper replied with such firmness that Shad looked puzzled, but his manners were too good—or perhaps he also had heard rumors about Lady Melina—for him to ask. "What does Jet do?"

"Jet is a problem," Sapphire sighed. "He conducted himself well enough in the battle. Elise, however, has petitioned her father for permission to break the engagement. Baron Archer has asked Elise to wait until the current negotiations are ended and she agreed—but only after insisting that the king be told informally that the alliance is ended. So now Jet is questing around, looking for someone or something to which he could attach himself. I really don't know what to do with him."

Shad laughed. "In my country we'd send him to sea on a 'prentice cruise. It's amazing how quickly ambitious young aristocrats learn just how little they matter when pitted against a hurricane."

"That's not a bad idea," Sapphire reflected. "There's good in Jet, but he's been too influenced by Mother."

She brushed her fingers along the snow white mark on her forehead as she said this, a tacit admission to those who knew her history that Jet was not the only one who must overcome Melina Shield's influence.

"And peace?" Firekeeper said. "Is peace found?"

"The talks continue," Sapphire replied, "but in great secrecy. King Tedric has not even called in his counselors."

Derian demurred. "That's not quite correct. He calls us together every afternoon and again every evening. However, I agree wholeheartedly with his decision not to take a huge entourage with him to these meetings. Forgive me, noble friends, but I have never heard anything like dukes and duchesses, earls and . . ."

Here Derian paused for a moment, for the title for male and female Great House heirs was pronounced the same, though spelled differently. Then he shrugged and stormed on, "And earles all arguing for positions that—no matter how they are worded—are meant merely to advance their personal causes."

Sapphire didn't look offended, neither did Shad. Derian reflected that what he had said was no news at all to scions of Great Houses. How had he ever been so naive as to believe that those noble born were any different from the lowliest farmer or cobbler?

Derian continued: "And matters become worse the longer we remain here. Queen Gustin's entourage has been fattened by representatives of all her Great Houses. King Tedric already had members of most of his here, but those who felt they were not represented by someone of high enough rank have sent along someone else. The only ones who benefit from this proliferation are the merchants in the twin towns. Hazel Healer said that profits are up so high that even rumors that changes are in the wind bother no one."

"Changes," mused Shad Oyster. "My father has told us to expect such. I fear that no matter how these negotiations are resolved, I will never again stand on the deck of a Bright Bay ship. Father has made the queen his enemy."

Given that such rumors had been current for several days now, not even Firekeeper looked greatly surprised.

"This feels," the wolf-woman said somberly, showing a greater understanding of the situation than Derian would have given her credit for, "like the prickle that fills the air before a thunderstorm. We shall either see battle again to make the battle before as nothing or . . ."

"What?" Shad asked, as transfixed as if she spoke prophecy.

"I don't know," Firekeeper said, wincing as she leaned back against her pillows. "I am only a wolf."

XXVIII

DUKE ALLISTER SEAGLEAM feared that despite his best efforts Bright Bay would soon be at war again. The question was with whom?

The ministers from Stonehold had arrived several days before with the promised compensation payment. However, doubtless informed by their spies of the tension between Hawk Haven and Bright Bay, they were being remarkably coy about handing the money over and clearing out their army.

The ministers' excuses were ever so polite and ever so practical. Stonehold's wounded could not yet be moved. The army was short of horses to pull their wagons. They needed to purchase supplies for the march home since Queen Gustin would not permit them to bring over supplies from Stonehold.

Neither Duke Allister nor Queen Gustin was fooled by these excuses. What Stonehold's ministers were really waiting to see was how much longer Hawk Haven would continue to support Bright Bay and, indeed, how much longer could Queen Gustin keep a hold on her increasingly unhappy populace.

The degree of that unhappiness had been a surprise to the young queen—although perhaps it should not have been. Crown Princess Valora had ascended the throne of Bright Bay eight years before, on the death of her long-lived father, Gustin III. Hers had not been an easy ascension, complicated by events from many years before her birth.

Duke Allister, seventeen years her senior and the result of much intrigue himself, clearly recalled those events and the history that had seemed to make them inevitable.

The net of intrigues, likes, and dislikes within the noble families of Bright Bay was no less complicated than that within Hawk Haven. At the time he established his new kingdom, Gustin I had created five Great Houses. From the start, these had relinquished their original family names and assumed new ones: Oyster, Dolphin, Pelican, Seal, and Lobster. The members of the newly created Great Houses had been encouraged to think well of themselves, to design elegant coats of arms, to build fine estates.

This had almost certainly been because Gustin Sailor—unlike Zorana Shield—craved pomp and circumstance. Indeed, at the same time that Gustin I was giving names and titles to his Great Houses, he had renamed his own family, shedding the pedestrian trade name Sailor in favor of the lofty and poetic Seagleam.

But beneath his flourishes, Gustin I was practical when it came to securing his ambitions for his young family. Before the end of the Civil War, his wife Gayl Minter—later Queen Gayl—had borne him two children. The eldest, a son named Gustin for his father, was designated crown prince. The second became Princess Merry. A year or so after the war had ended, Princess Lyra was born, the first child to be born into the Seagleam name.

Gustin I would have rested content had not Crown Prince Gustin died of pneumonia shortly after his sixteenth birthday. Driven nearly mad with grief, Gustin I confirmed Princess Merry as his heir, but decreed that upon ascending the throne she would be known as Gustin in memory of her brother—and, the cynical said, of himself.

King Gustin died five years after his son, an embittered man of sixty-five whose many successes could not console him for his one great loss. Crown Princess Merry, aware that the first succession in a monarchy is always the most uncertain, followed her father's commands and changed her name to Gustin, although she had been heard to protest about being forced to bear what before had always been an exclusively male name.

Although the new monarch was only nineteen, she was a strong-willed woman. Queen Gustin II used her unmarried state to explore the internal politics of her Great Houses and six years after she had taken the throne she married wisely and well to Lord Amery Pelican, a second son of that house. Their first child, a son, was born less than two years later. Contrary to expectations, the queen named the boy Basil, saying that two Gustins was too many. In this way she unintentionally established the custom that the name Gustin was only to be used by the monarch.

Queen Gustin II bore two other children, Princess Seastar and Prince Tavis. Then she concentrated her efforts on ruling her kingdom, efforts which included the idealistic but doomed marriage arranged between her son Prince Tavis and King Chalmer of Hawk Haven's daughter Princess Caryl Eagle.

When he was twenty-six, Crown Prince Basil married Lady Brina Dolphin, a union that was to have serious consequences for Bright Bay and for Basil's own unborn heir.

The marriage was unblessed with children. When this became evident some suggested that Crown Prince Basil adopt an heir. Several Great Houses thrust forth candidates—one of whom was young Allister Seagleam. With an egotism suggestive of his grandfather, Gustin I, Crown Prince Basil refused to settle for anything but an heir of his body. His mother frowned upon a divorce—not wishing to anger the Dolphin family, which had already been offended by her marrying of Tavis to Princess Caryl—as it had suggested to them that the children of their Brina might not succeed their father to the throne.

But the Dolphins' Brina bore no children and when at the age of thirty-six Crown Prince Basil became Gustin III, he set about finding a new wife. He did not do this quickly. Indeed, some said he enjoyed sampling the eligible noblewomen quite freely. Others said that his reasons for delaying were more practical—he needed to gather support from the rising nobles of his generation before declaring his divorce.

Whatever the reason for the delay, seven years after ascending the throng Gustin III took the formal step of divorcing Queen Brina—who reassumed her family name and title. Before the next year ended, King Gustin III had married Lady Viona Seal, a woman of only twenty— twenty-four years his junior.

Rumor said that the new queen was pregnant with the king's child when marriage oaths were exchanged. Rumor further reported that Queen Viona miscarried shortly thereafter. Whatever the truth, Queen Viona did not succeed in bearing a living child until seven full years after her marriage to the king.

The birth of Crown Princess Valora was publicly celebrated with dances, feasts, and songs. Privately, it was the source of much wrath. The newly made Grand Duchess Seastar—for as the king now had an heir she was displaced as Crown Princess—was wrathful. Although of late Grand Duchess Seastar had ceased to believe she would succeed her brother, she had come to believe that King Gustin III *must* adopt one of her sons as his heir.

Nor was she the only one of King Gustin III's nobles to feel that the baby girl was too little too late. Some muttered that Crown Princess Valora was not legitimate—that Gustin III's seed, not Lady Brina's womb, had been at fault for their childless marriage and that young Viona had in desperation found another man to father her child.

Others, unwilling to publicly question Viona's honesty, had questioned the validity of Gustin III's divorce. Still others had urged the claim of Duke Allister Seagleam, saying that he had been born to assume the throne and that the long delay in the king's producing an heir had been an omen in his favor.

All in all, Valora's birth had awakened much spite, but King Gustin III had turned a deaf ear to the murmurings, distracting himself by watching his daughter grow and his people with military ventures against Hawk Haven.

Crown Princess Valora proved to be a healthy child, astonishingly free of whatever flaws had slain her brothers and sisters while still in the womb. She grew strong, intelligent, willful, and even beautiful. Her dot-ing father was too wise to permit her to become quite spoiled, but from the time she could talk, Valora knew she would be queen. Unlike King Tedric, who could threaten to disown one of his children, Gustin III had no such option—even should he desire it. Nor did the crown princess ever believe her father *would* wish it. He had striven too hard for her birth.

As Crown Princess Valora grew, the ambitious still dreamed that a way to power would be opened to them—that King Gustin III would die while his daughter was still too young to rule without a regent and they could assume that privileged post. Yet King Gustin III defied them all, remaining sound of mind until a weak heart claimed him at seventy-one. By then Crown Princess Valora had passed her twentieth birthday and was safely beyond any challenge that she was disbarred by age from taking up her crown.

At the time of her coronation, some raised the old complaint that Valora was not a child of Gustin III's body, but this was a weak argument by now. From Gildcrest, Bright Bay had inherited the custom that an adopted child could inherit with the full rights of a naturally born one. Even if Valora was not Gustin III's daughter, he had clearly raised her as such and the will of a king served as adoption enough.

So Crown Princess Valora ascended the throne. In the pattern of her grandmother, Valora continued the tradition of taking the male name Gustin. Like her grandmother, she waited to marry until each of her Great Houses could present its claim—and its best candidate. Two years after becoming queen, Gustin IV married Lord Harwill Lobster, a handsome, but untried man slightly younger than herself. Some said that Harwill's relative youth and lack of achievement had been part of his attraction, for Queen Gustin IV would accept no rivals. Others were kinder and said that there was real affection between the two.

And yet how quickly our queen forgets, Duke Allister thought, *how her very birth was resented, how her own aunt saw her as a squatter on a throne destined for other—better—people. Perhaps she doesn't want to remember, but prefers to believe that these eight years have erased ambitions that had over thirty to grow.*

Whatever the reasons for her way of thinking, the queen's lack of de-cisiveness in this recent action has not helped her position. Indeed, I think that noble and commoner alike would support me over Gustin the Fourth if their choice was me as king or more war to keep a woman who many think should never have been born or ascended the throne.

Indeed, once rumors had been spread that Allister had requested the queen name him her heir, representatives of several of the Great Houses—starting with Pearl's own brother, Reed, Duke Oyster—had approached Allister, offering him their support if he wished to force the queen to step down. King Tedric had also shown his support for Allister—not publicly where the Stonehold ministers might claim it invalidated agreements made with Queen Gustin IV, but in a private meeting with Queen Gustin IV.

The queen had not been pleased, but no one was certain what shape that displeasure would take. Would she force a war that might lead to her kingdom's destruction or would she step down?

Duke Allister didn't know, but he suspected that the closed meeting which had been called for this very morning at the Toll House would resolve the question.

THE MEETING ROOM WAS CROWDED, for the Toll House had not been designed to accommodate such events. However, the international nature of the invitation list demanded that the conference be held on something resembling neutral ground.

Both Bright Bay and Hawk Haven were represented not only by their monarchs but by a single representative for each of their Great Houses. Duke Allister Seagleam, although technically not a representative of any Great House, was also present. Whether his Bright Bay title, his relationship to King Tedric, or his recent victory gave him the right was moot—not even Queen Gustin IV at her most autocratic would have dared exclude him.

In addition to these fourteen people, there were bodyguards for the monarchs—a matter, most hoped, of etiquette rather than of necessity.

There were a handful of secretaries and clerks to take notes or to supply documents as needed.

The crowding of not quite two dozen people made the stone-walled room close and heightened the air of tension. Duke Allister Seagleam, seated beside his brother-in-law, Reed Oyster, tried hard to look impassive though his heart was beating at a frantic rate.

King Tedric, as befitted his years, made the opening statement.

"We have gathered here," the king said, "to resolve certain matters that have arisen out of Stonehold's attack on Bright Bay. My kingdom came to Bright Bay's aid when she was attacked by her supposed allies. Although Bright Bay has settled with Stonehold, she has not fully settled with me. Until this is done, I do not believe matters with Stonehold truly have been resolved."

Queen Gustin IV, her red-gold hair cascading loose over her shoulders from beneath her crown, looked pale and stern as she stood to make her reply. As had King Tedric, she addressed her remarks to the gathered nobles rather than to her fellow monarch.

"Bright Bay has offered Hawk Haven a half share of the monies to be received from Stonehold as compensation for her assistance in defending our lands. We believe this fair and even generous for although both of our armies fought, Bright Bay's lands alone suffered damage. We have taken more than half of the injury, yet we are prepared to give over a fair half of the compensation in thanks to our recent ally."

Whereas King Tedric's speech had been met with neutral silence, when Queen Gustin stopped speaking low, angry muttering could be heard—mostly from where the Hawk Haven delegates were seated.

No wonder, Allister thought. *Their people died in her defense and yet she belittles their sacrifice. She doesn't even repeat the thanks she offered publicly and grudgingly upon her arrival after the bloodshed had ended.*

He noticed, however, that not all the Bright Bay delegates were neutral. Arsen, Duke Dolphin, no great friend of the queen and enough years her senior that he felt secure speaking out, stood to be recognized. Gustin did so with a formal nod of her head.

"I wish to call to Your Majesty's attention," Duke Dolphin stated with equal formality, "that according to the heralds' counts *more* of Hawk Haven's soldiers died upon the field than did our own. True, the number was close, but *their* valor in giving up their lives for the security of *your* kingdom deserves more than mere monetary reward."

Duke Dolphin's sly but certain emphasis of the phrases "their valor" and "your kingdom" served as a pointed reminder that Queen Valora had not been present to defend her lands. The queen's eyes narrowed, but her color did not rise.

"We thank Duke Dolphin," she said, "for his reminder. We had not forgotten this fact, but the matter remains that we had not asked for Hawk Haven's aid. We feel she should accept what reward we have to give, not barter like fish sellers in the marketplace."

This time the angry exclamations were more general and less restrained. King Tedric, however, merely raised to his hand for silence and said:

"Indeed, Hawk Haven was not invited initially, but after the Battle of the Banks, Duke Allister did thank us and formally request our continued assistance. It is my understanding that, although Your Majesty was too busy to come and assess the situation for yourself, you did feel comfortable designating Duke Allister your representative, even to the point of urging your officers to support him."

"I did," Queen Gustin said stiffly. She might have said more, but King Tedric continued with a smoothness that made his overriding her not even seem rude.

"We came to Bright Bay's aid," Tedric said, "without any formal contract, nor did we come as mercenaries. We came because I wished to support those who shared a heritage with my people against a foreign aggressor. Moreover, Duke Allister Seagleam is my own sister's son. I could not face my ancestors in good conscience if I refused him aid."

"Yet," Queen Gustin said bitterly, "you have not worried about your ancestors' reaction to the many battles you have fought against my people in the past."

"Those," King Tedric said, "were family squabbles such as the ancestors themselves have fought. No doubt you planned to instigate a few yourself, perhaps once this old king was gone and a monarch less certain sat upon the Eagle Throne."

Queen Gustin's cheeks flared sudden, unguarded red.

So that is what she did intend, Allister mused. *Good tactical sense, really, if anyone thinks about it, but her blush—whether angry or embarrassed—makes her appear a 'prentice caught plotting to steal from the larder.*

Duke Dolphin took advantage of Gustin's momentary silence to comment rather more loudly than necessary to his closest neighbor, Earle Pelican:

"In my father's day, our wars with Hawk Haven truly were a continuation of our Civil War. Gustin the Third was the first king to become dependent on foreign mercenaries. His daughter, our queen, has continued the dependence."

Wisely, Queen Gustin did not respond to this unofficial commentary. However, as she did not seem quite prepared to speak, King Tedric added:

"As I was saying, I sent my soldiers to Bright Bay's aid because I did not wish to see her fall to a foreign aggressor. Whether or not I believe the compensation Your Majesty has offered to us is just is not the real issue. The issue as I see it is, what do you offer us to remain your allies?"

Queen Gustin had regained her composure and her reply showed even a touch of humor.

"I don't suppose that you'd continue to support us out of kindred feeling?"

"My personal family feeling would not be enough," King Tedric replied. "My noble counselors do not have nephews among your Great Houses. I would need to be able to offer them something more if they were to send their sons and daughters to fight on your fields."

Queen Gustin glanced down at some papers in front of her, as if consulting them. Then she said coolly:

572 / JANE LINDSKOLD

"Stonehold found the benefit of money earned and a place to train their forces compensation enough. In addition, we gave their ships use of some of our ports. Would you consider a similar contract?"

King Tedric shook his head.

"My people are my greatest treasure," he said. "I cannot sell their lives for mere monies. Moreover, New Kelvin and Waterland are not as aggressive neighbors as those Stonehold might find challenging their southern frontier if the Rocky Band were not so well-trained. We have a port of our own, poor when compared to the water wealth of Bright Bay, but serviceable, and Waterland freely shares the northern oceans with our vessels."

"I heard," Queen Gustin said acidly, "from well-informed sources, that neither Waterland nor New Kelvin were pleased that you had come to Bright Bay's aid. Perhaps your borders and vessels are not as secure as you think."

King Tedric shook his head. "I am certain that if we offered due apology and promised never to aid Bright Bay again—no matter which foreign powers threatened—New Kelvin and Waterland would forgive us. Waterland in particular might have other ventures to occupy her time."

You walked into that one, Valora, Allister thought, listening to the murmured consternation from the Bright Bay representatives. *That old eagle was playing such games when you were floating toy ships in a garden pond. Now your own people see our increased vulnerability.*

For the first time, Queen Gustin looked momentarily panicked, perhaps envisioning a Bright Bay embattled on land by Stonehold—with or without Hawk Haven's aid—while Waterland preyed upon her from the sea. Until this point, Bright Bay had been a fair match for the neighboring sea power precisely because of Stonehold's support against Hawk Haven on land.

Gustin has been so busy concentrating on the immediate picture, Allister thought, *that she did not realize what other sharks would start circling once they smelled our blood and thought us wounded. Yet, if she had come to fight this battle, she would not find herself needing to grant concessions. It is her own cowardice—or prudence—that brought her to this point.*

For a fleeting moment the duke wondered what ultimatum Stonehold had offered Queen Gustin that war had been preferable to reply. Despite how attentively his spies and those of his allies had snooped about, no one knew for certain. The best any could say was that Stonehold's letter had to do with events dating back to days of Gustin Sailor.

Looking at the queen, sitting stiff and haughty in her high-backed chair, Allister Seagleam was certain of one thing. The ultimatum—no matter what it entailed—had meant less than the fact that it had offended Gustin's pride. She would not rush to Stonehold's bidding like a servant to cook, as she had put it in her letter to him, no matter what the cost.

Although there was still a small glimmer of fear in her eyes, Queen Gustin found her voice and addressed King Tedric:

"Your Majesty then agrees that what compensation we have offered Hawk Haven for her assistance in the battles of these few days past is sufficient."

Tedric replied carefully, "I have said we will accept it—I do not wish to discuss whether or not I consider the compensation sufficient, not when there is a larger question to settle. I ask you bluntly, Your Majesty, do you wish to continue in alliance with Hawk Haven and if so, what is that alliance worth to you?"

Queen Gustin hedged, "You have said you will not take money nor use of harbors, that your troops need no training. What is the price of your aid?"

"Nothing," King Tedric said, "that you must personally pay. I only ask that you name as your heir my nephew, your cousin Allister Seagleam. I believe that he will work toward the union of both our kingdoms, so that never again will such word as 'alliance' need be used to define our relationship to each other."

"You say," Queen Gustin said, her voice rising, "that this is no price to pay!"

"I do not ask that you step down," King Tedric said reasonably. "Only that you name Duke Allister Seagleam, son of Princess Caryl Eagle and Prince Tavis Seagleam, your heir. You have no son or daughter nor younger sibling. I am not asking you to disinherit anyone, only that you choose Duke Allister out of all those who could raise a claim to the throne and that you assure his—or his own heir's—succeeding you even in the instance that a child is born to you."

Duke Lobster, father of King Harwill and thus grandfather to the yet-unconceived child of the queen, spoke out without bothering to be recognized:

"Even if the queen has not yet born a child, there are those within Bright Bay's own nobility who should follow her. Grand Duchess Seastar's eldest, Culver, holds the title crown prince, though all understand that he will step down gracefully when Queen Gustin the Fourth bears a child."

"Then I," King Tedric replied, smiling slightly as if acknowledging Duke Lobster's unspoken advocacy of his potential grandchild, "am merely asking Crown Prince Culver to be gracious a bit sooner than was planned."

A few people laughed and Duke Allister noted that not all those who laughed were from Hawk Haven.

Queen Gustin was not laughing, despite the fact that this proposal came as no surprise. She had heard it before, both from Allister and from Tedric—and probably from others. Her request that King Tedric tell her what he wanted of her in return for his support had been for the benefit of those representatives of her Great Houses who might not have heard Tedric's demands—and who hopefully would be offended by them.

Doubtless what made the queen's face so stern was that Duke Lobster was the only one to raise a protest. There was no offended hubbub as there had been when she slighted Hawk Haven's contribution to the recent war, only thoughtful silence.

Duke Allister was not so naive as to believe that this meant there was near universal support for him. King Tedric's people were prepared to support him because of the near certainty that Stonehold would withdraw once Hawk Haven and Bright Bay showed a united front. Hawk Haven, therefore, would have won a victory none of their armies had in over a hundred years—the promise of unification—with no further bloodshed.

Among Bright Bay's assembled Houses, Oyster and Dolphin would support Allister's claim with enthusiasm. Oyster because of the prospect of seeing Pearl made queen—and the satisfaction of seeing their long shot in giving Allister a bride pay off. Dolphin would support Allister because of the old insult to Lady Brina—an insult that still rankled so strongly that Dolphin had risked its own interests to hinder those of the past two Gustins. Dolphin had long ago forgiven Allister for the earlier offense of his parent's arranged marriage in the light of that greater insult.

Lobster would support the queen. They must because King Harwill was of their family. Pelican and Seal were more problematical. True, Queen Gustin's mother was a Seal, but that House had old internal conflicts dating back to Viona's marriage to King Gustin III. Moreover, the Queen Mother Viona had not kept friends with all of her kin. Pelican owned lands along the Stonehold border and should be grateful for Hawk Haven's support, but they might prefer reconciliation with their closer neighbor.

Do I really want to be Gustin's heir? Allister asked himself. *Do I really wish this kettle of fish on Shad?*

He nodded to himself. He did. The problems would exist whether or not he was in a position to do anything about them. This way, he would have some control. Indeed, Gustin would need to work with him—or at least with Shad, as he would be her more probable successor—from the start if she wished to see any of her projects carried out.

"I am certain," Queen Gustin said, seeing that no one else was going to speak out in favor of her, "that Crown Prince Culver would be gracious. I, too, wish to be gracious, but this is much to ask."

"Still, I ask it," King Tedric said firmly, "and I am making demands not only of you. I will expect Duke Allister to prove his good faith to my people by wedding his heir to my heir."

There was murmuring at this, especially among the Hawk Haven contingent. King Tedric had remained stubborn in his refusal to name his heir in anything other than his sealed will. This last statement offered some slight clue to who that heir might be for Allister's own heir was widely recognized to be Shad, so Tedric's heir would need to be female. However, as there were three female candidates, this was hardly decisive.

Queen Gustin said silkily, "Duke Allister's heir is engaged to be married. Are you suggesting he name another child his heir or that he break the engagement?"

"That," King Tedric said, "is not my problem. To satisfy my belief that I am securing peace with Bright Bay for my kingdom, Duke Allister must wed his heir to mine. How Allister chooses to arrive at this end is his choice."

Earl Kestrel, quivering like his namesake bird about to launch after prey, stood and was recognized.

"Your Majesty, does that mean you will name your heir here?"

"If," King Tedric said deliberately, "Queen Gustin agrees to my terms, I will be naming my heir here so that everyone will know how the succession is to be established."

Earl Kestrel bowed and sat, glancing at Allister as if wondering how the duke would take to wedding his son to a feral woman who apparently thought she was a wolf.

I would wed Shad, Allister thought, *or Tavis, if Shad's engagement cannot be broken—to any of the three young women from whom King Tedric would select his heir and he would choose a young one rather than his niece Zorana, of that I am sure. The male candidates please me less since young Purcel Archer was killed, but I do not think the king will choose one of these. Baron Archer would not divorce his wife to marry an eleven-year-old; Rolfston Redbriar is dead, and Jet Shield is disgraced.*

Judging from the expressions on the faces of the Hawk Haven representatives, similar conclusions were being reached. The representative for House Goshawk looked vaguely disappointed, but those for Peregrine, Kestrel, and Gyrfalcon were quite alert.

"Queen Gustin," King Tedric said, "what is your answer? I have given Bright Bay ample time to consider my offer. Although this is the first time my terms have been mentioned in this company, it is not the first time you have heard them."

"It is," the queen said, "a monumental decision. Although this is not the first time I have heard your offer, it is the first time some of my Great Houses have been informed. I ask to have time to consult with them in private."

"Take that time," King Tedric said rising, "but know this, I will not wait beyond this hour tomorrow. Moreover, I do not think that Stonehold will wait. Already they see Hawk Haven's support as a negotiable commodity. I have given you the chance to win our support, but it does not mean that it is not valued by others."

With these stinging words, the king pushed himself to his feet and turned to go, escorted by his guards. His nobles rose in respect and followed him from the room, trailed by the clerks for Hawk Haven.

The words that had been kept back lest Bright Bay look less in the eyes of a nation that had been enemy, ally, and kin now flooded forth. Representatives of the five Great Houses surged to their feet, shouting, without waiting for recognition. Allister Seagleam listened to the noise in consternation.

Here, now, at last, it will be settled.

XXIX

FROM HER COT HIGH ON A SUNNY HILL, Firekeeper saw movement around the pavilion in which the negotiations had been being held. The cleared area around the pavilion, meant to keep eavesdroppers at bay, suddenly swarmed with those privileged few who had met with King Tedric, Queen Gustin, and the two ministers of Stonehold. Everyone was visible but Queen Gustin and King Tedric. They emerged some minutes later. Through the long glass, Firekeeper saw that the faces of both were grim and fierce.

"Now it comes," she said with certainty to Doc. "Soon the call comes."

"Call?" Doc said, looking up from the notes he had been making on a bit of paper. "You mean they've settled it all? Are you certain? I thought that was what yesterday's meeting at the Toll House should have done."

In response, Firekeeper handed him the long glass and motioned below.

"If I have learned anything of humans," the wolf-woman said, "I have learned that when counselors look upset and monarchs serious, a decision has been reached."

The bright call of a trumpet followed almost as she finished speaking and a herald's voice was heard announcing:

"Peace is made! Peace is won!"

Cheering followed these simple words, drowning out what the herald said next so that he must stop and wait. Firekeeper watched as men and women smiled or wept, pounding each other on the backs, embracing. She wondered at their simple joy. Couldn't they smell the blood that had been spilt? How could they rejoice at a peace following a war that should never have been?

Once again she resigned herself to accepting that perhaps for humans that battle did need to happen. Dangling her hand from the edge of the cot, she felt Blind Seer lick her fingers.

Doc lowered the long glass, saying: "The herald has given up trying to say anything more. I'm going to run down and learn the terms."

Firekeeper did not stop him, having plans of her own. As soon as the physician was gone, she said to Blind Seer:

"I smell Patience not far away."

The wolf grunted agreement.

"If you bring the horse to me, I will not need to walk all the way down the hill."

"Who said you are getting out of bed?" the wolf growled.

"I have," Firekeeper replied. *"And as you cannot stop me without hurting me further, I think you will get Patience."*

The wolf snarled something about stupid, impulsive humans, but by the time Firekeeper had sat up and swung her feet to the ground, he was back, driving the snorting grey gelding in front of him. Patience wore neither bridle nor saddle, but Firekeeper said to him:

"Kneel down so that I may mount or I will bite you."

A bit awkwardly, Patience complied, having no doubt at all that Firekeeper was completely in earnest. Wrapping her hands in the horse's mane and using the strength of her arms, the wolf-woman hauled herself astride. Despite the pain, she kept her expression carefully stoic, for she knew that at the first sign of weakness Blind Seer would realize he could stop her without retaliation.

She must have succeeded in hiding the pain that stabbed her back and groaned in the healing muscles of her thigh when she stretched it around the horse's barrel, for the wolf contented himself with grumbling:

"If Elation had not so taken to Derian, I would have her fetch him here. He could stop you."

"I doubt it," Firekeeper said cheerfully, adding *"Up!"* to the horse. Patience rose stiffly, muttering complaints about mad wolves. Firekeeper felt so good to be up and moving she let the gelding have his say.

"Down the hill," she said, slapping her steed's neck, *"to where the people are gathering. I want to be there when the king makes his announcement."*

"What announcement?" Blind Seer asked, trotting alongside.

"Why, his heir," Firekeeper replied blithely. *"I feel in my bones that now is the time."*

"Do you expect him to name you?"

"No, but I am no less curious for that."

"Curiosity is a puppy's vice."

"And a human virtue."

Doubtless because Blind Seer moved to pad a few steps in front of the grey gelding, a path cleared for them as they passed through the army camp. Firekeeper sat as straight as she was able, but she feared that she must look rather less than herself. Still, sporadic cheers and friendly greetings met her progress.

The news of her coming must have flowed ahead of her, because as she reached the area near the central pavilion Elation soared screeching out of the sky, heralding Derian's arrival a few moment's after.

"Firekeeper!" Derian exclaimed, the word protest and question all at once. She realized how much she had learned in that she could understand this. Once she would have thought it a simple greeting.

"I wanted to hear the king's announcement," she replied blandly.

"How did you know there was to be one?" he asked teasingly. "Isn't the herald's news of peace enough for you?"

Firekeeper replied as she had to Blind Seer, "I felt it in my bones." How else could she explain her growing awareness that humans revealed their thoughts and intentions through little signs even as wolves did?

Humans might lack tails and decent ears, but the signs were present nonetheless.

Derian might have teased further, but he was too concerned about her health and comfort. Given his height, he had no trouble checking both the sword wound to her back and the stitches on her leg without getting her down from Patience's back. When he had contented himself that she was not bleeding afresh and nothing seemed to have pulled loose, he grunted:

"Well, you are here, you might as well stay. Are you comfortable up there?"

"Enough," she replied. "Though Patience has a sharp backbone."

Derian remedied this by commandeering a blanket to make her a pad. Firekeeper leaned with her arms on Patience's withers while Derian slipped it under her. They'd just finished when Doc joined them, glowered at Firekeeper, but said nothing more. He was followed a few moments later by Valet, Race, and Ox. The latter explained:

"The king has called most of his nobles to him. That's where Earl Kestrel has gone. Shouldn't you be there, Firekeeper?"

She shrugged. "I am comfortable here. If they want me, I am easily found."

But no one came for her and when the herald emerged from the tent and the crowd fell silent she remained just one among many. After the herald made a completely unnecessary call for quiet, he continued:

"His Majesty King Tedric and Her Majesty Queen Gustin the Fourth have several very important announcements to make. They demand your complete and obedient attention."

At this, the monarchs emerged from the pavilion. Each was trailed by a small herd of nobles, each dressed in the best that could be found at short notice. Earl Kestrel and Baron Archer, like most of those who had seen recent military service, wore their uniforms. Standing next to Sapphire Shield who was wearing her battered blue armor, Lady Elise looked tranquil, if rather frail, dressed in the same gown she had worn to the ball.

Firekeeper wondered if hers were the only ears sharp enough to hear the sigh of longing and admiration that inadvertently slipped from between Doc's lips as he gazed at the young noblewoman. Something about the slight but definitely compassionate twinkle in Valet's eyes made her think that hers were not.

A raised dais a few feet high had been hastily constructed and side by side with measured tread, rival king and queen mounted to stand where all could see them.

Courage, Firekeeper thought with admiration. *Until Prince Newell's attack on the king, I never realized the risks these human Ones take whenever they are in public. Queen Gustin is not loved here. How easily an arrow shot from afar could end her life! Yet she stands there cool and even arrogant, like the senior doe of some great herd.*

This was the first time she had seen Bright Bay's queen close up and Firekeeper took a deep breath, hoping to catch something of her scent. All she got was that of horse and hot humans, but she did not doubt that the elegant young woman before her was scented like some rich flower or perhaps an exotic spice.

The queen, Firekeeper decided as the herald blatted out a completely unnecessary recitation of titles and honors, was furiously angry but knew herself in no position to express that anger.

After the announcement of titles, King Tedric began to speak. His every sentence was echoed by the herald so that even those at the far reaches of the crowd could hear, but Firekeeper was close enough to hear the old voice projecting with strength despite the shrillness of age.

"Good people. As was announced a short time ago, we have achieved peace between those who so recently contended upon the field just west of this point. Stonehold has paid the promised compensation. They will begin to withdraw their troops tomorrow morning."

He lifted a hand to forestall the cheer that began almost inadvertently and continued:

"Compromise is the weapon of peace. As many of you know, I first came here on my quest for a fitting heir. Part of my compromise for peace was agreeing to name that heir publicly. But before I do so, Queen Gustin has an important announcement of her own to make."

As the queen moved slightly forward to take over, a low murmur rippled through the throng to be instantly quelled by her gaze.

"As Stonehold's perfidy has demonstrated," Queen Gustin said in a firm yet musical voice, "neither Hawk Haven nor Bright Bay is strong enough to exist alone. My greatest wish is for an alliance between our kindred nations. In token of this, I am stepping down as queen of Bright Bay in favor of my cousin, Duke Allister Seagleam. As he was born as a pledge of our land's desire for mutual peace, I can think of no better proof of Bright Bay's goodwill toward Hawk Haven."

Nothing could stop the noisy roar of acclamation that exploded almost before her words were finished. Duke Allister nodded solemnly, but something of how deeply he was moved showed in the line of color that crept up from his collar to flush his cheeks. His wife, Pearl, was less composed. When she burst into joyful tears, Duke Allister was able to take refuge in comforting her.

The herald shouted the crowd to relative silence, and Queen Gustin continued, her tones now icy:

"My cousin has agreed that I should not make this great sacrifice for my people's good without some fitting reward. Therefore, the islands that have to this time been part of the nation of Bright Bay will become my new realm. To guard and protect the islands, I shall be taking with me a portion of Bright Bay's fleet. I hope that relations between my new realm of the Isles and her sister nations shall be characterized by mutual accord."

That last, Firekeeper thought, *is as true as if Blind Seer said he wanted all his fur shaved off. I doubt either King Tedric or Duke Allister believe her. Neither are fools.*

King Tedric stepped forward and resumed:

"I thank my noble sister and I shall devote my strongest efforts in these last years of my life to maintaining mutual peace. In the interests of this, I have decided that I can no longer delay announcing my heir. At one point I had seriously considered Duke Allister, but his new role as king of Bright Bay will heavily occupy his time.

"I wish to state that my naming of one person as my heir should in no way be taken as a slight to those who were not selected. All of the men and women I considered had qualities that might have made them good and able monarchs, but in the end, I could only select one person. Unlike Stonehold, my nation cannot be ruled by a committee.

"In the interests of furthering an alliance with Bright Bay, I decided to pass over my niece Zorana Archer and my nephew Ivon Archer. My other nephew, Lord Rolfston Redbriar, bravely gave his life on the battlefield before this decision was resolved, as did my grandnephew Purcel Archer.

"The next generation holds many fine young men and women. However, in choosing between them I let my desire for peace between Bright Bay and Hawk Haven dictate my choice to a certain extent. Duke Allister has four children. His eldest and his heir is a young man, the heroic Shad Oyster.

"My desire was that the reunification of our nations be delayed no longer than absolutely necessary. Therefore, my heir must be someone who could wed Shad Oyster. Together, they would rule Hawk Haven after my death and—with Allister Seagleam's enthusiastic concurrence—upon Allister's passing to the ancestors, they would also rule in Bright Bay.

"This narrowed my choices considerably, for only two women of near marriageable age are among my potential heirs. Both young women have shown true courage and fortitude in different ways during the battle. One of these candidates, Lady Archer, is the sole heir to her family duties. She is also just eighteen—not quite of marriageable age. However, these difficulties could have been overcome. What made me decide to select Elise's cousin, Sapphire Shield, over her was an event that is already becoming legend.

"By now all of you have heard how during the final battle of this recent war, Sapphire risked her own life to preserve that of Duke Allister and how, when Shad Oyster fell defending his father from further attacks, Sapphire herself carried him from the field. Such events forge deep bonds. I am not such a fool as to ignore the promptings of the ancestors. Therefore, I here name with all of you as my witnesses, Sapphire Shield the crown princess of Hawk Haven!"

Now, clearly, was a time for cheering and none attempted to restrain the thunderous applause that arose as Duke Allister led forward his son and his daughter-in-law-to-be. As the young couple stepped decorously forward to receive the acclaim of those who would someday be their subjects, they clasped hands tightly. Firekeeper was pleased to note that this was not mere form. From her elevated perch she could clearly see that the knuckles on both hands were white from the tightness of that grasp.

When the shouts and cheers faded to a happy murmur, King Tedric continued, "My voice is old and weak. Therefore, I ask my nephew, Allister Seagleam, to continue explaining the terms of peace."

Allister stepped next to the woman he had deposed and offered her a deep bow. Queen Gustin IV, soon to be Queen Valora of the Isles, was gracious enough, but the tight lines around mouth and eyes could not be smoothed away by mere intention.

Allister held up his hand for silence. When he spoke, his strong voice seemed emblematic of the promise of the new days to follow.

"My good people, tomorrow morning I shall depart for Silver Whale Cove, the capital of Bright Bay. There, with the full agreement of these nobles and the families they represent . . ." Here he paused to gesture at the gathered representatives of Bright Bay's five Great Houses. "I shall be crowned king of Bright Bay. However, I will not be made King Gustin the Fifth. The name Gustin shall be allowed to rest. Nor shall I be King Allister Seagleam. Instead, the name I will take is King Allister of the Pledge, chosen as a reminder of what has brought us all to this point.

"My son and heir, Shad, and Crown Princess Sapphire will be married soon after, also in Bright Bay. Thereafter, together, they will travel to Hawk Haven and renew their vows before their new countrymen. When I pass on to the ancestors, Shad and Sapphire will reunite the portions of our severed people. At that time, Bright Bay and Hawk Haven will cease to exist, becoming instead a new nation embracing the best of our peoples. To commemorate that change, a new name will be taken. Uncle Tedric has suggested we call our new country Bright Haven. What say you all?"

Firekeeper thought there could be no doubt of the people's approval. In keeping with the general festive atmosphere, even Blind Seer threw back his head and howled enthusiastically.

"I want you to know," Allister said, "that this union of our kingdoms is not contingent upon chance. If something takes Shad before me, Sapphire shall still follow me and reunification continue. The same is true if Sapphire dies suddenly. Shad is her heir, even as he is mine. The child of their bodies will follow them—either of them—to the throne. Their lives will not be easy for they must learn to govern wisely not one, but two peoples. Yet our dream is that by the time Bright Haven is born the people of that nation will no longer be two but one.

"I have spoken long enough. You gathered here have seen history made. The realm of the Isles is born. Bright Haven is conceived. Each one of you is witness to those births. Guard that responsibility as you would any newborn child, knowing that you stand as ancestors to those great events. Blessings on you all!"

As Duke Allister stepped back, Firekeeper joined in the new wave of acclaim, a thunder of cheering and shouting that lasted until the noble party had retreated from the dais. As the joyful noise faded, the crowd surrounding them began to break up, flowing about their little wolf-guarded group like a stream parting around a rock. Looking down from her seat on Patience, Firekeeper saw that Derian was looking at her, a quizzical expression on his face.

"You look awfully happy for someone who just learned she isn't going to be queen," Derian said.

"I know that I wouldn't be for a time," Firekeeper replied. "I was glad then and am gladder now because now Earl Kestrel won't look at me that hungry, hopeful way anymore."

"I wonder what he will do about you?" Derian asked.

Ox spoke up for his employer. "Kestrel adopted her. The earl won't dump her. He has too much pride of house for that."

Valet nodded agreement. "Firekeeper will never need search for a home. She has one in Kestrel."

Firekeeper thought about this as the group returned to the Kestrel camp. On threat of Doc's wrath, she was immediately returned to a cot. The others began breaking down the tents and storing the gear.

Some of Hawk Haven's army—Race among them—would remain in Bright Bay to make certain that Stonehold left as scheduled, but Earl Kestrel had been released from his command to tend his other duties. Immediately, he had arranged for a suite of comfortable rooms at one of Hope's better inns. Valet was openly pleased.

"What if," Firekeeper asked the five men, "I already have a home? Am I to be Kestrel's prisoner?"

Derian looked embarrassed, Ox and Race puzzled, Doc carefully blank, but Valet understood and reassured her.

"You should have freedom to come and go," Valet said, his hands busy stowing polished cookware. "Even if you are still nearly a child by Hawk Haven's standards, you have lived a very different life and Earl Kestrel will not wish you to be unhappy. Tell me, do you intend to return to the wilds?"

Firekeeper shrugged. "Winter is hard in the wolflands, but someday I would wish to see my pack, maybe in the spring. Then you found me; then I could return."

"Forever?" Derian's voice sounded oddly choked. He turned away and made himself busy stacking some blankets.

"Forever?" Firekeeper laughed. "After I go to all such trouble to learn human ways! Of course I come back."

"I'm glad," a new voice entered the conversation as Earl Kestrel walked into the camp. His followers sprang to offer him proper bows, but he waved them down. "Be at ease.

"I am glad," the earl repeated, turning to Firekeeper, "to learn that you plan to come back to us. Can I encourage you to stay through the winter?"

Firekeeper nodded. "I was thinking that food is hard to get in winter and, even with Doc's help, I will be some time yet making these cut muscles strong enough to run and hunt."

"Very good." Earl Kestrel beamed generally. "Before I left the king's presence, the new heir spoke with me. Sapphire asked me to counsel her on the needs of my house. Very prettily, she told me that until now she has concentrated solely on those of her birth house."

Earl Kestrel looked more serious. "Crown Princess Sapphire also wished to make certain that I would not hold any resentment against you, Blysse, for not being chosen as heir."

"Do you?" Firekeeper asked bluntly.

"No," replied the earl with equal directness. "Given the situation, the king could not have chosen anyone about whose heritage there was the least doubt. Moreover, as a public sign of her favor, the heir has asked if you will be an attendant at her forthcoming wedding."

Firekeeper frowned. "Wedding attendant?"

Earl Kestrel actually laughed. "It is a formal-attire occasion of the highest honor."

"More honor than the ball?"

"More than a dozen balls," Earl Kestrel assured her. He glanced at Derian. "I believe that Counselor Derian could teach you what you would need to know. Lady Archer will also be attendant upon her cousin. I believe that the crown princess wished to publicly demonstrate their amity."

Firekeeper shrugged away the unfamiliar word, more concerned about this new social challenge.

"Will you teach me, Derian? You and Elise?"

Derian nodded, pretending dismay. "I seem fated to act as lady's maid," he said in resigned tones, but Firekeeper saw the sparkle in his eyes.

Blind Seer saw it also. *"More kings,"* the wolf grumbled, *"and queens and formal attire. What shall I do?"*

Firekeeper scratched his great grey head. *"Be with me. Guard my back. There will be dangers there also."*

"Despite what Duke Allister implied today," Earl Kestrel said, unaware of the wolves' conversation, "the wedding and coronation cannot be held for some weeks. Queen Gustin must be permitted to move her belongings from the royal dwellings at Silver Whale Cove. Nobles from both Bright Bay and Hawk Haven must be given time to prepare for the festivities. Duke Allister will take up his responsibilities as monarch immediately—indeed, the last thing we witnessed before the meeting ended was a representative of each of Bright Bay's Great Houses swearing loyalty to their new king—but further formalities will wait."

"I must return to Eagle's Nest" Earl Kestrel continued, "and then to the Norwood Grant. King Tedric has asked that I take Prince Newell's servant Rook into my custody. Apparently, Lady Zorana wants him executed, no matter what promises he was given in return for his confession. King Tedric might have given Lady Zorana what she wished but this Rook claims that he is not the one who took such liberties with Lady Zorana's person—he says another man, named Keen, was responsible."

"I think," Firekeeper said slowly, "that Rook tells the truth. I did not see faces, but I did see shapes and hair and such. The man who pawed at Lady Zorana was not Rook. He was the one who later I cut beneath the eye. I did not recall this at the time, but once or twice I saw one who could have been this Keen near Prince Newell's tent."

Earl Kestrel looked interested. "I doubt that such information would change Lady Zorana's feelings. She would simply say that Rook stood by and permitted this Keen his abuses. Still, I shall pass your report on to King Tedric. For whatever reason, King Tedric is standing by his promise to Rook and has asked that I secure the prisoner in the Norwood Grant, where Lady Zorana would find it more difficult to do him injury."

"My thought," the earl went on, "is to have Lady Blysse remain here in Hope to recuperate from her wounds. Not only would it spare her a trip in a jolting wagon, but when she feels better she will have woodlands near for her pleasure. I must take Ox and Valet with me, and Derian will certainly wish to visit his family and tell them about his new honors, but I thought that you, Jared, might be willing to look after my ward."

"That's a good thought," Doc said. "I'll stay and keep Firekeeper and Blind Seer out of trouble. No one is waiting for me in Eagle's Nest."

Firekeeper heard the sadness in his voice. If Earl Kestrel did, he didn't comment.

"I may be speaking out of turn, Cousin Jared," the earl added, "but I was given the impression that you will be invited to the wedding celebration in Silver Whale Cove—as well as to the one in Eagle's Nest. Shad Oyster appreciates how your talent sped along his healing and that of his father. He wishes to offer you this mark of favor before his people."

Sir Jared's smile glowed. Firekeeper knew why. Elise would be at the wedding. The prospect of that meeting—not the royal invitation—was the honor that lit his soul.

Firekeeper shook her head, wondering if she would ever feel so intensely about a human. She could be fond of humans, yes. She was fond of Derian, of Elise, of all those she thought of as her human pack— even of Earl Kestrel. She would die for King Tedric as she would for Blind Seer.

Her hand curled tightly in the wolf's ruff, knowing that her silent wish was impossible, wondering nonetheless if somewhere, somehow, there was magic that would transform her so that she might run beside Blind Seer, wolf and wolf.

GLOSSARY OF CHARACTERS[1]

Aksel Trueheart: (Lord, B.B.) scholar of Hawk Haven; spouse of Zorana Archer; father of Purcel, Nydia, Deste, and Kenre Trueheart.[2]

Alben Eagle: (B.B.) son of Princess Marras. In keeping with principles of Zorana I, given no title as died in infancy.

Allister Seagleam: (Duke, B.B.), called the Pledge Child; son of Tavis Seagleam (B.B.) and Caryl Eagle (H.H.); spouse of Pearl Oyster; father of Shad, Tavis, Anemone, and Minnow Oyster.

Amery Pelican: (King, B.B.) Spouse of Queen Gustin II; father of Basil, Seastar, and Tavis.

Anemone Oyster: (Lady, B.B.) daughter of Allister Seagleam.

Aurella Wellward: (Lady, H.H.) confidant of Queen Elexa; spouse of Ivon Archer; mother of Elise Archer.

Barden Eagle: (Prince, H.H.) third son of King Tedric of Hawk Haven. Disowned. Spouse of Eirene Kestrel; father of Blysse Eagle.

Basil Seagleam: see Gustin III.

Blind Seer: Royal Wolf; companion to Firekeeper.

Blysse Eagle: (Lady, H.H.) daughter of Prince Barden and Eirene Kestrel.

Blysse Kestrel: see Firekeeper.

Brina Dolphin: (Lady or Queen, B.B.) first spouse of Gustin III, divorced as barren.

Brock Carter: (B.B.) son of Colby and Vernita Carter; brother of Derian Carter.

Caryl Eagle: (Princess, H.H.) daughter of King Chalmer I; married to Prince Tavis Seagleam; mother of Allister Seagleam.

Chalmer I: (King, H.H.) born Chalmer Elkwood; son of Queen Zorana the Great; spouse of Rose Dawn; father of Marras, Tedric, Gadman, and Rosene.

Chalmer Eagle: (Crown Prince, H.H.) son of Tedric Eagle and Elexa Wellward.

Citrine Shield: (H.H.) daughter of Melina Shield and Rolfston Redbriar.

Colby Carter: (H.H.) livery stable owner and carter; spouse of Vernita Carter; father of Derian, Damita, and Brock.

Damita Carter: (H.H.) daughter of Colby and Vernita Carter; sister of Derian Carter.

Derian Carter: (H.H.) also called Derian Counselor; assistant to Norvin Norwood; son of Colby and Vernita Carter; brother of Damita and Brock.

Deste Trueheart: (H.H.) daughter of Aksel Trueheart and Zorana Archer; sister of Purcel, Nydia, and Kenre Trueheart.

Dia Trueheart: see Nydia Trueheart.

Dirkin Eastbranch: (knight, H.H.) King Tedric's personal bodyguard.

Donal Hunter: (H.H.) member of Barden Eagle's expedition; spouse of Sarena; father of Tamara.

Eirene Norwood: (Lady, H.H.) spouse of Barden Eagle; mother of Blysse Eagle; sister of Norvin Norwood.

---

[1]Characters are detailed under first name or best known name. The initials B.B. (Bright Bay) or H.H. (Hawk Haven) following a character's name indicate their nationality. Titles are also indicated in parenthesis.

[2]Hawk Haven and Bright Bay noble houses both follow a naming system where the children take the surname of the higher ranking parent, with the exception that only the immediate royal family bear the name of that house. If the parents are of the same rank, then rank is designated from the birth house, great over lesser, lesser by seniority. The Great Houses are ranked in the following order: Eagle, Shield, Wellward, Trueheart, Redbriar, Stanbrook, Norwood.

Elation: Royal Falcon, companion to Firekeeper.

Elexa Wellward: (Queen, H.H.) spouse of Tedric I; mother of Chalmer, Lovella, and Barden.

Elise Archer: (Lady, H.H.) daughter of Ivon Archer and Aurella Wellward; heir to Archer Grant.

Farand Briarcott: (Lady, H.H.) assistant to Tedric I, former military commander.

Firekeeper: (Lady, H.H.) feral child raised by wolves, adopted by Norvin Norwood and given the name Blysse Kestrel.

Gadman Eagle: (Grand Duke, H.H.) third child of King Chalmer and Queen Rose; brother to Marras, Tedric, Rosene; spouse of Riki Redbriar; father of Rolfston and Nydia.

Gayl Minter: see Gayl Seagleam.

Gayl Seagleam: (Queen, B.B.) spouse of Gustin I; first queen of Bright Bay; mother of Gustin, Merry (later Gustin II), and Lyra. Note: Gayl was the only queen to assume the name "Seagleam." Later tradition paralleled that of Hawk Haven where the name of the birth house was retained even after marriage to the monarch.

Grace Trueheart: (Duchess Merlin, H.H.) military commander; spouse of Alin Brave; mother of Baxter.

Gustin I: (King, B.B.) born Gustin Sailor, assumed the name Seagleam upon his coronation; first monarch of Bright Bay; spouse of Gayl Minter, later Gayl Seagleam; father of Gustin, Merry, and Lyra Seagleam.

Gustin II: (Queen, B.B.) born Merry Seagleam, assumed the name Gustin upon her coronation; second monarch of Bright Bay; spouse of Amery Pelican; mother of Basil, Seastar, and Tavis Seagleam.

Gustin III: (King, B.B.) born Basil Seagleam, assumed the name Gustin upon his coronation; third monarch of Bright Bay; spouse of Brina Dolphin, later of Viona Seal; father of Valora Seagleam.

Gustin IV: (Queen, B.B.) born Valora Seagleam, assumed the name Gustin upon her coronation; fourth monarch of Bright Bay; spouse of Harwill Lobster.

Harwill Lobster: (King, B.B.) Spouse of Gustin IV.

Hazel Healer: (H.H.) apothecary, herbalist, perfumer; resident in the town of Hope.

Holly Gardener: (H.H.) former Master Gardener for Eagle's Nest Castle; possessor of the Green Thumb, a talent for the growing of plants. Mother of Timin and Sarena.

Hya Grimsel: (General, Stonehold) commander of Stonehold troops.

Ivon Archer: (Baron, H.H.) master of the Archer Grant; son of Purcel Archer and Rosene Eagle; brother of Zorana Archer; spouse of Aurella Wellward; father of Elise Archer.

Jared Surcliffe: (knight, H.H.) knight of the Order of the White Eagle; possessor of the healing talent; distant cousin of Norvin Norwood who serves as his patron. Widower, no children.

Jem: (B.B.) deserter from Bright Bay's army.

Jet Shield: (H.H.) son of Melina Shield and Rolfston Redbriar; brother of Sapphire, Opal, Ruby, and Citrine.

Joy Spinner: (H.H.) scout in the service of Earle Kite.

Keen: (H.H.) servant to Newell Shield.

Kenre Trueheart: (H.H.) son of Zorana Archer and Aksel Trueheart; brother of Purcel, Nydia, and Deste Trueheart.

Lorimer Stanbrook: (Lord, H.H.) spouse of Marras Eagle; father of Marigolde and Alben Eagle.

Lovella Eagle: (Crown Princess, H.H.) military commander; daughter of Tedric Eagle and Elexa Wellward; spouse of Newell Shield.

Marigolde Eagle: (H.H.) daughter of Marras Eagle and Lorimer Stanbrook. In keeping with principles of Zorana I, given no title as died in infancy.

Marras Eagle: (Crown Princess, H.H.) daughter of Tedric Eagle and Elexa Wellward; spouse of Lorimer Stanbrook; mother of Marigolde and Alben Eagle.

Melina Shield: (Lady, H.H.) reputed sorceress; spouse of Rolfston Redbriar; mother of Sapphire, Jet, Opal, Ruby, and Citrine Shield.

Merry Seagleam: see Gustin II.

Minnow Oyster: (Lady, B.B.) daughter of Allister Seagleam and Pearl Oyster; twin of Anemone Oyster; sister of Shad and Tavis Oyster.

Nanny: (H.H.) attendant to Melina Shield.

Newell Shield: (Prince, H.H.) commander of marines; spouse of Lovella Eagle; brother of Melina Shield.

Ninette Farmer: (H.H.) relative of Ivon Archer; attendant of Elise Archer.

Norvin Norwood: (Earl Kestrel, H.H.) heir to Kestrel Grant; brother of Eirene Norwood; spouse of Luella Stanbrook; father of Edlin, Tait, Lillis, Agneta, and Blysse (adopted).

Nydia Trueheart: (H.H.) often called Dia; daughter of Aksel Trueheart and Zorana Archer; sister of Purcel, Deste, and Kenre Trueheart.

One Male: ruling male wolf of Firekeeper and Blind Seer's pack.

One Female: formerly Shining Coat; ruling female wolf of Firekeeper and Blind Seer's pack.

Opal Shield: (H.H.) daughter of Melina Shield and Rolfston Redbriar; sister of Sapphire, Jet, Ruby, and Citrine.

Ox: (H.H.) born Malvin Hogge; bodyguard to Norvin Norwood; renowned for his strength and good temper.

Pearl Oyster: (Lady, B.B.) spouse of Allister Seagleam; mother of Shad, Tavis, Anemone, and Minnow Oyster.

Purcel Trueheart: (H.H.) lieutenant, Hawk Haven army; son of Aksel Trueheart and Zorana Archer; brother of Nydia, Deste, and Kenre Trueheart.

Purcel Archer: (Baron Archer, H.H.) first Baron Archer, born Purcel Farmer, elevated to the title for his prowess in battle; spouse of Rosene Eagle; father of Ivon and Zorana.

Race Forester: (H.H.) scout under the patronage of Norvin Norwood; regarded by many as one of the best in his calling.

Riki Redbriar: (Lady, H.H.) spouse of Gadman Eagle; mother of Rolfston and Nydia Redbriar.

Rolfston Redbriar: (Lord, H.H.) son of Gadman Eagle and Riki Redbriar; spouse of Melina Shield; father of Sapphire, Jet, Opal, Ruby, and Citrine Shield.

Rook: (H.H.) servant to Newell Shield.

Rose Dawn: (Queen, H.H.) common-born wife of Chalmer I; his marriage to her was the reason Hawk Haven Great Houses received what Queen Zorana the Great would doubtless have seen as unnecessary and frivolous titles.

Rosene: (Grand Duchess, H.H.) fourth child of King Chalmer and Queen Rose; spouse of Purcel Archer; mother of Ivon and Zorana Archer.

Ruby Shield: (H.H.) daughter of Melina Shield and Rolfston Redbriar; sister of Sapphire, Jet, Opal, and Citrine Shield.

Sapphire Shield: (H.H.) daughter of Melina Shield and Rolfston Redbriar; sister of Jet, Opal, Ruby, and Citrine Shield.

Sarena Gardener: (H.H.) member of Prince Barden's expedition; spouse of Donal Hunter; mother of Tamara.

Shad Oyster: (Lord, B.B.) lieutenant, Bright Bay navy; son of Allister Seagleam and Pearl

Oyster; brother of Tavis, Anemone, and Minnow Oyster.

Steward Silver: (H.H.) long-time steward of Eagle's Nest Castle. Her birth-name and origin have been forgotten as no one, not even Silver herself, thinks of her as anything but the steward.

Tavis Oyster: (Lord, B.B.) son of Allister Seagleam and Pearl Oyster; brother of Shad, Anemone, and Minnow Oyster.

Tavis Seagleam: (Prince, B.B.) third child of Gustin II and Amery Pelican; spouse of Caryl Eagle; father of Allister Seagleam.

Tedric I: (King, B.B.) third king of Hawk Haven; son of King Chalmer and Queen Rose; spouse of Elexa Wellward; father of Chalmer, Lovella, and Barden.

Tench: (Lord, B.B.) born Tench Clark; right-hand to Queen Gustin IV; knighted for his services; later made Lord of the Pen.

Thyme: (H.H.) a scout in the service of Hawk Haven.

Timin Gardener: (H.H.) Master Gardener for Eagle's Nest Castle; possessor of the Green Thumb, a talent involving the growing of plants; son of Holly Gardener; brother of Sarena; father of Dan and Robyn.

Valet: (H.H.) eponymous servant of Norvin Norwood; known for his fidelity and surprising wealth of useful skills.

Valora Seagleam: see Gustin IV.

Vernita Carter: (H.H.) born Vernita Painter; an acknowledged beauty of her day, Vernita became associated with the business she and her husband, Colby, transformed from a simple carting business to a group of associated livery stables and carting service; spouse of Colby Carter; mother of Derian, Damita, and Brock Carter.

Viona Seal: (Queen, B.B.) second wife of King Gustin III; mother of Valora, later Gustin IV.

Wain Cutter: (H.H.) skilled lapidary, or gem cutter, working out of the town of Hope.

Whiner: a wolf of Blind Seer and Firekeeper's pack.

Yaree Yuci: (General, Stonehold) commander of Stonehold troops.

Zorana I: (Queen, H.H.) also called Zorana the Great, born Zorana Shield. First monarch of Hawk Haven; responsible for a reduction of titles—so associated with this program that over-emphasis of titles is considered "unzoranic." Spouse of Clive Elkwood; mother of Chalmer I.

Zorana Archer: (Lady, H.H.) daughter of Rosene Eagle and Purcel Archer; sister of Ivon Archer; spouse of Aksel Trueheart; mother of Purcel, Nydia, Deste, and Kenre Trueheart.